Guy of Gisborne
Book 1: Crusades

L. J. Hutton

Copyright 2018 L. J. Hutton

This book was previously published under the title of
Much Secret Sorrow in 2013

Copyright

Acknowledgements

Thank yous are due in several areas for helping to make this book possible.

Firstly I need to thank the staff at the University of Birmingham. I went there as a mature student to do a degree which is sadly no longer on offer, Medieval Studies. This degree covered not only the history of the period, but literature, art and archaeology, and I was lucky enough to be taught by some truly amazing people who knew their subjects inside out – in particular Dr Philippa Semper who not only fostered an enthusiasm for Old English but also became a valued friend. I then did an MPhil in Medieval History, and was again fortunate in my tutors, in particular Dr Steve Bassett whose attention to detail was legendary and who insisted on the same from his students. If I learned good habits for editing they are down to his influence, and this book would not have been possible without the research skills I learned from that master's degree, for which I am very grateful.

Thanks are due to Rowan and Callum at Drudion re-enactment for perceptive comments – especially about archery and rabbits!

I also need to thank my faithful two readers who get the raw material and make perceptive comments. Karen Murray is expert at keeping my inner historian under control, and reminds me that I am writing fiction and not a thesis when I get too engrossed! Teresa Fairhurst has offered endless encouragement and a good deal of Italian food along the way. And it is to her mother, Clelia, that I owe thanks for the recollections of the dog bread still made in the twentieth century for hunting dogs on rich estates in Italy, and how good it tasted. Also thanks to Mary Ward, scholar and friend, for her support.

Evesham Greyhound and Lurcher Rescue deserve a mention – Guy's dogs come from direct experience of living with the long dogs we've had from them for nearly twenty years now! My lovely lurchers Blue and Min have kept me company during the writing of this, while our much loved Raffles didn't quite make it to the finished product, but is in here in spirit.

Finally, thanks to my husband John who has yet again put up with living with someone who spends an awful lot of her time in another century.

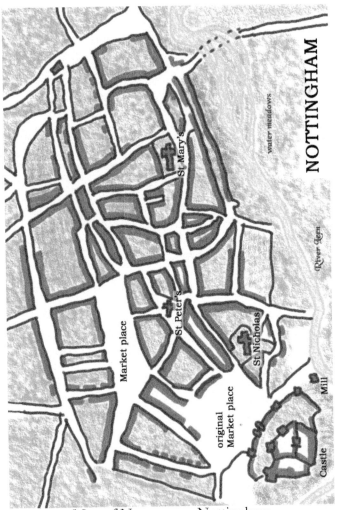

Map of Norman era Nottingham

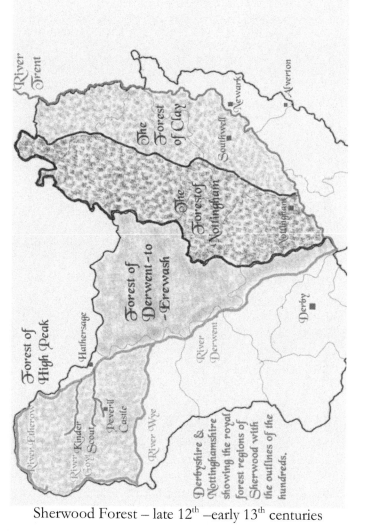

Sherwood Forest – late 12th –early 13th centuries

The ancient Forest of
Nottingham,
with the three keeperships of
Leen to Dover-beck,
High Forest, &
Rumwood, with
the hays,
parks, and
nine bailiwicks

River
Trent

CARBURTON HAY
Roomwood
& Osland
BUDBY HAY
Birkland, Bilhaugh
BIRKLAND & Clipstone Scroggs
HAY
Edwinstowe
Ollerton
CLIPSTONE
Clipstone PARK
Rufford

BILLAHAUGH
HAY

Mansfield
Woodhouse
Mansfield W
Nomans Wood
Mansfield
Mansfield & Lindhurst
Lindhurst

Blidworth
? Langton
Blidworth
Sutton
Blidworth &
& Highwells
Farnesfield
Kirkby
Kirkby & Sutton
Annesley
Newstead
Huckpall Papplewick
Newstead &
?LINBY
Papplewick
HAY
?WELLEY ?BESKWOOD
HAY
River
Leen
River
Erewash

Farnsfield

River
Greet
Southwell

Newark

Dover
Beck
Cocker Beck

Arnold

Calverton &
Arnold Hill

Nottingham

Map of old royal Forest of Nottingham

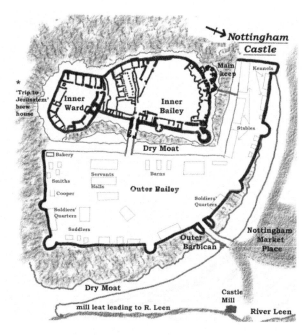

Plan of Nottingham Castle

(all maps and plans © L. J. Hutton)

Confiteor

I confess to Almighty God... to all the angels and saints, that I have
sinned exceedingly in thought, word, deed:

My name is Gisborne, Sir Guy of that same. You may have heard of
me. Most of it will have been lies or tall tales. I care not. I shall tell my
version of events now, for my confessor insists I hold nothing back for
fear of imperilling my immortal soul.

I know what his abbot thinks I shall confess to, here and now when
my deathbed looms. I wish I could write this all in my own hand so that
for once, at least, the full tale will not be edited by those who lack the
courage to hear the truth. Instead I shall have to trust to my scribes' vows
and honesty, and in God, that in his mercy he will allow the truth to
come out. May Dewi Sant and Saint Issui intercede on my behalf one last
time.

No Brother Gervase, do not look so askance. You have no idea of
what I shall tell, so do not judge me yet. If other readers like it not, that is
for them to argue over with their confessors and their consciences. Mine
is clear. If you think I lie, well then, you may believe me condemned in
the afterlife if it comforts you. I, however, have no such doubts of what
lies ahead. This is the truth, as I swear to it by Almighty God, who has
seen all already and knows my fate better than me. I entrust my soul to
his care, and once that has fled my body, what happens to this frail shell
is of little consequence. If some wish to dance or even piss on my grave I
shall be past caring.

So, where to start? I know what you, my confessor Gervase, and any
other reader who later on digs this out of the dusty monastic scriptorium,
wants. You want to hear about him. About Robin Hood. It is nothing less
than I expected. After all, to all of you our stories are intertwined and his
is the legend – I only catch your interest for his sake. But I have a mind to
make you wait a little. We shall get to him soon enough! You must bear
with me and my story for a while yet. First you must hear about how it
all began, what happened to our family – oh yes I do say <u>our</u>, dear
Brother, for a connection is there – and what set us on the road to
unexpected infamy. Only then may you judge whether I deserve my
reputation – a reputation, I might add, which has only come about long
after the events happened, and from the mouths of those who were never
there.

Yet one point I must dispel before we start, for it irks me mightily. In
these latter days a foolish rumour has arisen that the great outlaw was
also a great earl. Some even hint that he was of noble Saxon lineage,
although surely even the most cloistered monk knows that no lords of the
former English retained such power and office by our day. No! A pox on
such nonsense! ˜Robin Hood˜ was never an earl! What need would such a
man have had for taking to the green-wood? Even in the days of my

youth those great men were never simply ˜Englishmen˜ any more than they are now when our French lands have been long lost. All the men of such rank and substance also held lands in Normandy, Brittany or Aquitaine, quite aside from their estates here. Even in more recent times when King John in his folly lost our lands across the water, they could still easily retreat to France by the simple expediency of swearing fealty to the French king when they fell foul of their English one – which many did over the years.

Or if they lived nearer the borders, then the Welsh princes and Scottish kings were also only too willing to welcome the enemies of their powerful neighbour – as my father witnessed and suffered for. Did not King Henry I move against Robert of Bellême, Earl of Shrewsbury – the son of Roger of Montgomery – for just such an alliance? In 1112, if you recall our not so distant past, after imprisoning the rebel earl, he seized not only Bellême's land on the Welsh border but also the family lands of Mortain in Normandy. And Mortain you should know of as staying in royal hands, since John was Count of Mortain long before he was king! If ˜Robin Hood˜ had been such a man, do you truly believe that even absent King Richard's hapless governors, let alone the more resident King John, would have left him to be dealt with by a mere local sheriff? No! That tale is utter nonsense!

And as for being the Earl of Huntingdon, ah me! Do not make me laugh, for it makes me wheeze these days. Have you no memory for such things? The true Earl of Huntingdon was brother to the king of Scotland, no less. Indeed, David of Huntingdon, with his brother King William of Scotland, and the king we never had – Richard and John's oldest brother, Prince Henry – took control of Huntingdon early in the great rebellion of 1173 to '74. Ah, I remember that well, being very disgruntled to be left behind when my not much older cousins went off to fight.

But you are distracting me already! Patience, Brother Gervase! Recollect what happened then, for it is all pertinent. King Henry II sent his army north and resoundingly defeated the lot of them, with King William of Scotland being sent to the leonine Henry at Northampton in chains. That is what happens to earls who defy kings! It took ten long years for Earl David to get his hands back on the Huntingdon estates, and then only after King William had bound himself to Henry and acknowledged his over-lordship of Scotland. Do you seriously think that even in his dotage Henry, or his lion of a son, Richard, would have stood back for a heartbeat while such a man defied their family again? And in nigh on the same shires, no less? For truth, no! And do not forget, our legend was well established long before John took the throne and had to deal with his rebellious earls. Robin Hood was not, nor ever could have been, this man or his heir. Besides which – just to throw you a bone to tease – I met and came to know David of Huntingdon, so I can tell you from personal experience that he was nothing like ˜Robin Hood˜ in looks or manners!

There, I have had my say on that matter. As for the rest, will you believe me? Or will you think I am simply lying to make myself seem a better man at this last stage of my life? This whole saga an aggrandisement of myself at his expense? Me, the dreaded Guy of Gisborne. Gisborne the jester stealing the king of Sherwood's crown in death, as I could not do in life? Or will your mind remain unclouded enough to read these words and sense the truth behind them? And will you recognise him when he first appears? Will you see him as I saw him, before the legend entwined itself around him? So I challenge you, my reader, now that I can no longer ride in the lists and take up challenges by right of arms. I challenge you with the point of my quill pen – ha, there is a pretty image! I challenge you to read this with an open mind. Only when a line has been drawn beneath the last words may you say Gisborne lies and is no better than you thought him.

So, dear brother, we will begin in earnest in the morning, and you may judge my unshriven soul for yourself.

Welbeck Abbey, Nottinghamshire, in the reign of Henry III.

A h, I dreamed such a dream last night, Gervase. It must have been your exhortations to tell all and tell the truth, for when I lay down in my bed my mind was all of a whirl. Either that or it is the effects of this dreadful ague I suffer, after the drenching in the cold and rain I received coming here! For you should know that while I am deeply grateful for the attentions of your infirmarer, I would not willingly have come back to stay in this where I lost so many of those whom I held dear. My intent was only to spend a single night near to Nottingham and then return north to my home. Indeed, had I not felt it incumbent upon me to honour the last wish of another of those cherished few, at my age I would not have made the long journey and be here now. The years weigh heavily on me in this familiar landscape, and already I feel that if I could just walk out of here and turn a corner, I would walk through an invisible veil and step back to those years of my prime. So as I scoured my memories in those last moments of wakefulness, here in this bed, they shifted into dreams which took me back all those years to when it began – before the legend wrapped itself around us, and, had we known it, when we were all standing on the brink of the greatest adventures of our lives.

In my dream I was riding like the wind through that Derbyshire vale, the winter landscape sharp and crisp around me, and down below me I could see the fight unfolding. Little John was facing Robin Hood with swords drawn, and there had clearly been an exchange of blades already. Then Robin went flying backwards as his heel caught on a fallen branch. His sword flew out of his hand and Little John closed on him, although I knew that John would never maim, much less kill, unless he had no other choice. Then a thrown knife from Will Scarlet's hand skittered along John's blade right by the guard and John dropped his sword too. I remember digging my spurs into my horse's side, determined to get there and stop this madness, and vaguely registering that there were other men surrounding the fight, all of them mounted. Up with me, two other horses were pounding alongside mine, and I recall their smell on the crisp winter air and the sound of their hooves breaking icy puddles as we plunged down the slope.

I recall thinking as we rode, and the freezing air blasted my face,

~There are three of us here with a boy, and three more of mine down there. Can we take six experienced fighters like them if it comes to a fight? Sweet Jesu, we have to! I have to take them. I cannot tell the sheriff I let so many well-armed ruffians go free to ravage as they pleased! ~

I saw Robin roll and come up with a knife from his belt in his hand and make a swipe at Little John. I remember thinking back then,

~By Our Lady, he means it! Blood will be spilled this day!~

And so it was in my dream, so vivid, so fresh!

Someone off to their side tried to dismount to join in the fight, and an arrow from one of my men stopped him in his tracks.

~Good for Thomas~ I heard one of my fellow riders give praise, and gave thanks myself for the range and power of the great wyche-elm longbows.

I saw Brother Tuck reach out and restrain one of the other strangers, but we were still too far off for me to see how successfully or not he was in holding on to the man. However I heard him call out in his strong Welsh voice,

~Stop! In the name of God, I command you, stop!~

And then I was shouting as loud as I could,

~Stop in the name of the sheriff of Nottingham!~

As a forester and a man of the sheriff, I had full authority there and intended to use it against these vagabonds. Whether that would be sufficient, or whether I would end up making an utter fool of myself, I had not the time to consider.

I rode up to this man I was to come to know as Robin Hood, standing there tall and dark, with a soldier's readiness to pounce, and looked into dark brown eyes as feral as a wolf's and every bit as dangerous. I heard another great bow sing and felt the thump of another long arrow hitting the ground nearby. Another warning shot no doubt, but I was not so foolish as to break my gaze upon this outlaw to turn and look. If I could not subdue him, then those arrows would soon be taking flight in anger!

~How dare you attack my men! ~ I snarled at him, and he stood his ground and stared back at me with insolent arrogance. He was not in awe of any sheriff's man then any more than later.

I recall Little John getting up and backing off from him but watching me warily too, as did the others in my party, all waiting for my signal to attack these sunburned strangers, who had the appearance of Templars even if they were acting like outlaws. Experienced fighters every one, they were the most dangerous men I had seen in years. Not since my time fighting the Welsh had I seen soldiers of this calibre.

˜I will not tolerate you marauding your way through this shire!˜ I threatened them, and hoped it would be enough, for I can still recall the feeling of my pulse racing and the blood singing in my veins, as it does when time seems to slow in that moment before chaos erupts, and when everything changes.

I see us all still, both in my dreams and now in my memories, frozen in time there amongst the trees like in some religious tableau. Me up on my big horse. Robin full of fire and fight on the ground before me. Little John standing a few paces off but no less ready for a fight, and Tuck on a shaggy carthorse trying to bring a calm to the situation and yet still ready to join in if things turned nasty. The four of us and the man you know of as Will Scarlet, plus others who would be part of the famous outlaw gang, all lined up as if for inspection by some unseen divine being who was still contemplating what to do with us all.

These dreams still come to me, Brother, and in them I cannot help but feel a higher guiding hand even if that thought scandalises you. Wise men have told me that dreams and visions are closely related, and that just as in the religious vision, a dream may illuminate the workings of the divine to mankind in a way we would not see in this real world. I do not claim saintliness for myself or those others, Brother, so you need not purse your lips so hard in disapproval. No, I am saying that in those dreams and in the memories they refresh for me, I now see a force outside of ourselves pushing us in ways we might not have gone of our own accord. I believe that Robin Hood, the legend, came to be because someone more than mere men decided that there <u>needed</u> to be someone like him. That greatness was thrust upon him and those around him, and that is why the tales have lingered so in the minds of folk who have never even been to Sherwood or Nottingham.

However, to return to my dream of last night, you need to hear much more of our earlier lives in order to see that divinely preordained confrontation in the same light as I do now. To see how we came to that point when Little John and Robin Hood were having their first encounter, and that it was a fight where one or other of them might have died if things had gone differently! You see? Such are the pivotal moments legends are made of! So let us begin while I still have breath to tell the tale.

Chapter 1

I shall not bother you with the tedious years of my early childhood.
There is nothing there which needs to be written down for posterity,
or warrants confessing, since those paltry confessions were wrung
out of me back when I was innocent and afeared of priests! Suffice it to
say that I was born at Alverton in Nottinghamshire in the year 1160, the
first and only surviving child of my parents, although my mother already
had a son, Audulph, by her first marriage, who lived with us. My mother
was the sister of Sir Fulk fitz Waryn's wife, and my father a distant
cousin of his, which was how come my half-brother and I grew up
playing with our cousins – fitz Waryn's sons, plus two others. There, you
see, Brother Gervase? An utterly unremarkable beginning! Do you want
to hear of how I climbed trees and skinned my knees? No, of course you
do not! So let us move to the first event which shaped my life in the
spring of my seventeenth year.

Oh come, Brother, do not heave such sighs. What? You thought we
would go straight into the tales of Robin Hood? No, that cannot be.

You want the truth of the great man and why, as you no doubt think
at this stage, I fought against someone who did such good? Oh, Brother it
was not like that, and I cannot fall straight into the telling of Robin's
daring deeds, for then you will still not understand my part.

Beware of the sin of pride!~

Of making too much of myself at this hour when my soul may be in
peril?

No, Brother, it is not pride which draws me back from the excitement
of the legend to my own life. Despite what you may think, I would not be
so arrogant with any confessor. I promised the truth and that is what you
will get, but to do that you must first learn who Robin was in his youth
too. Of what he was to me long before greatness enveloped him. If I do not
tell you now, then I shall have to stop in the middle of a thrilling tale
when you ask me how such and such a thing could be. Or how I could
know this thing, or that.

For at some point, for all this to make sense, you will have to know
how it all began. What our real relationship was founded upon, and
therefore how we could argue like cat and dog at times and yet still care
deeply about each other. For this is no simple tale of good against evil,
despite your monkish desire for such things. I was not wholly the wicked
villain of the plot and Robin no saint either, and yet I loved him like a
brother and him me. Ah, that has made you sit up and take note again!
Good! Now bear with me and listen as I take you through our early days,
for it will save much delay later on when you will be hanging onto my
every word with far more relish. That I promise, Brother! Does that
satisfy you? Good.

Now in the name of the blessed St Issui, let us get on before I die of old age with my story half told! Excitement aplenty waits us along the way, dear Brother – even enough for you! – and I promise devoutly that I shall not delay you unnecessarily.

The manor of Alverton in Nottinghamshire April, the year of our Lord 1177

"You're going *where?*"

The seven of them were standing at the grave of Fulk fitz Waryn senior where he had been laid to rest a month ago. The grass had yet to begin to grow over the mounded earth and its cross had only just been set into place. The young Sir Fulk was standing at the head of the grave, filled with a sense of his own importance. He was, after all, the lord of the manor now – even if that manor appeared to be rapidly disappearing out of the family hands. At the moment he was flanked by the second fitz Waryn son, Philip the Red, and Audulph de Braose, his cousin.

"You're going where?" Guy demanded again.

It was strange, he reflected, that although both he and Philip had been born in 1160, Philip – having been born in the January – had always been part of the older threesome. Whilst he, having been born in the May, had always spent his time with the younger members of the family. Yet even that wasn't quite accurate. For John stood beside them. Born in the July of 1159, a scant six months before Philip, he was the bastard son of old fitz Waryn, foisted on a reluctant family by the old man's strength of will. Despite that, Fulk and Philip had always made it clear that they thought John wasn't admissible to become one of their clique and so John, having appeared in their midst as a robust four year-old, had swiftly found life as the family cuckoo much more comfortable with the less judgmental youngsters.

Maybe that was because Audulph, too, had always thought himself above his half-brother, Guy. His father might have been the youngest child from a second marriage of someone who was already a younger son in a cadet branch – and therefore in line to inherit precisely nothing – but Audulph had the de Braose name, and to him that was everything. No matter that, when his mother had been widowed when he was but a babe in arms, he would have starved if it had been left to the de Braoses to find them a home. Guy's father, Giles of Maesbury, as a mere knight in service to the fitz Waryns despite being old Fulk's cousin, was – in Audulph's eyes – an altogether less worthy man, even if he had put a roof over Audulph's head, and fed and educated him.

The others present were Baldwin de Hodenet – the fitz Waryns' other cousin on their mother's side, and therefore also Guy and Audulph's – and Allan fitz Waryn. At twelve heading for thirteen in a couple of months, Allan was definitely the baby of the group, but Guy, Baldwin and John tolerated him in a way the three others never would. And now Guy was beginning to have some very dark suspicions. Occasionally he had heard rumours that Allan was in fact Lady fitz Waryn's bastard – her son by a brief affair which the old man had consented to keep hushed up in order to protect the family name. Now, like John, Allan had been excluded from the reading of old Fulk's will – a reading which Hawyse fitz Waryn had emerged from even more pale and drawn than when she had entered the closed room. Moreover, a reading since which there had been a marked change in attitude towards Allan by Fulk and Philip.

The miserable old bastard's cut Allan out of his will! thought Guy savagely now. *Would it have been so hard to throw the lad some crumb from the table? Fulk and Philip could still have had the lion's share.* For Fulk had just made an announcement. He, Philip and Audulph would be leaving to find their fortunes elsewhere.

"Where did you say you were going?" pressed Baldwin.

"To join the Earl of Chester," declared Philip loftily for his brother. "He must surely be recruiting now that he's been released from prison by the king. There'll be plenty of opportunities for young men of good families."

"*Why* are you going, though?" a bemused John was asking before Philip had barely finished. "You have estates right here! You should be looking after them, not gallivanting about in foreign parts!"

"Don't you dare tell me what to do, John!" snarled Philip, and Baldwin and Guy sighed and exchanged glances. With Philip it was always a touchy matter that John was the older of the two, regardless of issues of legitimacy. It made it grimly inevitable that he would take offence at everything John said, even when none was intended.

"But John's right," Baldwin said hurriedly before a fight could start. "What's happening about the family estates?"

"Oh, the family estates!" Fulk pronounced with withering sarcasm. "And with what would you propose we *pay* King Henry to allow us to keep them?"

"Pay? They're yours by right!" Baldwin protested. "You shouldn't have to *pay* anything!"

Before Fulk's notoriously short temper could explode, along with Philip's, Guy steeled himself and cut across them all. "The King needs money. That's it, isn't it, Fulk? You've not yet reached the point where you're considered useful enough as a baron in these parts, because you're not even twenty yet."

Fulk clapped his hands slowly. "Oh well done! Clever Guy, as ever! Yes, my dim little cousins! That's precisely it. Our beloved king is selling the estate to the baron with the deepest purse."

Guy and Baldwin exchanged weary glances again. Fulk always tried to make out that he, Philip and Audulph were seasoned warriors, and it didn't go down well that Guy had latched onto the problem so accurately. Three years ago, in the July of 1174, the senior trio had gone as part of the levy of men who had defended the realm against the Scots in King Henry's absence. Granted they had seen real fighting, but with Fulk and Audulph only sixteen (even if Fulk had been only a week or two off his seventeenth birthday), and with Philip a mere fourteen-and-a-half, they had been very much the young squires and not the knights at the forefront of things. Not that anyone would have known that to hear them talk of it. So Guy knew that being dismissed as youngsters a full three years further on must have rankled terribly. Maybe that was why Fulk was so angry, but it didn't excuse the way he was speaking to them at the moment.

"But what of your mother?" Baldwin asked anxiously as John cried,

"Lady Hawyse? What will become of her?"

"Kirklees Abbey," declared Fulk flatly, with as much detachment as if he had been deciding which cow to slaughter for the winter.

You cold-hearted bastard! Guy fumed inwardly. *She's your mother, for God's sake! By Our Lady, I hope you live to regret this day! She's not responsible for the slight against you any more than we are. And I dare say that will mean Mother will be going there too – she can hardly hope for a new lord to look after a widow of no consequence.* And 'cousins'? That had to mean that Fulk and Philip no longer recognised Allan as their full brother. Allan still had a claim to be the cousin of the two older fitz Waryns, as well as his and Baldwin's, because their mothers had all been sisters and nothing could change that, but this smacked of a distancing with regard to Fulk senior as the father. Subconsciously Guy reached out and drew the younger lad to him.

"What of the rest of us, then?" he forced himself to ask calmly, even though he dreaded what the answer might be. "If the estate's to be sold, and Lady Hawyse consigned to a nunnery, where will the rest of us go? What of Audulph's mother, of Lady Alice?" He was careful to put his mother in that context and distanced from himself, knowing that it might be the only way he'd get any information.

For the first time Fulk had the grace to look uncomfortable, although it was Guy's half-brother Audulph who blushed scarlet with the shame of what was to come.

"Your mother has elected to follow her sister to Kirklees. Baldwin will be returned to his father. There's hardly anyone who could continue to foster him here now. You, Guy, will go to serve the fitz Alans at Clun. As hereditary Sheriffs of Shropshire they're our best chance of getting the family lands back. John will serve as a household man to whoever takes on this estate. We could hardly ask for more for him from anyone else and we can hardly take him to Chester! Even you must have the wit to see that! The same will go for Allan since he's too young to be capable of offering any real service to a lord. If whoever that turns out to be doesn't want them, then it will be up to my lord Giendara to decide what happens to them."

A stunned silence greeted his pronouncement. Guy thought he'd never seen Audulph look so miserable, but Philip was standing boldly with a sneer of satisfaction on his face. *So you think you've had your revenge on us,* Guy realised with a flash of insight. *All these years it's galled you to be with those of us you see as lesser cousins, half-brothers and bastards, and now you think you're free of us. You think you've risen above us at last. God rot you, you've not given a moment's thought for what this will mean to any of us! Baldwin and I will no doubt cope. But what of poor John?* John's mother had been married to one of the Peverels; but given that the leader of that house had fled England twenty years ago having supposedly poisoned the previous earl of Chester, young John Peverel (for he had an official name if only to save the old man's face) would have been in serious danger going to the heart of the Chester lands. Guy didn't dispute that. It was the lack of concern which he found unforgivable. *What if the new lord doesn't want a household man? What if he brings his own men with him? Where will John go then?*

And what of Allan? he thought. *There'll be no fostering to a family we're friends with, the way old fitz Waryn sent you three to Baldwin's father after you came back from the north. And he won't be able to come home for the winter when his service is done for the season as you all did, either! That's a luxury Allan's never going to have now you've robbed him of anywhere to call home, whatever happens. May God forgive you, Fulk, because I can't at the moment! Sheriff Giendara is a vicious, murdering pig who'll no more think of the results of his actions than you have. You've condemned them both to the life of lackeys, dependent on a lord's whim! Worse than the lowest peasant!*

The fate of his two cousins choked Guy more than anything for himself. Far more than the fact that he realised he was being used to help pay off the family's debts of service, incurred even before he was born. John was a kind soul, and Allan had always been a sensitive boy, more given to spending time with a quill or lute in his hands than the sword and lance. Guy had only seen the new sheriff of Nottingham once when he was on his way in to claim his post a month ago, but Serio de Giendara had looked more like a hardened mercenary than a man of culture. And Giendara didn't even sound like a Norman name! So God alone knew where he'd originally come from and where King Henry had found him.

Certainly some horrific stories were already creeping out of the castle of the new sheriff's heavy-handed attitude to all around him. One former soldier who had served with fitz Waryn had turned up two weeks ago to beg help from him, only to find it was too late and fitz Waryn being wrapped in his winding sheets. But Lady Alice had dressed the man's appalling lash wounds with Guy's help, and had given him food and money to help him on his way. The memory of the soldier's lacerated and festering back – and all for a dropped sheriff's sword! – wouldn't leave Guy's mind now it had been connected with John and Allan being in the same sheriff's hands.

"You're selling them off like slaves," an appalled Baldwin finally found the voice to protest.

"I'm dealing with them as their lord and master," Fulk responded nastily. "If I don't have the estate, I don't have the responsibility to any of you either. ...So think yourselves lucky that I've made these enquiries on your behalves! Philip and I could have walked away and done nothing. We could, you know! So consider that before you're so quick to complain."

John edged closer to Guy and Baldwin and whispered softly, "Sounds more like Fulk's trying to convince himself, if you ask me."

Baldwin sniffed derisively. "Phaa! 'Could have done nothing'," he mimicked Fulk softly. "He hasn't done anything! He's just turning his back!"

By now the three would-be knights had turned on their heels and were walking back towards the manor house, although Audulph trailed behind the other two with his head hung low.

"Your brother doesn't seem overjoyed at the prospect," John added to Guy.

"Too easily led by half," Guy observed dryly as Baldwin too came to embrace Allan. "Audulph's a decent chap but we might as well wait for Hell to freeze than expect him to face Fulk and tell him he's wrong."

The full impact of what had been said had begun to sink in on Allan and the youngster's eyes were filling with tears. "What did I do wrong?" he whimpered to the three who remained with him. "Why are they leaving me behind? Why do Fulk and Philip hate me now?"

John, Guy and Baldwin exchanged glances over Allan's head. How could they tell the lad that his older brothers had probably never loved him much in the first place? As John now pulled the sobbing boy fully into his embrace to comfort him, Baldwin and Guy stepped to one side.

"What are we going to do?" Baldwin fretted. He didn't need to say what he meant, for his eyes had never strayed from John and Allan.

Guy sighed and scrubbed his hands through his thick dark hair. "By Our Lady, what a mess! It would help no end if we knew who was interested in the estate. A good lord might mean it's not such a bad fate for those two..."

"...But a bad one?"

"Aye! There's the rub!"

"The good thing is that it's a small estate," Baldwin said, desperately trying to find some positive note. "It's not the kind of place an ambitious man might want, ...is it?"

"No, not an ambitious one. But the sheriff might want it for one of his men – maybe some foreign fellow countryman – which is a ghastly thought! Blessed Virgin protect us from two such as him in the neighbourhood! ...Oh Lord, Baldwin, all I can think of doing is to start asking as soon as we get into our allotted roles. See if there's anyone who looks like they might be kind-hearted enough to take one or the other of those two in, so that at least they'd each be with one of us."

Baldwin nodded and they stood in silence for a moment, the only sounds being Allan's stifled sobs coming from the front of John's jerkin.

"At least we're going home," Baldwin said eventually with his best effort at a smile.

"*Humph*! The Welsh borders are hardly my home as they're yours!" Guy snorted disgustedly.

The fitz Waryn family had had an illustrious start to their life in England when they'd arrived in the wake of William the Conqueror. The family founder had built Oswestry Castle on the Welsh borders and handed it down, but the main line had faltered and Oswestry had passed to the fitz Alans, leaving the fitz Waryns with the lesser holding of Whittington Castle as the fitz Alans' tenants. Not that it was a mean place to have. There had been enough land for Guy's predecessors in their turn to hold the goodly manor of Maesbury from the fitz Waryns, as had many similar lesser knights with the other manors in the fitz Waryns' care.

Yet as ever the problem was the Welsh. In 1148 the men of Powys under their lord, Madoc ap Meredudd, had seized Oswestry and the surrounding area, forcing all the families to flee. By the end of the 1160s King Henry had forced the Welsh back enough to be able to re-fortify Oswestry. But life in the Marches was always precarious and Henry wanted his own men out there instead of hereditary lords, who tended to try to build their own empires at his expense. That meant that the elder Fulk had pleaded and protested for his lands to be returned to him all to no effect. Currently the fitz Waryns still languished in the Nottinghamshire manor they had been allowed to hold as supposedly temporary compensation, and now it looked as if they were even going to lose that.

As for the other side of Guy's family, Audulph's father had held Meole Brace Tower, on the opposite bank of the River Severn to Shrewsbury, as castellan on behalf of the senior branch of the de Braose family – when the Welsh allowed. Yet it was no place for his widowed mother to hold alone, and she (if not her son) had been glad of the offer of marriage and a home in Nottinghamshire, away from constant danger, with the dispossessed knight from Maesbury. And Nottinghamshire had been where Guy had subsequently been born after his mother had married Giles of Maesbury in the little church down the road in Kilvington.

Whereas in Baldwin's case, his family still had their modest castle of Hodenet closer to the Cheshire border with Shropshire. Yet they were hardly leading members of Marcher society, and there had been a limit as to whom they could ask to foster their third, and by far the youngest, son. Their fitz Waryn former neighbours, and relatives by marriage – by virtue of Matilda de Hodenet being the youngest sister of Hawyse fitz Waryn – had been the clear choice for Baldwin. More recently Fulk and Philip, along with Audulph, had gone to Hodenet in the summer months in return, to help provide the knights' service due to the sheriff for patrolling the border alongside Baldwin's older brothers.

Yet like Guy, Fulk and Philip, along with John and Allan, had all been born in Nottinghamshire within the time of the extended family's exile from their estates. Even Audulph had been little more than a toddler when he'd left the Marches. Only Baldwin of all of them had spent enough time in the Marches to have any memory of what he was going back to.

"I dare say my father will be glad to have me back now that I'm big enough to fight," Baldwin said more with hope than a real expectation of it happening. He knew it was more likely that his father would be appalled at having another mouth to feed for the whole year again. When Fulk, Philip and Audulph had been there during the last two summers, they'd spent most of their time following in the wake of the sheriff's knights, not residing at Hodenet. But having had his fifteenth birthday only last week, Baldwin was still too young to be of much use to the sheriff. And it was hardly as though his father was lacking in heirs. For such a small manor finding a living for even a second son would not be easy. So as the third son, and coming from Brian de Hodenet's second marriage when the heirs from the first were already men looking out for their own interests, Baldwin's prospects had always been limited.

"Ah, you never know," Guy tried to stay positive even though he worried that Baldwin's reception might be frostier than his cousin was making out. "You might end up at Clun with me!"

"That would be good," Baldwin sighed wishfully. "But it still doesn't help us over John or Allan, does it?"

Meanwhile John was gesturing them to follow as he turned back towards the manor. "Come on!" he called. "We're going to get the horses!"

"Where are we going?" Guy called as he and Baldwin jogged to catch up.

"Out of here for a start!" John replied bitterly.

The four of them saddled their horses and, with two vegetable pies commandeered from the manor's kitchen, rode out. Even in the brief time they spent in the building, Lady Hawyse's sobs followed them wherever they went, and, however much they wished they could do something for her, their helplessness in the face of this crisis made listening to her grief too much for them. Once, Guy heard his mother's voice trying to console her distraught sister, doing as she always did and making the best of a rotten situation. He had a sneaking suspicion that she, at least, would find the quiet life in a convent a blessed relief. The prospect of living on someone else's charity as a widow yet again was bleak – a life of constantly walking on eggshells – and in private she had already told him that she was contemplating such a move. She didn't like the way Audulph was turning out, but without a way to extract him from Philip and Fulk's company there was nothing she could do or say.

"Promise me you won't follow them too," she had begged Guy. He would have only gone somewhere with those two under obligation and duress from old fitz Waryn, he'd told her. Well at least Lady Alice should be happy about that, he thought with a smile, since there was no earthly possibility that he could now be pressurised by the old man, nor of young Fulk taking him willingly. She certainly sounded calm enough despite the events of the day so far. Thanks be to God, then, that he didn't have the care of his mother to worry about as well as that of John and Allan!

Later that afternoon found them sitting on the bank of the wandering River Smite, which drained into the Trent to the north at Newark, sharing the pies and watching the water drift by them. Alverton sat on a small rise in the flat lands, bound on the west side by the Smite and by the even smaller Devon on the east, but down here by the river they were in a flat land of high rushes, and even their ponies would be out of sight except from the river itself. A sudden burst of warm spring weather meant that they were basking in sunshine and with not even a whisper of a breeze to disturb the burgeoning vegetation. High overhead a goose flew past, searching for the rest of its flock, and somewhere off in the reeds an amorous drake was pursuing females and challenging a rival, but apart from their noisy quacking there wasn't a sound to be heard besides the ponies' enthusiastic champing on the fresh waterside grass.

Allan took another bite of pie and with less enthusiasm sighed mournfully. "It's all beans in here, isn't it," he complained.

Of all of them Allan really loathed the re-hydrated dried beans and peas with which the pies were filled. Despite it being April this was the lean time for the manor's supplies, as it was for everyone. The fields might be burgeoning with new growth, but it would be several weeks yet before anything really started to crop well. In the meantime, they were living off the last of what had been put down to get the manorial household through the winter, which meant a lot of salted meat and dried vegetables. The only consolation was that, with the large flocks of sheep penned close to the manor for the safety of the lambs, there was plenty of fresh sheep's milk cheese available, and even some of last year's hard sheep's cheese. Luckily their cook was good at using it with seasoning to make what she could of the limited variety she had to use in the way of staples.

"Here you go, Allan," John said, fishing a lump of melted cheese out of his own half-pie with a piece of pastry, "you have that."

He handed the piece to Allan who brightened immediately, prompting the others to break open their own remaining portions and find similar lumps. With John coming up eighteen, Guy a few weeks from his seventeenth birthday, and Baldwin still older than Allan by two years, the youngster tended to get indulged by them when no-one else was around to protest. And after this morning's proceedings they were all anxious to do anything they could to cheer him up. Clearly worn out by the emotional turmoil, once full, Allan was soon fast asleep in the warmth of the sun, and the others edged away a little to talk.

"What I don't understand is why they're being so foul to Allan," Baldwin whispered in bemusement to Guy and John. "I mean, I can just about see how in Fulk's twisted mind you aren't worth bothering about, John. You're a reminder of his father's fall from grace, and Fulk always did idolise the old man. But Allan's his *brother!*"

"No he isn't," John said softly, his voice heavy with sorrow.

"What?" Baldwin gasped only to be shushed by Guy before he woke Allan.

John shook his head despairingly. "You're too young to remember, Baldwin, but Guy does, don't you?" Guy nodded tensely. "When I came here I was brought by the man I thought was my father. Old fitz Waryn was away at the time. By Our Lady, I remember it well, even though I was only a small lad myself. He dragged me into the solar where Lady Hawyse was sitting and said she could have her husband's by-blow. That he wasn't going to bring up some bastard forced on his wife by another man when he had enough mouths to feed already. There was a lot of shouting and then Lady Hawyse slapped him, and then he dragged her to the couch. Well nine months later Allan appeared, and even old Fulk could do the counting on that one! Especially when he'd already been gone for four months and didn't come back for another three. Luckily for Lady Hawyse, the servants told Fulk they'd pulled my 'father' off her, and they all backed up her story."

"What happened then?" Baldwin was agog. This was all news to him.

"There was a duel," Guy told him. "I don't remember Lady Hawyse's assault, but I do remember John suddenly being there with us, and then Mother and Aunt Hawyse telling us that he had to stay now because his 'father' was dead."

"Why did old Fulk accept that?" Baldwin was still puzzled. "He was never one to let an insult go!"

John gave a soft bitter laugh. "For once he had no choice! If he'd sent me back he would've had to do some explaining – especially given that my lady Peverel was like to scream to the sheriff fit to wake the dead if I'd reappeared at her door once more. She already had much sympathy as the wronged widow, so with the possibility of her as a neighbouring noble lady accusing fitz Waryn of rape, and pointing to my clear resemblance to old fitz Waryn as proof, it was a very dangerous position for him to be in! After all, she was no mere serving wench he could tup at will! And he would've also had to admit that his own wife had had a child by another man to explain his excessively vengeful actions, if anyone started taking too great an interest – a man who was then suspiciously and conveniently dead, as a result, and whose widow was unlikely to keep quiet.

"Come on, you knew old fitz Waryn! Accepting me was nothing. He could have shoved me off into service somewhere and never looked back – probably still intended to in a year or so's time, even if he hasn't done it before now. But what stuck in his craw was having Allan fathered by another under his own roof. That was an insult he would never let go! *That's* why he fought the duel and killed Sir Edmund, not over his wife's supposed rape, or me. Well the old sheriff used to take a dim view of men taking the law into their own hands, Baldwin, and while he'd turn a blind eye sometimes, it was only when something could be quietly swept into a dark corner and forgotten about. And this one wasn't about to go quietly unless old Fulk accepted me to make it seem as though Sir Edmund challenged him, and with a false accusation, not the other way round. But he never did love Allan as he did Fulk and Philip.

"You see, what my 'father' said on that afternoon in the solar was that his wife couldn't bear to have me around anymore because I reminded her of what Fulk had done. I think that was so, because she was never kind to me, but I think the unbearable insult was more on Sir Edmund's part. But even that's not quite the full story," John astonished both of them by adding. "Oh they said Lady Hawyse was raped, but I was there. As a child I didn't understand what I was seeing, but I do now! Sir Edmund didn't rape her, they'd been lovers before – and I'm sure part of the rub for him was his *own* guilt at knowing that he'd provoked someone as brutal as old Fulk. It was *their* affair five years before then which had prompted old Fulk to storm in and rape Lady Peverel in a vicious act of revenge. He'd found out he'd been cuckolded by his wife and Sir Edmund before I was even born!

"So the final insult was having his revenge rebound, and finding me brought to his doorstep and then Allan appearing – or at least the bump in Lady Hawyse's middle which would become Allan! It meant back then that Fulk was beside himself with rage, because he saw himself as the wounded party – and twice over! – not the other way round. He'd acted to take his revenge for them making a fool of him the first time, by raping my mother. And then Lady Hawyse went and did it again! By then he wasn't even sure that Philip was his. That's why he fought and killed Sir Edmund! The trouble was, he couldn't very well tell the sheriff that not only was his wife unfaithful twice or maybe more, but that he didn't even know if his heirs were really his. 'Big' men like him don't like to appear fools in public! Of course, as Philip grew up with all that flame-red hair, and with his height and build he couldn't be anyone else's but Fulk's, but by then it was all a bit too late."

Baldwin, eyes wide in astonishment, began nodding. "Of course! Even though our Fulk isn't as flame-haired as Philip and the old man, there's still a lot of red in his colouring, and he's big too, like old Fulk."

Guy was nodding now as well. "And you've inherited the fitz Waryn build, John, but you're jet black. Is that your mother's colouring?" Lady Peverel had been dead for many years by now, having only lasted a year after her husband's death, and Guy couldn't remember her at all.

"As far as I can remember, yes. But Sir Edmund, Allan's natural father – and my supposed father to most of the outside world – was a smaller, fair-haired man, and with Lady Hawyse being petite too, you can see why Allan's on the short side for his age. The old bastard must've written it all down in his will, and yesterday when that got read was when Fulk and Philip knew for sure what had happened. No doubt old Fulk couldn't face the shame when he was alive, but once he was dead and past caring he must've been determined that Lady Hawyse would pay. He had nothing to lose sending her to a nunnery once he was gone. And the way King Henry's behaved these last years must have made him see that the estate would never pass intact to young Fulk, if he inherited before he'd proved himself, so why not have his revenge?"

"And now his sons are doing the dirty work for him," Guy added bitterly. "Damn them, can they not see that it's not Allan's fault? If I were in their place I might be angry with my mother, but not with the little brother who'd had no say in the matter."

John smiled weakly and patted Guy on the shoulder. "Aye, but you're a different person to them, Guy. But now you'll understand why I've made my decision." He took a deep breath. "Tomorrow morning I'm going to take Allan and we're going to ride to Southwell."

"Southwell?" Baldwin was now completely confused. "Why Southwell?"

"Because there's the Minster there," John explained gently. "Look, someone has to be able to look after Allan. You and Guy can't because you're being sent away. Let's face it, Baldwin, you aren't any too sure of your own reception! You can hardly turn up with Allan in tow as well. And you, Guy, you're being used to pay off some of the family obligations by being sent to the fitz Alans. They'll have no use for a boy who's barely coming up thirteen in a Marcher castle – they've enough of their home-grown scullions and the like without another one – so he's too young to do military service, and too poorly connected to warrant the expense of training. I presume you are going?"

Guy nodded grimly. "What else can I do? I daren't refuse in case they block Mother going to Kirklees with Lady Hawyse. It's what she's secretly wanted for years now, and I can survive roughing it, but Mother can't. I daren't risk her being made homeless and with her reputation ruined by one of Fulk's nasty rumours."

John nodded. "He'd do it too, curse him, if he thinks he's been spited. That's why I want Allan and me well out of the way as fast as possible, before Fulk and Philip have the chance to cook up some new way of humbling us even further. So I'm going to take him with me to the monks at Southwell. They've got that huge new church and the endowments to go with it. They must need laymen to work for them. It's not a nobleman's occupation, but now neither Allan nor I can expect anything of that sort. What's important is that there's always plenty of food there, because the surrounding land is good – so we won't starve! And if the accommodation isn't luxurious at least we'll have a roof over our heads. We'll be out of the elements in the winter in a good stone building, or at least a solidly built wooden hall, not huddled in some leaky hovel of a lean-to by a peasant's cattle pen which the lord can't be bothered to have repaired. The work the king wants done at Nottingham Castle is still under way, don't forget. If we stay here, the likes of Allan and me will most likely end up breaking stone and hauling mortar for the masons. We won't get anything better! And I for one don't want to die in the next year or so, falling to my death when some rickety bit of scaffold gives way under the weight of me and the load I'm lugging."

Guy sighed. "Oh Lord, I'd forgotten the king's building work. The new outer walls and keep might be more or less finished but there's lots still going on. ...Oh, Mother of God, I forgot! The king is coming to Nottingham later in the summer, isn't he? Oh, Heavens, in that case Giendara will be flogging the workers day and night to have the work finished. Of course, you're right John. That's where you two would end up – especially with you being strong! You'd be hauling rocks all day! And it's not only you who would end up falling to his death. With Allan being so little they'd be bound to put him up working on the roofs because he's light, and we all know how clumsy he is at the moment! He wouldn't last the month!"

He squared his shoulders. "Very well, we'll come that far with you. It'll add more weight to your request to be taken in if we come along. We'll tell the prior that it was Baldwin's father who died, not Sir Fulk, and that he and I are going to his uncle rather than to his father. We can say that a small house over here is being sold, and that we need to find a position for our two household men. If we pass you two off as yeomen to start off with, if Fulk and Philip do start looking for you they'll be thrown off the scent. They'd never ever let go of their names so they won't even begin to think that you would."

"But that's lying, and to monks!" Baldwin protested. "And why would Fulk and Philip look for them? We've just said they don't care about John and Allan."

John shook his head. "Ah Baldwin, better to tell a few small lies to the monks than end up dead. And as for Fulk and Philip, no they don't care. But there's a difference between not caring and seeing a way of getting money! With no-one to stand up for us except you two, once you're gone what's to stop Fulk saying we were really his serfs? There aren't that many men left of such low status these days, I know, but even as lowly peasants we'd be at his mercy to do with as he fancied. If the sheriff is willing to pay for men to work on the castle to earn favour with King Henry, then we'd be foolish not to expect Fulk to see us as a way of getting cash, if not favour for himself."

It was the sad truth that Alverton was a small estate of the kind which few people but its immediate neighbours took any notice of. The kind hundreds of which could be found the length and breadth of England, and with no outstanding features. All four lads knew that if Sheriff Giendara questioned any of the local worthies as to who lived at Alverton, beside Fulk and his heirs, no-one would have a clue as to who the rest of them were, or be in any position to contradict Fulk and Philip's version of the truth.

However that also worked in the lads' favour, and Guy and John could see the reality that if they said the name of Alverton to the prior at Southwell it was unlikely to mean anything to him. Oh, he might have heard that the lord of such a place had recently died, but given that any death duties in the form of burial fees and the like would go to the great church at Newark, he would probably have dismissed it from his thoughts already. Alverton manor house itself was a good sized house built of stone, and had commodious stables and outbuildings around it, but that didn't make it a noteworthy estate. Therefore their deception had a good chance of succeeding.

So the next morning, while everyone else was barely getting up, the four of them rode out with packed bags. Guy and Baldwin had decided that they would ride straight on for the Welsh Borders once they'd left John and Allan behind. Neither of them trusted themselves to face Fulk and Philip and lie convincingly, and the thought of facing Lady Hawyse was too much to even think about once she knew her beloved Allan was gone – for in stark contrast to Fulk senior's disdain towards him, Allan had always been her favourite son by far. Guy simply left a message for his mother to say that he'd gone with all speed to avoid Fulk changing his mind. He knew she'd understand what he meant. They also only took the shaggy work ponies usually used for baggage hauling – the last thing they wanted to do was provoke a chase set up by Fulk by claiming they'd stolen valuable horses, even though one of the best in the fitz Waryn stable was Baldwin's by right. Hopefully they'd view one well-bred palfrey a fair exchange for four shaggy ponies.

By mid afternoon they were riding up to the great Minster church at Southwell.

"Look at the size of it!" Baldwin gasped.

The honey-coloured stone glowed warmly in the spring sunshine, and, seeing how much money must have been spent to create the elaborately carved corbel table around the roof alone, for the first time Guy fully began to believe that John was right. Taking their mounts round to the stables they requested an audience with someone senior and were soon talking to the prior. As a man of some standing, given the eminence of the foundation, he was haughty but not unkind. The two youngest left the talking to John and Guy, not only because as the oldest they would be seen to be the ones having authority, but also because they would carry the lie off best. Baldwin was hopeless at telling untruths, his deception was always written all over his face. So he allowed his genuine distress at parting from John, Guy and Allan full rein, and Guy covered it with an explanation of him still grieving for his 'dead father'.

To everyone's relief John and Allan were found a place, although it was to be as shepherds on a distant grange rather than in the Minster complex.

"Will you be able to carry it off?" Guy asked John softly as they shared a final meal together in the poorer end of the monastic guest quarters. "You two are hardly experienced stockmen and you'll be alone up there for days on end. Will you cope if a sheep gets sick?"

"By Our Lady, I hope so!" John whispered back fervently. "At least I helped out with lambing and stuff back home. Allan will just have to learn quickly!"

In the last of the evening light they walked around the outside of the church and admired the carvings while the monks were at prayers. The great arches of the doorways were the most elaborate, with fanciful faces biting the rolled edges of the layered arcs of decoration on the main door. Heads which looked as though they belonged to some kind of mythical big cat vied with strange beaked creatures, which were neither bird nor beast, to glower ferociously down on them.

"God's wounds! The man who did this had some imagination!" John breathed as he stood with his head thrown back looking up at the faces staring down at him.

"They aren't real are they?" Allan asked worriedly. "I mean, not *them*. I know they're only carvings. But they're not taken from some real creature's likeness are they?"

"I hope not, Allan. I do surely hope not!" Baldwin answered with a watery smile. Given that he was the most recent addition to the extended family, strangely he was finding it even harder than Guy or John to reconcile himself to its break-up. Maybe because he'd never had brothers the same age as himself but far older, he'd formed a particularly strong bond with Allan, and it was tearing him apart now.

Nor was it any easier come the morning, even though they'd tried to say their real goodbyes in private the night before.

"Write to us," pleaded Allan.

"We will," Guy promised.

"We won't forget you," Baldwin choked out, then found some inner strength from somewhere. "When I come into my inheritance I shall send for you! We'll be together again! You'll be my loyal fighting men and we won't be separated by any lord or master ever again!"

"Promise?" Allan whispered, clutching John's hand tightly as if he feared he too might suddenly disappear.

"Promise!" Baldwin replied firmly and Guy nodded his assent too, even though he could see that John, like him, doubted that would ever be possible.

We parted company, Baldwin and I, at Bridgnorth. It was the farthest we could go in company, for had I ridden on with him to Hodenet, I would have had a much longer journey alone and going through some very wild territory. As a lone English rider I would have been easy prey for Welsh raiding parties. So he turned north for his home, and I rode on west for Clun, keeping very much on the English side of the border for now. I had left behind the patch-worked countryside of neat fields and tidy hedges, of big trees and big skies, and had come to something far wilder, and potentially more dangerous, where there were places for lawless men to hide in the folds of the land.

The day I caught my first sight of Clun Castle was a day of strange lights. Steel grey clouds hung in a flat blanket low across the sky, occasionally brushing the tops of the ridges which surrounded Clun, yet there was an eerie yellow glow about the valley speaking of hidden sunlight. I remember that day clearly, Brother, because it was my first glimpse of a far wilder countryside than any I had seen so far. It seemed pagan and feral to my young, impressionable mind. A place where anything might happen. After all, as boys we had all listened with bated breath to the travelling jongleurs and minstrels singing of green knights or men – invincible lords of wild woods and hills such as these – who would exact a high price from any traveller wandering into their demesne. At the age of seven or eight it had been thrilling to listen to a knight risking beheading at such unearthly hands, now ten years later and faced with a reality which bore an uncanny resemblance to my youthful imaginings, excitement was not quite the word I would have used to describe my state of mind!

I had been following the thickly wooded slopes of the Long Mynd to get here, but they had only been on one side of the road, leaving more scattered woodland and open skies on my left. Now, however, I was enclosed in a land of rich, deep greens, and with a soft moistness in the air which was not quite rain, but still had me soaked to the skin. So I arrived at Clun looking more the drowned rat than a promising young knight. The weather somewhat suited the circumstances too, for now, Brother, I learned of the depths of my cousins' disinterest in me. No-one at Clun was expecting me! Fulk and Philip – not to mention Audulph – had failed to tell me that the William fitz Alan to whom old Fulk had been beholden was already long dead. Indeed the old man had died around the time I was born! The current leading member of the fitz Alan family was another William, but barely a year or so older than me. They could not have been unaware of this, having travelled this way in company and having met the acting sheriff, and were no doubt currently laughing snidely at my imagined discomfort – I was not.

In young fitz Alan's stead a man called Guy le Strange was handling the affairs of the family, and in particular was acting as sheriff until such time as young William would come of age and take charge. As precarious circumstance went, things could hardly have got much worse, and I confess that I felt very sorry for myself. Baldwin might not be welcomed home with much enthusiasm, but he would not be turned out, while John and Allan had taken a drastic reduction in their circumstances but at least had a roof over their heads. I, on the other hand, was in serious danger of being turned out into the wilds, lord-less and homeless, and with few skills to recommend me to anyone to take me in.

Mercifully, the lesser men were more kindly inclined than a great lord might have been. Down at an alehouse in the village which nestled at the feet of the castle's great earthworks, I was given some advice that night by a couple of fatherly men who took pity on me. Guy le Strange was absent at the moment, which they now told me was a good thing since it would allow me to present myself to him in a very different guise to that which I had intended. The vast Honour of Clun was no mean border lord's manor, and they had great need of ordinary men as well as knights. The pair advised me to meet them at the gatehouse again the next morning, and I would be taken in to meet the man in charge of the huntsmen, and the other men who did all of the multitude of tasks which kept such a large place working besides the soldiering.

They counselled me not to even try to play upon my noble birth, given how low down the order of knights my father had been. Le Strange had knights aplenty, they told me, especially young men with little experience of doing exactly what I had anticipated my tasks would be; that of fulfilling their family's obligations to send someone – anyone – however useless that lad might be in reality. I would be turned away in a heartbeat, I was told, given that le Strange had no knowledge of the fitz Waryn ancient obligation, and therefore had no need to honour his part in it. Particularly as I did not even possess my own hauberk of linked chain, much less all the other accoutrements of a young knight, such as a trained war horse – for a work pony was no substitute for a well-bred day-to-day palfrey, let alone a fully trained destrier fit for war! And no-one knew what changes the young Sir William might soon want to make to put his seal upon his newly acquired lordship to make it more his own. Much better, and safer, to allow myself to be taken on by the household's seneschal, and simply be registered as a new addition to the household.

A more arrogant young man than I might have scorned to stoop to a lower station, but I had sufficient common sense to see that it was this or starve, and I accepted their offer if not with great enthusiasm then at least with heartfelt thanks. I also tell you all this for good reason, Brother, for it was a salutary awakening for me. I had so far lived the privileged life of any well-born young man of Norman lineage, and as such I had never really taken any notice of those beneath me. Oh, I knew full well how far below the salt my family sat at the grander gatherings, but how my life compared to those of men who were not nobly born was a matter which had never entered my young head.

Indeed, when the four of us rode out of Alverton that fateful morning, I doubt any of us had the faintest idea of what sort of life John and Allan would be leading from then on. Just how hard it would be for them at times, and those things that they would be doing without which had been commonplace until then. Or that the grange they were going to might be no more than a freeman's single-roomed farm cot, not a stone manor such as we had lived in, nor even an oak-timbered longhouse. Now I, like them, was suddenly catapulted into the world of the lowlier men, and what I experienced irrevocably destroyed my belief in the certainties of life, as well as radically altering my views. I was now one of the lowly, the common herd, and could not afford noble airs and graces. The first time I had to lower my head as le Strange rode by I thought I should die for the shame of it!

However, I clearly survived my rude awakening since I am here to tell the tale, and I shall not bore you with the early details of life at Clun for it is but a stopping place along the way. I now know that my life was one of any other young man of modest station at that time. I was trained to various tasks, on one occasion we fought a Welsh raiding party alongside the soldiers, and in the depths of that first winter I was very lonely. Letters came a couple of times from Baldwin, and I wrote to him and to John when I could beg a scrap of parchment to reuse. I would carefully scrape the words of its last use off, and cram a few lines of my own on in ink which bled badly on the unfinished surface. Whether they ever got to their intended destinations I never knew then, but I was right to be pessimistic. Much later I found out that only Baldwin had ever heard from me. Then I had a message back from him. It was brief but its news chilled me to the bone. His father was sending him to the Templars.

Of course even out on the Welsh borders we had heard the news from the Holy Land. The king of Jerusalem was not even of age and yet was seriously ill with leprosy, and unlikely to live many more years. And names of men like Reynauld de Châtillon were already known to us, even if they had not yet achieved the notoriety they would later on. For a while I harboured the hope that Baldwin would end up at Garway, the Templars' wealthy grange and preceptory further south in the Welsh Borders. After all, there were few Templar holdings in England in comparison to France, and so in my youthful optimism I believed him safe. He could not possibly be in the Holy Land, I told myself, and did it so often I came to believe it for the truth.

Instead, John and Allan still occupied my prayers in full measure whenever I made my way to the chapel although, for all that I was living in a major castle, my life was far from idle and my visits there were limited. There was a brief moment of hope only a few months later in August when we heard that King Henry was meeting the Welsh princes to discuss some kind of pact at Oxford. In my innocence, I hoped and prayed that this would mean that the fitz Waryn Marcher estates would be given back if there was no longer any threat of invasion. What naivety! My dreams of us all returning and living happily ever after were barely born before they were dashed. If King Henry could not be bothered to wholly conquer Wales, he was certainly making sure the Welsh princes swore fealty to him, and the bargaining tools he used were the gifts of lands. Not that he would have given a Welshman any estates close to the border! But with land having to be found for them elsewhere in his kingdom, he was not about to hand out manors to callow youths with no experience, and I heard nothing from or about Fulk, Philip or Audulph. For all I knew they might have been dead already.

Yet my own situation was also still precarious. As a young and desperately inexperienced fighter I was hardly considered of any value, and as a mere serving man I soon realised I would have little control over my life. Norman blood alone would not save me from starvation, and I swiftly realised why so many men put up with high-handed lords, for to *be alone and adrift without the protection such a lord afforded was a terrible fate indeed! The Marches were a law unto themselves then even more than now, Brother, and a man did well to take notice of who was in favour and who was not. With only a handful of great families ruling the area, and a constant threat looming from the Welsh princes, a wise man took notice of the affairs of those above him, and I observed that the fitz Alan heir was not yet so secure that he could not succumb to the machinations of his neighbours, and might yet lose all. If my life in our enclosed little world out on the edges of civilisation was not to be one of being blown on the political winds like some kind of human dandelion clock, I knew I had to find a way to acquire a more secure position in a more established household.*

Chapter 2

$\mathbf{S}$o after barely two years at Clun I was soon to be on the move again. In those years I had come to adulthood and was in most respects considered a man. Are you waiting for some salacious piece of information now? Ha, no dear Gervase, I shall disappoint you, for I am in a mischievous mood this morning! But if you think I went to Clun a virgin, you are sorely mistaken! That was one piece of growing up I had done long before leaving Nottinghamshire. However, her name is a secret I shall take with me to my encounter with St Peter and it is not for your ears! I shall take my chances on not confessing that first lady's name since only one of us was an innocent, and it harmed no-one. So shall we continue with less titillating information?

I was quite content to work under Guy le Strange, for he was a hard but fair man, but with his return from the Easter sheriffs' gathering of 1179 there came some disturbing news. The young William fitz Alan had, like me, come of age but was considered by all to be something of a wastrel, and it was no surprise that the king did not believe him up to the job of acting as his sheriff in a major border shire. However, most of us had expected le Strange to carry on doing the job he had been doing – and doing very well – since 1170. It therefore came as a bolt from the blue to discover that the sheriffdom was to pass back to the family, not however to the flighty William, but to his sister's husband.

I tell you, I was appalled, Brother, for Christina fitz Alan (as she had been) and her husband, Hugh Pantulf, already lived not far away, and we knew them and their ways all too well. Whenever they had come to Clun it had been a misery for all concerned, for they both stood on their dignity and let it be known to everyone that they considered they should have been the rightful heirs to the castle, and all its attached titles and rights. Now that acquisition was to happen at the coming Michaelmas court, when all sheriffs had to go and present their accounts to the king's Exchequer. Guy le Strange would present the accounts for the year of Michaelmas 1178 to Michaelmas 1179, and would then not return, while the dreaded Hugh Pantulf would be sworn in and come back in what we all expected would be smug glory. The young lord William fitz Alan would still live at Clun but under his sister and brother-in-law's watchful eyes, and the whole household feared that this would be setting the stage for many battles of wills, as each tried to demonstrate their control over this or that area of the castle.

So in a complete panic I began casting about to try and find another position. My fear, you see Gervase, was that anyone taken on by le Strange might be seen by the Pantulfs as tarnished, and therefore would be dismissed. For many of the men that would be a sad blow, but most had been pulled from families in the area and could go back to helping working the family farms, if nothing else. I, on the other hand, had *arrived under the most precarious of circumstances and was not prepared to be cast out to repeat the experience! However, this time I had one advantage, for by now I had discovered I had a talent – I was good with dogs. Also, I could track a trail better than any other man in the castle, and that was how I intended to find my new role.*

Any castle of a decent size still employed a wolf-hunter to keep the surrounding area safe – a job which survived in name only in the more inhabited shires of England, but was still essential in the wilder borders with mountain refuges close by, and at Clun I had become friends with that person. Already an old man, he was glad to have someone younger and fitter to learn some of the tricks of the trade in return for doing the more mundane physical work. I had given up on the idea of getting any advancement with the head kennelman, and was stuck with simply doing the essential chores, for the man had a son whom he intended to inherit the role after him, even though the boy was too stupid to catch cold, and too heavy-handed with the hounds for them to ever obey him properly. So I cultivated the wolf-hunter instead, and learned that in that role at least I could hope to earn three shillings a year – nothing like enough to make me a rich man, since it would just about pay the rent on a meagre cottage for a year, but not my keep as well. So those wages would be spent on whatever I could not gather from the common stores at my next castle, and not luxuries either! However, it would be something which was mine and it would set me aside from the rest of any garrison.

That idea suited me, for by now I had become a solitary soul. Part of me still sorely missed my cousins, and part of me was too scared to make any further close friendships for fear of the pain returning when they were broken. The dogs were much safer company! – Ah! Did you not expect such a confession, Brother Gervase? Did you think I would never admit to such tender feelings? Me, the hard and cruel Sir Guy of the stories! Well it is the truth. I did miss my family, and not just my cousins. Just because my mother was in Kirklees Abbey, it did not mean that I missed her good counsel and company any the less. I found it harsh when she wrote to me telling me that this would be the last letter she would be allowed to send me, and that her vows would take place shortly. The young man that I was understood with his head, but not with his heart.

Indeed, Brother, I now felt most profoundly orphaned and alone, and also fallen a very long way below the station of my birth. I was now no nobleman's son to the outside world, and the day to day necessity of survival meant that I had found it better to not dwell on such matters, and to harden my heart to the realities of life. You chastise me, saying I frequently talk down to you and that you know as much of the world as any man, but you do not. Not immured here in your cloisters for all your life, with all of the basic wants of life found for you without you ever lifting a hand. Men are not born hard, Brother, it is life that makes them so. And so it was with me – but you shall not get me to rush my story and skip to the hardened and devilish Sir Guy, as you so anticipate! You must have it all or not at all! So...

The standard huntsman's pack was of around twelve couple of hounds and eight greyhounds, and at Clun the young lord fitz Alan enjoyed his hunting and had many packs, meaning that even with the head kennelman and his son, there was plenty of work for me and two others. I enjoyed the rough and tumble of the hound pack, but I adored the greyhounds and they me. Yet an elegant greyhound was of scant use over such rough territory as I covered when we went hunting in our specialist role. So with the wolf-hunter's blessing, I managed to circumvent the kennelman and regular huntsman and petition my lord le Strange directly to acquire some deerhounds. The fitz Alans had Scottish connections enough so that it was a simple matter to request some pups, and when they arrived I threw myself into training them. Happily I was able to keep them separate from the main packs, as the kennelman disdained to have anything to do with them, so they were all mine! The rugged, thicker-coated deerhounds took to the misty hillsides of western Shropshire as though they were natives, and we were soon a formidable team, supplementing the kitchens with a plentiful supply of hares, and some roe deer as well, for which we were very popular!

Yet even in those days wolves were hardly in such great numbers in the area, and with young fitz Alan regularly hunting with his lordly friends over the hills around Clun, few wolves ever showed their noses, let alone bothered us. They preferred quieter areas. Lands where all they had to contend with were a few shepherds' lads. Land which fell under other wolf-hunters' jurisdiction than ours at Clun. This meant that I would always be expected to fulfil my more regular duties as one of the lesser huntsmen first, but as a man-at-arms within that great garrison as a very close second – and as a man-at-arms I was a very lowly person indeed! My ring-mail hauberk and coif were from the common store at Clun, as was my sword and even the padded gambeson for beneath the mail. Only my long huntsman's knife was my own. I was definitely no-one in particular at Clun!

Therefore, when le Strange's men returned with him that Easter with, amongst other news, word that the head of the de Braoses, Earl William, wanted a huntsman who could deal with wolves for the holding of the Three Castles (or the Honour of Grosmont as it was anciently and properly called), I begged to be allowed to apply to him. Earl William de Braose, as sheriff, was the person in charge of the Honour as a whole and dealt with the higher affairs, while the castles were kept by their respective keepers. I admit it, this time I shamelessly played on my half-brother's name! He was a de Braose, after all, albeit a very insignificant one! Audulph had left me behind to moulder without a thought for how I would fare, and so I felt no remorse at using his name in vain in return. Who else was to know I lied when I said I wished to serve the de Braose family out of loyalty to Audulph? – There, are you happy now, Brother? A little confession of ill-doing to be weighed against my shrivelled soul on Judgement Day! Is that more what you wanted? Are you rubbing your hands in expectation? Patience, Brother!

Clearly I had made little impression one way or the other on le Strange or young lord fitz Alan, since they were indifferent to my leaving, and something I wrote must have impressed Ralph of Grosmont, the seneschal who was in charge of the hiring, for I was soon on my way south. For me, though, the world had become a little brighter. The Three Castles were Skenfrith, Llantilio and Grosmont, tucked away in southern Herefordshire, but most importantly to me, they formed three points on

*an approximate square, the fourth of which was the Templar's Garway –
and if I could visit Garway I dreamed that I might be able to see Baldwin!
If Audulph was rapidly fading from my brotherly affection, Baldwin,
John and Allan never did.*

There, Brother, that is the truth!

The Honour of Grosmont, Herefordshire
May, the year of Our Lord 1179

"You have *how* many hounds?" Guy stared at the teaming kennels.
They were far more extensive than he'd expected for somewhere
which was much smaller than Clun.

"Oh, about seventy if you count the pups and breeding bitches,"
the weather-beaten older man said with a gap-toothed grin. "Mind
you," he added admiringly, "yours are a handsome bunch!"

Guy felt no guilt at the deception he had perpetrated on his
former lord. Half a dozen pups had arrived at Clun from four
different litters courtesy of the fitz Alan's family in the north, clearly
because they'd expected some of them to die before they reached
maturity. They hadn't reckoned on Guy. Every one of the
deerhounds had grown to become beautiful, big strong beasts, and
Guy had trained them all. So when he'd departed he had left behind a
dog and two of the bitches with the old wolf-hunter, but he'd also
brought the same combination with him, telling the incurious
kennelmen of Clun as he departed that they were a gift from one
sheriff to another. Once at Grosmont, though, he'd changed his tale
to the dogs being his and the last of the animals bred by his own
father. He loved his dogs, and these three in particular, and had no
intention of risking their being killed by some thoughtless lord's folly,
for he knew those left behind were safe but not what he was coming
to. He'd lost his human family, he wasn't about to lose his canine one
so easily. Survival was teaching Guy to be economical with the truth!

"You won't find better!" Guy said with pride. "You're a clever
boy, aren't you Blue," he added, ruffling the ears of the big, steel-grey
dog who promptly leaned into Guy's hand with a grunt of
satisfaction.

For a moment the old man's expression had darkened at what he'd first seen as Guy's arrogance, but the instant he saw that it was the dogs Guy was crediting his frown softened again. If this lad thought that much of his hounds then there wasn't too much wrong with him. Yet he still had his reservations.

"Don't take this wrong, son," he said easily, "but aren't you a bit young to be a wolf-hunter? We were expecting someone a mite older, to be honest. How old are you?"

"Twenty," Guy lied. His nineteenth birthday was due next week but he thought it would sound better if he claimed he was at least out of his teens. However, he'd learned the hard way that stretching the truth was best kept to a minimum, or at least to what was plausible. And his own well-honed sense of survival was now telling him that he needed to keep on the right side of this canny older man. Swallowing his pride he forced himself to relax as he confessed,

"But you're right, I am young to be a wolf-hunter. I did the job at Clun because I could track better than anyone else there, apart from the old man who couldn't run with the dogs anymore, not because I'd knew much about the actual killing. That and the fact that the huntsman and his main assistant thought wolves a little beneath them! They preferred the hunting of the deer with the young lords – much more chance to show off for their master then, you see."

"Had much trouble with wolves up there?"

"Not much. This last winter we had them come down to the stock pens in the worst of the snow, but they were poor half-starved things that didn't take much catching. The one was a big brute, but he was old. Really old. It wasn't just his muzzle that was white. His face was snowy right up to his ears. Lord, but he gave me a turn when I first saw him in the half-light! He seemed almost ghostly! There was this white wolf's mask seeming to be detached and moving in the shadows!"

The old man chuckled. "Ay, it fair loosens the bowels seeing something like that, doesn't it! I saw one like that many a long year ago. She was a venerable old wolf bitch, too. So did you kill him?"

Guy nodded, but wasn't able to conceal his sadness at the memory.

"Ah, not a good kill, then?"

"No. When we were almost upon him I could see that he was running with a limp. I doubt he'd brought down his own food for some time. That must've been why he was after the stock – the penned animals were all he could catch." Guy paused wondering whether to share the next part. He desperately wanted to unburden himself to someone, but someone who wouldn't laugh and think him fanciful or stupid. Yet there was something in the way the old man was still looking at him that made him think that at last he'd found that person. "I think he let us catch him," Guy confessed. "I think he'd had enough and was in pain, and wanted it over with. It let him go out quickly, not some lingering death slowly starving. Does that sound fanciful?"

"No, son. Some who might not know animals might think so, but not me. Wolves are closer to dogs than most folk are comfortable admitting, and I've been around dogs all my life. They're not so different from people. Some are foolish, some are stupid, but others are smart and knowing. And wolves can be the same. Yes, I believe you."

What he didn't say was that he thought a lot more of Guy for the admission. Too many young men would have bragged about how they'd brought down a big old pack leader to make themselves seem good. He was rapidly coming to the conclusion that if Guy wasn't quite the experienced wolf-hunter he'd hoped was coming, at least this was the right kind of young man for the job. Someone who worried about doing it right. Not some firebrand, all too eager to make a name for himself. That kind of man got valuable dogs killed without need, and the old man really hated his hounds getting maimed or worse.

"What of the others? You said 'them' so I'm guessing there was more than just the one."

Guy straightened and shook off his regrets. "Oh yes, but I think they were both runts of the litter," he said with more detachment. "Both small and very young. I think they'd failed to keep up with their pack and were just after anything they could get. Blue, here, took the one down all by himself, didn't you boy?" The deerhound's ears pricked and he grinned up at Guy, his tongue lolling out of one side of the panting jaws. "I know Blue's a big dog and weighs as much as some men, but I don't think he'd have had such an easy time with an experienced wolf in prime condition."

The old man nodded, again partly in approval of Guy's attitude as much as agreement. Not overly sentimental about catching wolves, then. That was good. It wasn't a job which had to be done that often these days, but when it needed doing it really had to be done. Wolves who came that close to humans were either sick or had lost their fear of man, and the latter made them very dangerous indeed.

"You'll do, lad. Come on. I'll show you the rest of the kennels and then we've got a job to do."

"What? A wolf already?"

"No, just a couple of foxes who've got fearless and keep getting into the chicken coops! The running-hounds aren't much good in close conditions and these two are hiding in that copse you can see just round the bend in the river. If I take the hounds round the back and let them flush the beggers out, can your three do the killing?"

Guy grinned. "You just watch them!"

As they turned to the low building where he would be sleeping, which butted on to the kennels, he permitted himself the spark of hope that he had, for now, found a home.

"So does my lord de Braose stay here often?" he ventured to ask. "My last lord was at Clun more often than not."

"Oh de Braose isn't your lord," Ianto corrected him swiftly. "The man who brought you here is Ralph, the castellan, but he and all of us attached to Grosmont are really the king's men. De Braose has his own lands closer to the Welsh, and he lives in his castles over there when he's not out and about."

Guy was embarrassed at his naivety as well as his stupidity for not having enquired more carefully. So much for a new home! He might just have jumped out of the pan into the fire.

"So de Braose isn't my lord, then?" he quizzed Ianto.

The old kennelman sniffed. "As a matter of law? No. You're the king's to do with as he wishes, should you ever have the misfortune to come to his attention. However, the king never comes this far west unless he's hunting the Welsh princes, so the chances of that happening are beyond remote. What you should never do is say as much to the earl! It's a sore point with him that he does the king's work on this land but has no ownership, yet he needs to stay on the good side of King Henry or risk being supplanted as sheriff, and have some other lord watching him on the king's behalf. That would really piss him off! He's a bloodthirsty bastard, and king or no king, he's as likely to have you beaten to a pulp if you cross him. So for God's sake don't bring the subject up! If I were you I would bend your knee to him when you have to and stay clear of him if at all possible – I do!"

"Thank you!" Guy said from the heart. What a trap he had nearly fallen into! On the other hand it didn't sound quite so bad if de Braose wasn't likely to be here for weeks on end, and no other great noblemen either. Life might be comfortable after all.

Over the next few months Guy also came to realise what a good move he'd made in befriending the kennel-man, Ianto, who wasn't as old as he appeared. He was listened to and respected, and if he had little influence inside Grosmont's main building, he was a law unto himself outside in the fenced-off area of the kennels. Ianto's domain was the wedge of land sandwiched between the castle's earthworks and the western bank of the Monnow, for the stables were further round to the south where there was a bit more room to move. Even the guards rarely patrolled this bit of bank since the dogs were quick to let anyone know if there was a whiff of a stranger about, and the castle walls looked out above them over the wider expanse of the Monnow's course to watch for larger bodies of men approaching beyond the river. This meant that if Guy wanted space from the other men-at-arms he only had to get to the kennels and he would be left alone. Not that he was bullied by the more established men. They only ever tried that once with Guy, at which point they discovered that he was more than capable of standing his ground and acquitting himself well in any rough jesting which took place. Had he wanted it, he could have become a popular member of the coterie of men-at-arms who lived at, and rode out from, Grosmont and the other two castles. Instead he was well-liked enough and distant by choice.

It was a choice Ianto commented on once they'd got to know one another better. "Why are you hanging around here with an old man like me?" he once quizzed Guy as they sat enjoying the late summer sun one evening. "I'd have thought you'd be off with the other lads down the alehouse! You're not shy, so what's stopping you?"

Guy gave a small, wry smile. "I find it hard, being with the lads. I'm not quite one thing or the other, you see Ianto. I grew up expecting to do all the things a knight's son should do. My childhood was nothing like most of the lads who are men-at-arms here. I've never worked the land. I've never loaded hay onto a cart at harvest. Oh my cousins and I were expected to look after our own horses and dogs because the manor wasn't big enough to have that many servants, but the expectation was that we would become fighters, not farmers. At best I did some helping out at lambing times, and then only with those of the folk who were down by the manor."

He blushed at a memory. "I made such a fool of myself when I first went to Clun. Several of us were acting as beaters for my lord, flushing the deer out of the woods into the open fields. One of the farmers came out and made such a fuss that we'd driven a herd of deer out through a field, and then my lord and the hounds followed trampling what was left. I couldn't understand it! Honestly, I didn't Ianto. The field looked fallow to me and I said as much. All the other beaters went from taking the piss out of the poor farmer to mocking me. How could I be so stupid as to not know mengrell growing when I saw it, they taunted.

"So then I had the shame of admitting that I'd never seen it before, at which they called me a liar amongst other things! But the truth is, Ianto, I really never had seen a mixed crop before! Our lands around the fitz Waryn manor were all on deep, rich, fertile soil. You could grow anything in that good earth! So of course it was all laid to wheat, as I now realise, because it could be taken to market for a good price."

"What did your beasts eat, then?" Ianto wondered. "Surely you didn't waste wheat on them?"

"Oh no! But all the fodder came in by cart. The steward or one of his men went off to market with a wagon full of harvested wheat or grain, and came back with one filled with fodder for the horses and plough oxen." Guy drew his long legs up and wrapped his arms around them so that he sat with his head resting on them, staring mournfully out into the distance. "Of course, once I saw the mengrell in its harvested form and bundled into bales or in sacks, I knew what it was. It's just that I'd not seen a field with that mixture of oats and peas and beans and vetch all growing together on purpose before. ...By the time the winter sowing came around I made damned sure I watched what they sowed like a hawk, thinking that I wouldn't be making such a fool of myself again. ...Didn't save me though. When I recognised that wheat and rye was the maslin used for bread, and the wheat and barley was the mixtil used for ale, I got another rough ride. The word had spread by now that Guy pretended to have airs and graces, so all the lads I should have been friends with thought it huge fun to call me a liar, or to mince around mimicking the fine lords and calling out to me in silly voices. Not to mention the fights in the barns when no-one in charge was watching!"

He turned a baleful eye to Ianto. "I suppose you think I'm a fool for not just letting it go, but it went on from harvest until Christmas that first year, and that's a long time to put up with such taunts and punches! It certainly means I don't have any friends back at Clun from among the lads. Any who would have been friends were soon put off when they saw me taking the brunt of the ring leaders' japes!"

"And you don't like being called a liar, either," Ianto observed perceptively. Guy just shook his head, still too lost in the past to take much notice of the comment, but Ianto marked it down as another point in young Guy's favour. His new young friend was clearly honest by nature and was bothered by accusations he might be otherwise. Ianto also thought that it might be no bad thing that Guy had experienced what it was like to be on the receiving end of bullying, albeit for only a short time. He still had some growing and filling out to do yet, but the indications were that Guy would be a big man once he came to maturity. If he therefore decided to start throwing his weight around with the lesser folk whose homes surrounded Grosmont, then there would be few who could stand up to him – and Ianto had known one or two young men in the past who had vented their frustrations at not climbing as high as they would have liked upon those whom they saw as beneath them. Thank Dewi Sant, then, that this was one problem he wouldn't have to deal with here! And Guy might even become a steadying influence on some of the other young firebrands amongst the castle guard once he'd rediscovered some self-confidence, for although Grosmont wasn't as vast as Clun, it still required a regular garrison.

Grosmont itself was a substantial castle built upon a series of earthworks, and protected on its eastern flank by the River Monnow, but it was built of wood – unlike Clun which was all of stone. However, still large by most castles' standards and highly defensible, Grosmont was a prestigious enough place considering that it served as the administrative centre of the narrow corridor of land leading into the southern Welsh territories. The kennels and stables were contained by the outer earthworks, but there was a deep dry-moat around the castle itself, a large wooden gatehouse with firing platforms for archers to protect the gate below, and the castle's wooden curtain wall was no flimsy affair, also having firing platforms all around its perimeter. More than any mounted knights, what kept Grosmont safe were the local archers who served the king here, and Guy discovered a new pleasure in learning to use the big Welsh longbows made of wych-elm. He already had the strength to pull a good sized bow, and happily joined in the practice at the archery butts when he could until he too could hit his target at 250 yards, even if he wasn't quite up to firing one every count of ten with deadly accuracy as the locals who'd been doing it from boyhood could.

Within the walls, the inner ward was of a goodly size with plenty of room for a great household to be accommodated, a large kitchen, and a substantial wooden hall on two floors, having a solar and hall on the first floor as well, besides the general assembly hall below. In which respect it would have made a fitting residence for Earl William had it been his to have and not the king's. Instead, he had many more places to oversee, including his own strongholds of Brecon and Abergavenny. The real fortress of the three in the Honour's danger zone was Llantilio, with Skenfrith also sharing the line of defence, while Grosmont sat closer into Herefordshire at the apex of the triangle. The keepers of these three kept in touch with one another and exchanged services, so that Guy's new world turned out to have broader boundaries than he'd anticipated.

De Braose himself came and went with speed during that first summer, constantly moving between the family's holdings and the king's with his personal retinue, and Guy rarely saw him – which was a good thing since he had no wish to discuss his tenuous link to the family with its leading figure. Also the way the earl took his temper out on anyone who irritated him, whatever their station, made him feared by the castle's inhabitants and they took no time in reiterating Ianto's warnings to Guy of this, making him glad to keep out of the earl's way for reasons other than his family. United by their fear of their lord, the occupants of Grosmont were much more kindly in their warnings to Guy than those who had wanted to exploit their immature lord's favours up at Clun.

The first time Guy saw the earl's ferocious temper for himself it shocked him to the core. Why de Braose was in such a foul mood was a mystery, but the poor stable lad who brought the earl's horse to him had committed no greater crime than to stand at the wrong side of the horse's head to provoke de Braose's wrath. Swearing incomprehensibly in his bastard Norman-French, de Braose punched the lad so hard he was thrown against the gatehouse stone wall. Yet it didn't stop there, for de Braose picked him up and punched him again and again, until the lad's face was a bloody pulp and he was insensible. Only then did the heavily blood-bespattered earl turn on his heels, mount up, and ride out as if nothing had happened.

Guy and Ianto were amongst those who ran to pick the lad up the moment de Braose was gone. A week later the boy died, and Guy was appalled at the way he was buried in a hurry and without comment. He had been the one taking his turn to sit holding the poor lad's hand at the point when he died, and it was his first experience of a violent death that close to. It sickened him to the point of being off his food for several days, but also confused him. Seeing someone whose station his upbringing had taught him to revere behaving with such thoughtless brutality shook him more than he could express – even to Ianto. What of a lord's Christian duty? The very thing old fitz Waryn had dinned into them as boys. Did de Braose think nothing of his immortal soul? Or did he think he could buy his way into Heaven with generous donations to the Church? A string of monks in chantry chapels saying prayers for his soul to ensure his afterlife wasn't in Hell? Was that the plan? Was that why he acted with such cruelty? It was inexplicable to Guy.

It was also the first time he'd had intimate experience of just how much control a man like de Braose could have over the ordinary people – even when they weren't his personal tenants. Over their very life or death! Yet of itself that still didn't explain such wanton squandering of life. He'd seen as much control at Clun under le Strange's warden-ship, albeit rather more distanced from it, but it hadn't been randomly vicious or wasteful. And back at Alverton, every man had been needed to work the manor's fields and tend the animals, and therefore even a lord as volatile as fitz Waryn had kept some kind of restraint in place. But then Alverton was tiny by comparison with his current location, and as a manor its needs were very different – as well as its local people being well represented in the local Hundred Court. There was no such court as empowered so close to Grosmont, the nearest being eastwards in Archenfield, and their writ ended at the River Monnow. This hard on the Welsh border such Saxon institutions' hold had always been more sporadic, yet despite that at Clun they had still been a minor force for good, and belatedly Guy found himself wishing it here.

Out here the administrative hundreds were vast in acreage in comparison to the tightly packed hundreds of the fertile Trent valley which Guy was familiar with, and here half the freemen within one were so scattered they could hardly know the others beyond a few nods and comments in the court. Certainly not well enough to band together trustingly to risk standing up to a lord of de Braose's standing, let alone with him being sheriff as well. And definitely not to be the irritant to a Norman lord that fitz Waryn had believed the Newark hundred, under its old Danelaw name of the wapentake, had been. Yet fundamentally, it was the wastefulness, and the simultaneous imperilling of a soul that went hand in hand with de Braose's brutality, which remained incomprehensible to Guy. Did de Braose not lose enough men in fighting the Welsh that he could afford to lose more? Men who could have manned Grosmont's walls? Whatever the reason, Guy was desperately thankful that he had been forewarned about de Braose! Only in his subsequent nightmares following the boy's death did it cross his mind to confront the earl!

Summertime was thankfully not the hunting season for the nobly born, allowing Guy time to order his thoughts again before having to earn his keep alongside de Braose in the hunt. Other more pressing matters, such as cross-border raids, were far more the seasonal concerns of the sheriff, as was keeping an eye on the political machinations going on in the fight for the throne of Gwynedd, allowing de Braose a legitimate venting of his warlike spleen without including Guy. It was still only two years since King Henry had made the Welsh princes swear fealty to him, and de Braose had long since earned himself an evil name amongst the Welsh, thus making him an ideal threatening presence on Henry's behalf on their border should any of them get ideas above their station.

As he got to know more people within the castle, Guy heard of how a mere four years ago, in 1175, Earl William's father, and then sheriff, had lured Seisyll ap Dyfnwal and his men to Abergavenny Castle – the premier de Braose holding – and massacred them. The elder William de Braose had then taken his men to Seisyll's home and murdered the Welsh women and children too, for which wholesale breach of hospitality in both cases King Henry had removed the old man from the sheriffdom in favour of his son. Word around the castle, though, said that their current lord had been there murdering alongside his father, and that the reason why the king had merely handed on the sheriff's role to the next generation was because the dismissal was a formal gesture he had to make, rather than inciting his heartfelt disapproval. The old man now sat and whiled away his old age elsewhere, but that didn't stop his son continuing to emulate him. Clearly a father who could brutalise his enemies in such a way had not been an easy parent, and either the young William had been hardened at an early age or had simple inherited the family brutal steak. Whatever the cause, the sheriff sometimes acted as though his own household were the enemy, and as if his father was watching him from some hidden vantage point.

Yet in Guy's mind he still couldn't imagine fitz Waryn – still the main yardstick he possessed to date against which to measure knightly behaviour – going so far as to kill just to prove a point, whether to the king, his father or anyone else. If he couldn't quite forgive the old man yet for how he had treated Allan and John in his will, he was certainly revising his opinion of him as a brutal master when it came to the manor. Fitz Waryn had been nothing compared to de Braose!

As a result, although Guy wasn't squeamish by any stretch of the imagination, he rapidly decided that he wanted no part in such honourless dealings, should de Braose find another such means to flex his muscles. Fighting bloodthirsty Welsh warriors was one thing, and an experience which Guy was quite looking forward to – in a nervous kind of way – as a means of proving himself, but the thought of slaughtering unarmed women and children turned his stomach. The tales the older soldiers told in the evenings sometimes, of de Braose rampaging through the Welsh hall, besmirched with blood, and laughing like some fiend from Hell as he savaged tiny children, froze Guy's blood merely at the thought! As yet he hadn't been around when de Braose was mustering men, but he privately vowed to establish his role as a hunter not a fighter, and if necessary he would remove himself to one of the other castles before his lord appeared, should political thunderstorms begin brewing.

With that in mind he set to culling the local fox population with a will. Once he'd stopped the predations on the chicken pens around Grosmont, he asked Ianto if he could go and do the same for Skenfrith and Llantilio, a request which Ianto passed on to Ralph the castellan, a quiet and sensible man whom Guy, to his own surprise, got on with well. Given that Guy was thought to have swiftly proven himself reliable and trustworthy enough to be let off alone, July therefore found him riding out on his own with the dogs. His first call, though, was not to one of the other castles but a short ride westwards to the Templar preceptory of Garway. Ianto had heard that they were suffering from a family of foxes and had thought to volunteer Guy's services as a way of keeping on de Braose's good side, for the earl was known to have strong feelings on the need to retain control of Jerusalem – as did the king, their true employer – and both therefore vigorously supported the Templars.

Guy covered his excitement at going to the one place he wanted to visit most of all by revelling in the tales of the Templars' exploits told at mealtimes in the hall at Grosmont. It had been quietly driving him mad to stand on the walls at Grosmont looking at the ridge known as Garway Hill, and yet not be able to go beyond it to Garway proper, for in the main the Templars looked after their own lands as a quite separate unit from the castles. He hadn't know whether to be disappointed or glad when Ianto had told him that Garway was hardly packed to the brim with fighting men. After all, most of the Templars' great wealth of lands lay in France, not on the distant western borders of England, and Garway was more of a farming estate and retirement posting than a great training ground for knights. As he rode over Grosmont Bridge and then followed the road above the north-east bank of the River Monnow down to Garway, Guy still felt almost optimistic about the chances of finding Baldwin. If his cousin had been sent to the Templars then this was the nearest place of any consequence, and he dreamed that he would find Baldwin tending horses or cattle, bored stiff but safe.

It was the kind of balmy summer day to inspire such daydreams. In a field down below him cattle grazed contentedly on the rich grass, and bees buzzed at the wayside flowers. The hot sun beat down on them and the dogs soon had long tongues hanging out as they padded along beside his horse. For their sakes Guy kept the pace at a steady plod. It wasn't as though it was going to take them long to get there, and on this side of the river there was little chance of anyone trying to waylay him and so requiring him to stay alert. Safe enough, indeed, that he had felt no need to draw a gambeson from the stores to swelter in, let alone a ring-mail hauberk – his linen shirt alone felt hot enough in this weather! By mid-afternoon they were climbing up out of the river valley to where the preceptory and its church nestled in a fold in the ridge. Unlike the castles, the preceptory was hardly noticeable above the trees until he was almost upon it, but once up on the elevated position and looking back the way he'd come, Guy now saw thick, dark thunder clouds swelling up out of the southwest.

"Looks like we made it just in time," he said to Aethel and Blue as he dismounted and led them into the yard of the grange farm. Meg, the other bitch, was in pup and rather than over-tire her Guy had left her in Ianto's care. He was greeted warmly enough by a stolid-looking groom and taken into the main living quarters, once his horse was stabled and the dogs were found a corner of a stall to bed down in. Given that he was here on business it took some time before Guy felt he could ask about Baldwin. The problem of the foxes and the hen-house, and where the foxes' lair might be, all had to be aired, and so it was only as the bell rang for the evening prayers that Guy dared to broach the subject.

"A cousin of mine was sent to join your Order about a year ago," he said casually to the elderly Templar veteran who escorted him towards the church. "I wondered if he might be here? His name's Baldwin de Hodenet. He's seventeen years old. Do you know him?"

The Templar frowned but shook his head. "...No. ...No, I can't think of anyone that young who's passed through here of late. Do you know where he joined the Order?"

Guy sighed. "No, not really. I assumed at first that it would've been somewhere close to his father's lands, which are up in north Shropshire. Before I moved to Grosmont I'd already managed to inquire at your preceptory up at Chatwell, which was the nearest, but they've never seen Baldwin. That's why I thought he might have come here, because there aren't that many preceptories over here in the west of England."

"Hmmm. Well unfortunately it's more likely that he was sent to London, or maybe Norfolk or Yorkshire. We do have another preceptory over on the Gloucestershire border, but you're right, other than that it would be us he came to if he was staying in the region."

"London?" What little Guy knew of the teeming capital city made him think that it was no place for someone like Baldwin. His young cousin had always been far too trusting for his own good. He forced himself to remain calm and tried to find a bright side. After all, he was here as a guest and it wouldn't do to suggest that Baldwin was in danger in another of their places. "Not the Holy Land then? That's good!"

The older knight took in Guy's expression and guessed at what lay at its root. However, he was not about to start handing out false hopes. "I can't guarantee that. There's a distinct possibility that he's in the east, or at least on his way there." As they entered into the round nave of the recently built church and stood waiting for the priest, the knight leaned closer to speak more softly to Guy. "Things are ...complicated ...in Outremer. Three years ago we should have had a strong king to succeed King Amalric in Jerusalem, but we got a thirteen year old boy. And to make matters worse, young King Baldwin has leprosy! He's unlikely to live long with that! Nor is he likely to sire an heir, so it's a good thing that his sister Sybilla has given birth to a son, but may God ensure that the babe doesn't have to take over from his young uncle any time soon! There are too many trouble-makers out there as it is without having a regency to be exploited, and the last we heard there was war brewing anyway. It may already have started for all I know. But if it has, be prepared for your young cousin to have been sent out.

"On the other hand we've got a new preceptory being built up in Yorkshire at Foulbridge. That's the kind of place a new recruit might be sent, because they'll need plenty of extra hands for the time being. Apparently it's somewhere between what they call the Moors and the Wolds..."

"...I know it!" Guy exclaimed with as much restraint as he could manage given that they were now in the church. "We used to live over that way. It's in the valley of the River Derwent. Oh I do hope he's gone there! It would be like going home for him!"

"Well don't get your hopes up too much. As I said, it's only a possibility. He could equally have gone to London or the Holy Land." He took in Guy's crestfallen expression and realised how deeply Guy's concern ran. "I tell you what, lad, leave it with me. I'll try to find out. It won't be quick, mind you! But at Michaelmas we'll be riding up to London to take goods up to the New Temple, and someone from Yorkshire is bound to be there. I'll ask around for you. No doubt you'll be back here with those dogs of yours when the weather draws in and the beasties get more hungry, and see our chickens and sheep as a tasty option! Come and see me then."

Then the priest appeared and the observances began, halting the conversation, yet Guy's mind was in turmoil. As he stood staring at the beautifully carved and painted chancel arch whilst following the knights in their obeisance, his prayers went out on Baldwin's behalf. It seemed like some horrible twist of fate that his cousin should share the same name as the young king of Jerusalem – and he only just refrained from groaning out loud as he realised that they were also the same age. Was his Baldwin fated to die in some barren desert to preserve the sick monarch? He shuddered, for at the moment that the thought occurred, a great clap of thunder rattled almost directly overhead. They'd been aware of its progress towards them, but there'd been a gap in the thunderclaps between those in the distance and this one, making it all the more startling. It seemed too much of a coincidence to Guy, as though the Almighty had read his thoughts and was crushing all hope.

Come the morning he was glad to get out with the dogs, although there was little he could do. The deluge had gone on deep into the night and any scent would have been washed away as would any tracks. Not that the fox had ventured anywhere near them on such a filthy night, and all the fowl were safe and sound. Suddenly Guy wanted to be out of Garway as soon as possible. Promising to return when there would be more chance of tracking the chicken thief, he retrieved his pack and rode out heading for Skenfrith. This was an even shorter ride than the last day, and he was there nicely in time to shelter from another burst of heavy rain sweeping in.

Despite another thundery night he felt rather more relaxed at Skenfrith, possibly because this was a wooden-keeped motte and bailey castle of the kind he was getting used to at Grosmont. The Templars had been friendly enough, but his fears seemed to press in on him too much in their presence. Here there was just the normal castle banter going on in the crush to get a helping of the evening meal, and for once Guy was glad of such company. As it happened they'd had little in the way of fox trouble and so he was on his way westwards the following day. With the heat slacked by the rain he was able to set a brisker pace, and, although he achieved little at Llantilio either, it had at least allowed him the chance to familiarise himself with the countryside beyond Grosmont.

However, his leisurely ride to Skenfrith had also provided a different kind of distraction. Having got there at barely midday, and with nothing to do once he'd reported to the leading knight, he had left Blue and Aethel in the cool of the stables and went to walk along the Monnow. The waters were low at this time of the year and the meadows were lush and fragrant, steaming in the summer sun after the heavy shower, so that he'd wandered daydreaming further from the castle than expected when a woman's voice called to him. He found himself being confronted by a very comely young woman with dark hair and pale grey eyes who introduced herself as Megan, the farmer's wife – a farm she gestured to further up along the valley.

"Brought some eggs to the castle, see," she said with a coquettish smile, and winking at Guy.

He was suddenly very aware of just how long it had been since he had enjoyed any sort of female company and of a very deep and urgent lust. There were plenty of women at the castle, and a simple young pig-herder from Grosmont village, named Bethan, had taken a shine to him along with two others of the village girls, but none were women he dared be intimate with for all sorts of reasons. Any fears he might have had of forcing his attentions on an unwilling woman, in this instance however, were quickly dispelled as Megan loosened her bodice, revealing a substantial amount of her full breasts. Beyond thought or restraint, Guy found himself pulling off his own clothes and hers, and the two of them falling into the soft grass to satiate their desperate need. When they lay panting beside one another a little later in the damp grass, and not just from the sultry heat of the summer day, it belatedly occurred to Guy to ask after her husband as he watched another thunderstorm brewing on the horizon.

"Oh he won't notice," Megan sniffed with a roll of the eyes. "Too busy with his bloody prize bull! A bit more of the bull in him would be nice!"

Guy had to wait until after their second and rather more leisurely sexual encounter to hear more. What he heard, though, made him feel less guilty at what he'd done with another man's wife. (Although far from fanatical in his faith, Guy still had a healthy respect for the Ten Commandments!) However, Megan had been married off at a very young age to a much older man, both to cement a deal over some fields and also supposedly to keep her out of trouble. Guy could imagine her sultry looks causing her father and mother some worries as they watched her develop. However, for Megan the marriage had proved little short of a prison, with a great deal of work and little play. Even worse, given that she was of an age when such a thing might be expected, her mother and most of the other women of the valley had been watching her like a hawk for signs of a pregnancy. Megan had done her best to hint at her husband's lack of interest, but as her husband was still a fine figure of a man, no-one really believed that he was lacking in his husbandly duties.

"At first I didn't mind," Megan admitted. "Kept him away from me, see, and I wasn't that taken with him. But now I want babies of my own," she sniffed and Guy could see real tears in her eyes as she added, "And it's bloody humiliating when all the girls of my age round here have at least one, and most are on their second or third. I keep having to bounce everyone else's babies on my knee and try and smile while I do it."

"So you've been trying your luck with the other young men?" Guy guessed. Then was shocked by her vehement response.

"Dewi Sant, are you mad? In this little place? By St Heledd, the first time I lifted my skirts to a local man it'd be known the length and breadth of the valley before the sun rose! I've no wish to be cast out as a whore, or dragged before the priest! One travelling merchant, that's all I've risked so far. But you're not local, are you?" Now she smiled shyly. "And you are very handsome!"

Guy found himself suddenly realising that here was a God sent opportunity to salve a little of his loneliness, quickly telling her that no, he wasn't local, nor likely to be sent to Skenfrith permanently, but that he would be coming here several times a year. To his delight, Megan immediately began working out a way for him to send her a signal that he was at the castle the next time he came over, without it being too obvious, and when Guy left Skenfrith the next morning it was feeling more content than he'd been for many a year. He, too, had worried about forming too close an attachment in the immediate village at Grosmont. Without any security for himself he had no wish to force such a footloose life onto a wife and children, and he couldn't be so blasé as to not care about any child he might father.

In Megan's case, though, any child would be very welcome, and since she was as dark as he was, there would be little to give away the fact that her husband had not been the father. Moreover, although he had several moments of anxiety when he recalled John and Allan's fate as bastards born to the wrong side of a marriage, he could also see that here there was no great estate at stake to cause worries over bloodlines. All anyone in the valley would worry about was having a strong and healthy son to carry on working the fields when his father got too old to do it himself, and he permitted himself the hope that Megan's husband wouldn't want to look the fool in front of his friends by forcing attention upon the fact that he was ignoring such a comely wife. Consequently the promise of more assignations in the romantic withy beds, or in some hay-barn in the winter, cheered Guy mightily.

He also found that now that even the faintest chance of reuniting with Baldwin had been crushed, he was able to concentrate on his own fate more easily. In the first winter he proved his abilities with the hunt, and brought in two wolf pelts from animals raiding the sheep by the time he had his first face-to-face encounter with Earl William. That at least meant that no-one doubted his abilities, and as a consequence the sheriff saw Guy simply as a huntsman and not some hanger-on playing on a family connection. In fact, Guy doubted whether the sheriff had even recalled that there was a connection at all, and he was in no hurry to remind him. As a still very young man he was at the mercy of his lord's whims and favours, for until he had proven himself somewhere he had little chance of moving should he fall foul of the great man.

The first time he actually spoke to Earl William it was on a bitterly cold February morning. The previous day Ianto had informed him that their lord and master wished to hunt boar.

"Go and find a trail," the old kennel-man told him urgently. "Any bloody wild pig will do! Just give him something to chase after and work his ire out on! Poor Ralph's walking on eggshells inside in case the old goat takes a dislike to something out of spite. If he doesn't vent his spleen soon we shall all feel the backlash, and God forbid that he should write and complain of us to the king! A boar, my lad! Find him a bloody boar!"

Guy felt the first fluttering of doubt he'd had on seeing Ianto's worried expression fade. "I don't have to hunt far for that!" he sighed with relief.

"No?" Clearly Ianto thought he was bluffing.

Clapping his old friend on the arms Guy grinned. "No, seriously, I don't! When we were out after foxes a week ago I found some wild boar wallows, and there were signs of them rooting about a bit further up the hill. They're up in the woods on the east side of the road down to Llantilio. I'll go and check for fresh spoors, but I'm positive we'll be able to offer his lordship a hunt tomorrow morning."

Ianto's relief was plain to see. "I'll go and tell the sheriff's steward," he said thankfully, and when Guy was riding out he could see Ianto standing on the drawbridge to the castle proper in animated conversation with a harried looking man in courtly dress, who was flanked on the other side by the harassed castellan, Ralph. Giving them a cheery wave Guy set his horse at a brisk trot as Meg and Aethel loped at his heels along with Odo, one of the big, wattle-jowled lymers they used for tracking quarry. He hadn't thought things out that clearly when he'd moved here, but now, having learned more of the ways of the world regarding hunting he was glad he was in the western Marches where there were no royal Forests. If they'd been within Forest land there would have been nowhere for the Earl to hunt without royal dispensation, and Guy certainly wouldn't have had the chance to polish his tracking skills so much either. Mercifully the nearest royal Forest was at Dean, and that was many miles to the south, so the field was clear for a good hunt.

Before two hours were out he'd found the spots he remembered, and was happy to discover that there was further signs of disturbances by the boars. Clearly they were in the vicinity and not inclined to move just yet. With Odo quartering the ground, large ears flapping and jowls rattling as he whiffled his large and expert nose along, Guy soon had a route planned in his mind for the hunt. He would bring the main party in from the west – or more likely he would get Ianto to bring them. Once they were on the scent, the hounds would be able to follow it easily for the first part of the way. If they flushed a boar on that stretch it would be Guy's bad luck if the earl didn't get a kill, but he thought it unlikely unless a young boar got disorientated and ran the wrong way. He would be further up the hill where he could keep an eye on things with Odo and his companion lymers, Motte and Bailey. The heavyweight, doleful-eyed dogs were the best thing for such a hunt, for in the tangle of the woodland there was little room for his beloved deerhounds to show off their skills. The three lymers might not be quite as tall as the deerhounds but they had far more bulk, and muscle would be what was needed to bring down a boar if it got wounded, then made a run for cover where the hound pack could not be used.

However, Guy was hoping for all he was worth that Earl William would want to bring the beast down himself. Setting even a pack of dogs on a wild boar, especially if it was a big old sow or boar, was inviting the dogs to get hurt. The wild boars had incredibly tough skin, making it difficult for the dogs to get a grip on vulnerable areas, and the boars' tusks could inflict horrendous wounds if they turned and gored a dog. So Guy was hoping that all he'd heard about Earl William for once was true, and that the man had the kind of overarching pride that wouldn't allow him to back down in front of such a challenge.

In the watery morning light, part filled with chilly February mists, Guy rode out with two other men and ten of the hounds to complement the lymers. They found a sheltered spot out of the biting wind and huddled with the dogs and horses for warmth while they waited. Guy was almost beginning to panic, and think that Ianto had failed to find the trail he'd laid, when the sound of horns and men's voices drifted faintly up to them.

"Thank God for that!" one of the other men said from the heart as he stamped his boots. "I was beginning to lose the feeling in my feet!"

However Guy was already mounting up. "Come on," he said softly. "Best keep abreast of them or we'll get caught out, and you'll be meeting God quicker than you thought if you upset his lordship!"

The earl had been in a foul mood the previous evening, and Guy had been thankful that his lowly position meant that he could slip out of the great hall at the earliest opportunity – as did many others – leaving only the earl's close household to bear the brunt of his temper. Already one of the household knights was sporting the makings of a fine black-eye, and a servant had had his hand nail to the table with the earl's meat knife for spilling the wine when the earl had jostled him. De Braose's personal steward had tracked Guy down later on, desperately eager to receive confirmation that a hunt would be going ahead.

"He needs blood," the man had told Guy with a shudder. "Preferably buckets of it! He'll be better once he's slaughtered something. So for all our sakes make sure it's a pig that gets stuck or it might end up being one of us!"

Now the said pig was heard crashing through the undergrowth as it ran to avoid the main hound pack coming up the valley with the earl. A small one by the sound of it, Guy thought, but any boar was better than none at the moment. He could hear the horses in pursuit by now, and then the first of the hounds broke cover just a little below him, as it swung wide to harry the boar on its left. A moment later the boar broke out into a small clearing further along and Guy got his first sighting of it. Offering up a prayer of thanks for the fact that it was a decent sized beast, Guy put the horn to his lips and sounded it to signal that the boar was working its way to the right of the hunters. Then he let slip the few hounds he had with him to cover the bank and keep the boar from ploughing uphill. It had to go straight on for the earl to follow it, and that suited him fine, for there was a sharp drop off a steep bank not far ahead. The boar would either fall there and slow its flight, or it would stand its ground.

The earl was the first of the riders to appear, spear in hand and baying for blood as hard as his hounds. With Guy riding on the upper track he reached another small clearing just about the same time as the earl and three of his men, to witness the boar turning back to face them as it realised its escape was cut off. Guy whistled the lymers closer but kept them in check, hoping that it was the right move.

It was. Mindless of the danger, the earl vaulted from his saddle and hefted the spear in his hand to improve his grip. As the animal swung one way and then back again he shifted position, but in the end he stood straight before it as it charged. Holding the spear low he leaned into the impact, driving the spear deep into the neck of the boar. It gave an unearthly shriek and tried to raise its tusks to gore him. For a brief instant it seemed as though the boar would bowl him over. Then it faltered as the effects of the impaling took hold, and the earl was able to side-step as it wavered and then went onto its front knees before keeling over, still squealing.

The boar's blood was running out and Guy hurried forward with another of the huntsmen, for the blood by right belonged to the dogs and for such a purpose skins were carried to collect it in, along with the boar's innards. Given the freezing conditions, had they been further from the castle Guy would've got a fire going and cooked the blood up there and then, with it soaked in plenty of bread. The dogs normally needed something to keep them going after a hard chase, but this hadn't been long and they would be back at the kennels soon enough, so collecting was all he would do here.

With the beast now dead, the earl had turned away to be fêted for his bravery by his coterie – which was why he didn't hear what Guy did. It was the low rumbling growls from Motte and Bailey which alerted him, and he looked up from where he was working on his knees with a sharp knife.

"What is it lads?" he asked, wiping his hands free of the worst of the blood on the winter-wilted grass. Then he heard it too. Somewhere not so far away was another boar and it was a big one! Wild boars were every bit as bloodthirsty as the earl and could devour red meat just as readily. Guy was guessing it was the scent of the blood from the one he was gutting which was drawing the other one, and he hurriedly slopped the bits he needed for the dogs into the leather sack and drew the cord tight around it. He flung the sack up onto a gorse bush out of the way and called a warning.

"My lord! My lord! Another! There's another boar coming!"

The earl turned and fixed him with a steely glance, then followed Guy's outstretched arm to where he could see the bushes shuddering a little further up the hill. With a snarl of delight the earl hurriedly mounted up leaving his escort to scramble for their horses in his wake. It wasn't a moment too soon. The brush parted and a huge old male boar thundered in. One hapless courtier failed to wheel his horse quickly enough and the poor animal received the boars' tusks in its gut, falling and throwing its rider in the process. The courtier got a nasty gouge in his leg, but the boar was now trying to get away from the hounds nipping at its rear when it had no room to turn on them, for other men with spears were jabbing at it from the sides.

As it broke free of the men and dogs, the earl was on its heels, drawing his sword and then leaning down out of his saddle to plunge the blade in with a mighty downward thrust. The blade was wrenched from his hand and one of the men behind the earl immediately handed another to him. Another stab plunging deep into the enraged boar finally brought it down, but not before it had tossed and gored a young man foolish enough to dismount in a pitiful attempt to mimic the earl's previous kill with a spear.

"A feast!" the earl crowed exuberantly. "A veritable feast we shall have tonight!"

Someone passed him a leather flask of mead and he swigged from it heartily before handing it round. Not that the likes of Guy were included in the celebrations. Instead, once he had finished gutting the second boar, others stepped in and divided it up into rough joints to be taken back to the castle kitchens. If the earl wanted to eat his kill tonight there was no time for the beast to be cooked whole. And so a long, thin procession began to wend its way back to Grosmont, the earl and his chosen few in the lead, the two wounded men in makeshift stretchers, and everyone else following in their wake as their tasks and stations befitted.

Ianto was congratulating Guy as they came to the flatter ground of the river valley when there was a flicker of movement off to one side. Those who lived permanently at the castle never gave it a moment's thought, for everyone knew who it was. Earl William, however, was filled with bloodlust and mead and he let out a bellow.

"Ha! ...Look! ...A Welsh witch! See her familiar!" and he clapped his spurs to his horse's flanks and grabbed a spear from one of the retinue as he shot past the startled man.

"But that's Bethan!" Guy cried in horror. The simple-minded lass helped out herding the village's piglets in the woods, one of which she currently had clutched in her arms. It had been a late litter and one of them had clearly made a bid to explore the neighbourhood and was being brought back to the pen. She had taken a shine to Guy when he'd first come, and had brought him a circlet of daisies one day telling him he was her king. At the time Guy had been dreadfully embarrassed, but over the months he'd come to understand that she lived in a world of her own, and that she wouldn't harm a fly intentionally. When Meg had had her pups he'd been hard pressed to get Bethan out of the corner of the stable to give Meg some peace. But her adoration of the pups had cemented an odd friendship.

Now he was watching his strange little friend being ridden down by a blood-crazed monster. He drew in his breath to yell to her to get down on the ground, for there she would stand a better chance – too low for the rider to reach and unlikely to be trampled deliberately by the horse. As the first syllable was on his lips he was winded by a punch in his middle from Ianto.

"Quiet you fool!" the old man hissed. Still gasping for air like a fish out of water, Guy gestured frantically at Bethan. "I know, boy, but there's no way to stop hi..."

Earl William's spear hit Bethan and went straight through her, lifting her like a broken rag doll and flinging her arms wide, so that the piglet flew out of her arms and ran like mad for the nearest cover. By the time the earl's horse had turned the piglet was out of sight.

"Did you see that? Her familiar disappeared!" he roared. "Throw her in the river! No witch will be buried in my churchyard!"

Guy was on his knees, but Ianto and another man he couldn't see through the tears hauled him upright.

"For God's sake don't let him see you mourning her!" Ianto whispered ferociously. "I can't save you, boy, if he thinks you were friends with her."

The import of Ianto's words hit Guy, and he belatedly realised that Ianto had been right. As mere servants there was nothing they could ever have done to prevent Bethan's death. The earl's word was the law around here, and justice was his to dispense without questioning from those beneath him. Even had there been one around here, the Hundred Courts could only stand up to a sheriff so far – and witchcraft was a touchy subject which might or might not go to a bishop's court, or could be dealt with locally, which meant de

Braose. And, if crossed, it was well within the means of the earl to have Guy, and potentially Ianto too, killed as Devil-worshippers, and be able to justify himself to outsiders for his actions. Guy would be putting more than his own life at risk.

Odo came up and nuzzled his hand, whimpering mournfully, and it was the dog more than anything which brought Guy back to reality. The dogs had smelt Bethan's familiar scent, and were now distressed by smelling it mixed with that of her blood. Thrusting the skins of blood and sacks of entrails to Ianto, Guy turned to the other men.

"You four go with Ianto and take the hounds back to the kennels and get them fed with the others."

"What are you going to do?" Ianto demanded anxiously.

Guy's face was a mask. "The earl wants her thrown in the river? ...Then I shall be the one to do it," he said in a voice devoid of any emotion.

With Odo, Motte and Bailey lolloping at his heels Guy strode to the dejected corpse and when the earl turned back he saw his young huntsman, knife in hand leaning over the body.

"Good man, that," the earl observed to his two closest companions. "Gutting pigs or witches, it's all the same to him! Ha! ...Good man! ...Need more like that!"

What Guy was actually doing was cutting the spear out. It was all he could do to not be sick, and he had to stop frequently to brush the tears from his eyes so that he could see what he was doing. By the time he was done, the main riders were long out of sight, and the only ones left to see him were the already receding huntsmen with Ianto. All they saw was him hefting Bethan's frail body over his shoulder and setting off in the direction of the churning river in its spate, soon to be lost in amongst the trees and bushes, the three lymers still following.

Ianto shook his head sadly. "He had to toughen up sometime," he observed to the oldest of the men who nodded sagely, but inside Ianto feared what this had done to his young friend.

That night in the hall Earl William was fulsome in his praise for Guy. "By Our Lady, that was some hunt today, young man!" He gestured to the pile of steaming meat which had just been processed into the hall. "Here! Bring your plate and have some!" As Guy reluctantly came forward the earl speared a large chunk on the end of his knife and dumped the nauseatingly still-bloody chunk onto Guy's wooden platter. "You'll join us to hear the minstrel!" It wasn't a request but a command, delivered by the earl already half in his cups and farting noisomely, to the discomposure of the men to either side of him.

Guy inclined his head but his hatred gave him courage. "I fear not, my lord."

The earl's head shot up and Guy found himself looking into two eyes as bloodshot as the boar's had been. "You fear not!" Earl William mimicked. "What do you mean by that!"

Guy braced himself but held his ground. "My lord, I'd be honoured but I cannot."

"Cannot?" The earl was going a distinct shade of puce, but Guy was beyond feeling fear of what might happen to himself, he just wanted to thwart the earl in some way, albeit ever so small.

"My lord, I believe this hunt gave you much pleasure, and may I venture to suggest that this will mean that you may grace us with your presence for another before too long?" De Braose was now looking perplexed, frowning in mead-fuelled incomprehension as Guy plunged on. "But the skill was not mine alone. The dogs, sire. They must be tended to. I would be a poor servant to you if I gave you one such day's sport and then neglected my duties just to revel, thus depriving you of the means of further days' hunting if the dogs sicken for want of care. Therefore, if I am to be a good servant to you I must forego tonight's pleasures for the duties for which you pay me." Not that it was the earl paying, but Guy wasn't feeling that brave to say so!

The earl was temporarily lost for words, but then he guffawed heartily, echoing it with another thunderous fart. "A good huntsman who knows his place! I like that! By Saint Peter's balls, I do! Go on then, man, and I shall expect nothing less than the best from you the next time I come hunting!"

Bowing deeply Guy backed away from the top table and then hurried from the room, his presence already forgotten by the carousing earl.

So do you think I tossed my friend's corpse into the freezing deep waters of the River Monnow like a piece of carrion for the fishes, Brother Gervase? Well I did not! Away from the site of my savage lord's act of slaughter, I realised that her slight little body would be frozen in no time – long before she would normally stiffen in death. There was a small hollow in a bank not far away and I put her in there, laid her out properly, and covered her with bracken and some branches. Then I had to go back to the castle and endure watching that vicious murderer taking his pleasure with nary a thought for the suffering he had caused.

I tell you, Brother, if the opportunity had presented itself I myself might well have been confessing to murder now, for I could have killed him with as little compunction as he showed to Bethan. In my eyes he was an animal more dangerous than the boar he was now devouring, and one I would have willingly slaughtered for its lethal madness. St Thomas must surely have been staying my hand that evening, for my own control was all but gone! What I did do was leave the castle that night while they were all in their cups and busy congratulating themselves. I went to the pitiful hovel Bethan's family called their home. Someone had to tell them why their daughter had not come home. I was too late to break the news, but her father and two brothers came with me to fetch her. With a couple of picks we broke the ground in a corner of the wood beyond the castle sufficient to bury her, and put her in that shallow grave wrapped in old sacks.

A couple of weeks later a funeral was held for one of the old villagers. No-one said a word, but that grave in the little churchyard was dug very deep for just one old woman, and in the depths of night the four of us went to the wood and once more carried Bethan off. This time to the consecrated ground and a proper burial. We did not dare put too much earth in on top of her, but even so there was still a deep enough hole that any of the earl's cronies passing by would not pass comment – and anyway, a day later the whole thing was filled in once more.

That was my first experience of the quiet rebellion of the ordinary people. No feats of arms, no heroics, just a quiet denial of their oppressors' ability to rob them of everything. Whatever the earl might say they all knew the truth, and truth was that Bethan was one of life's innocents and would not have known what a witch was, much less been one. And as one of their own, and for the sake of that innocent soul, the villagers were not having her buried anywhere but on hallowed ground. They could not defy the earl directly but that did not mean that he had won.

Are you surprised at that confession, Brother? Did you think I would be on the other side? Did you think that I would ingratiate my way into the earl's good will to save my own skin regardless of the cost? Then maybe you do not know me as well as you think, eh? For that was just the first of many times when what my masters saw was less than the truth. Such a short time had been spent down with the common folk and yet those experiences had already changed my whole life, as you shall see. Yet for now there I was, still only nineteen (for my twentieth birthday was still three months away) and already breaking the spirit of my vows of service, even if I appeared to be carrying out the actions. A life already setting out on the path of deception, I can see you thinking! But is it the kind of deception you thought it would be?

Chapter 3

For the next few years I carried on at Grosmont. When Earl William was not there it was a comfortable enough place to be. When he was there I made sure that I had already got hunts marked out in advance, and made myself scarce if he was coming mustering war parties against the Welsh.

No, Brother, stop those looks! I was no coward, but de Braose's kind of war was not mine. The poor folk who scratched a living on the upland soils were no danger to us or anyone else, no matter which side of the border they lived on. The war bands came from deeper into Welsh territory and from the courts of the princes of Powys, who were every bit as bloodthirsty as de Braose. But I shall come to them again soon enough!

Every sign of boar and red deer I came across I made a mental note of, and made signs of my own on the nearest main track so that I would be able to find them again. As soon as the first of the earl's retinue would appear to prepare the place for his arrival, I also took it upon myself to warn the villagers of where we would be hunting – I never wanted to witness a repeat of Bethan's awful death, and my consideration made me a popular man with the villagers. Unfortunately the reality was easier said than done where the sheriff was concerned, for the man could hunt all day once his blood was up, and although I knew where we would start, where we ended was often more up to fate than my designs.

Twice more I saw villagers caught up in one of de Braose's bloody frenzies, and I cannot tell you whether I felt it was any less repellent knowing that they had at least not died, but were maimed for life by spear shafts through the leg. All I could see after those hunts when I closed my eyes at night and dreamt, was de Braose wiping his bloodied hands across his mouth to cuff the mead dregs away, and laughing with twisted glee as if he had never seen people in his path, but merely some kind of lowly animal barely worth turning from the greater sport for. In some of my dreams he even sprouted devil's horns, and I would wake up all of a sweat and shivering, hastening to the church with the dawn to pray that my dream had no basis in the real world. The boy I had been, who had aspired to one day become a great knight, was turning into a man who despised such men.

Yet my planning for my own future was, on the whole, less fraught and, because my ambitions had become far more lowly, more successful. I began to realise that I had made a better move than I had realised, for now I was officially an employee of the crown's – not of some wilful and whimsical local lord who could have made my life hell. (I was beginning to have the worrying thought that maybe de Braose was not an isolated specimen of the breed!) Mercifully, my lord de Braose might be our sheriff, but he only administered our area – which saved us at the castle more than once from the earl's wilder actions! The same could not be said *for his own lands, going by the tales some of the men-at-arms who came with him told us on the quiet. De Braose appeared to get some kind of perverse and morbid enjoyment out of baiting the Welsh with acts of terror, even if all he got for it was a bloody skirmish with a minor lord. One day, I believed, his actions would come back to haunt him, and you will hear later how right I was to believe that.*

King Henry, meanwhile, never came to the Honour, for he was far more engaged with his lands beyond the sea. Four rebellious sons were enough to keep even a king of his stature busy! ... Oh do not snort so, Brother Gervase! That is not treason! We all know now that England had a narrow escape in not having Prince Henry succeed instead of our lionhearted King Richard, but at the time it was never something we dreamed of. Back then chivalrous Prince Henry seemed like the future king we had all hoped and dreamed of, not the dissolute wastrel with a quick tongue for a lie, which was the reality. No Brother Gervase, if you must believe in something, then believe it was divine intervention which gave the prince the raging gut which saw him off, for it surely saved many other lives. The oldest of King Henry's sons might very well have been worse than his youngest, and even you cannot call King John good!

But back to our story... The reality of what happened to Baldwin was equally elusive to me in those days. My contact at Garway was good to his word, and when I went there to dispatch a mangy young wolf who in desperation had become too bold for its own good, he came and found me. Frère Edgar was a good man, and had done more than I had any right to lay claim to in the name of such a short acquaintance. Frére? Oh yes, Brother Gervase, the Templar knights are called brothers too, just like you monks, for they are a fighting monastic order. Did you not know that from here in your cloister?

Well, his lengthy inquiries had revealed that Baldwin had indeed gone to Foulbridge, but young men were of more use to the Order elsewhere than manning estates in a country so distant from their primary cause. So he had already been moved on to France by the time Frère Edgar had spoken with his friends in the north. He thought it might well have been to one of the great farms in France where the Order's horses were bred, and that at least was some consolation for me. Especially as Frére Eadgar said word from the Holy Land also told that Princess Sybilla's husband, William of Montferrat, would act as regent for their infant son if necessary. That hopefully meant that there would be a strong heir who was not one of the warmongers, to take over when the poor young leprous King Baldwin IV died. Surely that would keep the Saracens in order, I hoped and prayed? Without a war my Baldwin would have no reason to be sent east unless he was stupid enough to volunteer – and I sincerely hoped Baldwin's chivalrous nature did not extend that far! Of John and Allan I heard not a word, nor was I in any position to find out.

So I began to focus more on my own life. It was hardly thrilling for the most part, although in the summer months there were brief moments of excitement when the Welsh looked threatening, and in the winter, as I said, when the hunting season was upon us. I also had several more enjoyable encounters with Megan which resulted in her having first one son and then another. She was happy with our arrangement and so was I, and if her husband was in any way suspicious of her sudden fecundity then he was sensible enough not to say anything about it. Megan was bright enough to ensure that she at least tried to lure him to her bed within the month of my visits, although she did it when he was in his cups with ale and hazy of memory. She swore he took so little notice she might just as well not have bothered – and had it not been for any potential questions from the sharper women in the valley she would not have even made that much of an effort after the first time. But she would go to the alehouse and make much of fetching him home even if he did nothing once there.

Did I love her? Yes, in a way, but it was not a great passion, and had she suddenly become widowed I think neither of us would have hurried to make our relationship more permanent. It was an enjoyable means of both of us staying sane and keeping our reputations intact, and it harmed no-one. My unacknowledged sons in the valley were unlikely to suffer anything like John and Allan's fate, I was greatly reassured to discover. Emboldened by this realisation, as her ardour waned with the ties of motherhood, I found another married woman down in the village of Llantilio, whom I visited less regularly but in a similarly amicable arrangement. I was always very aware of the danger I presented to a young unmarried girl unless I wished to marry in a hurry – and I feared a life chained to someone I could hardly stand the sight of, just because I had been unable to control my bodily needs!

That is not moral cowardice, Brother, so do not tut over that either! I simply recalled how miserable Lady Hawyse had been married to fitz Waryn, and how much happier my own parents had been – whilst my father lived – having married out of genuine fondness for one another. I might not have had an estate to marry for, but it was clear even in the foolishness of youth, that a hasty marriage in poverty could be every bit as miserable as the mighty fitz Waryn's.

Gradually Grosmont became home, and I still have a place in my heart for the wild rolling countryside of the Marches. Grosmont sits in a lovely spot with views to the hills, and I often enjoyed watching red kites and buzzards wheeling high overhead in the early morning, or a red deer herd passing through the trees in the distance in the dusk, when I took my turn at lookout duties up on the ramparts. Skenfrith sat in a very different kind of location, for although it was only half a dozen miles farther down the Monnow's course, it sat low on the river's banks, not up on a rocky knoll like Grosmont. Yet it too was prettily situated, guarding the river crossing as it did.

The one of the three I was never entirely comfortable with was Llantilio. It might have been just my imagination, but I never liked the great flocks of rooks which inhabited the few trees near the castle. All manner of strange things would set them off, and then they would fill the air in a black cloud, tumbling and cawing in a wild mêlée before settling again. One old man-at-arms said they were the souls of soldiers dead before their time who could not rest and, in some ancestral pagan fragment within my heart, I could believe it. Fanciful I know, but those birds unsettled everyone. It was not helped by the land around the castle walls being kept empty (because Llantilio was that much further into potentially enemy territory), except for a lone lightning-blasted oak sticking its bleached white branches skyward, like some ancient priest reaching up to God in supplication. No doubt I could have moved there and gained a reputation as a soldier – for there was a good reason why later, in 1184, King Henry would order Llantilio's curtain wall to be upgraded in stone – but I was always glad to quit the place, and worked on being simply Guy of Maesbury, the huntsman, instead.

Oh do not look so disgusted, Brother! The truth is not always high drama. Would you rather I lied? ...No? ...Well then! ... Shall I throw you a trifle to keep you happy? A confession of my going behind a sheriff's back (albeit in the Marches and not in Nottinghamshire) in spirit if not openly? ...Very well, for it is more of my story in any case!

We are now a good three years onwards from when I had come to Grosmont and two beyond when Bethan was murdered, and I was twenty-two years old...

The Black Mountains, Brycheiniog, Wales: November, the Year of Our Lord 1182

For once Guy was a long way from home, deep in the Black Mountains of Wales. He'd been tracking this wolf for days closer to home and he currently had Motte and Bailey with him as well as Blue, Meg and Aethel. This wolf was no runt of a litter, but a large, cunning male who seemed to have a young female running with him. A large male who had lost all fear of men, and had already savaged one of the tenant farmers as he tried to protect his penned sheep. Guy normally mentally justified his job by telling himself he was doing the wolves a service by culling the weak and sick from the packs which hunted in the mountains. Today, however, he was doing the job he was really paid for and there was no room for sentiment, for this wolf had to be just a bit mad, and if it wasn't stopped it would lead others into dangerous habits. That's why he was taking no chances and had the two heavy lymers with him and all three of his deerhounds, even if the lymers' main job was what they were doing now – quartering the ground with their noses, following the trail.

They'd crossed the Monnow and headed up towards the monastic church at Abbey Dore at first, but the wolves must have doubled back, for the morning after they'd left the abbey's guest quarters, Motte and Bailey could only find a trail going back the way they'd come. They trekked up over one ridge, then down into the Escley valley before swinging north again. It didn't help that it was a bitingly cold day and had been like it for weeks. Far too cold for Guy to be camping out in order to follow his quarry unless he had absolutely no other choice, not only for himself but also for the valuable dogs' sake too. So that meant finding somewhere to lodge for the night as each evening fell, and with it being November he was losing usable daylight with every day that passed. However, going back unsuccessful was not an option in this case, and he'd slept in humble barns for the last four nights for want of anywhere better, kept warm by the presence of the dogs as they all dug deep down into the straw against the bitter nights.

"Good boy, Bailey," Guy praised the big black and tan dog as he began casting about again. Some men Guy had encountered would have been berating the dogs by now for not keeping to the scent, yet Guy could never see the sense in doing that. Far better to keep encouraging the animal to do its best, rather than worrying it so much that it was too fretful to focus. And once again Guy's patience paid off. Sudden Bailey was off, tail in a half-wag in time with his long swinging ears, as he plunged off down a steep track.

Motte joined Bailey, and together they led the other dogs and Guy at a brisk trot down one slope and then up the opposite side of the small stream valley. The whole area was criss-crossed with these little tributaries to the larger streams which eventually drained down into the rivers Dore and Monnow. It was a constant series of up and downs, which was tiring on the legs, especially as Guy had reluctantly foregone bringing a horse for the last three days as the terrain had got worse. As he puffed his way up to the next rise he realised that they had steadily climbed the mountains in their wandering path, for in the distance he briefly glimpsed Hay far below. The castle was nothing like as grand as the de Braose's main castles at Brecon and Abergavenny, but Guy was definitely well within the de Braose lordship, and it was possible that one of the family was in residence at the substantial fortress which guarded one of the crossings of the River Wye, for there seemed to be smoke rising from several fires within the castle walls. Or at least he sincerely hoped those were cooking fires!

Only that May, de Braose had been soundly routed by the Welsh at the battle of Dingestow, just south-west of Monmouth Castle, and then Llantilio had been stormed. On that occasion Guy had fought with the rest of the Grosmont garrison alongside de Braose's men in a counterattack to drive the Welsh off, and had been glad to do so. Coming up against seasoned warriors was not something he was shy of doing, and in the running skirmishes with the Welsh rearguard he became battle-seasoned and relieved to have proven to himself, if to no-one else, that he was no coward. He had then been in the thick of the hand-to-hand fighting to retake Llantilio, even if he didn't particularly like the place. That day the rooks had had plenty to feed on, and Guy was glad to have come out of it with nothing more than near-miss scratches from a few Welsh arrows, and a couple of gashes from swords, although when the padded gambeson came off he had some spectacular bruises showing where the ring-mail had been punched inwards by blows from swords, and the butts of spear shafts. At least the inter-linked steel chain had saved him from worse, though, and he vowed that he would do his best to get himself his own hauberk and gambeson to be kept in good repair against his involvement another such battle.

At times like this it was very clear that the Welsh could be a formidable enemy, and one he fought against without reserve or second thoughts. It was de Braose's tendency to then take his revenge upon the local population which stuck in Guy's throat, and he wondered many times why de Braose couldn't see how many unnecessary enemies he made in doing that. It antagonised local people who might otherwise have sent warnings of Welsh scouts, for the Welsh war-bands tended to loot as they went, and could be every bit as much of a nightmare for the little folk as de Braose. He'd seen plenty of cottagers desperately putting out flames as he'd ridden behind de Braose, frantically pursuing the raiders only to find that they had reached Abergavenny Castle ahead of them, and had used the castle ditch to hide in and then bring ladders to the wooden palisade. The garrison had been killed or taken prisoner – except for those who had retreated to the stone keep – and with the palisade burned down, de Braose had only the keep of his castle left standing by the time he got there.

However, the fires whose smoke Guy could now see down in Hay seemed far too controlled for fighting. It paid to be cautious, though – he didn't want to find himself a prisoner of some Welsh minor prince! If he hurried he might reach Hay by nightfall, and the lure of a warm bed and a decent hot meal were real temptations, for come what may, a steward and basic staff would be there. On the other hand he might well lose the trail again if he called the dogs off now. Groaning out loud at the thought of what he was missing, Guy hurried after the dogs, who were in danger of leaving him behind after his pause. It was small consolation to find that he'd been right about the dangers of losing the two wolves, for they now turned left and began following the ridge south again. By Guy's guess they were trying to head off into the higher range just beyond the Black Mountains, the nearest of which was Brecon Beacon. It made sense if you were a wolf, he conceded, for the Wye lay across their path and they would have to go further west first before they could go north. He was pretty sure the wolves must have caught his scent by now, and he wasn't about to underestimate what they might do as a result.

However, by nightfall he was no nearer to closing on them and resigned himself to his first night completely outdoors. It was still a bit early in the winter for snow, but nevertheless it was bitterly cold once the sun had gone down and with it what little warmth there had been during the day. A small, low-walled stone sheep pen was the best cover he could find which was man-made, and one he rejected in favour of a small, but snug, hollow formed by the upended root system of a great fallen oak. The huge old tree had torn a massive hole out of the ground, and although much of the soil had washed back in over the months, it still left a sizeable overhang of tangled roots and wood to provide something like a roof. The now desiccated smaller twigs and branches from its top made excellent kindling, and with some old dried fungus as the starter for his fire, he soon had a goodly blaze going at the front of the makeshift cave.

He'd allowed the dogs to hunt on their own account as the light had dimmed, and although Motte and Bailey were too slow to catch much, the deerhounds had soon provided hares for all five dogs, plus a couple which Guy spitted and began roasting over the fire for himself as soon as he had sufficient heat from it. With some rather stale bread and the last of a skin of small beer it was hardly a luxurious meal. On the other hand, few people must have hunted up here because the hares were large, plump, and lacking in the fear of dogs that those closer to home had. Allowing the fat to run into the bread as it toasted also made it far more palatable than it might have been.

Guy was so busy gnawing the last of the meat off the hares' haunches that he was unaware that someone else was around until Meg gave a warning low growl. Looking up he saw beyond the fire the shadow of a figure standing very still, watching him. The Welsh after him, he wondered? Using the cover of throwing the tiny bones onto the fire in order to move, Guy eased his long knife out of his boot leg, then worked his way into a crouch as he put a couple more small branches onto the fire. It all looked innocent enough to the observer, but he was now in a position to spring if attacked. Careful not to look into the flames and destroy his night vision, Guy glanced out of the corner of his eye in the direction the figure had been in. It had gone! Before he could relocate it there was a blur of fur as Blue, Meg and Aethel streaked past him. Too well trained to make a noise when hunting, the only sound was the scratching noise made by their paws disturbing the dead leaves underfoot.

Expecting a human scream as he launched himself to his feet to follow them, Guy was nonplussed to suddenly hear very canine snarling coming back, and then to realise that Motte and Bailey were weighing into the fray. Turning and seizing a burning brand from the fire, Guy waved it above his head and for the first time saw what was happening. The wolves were right here! Blue and Meg must have gone after the large male wolf, while Aethel drove the smaller bitch back into a tangle of brambles. Attacked on both sides the dog wolf was barely holding them at bay, and, when Motte threw his sizeable weight straight at it, the opening gave Blue the chance to go for the throat. In a tangle of paws and jaws the four went down in a heap, but Guy knew his own dogs well enough to know that it wasn't them shrieking in pain. They had no need of his help and he turned towards Aethel intending to aid her in bringing down the bitch wolf.

What he saw instead shocked him. As Motte pounded in on Aethel's left she moved around to snap at the wolf's flank revealing what she had been standing guard over. It was a small boy! And then Guy registered the taller figure he had seen outlined earlier darting back and forth on the other side of Aethel, trying to reach the child.

"Stand still!" Guy called out the command. "My dogs won't harm the child, but if they think you're threatening me they might attack you. Stand still, I say!"

The figure wobbled on its feet but then at least kept its feet still, even if it continued to paw at the air as if reaching out as an anxious reflex. Within moments the snarling and death-throe screaming of the wolves ceased and all that could be heard was the collective panting of the dogs, a soft sobbing from the shadowy figure, and closer to, a muffled whimpering noise. In three strides Guy had reached the little figure on the ground and bent down to place a reassuring hand on its shoulder.

"Steady now, you're all right," he said soothingly. Then got to his feet, stepped over the child and went towards the other figure holding his hand out, palm upwards, beckoning the figure forwards with his fingers. "Come here!" He kept his voice level and non-aggressive. "Leave!" he commanded the dogs more forcefully. It wasn't just the strangers he was talking about. The dogs could have the meat from their quarry but Guy needed the pelts as proof of a successful hunt, not to mention what they would fetch him in payment. He couldn't afford to take a mauled pelt back, but he needed to deal with these newcomers before he could begin skinning and gutting.

The dogs backed off and sat down, then subsided and began licking their fur clean of wolf blood, not remotely perturbed by the presence of the two strangers. That alone convinced Guy that there was no threat to him here, for Blue and Meg in particular would never have relaxed so quickly if there had been.

"Come here," he repeated his invitation, and the figure of a lad detached itself from the shadows. "Who are you, boy?" he asked. As maturity had gained on Guy he had become a tall, well-muscled young man, even if he was never going to become a truly huge man like his fitz Waryn cousins and John. Yet because he was mostly in the company of older men, even if only by a handful of years in some cases, he hadn't quite appreciated how much he'd grown in the last years until now. It was something of a shock to realise that the lad before him couldn't have been far off his own age, yet barely came up to his chin. "By Our Lady, lad, what are you doing out here alone at night? Those wolves could have eaten you! They've already killed bigger men! Why aren't you at home?"

"Please don't beat me, my lord," the lad whimpered instead.

"Beat you?" Guy was shocked. "Why in Jesu's name would I want to beat you?"

Frightened eyes flickered up to catch Guy's gaze and then dropped again. It was behaviour Guy had seen time and again amongst the lowliest peasants whenever anyone with any sort of rank was around. It was the mark of the utterly downtrodden and Guy hated seeing it. Maybe because it had never impinged on his small world back in the fitz Waryn estates, it had been glaringly obvious when he'd first encountered it at Clun. However, back there it had been just a few of the nearby villagers who had feared a beating, and in every case their plight had been at least partly their own doing, for they had been those least inclined to pull their weight in even the basic work. Only when he had moved to Grosmont had Guy seen real terror in the eyes of all the peasantry when de Braose and his thugs were about. Raise your eyes, or fail to bow low enough, and who knew what might befall you on such a lord's whim? No matter that the king was their lord and not the sheriff. The king wasn't the one handing out the punishments, and never likely to be as far as the local people were concerned. King Henry barely crossed their minds for the most part, but the brutish de Braose they knew only too well. Such panic and fear was written across the face Guy could see by the flickering fire light.

"You're the huntsman, aren't you?" the nervous young man was saying. "The one they said was coming hunting wolfsheads!"

Guy felt his gut lurch. Wolfsheads, not wolves? That meant outlaws! He'd been told his services were also needed over on the sheriff's estates before he'd set out, but in his naivety he'd assumed it was the normal run of animal predators he was being asked to deal with. It had never remotely occurred to him that he might be asked to hunt a human quarry. That was a whole new bundle of trouble, and it sickened him to think of what he might've walked into unprepared. For now, though, he forced himself to focus back on the figure before him.

"Well, I know nothing about that," he said as dismissively as he could manage. He didn't want this poor soul fearing for his life when he'd only just escaped being eaten by wolves. "Word might have been sent on ahead of me, but I've been on the trail of these two rogue wolves for a good week now, and they're the *only* quarry I've been hunting. So I know nothing about wolfsheads, and anyway, they aren't my business."

The lad seemed to breathe a sigh of relief, which prompted Guy to ask again,

"So why *are* you out here? I presume this little one is with you?"

"He's my brother, my lord. He followed me and then it was too late to take him back."

Guy looked back over his shoulder and saw a small boy of about seven sitting up in the leaf mould, hugging his knees and shivering.

"Mother of God, you're both frozen," Guy muttered despairingly and reached out and grasped the older lad's arm, briefly registering how thin he was. "Come over to the fire, both of you!" He towed his captive over to the fire and kicked it into more life. Pushing the young man down onto the bed of bracken he'd laid down, Guy went and picked up the child and brought him back too, then threw more small branches onto the fire to build it up. The dogs had followed him back and at a click of his fingers now settled down on either side of the two boys. The dogs wouldn't even think of hurting them, but Guy was hoping their presence would stop the pair from running off into the night in fright.

"When did you last eat?" he called to them as he dragged the first wolf body to the rising light of the fire.

"Yesterday," the older one mumbled, still only giving Guy flickering upward glances, and for the most part keeping his eyes firmly on the ground.

Guy was appalled. In these freezing conditions they wouldn't have survived the night at that rate. He began expertly skinning the wolf, and once he had the pelt off and rolled up, jointed the carcass up and gutted it. He had a pot which was permanently strapped to his pack and he now threw all the innards into it to cook up for his dogs. They needed some good food after the energy they'd expended, not to mention being given their reward for a clean kill. He did the same with the second wolf and then turned his attention to the pot. He dumped most of the stale bread from his remaining loaf into it to bulk it up for the dogs and to absorb the blood, but the best of it he set to one side and began slicing the meat off one haunch up into slivers which he then set to cook on his tiny skillet.

"Wolf isn't good eating," he said conversationally. "Certainly not something the highborn like on their platters! But happen it will keep you two alive tonight, I'm thinking. I'm sorry, but all the hare is gone, and it's too late to ask the dogs to hunt more."

Two pairs of startled eyes shot up to stare at him. This clearly wasn't what they'd expected. However, the youngster in particular was too hungry to argue. As soon as Guy piled the shredded meat and juices onto the bread and handed it over, the lad tore into it with gusto. His older brother was more wary, but when Guy handed over his leather water flask the last of his resistance seemed to collapse. As the famished pair gratefully chewed away, accompanied by the slavering of the eating dogs, it gave Guy time to think and a nasty thought crept forward into his mind. At the time of Bethan's death he had been too stunned to think overly much about how Sheriff de Braose had perceived him. However, since then Ralph at Grosmont had dropped him the hint that de Braose thought Guy was 'his sort of man', and the sheriff's comment about him hunting a witch as good as a boar had also found its way to Guy's ears.

Thoroughly revolted by such an idea Guy had shrugged it off, and his fellow inhabitants of the castle, seeing that he had no intention of capitalising on his favoured state with the sheriff, had let it pass. Now, though, Guy wondered whether the sheriff had forgotten it so quickly. De Braose's arrogance would ensure that he would never think there was another motive to Guy's actions other than the one he had ascribed to them. Therefore, if he had a problem in his own estates, he might well think that the man whom he perceived as a cold and calculating hunter might just be the man to sort it for him.

Guy shivered and offered up a prayer of thanks to the Almighty for having had this forewarning, for without it he might have walked into Hay or Brecon castles without an inkling of what was awaiting him. And once there he would've had the greatest difficulty in extracting himself without bringing the wrath of the sheriff down on him, and also onto those who were presumed to be in charge of him back at Grosmont. Now, though, the question was what to do with the pair he'd just rescued.

"Why did you think I'd be hunting you?" he asked the older brother as the youngster tottered into the back of the now warm cave-like space, and curled up between Motte and Bailey to instantly fall asleep. "You're a bit young for hardened outlaws, aren't you?" He kept his tone jovial and waited to see what it produced. "What's your name? Mine's Guy of Maesbury."

"Sir Guy?" the lad asked.

Guy hooted with laughter. "Lord, no! I'm not Sir Guy of anywhere! I'm just Guy the huntsman. My father was just a man-at-arms up at Maesbury then over in Nottinghamshire, not some noble." That wasn't entirely the truth. Guy's father had certainly been higher born than a man-at-arms with a manor of his own once upon a time, even if he hadn't been a leading knight of the realm, but Guy wanted the boy to trust him as one of his own.

The lad seemed to think about that for a second then said,

"My name's Gwillam, and that's my brother Dafydd."

"Well then, Gwillam, where do you come from?"

"Our da worked for one of the farms down on the Wye."

"Worked?"

"He died two years ago."

"I'm sorry. I know how hard that is. I lost my father when I was about Dafydd's age. How are you managing now?" Guy could guess that without a man in the family even the roof over their heads might be in danger of being taken away. The poor peasant farmers in this region didn't get enough off their land to be able to support a whole family who couldn't work. It wasn't callousness, just dire necessity.

"I tried to do Da's work," Gwillam confessed, "but I got sick in the spring last year. Old man Jonah left us alone as long as he could, he really did. But then the early harvest needed getting in and he had to hire someone else. Jonah managed to find a single man as a tenant and convinced him that Ma could keep house for him when he moved into our home, so that she kept the roof over her head and Dafydd with her."

"But what about you?"

"I was better by then so I went to Morgan's, the next farm, and got a bed in the byre."

"So what went wrong? ...I'm guessing something went wrong by the fact that you two are out here?"

Gwillam paused to burp as the warm food settled heavily in his empty stomach. "The new man had a brother who was one of the sheriff's men," he said despairingly. "He'd come around lording it over Ma and Daf. Trouble was, he'd eat their food too! His kid brother could only put so much food on the table, so when it was gone it was gone and Ma and Daf's hard luck if they hadn't had any."

He sighed and scrubbed at his eyes with his sleeve, which was when Guy saw the tears he was trying to hide. "I used to set traps for hares and anything else small I could catch when I got the chance, and I'd take them over for them. It wasn't much. We just about got through that winter, but it was in the winter when the brother started coming over regularly. I think the food got a bit scarce in the castle and he thought he could get some extra at his brother's. He kept telling Ma and Daf that they should be grateful and give it him, because when the Prince of Powys came raiding again in the summer we'd all need men like him to fight for us. Him, fight? Ha!"

"Not much of a hero?" Guy guessed.

"Na! Not him! Pumped up windbag!" Gwillam glanced back to make sure Dafydd was fast asleep. "Thing was... I couldn't understand why Ma was getting paler and thinner all through the summer." Guy's mind made the grim leap ahead to what had happened, but kept quiet to let Gwillam tell him in his own words. "I also started sneaking odd vegetables out with me when I crept off to see them at night. Morgan never moved out of his bed, and with me out with the beasts who was to hear my comings and goings? Who'd miss a few turnips or peas and beans from the animal feed? But no matter how much food I took her she still seemed to be sickening. I was worried stiff. If she died who would look after Daf? I couldn't have him with me, and there isn't anyone else!

"So I started trying to catch fish too. I'd got this eel trap down by the river. I even caught a few! Then one evening in September I managed to get away from Morgan's earlier than normal on account of him and his sons being off to market all together for once." He sighed. "It was a lovely autumn evening, warm and sunny. I was down in the river getting my trap out of the water when I heard someone coming, so I hid in the bushes at the water's edge. It was Ma with an armful of washing she was getting in that she'd left drying on the bushes. I was just about to call to her when that man turned up. Before I could do anything he'd knocked her to the ground and was rutting like a pig on top of her."

Gwillam sobbed. "But what cut me to the bone was the way she kept pleading with him not to do it again! *Again?* I couldn't believe what I was hearing! Then I understood why she'd been getting so sick. It was him! He'd been at her all summer! Raping her like a common whore! And if he got a child on her she'd have been thrown out for a slut and he'd not have cared." The hunted look came into his eyes again as he turned to face Guy. "I don't know what happened next. ...The next thing I remember is that I'm standing in the shallows with this rock in my hand and covered with blood and Ma's screaming."

"Where did the body go?" Guy asked gently, feeling nothing but sympathy for the lad.

"Already floating off downstream," Gwillam said wearily. "Trouble was, it had to go past the castle. So they spotted him and hauled him out. I'd have got away with it, 'cause at first they just thought he'd slipped and bashed his head on a rock. But his brother starts bawling and shouting. God knows why. He was treated like shit the same as us. You'd have thought he'd be glad to see the back of his bullying brother! Five weeks ago the sheriff came back and the brother begged him to deal with his brother's murder. He pointed the finger of blame at Ma at first, but anyone with eyes in their head could see she couldn't have hit him hard enough in her state, and even the sheriff isn't *that* stupid! So the finger of blame came my way and I made a run for it into the hills. For the first weeks I did all right 'cause the sheriff moved on. The soldiers at Hay couldn't find their arses with both hands!"

Guy had to grin at that. He'd met some of the Hay garrison and hadn't been impressed. They were clearly the ones who weren't fit for anything else but sitting behind a castle wall and keeping the gate shut. The real fighters were out on the move with the sheriff, especially this year when trouble was in the air, sometimes up at Builth Castle deeper into Wales, or at Pain's Castle, which was the small de Braose castle on the Welsh side of the Wye, only four miles west from Hay but infinitely more vulnerable. But of course now they were at the end of the raiding season, and de Braose had evidently begun to spend time closer to home. With hunting more on his mind, it had no doubt also turned to chasing down fugitives from his rough justice.

Gwillam wiped his nose on his sleeve. "My rough luck then that the real soldiers decided to have some fun. Twice this week I've only just escaped being ridden down. Then Daf came to warn me that a real hunter was on his way to find me," then he broke down completely and sobbed for several moment. "He told me... Told me Ma was dead too. ...Died giving birth too early to the bastard of that guard!" He sobbed and hiccupped a bit more. "I tried to take him up to the monks at Llantony. I thought he'd be safe up in the hills. But he wouldn't go, said he wouldn't stay. Said we had to stick together now."

"He probably had the right of it, if it's any consolation," Guy said sympathetically. Two lads suffering for the actions of adults, and rape at that, was striking a little too close to his own past for him to be able to take a detached point of view. "The monks at Llantony are close to the Abbey at Gloucester and that means a lot of noble patronage. They certainly weren't any too pleased to have to accommodate even the likes of me a while ago. And that's with the lord of next door Longtown Castle being young Walter de Lacy and the sheriff's brother-in-law! I doubt they'd take in an orphaned peasant boy! And if they got even a whiff of your brother being related to what they'd see as a common murderer, they might have tried to use him to lure you into the sheriff's hands."

Gwillam looked aghast. "They'd do that? But they're monks! I thought they had to give sanctuary?"

Guy sighed. "They do! But even sanctuary's not forever, Gwillam. Forty days is all you get! And at some point you would've had to leave, and they could've had the sheriff sitting outside the gate waiting for you."

"What are *you* going to do with us, then?" Gwillam asked after a moment's weighty silence.

Guy shrugged. "I have no idea, but whatever it is it won't involve handing you over to the sheriff, that you can be sure of."

"But why are you helping us?"

"Because ...because someone I grew up with was left with nowhere to go not so long ago. Someone whose mother had been raped by a powerful man, but my ...friend ...paid a heavy price too. Now get some sleep!"

Come the morning Guy had something halfway resembling a plan. He would have to go to Hay with his pelts if the sheriff was there, but first he would backtrack for a day. There was an old disused shepherd's hut off up in one of the little side valleys, and he planned to leave Gwillam and Dafydd there while he went to Hay. That way, if he met anyone on his way down into Hay he could say that he had come along the tracks from Llantony and not seen hide nor hair of the fugitives. However, he made a point of asking both lads for a distinctive piece of clothing, for he planned to tell the story as if he had not been on hand to save them from the wolves.

Armed with this evidence he hurried down into Hay two days later and, finding the earl himself there, asked for an audience with de Braose. The Earl was his usual ebullient self, overly fulsome in his welcome which was as false as the Earl's assumed gentility in the presence of his wife and daughter-in-law. Bertha, Lady de Braose, was every bit as formidable as her husband, and Guy guessed that she was cut from the same cloth as her aunt, the old Empress Maud who had caused so much chaos in her fight with King Stephen not so many decades ago. Daughter of the Earl of Gloucester, Lady Bertha was used to getting her own way in every matter where her husband could not overrule her, and Guy loathed her on sight. No amount of wealth would make her a likeable person. Her daughter-in-law, Lady Maud, on the other hand, was a very different woman, and had he dared Guy would have flirted with her, for she was a strikingly good looking young woman. Instead he noticed her occasional shivers and dared to offer her the pelts.

"I'm sure these would make a warming mantle for you, my lady, against this chill Welsh weather," he said, bowing as he spoke, and was rewarded with a smile. Going by the looks he was also getting, wherever her husband was he was certainly neglecting her of late despite the young family which he knew they had. Indeed the oldest – the third generation of William de Braoses and a strapping seven year old who could have dwarfed Dafydd – had come in, spotted Guy placing the pelts on the table before Lady Maud, and had grabbed one and was now whooping his way around the hall draped in it, getting covered in dried blood in the process and trying to make wolf-like noises, to his grandfather's clear annoyance. However, the sheriff forced himself to ignore his grandson and was reclaiming Guy's attention.

"I'm glad to see you were successful in ridding us of these pests," the earl growled in satisfaction. "Now then, I have another job for you since you are here."

Guy decided to pre-empt de Braose. "If my lord is thinking of my dealing with the wolves which have pestered closer to here I think they were the same ones," he lied smoothly. "You must have wanted them caught badly if they were savaging your peasants."

"Savaging my peasants?" de Braose was wrong-footed, which secretly pleased Guy.

"Yes, my lord." Guy pulled the rumpled clothing from out of his pack. "Saving your presence, my ladies, but I came upon the wolves too late to save these two. They'd already been feasted upon." Lady Maud gave a little whimper of distress or disgust, but Lady Bertha merely quirked a cynical eyebrow.

"Feasted?" Now de Braose was intrigued.

"Yes, my lord. A young man and a boy by the looks of the remains. Quite what they were doing up in the hills alone is beyond me, for I saw no sheep they might have been tending."

Guy was all innocence on the surface, but he saw de Braose's vicious smile and knew he'd been right to do it this way.

"Well, well, Huntsman, you keep on pleasing me!" the earl chortled. "Don't lose any sleep over those two! I was planning on having you chase them down too and bring them back for a good hanging. ...Seems the wolves beat me to it! Ha, ha, ha!" His belly-laugh had a false joviality to it, and Guy wanted to retch had it not been so dangerous to do anything but stand there with solemn blankness on his face.

"Have you any other business for me, my lord?" Guy asked, silently praying that no other poor unfortunate had crossed the sheriff of late. He wanted to get back to Gwillam and Dafydd, for he had an idea of where he might take them now.

Unfortunately, despite being prepared for the worst, it now transpired that Earl William had every intention of having a purge of his more lawless tenants. Men upon whom he had pronounced a death sentence in their absence at the eyre court in Hereford. Had they been elsewhere and the crimes been something which could have been pursued through the Hundred Courts, the fines the earl would have been urged to demand by those courts as an alternative punishment would have been owing from the leading men of the missing men's villages, and therefore the earl's bloodlust would have found no outlet. However, they were deep within the borders and these were severe charges (albeit trumped up, Guy thought), and so de Braose had had no hesitation in proclaiming the heaviest of sentences of his choice. He was already all the more irate at being foiled from carrying the sentences out at the time of pronouncement, and would clearly be deaf to any pleas for clemency. With his heart sinking at every word Guy listened as the sheriff gave him his instructions.

"Bloody Welsh tenants! Think they can get away with anything! I want proof, man, do you understand? A left hand for each of the miscreants! No right hands! I don't want you taking a pair from one man and making out you've dealt with two! Not that you would! Ha, ha! I've seen you hunt! ...No lover of the druids and their kind, are you?" It was a statement, not a question, for the earl believed he knew his huntsman.

"No, my lord," Guy said with as much firmness as he could force into his voice, although he was unable to feign any enthusiasm.

Hopefully the sheriff would think him such a cold fish that he never got excited about anything. "I shall need a horse, my lord, if I'm to go to Longtown and then on to Abergavenny."

"Of course," the sheriff snapped, irritated by such an obvious statement.

"What I meant my lord is that I shall have to take a day to try a horse out. Not all are happy having five large dogs right at their heels, and I have no wish to end up in a frozen ditch and unable to complete my hunt because my horse took fright at my own animals. Do I have your lordship's permission to try several of the horses tomorrow and set out the next day?"

Mollified, the sheriff nodded. "Yes, yes, do as you see fit – just bring me those hands!"

"And where should I come to, my lord?" Guy asked deferentially. "Will you be here for some time or should I make for another of your holdings when I'm finished?" Guy was silently praying with all his might that de Braose wasn't intending to ride part, or all, of the way alongside Guy with his retinue. If he did then there was nothing Guy could do to soften the blow which was about to fall on these unsuspecting folk.

However, his luck was in. "Humph!" the sheriff snorted. "We shall be riding up to Builth in two days' time, and thence to Knighton. Our king wants me to have words with Roger de Chandos who's developed ideas above his station! It may take some time, but if I'm not there then I shall have returned to Brecon." Then he paused as he went through the visibly painful process of thinking and farting at the same time. "You may take the hands to Brecon whatever happens. My lady will be going there ahead of me, and she can confirm your executions on my behalf. ...Remember, Huntsman, I want the arm off up to the elbow! I want proof these men dead, not crippled and using a hook for a hand! Dead!"

"Yes, my lord," Guy forced himself to agree, then extracted himself as fast as he could. Tomorrow he would have to ride back to the boys with whatever supplies he could scrape together, and then leave them to their own devices. They weren't fit enough to spend long days alone out here so he'd have to send them on somewhere, but somewhere away from the sheriff's eagle-eyed gaze.

As he left the hall and went to where the dogs waited for him he saw a small girl standing regarding them with a look of absolute dread on her small face. By the way she was dressed she had to be another of the young de Braose brood and so Guy felt it incumbent upon him to speak to her.

"Don't worry, miss," he said with a forced smile. "You can walk past them. They won't bite."

Two huge eyes turned up to him and in a hushed whisper she

said, "William says that I must con... conquer my fe... fear. If I don't he says father will find me a husband to beat it out of me."

Guy grimaced. What a charming child the heir was! Already happily terrorising his little sister! It didn't bode well for future generations of de Braose tenants. Then he realised she had cringed back from his grim expression and promptly crouched down to her level.

"Don't worry, lass. What's your name?" he asked with much more warmth and sympathy in his voice.

"I is ...I am Margaret," she said shyly, now blushing and looking tentatively up at him through thick dark lashes.

"Well you come and take my hand, Margaret," Guy said, and when the small hand pressed into his, he wrapped his other arm around her and held her close. "Here Meg!" he then called softly and the big grey bitch stretched leisurely and then ambled over to them. Young Margaret shrank back into Guy's arms, screwing her eyes up until Meg snuffled at her and then planted a big sticky lick on her pink cheek. A nervous giggle escaped Margaret's lips and then she cautiously reached out and touched Meg.

"Oooh, she's so soft!" she cooed, losing her fear to scrunch her small fists into the thick downy undercoat.

"See? I told you she wouldn't hurt you," Guy said, beckoning the others over too. "Dogs know when someone means them harm. If you're kind to them you have nothing to fear."

Margaret disappeared into the midst of the five dogs, all of whom were wagging their tails enthusiastically now.

"Margaret! What are you doing?" the high-pitched imperious voice of her brother broke into the laughter. "Where are you?"

"I 's here, Will'm!" his sister called out gleefully, emerging from under Blue's chin. "Look! I isn't afraid no more!"

The young heir's face turned sour in an instant. "You're just showing off!" he sniffed. "I could do that too!" and he marched towards the dogs.

The change was dramatic. Suddenly Blue's hackles went up, Meg stiffened, and Aethel's ears pricked as far as they could go, while from Motte there came a low rumble of warning. Guy had to bite his lip from hooting with laughter as Bailey gently took hold of Margaret's collar and pulled her back away from her brother as the three deerhounds' heads dropped into hunting mode. Clearly the dogs had made up their own minds that the little girl was in danger. As for young William, he froze in his tracks and suddenly looked more his age.

"Call them off!" he squeaked. "Call them off or I shall tell Father!"

"Of course, young sir," Guy said calmly, snapping his fingers and gesturing the dogs to lie down, "but you might find he'll tell you that you shouldn't be provoking big hunting dogs before you're old enough to handle them."

Young William glowered at him but turned on his heels and stomped off rather than arguing. Margaret, on the other hand, seemed to have grown visibly in confidence from the experience.

"I stroked the doggies and William couldn't," she said with almost breathless excitement. "I gotta tell Nana!" and she ran off, to tell the Nana whom Guy assumed would most likely be her nurse rather than her grandmother.

For himself Guy thought he'd had quite enough encounters with the different generations of de Braoses for one day, and took himself off to an early bed, relishing the thought of being warm again at least for one night.

Mercifully the next day dawned misty with a frosty dankness, discouraging men from venturing out too far. Guy had begged more bread than he really needed from the castle's weekly supply of dog bread, and now had three extra loaves and some other bits of food stuffed into a light bag over his shoulder as he rode out. Picking the horse had been easy, and he had no doubts about the dependable mare he was mounted on. She had the stamina to keep going in all conditions and was indifferent to the dogs' presence from the moment Guy had led her from her stall. This ride was a fiction for the earl's benefit, and once back in the hills Guy commanded the dogs to stay at their former campsite and rode on alone. There was no need to tire them with a long journey today.

As he rode up to the cottage he was glad to see that the boys had followed his advice and there was no sign of activity, although he could smell wood-smoke and guessed that the fire was not long gone out. Dismounting he called out,

"Fear not! It's me, Guy! I'm coming in!" and shouldered the door open, pausing in the light to let them see it was him and that he was alone.

A rustle from the corner announced the appearance of Dafydd from under a pile of old bracken and then Gwillam appeared from behind the door. Guy thrust the sack into his hands.

"Take this and listen! I don't have long before I'm missed so I have to be quick about this. You must keep to the high ground and head north. Cross the road coming out of Hay with care! The sheriff will be riding north for Knighton tomorrow, so you must be past that road today! Follow the hills as they come to an end and work your way around to the east until you can see the hamlet of Dorstone below you. It's a tiny place, not more than a handful of houses, so you can skirt it easily tomorrow night and cross the road down to the Monnow without anyone spotting you. Now I want you to go straight over the bridge and on towards the loop in the Wye. There's an old monastery at Bredwardine – it's no big abbey! Just a couple of buildings and a few monks. But they're the old kind. Men of faith living away from the world. They don't get involved with the high and the mighty. They'll take you in out of charity and ask no questions. Tell them I shall come back for you, but it might take a week or two because I have to go into Wales for the sheriff first."

"But where will we go then?" Gwillam asked worriedly. "The sheriff owns all the land around here!"

"I know some of the knights at the Templar preceptory at Garway," Guy reassured them. "You won't get much, but you'll have a roof and a bed and food if you'll help look after their huge flocks of sheep. You won't get any wages except your keep, but you'll be under their protection. Better still, the sheriff never has need to flex his muscles over their lands, so you're unlikely to even see him from a distance unless he decides to pay the preceptory a visit – and I'm sure you can be out in the fields if that happens, eh? Not that I can imagine a lord like de Braose remembering the face of some peasant he's barely laid eyes upon. Now come on! We have to get you out of here and on your way. Unless you get caught here and prove otherwise, the sheriff thinks you're dead anyway, so let's not give him chance to change his mind!"

With the boys out and on the tracks through the hills, Guy headed back to the castle and the next day set out for Longtown. Not, however, before he had conducted a little business of his own. Quiet inquires had revealed just who the man was who had fingered Gwillam to the sheriff, and Guy had a mind to see justice was done there too. Since the brother's death, Gwillam's bane had taken to hanging around the alehouse in Hay closest to the castle, where many of the soldiers went when they were able. The man wasn't popular, though, and Guy, having sat in the alehouse quietly watching and listening, saw him staggering out and weaving his way home alone.

Guy had picked his spot carefully. One which wasn't overlooked from on high from anywhere in the castle or other houses. Once the man was clear of the few who were also wending their bleary way back home, Guy called to him softly. Too drunk to think, the man followed Guy's soft calls and offers of more drink until he was in position. It was simplicity itself to drop him onto some straw and slit his throat, and for an expert huntsman like Guy butchering a corpse was nothing, for he'd felt more respect for some of his animal quarry than this weak and self-serving man. Guy had no doubts that the man's actions had had more to do with what he thought he could get in rewards and payments, than ever they'd had to do with genuine remorse for a lost brother.

Taking the left arm off at the elbow, Guy thrust it into a prepared sack. That was one trophy already, and that meant he could possibly save a second innocent victim of the sheriff's ire. The rest he divided into two piles. The bones and identifiable body bits would go into the pen-full of pigs who were waiting a little way off in anticipation of being needed for the lord's table themselves. As he dumped the grisly remains into the pen he couldn't help feel there was some strange kind of rightness to it all. He had made de Braose think the fugitives were dead, so de Braose was leaving early, which meant the pigs wouldn't be needed after all. That might just mean they could be slaughtered to feed their peasant owners' families instead, and save someone really needy from starving in the cold winter. For that Guy thought the pigs deserved a good meal.

However, he wanted every trace of the man gone, and there weren't that many pigs and they had already been fed. So the majority of less identifiable bits would go into the gruel he would mix up for the castle's dogs in the morning. He'd instantly got on with Ianto's counterpart at Hay, and had joined him that morning with the kennel routines, which meant the man would think nothing odd if Guy did the same in the coming morning. The bits which the pigs and dogs couldn't easily see off, like the man's shoes and his clothes, plus the de-fleshed and smashed skull, he managed to throw into the back of the fire which was already being stoked for the big communal bread-oven out in the castle's yard in readiness for the next day's bake. The old ashes had already been scraped out and the overnight embers were glowing gently, since a huge oven like that was never allowed to go truly cold because of how long it took to heat up again, and Guy made sure that what he threw in went further back than the starter for the morning's new fire. The scullion who tended that would be half asleep when he threw the first of the new fuel in during the dark of the early hours of the morning. It would be exceedingly bad luck if the bits were spotted, and Guy felt reasonably hopeful he'd got away with his first murder.

Riding once more into the Black Mountains it was less than a day's ride to Longtown, even keeping the horse at a slow pace to not tire the dogs. It was a typical large motte and bailey castle, but at the moment only with a skeleton garrison as its de Lacy lord was not in residence while the upgrading building work was in progress. They pointed Guy in the direction of the scruffy little Welsh village of Clodock close by, and furnished him with a description of the felon the sheriff wanted hunted down, then left him to it. There was a certain advantage to turning up with five massive dogs, Guy thought. Even if he'd been a midget with a squint, the men wouldn't have questioned his ability to hunt a man down, and a big man like him was clearly thought to need no help at all from them. It meant that he could ride down into the village and assess things for himself.

As he sat on his horse looking at the ring of sullen faces staring back at him – or at least those who dared to and weren't echoing Gwillam's downcast gaze – Guy decide to take a chance.

"I have to take back the arm of Rhodri the shepherd," he announced to the crowd.

"Oh? And how will you know it's *Rhodri's* arm?" a youth spat back sarcastically.

"Precisely..." Guy said, leaving the word hanging there in space. More heads gradually looked up at him until he was sure he had their undivided attention. "The sheriff wants an arm. Do you think he'll know what Rhodri's arm is like? Do you think he even knows what Rhodri looks like? His men have told him Rhodri is trouble. So, is Rhodri still here?"

A short, burly man of mature years stepped up to Guy's horse. "Don't be bloody daft, lad! He went weeks ago! The last we heard he was deep in Deheubarth with the sons of Maredudd. If the sheriff wants Rhodri he'll have to ask the Prince of Powys for him!" and there were soft chuckles all around at that. Madog ap Maredudd was giving the Mortimers a run for their money in the north, while the late Prince Maredudd's other sons were the current running sore in de Braose's side. A constant drain on the Marcher lord's resources they were never quite enough of a threat to bring King Henry and his army here away from his problems in France – not at least since the early days of his reign. If the sheriff wanted to deal with the Princes of Powys (of both north and south) he was on his own unless he could convince another lord to throw in his hand with him, and few were keen for a foray into such unforgiving territory. All of which Guy knew full well, and was counting on the villagers knowing too.

Now he leaned out from his horse to the man who was clearly the village headman, but spoke softly.

"Look, I don't care what Rhodri is supposed to have done. He could've done a lot worse than pelt the earl's friends with rotten eggs – was one *ever* a stone? – and blind one, and kill a man-at-arms, before I'd start bothering. And I'm not so much of a fool that I can't see that his supposed previous crimes are trumped up charges too. I'm a wolf hunter, not a man hunter. I've just come here and been saddled with this bloody job. A job I don't want! So I've got to take a man's arm back to keep the sheriff off my back too. Now, you tell me how we're going to do this? If you've got someone recently buried whom we can take the arm off and save the living, then I for one am not going to object. The dreadful thing is going to be alive with maggots by the time I get it to the sheriff anyway! But it has to be a left arm and a man's."

The man turned and looked around the assembled little group. "Go on, get out of here, all of you! Except you Hwel, and Madog." The other villagers looked at him curiously but went, while two strapping middle-aged men came closer. When there was only the four of them left, Guy dismounted and the head man spoke quietly.

"I don't want all and sundry knowing the details. Gwen couldn't keep her mouth shut to save her life, and Nesta is sweet on one of the young lads at the castle. Hwel, your cousins further on up the valley, have they buried Rhys yet?"

"Two days ago," the solid farmer supplied briefly.

"Then tonight we have to go and dig him up and take his arm off!"

The two looked askance. "What are you doing, Ivor?" Hwel fretted.

"Look," Guy hissed urgently. "I don't want to deprive you of another man to work your lands in Rhodri's place – because I dare not go back to the sheriff empty-handed, and if I was daft enough to, he'd be down on you like the very Devil with his men-at-arms and it would be all the worse for you! So I have to have *someone's* arm! Let's do this, then you can tell the earl's reeve that you've had to move someone else into Rhodri's cottage – even if it's his sons or whoever else of the family is still here. Moan just enough about losing an experienced pair of working hands and you'll be believed. Stuff along the lines of Rhodri being a pain in the arse but useful at lambing, harvest and ploughing. Tell him everyone's shocked at seeing Rhodri hunted down by the dogs."

"The dogs?" Madog had been absentmindedly ruffling Blue's ears and now snatched his hand away.

Guy grinned. "Don't worry! They wouldn't hurt you! But we have to put on a show for the castle back there." He pointed to the tiny timber motte-and-bailey fort sitting on the turn in the river bank (and which would undoubtedly be made redundant by Longtown when its expansion was finished), where a few soldiers idly watched from the walls. "From the top they can see a fair way down this stretch of river. So find me a lad about the right size as Rhodri and tell him to run across the ford, then through that copse of woods opposite of the castle. I'll chase him with the dogs until we're out of sight. We'll fake some screams as though he's being mauled. Let's do it around dusk when they won't see so well. Then tonight we get the arm. I won't go right back into the castle. I'll just ride close enough to wave the arm at them in the morning and then ride on. You must dig a grave then. Rhodri's accused of murder, so you must make out he's who you're burying. Not in the graveyard! Not for a murderer, and anyway the priest would have to know then."

"Oh you don't have to worry about our priest," Ivor the head man said blithely. "He's on our side! Appointed by Llandaff, not some English bishop! Brother Tuck is a good man. He'll help."

Guy felt more than a little sceptical about that, but kept his doubts to himself. At the moment he just wanted to convince the garrison he'd done his bit and hunted the fugitive down. If he couldn't get the arm then he'd have to come up with some other plan, but time was pressing.

As the light grew dimmer in the short winter afternoon, Guy mounted up out of sight and got the dogs ready. Sensing the excitement, they were full of curiosity and circled the horse restlessly. A young man wearing obviously borrowed clothes by the way they fitted where they touched came up to them.

"I'm Peter," he introduced himself. "They won't hurt me, will they?"

"The dogs? Lord no!" Guy reassured him. "Go on, stroke them, they won't bite."

Gingerly Peter reached out and warily patted Meg, who promptly covered his hand with licks and leaned against him for more fuss. Not to be left out, Blue and Aethel also began nudging him for attention, so that his fear was completely quashed.

"Now," Guy interrupted the fun, "start running through the ford and up to that wood where Ivor told you to! In a moment I'll let the dogs chase you. Don't stop! Go right round the wood out of sight, then sit down and scream like you're being mauled! The dogs won't harm you and I'll give you a good head start. ...Now run!"

Peter, now keen to play his role, took off like a scalded cat. Eager to join in this new game, the three deerhounds began howling in their excitement, which was just what Guy wanted. When he let them begin the chase, they took off yipping like excited pups, but to the uninitiated Guy hoped it would sound bloodthirsty and savage. How would anyone know that his dogs were silent when they truly hunted? In these valleys the sounds easily got distorted and as he pounded off, calling to imaginary fellow hunters on foot, he prayed it would look convincing from the castle. When he finally caught up with Peter it was to find the young man in a tangle on the floor with the dogs, all panting and all feeling very pleased with themselves as demonstrated by Peter's grin and the dogs' wagging tails.

"Was that all right?" Peter asked.

"Bloody marvellous!" Guy permitted himself a laugh. "By Our Lady! That was a realistic scream you gave back there! I thought for one horrid moment we'd chased you so hard you'd broken a leg in a rabbit hole or something!"

Then Hwel, Madog and Ivor appeared, also grinning widely.

"Right Huntsman Guy, let's introduce you to Brother Tuck!" Ivor declared.

And so we come to your traitorous fellow priest, Brother Gervase! For that is no doubt how you think of him, is it not? But he turned out to be a priest of a very different kind to you, Brother. I must confess that I had been struggling with what I perceived as the Church's role in society. My experience of men of the Church so far had consisted of the poor priests who tended to the ordinary people, such as our priest back at Kilverton in Nottinghamshire and who, to a man, were as downtrodden as their flocks. Or the personal chaplains of the great men who came to Grosmont, who without exception were unctuous and self-serving creatures, more attentive of the wine than their Psalters.

Where were the men of God, I often found myself asking? If peasants were put on this earth to till the soil and provide sustenance for all, and the nobility were there to fight and protect us from earthly enemies, where was the third side of the divinely planned triangle? The holy men whose role was to pray for all of our souls and protect everyone's immortal souls from demonic assaults? I could never imagine the poor priests' feeble prayers carrying much weight in the great battle against evil, and the chaplains only seemed to go through the motions of praying when there was someone watching! I had no doubts about the greatness of God, Brother, have no fear over that, but the more I saw of the Church the more it baffled me. Where were the men of vigorous faith, I wondered? Our champions of Jesus Christ in faith as the knights were on this earth? And then I met Tuck!

When we got to St Clydog's tiny church at Clodock I met the squarest man I had ever seen. Brother Tuck was nearly as wide as he was high, yet he was certainly not fat, and although he was a man of above average height the bulk always made him seem shorter. Even under his long monk's habit I could see that. He had shoulders like a bull, rising to a thick neck and tapering down to his middle in the other direction. Big feet showed beneath the robe's hem, and big, muscled hands reached out to greet Ivor, whom he clearly knew well. As Ivor explained why we were there I found myself staring into a pair of sharp blue eyes that were so pale they were like water crystals. But then Tuck was a sharp man. Nothing got past his gaze! And as I was soon to discover, his heart was as big as the rest of him.

He listened to Ivor without saying a word but looking me up and down all the time. Only in later years did I discover how touch and go it was for him to believe in me and my plan! Thank Jesu he did, though! ...Oh do stop tutting, Brother! We shall be here forever and I shall die unshriven if I have to modify every word to your picky sensibilities! ...By Jesu I gave thanks, and meant it, Brother, so do not regard me as some kind of blasphemer. Good Brother Tuck went and got his shovels and we dug like men possessed. When we got down to the woollen shroud and Tuck had cut it open, I sent the village men away to sit on the churchyard wall. There was no need for them to watch me ply my grisly trade on one they had known and cared for. Had there not been such grievous need I should not have been so keen myself.

I think it was at that point, though, that I realised that Tuck was made of sterner stuff. He watched me for a few moments then lowered himself into the hole with me. Without saying a word he took hold of the arm and braced it for me so that I could make the cut quicker and cleaner.

I confess the strain of the last couple of days was catching up with me by then, for suddenly the full import of what I was doing bore in upon me, and I had to make a dash out of the graveyard to be very sick. Oddly, that endeared me to Tuck more than anything. He told me months later that seeing me retching pitifully against a tree convinced him that I was not by habit or inclination so hard or heartless. He offered me shelter in the tiny house he had by the church for the night, and once we had laid the corpse to rest once more with earth and heartfelt prayers, I accepted. We bade farewell to the village men, and I entreated them to keep to our plan or else I would not be able to save them from de Braose's anger again.

That night I slept poorly and come the morning Tuck offered to hear my confession. At first I hesitated. After all, more than my life depended on Tuck not running to the sheriff or his bishop as soon as I was gone. But I was still a young man, and far from as hardened to the ways of the world as I became in later life. Initially with great caution and then with relief, I bared my soul to Tuck. Unlike many a priest I had met before or since, he was able to see beyond the act itself, and if he judged it was never without thought.

It made it so much easier to tell him of what had happened in Hay when I went back for the second night. Of how I had discovered that Gwillam and Dafydd's poor mother had been buried as little better than a garrison whore, unshriven and unblessed, and her lodger bragging in the alehouse about how he and his brother had used her. But even worse, how I had heard him bragging about how he had abused little Dafydd with perverted games – he made out it was Dafydd who had been corrupt in his soul and instigating what was done, but I saw through him if no-one else did, or was too scared to say so. At that Tuck gave a very unbrotherly growl and I knew he was as offended by it as I had been. You might not have given me absolution, Brother Gervase, but Tuck did!

And that might have been the end of it. He agreed to dig a grave outside the churchyard wall for the absent Rhodri, and to put a hay and wood stuffed shroud in so that anyone investigating would think they had found the woollen winding sheet. He would put it right down by the banks of the Monnow, he told me, so that the river, which rushed along his church's eastern boundary, could be blamed for a body purportedly swept away in winter floods, should anyone investigate further. He agreed wholeheartedly with me that taking Gwillam and Dafydd to Garway was the best thing to do. He even wrote a letter to the Templar's priest backing my plan, although it was on a very well-used piece of parchment and despite careful sanding beforehand the ink still bled badly. But if I thought I was done with Brother Tuck, he certainly had not done with me. As we shared a midday day repast of sweet apples, nuts and cheese, with some barley biscuits he had made on a griddle, he seemed to make up his mind.

˜You trusted me with your secret, Huntsman Guy,˜ said he. ˜Now I shall trust you with mine! For I have need of your help in return for giving mine.˜ And what a secret that turned out to be!

Chapter 4

I shall never forget that day, sitting in Brother Tuck's small cottage listening to his tale unfold. He had been given to the Church as a tiny boy as an oblate at the Benedictine monastery of Ewenny, down on the south Welsh coast, and then later had been a monk at Monmouth. However, the monastic life had not suited him, no matter how hard his teachers had tried, and for a time he had gone on a pilgrimage to the Holy Land. Despite not intending to fight as Baldwin's Templars' did, or the Hospitallers, nonetheless – as so often happened out in such perilous lands – he found it necessary to learn how to defend his body in the process of saving his soul. A dead body has no chance of redeeming its immortal soul without some serious intervention, he pointed out to me with a mischievous wink.

However, he had returned home with others of his order, convinced that there would never be peace in the Holy Land whilst so many men out there thought only of power. How right he was in that, Brother! Yet once back here in England Tuck had found it far harder to settle, not easier, for as he told me in his own words, once God had lifted the veil from his eyes to the injustices of the world he could not ignore them at the will of a mere abbot! ...Ah! You are scandalised again Brother Gervase! Well be prepared for another shock when you meet the Almighty, because he might just regard Tuck as being the more saintly of you two despite having been an outlaw, for Tuck was never afraid to have his faith in God tested the way you are. Ah me! And there you go again with your horrified sighs! Keep breathing, Brother! We have a long way to go yet and there will be bigger shocks for you before the end! ...But to return to Brother Tuck.

The good brother did not fit easily into the political world of a great abbey, and for both his sake and the abbey's, it was rapidly decided that he would be better used for God's purpose out in the world ministering to the souls of a more robust and less refined community. And so he was sent to his first flock on the de Braose lands at Abergavenny, not to the great abbey hard by the castle, but to a small church at Llanbedr up in the hills above the River Usk. Then when he had irritated the abbot yet again he was moved from Llanbedr – where there were regular pilgrims going up to the church of St Issui higher up the narrow valley, and where the Church therefore had vested interests to be kept free of a rebellious brother's interventions – to Clodock, where he could be watched more closely and visited by passing clerics without warning.

Yet by now Tuck had become good at avoiding the beady eyes of politically inclined priors and abbots, although he did moderate some of his practises whilst there – only later was I to know just how radical Tuck could be in his beliefs and assertions. Oh he was never less than totally devout, Brother, never doubt that. Tuck's faith in God, Jesu and Our

Lady, not to mention the saints as well, was the most steadfast of any man I have known. Rather, it was the form and the practice of his beliefs which raised many eyebrows.

However, to return to our tale, as a priest out in the community he had begun to hear things about a prisoner, in no small measure helped by the news from the regular passing traffic crossing the upper reaches of the River Monnow at Clodock's ford beside his church. There was a mysterious poor soul who had been immured at de Braose's pleasure for many long years in the keep at Abergavenny. These days I know how that must have piqued Tuck's insatiable curiosity! He could no more have ignored it than grown the extra foot in height to spread his girth out more evenly. Ah, Gervase, ...Tuck was good company and I do so miss him in my old age. Please God we shall be reunited when my time comes and I pass on, for I would love to hear his big laugh once more and have him remonstrate with me as he used to do, for he loved to argue a point and was knowledgeable about many things. And that knowledge served him well back then, too. For once he heard that the prisoner had been at Abergavenny since 1165 he began to put things together. By the time I came into his life he had not only discovered the man's identity – he had managed to worm his way into the castle and speak to him!

So who was this mystery man? Well you might remember the name Seisyll ap Dyfnwal, for it was his murder and the resulting massacre which had forewarned me of what a de Braose could be like when roused. But those actions in 1175 were only following on from earlier acts perpetrated by King Henry himself. For in 1165, after a failed attempt to subdue Gwynedd, the king had his many Welsh hostages blinded out of spite. Two of these hostages were the sons of the Welsh prince, Owain Gwynedd, and it was one of these two unfortunates whom Tuck had discovered still mouldering years later on in de Braose's castle. The de Braoses of all generations had clearly appealed to our late monarch as brutes who would not be swayed by compassion, even before the earl I served had enacted his worst upon Seisyll's family.

Now Tuck could never abide seeing a free thing tethered, and having seen what a resourceful soul I could be in an hour of need, he believed God had sent me to him in the nick of time to help. So there I was, Brother, a mere twenty-two years old and planning to challenge the king's wishes, no less, and in the company of someone who was to become a notorious outlaw!

The Black Mountains, Brycheiniog, November, the Year of Our Lord 1182

"I've been planning to get Maelgwn out for some time now," Tuck confided to Guy, as he sat on Tuck's floor putting a fine-toothed bone comb through Meg's fur to un-matt it. "And what happened this summer with that raid on the castle has only convinced me of the need to move faster. How would he have got out if the keep had begun to burn? After all he's stone blind! The problem, though, has always been where to take him. He can hardly fend for himself. And it didn't help that the bishop and abbot confounded my plans by moving me up here. When I heard of him first I was still at Llanbedr, with more chance of getting help from a Welsh rebel or two! I originally thought about the monastic community at Caerleon-upon-Usk. I was going to take him there – still might if I can. Not as himself, you understand. That would be far too dangerous! ...No. He would go as Brother Maredudd. ...It's a common enough name amongst the Welsh, and if anyone is left alive who remembers him from Gwynedd it's only as a boy. No-one amongst the Welsh have seen him since he's grown to manhood."

"Isn't Caerleon still a bit risky?" Guy wondered, giving up on a particularly tight knot and using his knife to gently raze the hard ball of fur off Meg's foot, before it got too hard and began making her limp. "I mean, Caerleon's rather on the route through to south Wales and the ports to Ireland. You know how keen the king is supposed to be about Prince John becoming King of Ireland. What happens if King Henry decides to march another army down there to ship across to Ireland, as he did last year? He might just stop at the abbot's house for want of anywhere else if he comes himself and doesn't want to pause at a castle. Can you chance it that the king of all people won't recognise this Maelgwn? Does he resemble his father the Welsh prince?"

Tuck growled in frustration. "Curses! I'd forgotten the king and Ireland! ...You're quite right, of course. That's why the Romans built their fort down there centuries ago, because it's smack in the middle of the access to the southern coast. Yes, of course King Henry would go that way to Ireland. I, in my confidence, had only been thinking that the southern principalities of Wales are now under the Plantagenet's heel, and unlikely to rebel as the princes of Powys have been doing. You see, Guy, God sent you here to help me! I've spent hours mulling this over and over by myself, and then you come along and put your finger right on the sticking point!"

Guy smiled and shook his head in amusement. Nothing he said was going to convince Tuck otherwise, and that his appearance had simply been good luck. Then he had a thought.

"Of course we could try to get him out by using that..."

"What on earth do you mean?" Tuck sat bolt upright and gave Guy a fixed stare.

"Well... If Caerleon is so obviously heading in the wrong way, ...do you think we could convince the Abergavenny garrison to hand the prisoner over to monks going to that monastery? Not actually take him there, you understand, but make them think that's where he's heading. Better still, let's make it your old monastery of Ewenny. Just in case the soldiers can tell Black Canons from Black Monks! It's further on into Wales anyway, so less likely to be proven false. ...Tell them that the earl has had enough of a blind old man cluttering up the place."

"Maelgwn is no old man, Guy! He's only just passed thirty."

Guy thought for a bit longer. "But is he hale and hearty? ...He's been a prisoner for nearly twenty years! He can hardly have been getting much exercise. Maybe his importance is more his birthright than what kind of man he is now, do you see?"

Tuck rubbed his chin in thought. "Hmmm. ...I see where you're going with this now. No, Maelgwn is only a frail man, very pale and quiet. Not much of a threat in himself."

"So could we say he was sickening and dying?" wondered Guy. "Have you any herbs which would give him a dire cough? Something like that? A raging gut isn't any good because he must be fit to travel. And it needs to be something which appears will give him a long, slow demise. Could you find such a thing?"

"Yes. But how would we get it to him?"

"I have to go down to Brecon to report back to de Braose. If I go straight to Abergavenny now, and call at the castle under the guise of this damned hunt the sheriff wants me to do ...hmmm ...I could use it as a pretext for checking on the prisoner. Especially since they haven't got the bailey fully secured again yet after the Welsh raid. If I could get to him, give him the herbs and then tell him I'll be back after I've been to Brecon so he's to take the herbs on a certain day...?"

"...Might work!"

They bounced the idea back and forth for the rest of the day, working out the kinks. In the end they had to assume that it would take Guy at least a week before he would be able to go to Abergavenny, and that was if all the other three men he was supposed to hunt down could be so easily accounted for as Rhodri the shepherd had been. They then thought it possible for him to take the time to go to the castle under the pretext of hunting one of the fugitives. That way, if anyone should mention his presence it would be seen as for legitimate purposes. Also the sheriff would be less likely to smell a rat over the speed with which Guy was accomplishing his tasks if he drew it out a little longer. And Guy wanted the severed arms to be in a further state of decay by the time he got to Lady de Braose. The last thing he wanted was for her to make too close a scrutiny of them!

He would give the herbs to Maelgwn and leave. Then Tuck would go back in two weeks' time. No point in going too quickly, they thought, for that might draw associations too. He would come bearing a letter authorising the now sick Maelgwn to be taken to Ewenny, and Guy would turn up as his escort. A man who could be trusted to hunt down fugitives would be sufficient to escort one sick man whom no-one cared about any more. And they were pretty certain no-one cared about Maelgwn anymore, because the sons of Owain Gwynedd's second wife had been quick to murder the remaining sons by his first marriage in the unseemly scrabble for power when Owain had died in 1170. Maelgwn was now the lone surviving son from that first family, so the fact that no-one had even bothered to find out if he was still capable of leading a rebellion surely meant that his half-brothers either thought him dead, or of no political significance. And if he was of no political use to the Welsh then he had long outlived his uses to King Henry. Guy and Tuck could only presume that the king had not conveyed this to de Braose, and so the sheriff was assuming he was still under royal orders to keep Maelgwn imprisoned.

"By Our Lady, Guy! I feel we shouldn't linger too long over getting him out now," Tuck confessed. "Now you've put my mind on that track I can't help but think poor Maelgwn wouldn't be long for this world if the king did recall he was still alive! I shall have him here with me. At least he'll be safe for a while and we'll have time to plan more thoroughly for his future."

And so Guy rode onwards. The briefest of stops at Abergavenny Castle gave him the names of the other fugitives he was supposed to go on and hunt from a harassed captain of the guard, and he was on his way once more. He also picked up further supplies there for himself and the dogs, while secretly eyeing the place up, and then set his horse for the road up the Usk valley towards Tretower Castle telling them he'd be back soon. This aroused no comment for they told him that two of those he hunted had taken refuge in the high valleys to the south.

When Guy got to the home of the first man it took no time at all to work out that this was just an ordinary farmer who had been pushed beyond endurance. The rape of his oldest daughter by one of de Braose's leading knights, and the act going unpunished, had been the final straw in a long line of callous acts which had been got away with out in this wilder landscape. Guy knew only too well that had this happened in Nottinghamshire or Yorkshire, the farmer would at least have had recourse to the local Hundred Court and the vocal support of many neighbours. Out here he was isolated and powerless.

"Have you anyone who might appear in your place if the earl sends his reeve out here? Pretending he's a new tenant in your stead even though you'd still be here, I mean?" Guy asked the farmer, after managing to convince him not to try braining him with the mucky shovel he'd had in his hands when Guy had ridden in.

The man shook his head. "My brother died, ridden down by those bastards when he got in the way of a hunt four years ago. Our two sons died before they had chance to become men. If you take me, my wife and daughters will starve to death!" and he brandished the shovel at Guy once more, eliciting more growling from the dogs.

"In Jesu's name, man, put that bloody thing down before you make my dogs attack you!" Guy pleaded. "I'm not here to make things worse! I've told that to one family already, and now I'm telling you, I hunt pests not people! Now listen to me! I can't stop the earl sending his reeve with a bunch of thugs back here. That's not in my power. If you had another man in the family who could make out he was still working the land and paying the earl's taxes, then you might have got away with staying here and just hiding when the sheriff's men came around. But given your circumstances, I think no sooner I tell him you're gone then he'll be over here with a new tenant. You can't fight that many men!

"Now then... That spavined old ox I saw in the far field. Is that yours? Good! Because we're going to slaughter it!" The farmer's wife began weeping. "No goodwife, don't cry," pleaded Guy. "We have to make a burial of something in your husband's place, because as a named murderer he wouldn't be allowed a burial in the churchyard, and the grave has to be big enough to appear sufficient for the remains to be of a man if they come along in the spring and dig him up, just to be sure! There's little enough meat on that old thing anyway and it's too weak to travel with you. For travel you must! Go west from here out of de Braose's lands. The difference is that you'll all travel together, and with a man still at the head of your family some Welsh lord will no doubt take you in. Even if you only work as a shepherd it'll still be a cottage and a garden of your own. It's not much of a chance, but it's a lot better than trying to stick it out here, him getting killed, and then having you women on the road unprotected."

The last statement seemed to finally get through to the farmer as to what Guy was trying to do. So while the family dug a mock grave out in a sad, stunted hazel coppice, Guy dealt with the ox. The biggest bones he saved for the dogs, for they would fool no-one into thinking they were human. He also skinned the beast, for its tough hide would take far too long to rot down into an unrecognisable state.

"Here you are," he announced to the family, taking them the best cuts of meat and the skin. "Take that to a tanner and get something for it. It won't be much. The rest will help keep you going until you reach safety." Then he left them packing while he went and arranged the bones as best he could in the mock grave, using a couple of lengths of tatty old linen as a makeshift winding sheet to mimic the shape of a body. It wasn't much, and there was nothing remotely like a skull, but he hoped it would satisfy some ignorant thug of de Braose's should they be suspicious enough to dig the body up. Those of higher knightly rank weren't used to butchering their own hunts, and so would be less likely to be capable of differentiating between types of remains the way Guy could – he could only hope that they would think some beast had made away with the head in that event!

"Blessed Saint Edmund," he prayed to the anciently sainted Anglo-Saxon king as he worked, "if a wolf could retrieve your lost, severed head as a miracle, please grant a smaller miracle this time for the reverse, and protect these poor souls in the process."

He and the dogs slept in the rickety barn, and in the morning saw the family off on the humble track road which led down to Merthyr Tydfil and then on into the heart of Wales. Once convinced that they wouldn't try to turn back and make a liar of him to the sheriff, Guy retraced his steps. Then decided to spend one more night at the farmhouse, for the family had seemed dreadfully reluctant to take their chance on the road despite the reality of certain death at the hands of de Braose's thugs if they stayed. Mercifully they didn't return, and Guy decided to enhance the appearance of decay by using his horse to pull at one of the roof timbers until the whole roof fell in at one end.

"St Tydfil, please look after your own! Make whoever comes here think that the women up and left in desperation," he prayed again as he turned his back on the gloomy little valley. At least he had the arm he had taken earlier from his first murder to fake the farmer's death with.

His next quarry was a very different man. At Guy's appearance in the tiny hamlet, the man had no compunction in putting his knife to a young woman's throat to warn Guy off. All the other folk around him pleaded to no avail, and by his behaviour he was used to bullying all of them. Guy's remaining sympathy totally evaporated when the woman's toddler broke free of restraint and ran to try and get to her, only to be viciously kicked by the thug. By now the practice at the butts had begun to pay their rewards and Guy was an expert shot with a small wood-bow, even if the massive Welsh wych-elm longbows were not yet his weapon of choice for accurate work. In one swift movement Guy had nocked and drawn the bow, and let an arrow fly straight into the thug's throat as the man had turned to snarl at the villagers. In a welter of blood the man went down and was dead within seconds. No-one cried for him. There seemed only relief at his passing.

With a promise to ask the priest in the next village to conduct a burial mass to ward off such an evil spirit, albeit not on hallowed ground, Guy left them with assurances that no further retribution would fall on them as far as he was concerned. It seemed to him that they'd suffered quite enough. It also meant that with the arm he had cut from Gwillam and Dafydd's persecutor he had three arms to satisfy Earl William that he had made three kills. With two innocent men's lives saved in the process, Guy was thinking things could have turned out a lot worse. His inner self was seemingly feeling the same, because the nightmares he had suffered over his first killing also abated with this knowledge, and Guy hoped that this was a sign that his mortal soul was less in peril after the greater good which had come about from his one ill deed.

Even better, his luck held as he rode back towards Abergavenny. He'd already decided to delay his hunt for the last man by a day or so when a chance remark overheard in a tavern led him to believe he had another blameless victim awaiting him. A quiet word dropped to the landlord left Guy with no doubt that the man would be nicely long gone from the village when he got there, as long as he took the long way round. So he rode into the castle making much of frustrating hunts and too many cold nights away from a decent fire. The garrison soldiers were welcoming enough, and Guy spent the evening chatting before the good hot brazier which warmed the guardroom. Only last thing did he bring up the subject of Maelgwn, and then as if something nearly forgotten.

"Oh dear Lord!" he muttered sleepily to the man who was directing him to a bench where he could spread his blankets out. "I near forgot! The earl said something about checking on a prisoner here while I was at it?"

His companion sniffed. "Which one? The earl's always dragging some poor sod in here for something! Bloody good job most of them don't last long or we'd be hanging them in cages from the rafters! By Our Lady, we were practically stacking them in the dungeon after the Welsh came in May!"

"Sounded like someone better bred than that," Guy said as if he didn't care, but desperately trying to jog the man's memory.

"Oh him! Poor sod's hardly a cause for us to worry about! He's as blind as a bat after the king finished with him. He can just about find the privy on his own."

"Oh..." Guy put on all disinterestedness. "Oh well, I suppose I'd still better see him in the morning. It'd be just my luck to not bother, and then he up and dies and the earl asks me why I didn't say anything."

"Aye, you don't want to cross his lordship!" the other guard sympathised. "The last man here who did that ended up feeding the crows for a week off the battlements!"

With the weak winter sun making a feeble attempt at cheerfulness, in the morning Guy ascended the stair to the tiny room in the thickness of the keep's wall where Maelgwn was held. There wasn't even a permanent guard, just a stout oak door and a big iron lock.

"Visitor for you," the guiding guard announced in a bored voice, opened the door for Guy, and then left after he had thrust the key into Guy's hand. "Lock up after you leave," was his parting shot, and Guy heard his boots clumping off into the distance.

"Hello," Guy said softly, not wishing to alarm the hunched figure he saw slumped in the chair near the brazier fire.

The head lifted wearily, and with resignation redolent in his voice Maelgwn asked,

"And who are you? Have you too come to see one of the dreaded Welsh princes? ...Am I not what you expected? ...Not quite the spectacle you thought? ...Should I rave a little so that you can tell his lordship that it was worth the payment you made?"

"Mother of God! He doesn't sell you to entertain like a fairground bear?" Guy was appalled.

"You didn't pay?" In his turn Maelgwn was surprised. "Why are you here then?"

Guy moved closer and squatted down on his haunches so that he could lean close to the seated figure. "Brother Tuck sent me!" he whispered urgently. "You do remember Brother Tuck don't you?"

Maelgwn sighed but smiled. "Oh yes! Dear Brother Tuck. So optimistic that he could save me. Yet as you can see I'm still here. How is the good brother?"

"Worried about you," Guy said insistently. "He's been watched by the bishop, which is why he hasn't been able to come and visit you lately. But he's never forgotten you, or given up hope of being able to get you out of here. ...Now you must listen carefully to me!" He pressed the small packet of herbs into Maelgwn's hands and was surprised to realise that with a little more exercise and food he would have been a fine figure of a man. "Take these one week from now! Tuck says all at once will do the trick, but it would be better if you take them over four days. They'll give you a cough. That's what we're going to use to get you out of here! We'll tell them that we're moving you to a monastery infirmary. ...Do you understand?"

For a dreadful moment Guy began to wonder whether the years of confinement had turned Maelgwn more than a bit simple. If he failed to understand what he needed to do, then Guy was out of ideas of how to help him. Then Maelgwn shrugged.

"Very well. I have little reason to trust you, but an early death would be better than existing like this. Maybe then they would at least allow me a priest to hear my last confession."

Trying to force a little jollity into this sad soul, Guy joked,

"Lord, sire, I would have thought there was little you could get up to in here that would warrant confession!"

A flicker of a smile twitched on Maelgwn's lips but was gone in a flash. "Maybe not, ...but I do have such thoughts... Such dreams..! Of girls I might have known... of the vengeance I might have taken if I'd not been reduced to this shell of a man... Such bitterness does not become a Christian... or so my lord's chaplain repeatedly tells me when he can be bothered to speak to me."

"Phaa!" Guy snorted derisively. "...'Becomes a Christian'? ...What would he know of such things! He's with the earl because there's not a monastery in the land would have him, even if only part of what I've heard is true! No, my lord, there's nothing unnatural in your anger at what was done to you. Any normal man would feel that way. It's just that having been sealed up here for most of your life you haven't met many of those. Well we're going to change that! ...Now I must be going. I shall report back to the castle at Brecon, and when I do I shall say that you seemed unwell to me. That should make your new illness all the more believable when they hear of it. Trust me, my lord, we will be back for you!"

Maelgwn passively let Guy clasp his hands, but gave a watery smile. "Oh such passion! You must still be a young man to believe so earnestly. And I'm not 'my lord'. That went when the king dispossessed me and took me from my family. I'm just Maelgwn now. Just Maelgwn."

Guy retreated shaking his head in sorrow. With that same youthful optimism, it tore at him to see someone not so very much older than him reduced to the state of a pitiful old man with nothing left to live for. As he was about to hand back the key it struck him that it would be useful if he could copy it. Finding some old candle wax he hurriedly pressed the key into it on both sides and then pocketed the wax. As soon as he was out of the castle he transferred the wax to his saddle bag where it would be cooler, and that night, as he sat in a meagre alehouse, he whittled a piece of wood until it was as fair a copy of the shape as he could make it. It was far from perfect, but he had hopes of what the smith at Grosmont might make of it – just in case they had to take Maelgwn by more forceful means!

For now, though, he had to find his fourth man. This time the villagers were too hostile for him to appeal to them to aid him in his deception. The only good thing was that the man was clearly long gone from the area. So when he reported back to the earl, Guy would have to make out that he had ridden in pursuit and hunted the man down. It peeved him, for it meant that he had to spend two more nights in makeshift shelters in order for his story to fit. However, he crept down to a small churchyard in the depths of the third night and robbed a recent grave for his last trophy. Already mouldering, the arm was in the worst state of them all, but Guy couldn't afford to be picky.

When he strode into the great hall of Brecon Castle, Lady Bertha was waiting for him with her most superior expression on her face. That swiftly changed when Guy deposited his gruesome packages on the long table to the side. The stench had been around Guy for so many days now that he was becoming immune to it. Not so the household hangers-on around Lady Bertha, or the lady herself.

"By Saint Thomas, take that disgusting mess out!" her factotum exhorted Guy as he gagged into a silk kerchief. Bertha herself was also waving him away vigorously as she clamped a hurriedly snatched lavender bag to her nose.

"Where should I take them, my lady?" Guy enquired with icy politeness. "Will my lord sheriff be wanting to inspect them?"

"God's bones, man, no!" the disgusted factotum shrieked. "The midden heap! Take them to the midden heap! At once!" He was clearly imagining the ghastly state the remains would be in by the time his lord returned. However, it suited Guy perfectly. In the midden heap with all the other detritus from the castle the rotting process would be hastened, thus disguising further the subterfuge he was perpetrating upon the sheriff.

Perfecting his guise as the heartless butcher, Guy picked up the sack wrappings he had spread across the boards, and the odd detached finger which had rolled Lady de Braose's way, and with a small shrug departed for the middens. By the time he had returned to the hall, Lady Bertha was gone, and one of her retinue had remained only long enough to tell him that his services were no longer required, and to pay him the extra he was due for his additional duties. Guy could hardly leave the same day, and it wouldn't have been fair on the dogs to travel hard again. So he was forced to overnight at the castle, but made sure he kept to the kennels rather than putting himself in the way of the guards. To the head huntsman at Brecon he casually mentioned that the prisoner at Abergavenny seemed to be failing and left it at that. Not something worth bringing to the attention of her ladyship, he implied, since Guy made out he had heard it more in passing than having made the effort to see Maelgwn especially.

The next day, though, he travelled as fast as the two heavier dogs could comfortably manage and made it to Tuck's cottage by nightfall. Having reported back to his fellow conspirator, he then made all haste back to Grosmont and tried to act as if all was normal for over a week. He made much of his disgust at the job de Braose had foisted upon him, but never let on that he had so openly defied the earl. That would have been courting disaster, for it would only take someone to let slip something in innocence and the blind would all fall apart – as would Guy's head from his shoulders, he had no doubt!

Yet the sheriff unwittingly played into Guy's hands, giving him the excuse to go absent again so soon after returning. Just as Guy was wondering what possible excuse he could give which would allow him to go and meet Tuck, the earl announced by advanced rider that he would be stopping at Grosmont within the coming days in order to be at Brecon in time for the Christmas festivities.

"I'm getting out of here!" Guy announced to Ianto. "Dear God, I want none of his lordship's manhunts again!" An explanation which Ianto accepted without question, for all of those living at Grosmont had been appalled at what Guy had been expected to do in cold blood, even the soldiers. It was one thing to butcher a man in the heat of battle, or when your own life depended upon it. To have to cut a man down as Guy had been charged to do turned all their stomachs, and even more so as Guy had made no bones of the fact that he had thought more than one an innocent man wrongly charged. An assertion which was borne out by the audible nightmares Guy still had on several nights when arm-less corpses pursued him through woods, their detached arms flying beside him beating at him even as he ran.

He left the dogs with Ianto with the plea to keep them hidden and out of the earl's sight, and rode off at speed. Able to ride harder without the dogs at his heels, Guy made it to Tuck's by nightfall.

"Well, this is it!" Tuck said, as they shared a hearty vegetable stew and dumplings. "I've borrowed the cart from the village. Luckily the horse is young and fit so she should keep up with yours."

"The cart was a good idea," Guy agreed. "When we first planned this, I thought we should be far quicker if I brought two of the horses from the castle under some pretext. But having seen Maelgwn, I don't think he'd stay on it if we had to go faster than a walk. And if we're going that slowly the cart is just as fast and steadier, and it lends more truth to the story that Maelgwn is dying."

At midday two days later they wandered in to Abergavenny Castle at a leisurely pace with an insouciance they were far from feeling inside.

"Come for the prisoner," Guy announced in a bored tone to the captain of the guard.

"Where's he going to?" the startled captain asked. "No-one's told us he's moving!"

"It's been decided that he should spend his last days with us at Ewenny," Tuck chipped in in his most unctuous tone, wringing his hands together and looking the picture of the humble brother. At Guy's insistence he had padded his middle out so that he now looked the archetype of the overfed, idle brother, near spherical and comical rather than muscled and threatening. It certainly worked with the guards who looked down their collective noses at Tuck and mentally dismissed him, even if not physically rid of him yet. Guy they remembered only too well from the reeking limbs he had inflicted on their presence only weeks ago, but in the role of a cold, hard hunter. Nothing about him hinted that there might be a compassionate side to him.

Shaking his head in resignation at the unpredictability of their lord who should order something and not tell them yet again, the captain led Guy and Tuck up to the room where Maelgwn was incarcerated. Before they got there they could hear his fearful, rasping cough.

"Poor bugger! I hadn't realised he was so bad," the captain muttered. "I don't mind admitting I've never liked what was done to him. He was only a tiny lad when he came here. If the king didn't want him around why not kill him and have done with it? I'll fight the Welshies with the best of them, but not putting out the eyes of a lad the age of my son now. Bloody cruel even for his lordship!"

"I thought it was the king who did it," Guy couldn't refrain from saying.

"King? Nah! King Henry's a vicious old sod but he doesn't get his hands dirty like that! That's why he keeps dogs of war like the de Braoses! No, it was the old man, with his lordship holding them down for his father who did the actual deeds. Sweet Jesu, but the earl gives me the shudders when the mood's upon him! You'd think his father losing the sheriffdom for what he did to Seisyll would have been enough of a warning, but it's never slowed his lordship down a jot. There's nothing he wouldn't stoop to once his blood's up. I tell you, I've put in to go to the lands he has down on the Gower. I want my wife and kids well away from him and his demon brood for as long as possible, and they don't go there as much as they do the other castles. I'm all for the quiet life these days! ...Here you go,..." and he threw open the door to Maelgwn's room.

The Welsh prince lay on his meagre pallet, his body wracked with coughing.

"Duw! Brother, brother!" Tuck exclaimed, doing a remarkable job of flapping his hands and looking ineffective. "We must get you to Brother Owen with all speed! There's a bed in the infirmary all ready and waiting for you. Come Huntsman! Help me get him into the cart!"

Guy rolled his eyes theatrically at the captain behind Tuck's back, earning him a sympathetic smile. Clearly the captain was already wearing of Tuck's effusive Welsh presence and was silently offering up thanks that it was Guy, and not him, who had been given the unenviable task of accompanying the prisoner.

Together they virtually carried Maelgwn to the cart and piled him in, covering him with blankets as he bedded down on the deep layer of hay they had lined the base with.

"Best be off," Guy declared out loud to anyone who was even half listening. "The sooner we get him to the monastery the better!"

"Good luck!" the captain wished him, and slapped the cart-horse on its rump to get it moving as Tuck flapped the reins about in a very inexpert manner.

Sighing dramatically, Guy heeled his mount up to the cart-horse's head and took a hold of one of the reins, then led it out of the walled enclosure through the huge gate. And that was it! Without so much as a blow being struck, they had managed to seize one of King Henry's own prisoners out from of the hands of his sheriff and out to freedom. As soon as they were well down the road and out of sight of the castle Tuck pulled over and nimbly leapt into the back of the cart.

"Here Maelgwn," he said, tipping a thick liquid from out of a small flask down Maelgwn's throat. It smelled strongly of honey and seemed to work with remarkable speed on easing the cough. "Take this and have a sip every now and then." Tuck then proceeded to strip his additional layers off, and used the thick blankets he had padded himself with as additional cover for the frail former prince.

The journey back to Tuck's took longer than it might have, for Guy led them up into the Black Mountains on unused tracks. They'd had to cross the Usk in front of the castle to perpetuate the myth of going into south Wales, and so had to work their way north and west to find another crossing coming back which was out of sight. They dared not use the regular roads going back north yet, in case someone saw them and remembered them later on. However, by the midday two days on they were back at Tuck's little house by the Monnow, and the horse and cart returned to its rightful owners. Tuck was quite clearly adored by his small flock, for not one asked why he had needed the cart or where he had been, and Guy began to realise that the burly brother must have stood up for them too in the past.

"Will you be all right if I leave you now," he fretted. "I'd stay to help guard you in case anyone comes looking, but I think I'd be more likely to bring suspicion down on you if I stay away from Grosmont any longer."

"We'll be fine," Tuck reassured him, for they had now decided that the only place Maelgwn could ever live in safety was with Tuck. The idea of it being a temporary arrangement had been abandoned in favour of permanence. "In a few days Maelgwn will be well again, and then I can start teaching him how to look after himself. Go! ...You've done more than I would have believed possible! ...And you're right, you'll be missed, whereas the villagers around here will just accept that I've had another brother come to live with me – especially when they see how he is. I'll spin some tale about how he's a lay brother who can't work for the monastery anymore."

"I'll come and check on you when I can," promised Guy, "and if I hear of the earl passing this way I'll try to send you a warning, if I can without making it more dangerous for you."

"Bless you!" Tuck intoned with genuine warmth and enveloped Guy in a bear hug. "Now go, brother! Get back to those dogs of yours, ...and try to stay out of trouble!" he added with a twinkle of mischief in his eyes.

"It's the company I keep, that's the problem with that!" Guy teased back, mounting up and riding off.

So there you are, Brother! A true rebellion and no mistaking it! And whatever you may say, I had no regrets about it then and never have done since. The change in Maelgwn in those first few months was a wonder to behold. It took me until well into the new year to get back over to see Tuck, for shortly after Christmas the sheriff sent some of his favoured lordlings over with the king's permission to hunt the forests around us, and so I was kept busy at my preferred task of hunting boar and deer, not men. Yet when I did get there, with a young buck I had taken on my own account on the sly slung over my saddle for Tuck's larder, I was astonished. Maelgwn had straightened from the hunched weakling I had met into an upright man with some proper colour in his face. By the time I went back again he was starting to put on some much needed weight, and was helping Tuck dig his little garden over to plant spring crops. Had I needed any thanks for what I had done I got it in seeing this man come to life again, for he took such pleasure in the simple things in life that only a twisted soul could have begrudged them him. And whatever you think of me, Brother Gervase, I am not that bad!

By the time summer had come around it was possible to teach Maelgwn some basic elements of self-defence. There was no point in teaching him how to use a sword or a bow and arrow, for his lack of sight made a mockery of such skills. However, a quarterstaff was an ideal weapon. At first Tuck taught him with a couple of branches we hacked down and trimmed up, but when he began to show a real aptitude with them I managed to smuggle a properly fashioned and seasoned one out of the weapons store at Skenfrith Castle when I was down there one time. I also got one for Tuck from Llantilio, for the good brother was enough of a realist to know that his habit and tonsure would not be enough alone to save him if his conspiracy was discovered.

For a whole year I held my breath every time the earl passed through our area, but to our intense relief both the sheriff and the king had other things on their minds than some ancient enemy. I still kept my ears open for rumours of an escaped prisoner through the summer of 1183, but nothing happened and slowly we relaxed. Quite clearly everyone except those left to the task of guarding him had forgotten about Maelgwn's presence, and now even they assumed he had died, if they thought about it at all.

And then there was an event in the summer which eclipsed all manner of things! For if you recall, Brother, the young Prince Henry died that June. It took a while for word to reach us, for there was open warfare between King Henry's sons in France and it was there, while trying to overthrow Prince Richard, that Prince Henry got the dysentery which killed him in a matter of days. Then all our worlds went into a spin, for no-one could work out which of his other sons King Henry intended to make into his heir. Some said Prince Richard had the right as the next oldest, but others wondered whether despite that the king would by-pass Prince Richard for the youngest, Prince John, who had always been the old king's favourite son. And we all wondered what the middle prince, Geoffrey, would say and do whatever happened, for he was always the least predictable of them!

I feared war would come upon us the way it had upon the unfortunate souls in Normandy and Aquitaine, especially when the king sent word the following year that he wanted Llantilio's castle walls upgraded to stone. However, it did do me some small favours, for in all the excitement there was an increased need for armed riders to go into Wales to the various Norman lords' holdings with messages. Since I had effectively got rid of all the major threats to livestock I was someone who could be spared my own duties to take on others, and so I added riding as a messenger to my growing list of uses. Now I know you will tut at this Brother Gervase, for you seem to take a perverse delight in being disapproving, but it at least allowed me to call in on Tuck and Maelgwn on a regular basis. All three of my lovely deerhounds were starting to show their age and so it served me well on their behalf too. I was able to leave them in the warmth of the kennels for more of the time in the winter, yet shortly after Christmas of 1183 my lovely Meg died and I was inconsolable in my private grief.

...There really is no satisfying you, is there Brother Gervase? When I demonstrate compassion for a fellow man you sigh over the circumstance, then when I declare my affection for my canine companions you purse your lips in disapproval at that, as though I were engaged in some unnatural practice with them! Oh dear, has that thought shocked you even more? Ha! Taunt me at your peril Brother! I may have need of your services, but that does not grant you licence to censure me at every turn for things which priests other than you have seen no ill in. I may be the old wolf but I can still bite, albeit with my tongue and not the teeth! I have no intention of dying quietly, and if you persist in provoking me you may be my last bit of sport!

Now where was I? Ah yes.... Dearest Meg died and within the year I had lost Aethel too, but at least by now their pups were growing into handsome beasts and proving as good as their dams at hunting. Around that time we heard that King Henry had summoned all three of his remaining sons to England from France, and was bent on forcing them to make their peace with one another. Such news I heard when the sheriff came our way once more, and it so happened that he was about to go out hunting on one of my boar trails when news came which would change my life in a way I could never have expected.

At the time, though, I was simply grateful that turmoil on the larger stage meant that Earl William had no time to persecute his less favoured tenants, which I regarded as another blessing. I had not had to repeat my grim hunt as yet, although I had been called upon to track other renegade men on two separate occasions. Men who mercifully were every bit as guilty as the sheriff claimed, and in their case it was simply to bring them back to Abergavenny and Hay castles respectively. I was never again the instrument of his perverse justice, thank Our Lady. Yet Ralph of Grosmont, our steward and household head man, assured me that sooner or later Earl William would get bloodthirsty again and his tenants would suffer. So any news which distracted him was good in my eyes.

However, to the news. ...King Baldwin of Jerusalem was believed to be in his last days, and the Patriarch of Jerusalem had travelled all the way to London to offer King Henry the throne of Jerusalem in a valiant attempt to secure a strong king for that turbulent kingdom. What was more, the king intended to hold a great council in March and all his lords were summoned to attend and debate the matter. De Braose declared there and then that he would be going, and instructed me to provide a goodly amount of game for his party to take with them.

Have you ever been to court Brother Gervase? Well I have seen more seemly bear fights than some of the places in London! A stinking, heaving mass of the worst of humanity and yet the most glorious of places too in parts. You might think it odd that the earl would cart his food all the way from Wales with him to such a place, but I can assure you it was necessary to think about providing some food of his own. Such a multitude of people all in the capital could not hope to be fed solely from the supplies there, or at least not to the satisfaction of a man of de Braose's tastes! Game was a good thing to take, for the days on the road allowed it to hang and become palatable. So out I went hunting as soon as the Christmas festivities were past to fill the cold store with meat, never thinking that I would be going to London too!

Chapter 5

o now we get to that most significant year, 1185 – a year when my life underwent another huge change and we draw closer to your heart's desire. Ah Brother Gervase, how one small act can change things forever! But at the time it never seemed so far-reaching.

As I told you, the earl was determined to go to London and the great council, and not to starve on the way, either! So as February came around I began to go out hunting for game. Birds were of little use for this sort of fare. They took far too long to catch enough to feed a large party, since a duck or goose provided barely enough for one man for a day. Partridge and grouse, meanwhile, were the preserve of the various castles' falconers to hunt and needed none of my skills with the bow, nor were my dogs fitted to retrieve them from less accessible places when they fell from the air. Instead I was after red deer and boar. Animals big enough that one hunt would provide us with plenty of meat for the lordly, and the means to make many lesser meals for the servants in the form of hearty stews and marrowbone soups. Huntsmen in de Braose's other holdings would be hard at work too, for in the time allotted, such a provision could not all come from the Grosmont area, but I had to play my part.

Meat was not all that would be taken, of course, but the rest was taken care of by the various castles' kitchen staff, for Abergavenny and Brecon would be contributing to their lord's progress to the capital, and I saw no part of those preparations. All I could think of at the time was that it was a blessed relief that the sheriff left me to it, rather than using it as an excuse to indulge his favourite passion. With so much meat needed, I had no time to guide him and his men on hunts of my choosing, and I would surely have had to leave him to his own devices – something I was loath to do, not only because of Bethan's legacy but for other reasons.

You see, Gervase, I had turned a blind eye to the small scale poaching which the local people indulged in. ...Ah, I see you have acquired some caution before expressing your disapproval, Brother! ...What were a few hares or the odd squirrel to a lord? Or even the occasional roe deer? He would have objected on the basis of having his peasants getting into land he regarded as his own hunting preserve, of course. Not that we lived in a royal forest on the Marches – the nearest one of those we had was the Forest of Dean, and that was still a goodly ride from where I plied my trade. I was to find out later how much worse royal forest life could be! Here there were no watchers in the form of riding foresters; nor were there verderers attachment courts to fine; nor agisters to collect rents from those unfortunate enough to live within the nominal boundaries of such a forest – and how I was to come to know all of these in the very near future!

Yet that would not have saved the ordinary folk from the earl's heavy hand had he come upon them taking what he saw as his. I, however, thought it perverse to complain of hares or deer destroying crops yet, on the other hand, prohibiting folk from killing them when they could be well used to save a worker's family from starving. Of course, a good many woodcocks and pigeons no doubt ended up in the poor folks' pots as well, but there were plenty of them and scant few cottagers to take them. Few cottagers could ever have managed to bring down one of the massive red deer beloved of our lord, but a roe deer lying in cover whist ruminating was somewhat easier prey for the crafty, even if so few were taken that a lord might not notice, and even a small roe deer was a good many meals for a poor family! So I had ignored all signs of such simple hunts, and consequently that winter I thanked God in his small mercy for being able to work alone, and if I had to work harder to fill the cold stores without the earl and his men, I did not complain.

It therefore made it all the more surprising when I was out one day with two of my young deerhounds, tracking a small herd of red deer, and heard the sound of many men. I called the dogs to me and stopped to listen. Ah me, Brother, that day is now burned into my memory! I can still smell the frosty air if I close my eyes, and remember the dank, chill haze which hung over that valley north and east of Grosmont. I thought it odd that poachers should make such a din, for they were making no effort to be stealthy. Then I registered that the voices were not calling to one another in the singsong accents of the locals, but in the French-accented voices of young noblemen brought up in Normandy, or at least at court.

Biting back my irritation at having to abandon the trail of the red stag I was tracking – for by his prints he must have been a big old beast of some 700lbs, but with a limp and therefore needing culling – I went to investigate, and there he was! The bane of the rest of my adult life!

The Welsh Borders, February, the year of Our Lord 1185

"God's balls, de Lacy! Catch the bloody beast!" a petulant voice screamed as Guy rode down the valley side towards the commotion. As he got closer and the frosty haze thinned, Guy could see several young noblemen attempting to spear a young female boar and making a right mess of the job. Over to one side a small, slightly podgy youth in opulent furs, and mounted on a superb horse he was clearly incapable of handling, was the source of the chivvying.

"Kill the bastard and bring it to me!" the youth screamed, going scarlet in the face as he did so. To Guy's amazement the young men seemed more afraid of the youth than the boar, for they all began to stab wildly at it with their hunting spears and swords. Not with any skill, but rather in desperation. Bemused, Guy nonetheless couldn't stand seeing the boar being toyed with, even though it was done out of clumsiness not by design. Kneeing his horse to the trot he positioned her neatly to come up behind the boar, as long as none of the effete young men got in the way, and hefted one of his sturdy spears into position. Cutting across two of the riders and coming up to the rear of the sow, he got alongside and then struck downwards with all his might. In one skilful stab he brought the terrified beast down, and it collapsed onto its front legs and then keeled over with a final squeal. Guy's momentum had carried him and his horse beyond the boar, but he easily reined her in and turned back to face a stunned group of riders all now looking at him agog.

"Christ on the Cross! Who in God's name is this damned whore-son peasant?" shrieked the boy of his party in general, all of whom tried desperately to avoid his gaze.

In his innocence Guy rode directly to the youth and declared,

"I am the huntsman in these parts, charged by my lord de Braose with the care of the game in these woods. And who might you be my lord that you hunt without my lord's permission?"

The two young men sat on either side of the fur-draped youth stared at Guy slack-jawed, as if he had lost his mind.

"Who am I? ...*Who am I?*" the youth screamed, positively apoplectic by now. "I, you *ignorant cur*, am Prince John! Do you understand that? *Prince John!* Or are you such an uncouth dolt that my name has eluded you? Because let me tell you, I shall give you a lesson for this that you'll never forget!"

For some reason Guy never did work out, he was never in awe of Prince John – not then and not later once he was king. Scared of him, yes! For John was unpredictable, and in one of his infamous tempers was capable of almost anything. But in awe? No, not even at that first meeting. Neatly vaulting from his horse Guy dropped to one knee on the frozen mud.

"My apologies, your grace," he said with a calmness he was far from feeling. "We had no forewarning that you would be in this area. Had I known that you would be coming I would have provided you with better sport than this paltry sow, as I'm sure my lord de Braose would have wished ...had he known." *There*, Guy thought, *now you know that even your father's trusted barons don't know you're here. You can strike me down, but you'll have to answer to someone as to why you were out here in the first place.* However, the prince's mood had switched again.

"Paltry sow?" Prince John spluttered. "Did you hear that you incompetent bunch of catamites? This man thinks this beast you were making such a by-Our-Lady mess of hunting was small fry!" His anger was deflected amongst the courtiers in general, and Guy offered up silent thanks to the same Lady for his narrow escape and the hope that his luck would continue to hold.

"Do you wish to hunt further, your highness?" Guy inquired with as much servility as he could muster. "For I might be able to direct you to better sport. Or would you like me to show you the shortest way to where you intend to stay for the night?" while silently offering further prayers that wherever that was it would be well away from Grosmont. Certainly they'd had no word to prepare for the arrival of an eminent guest of any description, let alone a royal prince.

He stayed down in the dirt on his knee, not so much out of respect, but because he reckoned that if the prince took a swipe at him with the fancy sword hanging at the royal hip, he could duck under the horse's belly out of the way. If he got up, there was no way he could avoid being cut down. He also kept his gaze as low as he could, but was watching the prince through the crazed reflection on an almost frozen puddle a few feet away. Prince John, however, took it as a sign of suitable obeisance and his considerable vanity was somewhat appeased.

"This man wants to know what I *wish*!" the prince crowed. "Do you hear that, de Lacy? De Say? De Clifford? A mere huntsman and he can offer me what you bunch of idiots cannot!" Guy felt the collective ire of the young noblemen turn his way and swore under his breath. Was there anything this young prince did which didn't offend someone or cause trouble? "What I *wished*," the prince was spitting petulantly, "was to enjoy some good hunting on my way to Ireland. But I'm now cold and hungry and what I want is to get *indoors* and be entertained! Do you all hear me? *Entertained!*" The last was screamed at them in another fit of temper, and Guy wondered whether it would be worth losing his head in the Tower to hoick the arrogant pup off his horse and wallop the living daylights out of him to teach him some manners.

"Where is the nearest castle, huntsman?" a slightly older young man asked civilly, if with a hint of despair in his voice. "We were due to overnight at Abergavenny Castle tonight. Are we anywhere near there?"

Guy rose to his feet and stepped quickly to the lord's side and well away from Prince John, just to be on the safe side. "Abergavenny? My lord, there's no way you'll make there before nightfall. You wouldn't make it in summer time, let alone at this end of the year. You're way too far north by now for that, and too far from the roads for a speedy journey. The nearest castle is Skenfrith, but that's a border fortress with little in the way of accommodation suitable for such ...august ...guests." Guy tried to phrase it as tactfully as possible, unable to imagine the prince coping with the austere conditions at Skenfrith. "However, Grosmont isn't that much further on and my lord de Braose has personal quarters there, which might suffice for his highness in such an ...emergency." He couldn't believe he was suggesting this, but it was the only alternative to leaving the royal presence out all night to freeze his arse off. Not something Guy cared about, but he feared what Earl William might say on the matter and he rather liked living here – too much to risk losing his job in a deliberate act of insolence.

"Mortimer? Are we ever going to move? Or am I destined to sit on this Goddamned horse until my balls freeze?" was the prince's next peevish demand, which cut across what Mortimer was trying to say to Guy, and the young lord was forced to sit in silence until the prince had finished his rant.

"I think we'd best make for Grosmont with all speed," Roger Mortimer finally said softly to Guy when he got the chance, with the faintest hint of humour twinkling in his eyes.

"Grosmont! Yes, my lord! This way, if you please," Guy responded, turning and vaulting onto his horse and directing the party up into the trees.

The prince's escort all turned and followed Guy, the young prince keeping up a constant flow of whining complaints to his entourage from somewhere in the middle of the group, while Lord Roger kept Guy company in the lead.

"Forgive me for asking, my lord," Guy said softly so that only Mortimer could hear, "But is he always like this?"

"May God forgive me for saying this, but this is one of his better days," Mortimer answered with a sigh.

"Dear Lord, you mean he can get worse?"

"Oh much worse! No-one has died yet today, and although he has his father the king's temper, he lacks King Henry's stamina. Or that of his brother, Prince Richard, for that matter. With any luck, once he's been fed, he'll retire to his chamber with some unfortunate wench and that will be the last we'll see of him until well into the morning. That's been our trouble, to be frank. The prince is far too fond of bedding the wenches! Noble or poor, singly or in collective orgies! So much so that our party has become strung out all along this route to the Welsh ports."

"Do you make for Ireland soon?" Guy wondered, desperate for some indication of how long they might have to endure the prince's presence.

"Aye, Ireland!" Mortimer shook his head in despair. "And supposedly with all speed, although the prince has made a mockery of that! The king thinks that now John is seventeen he can start playing a more active role in affairs. Nothing could be further from the truth!"

He lowered his voice even further, and leaned out of his saddle closer towards Guy. "Prince John is selfish, spoilt, immature and lethargic," he whispered confidentially, his frustration clearly making him forget that he was talking to someone who was a mere lackey in comparison to his own status. "All of which means that nothing short of a miracle will make him endear himself to the Irish princelings. God help Hugh de Lacy over there, for he'll have his hands full with the prince and his hangers on!"

Mortimer referred to the king's viceroy in Ireland whom even Guy had heard of. Hugh de Lacy had been doing sterling work, if all Guy had heard was to be believed, in bringing the native chieftains and princes around to the idea that they were better supporting King Henry, rather than fighting him. Hence the fact that one of the younger de Lacys from this side of the water would be escorting the prince across to Earl Hugh. Mortimer confided to Guy that he was infinitely glad that his part would be over once he had delivered the prince to the port and seen him on board ship.

"I shall be riding away as if the very Devil himself was on my heels, as well," Mortimer muttered, as another complaint was relayed forward from the prince. "If his bloody ship has to put back into port I want to be nowhere near there!" A sentiment Guy could well understand, especially since even he had heard how King Henry had been so fickle as to imprison this same Lord Roger for killing a Welsh prince, only releasing him after the Welsh raid which had assaulted Sheriff de Braose and Abergavenny. The young lord Mortimer must feel like he was dancing on hot coals all the time trying to keep up with the mood swings of the royal family, Guy thought.

The party got to the proper road to Grosmont, and then Guy made his excuses and galloped to the castle as though the hounds of Hell were at his heels instead of his own beasts, to warn them of the impending catastrophe about to overtake them. As Guy had feared, Prince John was far from being grateful at having a bed for the night. He stormed at and berated every unfortunate soul who got close to him, from the castle servants to his entourage, only giving up when he fell asleep at the table. Two of the prince's long-suffering companions carted the royal presence off to bed and everyone took a deep breath of relief.

"Would you like me to guide you in the morning?" Guy asked Lord Mortimer as he showed him to the room he would be sharing with several other members of the party, for Grosmont was not used to accommodating so many of high rank.

"I think you'd better," Mortimer said with another twinkle in his eye and a conspiratorial wink for Guy. "At least that way if he takes it into his foolish head to hunt again we can get it over and done with *and* get to Abergavenny without getting lost again!"

Leaving others from the castle with strict instructions as to where to find the two deer he had already brought down the previous day before meeting the prince, and had then had to abandon, Guy set out at the head of the royal party come the morning. To some quite blatant sighs of relief from the others, the young prince announced that he had had his fill of trying to hunt, and so they were able to make good time on their ride south. Despite setting out far later than Guy would ever have done to go on such a journey, they were getting close to Abergavenny in the afternoon when they heard a large party riding towards them.

"Not the Welsh, surely?" one of the young courtiers asked Guy nervously, clearly not fancying the idea of having to defend his prince against uneven odds.

Guy smiled reassuringly back. "Lord no, sire! Those are proper war-horses coming our way. The Welsh would be riding hill ponies, and you wouldn't hear them coming! No, my lord, I suspect this is your host getting nervous in case the king accuses him of losing the favourite heir!" As was indeed the case.

At the next sweep in the road as it followed the valley round they almost collided with de Braose and a well armed party of riders coming their way at speed.

"Huntsman!" de Braose exclaimed, recognising Guy. "What are you doing here?" Then the earl spotted the prince and immediately dismounted to bow to him. "Your Highness! We were worried!" The brusque earl seemed to be struggling to find a way to ask what on earth the prince had been up to without offending the notoriously touchy royal, and Guy decided he'd better step in before things took another turn for the worse.

"I found the royal party hunting near Skenfrith, my lord," he interspersed quickly. "His grace had become engrossed in the sport and had taken a wrong turn. The hour was late and so I led them to Grosmont where the prince has been overnight."

"God's cock, de Braose, how do you sleep in such a stinking piss-pot of a place?" complained the said prince before Guy could say anything else. "Does my father know you keep his castle in a state scarcely fit for a serf? It's a dung-heap! A midden! God's bollocks, I shall tell him so! I shall indeed!"

De Braose went a strange shade of crimson but managed to retain his verbal composure at the slight. Grosmont was very well appointed for a place of its size and was certainly as comfortable as many a larger castle, for de Braose didn't stint himself when it came to comforts. Nor was the king likely to be unaware of what a simple border castle could be like, even if it was his own. Henry at least would be realistic, and given that, would know that a piss-pot Grosmont certainly wasn't! The prince's habit of swearing on God and his private parts was also deeply offensive to those of a more religious persuasion, and didn't always sit easily with some of the broadminded either, even the earl.

"My lord," he ground out through clenched teeth, just about managing to convey some kind of vague agreement with the royal pronouncement, although Guy hoped like fury that the prince wouldn't push de Braose further.

"We have entertainment laid on for you, sire," a lighter voice hastily added, and Guy turned in his saddle to see that a younger nobleman had joined de Braose.

"Ah, de Blundeville!" John exclaimed in recognition. "What are you doing so far south? I had not thought to see you down here?"

"No, my lord, I would normally be preoccupied with my own lands, but the king, *your father*," he emphasised pointedly, "sent a message requesting that I join de Braose to ensure your safe passage to the ports, and to oversee that you had adequate troops for your venture to Ireland."

Guy looked askance at the newcomer who was evidently the young earl of Chester, then realised that the man was being diplomatic. It was blindingly obvious that the king would have made sure sufficient troops were dispatched, and that there was no need for the earl to do anything of the sort. More likely the king had asked Ranulph de Blundeville to come and aid de Braose in guiding his wayward son, but there was no way the earl of Chester could say that outright.

"We should continue, should we not, my lord?" Ranulph said tactfully to the prince, who was looking set to start pouting and bemoaning all and sundry again. "We have provided some more attractive company to relieve the tedium," he hinted heavily and the prince took the bait.

The extended column moved off, and de Braose waved Guy to the side until the prince's party had ridden off with de Blundeville.

"Christ sur le Croix! What the fuck happened?" he exploded once the royal behind had disappeared around the next bend in the road, and his whining voice could no longer be heard. For once de Braose was beyond formality, in itself an indicator of how much his patience had been tried by this episode.

Guy chuckled and shook his head. "By Our Lady, my lord, it was certainly a shock to me! I was hunting game in preparation for going to London, as you instructed, when I came upon them. I thought them some young nobles who'd strayed too far our side of the Wye. Maybe guests of the Earl of Gloucester or something. Well they were making a right mess of hunting a small wild boar sow, and I had to finish it for them before someone got hurt. Then when I found out who it was, I thought it best to take them to Grosmont for the night rather than trying to make for Abergavenny in the dark. At least the prince was safe there."

Then Guy risked making a comment. "To be frank, my lord, I doubt the prince would have made Abergavenny had I tried to lead them there. He was complaining about being cold and hungry, even though he was the reason they were so far off their route. He'd have barged in on the nearest place we came across that looked as if it had food, and God only knows what he might have done when it didn't satisfy him."

The earl's great frame shuddered at the thought. "No, Huntsman, you did right! ...You did better than right, you did very well. Very well indeed! By St Thomas, the prince out at night in the borders without a proper escort!" He shuddered again. "It doesn't bear thinking about what could have happened!"

"No, my lord," Guy agreed wryly, and heeled his horse to follow after the earl.

At Abergavenny the castle was heaving with folk and was surrounded by several grand tents too, and Guy thankfully took himself off to the sanctuary of the kennels, hoping to escape back home without comment the next day. However, he wasn't to be so lucky.

By nightfall some sort of contorted order had imposed itself on the assembled folk and everyone sat down to eat a hot meal, of a kind befitting each of their stations. Guy had no complaints over the vegetable and barley stew he got, for he got to eat it in much better company than those eating the haunches of venison in the great hall. Afterwards, he was proudly being shown a litter of pups Blue had sired on their last visit there, when he and the head kennelman heard voices outside. The kennelman rolled his eyes in despair at Guy – the last thing he wanted was some drunken lordling barging in and upsetting his nursing bitch – and so Guy signalled that he would go outside and fend off whoever it was. Slipping carefully out of the door to shed as little light as possible and reveal his presence, Guy moved towards where he thought the voices had come from. Then to his shock he realised that it wasn't drunk young nobles but some of the ladies, and one of them sounded very upset.

"You must come back inside, Heloise," one lady said urgently. "He's the prince!"

"Aye the prince, but he still has no right to misuse you!" a voice which Guy recognised as belonging to Lady Maud de Braose spoke up in disgust.

"But how can we stop him?" the first voice demanded anxiously. "Poor Heloise is still in mourning! She should be respected for that, even if Prince John thinks of nothing else."

"And I doubt his father would be any too thrilled at his son misusing a valuable heiress who's a royal ward for now!" Lady Maud added. "No, the prince must be made to see sense. His father might take mistresses as he wills, but he wants to dispose of the Cartmel estates to a favoured man, not insult whoever it is by offering them his son's cast off plaything."

Guy heard the one who must be called Heloise give a sob at this and wondered if any of the de Braose's knew what the meaning of the word tact was. To tell the poor lass to her face that she would be parcelled off on the king's whim, or that she faced being raped by his youngest son, was hardly going to cheer her up! He could now guess at who the distressed girl was, for it was known that since her father's recent death Heloise of Lancaster was the unfortunate heiress to a vast estate which extended right over to Yorkshire. But what was she doing here? Then he wondered whether the young earl of Chester might be making a bid for her hand. It would certainly make for a nice parcel of land adjoining the Chester estates, although it would also make the earl far too powerful and Guy couldn't see the king standing for that alliance.

Then he heard heavier boots coming towards them. "The prince wants you inside. Now!" The voice carried threatening undertones, and Guy heard a squeal and guessed that at least one of the women had been grabbed hold of.

He stepped out into the courtyard which was dimly lit by a couple of torches in sconces on the keep's walls. Lady Maud must have already gone in, for there was no sign of her. Instead, one of Prince John's less savoury servants had one of two young women by the arm and was trying to pull her towards the half open doorway.

"Let her go!" Guy snapped with more authority than he felt.

"Oh the bloody hero huntsman!" the man hiccupped, and Guy realised that the man was more than a little drunk. No doubt serving such a trying master as the prince would do that to the best of men, and this one was far from that. Besides which, Guy could imagine what de Braose's language must have been like when the bulk of the royal retinue had turned up without the prince! He would have verbally flayed the skin off them even if physically they were still intact. No wonder the men were bitter if they'd been blamed for the prince's folly.

"Piss off!" the man growled, and swatted at Guy with his free hand.

It took no effort on Guy's behalf to plant a hand on the man's chest and give him a good shove, resulting in him going backwards into the horse trough. As he overbalanced the man let go of his captive, and was then more preoccupied with trying to get himself out of the ice-cold water before he drank horse spit or drowned.

"Come on," Guy said gently to the two women. "You'd best go in or the prince will only send more like him out here. I'll come with you."

Poor Heloise was sniffing into a cloth kerchief and too distraught to notice, but the other shot him a look of gratitude.

"Who are you?" she asked him softly as they made their way into the crowded hall.

"I'm Guy of Maesbury, Earl de Braose's huntsman. Who are you?"

"Rohese, Lady Heloise's companion. My father is one of the knights at Cartmel."

Guy felt a small burst of happiness at that. A knight's daughter! Not so very different from his own station, then! And a comely young woman at that! For a moment he allowed himself the vague hope that he might have found himself a pleasant companion for the evening once her lady had been attended to. However, the prince seemed set to put paid to that dream. At the top of the great hall Prince John was half sprawled in the best chair, fumbling with a well-dressed young woman clearly none too pleased to be the object of the prince's attentions.

"Ah, my pretty bird!" he chortled as he caught sight of Heloise. "Come here, my lovely!" and he tottered to his feet. "I shall be retiring to my chambers for the rest of the night's entertainment!" he declared to all and sundry. "I do not expect to be disturbed!"

As the prince draped a tipsy arm around another girl and led the pair of them away, it was very clear what he intended to be doing. De Blundeville looked from the prince to Heloise and back again with a stricken expression, confirming Guy's suspicions. *You must rue the day you thought to bring her down here,* Guy thought as the earl made to protest.

"But my lord!" he spluttered, "Lady Heloise is still in mourning for her father! I brought her here to distract her from her grief!"

"The she shall be suitably *distracted!*" the prince guffawed callously. "Or shall I tell my father you defied me in front of this assembled host, eh, Ranulph?"

The horrified earl of Chester looked about him, caught in a cleft stick. De Braose attempted to intervene.

"Your highness, might I remind you that your esteemed father himself has expressed an interest in this young lady's disposal. He may be deeply displeased at your intervention here."

It was remarkably tactful for the earl, but it fell on deaf ears as far as the prince was concerned. "Well for once I shall have stolen a march on the old goat!" he hooted exultantly and exited the hall. The assembled lords sat staring at one another in grim disbelief. All knew how the branches of their families over in France had been forced to take sides in one royal spat after another, as King Henry's sons tried to carve out a place for themselves from his empire. But this was England! It wasn't supposed to happen here! And if the king couldn't control his sons across the water then there was little hope for a successful outcome in this case.

For his part Guy was thinking fast. Wrapping his strong arms around Heloise he propelled her with speed after Prince John, Rohese in their wake.

"What are you doing?" she hissed angrily.

"Hopefully saving your mistress," Guy flung back at her. "Tell him you have to help her ...compose herself! ...Look at her, Rohese!" He dropped his voice and whispered urgently to her so Heloise couldn't hear. "She looks a mess! ...So tell him you'll make her fit for a king and will bring her to his chambers after you've done ...well, whatever it is you girls do! That should buy us some time!"

Catching on, Rohese made the appropriate excuses, and seeing Guy – the callous huntsman he had been hearing de Braose extolling the virtues of – rather than the besotted Earl of Chester, Prince John demurred. Unable to contain his lust any longer, the prince was already fumbling up the dress of the first woman and clearly intended to take her the moment they were in his chamber, if not before. With him distracted, Guy was able to steer Heloise after Rohese until they came to a small chamber up on the next floor which had been allocated to the women.

As soon as they were inside the door Guy jammed the latch shut with his older hunting knife. The blade was no longer good enough for the precision work Guy sometimes did, but it was sharp enough to bite into the wood and hold the peg hard in the slot. Then Guy dragged a heavy oak chest across the door.

"That should hold them for a while!" he said with a grin at Rohese. "Now when they come tell them the latch has stuck! Don't mention I'm here! If they break the door in I want my presence to be a total surprise."

"What do we do now?" Rohese asked in awe.

"Well I think your mistress should get a good night's sleep!"

"And what about me?"

"I suppose that depends on how sleepy you are...!"

To Guy's relief the prince forgot about Heloise once he was being entertained by others – not only because he wasn't sure how he would cope with fighting off the prince's men alone, but because he was somewhat otherwise preoccupied for much of the night with Rohese. As soon as the servants began stirring in the morning they dragged the chest away from the door again and Guy went in search of the earl of Chester. He feared he would have to get past the earl's servants to wake him, but instead he found the young earl pacing the room below, haggard and still in the clothes he had worn the night before. By the time Guy explained what he'd done he thought the earl might collapse as the tension ran out of him.

"Now, my lord," Guy concluded earnestly. "I suggest *I* take the young lady north from here with all speed, preferably before the prince departs? You could both be at Brecon within the day, but that might be a touch too obvious if the prince sees you disappear off for the day and at the same time my lady vanishes. May I therefore suggest I take her to Llantilio?" It was big enough to accommodate the young earl's retinue when he returned, whereas Skenfrith certainly wasn't. "Prince John's never been there and I doubt he even knows it exists! When he's on his ship you can come home via the castle and collect Lady Heloise. If you stay with your men then the prince can't accuse you of defying him, and neither can my lord be accused of open disobedience if one of his men acts rashly and alone. Mind you, I doubt the prince would think of me, and anyway, technically I'm his father's man, not Earl de Braose's. So it would be an interesting point if the prince wanted to punish me! It couldn't be done without an explanation to the king."

De Blundeville's relief was visible. A way of saving Heloise and his earldom was not to be brushed aside. "Do it!" he instructed Guy. "Go now! I shall tell de Braose when he rises. Go! Go before the prince wakes!"

And so Guy found himself on the road in the breaking dawn with two pretty young women for company – a considerable improvement on his normal riding companions! Lady Heloise was subdued and said little, but as the day wore on she seemed to realise that she was finally safe. Rohese, on the other hand, flirted outrageously with Guy now that they were away from disapproving eyes, and by the time they rode into Llantilio he could barely control himself. For a week they remained at the castle. A week in which Guy got almost no sleep thanks to Rohese, and began to think it might be possible to have too much of a good thing – but not quite! It was even revising his feelings on Llantilio itself! He was so overwhelmed by her that he was half thinking of asking if it would be possible to move north and act as huntsman on the Cartmel estate.

That was until the earl of Chester rode in. Lady Heloise had rallied with each day, and had even confided to Guy that she was far more interested in a young nobleman called William Marshal than the earl. Moreover, she had high hopes that the king would approve of an alliance between her and William, which was something she could see he would never allow with de Blundeville, even if the young earl couldn't. With the reappearance of Ranulph of Chester she wilted again, but there was little Guy could do, for his lordship announced his intention to ride off within a day since he was accompanied by the young Lord Roger de Mortimer, and in company they were far safer than separate.

"We've heard Rhys ap Gruffydd is getting restive over in the west," Lord Mortimer confided to Guy. "If he and Gruffydd Maelor joined forces we'll be in real trouble without a proper army here. God knows how, but the Welsh rebels got wind of Prince John wandering about the countryside. Thank God and St Thomas you shepherded him back to us! I shudder to think what King Henry would have done to us if we'd lost the little shit! When I'm next at court I shall make sure the king is informed of what his son did. Henry might dote on the boy, but he won't excuse stupidity in the face of danger!"

Guy felt a certain glow of pride for the rest of the day for he was under the impression that he would be given full credit for his part too. But that night his fragile happiness was burst like a soap bubble. He hadn't expected to be able to be close to Rohese with all the lords about the place. She was, after all, Lady Heloise's maid and as such had to be with her lady. However, once the court had retired Guy risked creeping into the castle from his own quarters. Making his way to the tiny chamber he knew Rohese occupied, he expected to find her ready and waiting for him. Instead, as he softly lifted the latch to her room, he heard energetic rustlings from the direction of the bed. Some sixth sense made him freeze before he was fully inside the room, although his head was still wondering what kind of surprise Rohese was preparing for him that would take so much energy. That was until he heard her cry out in a way he knew only too well, and then moan,

"Oh my lord....!"

"My little rosebud!" a voice which Guy recognised full well as belonging to Ranulph de Blundeville panted lustily, and the bedclothes rustled even more vigorously. "Has my little bird been good while I've been gone?" Ranulph gasped raggedly. "You haven't been tempted have you?"

"Oooh no!" Rohese squealed, then paused to gasp twice before adding, "no-one could compare to you, my lord!"

Stunned, Guy staggered back from the door. He'd had no illusions that he was the first man in Rohese's life – she'd been far too experienced for that. But to hear her now it was clear that he'd been nothing but a distraction for her, and that hurt. Too shocked to look where he was going he'd only taken a couple of steps before he blundered into someone.

"Ah, Guy..." Roger de Mortimer's voice brought him back down to earth, and Guy realised that he'd walked straight into the young nobleman. For an awful moment Guy wondered whether he was going to have to find some reason for his being there, and then realised that he couldn't think straight enough to form anything like a halfway decent excuse. However, Lord Roger took him by the arm and steered him on towards the room he himself was occupying for the night. Once the door was shut Mortimer asked,

"Do I gather you fell prey to our young witch?" Guy nodded numbly, then found Lord Mortimer pressing a glass of rich red wine into his hand. "Here drink that, you look like you need it! And take a seat by the fire. ...Now I'm sure I don't need to tell you that you can't say anything about this to anyone?"

"No," Guy answered sadly. Then shook his head and regained some clarity. "No, my lord, I won't make any trouble for his lordship. It's just that..."

"You thought you were in with a chance?"

"Well... yes! ...God Almighty, sire, she can't honestly think he's serious about her, can she?"

Lord Roger was stood back in the shadows but Guy still saw him shake his head. "Who knows what the foolish girl thought. ...You're right, of course, he's only using her to satisfy his lusts until he can get his hands on Heloise. And if he does, she'll be out of the way pretty fast."

"Except that Rohese knows that Heloise doesn't want the earl, and has her own sights set on someone the king might well agree to instead," Guy informed him morosely.

However, that made Mortimer sit up in surprise. "Does she? Well now! That shows more intelligence than I'd credited Heloise with! That won't please Chester!"

"I suppose that just gave Rohese more hope that he'd fly in the face of convention and take her instead," Guy sighed. "And there was I thinking that because we're of much the same station that she'd be glad of the offer of a respectable union."

"Oh dear, you have been smitten badly!" Mortimer chuckled sympathetically. "Well if you'll accept a little advice from me that's kindly meant, Guy, consider yourself lucky to have found out now! Many a man's taken on a lass only to find that he's had his lord's cast-off foisted upon him, and often with a bastard on the way too! Rohese's not a girl to sit patiently at home waiting for you to return when your lord sends you off on some errand. You'd have been coming home to an already warmed bed more often than not, ...and as many men will tell you, that wears very quickly! It may not feel like it at the moment, but you've had a narrow escape, for this liaison cannot continue for very long and Chester will be looking for a safe place to get rid of Rohese to." And his pointed stare wasn't lost on Guy.

Lord Mortimer's words proved prophetic far quicker than either of them could have foreseen. As the noble party were mounting up in the morning, being seen off by de Braose who had ridden in with them, a rider hammered in with a message for the earl of Chester.

"It's from the king!" Guy heard Ranulph of Chester tell Lord Roger. "He wants Heloise brought to London with all despatch! He has a suitor arranged for her! ...No, this cannot be! She's mine!"

"Don't be foolish, my lord!" de Braose's deep growl sounded, cutting off the young noble's protestations. "You seriously thought King Henry would allow you of all people to take over the Cartmel estate? Fie, lad! Where are your brains? The king may tup every wench he can lay his hands on, but he never lets that rule his head. So he won't believe you are acting out of desire for the fair Heloise, will he? He'll think you're trying to cut your own kingdom out of the north, and who can blame him when he can't even trust his own sons not to do it to him?"

It was only many years later that I found out what became of Heloise of Lancaster. She was indeed betrothed to William Marshal upon her return to London but then the king, in one of his fickle moods, changed his mind and married her off to one of his Norman barons. Where the lusty Rohese ended up I know not.

Oh, Gervase, I was heartbroken in the way only the young can be! In recent years there had been little time to chase girls, and although I had had Megan and Mary sporadically for some company, it was far from love. It had also begun to dawn on me that most young men of my age were already married, and that at twenty-four, approaching twenty-five, I was rather trailing in the hunt for a suitable wife. Now, though, I possessed a steady position which I had settled into, and if I was not gaining advancement at any great rate, at least I could provide for a family. Therefore all that had stopped me, thus far, was the failed appearance of any available young woman I felt able to contemplate living with for years on end.

Yet now my heart had taken the lead for once, and I had given myself wholeheartedly if not wisely. So Rohese's lesson in betrayal hit me hard. Hard enough that I only just remembered in time that Fulk, Philip and Audulph had been heading for the earl of Chester to enlist with him. Being very much in Ranulph of Chester's favour at that point, I managed to pull myself together enough to ask about my cousins and half-brother, and at least if I seemed somewhat emotional in his presence that day he probably put it down to the fact that he knew nothing of them. In reality I was not upset that they had failed in finding a patron in the earl. Had I been less distraught on my own account, I would probably have gloated that they had seemingly misjudged their own prospects even more badly than those of Baldwin, John, Allan and myself. However, given the blow Rohese had dealt me, I could not summon the energy to pursue inquiries any further, and I could only assume that Fulk, Philip and Audulph must have had to find work elsewhere. Being jilted in love is an exhausting business for a young man!

Mercifully I was never the sort of lad to sit and sulk, or torment those around me with my moods and sighs, as some I have known since have done in their youth, and I certainly did not act like that as a grown man. That at least is not on my conscience. Instead I buried my feelings in the hustle and bustle of getting the sheriff's party ready to go to

London. I brought in deer aplenty, and several good-sized boar, so we were well provisioned for the trip to the capital.

However, I could not summon any excitement for the journey. In fact I was quite appalled when I discovered that Earl William intended me to travel with them. I had hoped that when they had all gone, I would be able to take some time to lick my wounds in peace and quiet back at the kennels. Moreover, I discovered, I would have to leave the dogs behind, and that tore at me terribly. London, I was told, was no place for my fleet-footed friends. Nor, Ianto pointed out, would it be wise to let the king see my handsome deerhound friends, for he was an obsessive hunter and if he thought them the best then nothing would do but he should have them. That depressing thought nearly did for me, Brother! I could cope with Rohese's departure, just about, but not losing the makeshift family I had created to replace my missing cousins.

And especially not the thought of my lovely deerhounds being run ragged by the ferocious king in pursuit of his own pleasures. A king who, by all accounts, had only ever cared for one person and that had been the beautiful Rosamund Clifford during her brief life. His sons were alternately his pleasure and his bane, and Queen Eleanor was always far too much of a match for his own strength of will for it to be anything other than a tempestuous match. Many had felt the lash of his fiery temper, and from knowing Maelgwn I knew how cruel he could be. No, I would not have wished such a fate on my beloved dogs!

So there we were by March, on the road to London. A long and wearing journey it was too, and one which gave me far too much time just sitting on my horse brooding over the injustices of love! I must have been a poor companion to my fellow travellers, especially at first, but then we drew near to the great capital and even I was forced to take some notice!

Chapter 6

L ondon! What a place! Now there, Gervase, was a town to lead a man astray if ever there was one! I thought I should go mad with the noise during those first days, for the whole place teamed with people – the worst of villains and rogues living scant streets away from the great and the good. The timber houses seemed to prop one another up, they leaned so close together – and sometimes seemed to be the <u>only</u> thing holding one another up. Knock one down and you felt they might all follow in its wake, to leave a jumbled pile of timber like the remnants of so many felled trees in a wood. Dark alleys gave access onto yards and workshops, and even gardens in the better quarters, but it was all a maze to me. Do not ask me where I went for the most part, Brother, because I have no more idea now than then.

It was an endless, confusing warren of streets where the only point of reference I ever managed to get some hold on was the great river which dominates life there. I had seen great rivers before, of course I had. But what made the Thames so different was the great mass of boats upon the water. Small water-men scurried hither and thither, transporting passengers by what was quite often the quickest way to get from one spot to another. Besides them, heavy cargo barges plied between the quays and some of the seagoing ships anchored farther out, or brought goods of their own to that heaving marketplace from further along the estuary or coast.

I walked about in a daze at first, although I had been warned of cutpurses well enough and kept my meagre pennies in a small pouch within my shirt. Everyone seemed in such a hurry, and I now understood why it was no place for the dogs, for I was often kicked at and cursed for not being swift enough to get out of the way, or for blocking some vital entrance which I was assumed to know better than to inadvertently stand in front of, albeit briefly. I tell you, Brother Gervase, it was an experience I shall never forget, but I have no wish to ever go back. Some love the excitement of being so close to the centre of the kingdom when it comes to power, politics and money. For myself I prefer to have a little more room to breathe and manoeuvre in. Space to see an attack coming, and places only I know about to use as refuges in case of times of dire need. No, London was not for me. Yet that time I was there it was to turn out to be the making of me in an unexpected way.

Once we had reached our appointed lodgings there was very little for me to do for the first few days. I saw nothing of my lord de Braose, for he was off at court with all the others whom the king had summoned. My job had been to help get him there, and perhaps would be even more vital to the getting back, for I would need to hunt daily then to replenish our depleted supplies. Most of the time the earl travelled with a much smaller retinue when he came from Wales to London, or went there from one of his other holdings which lay closer to the capital. Moreover, most of the *times he travelled there were for the set courts at Easter and Michaelmas, since those were the occasions when much of the country's business was conducted, with sheriff's rents being paid in and reimbursements coming out. This, on the other hand, was an extraordinary meeting of the great barons and advisors, and thus with far more men of means congregated there, which depleted the normal resources even faster than usual.*

For myself I cared little about the whys and wherefores. If King Henry was to accept the throne of Jerusalem, it was unlikely to matter to me any more than any other royal succession. I sat way too far down below the salt along the table of power for me to be affected any more than any others of the common folk. Since then I have often wondered whether the greater flow of history would have been significantly changed if King Henry had said yes. Would he have gone himself? I have debated this often over the years with friends at one fireside or another, and I believe he would have stayed in England even had his answer been yes. He would have appointed a regent in his stead whatever happened. We forget, because of his illustrious memory, that King Henry was no warmonger. He never fought at all unless there was no other way around a situation, preferring to impose his will on others by sheer force of personality, and in person instead of using an army. And also I think he loved his homelands too much – Normandy even more than England – to want to go to a land he had never laid eyes on. For let us not forget that although he was still robust and had four more years to rule yet, he was by now an elderly man worn down by his cares.

Send Prince Richard, you say Brother Gervase? ...Yes, I believe that was exactly the alternative he must have considered. Our beloved then-prince was already a formidable fighter and a man whom others in France and beyond feared and respected, and this was long before he was king in his own right and wielding such authority. But not just for that reason, Brother, oh no! I believe it would have fitted nicely into the king's plans under other circumstances. After all, he had tried to force Richard to hand over Queen Eleanor's Aquitaine to Prince John only a year or so beforehand. It had been an ill-advised move, as it turned out, and one which set the royal princes at one another's throats in the worst way.

I think the only thing which stopped the king pushing Prince Richard off to the Holy Land – whether as king in his own right or as Henry's regent – was the fact that the prince was in such disgrace just at the time the Patriarch of Jerusalem arrived in London. Richard had shown himself capable of taking on Prince Geoffrey and Prince John together less than six months beforehand. So King Henry must have wondered what his oldest son would do if he were ever to return from the east with an army of seasoned knights and Templars supporting him. The old king always did like to keep his sons close enough to keep an eye on them at all times, and Jerusalem was much too far away for that!

I suppose that, knowing what we know now, it would have made no difference in the long run if alternatively King Henry had passed the throne of Jerusalem to Prince John, in his search to provide him with an inheritance. Given that we seemed destined to lose not only Jerusalem but also any meaningful stake in the Holy Land, having such a useless military leader as Prince John would have merely hastened the inevitable. But it did not feel that way back in 1185. Much as many would have liked to see the back of the youngest prince, we all believed the Holy Land could be saved, and for that reason alone no-one would have wanted John to have the position.

But these are an old man's ramblings! Come, Brother, we must return to my story before I die with it half done! I was in London, a young man with my life ahead of me, and momentous events ahead...

The City of London,
April, the year of Our Lord 1185

Guy stared about him at the teaming river-front. It was his third day in the city and for the first time he had ventured further afield from their lodgings at Queenhithe. Now he was down river at Billingsgate, and standing with his back to a small waterside church watching the mad dance everyone so determinedly engaged in. How more folk never ended up in the river was a source of amazement to him, for the jostling and bustling was quite baffling to someone like himself. He felt sure that if he had to try to negotiate a path closer to the edge he would be into the swirling, murky water in no time.

"By Our Lady, look at them!" muttered his companion, a young Welsh lad named William Cosham but who everyone called Bilan, whom Guy had become acquainted with in the last few days as they had been thrown into one another's company. They had been warned by the earl's steward not to go out alone, and so the pair had decided that they should explore this manic place together. "Should we take some fish back with us for our supper, do you think?"

"We could..." Guy mused. "I have my skillet with me in my pack. I'm sure there would be enough heat in that little fire we have in our room for us to cook it on. We'll have to take enough for the others, though. If we make them live with the smell of cooked fish without even having the pleasure of eating it we'll be in for a lot of grief."

Together they managed to scrape together enough pennies for some good sized specimens (for Guy was not letting on that he had more about him than the barest funds) and approached a rough looking fishwife who was calling out her wares to passers-by. Young Bilan was the picture of fresh-faced rural innocence, and Guy could almost see the malevolent glee on the fishwife's face when he hurried up and asked her for fish. She lifted up two slimy objects and was about to dump them into a piece of muslin when Guy reached out and grasped her wrist.

"Not those two!"

" 'Ere! 'Oo are you to interfere?" she snarled, wrestling her arm free with more strength than Guy would have suspected she possessed. "If this young 'un wants these fish then 'e can 'ave 'em!"

"He's with me, and I'm paying," Guy said calmly, but in a tone that said he would not stand for being robbed. "So you can put those two stinking old things back! They're plump because they're bloated and rotten! Give them to the cat, if it'll have them!" He then gestured to two huge mackerel, their blue markings positively gleaming and clearly fresh from the sea. "We'll take those two and those three fish over there." He wasn't quite sure what the large silver fish were – they weren't cod, which he'd seen salted often enough, but thought they were probably whiting. Whatever the breed, he knew enough about fish to know that they too were fresh. He also hadn't appreciated how intimidating he could look to a stranger, for Guy's height coupled with his dark looks, sharp green eyes and hawk-like features made him seem dangerous even if he felt far from it inside. Few strangers apart from lords very sure of their position would pick a fight with Guy, but he hadn't yet been far enough afield since reaching maturity to know that.

The fishwife scowled at him and tried a last ditch attempt to argue that they weren't the best buy at all, but Guy was firm and stood his ground until she slapped them into a piece of less-than-clean muslin and held her hand out for the coins. As she pocketed the money Guy caught her looking away as if signalling to someone.

"Come on," he said to Bilan, grabbing the younger lad's arm and steering him briskly away.

"Wow! You upset her!" Bilan happily gabbled, clasping the fish bundle to him tightly. "But what was wrong with those other fish? How could you tell? They didn't smell off to me," then added, "mind you I can't smell anything here! Phew this river stinks!"

"It's all the privies that empty into it, I suppose," Guy agreed, for the river did stink something shocking. Especially to folks like Guy and Bilan who were used to the clear, clean running rivers of the wild countryside. "But surely you could see they weren't fresh? By St Thomas, the one fish was fit to explode it was so rotten! Didn't you see that?"

Bilan shook his head. "They just looked plump and shiny to me. I thought they were fine. I'd have bought them."

"Yes and you'd have kept me awake puking your guts up for the next two days if you'd eaten them!" Guy informed him acerbically. "But for now keep moving!"

"Why?" Bilan wanted to know as Guy propelled him along at an increasing pace.

"Because she's marked us down as a couple of country bumpkins, and her hired thugs are going to knock you on the head and addle what little brains you've got if we don't get out of here now! They'll take the fish back for her to sell again and whatever we happen to have in our purses, or anything of value, with them," Guy hissed in his ear. "If you don't want to wake up without your boots and coat, keep moving!"

Bilan turned a shocked face to Guy and then tried to look behind him, although it was impossible with the way Guy was shouldering him forward. Suddenly Guy yanked him sideways and they found themselves in the near darkness of a tiny alleyway, even though it was a bright and sunny day. Clamping his hand over Bilan's mouth Guy held him back against the wall, half-turned himself so that his dark hair and jerkin were facing outwards. In furtive glances Guy kept watch and within seconds was rewarded with the sight of two burly men hurrying past and then stopping to cast about them, clearly looking for someone or something. Quick as a flash Guy hauled Bilan to the opposite wall so that when the men turned back they wouldn't be looking straight at them. Moments later he saw the two shoving their way back through the crowd back the way they'd come.

By now Bilan's eyes were huge pools of surprise and Guy didn't need to hold him close, the lad was hanging onto Guy's arm like a vice.

"Can we go back now?" he asked in a small shaky voice.

Guy gave him a pat on the still tightly gripping hand. "Just a moment longer. Let's make sure they don't double back, eh? They might think we're daft enough to come strolling out the moment they're gone, and then they'd have us again. And we don't want that, do we?" he added softly.

Bilan's mute shake of the head froze as the shadow of the two men brushed across the entrance of the alley, and then both came closer to stand right in front of the alley, although mercifully with their backs to Bilan and Guy. Quiet as a cat on the prowl Guy drew Bilan further back into the gloom. Suddenly the sound of a bolt being drawn back came from right beside them and part of the wall seemed to move. Guy's quick reactions saved them, for he realised in an instant that they must be by a gate into one of the burgage plots at the back of the buildings, and that the gate was opening outwards. With his greater strength and height he lifted Bilan bodily off his feet and plunged them both backwards, so that when the gate opened fully they were behind it, rather than exposed by the fresh light which flooded into the alley.

They heard an elderly man's voice grumbling at the end of the alley, presumably remonstrating with the two thugs for blocking his way as he carried something out to a customer, who must have been waiting in the street. But the man's appearance and the evident lack of anyone behind him must have convinced the thugs that they had lost their quarry, for as the gate swung back closed there was no sign of the thugs any more.

"Phew!" Bilan breathed with relief. "By Our Lady, I'm glad I'm with you! They'd have had me for sure!"

Despite that, Guy had the feeling that Bilan still hadn't fully comprehended the dangers of London as a whole, or at least he hadn't until they had gone a little farther along the Thames' bank. Guy was still hustling his younger companion along when suddenly Bilan stopped altogether. Irritated, Guy turned back to him to see what had attracted the attention of the irrepressible lad, only to be surprised by seeing Bilan now completely white-faced, shivering and staring at the river.

"Oh Jesu!" Bilan whimpered, and then Guy saw what had shocked him so badly.

Drifting past them on the current with the other detritus and effluent, and heading for the sea, was the body of a boy, his corpse half over an old rotten plank and thus more visible than if he'd been wholly in the water. Like Bilan he had a shock of dark hair and pale skin. He might even have been the same age as Bilan, but he had clearly been severely in want of food for a very long time and was stunted and thin. However hunger was not what had killed him. That was the great slash which had opened his throat right up so that his head lolled at a strange angle upon the plank.

"Why does no-one do anything?" Bilan asked Guy in hushed, anguished tones whilst making frantic darting glances about them. Certainly no-one else around them was taking the slightest bit of interest. Some passers-by even appeared to look at the river without batting an eyelid, not seeming to register that there was something very wrong with the scene.

"Maybe it's too common an occurrence," Guy told him gently, his irritation evaporated and replaced with a sorrow of his own for the dead boy. "He's just one more peasant boy. One more beggar. Have you not noticed how many beggars there are around here? How they creep out of the dark alleys as soon as there's no-one around who might question who they once served? Or to drag them off to the sheriff, or whatever they have here in the city. Maybe he ran away from his lord in the country and came here to find work, who knows? And he might not even be English. There are a lot of boats tied up here. Fights amongst sailors who come ashore and get drunk must be a pretty regular thing. If he doesn't belong to a local lord and he's not trespassing on anyone's land, who would bother on his behalf?"

"That's even worse than de Braose!" Bilan said, shaking his head in disbelief, then whimpered, "Oh Jesu!" again as a further horror appeared.

As they stood watching the body drift further downstream, a huge black rat pulled itself up onto the plank and swiftly removed an eyeball. Within seconds others had joined it as the chance for an easy meal drew the scavengers of the river like moths to a flame. Guy spun Bilan and pulled the lad's head to his shoulder, guessing that the boy would have nightmares about this already without seeing the boy being consumed, but he himself saw one of the rats gnawing inwards from the cut neck making the jaw move as if still alive. The sight was truly macabre.

"Come on, let's get back before we're missed. It's getting late," Guy said, trying to put some normality into his voice. It seemed to work, for Bilan picked up his pace now, although Guy noticed that he studiously avoided looking at the swirling waters whilst they were beside them.

The wind had been taken out of the youngster's sails for the rest of the walk back, for he said very little in contrast to his normal stream of chatter. But that night, as Guy gutted and then cooked the fishes for himself and Bilan plus the six men-at-arms they shared their cramped quarters with, the men were regaled with the whole tale by Bilan and at great length, and his saving of Bilan took on heroic proportions. Luckily the men were old enough to recognise that Bilan was still reeling from all the excitement and frights, and rather than take exception at this elevation of Guy above them, simply indulged in some good-natured ribbing.

However, when Earl William's steward came the next day for someone to go to Swan Lane and collect some dyed cloth, all six promptly pointed the finger at Guy and he got landed with the task.

"Thanks a bundle!" Guy muttered ruefully to Bilan as they set out once more. "You know you've now saddled me with the reputation of being the one who can deal with snotty merchants, don't you! I'll be doing all the running and fetching for the rest of the time we're here unless the earl finds me something else to do."

However, Bilan was far from put off. Instead, he seemed to regard it as a treat to be able to come out with Guy again, or maybe, Guy belated thought, the lad simply felt safer with him after the shocks of the previous day. Mercifully they didn't have to go right to the water's edge this time and avoided both the worst of the stench and the sights. By the time they had got to the dyer's and collected the bolt of cloth, Guy had heard much of Bilan's life story, and he couldn't help but feel a bit sorry for him.

Bilan, it turned out, had two older brothers and had gained the nickname Bilan as the local word for 'spear' on account of being tall and thin. The family had been split up, though, after their father's death when the older brothers had been taken on as bowmen by de

Braose and enlisted amongst his soldiers. As the youngster, Bilan had been sent to the only place he could be useful, which was as one of the lowliest servants at Brecon Castle. It was his confessions over how much he missed his brothers which broke the last of Guy's resistance to his new friend. Especially since his encounter with Rohese he had longed for his cousins to talk to again. He knew John and Baldwin would have pulled his leg over mooning around over a girl, but it would have been done with a lot of sympathy and understanding of his hurt, for no-one knew him like they did.

So listening to Bilan made Guy wonder if he could do something for his young companion, and he resolved to see if he could get him moved to Grosmont as a kennel-boy. Yet before he could speak to anyone events took a surprising turn. As they got back to the earl's lodgings Guy was accosted by one of the senior men-at-arms.

"Have you got a decent set of clothes with you, Guy?" he demanded.

Guy stared at him in astonishment. "Decent clothes? No. ...In fact I don't think I've got anything anymore which could be described as decent. Everything I brought with me to this job that was any good I've grown out of. All my clothes are woollen homespun for working in. ...Why?" he belatedly thought to ask.

The man shook his head in despair even as he gestured for Guy to follow him. "Well we'd better get you something and fast then, hadn't we! Because you, my lad, are going to court tomorrow!"

"Me? Court?" Guy was flabbergasted. 'Lad' just about summed up how he suddenly felt about himself at receiving this bolt from the blue. Out on the borders, by now he had a calm confidence about his position and the authority that came with it, but here he was a fish out of water, and now it was as if he'd been instantly thrown back in time to being the callow youth who had marched up to Clun Castle. And with that thought came another, which said he should be fearful of the king. After all, it had been at King Henry's capricious wish that the fitz Waryns had been disinherited, and nowadays Guy's rank was even more lowly and powerless. "Why am I going to court?" he managed to blurt out.

"Don't ask me bloody silly questions like that!" the man answered with soldierly cynicism. "All I was told was to make sure that you were scrubbed up and decent when they come to get you first thing tomorrow. 'Court' was what his lordship's steward said, and he doesn't make mistakes, so I'm guessing court it is! ...Now then, we'd better kit you out from the spare uniform we've got with us if you've got none of your own. ...Here you go! ...These woollen hosen haven't got any visible holes or darns in them, ...and this tunic will have to do. Bit narrow across the shoulders and short, ...but that what comes of being a longshanks like you!"

The veteran soldier carried on rummaging through packs, pulling out items of clothing, and then replacing them with others as better fits came to light, until Guy had his arms full with a complete outfit. Back on the borders he regularly wore heavy duty woollen trousers, cut to the same pattern as his under-braes but weightier and tougher, but the sergeant informed him that such loose garments were regarded as old-fashioned in the city, despite being serviceable, and would mark him down as peasant if he went so dressed to court. Mercifully a few of the soldiers had invested in more fashionably cut clothes in the hope of attracting the girls when they came here with the sheriff, and so Guy had more than one set of hosen to chose from for a decent fit. Despite that, Guy wasn't too sure about the fastenings of the borrowed hosen, and hoped like mad that they wouldn't come adrift at a critical moment. Meeting the king with his underwear exposed and the hosen down around his ankles was not a happy thought! He vowed that if he was ever again to appear anywhere where the cut of his garments would matter so much, then he would get some properly made beforehand.

However, for now beggars couldn't be choosers. His braes and linen shirt undergarments were therefore still his own, but over that went the borrowed hosen with a smart pair of leather leg-wraps holding them firmly from the knees down, a smarter woollen tunic than he normally possessed, and a cloak which looked better than his own, although he doubted it would keep the rain off as well – his having been well felted by a Welshman who knew his wools. There was also a newish gambeson available, but both of them agreed upon reflection that it would be better not to look too ready for a fight at court!

The one thing they couldn't supply him with was boots, but then those at least had only recently been replaced, and with the best quality Guy could afford on his meagre pay. He'd found to his cost that few things were as miserable as ill-fitting and poorly made boots. Old clothes could be mended and patched, or let out where necessary, and layered over one another if the weather turned bad, but what went on his feet had to stand up to days of wear at a time out in all weathers, and so Guy treasured his boots. He kept them clean, and whenever possible he treated the leather so that they stayed supple and as waterproof as possible – even if that meant that the dogs got very excited by the smell of the goose grease and beeswax mixture he used for that!

"You'll do," the veteran said appraisingly when Guy had changed in order to be inspected. "At least you look like a working soldier and not some popinjay courtier! I doubt the king will object to that, nor Prince Richard if he's there, although expect some of Prince John's lot to turn their noses up at you for not having a silk pair of hosen."

"He's back at court? I thought he was in Ireland?"

"Not yet. On his way – yet again! – later this year if rumour is to be believed. Apparently, in all the ructions over what happened on his way to stay with our earl, word got back to the king and he was hauled back to London for strong words. The word amongst the soldiers is that the young prince has been sulking ever since."

"I think I can live with that," Guy answered with a wry grin, which elicited one in return as a response from his benefactor. Only later did it occur to him that Prince John's prolonged fit of pique might be the very reason he was being summoned to court and his initial qualms turned to out-and-out dread. If the prince had done what everyone said was his normal tactic of blaming anyone but himself, then the king might think Guy had deliberately led the youngest of his heirs astray. What the king might say to that gave Guy a very sleepless night indeed.

He was up at the crack of dawn, nerves all a jitter and pacing the hall below the bedroom rather than wake his roommates, so that he felt like he'd been up half the day already when the messenger came to fetch him. Together they rode through the warren of streets, for which Guy was thankful. If he'd had to find his own way to court he would probably have got lost ten times over, and possibly have been robbed of his horse and clothes to boot, when he wandered into one of the more lawless areas in his innocence. He was even more relieved when it became clear that they weren't heading for the great white-stone tower which he could see in the distance, and which in his ignorance he would have gone to for want of knowing anywhere else which looked like it might be royal.

When they finally dismounted, it was to find himself in an area which his guide told him was called Clerkenwell.

"Why are we here?" Guy whispered anxiously to his guide as the horses were led away by someone who looked very much like a Templar to Guy. "What is this place?"

"It's the house of the Knights of St John of Jerusalem," he was told.

"The Hospitallers? ...Why here?"

"The Patriarch is here." And that was all that Guy could get out of him.

He was left to cool his heels in a hallway while someone reported his presence, and the longer he waited the more he began to get worried. He was desperately trying to think what other dreadful sin he might have committed without knowing it, and could still only come up with his encounter with Prince John. After all, at twenty-five and living out in the wilds he'd hardly been overwhelmed with opportunities for mischief-making, and he was pretty sure that if it had been to do with Maelgwn's escape being discovered then Earl William would have dealt with the matter himself. The earl hardly needed a member of the royal family to hold his hand over something like that.

He was so lost in his own fretting that he failed to notice anything going on around him until a female voice said sharply,

"Are you going to stand there blocking the doorway all day?"

He spun round and saw a pretty blonde girl clutching a pile of what he assumed were laundered sheets.

"Oh ...er ...I'm sorry!" Guy babbled, disconcerted. "Here, let me get it for you!" and he pounced on the ring of the door latch only to find that it wouldn't budge.

"Oh for God's sake!" the girl sniffed, but Guy realised there was a twitch of laughter at the corners of her mouth. "Here! Hold these!" she ordered, thrusting the linen into his arms so that she could produce a key from the folds of her mantle. Evidently used to the quirks of the lock, she jiggled the key and Guy heard the lock on the other side of the door click open.

"What's a woman doing here in the Hospitallers' halls," Guy asked, then mentally kicked himself for being so clumsy. Had his experience with Rohese completely addled his wits where women were concerned?

"What's a country boy doing here in the city?" she quipped back, then looked him sharply in the eye as she snatched back the sheets. "If you must know I'm a sister of the Hospitallers."

"One of the knight's family? ...Here? ...I didn't think that was allowed?"

"No, you idiot!" she retorted with a glare, her good humour fading. "By St John! Why is it that you men think all anyone does in the east is beat one another over the head? Do you know nothing of what our order does?"

Guy desperately cudgelled his brains to work. "You take care of pilgrims," he said, carefully making it her order since that seemed to be what she was implying.

"We take care of any who *needs* us!" she corrected him firmly. "The sick, the infirm, or just the plain exhausted. Our hospitality extends to all. ...So do you imagine the brothers take care of the women and children pilgrims and travellers? ...Assist at difficult births? ...Even in the east?"

"Oh."

"Yes. Oh!" She looked him up and down again with now ill-disguised contempt. "So there are *sisters* among the order who tend to the sick as well, and I'm one of them! ...See?" She pointed at her clothes. "...A uniform! ...A clue, yes?"

"Yes," Guy replied humbly, feeling a right fool. "I'm very sorry. I didn't mean to insult you." He felt obliged to try and explain. "I'm not quite myself today. A young woman I thought..." How to explain without making himself seem hopelessly gullible? "I thought... I had reason to believe that she entertained the same feelings for me..."

"And she had some other chap lined up?" the girl finished for him bluntly.

"Yes."

Now it was her turn to be embarrassed as she took in the glint of a rebellious tear which had crept unbidden into the corner of Guy's eye. His head was hung in misery and if he hadn't been so tall she wouldn't have seen it. Making a rapid reappraisal of the man before her, the girl realised that actually he would be considered very good looking if he was smartened up a little, yet she hadn't noticed it until now because he didn't behave in the way she'd come to expect handsome men to do. Most of them knew only too well the effect they were having on the women around them, and out in the east she had taken a mischievous delight in cutting down to size those of their kind who came within her orbit. This man, though, seemed to need less of the cutting down than the building up.

"I'm sorry, that was sharp of me," she said sticking out her hand, "I'm Sister Marianne, by the way."

Guy looked down at her hand, not sure whether to kiss it or shake it as he would a man's, then back up at her. "Will you slap me if I kiss it?" he queried with some of his own normal good humour creeping back.

As his reward he got a throaty laugh which was so much more spontaneous than Rohese's giggle had ever been, making Guy think for the first time that Lord Roger might well have been right all along. It was a surprising relief to think like that after so many weeks of moping, and Guy belatedly realised that he'd actually got to the stage of being fed up with himself for feeling so wretched all the time. So he found himself returning Marianne's grin. That really transformed him, Marianne thought. Not quite her type, even given that her vows forbade any liaisons anyway – a bit too brooding and intense for her – but those green eyes were almost catlike in the brilliance of colour, which was unusual, and that smile came from inside, not just something painted on to watch for the effect of it.

"So, what are you doing here young master...?"

"...Guy. ...My name's Guy of Maesbury. I came here – to London – as Sheriff de Braose's huntsman, but for some reason I can't fathom I've been told to report here today. ...What about you? How do you come to be here? This doesn't look like a hospital."

Marianne wrinkled her nose in disgust. "I had to travel here with the Patriarch's party. There were some women returning with them from Outremer. Quite well bred ladies," there was no mistaking the sarcastic derision in her tone now, "and two of them are pregnant ...poor things. So that meant money was passed to the order for a nurse to accompany them." Her smile took on a forced jollity. "So for three months I've been treated like some cursed ladies' maid and worked ragged!"

"Will you return to the East?" Guy wondered. "I mean, there don't seem to be many folk around here wanting nursing, and outside of London most places in England seem to have some sort of hospital run by one order or another."

"I don't know. I expect that will depend on whether there's a place for me in the Patriarch's group again. I hope so. I don't feel like I fit in here in England anymore."

"Where are you from originally?" Guy asked, picking up on the remains of a northern accent in her voice. "Have you no family there?"

"I'm from Skipton," Marianne said with less bitterness. "I remember the hills and the cottage we lived in, but not much else."

"Why did you leave? That sounds as if you were quite small to be going so far afield?"

"Oh I was! Only eight! My mother was sick, you see, and father couldn't carry on the way things were, so he let his older brother take over all of the farm and decided to take us on pilgrimage to see if a cure could be found for Mother." Marianne sighed. "It's so sad. Knowing what I know now, I think that the dry warm air in the Holy Land would have helped her even if nothing else did, but she died in Cyprus without ever getting there. Father was distraught. He resolved to continue because at that stage there wasn't much point in turning back, and he wanted to say prayers for her in the Holy City. Well we got there and then it became clear that father hadn't ever thought about how we'd get back! I think mother must have been the sensible one. He just stumbled around for a few months and then placed me in the care of the order and disappeared.

"I'm told he said something about getting work to fund his passage back and then he'd send for me, but he's never been heard of since, so I think he must be dead too." She gave Guy a tight smile. "I can't really mourn them anymore because there aren't enough memories left. The people I'm missing most at the moment are the other sisters in Jerusalem. They were the family I grew up really knowing. I don't even know if the family up in Skipton are still alive, let alone what they'd think if I turned up on their doorstep unbidden! Anyway, I've taken my vows, and what I want to do is carry on helping the sick. It's what I'm good at!"

"Then I hope you get your wish," Guy replied. "I know what it's like to be cut adrift in a strange place, and it's no fun."

"Thank you." He was rewarded with a warmer smile. "Where are you from, then, Guy? Somewhere up north too, I can tell. It's nice to hear a familiar accent after all this time."

By now Guy was at his ease and answered without worrying about how he'd be perceived. "Oh I grew up on an uncle's manor in

Nottinghamshire. A middling size sort of a place. But he died and my cousins couldn't afford the price the king wanted. We all got split up – that's my cousins and me." Then a thought occurred to him. "Look Marianne, I have no right to ask this of you after knowing you for less than an hour, but if you get back to Jerusalem would you see if you can find someone for me? It's my younger cousin Baldwin. ...Baldwin of Hodenet. ...All I could ever find out was that he went to the Templars and that he's not in a preceptory here in England. The Templar brother who enquired for me thought Baldwin had been sent east. If you could find him would you ask him to write to me?"

Marianne had begun to look sceptical. "Jerusalem's a busy city, you know. Our hospital alone can hold two thousand people if needs be, and that's only a small part of the old city." Then she thought some more. "Mind you, there aren't that many Templars compared to ordinary people. I could ask, I suppose."

"Thank you!" The force of Guy's gratitude surprised her.

"You really care about him, don't you?"

"He's more of my brother than a cousin," Guy admitted. "I know we may never meet again, especially if he's out there, but I would dearly love to know that he at least still lives. If he could send word to the Honour of Grosmont, that's where I serve the earl." Then he had another thought. "And if I ever get back up north I'll try and find my way to Skipton and send you word of your family, if you like. What's the family name?"

"Shepherd," Marianne said with a grin. "Lots of them about! My uncle's name was Roger and my father's Walter."

Guy nodded, committing the names to memory. "Roger and Walter Shepherd, and Walter went to the Holy Land with his wife and daughter. That at least should identify them. I'll try to send word to the Hospitaller preceptory in Jerusalem if I find anything."

"If I get back there..."

"...if you get back there!"

They stood there grinning at one another, then Marianne sighed. "I'd better be getting on. The Patriarch needs clean sheets for his bed or there'll be trouble!"

"Good luck, Sister Marianne," Guy said, bending and placing a kiss on her cheek. "God speed!"

"And you Guy. God and St John keep you safe!" and she was gone.

Do you wonder why I even bothered mentioning her, Gervase? Is that why you have been fidgeting on your seat? What of interest could there be in a mere chance meeting with some girl? Ah, but you see I was to encounter Marianne again, and not so very far in the future. She, like Bilan, will return again in this story. Both of them have their parts to play in the greater tale, for I am not wandering so very from the path of the main story as you fear. I have not succumbed to age so much that my mind should dot about like some moth drawn to one candle after another in no particular order!

So do not be too hasty to dismiss my chance encounters, Brother! For now, though, let us return to the preceptory of the Hospitallers in London, for more of importance is coming hard on the heels of this last encounter.

Chapter 7

*S*o there I was, still kicking my heels in that strange place while others bustled about me on urgent business of one kind or another leaving me stranded in a strange limbo. My brief interlude with Marianne had relieved some of the tension from my mind, and if I was still worried as to why on earth I should have been summoned, at least my thoughts flitted back and forth between that worry and the rather more consoling thought that maybe I was finally getting over the flirtatious Rohese. Nor did I have much longer to wait before I was put out of my misery and the truth revealed, as I shall disclose to you now...

The City of London & the Marches, April, the Year of Our Lord 1185

Lost in his reveries Guy had found a small niche in which to stand out of the way, and was looking out of a window at some sparrows squabbling in the bush outside in the spring sunshine, fighting for the attentions of a female. So he ignored the booted footsteps behind him until a familiar voice spoke.

"Hello Guy!"

Near jumping out of his skin in surprise Guy spun round to see Ranulph de Blundeville, Earl of Chester smiling at him. With his heart beating like a drum, Guy had to swallow hard before he could return the earl's greeting and make the appropriate bow. Had Rohese said something to the earl, her lover, by any chance? No, for surely de Blundeville would not be so friendly then!

"My lord, I didn't expect to see you here."

The young earl quirked an eyebrow. "Well I'm here because of you, Guy. I'm here on the king's behalf. You won't be seeing him yourself, which I hope isn't too much of a disappointment for you."

Guy's heartfelt exhaling gave the earl a clue before Guy could summon the wits to speak again as his panic subsided a notch. "Oh no, my lord!"

"Really? ...I would've thought a young man might have relished the chance to further his career from such an opportunity? Put your plea to him in person?"

A nervous laugh escaped from Guy. "Plea? ...Me? ...in front of the King? Dear God, I hope not! If I may be frank, my lord, I think if even half that I've heard of the king and his temper is true I'm probably safer kept well out of the way. I've been worrying about what on earth I've done to warrant summoning here in the first place. What would make the king notice a lowly person like me? I'm not someone he'd normally even look twice at, so I can only assume that I've caused some offence. Under those circumstances I'd be downright terrified if I thought it was bad enough for the king himself to intervene."

"You don't know?"

Guy shook his head, just about stopping himself saying – in his nerve-wracked state – that if he'd known he wouldn't be asking, would he? In his turn the earl was satisfied that Guy was no opportunist, who would use the information he was about to receive with another party when the mood took him. The king had been most specific in his instructions – if Guy was genuine then the reward was his, but if there was even the faintest hint that he was untrustworthy, or had acted to deliberately worm his way into royal favour, then a much smaller reward would be given and the matter left alone.

"It's about the matter with Prince John," he confided in a softer tone, taking Guy by the elbow and steering him down the corridor to a quieter room, where he closed the door and drew Guy away from it. "The king was informed about your prompt actions and he's very grateful."

"Grateful? You mean Prince John hasn't sent some dire report of me that's angered the king?"

"Lord no! Prince John has kept uncharacteristically quiet about the whole affair – or at least he has in public. Which shows a rare dose of sense for the prince, given that any courtier worth his salt could tell you what the king was likely to say about his son gallivanting about the Marches with no escort but a bunch of noblemen's younger sons – saving Mortimer's presence – and not so much as a man-at-arms in sight! The reports the king received came from de Braose, Mortimer and myself, and told nothing but the truth of why the prince was not in Ireland at the expected time – we could do no less without risking the king's wrath upon our own persons! No, if the king is angry at anyone it's at the prince. ...Actually there's no *if* about it! He's spitting blood over the whole matter!

"What you didn't know then, and what you should never repeat, is that the king has since had intelligence that a small raiding party from Powys got wind of the prince's slow progress away from the expected route. Prince John laid himself open to being a target and the Welsh were quite prepared to seize it ...and him! ...Which is why the king is prepared to be very generous in his reward to you for saving the whole situation. If the Welsh had taken John hostage it would've been a political nightmare.

"Now do you begin to see? You didn't just save the royal personage from a cold and soggy night – which might have been no bad thing for John! You saved the king from looking impotent and having to ransom his son from his enemies, and giving others ideas he has no desire for them to have. Can you imagine the chaos? It's bad enough that the royal princes run to Philip of France at every turn, but if the Flemings as well – or the southerners on his border in Navarre, or even Aragon and Castile – started thinking that actually seizing a royal son was the way to carve a chunk out of the king's empire, ...*phut*! ...God knows where it would all end! So not a word about the Welsh from you, you understand!"

Guy nodded mutely, his innards turning somersaults at the thought of the larger web he had unwittingly got himself entangled in.

In return the earl's half-smile turned into a full blown grin. "De Braose was like a cat with the cream when he was singing your praises. Thought it reflected well on him, you see? What he didn't expect was for the king to insist on you getting a manor of your own. De Braose thought you'd be knighted and then be one of his retinue. Something about getting you out of the kennels once and for all, and fighting with him."

Guy felt his stomach lurch sickeningly again. All his careful planning undone by one rash act and no-one to blame but himself! He was so shaken that he nearly missed what the earl said next.

"But the king was most insistent. You are to be knighted and you have to have an appropriate manor! Seems he's making a show of knighting Prince John very soon at the end of Lent, to present an image of reconciliation to the world at large. Something to do with sending the right message to the Irish chieftains de Lacy is holding at bay, I believe. Around those of us within the inner court circle though he's quite bluntly said that, since he feels his hand is forced on this matter, he has no intention of raising up Prince John without raising up the man who saved him from his own folly as well. Well de Braose doesn't have a manor to give you. Or at least not without chucking one of his favoured men out, and he can't really do that – not even on the king's word – without weakening his standing amongst his fighting men. He needs his seasoned knights to keep his place as the king's guard-dog on the Marches. And if those men think he's fickle with his favours, the good ones would soon seek a place with a lord they thought more constant with his rewards. Not that Mortimer or myself would mind the addition of a few more experienced fighters, but De Braose can't risk that! I, on the other hand, have just the place and without throwing anyone out as my last man there has just died. It's not much of a holding, but it will suit you as a newly knighted man."

"Me? Knighted?" croaked Guy, still stunned.

"You are the son of a knight, aren't you? You asked me about your cousins, the fitz Waryns – a noble family even if they're not much in favour at the moment – so I assumed that you are nobly born? That's what I told the king, and from what I heard, the churchmen in Nottinghamshire confirmed that. The king's men are usually most thorough in such investigations."

The king had based Guy's reward on the received knowledge that he was nobly born, even if not particularly nobly employed at the moment. If he turned out to be some peasant's son, Ranulph would have to refer back to the royal household. It wasn't mere prejudice, an estate needed managing and they'd assumed that Guy would have picked up such experience at his father's knee, or at least his uncle's. No-one had the time or inclination to nursemaid a man who would struggle to separate himself from his new tenants if he hadn't. Luckily Guy was gathering his wits and managed to recover himself, and his recollections of who he had once been before old fitz Waryn and his father had died.

"Yes, my lord. Father was Sir Giles of Maesbury, one of the fitz Waryn enfeoffed knights on the Welsh border, and then in Nottinghamshire. That's how I ended up in Herefordshire – I was fulfilling part of the fitz Waryn obligations to help guard the Marches ...for that first year, at least. My mother and Lady fitz Waryn were ...are ...sisters, so I'm truly related to young Fulk, who's the current head of the fitz Waryn family."

Guy had a sudden nasty thought that between the king and Earl Ranulph he might yet find himself serving alongside Fulk and Philip. How could he tell the Earl of Chester to his face, and the king indirectly, that he wouldn't want to be reunited with those members of his family, when they thought they were doing him a favour? So he was even more thrown by the earl's next words.

"Splendid!" The earl was positively ebullient at Guy's confirmed status. "You won't mind going *back* to Nottingham, then!"

Guy felt the world spin around him and had to grope his way to the wall and the small stone-ledge seat. As he sank gratefully onto it and rested his head back against the thankfully solid cool stone, the earl cocked his head on one side, bemused.

"You really had no idea of this, did you?"

"No, sire. And to be honest it's all a bit of a shock. What do you mean, ...go back? If this place you speak of is in your earldom then why are you talking about Nottingham?"

"Oh, it's quite simple," de Blundeville said airily, coming to sit beside Guy. "You see, I have the manor. But it lies in the Royal Forest of Bowland right up by where that woodland starts to climb as it heads up into the Pennines. Now I watched you, Guy, while we were riding in company. You're no coward, and you're more than competent with a weapon, but you're also not the stuff great soldiers are made of. On the other hand you are a *very* good huntsman, and I think you'd make an equally good forester. The only trouble is, I've got enough foresters to deal with anything that crops up in Bowland. It's a place the king never bothers to go hunting in, for all that he owns so much of it, and there isn't much time for me to hunt there. I also have very few tenants there, meaning poaching isn't much of a problem. So my foresters have a pretty easy life most of the year!

"The sheriff of Nottingham, however, is in dire need of a good man to help deal with the vast expanse of royal forest he has under his jurisdiction in Nottinghamshire and Derbyshire."

"Isn't there a hereditary forester for Nottingham Forest?" Guy wondered, thinking back to when he'd last been in his home shire.

"Ah, you're thinking of Ralph fitz Stephen! Yes, he has the care of the old forest, but did you not know that the king had afforested the eastern side of the shire right up to the Trent?"

Guy blinked in shock. "No! When did that happen? I left Nottinghamshire in the spring of '77."

"Then you just missed it all," Earl Ranulph told him, now beginning to understand Guy's ignorance. "Hmmm, ...you'll find things much changed when you get back up there. That swath of farms and woodlands from the edge of the old forest across to the Trent is now called the Forest of Le Clay, but that's not all that the king claimed. He's also added the strip of land to the west of the old forest as well, bringing in the land between the Erewash and Derwent rivers. So except for the bit of the shire on the eastern side of the Trent the whole of Nottinghamshire is now under royal forest law."

"Good grief! No wonder the king needs more men there!" escaped from Guy's lips before he'd thought of who he was speaking to.

"Indeed!" Ranulph agreed with a dry laugh. "I wouldn't want the responsibility of looking after that lot! It means the sheriff now has to implement the royal writs over huge swathes of land which, up until eight years ago, had never felt the weight of the forest laws and taxes, and believe me, there's some resistance to those laws!"

"I can believe it!"

The young earl continued, "I think the king thought it would be more convincing if the forest as a whole had a new name, so he decreed the old Forest of Nottingham and Le Clay, and that whole

L. J. Hutton

swathe in the west which runs right up to the other royal forest of
High Peak, will be called the Forest of Sherwood from now on."

"The Shire Wood, how appropriate when it covers the whole
shire," Guy breathed in awe. When King Henry made a grand gesture
he certainly did it in style! "But why Nottinghamshire? There must be
other royal forests closer to the royal courts and easier to govern if he
wanted more land for himself?"

"Ah, but it's not for him!" Ranulph revealed.

"Oh Blessed Virgin! So the rumours that he was spending money
on the castle with an eye to giving it to Prince John were right!" Guy
gasped.

"And not just the castle at Nottingham. The old royal hunting
lodge at Clipstone has had a small fortune spent on it. Two hundred
and ten pounds just on the fish ponds, would you believe?"

"*How* much? By St Thomas! He intends the lad to live in some
rare kind of style!"

"That he did! And the king's been keeping a personal eye on the
goings on up there ever since, although not so much as in the early
stages now that he's pushing John towards Ireland."

Guy exhaled heavily and rubbed the back of his neck to relieve
the headache which was beginning to press upon him at all of this
news. "Aye, the king came a year or so before we left, which I
suppose is when he started putting his plans into place. He must have
been checking the whole area over to see if it would suit. I remember
being taken to see him! From a distance, of course. All the courtiers
and the hangers on – it was quite a sight! Has he been back since?" A
dread thought came hard on the memory's heels. "And does the
prince spend much time up in Nottingham?" He didn't much fancy
the idea of running into the prince any time soon if the king had
rubbed the young prince's nose in the dirt by reminding him of what
he owed to the actions of a mere huntsman. The king might be
grateful, but it was a fair bet that gratitude wouldn't be high on Prince
John's list!

The earl laughed, guessing why Guy had asked. "Oh don't fear
that! He's going to be kept pretty busy by his father for the
foreseeable future! He won't be bothering you. You'll be under the
sheriff's control not his."

Guy breathed a sigh of relief, but then wondered, "But you said I
would make a forester, not a soldier. Surely that still means I'm
answerable to my lord fitz Stephen?"

But Earl Ranulph shook his head. "You'll see more of this once
you're up there, Guy, but it's more profitable for the king if a sheriff
collects the moneys for a royal forest. Now the king wouldn't deprive
a loyal, old servant like fitz Stephen of his income. But the money fitz
Stephen pays for the *ferm* of the old royal forest is far less than the
yield from the fines and taxes for the rights and privileges, which have

142

to be paid for in the royal forest. So fitz Stephen keeps his hold on the old Forest of Nottingham with his men, but all of the newly afforested lands are under the sheriff's jurisdiction, so *all* of the money goes directly to the king, and that's where you'll be.

"That's why we needed to find you a manor from which you can pay your knight's fee from. You won't be a *forester-in-fee* like fitz Stephen's men, with lands and a home you could pass on to a son eventually along with the job. Your job as a forester will be completely separate from the manor you'll hold from me. That might make things a bit difficult for you, because you'll have to make some trips back to the manor to keep an eye on it – after all, I too need to pay the king my *ferm*, and that money comes from my tenants like you! But most of your time you'll be in Nottingham. And it's not going to be like you'll be owing forty days' fighting service to the king for your *fee*, as if you'd been made into a regular knight."

"Not quite so grand," Guy said with a wry, understanding smile. He'd been elevated but not that high above where he'd been before, and not even as high as his father had been if he wasn't going to have a proper *fee*.

"No, not grand," agreed the earl, "but secure! So this is the way it's going to work: the king suggested – and when he does that we tend not to argue – that if I were to provide you with the modest manor at Gisborne, then he would graciously consider the service you'll be giving to the sheriff at Nottingham as a forester as the fulfilment of my own obligation to the royal person, for the half-a-knight's service I owe him from my Gisborne manor. Do you see?"

Guy shook his head to try to rattle some sense into it. "So what you're saying, my lord – if I may be so bold as to clarify the matter – is that by giving me the Gisborne manor whilst I work elsewhere, I've saved you from having to provide the king with a fighting man for France, or if not a man, then giving him the money to purchase a fighter. And at the same time, by me going to work for the Sheriff of Nottingham, I'm saving *that* sheriff having to find and provide for another forester to oversee the king's laws and rights in the royal forests there – especially when the king has dumped a vast new area in his lap to be cared for! ...Heavens he must be desperate for more men!"

"That Sheriff Murdac is!"

"So you give me a minor manor which earns you very little anyway, the sheriff gets a man to get the job done – even though he's got nowhere in Nottinghamshire for me live off – and the king gets just what he wants. Is that the right of it?"

"You've got it!" the earl said cheerily giving him a hearty clap on the shoulder for emphasis. "And besides, we all know how passionate the king is about his hunting rights – and about getting money out of his royal demesnes when he can impose the laws and fines himself! Now as to the matter of your knighting...!"

A little over an hour later Guy tottered out into the watery sunlight to find his horse. He was still having trouble believing what had happened to him. The earl had taken his sword and knighted the shaken young huntsman, clearly enjoying every minute, which was more than Guy could say. Then he'd given Guy a signed and sealed deed to the manor and his new orders. Guy was to leave as soon as he'd gathered his things together, for the earl warned that de Braose was in a foul mood at having been out manoeuvred by the king.

"You must be quite the favourite, Guy!" the earl had teased as he'd led Guy out to the hallway. "I've rarely seen de Braose so vexed!"

"Oh I'm no favourite, sir!" Guy was swift to disabuse the earl of such a notion. "I just don't think the earl likes not getting his own way. You were right when you said I'm no soldier – or at least not the sort of soldier my lord de Braose wants and thinks I should be. I can't be like him, and if I tried then I couldn't face going into a church to make my confession and not be utterly honest. But the earl sees what he wants to see, and somehow he's got the idea that I have murderous leanings where there are none."

"Hmmm...," the earl hummed. "Would that be a careful reference to the goings on a few years ago at Abergavenny and the like?" Guy kept silent but nodded. "In which case you're a politic young man for your tact, and a sensible one for not wanting to get drawn into the earl's feuds. Never repeat this, Guy, but your former lord may one day bring down royal retribution on his head if he wrecks one of the carefully laid royal plans by his headstrong actions. King Henry likes men of action, but not thoughtless hotheads, and he was swift enough to let old de Braose know that! Yet our current earl seems incapable of learning the family lessons! You, on the other hand, seem like you'll do very well indeed for what the king intends."

Quite what the king might intended for him, beyond service as a riding forester at Nottingham, Guy didn't feel capable of pressing the Earl of Chester on, but clearly he'd been earmarked by the king as his own. It was only somewhat belatedly in the head-spinning turn of events, after he'd parted from Ranulph de Blundeville, that Guy recalled that as the huntsman at Grosmont he had already been the king's and not de Braose's, even if the earl was the one whom he dealt with in all practical respects. As he allowed the horse to plod back at its own pace, Guy mused on whether he had been used not so subtly by the king to remind the forceful earl that he still had an eye to keeping control of his more distant land-holdings.

That would explain Earl William's foul temper better, for he wouldn't like being reminded that the king could take away the power he held so dear, just as had been done to his father. De Braose might be very useful to King Henry, but he was still a royal subject, and his proposing to cut out one of the king's men and take him into his own service clearly hadn't gone unnoticed, or been taken to kindly. What a bitter pill to swallow! And Guy now cringed at the thought of how the king had used him as a stick to beat both his errant sheriff and errant son with at the same time. In one fell swoop, and without every doing anything to deserve it, Guy had had enemies made for him of two exceedingly powerful men, and there wasn't a damned thing he could do about it!

Back at the lodgings it was a measure of Guy's popularity that there, at least, the men were happy to celebrate his good fortune with him, rather than take offence at his new elevated status. Even Bilan managed to join in the celebrations, although after several ales he admitted he was miserable at the thought of having to go back to Brecon, and at not seeing his new found friend even once in a while once he got there.

With a thumping hangover from an evening of far too many strong ales, Guy gathered together his few possessions the next morning in readiness to ride back to Grosmont. Before setting off, though, the kindly sergeant who had kitted him out the day before marched him over to an armourer within the city.

"You'll need your own gear, now Guy," the sergeant prompted him. "No knight but the lowest draws his armour and weapons from the castle's common store, and you'll only get to make your first impression on the sheriff once! There are good metal workers up in Nottingham, so I wouldn't worry about getting yourself a hauberk until you get there – it's not as if you'll need it yet anyway. This chap here, on the other hand, has the best fighting swords I've ever come across – not flashy like for some popinjay courtier, but great for keeping you alive – and he won't cheat you on price."

Clearly the sergeant had brought the sword-smith custom before, and Guy soon found himself the proud owner of a sword which looked simple, and lacked any ornamentation on the pommel or guard, but which was beautifully balanced and a pleasure to wield.

"Get yourself a gambeson on the borders, though!" the sergeant advised. "Welsh wool is more than good enough! In fact there you'll get plenty of padding to stop an arrow, 'cause they're thinking of Welsh longbows as well as our crossbows! If you wait until you get to Nottingham they'll charge you the earth, because every scrap of wool there is considered of fine quality, and you won't get the thickness short of paying the earth. A Welsh gambeson and a Nottingham ring-mailed hauberk, my lad, and you'll live through most things!"

This cheery assertion was meant in good heart, but Guy felt his heart sink a bit lower again at the thought that he might be expected to fight like a knight. He'd only done the bare minimum of practising with a sword at Grosmont in order to try to look less of the soldier and more the hunter. Being tall he didn't want to seem too competent as well, for that would surely have attracted de Braose's attention. Even worse, in some respects, the one weapon he was now truly expert with was a small hunting bow, and he was getting pretty good with a Welsh bow as well – but neither were a knight's weapon at all!

Now, though, as his horse plodded back along the long and lonely roads westwards, Guy spent much time trying to remember all the tactics and moves he had once rehearsed over and over with John, Baldwin and the others. His right arm began to ache with the practice swings he made himself do with the new sword every morning and night, but at least he hoped that if this new sheriff decided to have someone put him through his paces, then at least he wouldn't drop the blessed thing after the first exchange, or come across as some kind of lanky, country bumpkin and make himself a laughing stock.

By the time he got back to Grosmont he'd thought himself into, and out of, so many predicaments that he was almost ready to ask for parchment to write and decline the king's offer – almost! It tore at him cruelly to be leaving his friends and the place he'd come to regard as home, but Guy was no fool. He'd taken in the Earl of Chester's warning and knew if he remained here, that when de Braose got back, he would be sent to Brecon in a heartbeat, for the king would then be a long way off and in no position to argue over something he knew nothing of. And if there was one thing Guy was adamant that he didn't want, it was to become one of de Braose's henchmen against the poor folk of the border.

Saying goodbye to Ianto was the worst thing. Both of them had assumed, without ever discussing it, that Guy would take over when Ianto got too old to work – and that day wasn't very far away. The previous winter the old man had been crippled with rheumatism, and Guy had taken over the running of the kennels in all practical respects except the making of the dog bread, which was a chore they'd enjoyed sharing beside the fire at night. But Ianto had also become a deeply valued friend, and Guy had few enough of those to be able to face losing him. Nor was the whole matter helped by the knowledge that he would be going a long way from where Brother Tuck was too. Albeit a newer friend than Ianto, Guy had quickly taken to the muscular cleric and his robust sense of humour.

With the earl not due back for at least another couple of weeks after Guy returned, he felt he at least had time to ride over to Tuck's cottage and say farewell in person. So he used the excuse of going to get a gambeson made from a man recommended by the captain of the guard at Grosmont, and set out. The gambeson was sorted even more quickly than Guy expected, for the man at Hereford already had one which only needed minor adjustments for Guy. One of the knights with Earl Mortimer had commissioned the thing and then had never reappeared. So the merchant was doubly grateful for Guy's custom for giving him a return on something he'd feared he would be taking apart, needing to shorten it just to find a buyer amongst the ordinary soldiers, much less someone willing to pay the full price as Guy was, and time was money let alone the materials.

Yet despite being able to head for Tuck's with greater speed than expected, it did little to cheer Guy. He had a very heavy heart when he crossed the ford on the Monnow and trotted up to the hurdle fence around Tuck's vegetable plot, but was jolted out of his misery by an extraordinary sight.

Tuck was shouting at another cleric, while two hefty men seemed to be emptying the contents of Tuck's cottage out into the road.

"You have defied the abbot and the bishop time and again!" the new priest was saying with great pomposity. "You cannot be surprised, Tuck. You've had warnings enough! You treat these villagers as if they were your own to do with as you wish."

"I treat them as God's children!" Tuck bellowed. "If they can't pay their tithes, I have the wit to understand that it's because to do so would leave them and their families starving!"

"Oh don't be so dramatic!" the new priest sniffed. "They've taken you in, Tuck. They're cunning, these peasants. And if they haven't fooled you, then you should be asking why God has forsaken them so much that they're in such a state. Bring them to grace and the rest will surely follow."

"Grace? What use is grace, you fool, when the earl's men trample their crops?"

"Blasphemy! Do you doubt the power of the Almighty? Phaa! The bishop is right! You need time back in the cloister and doing some serious penance to bring you back to your senses!"

"On a cold day in Hell!" Tuck growled. "You try making me!"

"Oh I'm sure Cedric and Miles will be able to guard you as they return," the priest sneered. The said men had evidently finished turning Tuck's stuff out and now came to flank him.

"Your things are inside now, Brother Horace," the one reported in a flat voice devoid of any emotion. Clearly this was all in a day's work for him, and he and his partner looked more like hired thugs than lay brothers from a monastery. "We'll take care of this one from now on."

He went to seize Tuck's arm, clearly expecting Tuck to try to make a run for it. What he didn't expect was for Tuck to turn to face him and drive his huge fist into the man's gut. With all the air driven out of him Cedric or Miles, whichever one he was, doubled over and started making fish-out-of-water noises. Tuck, in the meantime, turned with a speed his size belied and grabbed a handful of the priest's garments at the front. Pulling the taller, skinnier man down towards him, Tuck head-butted him hard, collapsing his adversary in a heap. But the other lay brother wasn't standing by. He too turned, but to pounce on something which, when he swung back, was revealed to be a thick blackthorn cudgel which he raised in the direction of Tuck's back and head.

Guy never thought, he just acted. Heeling his horse to jump the low fence, he kicked his feet free of the stirrups and, as the cudgel began coming down, he launched himself off the horse at the man. Together they went down with a crash, the man beneath Guy and deflecting the cudgel far from Tuck. A fist to the chin from Guy finished the man's struggling, and as he staggered to his feet he saw that Tuck must have dealt another blow to the man he'd winded, for he too was now unconscious.

"Guy! My dear friend! You are most welcome! What good fortune!" Tuck boomed coming to hug Guy in welcome. "God does send you at the most opportune moments!"

"Maelgwn? Where's Maelgwn?" Guy asked anxiously as he disentangled himself from Tuck's bear-hug. The thought of what these bullies might have done to the blind man was tearing at him.

"In the woods safe," Tuck hastily reassured him. "These three started bawling and shouting before they even knocked on the door. I had time to get Maelgwn out through the back window and send him into the woods out of sight. Of course I didn't think it would get so rough! I thought I'd just have a shouting match and send them packing with a flea in their ears."

Even as he finished they heard the tapping of a cane and Maelgwn appeared around the corner of the cottage, his face creased into a worried frown.

"Tuck? ...Tuck? ...Are you all right?" The blind Welshman groped his way along the tiny cottage's wall towards them as fast as he could go.

"I'm fine," Tuck called, hurrying to take the outstretched hand. "My dear friend, you forget I went to the Holy Land once. I'm far from unused to defending myself, and our friend Guy happened to call by at just the best of times to help me."

"Guy?" Maelgwn transferred the long, lightweight stick he used to find his way about to under his arm, and reached out for Guy's hand with the one not holding Tuck's. "Blessed be! You save us again!"

And suddenly Guy knew what he was going to do.

"I think we should load your stuff up onto that cart they brought and get moving," he said with a grin. "Let's get out of here before those three wake up and I can tell you my news on the way."

"Where are we going?" Maelgwn fretted.

"To my new manor!" Guy declared triumphantly.

With Maelgwn on Guy's horse being led, and Tuck leading the mule which pulled the cart, they set off at a smart clip, heading off down narrow tracks they knew far better than the newcomers would.

Both were as stunned as Guy at the news of his sudden elevation, as he filled them in on his last few weeks as they hurried along.

"Sir Guy of Gisborne! Who'd have thought it!" Tuck chortled happily. "And coming at such a fortuitous moment, too! The Almighty has been good to us, I think, my friends."

Guy felt happier than he had done for days as well. To be able to take at least two of his friends with him this time he was moving made all the difference as to how he now felt about going so far away. He had asked the Earl of Chester how he could hope to manage his manor if he was off in Nottingham, and had been assured that the king had already informed the sheriff that Guy would need time to go to Gisborne at regular intervals. If things worked out he might even be seeing Tuck and Maelgwn more often than he did at the moment, and that was definitely a good thing to hold onto.

They agreed that Guy could hardly take them into Grosmont Castle for the couple of nights he had remaining there, but Guy had by now made enough friends in the village to be able to ask for lodgings for them there. In part the dog bread had been responsible for this. Technically the bread should have been made in the castle's kitchens along with the other bread. However, Ianto had felt it unfair to burden the few regular kitchen servants with the need for enough rough bread to feed as many hounds as he had in his care. Also, he had his own recipe which added seeds and herbs to the rough grain, made from the mengrell crop, to suit the dogs. Therefore he and Guy regularly kneaded up the loaves in their shared cottage of an evening and merely took it across to be baked in the castle's big oven. It had been when Guy had been coming back with an armful of warm loaves that the first encounter had taken place. He hadn't been walking particularly fast and became aware of a strange tugging sensation on the one side. Finally jerked into turning to investigate, he'd found a small urchin from the village standing staring up at him in dread with a broken off nugget of bread in his tiny fist.

Guy was astonished. "It's dog bread, lad!" he'd said in bafflement. "It's full of seeds!"

The grubby little lad had nodded but had quickly munched his way through what he held. Belatedly it occurred to Guy that the lad looked terribly underfed.

"Would you like some more?" he had asked and was answered with wide-eyed vigorous nodding. So the lad had trailed him back to the cottage and been sent off with a quarter loaf, but at the next baking he had been back with an even smaller little girl. That had been the start of a long relationship, for Guy and Ianto had discovered that their mother was a young widow with two even younger children. The five of them lived in what amounted to a single-roomed shack tacked onto the side of a smallholding's cottage which belonged to her brother, but without a man to do the extra work needed to support the additional family they were quietly starving.

From then on, every time bread was baked for the dogs an extra couple of loaves found their way to the poor family, and to Guy's embarrassment so did word around the village. What had started with one loaf had rapidly expanded to loaves for the five hardest pressed families. It wasn't a lot, but it made the difference between near starvation and reasonable health for the children. Over the years he had become more relaxed with the families' gratitude, but it meant that when he asked for a place for Tuck and Ianto to stay he knew that he wouldn't be refused, and that no-one would say a word to the sheriff.

Parting from them on the edge of the sprawl of simple houses at one of the barns, he led his own horse up to the stables expecting his presence to go uncommented upon. So he was once more taken aback to find a normally friendly groom glowering sullenly at him and refusing to speak to him. Totally confused Guy hurried to the kennel's quarters and there found the simple cottage he shared with Ianto crammed with people.

"Oh Sweet Jesu! Is Ianto all right?" he called out as he tried to get in, fearing that the older man had suddenly been taken ill.

"No he isn't! And it's all your fault!" one of the household men snapped back at him, although letting him through.

As Guy got into the room he found himself staring at a pale and distraught Ianto and the castle steward.

"What's happened?" Guy pleaded.

"Oh, you're back!" Ralph the steward snorted.

Ianto lifted his head, looking like old age had caught up with him all in one go. "Stop it, please, it's not Guy's fault. He only did what any of you would have done. It's not his fault the earl's in a temper over it."

"The earl?" Guy felt a growing sense of impending doom overtaking him. "What's the earl done?"

"He's replacing Ianto," the steward said with weary resignation. "A messenger hammered in here this afternoon. The new huntsman's already been chosen, and Ianto's to get out of the cottage immediately to make way for him."

"But Ianto's post is his own! Not mine! And where's Ianto to go?" a horrified Guy gasped.

"Cast out!"

"Cast out? But he's been a faithful servant to the earl ...no, to ...to the king ...for decades! ...That's not just unfair, it's cruel at this time of year! What's he supposed to do for lodgings and food?"

The steward's demeanour softened a little towards Guy as he registered that Guy had never anticipated that his actions would rebound so drastically on those around him. "Seems the earl is angry at being outmanoeuvred by the king. It looks like he never bothered telling the king that Ianto was still the head kennelman here. Instead the messenger said that from what others told him, Earl William told the king he had better appoint another huntsman to look after the hounds if he was snatching you away. The king put it in the hands of one of his stewards who had a man in mind before the ink was dry on the parchment. It's petty, but it's the earl's revenge on you for defying him and thwarting his plans, even if you personally never did anything wrong."

Guy sank onto the bed beside Ianto and put an arm around his hunched old shoulders. "By Our Lady! I could throttle the earl with my bare hands for this! Ianto, I'm so sorry! When I went to London I had no idea this was coming my way. In fact, I told the Earl of Chester that I thought I was going to be punished not rewarded, because I thought Prince John had taken offence. Now it looks as if the earl intends it to be a punishment anyway."

"It's all right, Guy," Ianto said wanly. "I know you too well by now to think that you tried to curry favour with the prince, or that you sucked up to them at court just to get above us. I'll find some work somewhere. I'll be all right, you'll see."

"Yes you will be all right!" Guy declared emphatically. "Because I'm not letting the earl win with his spiteful schemes!"

Ralph shook his head, anger totally evaporated now. "You can't change things here, son. You might be a knight now, but you've no authority in this castle."

Guy grinned up at him savagely, green eyes flashing dangerously. "Oh I know that! But he's dismissed Ianto from his service hasn't he? Not just moved him to another job on the estate. Ianto's service has been totally severed. So in that case there's nothing to stop him going wherever he likes!"

"But Ianto's got nowhere to go!" an irritated voice from amongst the others snapped at Guy.

"Oh yes he has!" Guy declared triumphantly. "The whole reason why de Braose's in such a temper is because I've been given a manor of my own, not just been made up to a household fighting man. It's a tiny place by all accounts, but it's mine and it's a long way from here. Well, I'm going to be spending most of my time in Nottingham. That means I'm going to need someone I can really trust to live at Gisborne and make sure that the taxes get paid and the like. I'm going to need a steward! How would you like to be my steward at Gisborne, Ianto? It's not much by the sound of it, but you'd have a place in the manor house and a share of whatever food there is and a good fire in winter."

There was a stunned silence as everyone took in what Guy was proposing.

"Well? What do you say, Ianto? There's nothing to stop you now. The only reason I didn't ask before was because I thought the earl would never let you leave with me, and would cause all kinds of trouble for us both, but he's broken that chain all by himself and without any asking."

"God bless you, lad!" a choked Ianto mumbled and hugged Guy hard.

Suddenly the whole mood in the room had changed and men began laughing as they turned to wander out until there was only the steward, Ianto and Guy left.

"You'll be making an enemy out of the earl," Ralph cautioned Guy. "He's not a man to let a slight go. He'll bear a grudge against you to his grave."

Guy shrugged. "I can live with that. My manor isn't on his land or anywhere near it, and I'll be working even farther away. And as far as carrying a grudge goes, if you ever feel brave or have nothing to lose yourself, you might tell him that he made an enemy of me the day he rode Bethan down. I was never going to creep to him for favours, and he might have a shock if I ever told him how many ways I've turned his savage orders back on him."

"Back on him?" The steward was stunned. "What on earth have you done, Guy?"

"Oh, nothing so terrible. But when he's sent me off hunting down poor men who'd done nothing but try to stop their families from starving to death, let's just say that only a couple of them ever died by my hand. I found other ways to give him his proof, and if he was duped, then ever serve him right for issuing such an unjust order in the first place!"

"Lord save us!" the shaken Ralph said with a laugh. "Quite the little rebel under that mask, aren't you! But you've done the decent thing by Ianto here, so your heart is in the right place, even if I'm having my doubts about you living to old age if you carry on like this!"

Well, Brother Gervase, here I am, so I survived despite his gloomy prophecy. Since Ianto had to be out by the next morning we packed up our things as fast as possible – and of course collected my beloved dogs, plus a favourite pup of Ianto's whom none but we would have missed – and then spent one last night in our beloved cottage. At the crack of dawn we went and found Tuck and Maelgwn, intending to set out before anyone in the castle could see that our party had doubled in number

overnight. The last thing I wanted was for someone to let that slip and excite the earl's curiosity. If he thought I had made off with some of his tenants then he would be far more likely to come in pursuit. That thought, and that alone, stopped me from leaving word for young Bilan to come and join us – I would have been risking all the others' lives to help him, and he was young enough that there would hopefully be other chances for him to get away from Brecon Castle and the de Braoses, and he might yet get to join his brothers.

However, my young friend who had started off the bread donations was now a lad of twelve, and his mother pleaded with us to take him with us. At first I refused, for it would be a fair certainty that he would never see his family again given the distance we were going. Yet it was Tuck who talked me into taking him. The earl had yet to spot the boy, he pointed out, but when he did he would be dragged into a life of drudgery, whereas we might not know what we were going to, but whatever it was like, de Braose would not be there – something I could not argue with. That discussion swiftly made Ianto friends with Tuck and Maelgwn, and all agreed that young Elyas could become Maelgwn's guide. So it was a far more cheerful journey to our new home up in Lancashire than ever I had expected.

What was it like, this manor I had been given? Well luckily I had not imagined a grand place, for it was far from that. It sat in a fold in the land in a sheltered enough spot, but the lands about it were meagre and poorly farmed, which we commented upon. However, the house itself was a sturdy if unimpressive longhouse. It was built of local stone and had a roof of stout shingles, and looked as though it was well able to fend off the worst the weather could throw at it in those northern parts. Ianto expressed his thoughts that they would be comfortable enough in this place, and we went to introduce ourselves to those within.

We found a cowering middle-aged couple, fearful of finding themselves being turned out in a worrying echo of Ianto's situation. The previous tenant, it seemed, had had a very inflated idea of what it meant to be a knight. He had assumed that the servants would run the place for him, and without a guiding hand the estate had rapidly declined in his ten years there. A seemingly fortuitous fall from his horse whilst in his cups had seen him off, and none of us doubted that the horse had been deliberately spooked when we were taken to see it in the process of stabling the cart's mule – the only beast apart from my Blue, my two male pups and Ianto's hound puppy, we had dared bring from Grosmont. She was a placid mare who briefly looked up at us with baleful eyes before turning to gaze at her manger hopefully. Hardly the dashing charger, she gave no sign of being nervous or excitable, although she would have to do for me for now, I decided, for I could hardly afford a horse of quality.

I will not bore you, Brother, with the details of what happened next, for I am sure you are content with simply knowing that I had now come into the name I was to become infamous with. Suffice it to say that we arrived at the beginning of May, and I had a few weeks to set things in order before setting off for Nottingham. In that time our household soon sorted itself out. Mary was to continue as cook, and once Thomas had handed over the estate to Ianto and Maelgwn, he would help her get the house back into some kind of proper order. I made sure that they were reassured that the room behind the kitchen was still theirs, and installed the rest of us in the bigger room at the other end of the house. The hall was hardly large, but once swept out, the stone floor washed down, and new rushes installed, it was a good place for the day to day business to be conducted in. It had a moderate sized grate, big enough to warm the room thoroughly, but not so huge as to gobble up what precious fuel we had. On the other side of the bisecting corridor, the kitchen was also a sensible size, and on those days when it was unlikely that anyone would call on manorial matters it was where we all took to congregating by the range, to conserve the logs until Tuck had time to start laying down a good supply.

Of all of us the biggest change was in Maelgwn. Suddenly he was back in a world he was familiar with from his childhood, and we were all surprised by the extent of his knowledge. By the time I was getting ready to go it was clear that it would be he who was really in charge, with young Elyas being his eyes and Ianto the voice of experience on practical matters. Tuck, surprisingly, remained reticent about getting too involved.

We walked for miles visiting tenants, for Maelgwn had advised me to get out and see the farms for myself. It was good advice I was to put into practice many times after that, Brother. Never underestimate the fear a change of lord can instil into the heart of a simple peasant farmer! Many a man I have since encountered has been too scared to speak up and say that what has been demanded is nothing less than impossible. What I saw on my tour around the countryside soon had me making lists of things which needed doing, and as soon as I had got myself kitted out to do my job in Nottingham, I could see that I would be sending much of what I earned back here for a few years to come. Getting this land back on its feet was not going to be a quick task, I believed, although Maelgwn was to quickly prove me wrong on that count, had I been able to see into the future.

Yet all too soon the day came when I had to leave my friends to continue without me and make my way to Nottingham. Ah! You sit up eagerly, Brother Gervase! This is where it begins for you, is it not?

Well I rode into Nottingham on my old swaybacked mare with the two pups at her heels, full of trepidation and with a head full of questions, and presented myself to the sheriff. My dear old Blue had remained at Gisborne, for he was a very old dog by now, and it was hardly fair to make him work hard for his dinner any more. He would provide hares aplenty for the pot back there, but the youngsters were ripe for training up and so I took Fletch and Spike with me. The castle sat on a natural knoll reinforced by great fortifications and was bigger than any castle I had been in as yet – even Clun. The massive twin-towered gatehouse was just the first line of defence, and once through it I entered a bustling, seething mass of people, and the place that was to be my home for years to come.

The dreadful Serio Giendara of my memories had not lasted much over a couple of years, and his successor, Ralph Murdac, had been sheriff since 1180, so he was well established by the time I got there. I would be lying if I said I was ever close to him, but in comparison to some of the others I would later work under, he was a decent man. Unimaginative yet thorough, he dispensed justice with a fair if heavy hand, and looking back I can see that I learned a huge amount from him. He was no William de Braose, that was for certain, and I was much relieved to find that my duties were far less gory than they surely would have been in the Marches. My battered appearance caused much mirth amongst the men at first, but as I relaxed my guard and talked more in the castle's guardroom, there were many shudders at the tales of told of my previous experience of a sheriff.

As they came to realise that I had had little choice but to make do and mend the jokes stopped, aided by the fact that I strove hard to use my meagre wages to improve myself. Murdac was an honourable man in other ways too, for my leave to go to Gisborne was honoured, and if my visits were not frequent, I had at least managed to go there three times by the time the change of the year came around. Apart from that, I had my own space in the great castle – not in the better rooms where Sheriff Murdac lived, but not down in the kennels any more either.

Since Ralph Murdac had been in residence, the king had ordered a new great hall built, the keep had been spruced up and new floors put in, and additional chambers had been built, along with an almonry for the distribution of alms, and a mews for falcons. The king's extensive preparations for his son's royal residency therefore meant that I lived in considerably more luxury than I would have done in many another castle. What had been the main chambers, once upon a time, were now relegated to secondary uses for the likes of me and the other knights and foresters, and if we were sleeping several to a room then at least we had space to move, and chests where we could store personal items in security. Moreover, I had letters from my friends at Gisborne and they were working wonders at getting the place back on its feet. The first set of taxes had been sent off to the Earl of Chester without a hitch – for the first time in years if the locals were to be believed – and so my overlord for the manor was more than happy with my performance.

All in all, therefore, I was unexpectedly content with my lot – even more so, in one way, than at Grosmont, for I no longer looked over my shoulder in dread anticipation of William de Braose appearing over the hills to disrupt our peace. However I did still have qualms, and having adapted to life as one of the ordinary folk, at times I found it even harder than expected to reverse the process. There were moments in those first weeks when I only just managed to stop myself from speaking out against the very knights I was supposed to be one of again. However, I slowly got a grip on myself and learned how to dissemble well enough not to reveal my true feelings to all and sundry. Only when I was back at Gisborne did I allow myself to vent my frustrations to the sympathetic ears of my friends.

So all in all, I began to feel that I was in control of my destiny at last. Oh what folly that was!

Chapter 8

hat was Nottingham Castle like if it was so grand, you ask? Ah Brother, there you belie your claim to worldliness once more! Had you travelled about more you would know that many so-called castles are little more than a stout wooden keep up on a motte of piled up earth – secure enough from minor attacks to be sure, but not great fortifications. Nottingham, on the other hand, was a true royal stone castle guarding the royal interest in a fertile and productive shire – bigger even than Clun Castle, and I had thought that huge.

The massive half-moon of the outer bailey all by itself was a bigger enclosure than some whole castles I had seen on the borders. The palisade around it had five stout defensive towers in its circuit as well as the towers at each end, plus the twin-towered central gatehouse on the north-east side, all set high above the town on a natural rise – and that was before you even got to the motte! After you had negotiated your way around the milling people in the mêlée of the bailey, with its wood-built workshops, kennels and stables, and the quarters wherein the ordinary folk carried out the day-to-day tasks, you came to a dry moat – a relic of the days when the castle's defences had started there at the bottom of the motte, and a motte of natural rock, I should add, not pounded earth! Yet that stone motte was not the defence I thought at first sight, as you will discover when we move on a few years. There, I am throwing you a clue, Gervase! That seemingly impregnable castle had its weak points, and they were not of the same kind as most normal castles, but I shall not digress further at this point and you must bear with me for now.

Even on my first approach I realised that Grosmont's outer earthwork defences were paltry in comparison to Nottingham's great stone perimeter, and had I been a huntsman here, Ianto and I would not have had our own little area outside of the proper castle as we had had back home (as I still thought of it at that stage). We would have been jammed in right amongst the hustle and bustle of other folk, and under a good deal more scrutiny! No smuggling of dog bread was going to happen here, I immediately thought regretfully, for I saw several urchins who resembled Elyas as he had been when I first met him. Moreover, I had no ready ally in the form of another Ianto to work with and I would be lucky to find a place for my own dogs, for I belatedly realised that I would be living in the castle itself. I almost wished I had left Fletch and Spike behind at that moment, for their sakes if not mine – better to go friendless to a new place than lose the ones who had come with me. It all made my heart sink nigh into my boots as I realise how much more forbidding stonework lay beyond the bailey, I can tell you.

An equally substantial second gatehouse guarded the bridge over this dry moat around the steep slope of the motte. It had once been the main entrance to the castle and it showed! For here were the murder holes and the additional guard rooms, as well as a double portcullis. Beyond it, if you came as a friend, you come into the inner bailey – I knew of only one who got beyond there as an enemy of the sheriff, but that is in the future at this point! ...Ah I do love to tease you, Gervase, for it is too good a sport for me to resist! He is coming, dear brother, he is coming! And his friends even sooner, if you need a further pacifier!

On the left as you entered, on the southern side of the inner bailey, there was a whole new range containing a very grand hall, all built at King Henry's order against the day when his beloved John would be staying there. Around the rest of this inner bailey there were grand rooms and to the north a very impressive tower keep – recently upgraded as I knew from back at Alverton when we had been planning John and Allan's future. And as if that was not sufficient, there was still the oldest part of the castle tucked away on the southern side beyond the new hall.

These ancient works wrapped themselves about a comparatively tiny inner ward, and by the time I went there it was no longer possible to bring horses into this area since it could only be entered by getting around the new buildings cluttering the inner bailey. Furthermore, this oldest part sat perched upon the very highest point of the rocky knoll on its very own extra motte, seemingly impregnable and unassailable. And although many of my fellow knights would sniff at being quartered here in the old works, I always had a soft spot for these unpretentious old walls – they formed a fortress, nothing more nor less. It was in this oldest part of the castle that I was to be accommodated, sharing a chamber with other knights. This first castle had no massive keep as the main part now did, but there were still three small, tower-like points on its tight circle of walls, rising at least one floor above the rest of it. What passed for its keep was a fourth small tower, now wedged up against the junction of the newer workings and overlooking what little space there was left between the old and the new castles.

I tell you, Brother, properly manned, Nottingham Castle could have withstood a siege for ages, for that oldest part of the castle was at the crest of the natural rock which rose high above the little River Leen, and to get to it any attacker would first have had to fight his way into the outer bailey, then through to the newer ranges of the castle proper and its inner bailey, before they could even get close to the oldest part. Even this oldest castle was the size of Grosmont's main works and in stone, not wood! I was in complete awe for the first few weeks, and once I was up off the ground floor I kept getting disorientated. God be praised that this time, however – unlike at Clun – I managed not to make a fool of myself before anyone had got to know me.

So, here I was, back in the northern midlands and with a new job to learn. Oh I knew a fair amount, Brother. But where my skills lay was in the practical matters of the keeping of game and the removal of those beasts that preyed upon it. Yet here I was in a royal forest, and that is a very different thing, my friend! There are forest laws which pertain to royal forests which are unheard of elsewhere. It is no coincidence that of all the royal privileges these forest laws provoked the greatest clamour against them.

The royal forests provided huge amounts of revenue for the king, and I should know, for I had the collection of those moneys to deal with for most of the rest of my life. Moreover, the implementing of these forest laws had nothing to do with the manorial hundred courts, or the higher courts of the land. They were a matter of royal decisions by the king, and as such were utterly arbitrary and almost impossible to appeal against. King Henry's head forester was therefore always a hated man, even by other noble lords, and that before you reckon with many of them being thoroughly unpleasant men by anyone's standards. Such a man had powers even the great magnates could not overrule! However, a king's head forester could not be everywhere at once, and so we lesser foresters had much work to do collecting fines and checking for infringements of the laws.

Rarely overly large in terms of their value, the fines were a burden by the sheer number of them. If you have never heard this before, Brother, I can tell you that they were for crimes as simple as the collecting of firewood. You are surprised? Oh yes, Brother, the taking of timber for building is subject to strict regulation, which you might expect, but you should not forget that all those soldiers King Henry regularly made use of had to be armed. For arms and armour you need steel, and iron has to be heated to create steel – not over simple fires but over charcoal, and it was this charcoal which the lesser woods were needed for.

No matter that many of the little folk went cold and lived in shabby huts. If the king needed more arrowheads or spears or ring-mail, then the smiths were working like fiends in the pits of Hell, and Nottingham had the advantage or the bad luck – depending on how you see it – to be advantageously situated for the raw materials. And the bark of the felled mighty oaks of Sherwood also had a use of its own, for it provided the essential tannin for the tanneries which made the leather accoutrements which went with all that armour. Wood was living gold in Nottinghamshire!

Do I sound bitter? Well that might be because I saw much of the suffering, and little of the benefits, from those foreign struggles coming back to us in England. You are not the first man to chastise me for not trumpeting the virtues of trying to hold onto the Holy Land and King Richard's crusade – and one was your hero! But tell me this, Brother, what good did it do the ordinary people? The Jerusalem Tithe and the Saladin Tithe broke many a good family with their burden. For ten years we paid and paid in one way or another for something I've been told was a position we could never win, ... Ah but you are at it again, Brother! Are you sneakily trying to trick me into skipping ahead by getting me talking of things which still burn in my heart? Oh do stop the wide-eyed look of innocence! Craftier men than you have failed to pull the wool over my eyes with such dissembling! Come let me introduce you to life in Nottingham, for this is where our adventures will take place!

𝕹ottinghamshire,
𝕾ummer, the year of 𝕺ur 𝕷ord, 1186

Guy had presented himself upon arrival at Nottingham to a man he would come to know well, Robert of Crockston, who was the constable of the castle and who turned out to be a reasonable if blunt sort of man. Guy swiftly realised that he would never make a friend of him, but could work alongside him without the kind of fear and trepidation he had felt towards de Braose. Of Ralph Murdac, the actual sheriff, Guy saw little in the first weeks, for Murdac was down in the south presenting the shrival accounts for the half year along with all the other sheriffs, and then had other business acting as a justice out on eyre in another shire. Later he discovered him to be just the sort of man he imagined King Henry wanting in a key shire – tough enough to stand up to the nobles and to collect the substantial revenues of the wealthy shire, but not someone who would cause trouble by throwing his weight around unnecessarily. The third man in the chain of command in the castle was Robert of Crockston's aide, Alan of Leek, a young man of an age with Guy, albeit from a rather more wealthy background, and it was Alan with whom he had the most dealings in the early days of his life in this new castle.

Through the summer the ordinary knights of the shire came and went as they provided their forty days' service to the sheriff for their fees, and these were Crockston's duty to deal with. At any time, Guy finally realised, there would be about twenty knights accommodated within the castle, or out and about with the sheriff. Alongside them there were twenty-four sergeants-at-arms, and a similar number of fighting men who could use a crossbow with reasonable accuracy, all of whom also had to be quartered and fed, along with any men the knights brought with them.

However, as a subset under Alan's day-to-day authority, the foresters formed a much more stable community within the castle. They were roughly divided into two groups, not by rank but by the areas they were working in. Guy, along with the other less experienced young foresters, dealt with the newly afforested area of Le Clay to the east of the old Forest of Nottingham. The more experienced men tended to be assigned to the equally new Derwent-to-Erewash royal forest, perhaps because with its being more wooded there was a greater need for an experienced eye to spot ill-doings, or just a heavier hand with more infringements, Guy couldn't tell at first.

Of his fellow riding foresters, Guy soon became acquainted with Giles, an affable but dim young man of around his own age, whom

Alan of Leek never seemed to send too far afield. Similarly, Simon, a rather timid young man of barely twenty, was always given the tasks which were closer to home, and Guy swiftly realised that this was because he often had to return for additional support in order to extract fines and payments from any but the humblest peasants. The pair of them still had to ride beyond the immediate villages by Nottingham, though, for these were the subject to another knight, Sir Edward, who was the riding forester for the original royal forest still surrounding the town, which came under the authority of Ralph fitz Stephen (the king's forester), not the sheriff's. Simon and Giles were therefore something of a trial to their seniors!

So, too, was the fourth in their communal bedroom squashed into a tower in the old castle. Jocelin was the youngest son of one of King Henry's favourite knights, but a young man who had received one too many blows to the head in weapons' training, Guy guessed, for his head was rather flattened on one side and he was always the last to catch on to any joke or quip. Had Jocelin been born into a poor family he would probably have been a contender for the village idiot, but being the wealthiest of all of the forester knights, he was allowed this position even though he was befuddled much of the time and struggled to carry out orders, much less instigate instructions to the lower-born foot foresters they worked with. So these were Guy's immediate companions, but four more riding foresters for Le Clay occupied another room on the same floor of the old castle, all of them very lowly knights of a similar station to Guy – Mahel, Hamon, Philip and Sewel – and together they attempted to enforce the king's forest laws imposed out of the blue onto the reluctant folk of eastern Nottinghamshire nine years ago.

During that first summer of 1186 Guy had very little to do with the knights who policed the other new royal forest of Derwent-to-Erewash on the far side of the old forest, which linked the recently created whole of Sherwood to the other royal forest of High Peak over in Derbyshire. However, of the eight of those, two made an impression on him because they spoke almost no English and kept a hostile distance from the rest of the foresters. Fredegis and Walkelin had been mercenaries from the Low Countries who had pleased the king in some way and been elevated to the knighthood and to these positions in Nottinghamshire. Along with the resident two bullies among the forester knights, Sir Henry and Sir Eric, they seemed to be kept as the hammer which Sheriff Murdac used to batter the worst tenants into submission.

However, as with bullies everywhere, the latter two couldn't refrain from trying to dominate their fellow foresters too, and Guy had a rather heart-stopping moment in his second week when he punched Sir Eric across the stable yard. It had been an instinctive reaction when the older knight came up and thumped him in the back without warning, but within the day Sir Eric had a magnificent black eye and a lump the size of a duck egg on the back of his head from hitting the stable cobbles! For a whole night Guy fretted sleeplessly over a potential dismissal, until the next morning when Alan of Leek quietly told him that no such reprisal would be taken unless Guy turned out to be an unrepentant brawler.

Luckily Sir Eric just scowled at him from then on, and Sir Henry decided that Guy wasn't anything like the easy target he'd expected and didn't try anything similar; but to his embarrassment Guy found himself appointed the unofficial guardian of young Simon and Giles. With Guy in the shared room, they gratefully now revealed that they were finally getting some peace from the older pair coming in and haranguing them at night. It meant almost from the start, though, that Henry and Eric were Guy's enemies, and they, like Fredegis and Walkelin, weren't men to be crossed.

It was therefore a great relief to Guy that he didn't have to work with them, and that the nominal leader of their group was an older knight named Sir Martin, who shared a room with the other senior knight who likewise ran the western group, Sir Walter – both men permanently attached to the castle. The other man in their room was the royal forester's man, Sir Edward, who gave himself airs and graces as a result and whom no-one spoke to much. However Sir Martin and Sir Walter were in their forties, astute and very experienced, and if Alan of Leek was nominally in charge of the foresters then it was these two who actually made things work. Happily, Sir Martin seemed much relieved that Guy was a young man of intelligence – not another Simon or Giles – and someone who was actually making an effort to learn his job, and therefore Guy found himself swiftly earning the older knight's approval.

Having had to learn the ropes of the routine of a castle's kennels as his first experience of life away from home, it had never occurred to Guy not to try to learn the role of a forester. It was therefore something of a revelation to find that time and again many of the foresters who had been at the job longer than he still had to be told what to do. Another shock which he struggled to keep hidden was the fact that very few of the other knights could read. His mother had taken it upon herself to ensure that all of the cousins had their letters at an early age, pointing out to her brother-in-law fitz Waryn that reliance upon a poorly paid clerk was no protection against being defrauded of funds or lands. That Guy could actually read was something which swiftly got passed up to Sir Robert and to the sheriff himself, and to his amazement Guy soon found himself being given special jobs since he could be sent off without having to find time to send one of the hard-worked scribes with him. It alienated him further from Sir Henry and Sir Eric, but sealed him into his role as the unofficial leader of the younger foresters within weeks of arriving.

On the fateful day Guy was therefore riding alone as he reined in his horse and looked west. In the distance and barely visible was the great minster at Southwell. It wasn't a particularly long ride from Nottingham, and he had already been there as soon as he could combine it with one of his authorised journeys. On that earlier day he had felt barely able to breathe with the anticipation of being reunited with John and Allan. Yet to his horror he had found that the monks hardly recalled the two young men who had arrived at their door over eight years before. The two had indeed been sent to a northern farm in the Minster's holdings, but what had happened to them after that was clearly a matter for the man in charge of the lands up there, not recorded at Southwell itself. All the unsympathetic monk, whom Guy had spoken to, would say was that they had the numbers of men in any given location for taxation purposes, but that they had little interest in keeping track of names unless the man in question had fallen foul of the sheriff, or others, and been hauled before one of the courts.

That hadn't happened to John or Allan, of course, and Guy couldn't imagine any but the worst of circumstances under which it would have. John had gone with the intention of staying out of the reckoning of the sheriff and had clearly succeeded. However, it didn't stop Guy from stopping every time he was out this way and casting a longing glance the way of the great church. It hurt him with a strange keenness to know that he'd managed to find his way back here against the odds, only to find himself still alone, and those he had built such fragile dreams of being safe and sound maybe being in peril after all.

On this particular day he was on his way to the Templar preceptory of Mere just south of Lincoln with, amongst other business, a message from the sheriff to the knights there concerning some tenements they owned in Nottingham and Newark. Guy had no curiosity over what the message might be about – if he needed to read it he would find out soon enough. In the scant months since he had begun working for the sheriff the amount of bureaucratic parchment the castle generated had first overwhelmed him, and then squashed any curiosity he might have once had over how a sheriff conducted his business. Today while at Mere he was also supposed to collect some fines, one for the butchering of a roe deer, even though it had already been dead when found; another for a tree felling on the Templar's lands, but nonetheless within the royal forest and subject to forest law; and several bills for the right to pasture pigs in the king's forest issued by the agister for that area. Normally an agister would be living closer to the source of his work, but such things were still being worked out in Le Clay, and the last resident agister had been dismissed under something of a cloud, forcing the work onto the sheriff's scribes for now. Hardly the exciting stuff of great government, but every penny seemed to matter when it came to the king's exchequer.

All of which meant that today Guy felt as though he was getting little relief from what he saw as the dirty side of his job. The truth was that he was disillusioned and more than a little depressed. He'd come all prepared to put his woodsman's skills to the test, tracking wolves and other troublesome animals. Instead, he was discovering he was little but the taxman's junior helper, and he'd already got such day to day work learned and off to a fine art, to the extent that it provided no stimulation at all. Meg's pups, Fletch and Spike, still trotted at his horse's heels whenever he rode out, yet Guy had so far only had the chance to train them to take foxes and the odd wildcat, and most of the time he brought them along simply to give them a chance to have a good run and keep in trim. Dab hands at catching hares, and any farmed rabbits which had escaped from the warrens, Fletch in particular was in danger of putting on too much weight, revealing his sire as being Guy's much missed lymer, Bailey.

To top it all a letter had come from Tuck this week telling Guy that his beloved Blue had died. The old dog had simply gone to sleep in his favourite spot by the kitchen range one night and not woken up, but Guy was bitter that he had not been there after all the years they'd been together – he'd owed Blue no less. No human here had such claims on his affections, and it had brought on this bleak mood which was now cemented by recollections of his missing family.

Guy leaned out of the saddle and Fletch immediately lifted his big black nose up to nuzzle Guy's hand.

"Oh Fletch ...I wish you could track John and Allan with that wonderful nose of yours," sighed Guy mournfully. Spike had vanished into the undergrowth and now came out with a large young hare in his jaws. "No, you can't sit and eat that now," Guy remonstrated with the leaner of the two dogs, but with little energy. He dismounted and took the hare from Spike's mouth, stuffing the limp thing into his saddlebag. "You can eat that later when we get to Mere! Come on, lads, we have to be going. ...Spike!" But the dog had already disappeared again and Fletch with him this time. "Bloody Hell, you villains, get back here!" Guy fumed, and moments later the two dogs appeared sheepishly, but despite that with another young hare each. They were pushing their luck, he knew, because they'd sensed his apathy and that his voice lacked the usual masterful tone, yet he couldn't summon the will to be more assertive. "You'll get fat!" Guy told Fletch wagging the hares warningly, but all the pair did was sit licking their lips hopefully and wagging their tails so that they batted the dandelion clocks into the air, surrounding them all in white fluff which made Guy sneeze.

He managed to chivvy them onwards but twice more they shot off to hunt the new season's leverets, so that by the time he had passed Newark he'd had to pull a linen sack out of his pack and transfer the hares to it for want of room anywhere else. Four he made a gift of to the old ferryman who took him across the River Witham, but he was still well laden as he rode on towards the preceptory. When they happened upon two shepherds with a small flock of sheep, Guy dismounted and slipped a leash onto the hounds. They were still young enough that occasionally they forgot their training and thought sheep were to be chased too, and with the way they were taking no notice of him today he was taking no chances. Leading his horse and the hounds into a field gateway, he waited patiently for the shepherd to drive his flock onto a wide verge where they began to graze. He couldn't summon the will to rush.

"Thank you kindly," he said to the shepherd who knuckled his forelock as he passed.

"No, sire, thank you," was the shepherd's surprising reply. "Many a lord rides through us or lets his dogs have their sport and to the devil with the sheep."

Before Guy could respond, a bitter voice came from the other side of his horse.

"Why are you thanking him? You think he gives a dog's turd for you or the sheep?"

"Quiet Allan!" the shepherd gasped anxiously, but it was the name which made Guy look again at the first shepherd.

The other voice wasn't to be silenced and was carrying on regardless of the potential danger he was in. "Look at that filled pack! We haven't had meat in two weeks. Bloody turnips! I'm sick of bloody turnips and beans!"

Unable to keep the glee from his voice Guy chuckled. "You never did like root vegetables, Allan! But I'd have thought you'd be raiding my pack for cheese more than leverets?"

The second speaker had just appeared around the front of Guy's horse, but halted in slack-jawed astonishment at the words. He was even more amazed when Guy reached out and pulled the first man into a hug.

"By Our Lady, John, it's good to see you! So good!" and Guy's voice cracked with emotion.

"I fear you've mistaken me for someone else, sir," John's still familiar voice said in his ear, redolent with worry.

Guy pulled back and held him at arms' length. "Do you not know me? ...It's me ...Cousin Guy!"

John pulled back and then peered harder at the tall, dark and handsome man before him, brow furrowed in confusion. Suddenly his face broke into a huge smile and he now pulled Guy to him even harder than he'd been hugged.

"...Guy! ...Sweet Mother of God! It *is* you!"

With his nose smothered in John's shoulder Guy registered that if he'd grown into a tall man, John was even bigger, and in every way. John definitely had the fitz Waryn massive build even if Guy could feel every rib, revealing that the two cousins were indeed having a lean time of it. When John released him, Guy turned to Allan to hug him too, but the younger man stepped back beyond his reach.

"Where have you been, then?" Allan challenged him. "Doing all right for yourself by the look of it. Don't suppose you gave a backward thought for me and John, did you?"

Guy stopped in his tracks, slack-jawed with shock even as John remonstrated with Allan.

"Hush lad! What are you saying?"

Guy shook his head. "No John, it's all right. ...By Our Lady, Allan, is that what you thought of me? That I've been warming myself by some castle fire in idle luxury while you and John starved?" He was incredulous. "Do you not know me better than that? And did you not understand what happened to Baldwin and me?"

Allan pouted, an expression which had been so typical of the boy Guy had last seen but which now looked incongruous on a young man. "Maybe," he said with a shrug which was clearly supposed to demonstrate that he cared little what Guy thought of him in return. "I knew you once, but it was a long time ago. People change." Then the chin came up with a defiant sneer. "You certainly never came looking for us, did you?"

This was too much for Guy. After all the anguish he'd suffered on their behalf, to be accused of not caring was an injustice he could not let go. All the emotions he'd kept bottled up for so long welled up to the surface, and he stepped up to stand right in front of Allan, who had not grown so very much and now was easily a head shorter than Guy.

"Never came looking? God's wounds, Allan! I was sent as the lowliest of enfeoffed knights to the Welsh borders! Not just down the road some place – nearly into bloody Wales! How in the name of all that's holy was I supposed to come back? My every hour was ruled by the duties I had to perform. From the moment I got up to the moment I went to bed, I was under someone's watchful eye in those first days. Later I got a bit more space to breathe in, but if I'd ever been stupid enough to think about riding off I'd have been dragged back by the soldiers and flogged, or some other punishment, and by Jesu what a punishment it would have been!"

He glowered down at Allan, growing more furious as he recalled the last few years. "You might have had it rough in one way here, but you at least have never had Earl William de Braose to deal with! By God you would've known about it if you had! You think things are bad here? I've had the men I work with now going pale with some of the stories I've told them of things I've witnessed that sheriff do! Sheriff Murdac might be hard but he's fair – that's something no-one would ever be able to say of de Braose!"

"Oh ...the sheriff's man, are you?" Allan sneered with bravado, and it was only John stepping between them that stopped Guy from punching his younger cousin very hard.

"That's *enough*, Allan!" John said forcefully, and with a clear expectation of being obeyed going by the expression on his face. "Guy, I'm so sorry, our reunion shouldn't be like this!" and John clearly meant that too. Turning back to Allan, John told him to start rounding the sheep back up.

"We're only taking the sheep to the farm at the end of the next track," he explained to Guy. "Then we'll be turning back for home. Where are you going?"

Guy swallowed hard and fought his temper under control. John didn't deserve to be snapped at, and it was beginning to look like Allan had been a burden beyond anything they as boys could have dreamed. "I'm heading for the Templars at Mere. They don't have any preceptories in Nottinghamshire or Derbyshire which our sheriff can collect fees and fines from, so one of us has to ride up to by Lincoln to collect dues for the lands they hold in our area."

"Bloody taxman!" Allan muttered under his breath but still very audibly, and throwing Guy a very black look.

"I didn't make the laws!" Guy snapped back. "Someone is going to come for them no matter how you wish it otherwise..."

"...oh and it just has to be *you*...?"

"...and you'd rather it was some thug who enjoys going it...?"

"...ha! And *you* don't...?"

"...no I damned well don't!"

By now John had marched up to Allan, caught hold of his arm and was shaking him. "Stop it, Allan! By Our Lady, what's got into you these days? Your sharp tongue will one day get you into some trouble I *can't* get you out of!"

Guy's sharp senses might have been a little dulled that day, but he was still alert enough to pick up on that. How often in these past years had John had to sort out problems Allan had caused, he wondered?

John was gripping Allan so hard that the younger man was wincing with pain, causing him to writhe like a fish caught on a line, but at least he was distracted from hissing at Guy, allowing John to speak.

"We're going up to Mere ourselves, as it happens. We'll be stopping there overnight on our way back. If you can wait for us to deliver these sheep we could walk with you? If you're not in a hurry that is?" Poor John was clearly worried that Guy was going to leap on

CRUSADES

his horse and ride off, leaving them eating his dust and never to be seen again.

"Of course I'll wait!" Guy told him warmly and not having to force a smile for John. "After all this time did you think for one moment that I'd ride off and leave you? The sheriff's constable gets good service out of me for the most part, so he can wait a little longer this time. I'll find some excuse – I've never done it before so he's not likely to be suspicious. There arc others whom he's watching much more keenly than me."

John breathed a sigh of relief. "We're only going up to that farm on the rise," he said, gesturing to where a small farmstead huddled low on the top of a hillock not a mile away. "We won't be long!" And with that he set off, towing Allan with him like a naughty puppy, while whistling at the sheep and chivvying them with the crook in his other hand.

Once the sheep were round a bend in the lane Guy let the dogs off again. "Go on, then, you fiends! You can bring mayhem and slaughter to the local hares tor a bit!"

With joyful wags of the tails Spike and Fletch bounded off into the meadows of the River Witham which was only a couple of fields away. By the time John appeared striding back around the bend there were so many dead leverets Guy was wondering how he was going to carry them.

"Good grief, they're pretty expert, aren't they?" John whistled in awe at the heap of small corpses.

"I hope you like hare," Guy said, looking up with a grin from where he was stringing them together for ease of carrying.

"Lord, yes!" John answered with a matching grin. "We don't get meat that often, so anything's welcome."

With Spike and Fletch's hunting instincts satiated for the day, they all set off north again, John and Guy walking side by side as Guy led his horse, the two dogs questing in front, and Allan slouching along behind grumbling to himself for want of any other audience. Guy had offered to let him ride the horse in an effort to mollify him, but Allan was having none of it, preferring to retain his martyr status and complain.

At first John pressed Guy to tell his story, although Guy noticed that John made many backwards glances towards Allan. Clearly he was hoping that if the youngest cousin could hear that Guy's life had been difficult, then some of his antagonism might fade. John even deliberately slowed their pace further as Guy told him about de Braose riding Bethan down and his anguish over her death. However, Allan was resolutely trailing too far back to be able to hear much if anything of what Guy was saying, and finally John seemed to give up hoping.

167

"Is he always like this?" Guy plucked up the courage to ask, putting as much sympathy as he could into the question when the gap between them and Allan had widened once more.

John sighed. "Oh this isn't bad for him!"

"By Our Lady, John! What in Heaven's name has happened to you two to turn him into this? Has it been so very bad for you?"

John shrugged. "It's not been a bed of sweet-smelling roses, no, but it could have been an awful lot worse." He took a swig from the water skin Guy proffered, then took a deep breath and began. "I don't think he's ever really got over being disowned, to be honest Guy. The first few months he was in such a state, it was probably a good job that we were out in the fields far from anyone. That way they didn't see that he did nothing all day. I suppose I should have put my foot down earlier, but I was more than a bit shaken myself, and I think I thought that he would grow out of it. I mean we could all be sulky at that age!

"But then he got to fourteen, and the age when you and I were shouldering some pretty big burdens of our own, and he wasn't improving. Oh, I'd had to force him to pull his weight with the chores long before then, of course, I'd had no choice. Nevertheless, I did most of the work with the animals because it became pretty obvious that he had no patience with them. But I did insist that he helped with everything else, and at times like shearing and lambing he's had to do all of the other jobs because I was too busy working, sometimes through the night."

Guy nodded sympathetically. "When I was on the Marches the sheep governed the farming year – let's face it, for most of the folk they were the one chance they had of making a bit of money. That's no small part of the reason I got on so fast – not from starting at the top! Fulk and Philip left me all but destitute, and I had to start from the bottom! The dogs and I kept the flocks safe, and the longer I was there the more I came to realise how much that meant."

"Aye, it's a disaster if you only have a few sheep and then you lose your lambs to a fox! Mercifully we no longer get wolves in this part of England. I shudder to think what they could do to a flock if they got the taste for it! ...The thing is, we did all right for the first couple of years. The brothers left us to it as long as we showed the estate reeve that we were doing all we should be, and if the fleeces went to the tithe barn in time for the merchants to come."

"So what went wrong? I assume something did go wrong? It wasn't Fulk or Philip wanting their pound of flesh was it? They didn't set the sheriff after you?" Guy's blood suddenly ran cold at that thought, for if so then he could well see how Allan could feel abandoned.

John's expression became downcast. "No, not Fulk or Philip – although we did hear rumours that they had sent men looking for us.

That was no problem, though, because they'd assumed we'd all stay together, so at first they were looking for four young men, and mounted at that. Then word must have come back that you and Baldwin had got to where you were supposed to be. At that stage I'm guessing that they thought we two must be further afield too, because the search finished." He dropped his voice a little. "No, our problems were brought down on us by Allan alone."

"Allan?" Guy breathed softly, resisting the urge to look backwards and give Allan the idea he was being talked about. "Blessed St Thomas, John, what did he *do*?"

Grimacing, John replied bitterly. "Oh, I'd told him to go into Southwell village, and take some wool to the market that I'd managed to card and spin into twine in the evenings from bits I'd gathered off hedges and hurdles. It wasn't much, but it was good quality of the kind the villagers wouldn't be able to afford a whole fleece of – the monks have top quality livestock and our pasture is good too, so our fleeces are amongst the best in the county. The freemen's wives love to get their hands on those bits, to spin out themselves if necessary, and then knit into soft scarves and the like – only little things, but they give them the illusion of being better off than they are – so the Lindsey wool gleanings fetch a fair price if properly prepared. There were one or two other things, like eggs and some honey, to trade too.

"The first I knew of it was when I got home and there was no sign of Allan. Then the bailiff came out to our cottage and informed me that Allan was in the stocks for cheating at dice. He asked me if I could afford to pay the fine, and I had to explain that all we had had gone into Southwell with Allan. He was a good man, Guy, and he understood that I'd had no idea of what was going on, but he told me that it was far from being the first time – just the first time that Allan had been caught in the act. Apparently the little fool had been using his youthful looks to fool visiting traders for some months.

"He'd start betting with what we traded, pretending to lose some, and then he'd clean them out of their money. With most of them not being men of much importance there were just grumbles and no proper complaints, most of them being the sort who knew when to stop before they lost more than they could afford. The trouble was Allan got over confident. Started thinking he would never get caught, and then of course he did.

"I went into the village the next day to talk to him. He was far from repentant! Instead he kept telling me to pay the fine to get him out. Yet I had little choice but to leave him there for another four days to cool down. But on the way home I began thinking. Whenever he'd come back from town he'd only given me what I'd expected to receive. So where had the rest gone if he'd been so good at winning? He'd never come home with anything like new clothes, and the bailiff had said he wasn't that drunk, which made me think he wasn't spending it all on ale. It was only the next morning it came to me that he must have stashed it somewhere. That's why he thought I could pay the fine! Typical of Allan, though – having never told me of the money, it never occurred to him that I wouldn't know where to find it.

"Well, I went out to work with the flock that day, but when I came home that night I turned the cottage upside down looking for his stash. In the end I found it outside at the base of the chimney stones. Lord, Guy, I came over all cold when I saw how much he'd got. I mean it wasn't a fortune, but it was far more than two simple peasant shepherds should have had if anyone had come across it. There was me trying to keep us out of sight, and he was going and drawing us into danger! I'd brewed some mead from our honey and I tell you I needed it that night! I sat on the front step and thought long and hard. There was no point paying the fine now. Allan was due out the next day anyway, and folks would ask where I'd got the money from all of a sudden.

"Instead, I decided that before I went to collect him the next evening I would speak to the reeve and ask if there was somewhere else we could go. I spun a good tale about feeling rotten about what Allan had done to our neighbours and he believed me. He said he thought it would be a good thing if we moved too, and that there was a vacancy for a shepherd with the Templars over the border in Lincolnshire.

"So at first we went to work at Aslackby, out in the fens. It's a sweet enough place in the summer, Guy, but by St Thomas, it's bleak in the winter! The wind comes straight in off the sea and cuts like a knife! Mercifully we were only there for a little under a year, because the flock was in need of more than we could supply between us, and we'd only been sent there because the old shepherd's son fell into a drainage ditch and drowned, and the old man couldn't carry on alone with one other son who was a bit simple and their serf. We got replaced by a retired Templar who had a brother and two strapping nephews to help out. The Templars have been good to me. I think the Master for Lincolnshire has Allan weighed up, because he asked me if I would like to work close by the preceptory at Mere so that Allan could be put to work in the Templars lodgings, maybe in the kitchens."

John sighed and shook his head, this time taking no trouble to disguise his expression when taking a backwards glance at Allan, who by now was slouching along far behind, sullen and resentful. "I had to tell him that while I was very grateful for his consideration, I didn't think that it would be a sensible move. I mean, what would we have done if Allan had started playing his tricks on the Templar's guests, or on the other laymen who work for them? The master would have had no choice but to punish him, and severely."

"He hadn't learned his lesson, then?"

"Lord, no! I burned dice every time I found them, and every time he whittled more! In the end I realised that all I was doing was making him more expert at making dice weighted at one end to be used to his own advantage. Even worse, he'd been forced to be good while we were at Aslackby because there wasn't a town of any size close to for him to escape into and cause mischief. But we were only at Temple Bruer for two weeks, and in that time we went to Newark shepherding flocks to market twice, and both times I lost him in the town and then met him out on the road when going back. The first time he had such a smug look on his face that I knew he must have played and won. The second time he was hiding in the bushes much further on looking scared stiff, and the next day he was sporting a lovely black eye."

"Cheated someone and they'd thumped him and maybe threatened worse?" Guy surmised.

"I reckon so. Which was why I took up the master's offer of a remote shepherd's cottage up in the wolds, but answerable to the Willoughton preceptory. Not a grange, much to Allan's disgust! I think he had grand ideas of becoming the lord of even a small manor or farm, and then working his way back up to what he thinks is the life he should lead. And of course, that's why I couldn't accept a post attached to Mere preceptory. That close to Lincoln with all the traders and merchants who go through there, Allan would have been in the stocks within a week or so, and strung up by the sheriff before the year was out as a habitual gambling thief. He hates where we are, and even so there are times when I'm stuck with the choice of leaving him at the cottage – but knowing that he could be off in a flash with some harebrained scheme for getting rich quick – or bringing him with me and exposing him to the temptations of more peopled places."

Guy placed a sympathetic hand on John's arm. "By God, John, you've done more than enough! I've been around men long enough now to know the type of man Allan's turned into. We had one at my last place. He'd have gambled his own mother away on the off-chance of winning a bet! There's nothing you can do for him. Either he'll wake up and see what he's doing to himself and you, and recognise that the best thing he can do is never go near an alehouse or place where the temptation to gamble is strong, or he'll stay as he is, but only he can make the change. I'm just so sorry you've had to shoulder this burden alone. But did you know that Baldwin was sent to the Templars too?"

John's jump of shock was answer enough. "Yes," Guy told him, "not that long after he went back to his father's. Looks as if his prediction that there would be too many mouths to feed in the family castle was all too true. I made inquires through a kind Templar from

Garway, but it looks like Baldwin might be in France or even further afield."

"But they don't accept boys as gifts to the order as the monks do," John said in surprise. "He couldn't be an oblate when the Templars don't allow such practices. How come they took him?"

Guy shrugged. "I don't know for certain, but you remember Baldwin! He'd have felt dreadful if he knew he was putting a strain on his family. I suspect his father dropped a few very heavy hints – maybe giving him the choice between going voluntarily to the Order or unwillingly into the Church."

"Lord, I can see what you mean! Baldwin would have chosen the Order in a heartbeat! And of course, being young and single, with no family attachments to worry about, if they thought he was coming of his own accord they would've gladly taken him in."

"Absolutely. What worries me, John, is that Baldwin was so full of romantic ideas that he might just have volunteered for an expedition to the Holy Land."

"Saints preserve him!"

"Well I hope they do! You've heard how things are out there now?"

"Bits through those few fighting Templars whom we see who've come back to England. King Baldwin the Leper is dead, isn't he?"

"Yes, March or May last year if the reports are right. Poor soul, he was only twenty-four – bless me, it was our Baldwin's twenty-fourth birthday not so long back! Would we know him now? Would we recognise the boy in the man? But to be the young king, living with bits of you rotting off? ...Urrgh! ...It can't have been much of a life."

"No, and his sister's now queen, a widow with a son and like to marry Guy de Lusignan, so I've heard, or is she married to him already? Whichever, it sounds like a recipe for disaster even with my limited knowledge of things."

"Let's just hope our Baldwin is well out of the way, then!"

For the rest of the journey back to Mere, Guy and John chatted companionably, with them both relaxing more in each others' company with every mile, so that by the time they reached the preceptory gates it was as though the years in between had never happened in one way. Only when Allan had to rejoin them did the atmosphere become tense again.

Luckily the youngest cousin slouched off to his bed early in a sulk, and Guy and John were able to continue their catching up in a walk around the infirmarer's garden while evening prayers were being said. It was therefore to their intense delight to discover in the morning, that the master was requesting Guy to ride on to Willoughton in order to collect some horses he had promised to Sheriff Murdac on a previous occasion. Even better, he was asking if

Guy would take three other horses up there to be put out to stud. So John and Allan would be able to ride once they were out of sight of the brothers. They still didn't dare confess that they were all cousins, for that might have excited comment, so Guy had invented a story that John's father had been a steward on lands his own father had possessed. The Templars weren't that curious, anyway, and so no further elaboration was needed.

A day later therefore found them riding at a brisk pace in a manner reminiscent of their old lives. Even Allan was unable to keep his pleasure hidden at being able to ride again, and on a good horse at that, and finally he seemed to be acknowledging that Guy had had no hand in their fate, nor possessed the ability to change it.

I did offer them the chance to go and live at Gisborne – or to be more precise, I offered John the chance during our evening walk alone. It was not ill-feeling towards Allan, Brother Gervase, so do not wrinkle your nose so! Yet already I was a good enough judge of men to foresee potential conflicts if I exposed Maelgwn, Tuck and Ianto to Allan's pouts and tantrums. My youngest cousin was a difficult person to visualise in the quiet backwater of my tiny manor, for I could see that the merest mention of the word manor would create in him expectations of something far grander than anything I possessed. What would then happen when he got there and discovered an old-fashioned longhouse, and still sharing his bedroom with those he would see as servants, was something a bad nightmare could be made of. Yet John knew him better than I in those days, and I also felt I owed it to John to offer him some respite from a role as surrogate father he could never have imagined going on for so long when we had last met. However I will now confess to you, Brother, of my guilty feelings of relief when John expressed the same reservations I had been thinking, and said that if there was ever a time when he could go there alone he would be very grateful. But not with Allan! Not ever with Allan.

In my turn, though, I pointed out that Allan was now twenty-one years old and would be twenty-two come November. He was already a man in the eyes of the law even if he resolutely refused to behave like one. Because he was still small in comparison to both of us, it was easy for us to still think of him as the little lad, but that, I pointed out to John, was not how anyone else would see him! How long could either of us continue to hope that we could keep him on sufficiently short a rein to prevent him from destroying himself? Should we maybe try to get him into the army of some lord? Much as I hated the idea of our little cousin being in the midst of some deadly fight in Normandy or France, I pointed out to John that he would have little chance of getting into trouble in such circumstances. And maybe a few beatings from his fellow soldiers if he cheated them might affect what all of John's patience had failed to do. Harsh? Yes, Brother, it would have been, but as we saw it back then, better a life such as that where he would have a passable chance of surviving than the sheriff's gallows. A chance he was less likely to have here unless he remained with John.

However, for the time being John believed that he and Allan should continue as they had been doing. He would find a way to convince Allan that, given that I was living as a man of the sheriff's, there was little I could do in the way of providing better accommodation for them. It was a lie, but only a partial one given that it was the truth regarding my day to day life. I might be a knight, but I was not so high as to warrant a room all to myself, and with three of my fellow knights crammed in with me, even rooms as spacious as the castle's were cramped. When we got to Allan and John's homely cottage in the wolds I was able to say with genuine sincerity that Allan had more room than I did, for it was the truth. At first Allan thought I lied, but once I had paced out the tiny space I had in my shared room he began to believe that my life was not so luxurious after all. When I had convinced him of how lowly my manor house was, with no more room there either, for a brief time I saw some shade of the cheerful boy I had once known.

Yet I could not tarry long with them. All I could do was stay the one night, but at least I helped John skin and preserve the quantity of hare-meat the dogs had supplied, and we set the skins to curing so that they would both have warm fur hats and mittens come the next winter. As it turned out, I was able to make the detour to see them again on my way back to Nottingham, and promised them that I would come to see them whenever I was granted time to go to Gisborne. They would not be long visits, I warned them, for I really did have to go and check on my own lands, if only to show my face and assure my tenants that I still lived and wanted their taxes. However we would not be separated from one another as we had been in the past, and for both John and myself this felt like a substantial blessing. My beloved cousins were once more a part of my life!

Chapter 9

You are fidgeting, Brother Gervase. Does my story not move on apace sufficiently for you? Does the detail of my daily life as a lowly forester bore you? If it does then you have not been paying attention, for you have had much important information already. What say you in such wearied tones? That I doubtless have much to confess, but will we ever get to hear of Robin Hood? My dear Brother, what of your much vaunted virtue of patience? No, I do not mock you. I am merely pointing out that if you want the <u>real</u> story and not some foolish twisting, made up of bits of legends and scaremonger's stories, then you have to have it all as it came about. You have to be able to see it as I saw it if you are not to condemn me out of hand. But if this will console you, shortly you shall begin to see the coming together of the famous band of outlaws, for Robin Hood's legend was as much about his men as it was him.

So, I am sure you have realised that my dear friend Tuck became the notorious monk of legend, although it maligns him greatly if you believe him to be some brawling, fat glutton of few principles. Tuck's principles were of the highest, and because of that were frequently the cause of his getting on the wrong side of powerful men whose morals were dubious, to put it politely. Likewise, my dearly loved cousin John has been written about so much that the real man has been lost sight of, but you will have to wait just a little longer to discover just who first called him Little John. That person is not yet part of our tale, although he is not far off. However, the first of these coinciding events is about to take place in our story, so sit still and pay attention, Brother, and you will be rewarded. And Allan? Ah Allan will have his part to play too in the birth of the legend, both sooner and later!

So 1186 moved on into late summer and then to early autumn, and unbeknown to us events were also moving on in the Holy Land which would eventually impact upon our lives here in England. For the infant king, Baldwin V died within a year of his poor leprous uncle, throwing the area into turmoil. Nor, as a result of their actions, were the infant Baldwin's mother Sybilla and her second husband, Guy de Lusignan, to reign for long – but then we did not know that in 1186, although the future for the Kingdom of Jerusalem looked bleak, albeit for different reasons. Because even worse than the kingship crisis, that dreadful warmonger, Reynauld de Châtillon, launched an unprovoked raid on an Egyptian caravan, destroying all the hard work Baldwin IV had done to secure a peace in the east. But all this was news which took its time to get to us, as did its personal repercussions, unlike the other portentous event of the year.

The king's third son, Prince Geoffrey, died in the summer during a tournament, finally making Prince Richard the heir to the throne and *sealing our destinies if we had but known it. No, Brother, I was no admirer of Prince Geoffrey's, not that I ever met him. He was by repute a glib liar and as slippery as a snake, and many now acknowledge he had little to recommend him, but the one thing he was better at than his younger brother, Prince John, was ingratiating himself with his nobility – and we now know what that led to at the end of King John's life! Also let us not forget that it was Geoffrey who – following the death of their oldest brother Henry – now had that most eminent knight of the realm at his side, William Marshal, and him I had the utmost respect for. The same William Marshall whom Heloise had hoped to wed!*

You see, Brother, I no more condemn every great baron any more than I excuse every outlaw. However, King Henry's sons all had their serious failings when it came to being future kings of <u>England</u>, and I have no doubt that the Robin Hood legend would undoubtedly still have come about under a King Geoffrey, but it would certainly have been very different in the detail had Marshal become England's chancellor on Geoffrey's behalf.

However, to return to my story, the death of Prince Geoffrey caused me some worry, for I feared that Prince John, as the heir in waiting so to speak, might now come to live at Nottingham, and that I feared greatly! I could not count on the prince having forgotten the face of the man who had hauled him ignominiously out of trouble in Wales, for I was sure King Henry's rebukes would not be so easily dismissed! And if so, would the prince think it good sport to make my life a misery if he came here? I could not be sure, but on a happier note I managed to visit Gisborne not long after my reunion with John and Allan, and was able to share my joyful news with my dear friends. All three were truly glad for me, but also understood my concern over Allan. However, like me they thought we had time to plan for the future – how wrong we were.

I went back again to Gisborne at harvest time and found all well there, and Maelgwn and Ianto thriving in their new roles. Looking back on it, I was later to realise that Tuck was finding it much harder to fit in with his new life. The neighbouring church had a good and kindly priest who took his duties seriously, and so there was nothing for Tuck to do in terms of tending the souls of the needy. He could satisfy the need to expend his great physical energy in helping to put the lands back to rights, but his spiritual questing was stagnating in Gisborne's quiet backwater. So that for all his gratitude at having a roof over his head – and even more for the home I had provided for Maelgwn – Tuck was restless. Given the way he had asked most carefully about where John and Allan were, I suppose it was inevitable that one day I should find that he had made his way there. However, I could not have remotely begun to anticipate the circumstances under which it actually happened.

Yet I must recount a minor incident which had occurred early in my life at Nottingham Castle before we go any further, for it will impact on what you are about to hear. As I told you, I feared for what life my beloved Fletch and Spike would have once I had seen the place, and at first it seemed as though my fears would become a reality. My pair were grudgingly found a corner of the stables to live in when they could not be with me, for the head kennelman instantly refused to have them in amongst Sir Ralph's prized hunting hounds. So they were just about tolerated for the first fortnight. But then I went down to feed them one morning and found them already gnawing on a large bone each, and a smiling stable-lad making much fuss of them. Mystified, I went into the stables. Inside there was much excitement and people milling around at the far end where there was a large loose-box. This I knew already contained the sheriff's best-loved hunter, a beautifully marked dapple-grey mare who was heavily in foal. ˝Has the foal come?˝ I asked Harry, the head stableman as he emerged and came towards me. I was expecting the usual curt reply and so was amazed at being greeted with a warm grin. Even more astonishing was his answer that yes the foal had come thanks to my dogs.

As I stood rooted to the spot with surprise, he told me that in the early hours the mare must have gone into labour. Fletch and Spike were tolerated in the stables because when I told them to stay in one of the stalls they did so and did not trouble the horses. Yet my clever hounds had realised that something now was amiss! Consequently Spike had somehow got up the ladder to the hayloft and then out through the open hatch. He had then gone straight to where Harry slept and had barked until someone opened the door. Running in to Harry, Spike had then tugged at him and kept running back to the door until someone realised he wanted Harry to follow him. When Harry and two others got to the stable they found Fletch in the stall with the mare, who was on the floor, not bothering her but trying to gnaw her halter free where it had caught on the stall door. It was holding her head up at an awkward angle, and the rope gave way just as Harry and the others arrived, allowing her to lie down fully. Given that everyone knew that Sheriff Murdac adored the mare, Spike and Fletch were heroes of the day, for she needed serious help to deliver the foal which had got itself facing backwards in the womb, and with its cord entangled too, and no-one wanted to have to tell him that they had lost both foal and mother!

From then on I was always welcome in the stables and became friends with Harry in particular, so that when he came to me with a request for help with a family problem, I was sympathetic and willing to do what I could to help. That desire to help another ordinary family is, as you will soon see, part of a greater tangle I got embroiled in that autumn!

Nottinghamshire, Autumn, the Year of Our Lord, 1186

Guy grimly regarded the young lad his two hounds had pinned up against a tree.

"In Jesu's name, boy, what possessed you to come out trapping hares and squirrels today?" he demanded in frustration. "Did I not ride out through your village in full sight of everyone? I do my best to give you what unspoken warnings I can that the foresters are out and about, but I can't protect you from your own stupidity! Now I shall have to take you in, and your dog too."

"No sire, please sire, not my dog!" pleaded the lad. "They'll clip his toes! He'll die of the pain! He's only little! Please sire let him go!"

"You bloody fool, I can't!" Guy hissed at him, as he clutched the squirming terrier under his arm. "There are four of the sheriff's men within hailing distance of me and all armed with bows, and four mounted men-at-arms not far off either. If I let him go he'll be traced by his yapping and they'll shoot him without a second thought! At least this way he'll live!" He snapped his fingers at Spike and Fletch who moved behind the lad making soft growls which only Guy knew they would never follow up with their teeth. As the lad started forward in fear Guy clipped him round the ear for good measure.

He hated having to bring any of the villagers in to the sheriff, but if he was known to be letting people go for poaching he would be heavily fined more money than he could easily hope to find, and that would only be the start of it. If he lost his job then he would most likely lose Gisborne manor, and that would put more than just himself out into the wilds, homeless. His was a very different lot to those knights who held their lands by well established hereditary right. As he'd said, he did his best to forewarn the villagers that the foresters were out on any given day, but he couldn't protect them if they were daft enough not to heed that warning.

Grabbing the lad by the arm Guy marched him off, whistling his horse to follow. Guy's ability to get his horses to behave was the envy of the rest of the knights and foresters, who never seemed to connect that to the fact that Guy spent a good deal of time in the stables and was kind to his beasts. Something which Guy had given up trying to explain, and so reluctantly he accepted their cockeyed admiration since he couldn't change their ways. As he called out, two of the men-at-arms who were acting as walking foresters on this patrol came battering their way through the scrubby undergrowth, and took the lad from Guy so that he could mount up.

"Get some men to bring him to the sheriff, then you and the others go and tell his village," he ordered with weary resignation, and then heeled his horse forward with the terrier still pinned under his arm. Once out of earshot of its wailing master the terrier calmed down. "Good boy," Guy told it, ruffling its ears and getting a wagging tail and a sticky lick on the hand for his reward. "Now then, where are we going to put you out of mischief for the time being? Daren't take you back to the village. After all I can't show my face there alone and tell them the lad is likely to cost them all what will be a fortune for them in fines for his idiocy. I'd be likely to be pelted with rotting vegetables and sheep shit if they think I'm unaccompanied, and I'm not waiting for the others! Are you a good ratter? Bet you are! Let's see if you can work in the castle stables for a bit."

Days like today wore at his very soul. If it hadn't been for the need to hold onto this job for the sake of someone other than himself, he doubted whether he could have kept up the pretence. Had he been as alone as he'd been when he first went to the borders, he would have packed his bags, rounded up his dogs, and taken his chances living in the wilds further north rather than do this. Now, though, he had to stick at it. It didn't help that Giles had told him that things had tightened up in the last year or so. The old chief forester, Alan de Neville, who had governed the royal forests in the king's name for much of King Henry's reign, had stood down and Geoffrey fitz Peter had taken over last year.

No doubt intending to show that he could match his infamous predecessor, fitz Peter had toured sixteen counties in 1185 dispensing justice at the forest courts, or eyres as they were called in a mimic of the regular courts, despite being nowhere near as just. Guy had missed that tour over in western Herefordshire, and by the time he'd arrived in Nottingham they'd passed here too. Yet Sheriff Murdac was now keen to demonstrate that he was not shirking in his duties to the powerful and influential fitz Peter. Alan de Neville had been an old man by the time he'd departed as chief forester, and so had been unlikely to venture this far north in person anymore. The same could not be guaranteed for fitz Peter's possible return!

So Robert of Crockston, in his role as their own head forester, was now clamping down on the infringements of the laws. In the pursuit of this he'd had Guy and the other knights, plus the woodwards of the private parks, out all summer scrutinising the locals for any infringements or misdemeanours. The verderers' courts of attachment at Calverton, Linby, Mansfield and Edwinstowe had been kept equally busy, holding inquests into those deer found dead in the forest, and calling the neighbouring villagers in to swear as to the circumstances of those deaths. Luckily all the ones Guy had had personal dealings with so far had been proven to be natural deaths, or in two cases, acts of poaching by the sons of wealthy tradesmen from Nottingham town who would have no trouble paying the fines when the next full eyre came around. He really didn't want to be involved in persecuting poor villagers for taking meat they honestly needed – that had rather too many echoes of life under de Braose! Indeed he'd hoped that today they would've been doing nothing more than tracking down some illegal felling by one of the local land owners – hence the men-at-arms in case the curmudgeonly old knight chose to set his own men upon the foresters – and checking on a rumour of sheep being grazed where they shouldn't.

Given that they were already well out of the true forest woodland and therefore the habitat of the all-precious deer, Guy personally couldn't see why the locals shouldn't be able to clear land for valuable sheep farming, for here the land resembled the more open farmland around the Trent he had grown up in. These lands were subject to the king's forest laws by virtue of the king's broader legislation, rather than by possessing any large, dense woods. He therefore suspected that the grievance was more that the sheriff's agisters were put-out that the fees demanded for such new grazing hadn't been paid back on St Cyril's Day, at that swanimote gathering in July. Come the Michaelmas swanimote in late September, Guy could foresee some hefty fines being demanded from the two villages of Tollerton and Cotgrave, given the level of assarting he'd found and not a penny paid for all the felled wood to the court. He felt it altogether wrong that people had to pay to clear land and then not be able to keep the wood, then to add to the insult, to have to pay again to buy in wood from further afield. No wonder the people of eastern Nottinghamshire complained mightily of this new forest imposition! They had every cause, and Guy had winced inwardly if not openly when he'd finished calculating how much they would now be fined.

It had set him in a grim mood, for had Simon been doing his job the village would have been alerted by him to the fact that the progressive felling was being noticed, and could have paid some money already. Had it been Guy who had passed through here weeks ago, he would have dropped a quiet hint not to do the clearing all in one go. That way it would have been harder to tell how many trees had gone at any one time, and the fines due would have been more manageable.

Unfortunately it was just when the men and Guy had been making their way back towards Nottingham that they had come near to Lamcote, and discovered the lad poaching, thus putting the cap on Guy's internal disquiet. At least today was better than some, sighed Guy inwardly, for Lamcote was near to Nottingham and the castle. That meant it was close enough to leave the men-at-arms to make their own way back, while the two walking foresters who had been with them earlier could disperse to their own homes. He truly hated having to ride for days with some poor soul being dragged along behind him as they made their way back to the castle – as had happened when he'd been sent up into the north of Sherwood to check on the lands of the Le Clay afforestation which came within the Edwinstowe swanimote's purlieu. Those confirmed as poachers at that inquest still had to be brought back to Nottingham to await sentencing by the justices at the court of eyre, and that might mean a long wait in gaol, as well the caught men knew. One day he feared that his nerves would give out on him on those trips, and he would reveal where his sympathies really lay when they had to camp overnight, listening to a prisoner sobbing for the home he was leaving behind.

The beginning of the week had already been trying enough, bringing its own complications in a different way, for they had been acting upon a tip-off and patrolling around Clifton on land which was owned by the Bishop of Lincoln, even if it lay within royal Sherwood. There they had arrested four woodsmen who claimed that they were felling trees for building work the bishop wanted done. There was nothing like a member of the royal family as a bishop for being highhanded, and the bishop of Lincoln was King Henry's bastard son. With young Jocelin and a belligerent Sir Eric – smarting from some chastisement inflicted by Sheriff Murdac himself, and consequently temporarily with them as some kind of punishment – at his back, as well as four walking foresters from nearby, Guy could hardly step in and protest.

Yet he knew that the men were innocent in their intent, and were caught in a political trap like so many others. Disobey the bishop, their liege lord, and they would be heavily punished or maybe even flogged. Disobey the king's forest laws and fell trees without permission, and they would be imprisoned while the bishop argued it out with the sheriff and the head forester. It wasn't much of a choice, Guy thought. Therefore, as of yesterday the unfortunate woodsmen were languishing in the depths of the castle for a crime they hadn't known they were committing. He'd really hated yesterday!

At least today he had the little terrier safe. As rescues went it wasn't much, but it made him feel that all wasn't quite lost. He was just relocating the small dog in its new temporary home with the stable lads, who were very glad to have the minute assassin around after he'd caught a rat within the first five minutes of being in the yard, when he heard his name being called. Hurrying out of the stables so that the terrier wouldn't be seen, he nearly collided with Robert of Crockston.

"Ah Guy, there you are! The guards said you'd ridden in. Change of orders for you tomorrow – you're to ride to Lincoln for the sheriff."

"The four woodsmen?" Guy guessed.

Robert gave a half-hearted snort of disgust, and steered Guy towards a room on the ground floor of the old castle off the inner ward, where he endeavoured to keep some semblance of order in the chaos which was the castle and forest administration. Once inside, with the door shut, Robert flopped into a leather chair behind a table piled with parchment left by the scribe and gestured Guy to the window seat, where a tapestry cushion did its best to fend off the chill of the stone for the sitter.

"Bloody mess!" Robert growled. He was a pragmatic man, and while he could just about stomach the laws of the forest, whose fines were as much at the whim of the king than relating to any law of the land, the petty squabbling of the great lords irritated him immensely. "What possessed Geoffrey Plantagenet to send his men to chop down five bloody great oaks all clustered together right where we couldn't miss what was being done? It was just asking for trouble! Or maybe that's what he wanted? Who knows with that brood! Never a thought for the poor sods who have to sort the mess out when they quarrel!"

"How are the men?" Guy dared to ask, for in a normal year the men would have been put into the town gaol, which had appeared as part of King Henry's other building works nearly a decade ago, and where they could have hoped for some sympathy from the local men who guarded the place. Currently, however, the sweeps of the forest had resulted in the gaol being jammed to capacity, and along with some other poor souls, the woodsmen were incarcerated in the castle's dungeons – a grim fate indeed! However Robert was a fair man and unlikely to vent his frustrations at the inconvenience of having prisoners within the castle walls upon the men themselves.

"Oh, I've made sure they were properly fed and had clean straw put in the cell," Robert told him in his matter of fact way. He clearly wasn't about to make the bad situation worse by allowing the bishop to complain of the treatment of his men. "The thing is, Guy, the sheriff needs someone to go in person to the royal bastard and get the money. Sheriff Murdac is reluctant to simply write to him. He feels, and I agree, that we could be exchanging letters for months, and in the meantime the men are cluttering up our dungeon when we could be using the space for real felons. ...So, ...he wants one of his knights to ride to Lincoln, with the four men under guard, and personally receive the money."

He saw Guy's look of concern, which was perfectly understandable given the personality of King Henry's warmongering, illegitimate son, and smiled. "It's all right, Guy! We're not expecting you to fight his men to a standstill for it! It's a merely a display of authority. But if the bishop refuses the *personal* representative of the king's forester, then the sheriff can pass it all on to Forester fitz Peter to deal with at the next court and it's out of our hands – and nothing would please Sir Ralph more than that! The last thing he wants to do is get embroiled in a lengthy argument with a bishop who has aspirations to become king!"

Guy realised that this was a chance to do something a bit more positive than harrying hard-pressed peasants and thought quickly. "If you don't mind I'd like to take Wulfric and Alnoth, two of Verderer Henry's own men who know the area," he said. "They can testify to the fact that the spot where we found the men is now, as a result, officially deforested enough to be classed as wasteland. I'll take Thomas and Siward with me, too. There's a small open coal mine started up over by Leverton and Fenton, but we've had some conflict over the payments due from it, so we can go and accurately assess what's due. Thomas and Siward both have family who mine in the forest, so they'll be able to tell me what's realistic in terms of the mine's production. We might as well get it right from the start, rather than having appeal after appeal that the charges aren't possible. It's nearly on our way back, so we can combine the two jobs. It's not as if those men of the bishop's are going to need much guarding when we're taking them back home, and I doubt they'll chance running with my dogs at their heels!"

"True," Robert agreed, thinking that he'd been right to give Guy this job. He liked the newest of his knights for the way he never tried to puff himself up and be self-important, and it was typical of Guy that he would think of something else which needed doing so that it saved them a second job. Sheriff Murdac had been sceptical of Robert's choice of Guy for the job, but Robert knew the sheriff would be pleased when he was told of Guy's response.

For his part Guy was glad that he'd managed to get away with only taking two of the walking foresters with him and those of his choosing, for the verderer's men were really only servants and merely with him to make a display of authority. They'd be pretty useless if it came to a fight. If he took Spike and Fletch with him the bishop's men were unlikely to make a run for it, even to escape the bishop's wrath – which Guy wouldn't have blamed them for. However, the bishop's response was something he couldn't predict and had no means to influence either, which salved his conscience. So with any luck it would be a pleasant outward journey, even if his reception by the bishop was likely to be anything but welcoming. Yet he had another reason for tackling this job with some relish. Harry had taken him on one side only a week ago and asked with gruff embarrassment if he could ask for Guy's help.

"My family are mostly miners a bit north of here," he told Guy softly, keeping an eye open for anyone listening in on their conversation in the cramped confines of the bailey. "Now my brother found this seam of coal right up near the surface and applied to start working it. Seemed all right at first, but then that Sir Mahel of Screveton comes riding by and says they should be paying more. Well they'd hardly started getting anything out yet, so our Walter said he'd be happy to pay on what they got out, but not yet on account of there being nothing. That didn't suit, though, and Mahel's family are powerful up there, so Walter's family scraped together what funds they had and paid him five shillings to see them through to Michaelmas."

"Five shillings? That's a lot for a mine which hasn't produce anything!" Guy had gasped, for it was. A good mine might pay more, but for something which hadn't any record of what yield it might give it was a lot to ask.

"Oh it gets worse!" Harry had added grimly. "When Sir Giles came through a month later for the next attachment court up at Edwinstowe he told Walter there was no record of any payment!"

"God's wounds!" Guy had sworn, "Mahel's pocketed the money, hasn't he!"

"Looks like it! The thing is, Guy, they've got two more verderers' courts to get through before they can hope to appeal to the sheriff when the formal rents are due at Michaelmas. Can you try and be the one who goes up to that swanimote next month and see what you can do?"

Guy had promised to do what he could, but had admitted that it might take some engineering to get Alan of Leek or Sir Martin to let him pick his route. The only thing he could think of doing for the miners was to get there by one means or another and then take sworn statements in the local hundred court that the money had been paid. He'd still been mulling over how he was going to get there, though, when Sir Robert had pre-empted his request and unwittingly put him on the right road at the right time and with official backing to interfere, however contrived! It was therefore with great relief that he set out the following morning with the four woodsmen, the verderer's men, and his chosen two walking foresters – men whom he knew to be reasonable, and rather more importantly no friends of the rather imperious Mahel. The business with the bishop would have to be seen to first, but Guy had high hopes of being able to do some small good on the way back and help a friend in the process.

By the time another two full days had passed, he was climbing into bed in a small chamber in the guest house of the monastery attached to the great cathedral, the woodsmen were back with their families, and he had a night's grace before he needed to argue the matter with the bishop, whom he hadn't seen yet. He'd already presented the evidence to the prior of Lincoln, and had had the verderer's men's evidence written down by a scribe, so at least that was now a matter of record, whatever the bishop might say to try to wriggle out of the charges. Part of the job was therefore already out of the way, thanks be to God. As he rolled over and pulled the blanket up against the autumn night chill he soon felt his eyes begin to close. That was until he heard the latch on his chamber lifting quietly. Surely no-one would be trying to rob him in the bishop's guest house? He would never have believed such a thing could happen, and the proof of that was that his knife was on the chest by the window and out of reach.

He was just tensing himself to roll over and spring for it when a familiar voice whispered softly, "...Guy? ...It is you, isn't it?"

Sitting bolt upright, Guy stared through the gloom at the speaker. "Tuck? ...What in the name of all that's holy are you doing here?" Surely Tuck hadn't forsaken Maelgwn and Gisborne manor to come and rejoin holy orders? Yet he could think of no other reason for Tuck to be in Lincoln of all places. However, Tuck's next words took his breath away.

"Thank the Lord! I was coming to Nottingham to find you. It's Allan, Guy. He's being held by the Templars at Faxfleet. Apparently he tried to pull some sort of trick on some of them at Barton market and they've caught him."

"You what?" Guy was instantly out of bed and striking the flint from his pack to light the solitary candle in the room. As it flickered into life he could see Tuck's face more clearly and there was no mistaking the concern written across it. "What on earth enabled you to discover that!"

Tuck shrugged ruefully. "I needed to stretch my legs. Get a bit of weight off!" He patted his considerable middle but Guy wasn't fooled. Most of that was solid muscle, not fat, especially at this time of year when Tuck would've just finished getting the last of the summer wheat harvest in. If Guy had been a betting man he would've put money on Tuck doing the work of three men, both in the fields and in the barns stacking the hay and straw.

"What you mean is that you've been pacing the manor like a caged lion," he said with good humour. "Don't worry, Tuck, you don't have excuse yourself to me. I could see that Maelgwn and Ianto have formed a formidable team in managing my little estate for me, and Elyas is becoming a good apprentice to them. That sort of work is no more your forte than it is mine."

A flicker of a smile played over Tuck's face. "Thank you, Guy, you're always understanding."

"So ...what? You decided to stroll over to Yorkshire and see what my new-found cousins were like?"

This time Tuck had the grace to blush a little, but what he had found clearly overwrote his own embarrassment. "Well, yes... It was wonderful walking over the Pennines. I felt I had room to breathe again. I don't think I'm cut out for the domestic life, Guy. I'd intended to take it at an easy rate, but once I got the road beneath my feet I found myself swinging along at a goodly pace and before I knew it I was coming down to York."

"Phew! By St Thomas, you did take the long way!" Guy whistled. "I usually go between the mountains and the high grounds, and travel through Chesterfield, Barnsley, Shipley and Skipton."

"Yes, but I had a mind to see the Minster at York. What a building! Four storeys high, Guy, and that not counting the tower at the crossing! And inside …the arches and windows! All to the glory of God! What an undertaking and what dedication! Those first Normans under King William may have brutalised the north, but Archbishop Thomas of Bayeux certainly knew his business about building a house of God – no wonder he has such a grand tomb there! I attended mass while I was there and I could see right up into the heights of the domed apse and hear the chants echoing there!"

Guy now noticed that Tuck's tonsure was freshly shaved again. When they'd first gone to Gisborne he'd let it grow out and Guy had wondered at the time whether he'd turned his back on the Church, even though there was no question of his faith waning. He'd certainly had cause given the way the Church had treated him in recent years. Clearly Tuck had resolved whatever inner conflict had been going on, though, and was now proclaiming his vocation again. Tuck saw his gaze and nodded, his momentary rapture over the grand cathedral gone.

"It was a good thing I redid the tonsure at York. It meant that when I got down to the Humber and wandered into the Templar preceptory at Faxfleet, looking for a bed for the night and hoping to get a ride on the ferry they ply across the river, I was immediately marked down as respectable."

"So what happened? Did you go to John and Allan's home?"

"I never got the chance! When I got up on the morning after I'd arrived, I could hear someone at the gate. Out of curiosity I went down to see what was going on. I saw a huge man pleading with the gatekeeper and guards to let him in to speak with someone. They weren't hard on John, just distant and resolute. Of course I didn't know who he was until I got to talk to him. I asked the gatekeeper to let me go out instead of him coming in, so that I could offer some comfort to someone who was so clearly in distress. They let me because it eased the situation – so you see the tonsure had its uses. Well I took him around to where there was a bank we could sit on and asked him to tell me his story. You could have knocked me down with a feather when I realised who he was!

"It was also a good thing we were well out of earshot once I found out, because we were able to speak frankly. …Poor John, he's been having a hard life with Allan, I think. I doubt he told you all of it, for I didn't tell him who I was at first, and because he thought he was talking to a total stranger, and a priest at that, he was more open.

I suspect he feared what might happen if you'd decided to take Allan under your wing, you know. Not that you'd have been a bad thing," he added hastily seeing Guy's raised eyebrows of surprise. "More a worry of how quickly Allan would have cost you your job."

"Oh Lord, as bad as that?"

"I'm afraid so. John may have told you about how they came to be attached to Willoughton preceptory, but I don't think he said what's happened since unless you kept it from us in turn?"

"No, I told you all I know."

"Well your youngest cousin is a weak and foolish man. And he is a man now, although I can now see what you meant about John struggling to acknowledge that. The trouble started again about the time you three re-met, with a few scrapes when he went to market with John – poor man, he could hardly watch Allan every moment like a tiny child! That was at the weekly markets in Kirton. Several accusations of not quite honest dealings and the like, but I would guess that, like me, the locals responded to John and felt sorry for him. Apparently John says Allan came home with some unexpected bruises more than once, so I suspect a rough justice was handed out and no-one wanted to bother the sheriff's men. Unfortunately Allan seems incapable of learning a lesson!

"The first major bother came when Allan went off on his own one night without telling John. By the time he caught up with him a day later – having, by the way, had to do Allan's work as well as his own – things had already gone awry. Allan had made his way further off to Scunthorpe village, got into an early game of dice with some men passing through, won and got drunk on the proceeds, then had tried to play the same trick on some of the locals."

Guy groaned. "Scunthorpe? But that's the king's land! Dear God, Tuck, you're right, he is a fool! Bad enough to try that kind of lunacy on a manor or in a village with an absentee lord, but to do it on the king's land when the folk would go straight to the sheriff as their lord's representative? Whatever possessed him?"

"I think you might have to ask the Devil rather than God about that," Tuck answered sagaciously, "and I sincerely hope that's one conversation you never have the chance to have! The end result, however, was that Allan was clapped in chains in Lincoln while John found the money to pay the fine with."

"And of course the sheriff would have told their landlords, the Templars."

"Indeed. This was in the early summer. Luckily John still had the money he'd found from Allan's winnings, and so he just had to wait a suitable amount of time and then go and pay up."

"Not that Allan was a bit grateful, I bet."

"It didn't sound like it. John told me Allan was unbearable for the next few weeks. Especially when the midsummer fairs came around and John told him that not only could he not go, but that he wouldn't be having a new tunic, and fancy hosen instead of his patched trews, either. Allan couldn't seem to see that John couldn't be seen to be spending money on anything but the barest essentials, or else people would start wondering where he'd got the money to pay the fine with..."

"...and that would lead straight back to Allan and land him in trouble again!"

They both sat silently on Guy's bed for a moment, lost in bemusement at the insanity of Allan's actions and reasoning.

"And then what?" Guy broke the silence by asking.

Tuck rolled his eyes in exasperation just at the thought. "The little fool decided that it was all the Templars' fault! Three weeks ago he was working himself into a right froth. So much so that John refused to take him across to the preceptory when he went to take a ram to them to be exchanged with another from one of their other flocks. By the time John got back Allan was gone again. God bless John, he was feeling so guilty when I met him for having felt relieved that Allan was gone at that point. He said he thought that the lad had taken himself off and would be headed for London, or at least the south, where there would be more people to trick and fleece, but somewhere far beyond his own reach or ken. That was until a message came from Willoughton telling him that Allan was at Faxfleet. It seems that Allan tried to get some of the older Templars from Faxfleet into a game of dice at Barton market, and when they wouldn't play started a fight with them, bawled all sorts of wild accusations at them including some which they wouldn't be likely to let go lightly! ...I think one had something to do with sexual acts and sheep!

"John was told to take Allan's things to him, and that if he was ever found at the cottage again John would be turned out with him." Guy groaned and buried his head in his hands as Tuck continued. "This time the knights at Willoughton assumed that John wouldn't be able to pay given how quickly another fine had come round, and so had already replied to that effect to their brothers at Faxfleet. So John made the miserable journey up to the Humber, but when he got there the brothers took Allan's things off him and told him that Allan wouldn't be any concern of his from now on – which is where I came in the morning after. Allan's to be imprisoned at their pleasure and then will be cast out, but I suspect that the master at Faxfleet is just waiting for word back from the sheriff of Yorkshire to say that he can take Allan's hand off to mark him as a thief for life."

"We have to get him out," Guy declared although his voice carried little enthusiasm. "Not for his sake, the ingrate, but for John's. We'll do our best to get him out of the preceptory so that he keeps his hand – if it's not too late that is! But after that he'll be on his own, no matter what John says. I can't do this more than a couple of times – picking him up whenever he falls foul of authorities through his own stupidity – without arousing suspicions, and the cost is getting too high for John to bear."

"Can you leave tomorrow?"

"That rather depends on the bishop! But unfortunately, Tuck, I have another quest on my hands too," and Guy told him about Harry and the mine.

He was furious with Allan, he confessed to Tuck, for this would mean he couldn't really spend time going over the mine in detail if he'd already delayed his return to help Allan.

"Curse the wretch!" Guy muttered darkly, as he tried to get some sleep in the remains of the night. "Whole families might get turned out of their homes on his miserable account now! And what on earth am I going to say to Harry? That I chose my selfish pest of a cousin over his whole family? God rot you, Allan!" he said with a shake of his fist at thin air. "I never thought to say it, but I'm already sick of you and we've only known one another as men for a few months. Where did the loveable lad you were go to? Why have you forced me into choosing between you and everyone else? I can't be worrying over you anymore."

However, it transpired in the morning that Bishop Geoffrey was far off in York, although he could hardly be conferring with the archbishop since the see had been vacant for over five years now. Guy didn't need to pretend at venting his fury over not being told that upon his arrival, but it was uncannily fortuitous since it meant he now had a valid excuse to go further north. Had Tuck's and his prayers been silently answered already, he wondered? He immediately sent the four men who'd come with him on their ways back, on the basis that they'd done their job in escorting the prisoners. And so they were sent off to go the long way back via Sturton and Leverton, with strict instructions to ask the hundred court for those men owed frankpledge service to do their duty and swear as to the state of the mine.

"I would come myself," Guy said with absolute truth to Thomas and Siward, "but this damned matter with the bishop will have to be resolved or Sir Ralph will have my guts for his garters!" Then came the small lie. The twisting of the truth at its tail. "You know what Sir Giles is like," he said confidentially, but drawing the two unsuspecting foresters into the plan. "He says that the villagers swear they've paid up already but he has no record of it, but the previous forester to go over there was Sir Mahel, and he's not the best at keeping records straight either." Thomas and Siward were with him all the way by now, as pleased as could be at being trusted with such work, and secretly gloating that they might be putting right the mistakes of the dim Sir Giles and the arrogant Sir Mahel. "Get this straightened out, would you?" Guy pleaded with an expression so devoid of his actual intent it would have done the gambling Allan credit. "I shall tell Sir Robert and Sir Alan it was you who did the good work if you can."

That was it, the pair were hooked like fish on a line and set off with a will, especially when Guy made a point of telling the two verderer's men to inform Alan of Leek that his two under-foresters weren't dallying needlessly but doing important work. That Guy said all of this again in more tactful words before witnesses in the stable yard of the abbey, as they took charge of the horses they had been issued with for the journey, was even better. Being allowed to ride out and to be off alone on official business was a rare treat all four were clearly enjoying!

"Can you trust them not to mess it up?" Tuck whispered in Guy's ear as they watched them go.

"I hope so! I'm putting a lot of faith in the fact that everyone likes Giles, even if he is a bloody nuisance sometimes, whereas none of the under-foresters like the way that Mahel talks down to them and always rides off in front of them, never waiting for those of them on foot. So I'm just hoping that they'll want to rub Mahel's nose in the dirt for once, and with a legitimate excuse. And if what Harry's told me is true, then all the local men who'd be obliged to testify as to the state of the mine in the next formal hundred court will be glad to get at least one piece of business out of the way now. Damn Allan! It's the best I can do, given his foolish games!"

"You can only do what God allows," Tuck said sympathetically. "You can't save the world."

"Hark who's talking!" Guy snorted with amusement. "I've never known that stop you trying, Tuck!"

For his part, Guy declared to all and sundry in Lincoln that he would follow Geoffrey Plantagenet and his entourage to York and sort this matter out. Everyone knew that the king had ideas of forcing the reluctant Geoffrey into becoming archbishop in the north, and Guy made a point of hoping aloud that the very secular bishop would settle this dispute in Sheriff Murdac's favour just to get him out of the way, and avoid having yet another point to argue with his kingly father over. The rather more devout Bishop Adam of St Asaph was on his way to Lincoln, the prior now admitted, but he was only coming to perform those clerical duties which Geoffrey couldn't do, not having been ordained as a priest yet. Bishop Adam certainly wouldn't be in a position to sort out quarrels over forest law, they all knew, and so Guy's moving on appeared logical to anyone who cared enough to wonder.

Taking his leave of the monks, he joined Tuck out in the town, where Guy managed to stump up enough coins to buy two additional horses big enough to take John and Tuck's weights. Together they rode up the old Roman road of Ermine Street where they met John waiting hopefully near Kirton. He'd clearly been sleeping in the hedgerows, not daring to go back to his cottage in case he missed Tuck's return.

"You found him! And so soon!" was John's relieved cry.

Guy embraced his cousin. "Thank the Bishop of Lincoln for being an arrogant Plantagenet and crossing the Sheriff of Nottingham," he said in explanation. "Now, let's go and find Allan!"

Together they rode to the Humber getting there as dusk fell. "We'll have to go across on the morning ferry," Guy said. "There's no avoiding that. We'll tell the Templars' ferryman we're going on to York as I'm supposed to be doing. Then when we get out of sight we'll turn back and adopt our disguises." Luckily in Lincoln he'd also purchased a second-hand battered tunic with leather reinforcements, roughly stitched onto it by its mercenary former owner, and a much patched pair of trews to change into, for should they be seen it would not do for the sheriff of Nottingham's man to be recognised.

They spent a tense night of what seemed like endless hours, waiting for the first ferry to arrive. Once on the north bank of the Humber they rode past the preceptory and sized it up as they passed. It was hardly a castle in terms of fortification, but it was stoutly built of stone and rose to two floors with what windows there were up on the upper level. The double gates were strong and barred, and the whole place looked far beyond their limited abilities to storm.

"By St Peter and St Paul," Guy muttered darkly, "we're never going to be able to break him out of there by force. How are you at fighting these days, John?"

His cousin looked glum. "I haven't done a thing since we left home," he said miserably. "I worried that if I carried on practising that it would feed Allan's wild dreams of our being able to go home and live as knights once more. Anyway, it seemed better not look too handy in a fight if I was trying to pass us off as two shepherds, if you see what I mean!"

Guy looked back and forth between his two companions. "No disrespect to you both, then, but we're hardly equipped to fight our way in. Yes, Tuck I know you did some out in the Holy Land, but you've hardly kept your skills up any more than John has. It would be different if we were going up against three or four of the sheriff's local lads, most of whom are pretty inept against anything other than defenceless peasants. But these are Templars! I know most of the men inside that place will be lay brothers who've never raised a hand in anger, but there are sure to be a small but significant number of older men who once fought on crusade, and some of them might have come back not so very long ago that they'll be rusty just yet. There's no point in getting Allan out only to be killed ourselves!"

"But we can't just leave him there!" John gasped in horror.

Guy looked sympathetically at his cousin. "John, we'll do what we can, but look at the place! There's no way we can break down the doors or fight our way in, and the dreadful truth is that Allan is in there because of his own foolishness. At some point he has to be answerable for his own mistakes. We'll do the best we can, but one of these days our best isn't going to be good enough."

"He's right," Tuck agreed. "You've done all any man could for Allan, John. It's not your fault or anyone else's apart from Allan's. And even if we do succeed in getting him out of there, it's time to let him go his own way. You have to let him fall down without you being there every time he calls to pick him up, or he'll never grow up."

"Let him go?" John looked suspiciously from Guy to Tuck and back again. "What are you saying?"

"Think about it," Tuck said kindly. "What can you do? You've been told in no uncertain terms that Allan can't come back to the cottage with you – and if we get him out it certainly won't be long before someone comes looking for him, so you can't have him anywhere near the cottage! Not even in hiding! So he'll have to leave, but that's not a reason for you to go on the run too, John."

"You don't have to be the one to tell him," Guy added. "He half thinks of me as the bad sheriff's man already, so let me be the wicked cousin. That way, if he does sort himself out then he'll still have a home to come back to with you in a year or two's time."

John's face fell even further. "That's harsh on you, Guy. You've done nothing yet to make him hate you so."

"But it hasn't stopped him, has it?" Guy said pointedly, "So he might just as well have some good cause for his venom."

Then suddenly a bright idea came to him and he began to grin.

"What's got into you?" John asked, completely bemused at the switch in attitude, but Guy answered with a question.

"Tuck, did you see any of the sheriff's men in York? The knights I mean."

"Yes, a few. Why?"

"Were they dressed any differently to me? To a casual glance that is? Any distinctive markings or the like? Badges on their tunics?"

Tuck's face broke into an answering grin. "No! No difference whatsoever!"

"Right then," Guy declared, "I think we might have a plan! Only God knows whether it will work, but it's our only shot. Tuck, you'll stay here with Fletch and Spike and my horse." Guy was riding a distinctive bay of obviously fine quality, and he would bet that if the Templar's didn't remember his face they would surely recall the horse. The fine dogs had also been commented upon on the ferry, and so to go without them would further distance the party in the ferrymen's memory, should they be asked if any such group had passed that way afterwards. "I'll ride your beast, Tuck, since you can't realistically come with us. Any man of the cloth would be pretty memorable, and especially one whom they've recently entertained! I've got an old spare tunic in my saddlebags. I brought it thinking I was going to be returning through villages where I wouldn't need to impress someone like the bishop. If I put that on and ride this big furry fetlocked horse they'll think I'm a pretty poor knight, but that won't hurt. I don't think I need to adopt the disguise of a mercenary I bought in the market."

"I don't think the present sheriff of York keeps his men in many luxuries," Tuck added. "Now you draw my mind to it, the knights I saw looked much more roughly turned out than you, even allowing for the fact that you're dressed up to impress officially on behalf of Nottingham. If I were you, though, I'd swap your decent trews for the patched ones you bought. That'll make you seem even more threadbare, although still respectable after a fashion."

"And speaking of threadbare," Guy added, "it won't hurt that John now has several days' growth more beard since the gatekeeper laid eyes on him, and anyway, he'll be mounted and wearing the soldier's old tunic I bought. It's big enough, just about! We'd be very unlucky if he was spotted."

Their grins were now joined by John's who could finally begin to see where Guy was going with all of this. "What are you going to tell the Templars?" he wondered.

"Why, that Allan is a wanted thief in Yorkshire! Somewhere nicely out of the way so that no-one is ever likely to pass through it and check if we've concocted our 'reported crimes' out of thin air. I doubt the real sheriff's men would bother much about any prisoner of the Templars anyway, especially someone who's such small fry as Allan really is. We certainly wouldn't in Nottingham. They could dispense their justice as they saw fit when it was one of their own, as far as we'd be concerned. In fact, I'm guessing that the Templars will wait a long time if they're waiting for word from York, so hopefully Allan's still in one piece at the moment."

"Won't they think twice about Allan being a rogue, though, ...you know, a truly bad thief with a reputation, ...considering that they know he's a tenants of theirs from my landlords?" John asked. "Will you be believed?"

"Hopefully they'll be so sick of his whining they'll hand him over and worry later," Guy replied. "But if questioned I'll say that his family are indeed tenants of their brother Templars down at Willoughton, but that Allan's the wicked youngest son who hasn't long been back with them. That's why you're coming with me, John. If there are questions about being a Templars' tenant that I can't answer you'll chip in in the guise of being my man-at-arms. That at least will ring true, because two of us to fetch a cutpurse back to justice is about right. They'd send more for a known outlaw or the like, but not for some shabby thief."

"And then what?" John was clearly worried about what Guy intended to do to Allan once he got his hands on him.

However Guy was calm and clear in his response. "You, John, will ride with all speed back to your sheep. We can't have you associated with Allan's escape in any way, quite aside from our own plan. Your masters won't expect you to be riding back, so with a bit of luck, as long as they don't see you mounted up, it will only look as though you were slower than normal returning on foot. Keep the horse but out of sight in case you need it. Besides, this poor thing needs a bit of fattening up on some good pasture! Your masters were the ones who told you to go to Allan, so they can't complain too much over your absence, and they sound a decent bunch, so they should be sympathetic if you play up the wrench it's been leaving your little brother – or whatever you've called him, to them – even if he is a pain in the neck of the highest order. Tuck will come with me up to York, and Allan will come with us whether he likes it or not! Once there Tuck can see him out to the other side of the city walls on the road north. If we send him north, not south, there are fewer places he can come to grief in, and that's all we can do."

Guy took in John's mournful face. "No, really, John! It's his lookout if he turns back again. We're not sorcerers who can wave a hand and magic him out of trouble. God knows, my position is humble enough in the greater scheme of the castle! I can only do little bits of good when no-one is looking – and that isn't very often! Mostly I still have to do as I'm told! So I'll do my official business with the bishop in York to keep my cover intact, as well as me in my sheriff's good books, and then Tuck and I will ride back so that Tuck can come on to you. Can you give John a hand for a bit, Tuck, until he gets back on his feet? I'd also be grateful if you stayed so that if any of this does come back on John you can come and let me know."

It worked like a charm, Brother, my first attempt at breaking someone out of custody – for Maelgwn was hardly as guarded despite being in de Braose's castle. I rode into the preceptory with John at my heels and declared my intentions to the Templar's lay-brother who welcomed me. It was easy to coarsen my accent into broad Yorkshire, for we had had enough exposure to the local dialect as children, and I played my part modelled on a knight who had occasionally visited my father and old fitz Waryn. He had been a man full of his own importance at having risen

above his meagre neighbours, with no appreciation of how uncouth his manners seemed to those above him. So I in my turn became a growling, haughty knight who knew no better than to present himself on official business with his scarf still wrapped around his head against the dust of the road, filthy, and looking like some scruffy mercenary.

Why am I smiling? Because in those days it was exciting, and substantially more fun than I had had in a very long time! I rode up to the gate an hour or so after it had opened for the morning and the lay-brothers had gone out into the nearby fields. John sat like a stone on his big shaggy horse, towering over everyone, and we must have looked as if we meant business because no-one argued with us. We had rubbed some ash from our fire into his beard and hair to grey it and make him seem older, and the disguise worked. Certainly no-one batted an eyelid at him, and I was treated in such a way as to indicate that no-one queried who I was, nor thought me anything other than who I said I was.

As I had thought, the Templars were only too glad to get rid of Allan. I had to do a bit of negotiating, but I painted Allan as a real lowlife who had robbed the poor widow of one of the sheriff's men, and threw in that he had been caught trying to rob a local church but had escaped that time, albeit empty-handed, by knocking the priest on the head. All fairly minor misdemeanours, and ones which incited disgust rather than any more vigorous emotions. By the time I had finished Allan had become a long-standing pest who had forfeited any rights to leniency, but it was also a list of wrongdoing which far outweighed the Templars' claim on him. They never even asked me for a writ of authority. All I got told was to wait there in the yard and they would bring him to me – it was as simple as that!

We could hear his whining and moaning as he was dragged up from the cell where he had been kept, and every step seemed to be accompanied by some kind of gripe. The Templar who handed him over to me even went so far as to wish us good luck in travelling with such an ill-tempered prisoner. Of course our worst moment was always going to be when Allan laid eyes on us. Me he might not recognise in my more official capacity, but there was no way he would mistake John for a moment. In the end, for all that we had discussed what we should do at that point, John solved it by dismounting and coming to meet the two knights who hauled Allan along. As Allan's head came up and he saw us, John stepped smartly forward and thumped him with his huge fist, knocking him out cold. Allan folded up like crumpled parchment, and John simply bent and hoisted him over his shoulder, declaring that that should keep him quiet for a while.

That earned us some amused respect from the Templars and I rode out with Allan draped across my pommel, trussed like a chicken for the oven, and looking like a corpse heading for its funeral. No-one questioned our right to take him and no-one followed us. As soon as we were out of sight we met Tuck. He now kept the bigger of the bought horses and took Allan off me, I got my horse back, and John reluctantly left us and headed upstream to ride to the next ferry across the Humber to avoid contact with the Faxfleet ferryman again.

By the time Allan awoke we had stopped for the night near the village of Stillingfleet, which Tuck went into and bought us some food.

Allan was horrified to find himself bound hand and foot, and his curses were truly appalling. However, neither Tuck nor I were in any mood to be swayed by any utterance of his. I made myself as respectable as possible once more with a chilly bath in the nearby stream, while Tuck watched Allan with help from Fletch and Spike, who for some reason had taken against Allan this time in a way which was rare for them – maybe they sensed that he would do me harm if given the chance, for his foul words certainly left me in no doubt of his wishes. The dogs certainly guaranteed that there was no chance of him making a run for it overnight.

Then in the morning I went into York, while Tuck rode the circuit of the city walls and freed Allan out on the north road. He told me that Allan roundly cursed us all, and our youngest cousin was last seen stamping off up the old Roman road northwards, bemoaning his fate in an unjust world which constantly failed to acknowledge his rightful status. I am sad to admit that I was far from sorry to see the last of him, and I resolved not to waste time on worrying about what happened to him from now on. He would survive or die by hands other than mine.

I shall not bore you with the tiresome dealings with the bishop. As expected he refused to pay the fine and sent me away unsatisfied in any respect. Yet when I reported the same back to Sheriff Murdac he was far from displeased, for the Plantagenet bishop had played into his hands and now the king's chief forester would take over the matter. The bishop's absence from Lincoln, and my pursuit, satisfied Robert of Crockston that I had actually done more than expected, and so no-one questioned my longer than predicted absence, aided in no small part by the four other men returning ahead of me and preparing the ground for my tale.

Also, to my delight, it transpired that Thomas and Siward had done all I could have asked of them and some more, and had in their possession many testimonies written down for the miners on heavily reused parchment by an itinerant scribe. Indeed, it transpired that Sir Ralph was not around to praise me in person for what he saw as an excellent job done, Giles later gleefully told me, because he was busy tearing Mahel to pieces for his reticence in handing over the miners' shillings. Above all else Ralph Murdac was honest, and he could not abide an accusation of thieving being levelled at his office, or those acting under his orders. Therefore Mahel had bitten off far more than he had bothered to think about, and even better, I was completely excluded from the execution of his downfall, and could therefore not be blamed for being instrumental in it. If I came into it at all it was to earn Sir Ralph's praise for thinking to get the sworn depositions – no-one apart from Harry could have suspected that I had even a inkling that things were not as they should have been in Leverton!

As soon as circumstances allowed, I rode over to John's cottage and was delighted to find that Tuck was still there and that the two of them had become fast friends. That pleased me immensely, for I had realised that John had no friends anymore thanks to Allan. Tuck was an educated and knowledgeable man for someone of his upbringing – Welsh monasteries were clearly more fond of learning than some of our English ones – and he was someone whom John could talk to about all manner of things, raising John's life back up from more than just looking after sheep. Indeed it was visible how much of a strain had been lifted from John's shoulders. He and Tuck were even practising with quarterstaffs, and John's enjoyment at reviving something he had been good at back at home in Alverton was gratifying to behold. In my turn I wrote to Gisborne and reassured our friends there that all was well with Tuck, and explained why he would be absent for a while longer.

So there you have it Brother, the first time Little John, Friar Tuck and myself were involved in nefarious doings! Rescuing a thief, no less, even if he was one of our own. Yet can you now begin to see that we never set out to become law breakers? To see John so relieved of his worries made me feel that our deception had been worthwhile. There was no intent to repeat the process, or for me to continue subverting the laws I was supposed to uphold whilst maintaining the outward facade of dutiful knight. Indeed, I was most relieved that I had managed to resolve both matters without jeopardising my own position in the castle, and by telling the truth for most of the time too!

But if you wish for a bit more of an insight into my supposedly wicked life, Gervase, then I shall tell you this – I found it most often the best thing to do to tell the truth, for there was far less chance then of being caught out in the lie. It became what I was to think of in my own mind as telling the greater truth to carry the lesser lie, and that, I will confess to you freely, was something which I was to make far more use of than I ever suspected the first time on that trip to Lincoln and York. It also enabled me to use others to do the jobs I dared not, for they would act in all innocence, although again at the time I did not foresee that such manipulations would ever happen again. Only now, looking back, do I see that the desperate necessity of saving my cousin, and helping my friend's family, taught me things I would use often once I became embroiled in Robin Hood's affairs!

However, to the young forester I was back in 1186 that was all un-thought of and unanticipated. Instead, I went back to the grim but boring tasks of running the king's forest, and thinking back on that day as a brief but unrepeatable moment of excitement. Little did we dream at the time that there would soon come a day when we would be doing such things much more often, and with more at stake than just the loss of a hand and a few shillings!

Chapter 10

So, Brother Gervase, are you now all of a quiver? No? Oh, you think that if that was Allan's part in the story then it failed to live up to your expectations! Heavens above, Brother! You have missed the point if you think I was merely dwelling upon my family, for I did not spend my days mithering over one cousin who had treated another so badly! No, Allan will reappear again before my tale is done, but I am not going to delay further by telling you the whys and wherefores of his life as well as mine, or we shall be at this forever. Patience, Brother, patience! For now it all begins to come together. Just a little longer and our original band of merry men will be assembled for you to inspect. However, we still have one or two small matters to deal with, ends which need to be tied up.

Most significantly at this point, having proven myself to anyone who mattered at the castle in the episode I have just recounted, I got what in effect amounted to a promotion. Both Sheriff Murdac and Robert of Crockston now believed I was wasted just dealing with the mundane matters in the farmlands of the Le Clay side of Sherwood. Then when they found out how good I was at tracking too, they announced that I would move from working under Sir Martin and would shift across to attending to the densely forested area of Derwent-to-Erewash under Sir Walter's watchful eye. A knight from Sir Walter's eight foresters called Sir Harold, whom I had barely had two words with, had been summoned back to his family home upon the death of his brother, and hardly had the message come than I was in Sheriff Murdac's presence and being told the news of my move. The new knight who would need to be found to make up the numbers again, whoever he turned out to be, would take my place amongst the Le Clay knights.

I confess I found it a mixed blessing. It meant moving out of my room with Giles, Simon and Jocelin and into an even smaller room I shared only with Osmaer, a quiet young man of Viking and mercantile heritage, and therefore not exactly destined for higher things amongst Norman lords. We were never going to be close, for Osmaer was even more reticent than I when it came to making new friends. Time might have changed that, of course, but he was cold and unfeeling with it, and had a dislike of dogs stemming from being mauled when a lad, and nothing I could do was going to change his mind – not even encouraging him to get close to Fletch, who was as soft a dog as anyone would ever meet. Therefore I enjoyed an increased privacy away from the sometimes wearing boyish jocularity of Giles and Jocelin, and relished the challenge of the new work, for it required me to become much more conversant with the laws of venison and the realities of their application.

The less desirable side of the promotion was that now I was working side by side with the dreaded Sir Eric and Sir Henry – the only ones amongst us who insisted upon their titles when speaking with the rest of us – not to mention Walkelin and Fredegis. The other knights making up the Derwent-to-Erewash eight foresters were Humphrey and Thorsten, who shared an equally tiny tower-room next door to ours – men I was casually acquainted with, but had found nothing so far of common interest to create a stronger bond out of. This isolation was to work in my favour later, had I but known it, but the immediate repercussion was that I spent more time in the stables when I had a few free hours in the evenings. Harry and the rather more mature stablemen were far more comfortable company for me, and there was the added bonus that I could spend time with Fletch and Spike when I was down there. So many a night in the following winter was spent whittling red deer antlers into flutes with the dogs at my feet, and discussing the merits of putting one mare rather than another to stud with a stallion, instead of agonising over whose father had ideas of marrying them off before the possibility was even mentioned.

Come the turn of the year there was some excitement when King Henry announced that he would be collecting a tallage, for it was the first time in ten years that this extra tax had been collected. It became known as the Jerusalem Tithe since the Holy Land was where the money was destined to be spent – even though a tallage was a negotiated fixed amount rather than a true tithe of a tenth of a man's income, if you did not know that distinction, Brother. In Nottingham itself only the freemen would have to pay, but out in the countryside the demands would filter down to free and un-free alike. We foresters would not be involved in the collection, as we knew from the start, but it had an impact upon our work, for once the money had initially been given to the sheriff for the new tax, there was nothing left to pay the lesser taxes with regarding the forest levies.

Now I truly saw the burden of living within a royal forest and I can tell you, Brother, my heart went out to many of the poorest families. If you have not yet heard me rail so hard over the conditions of the ordinary folk of Nottinghamshire as I did over those on the Borders, it is because here the soil was richer and the crops generally much better, which meant that most folk at least earned a passable living off the land. But all that changed at the start of 1187, and for the first time here in the midlands I saw the burden of scraping together enough money to hold a family together descend on the peasant folk. Yet there was nothing I could do to help their situation as one man on his own – I was more powerless than I had been in de Braose's domain for all that I was now a knight! More than any other of my fellow knights I knew the reality of living like that, yet despite that I had to harden my face, if not my heart, in order not to show what would be perceived as weakness – especially when in the company of men like Walkelin or Eric!

In other respects, though, I throve on having work more suited to me, for this was truly being a forester in dense woodlands, and I was back in an environment I felt happy in. I am no more inclined to idleness in my mind than in my body, Brother, and the one thing you cannot level at me is that it was the Devil finding mischief for idle hands which led me into my life of deception! So I happily rode out to track the plentiful herds of *red deer and note their numbers for the sheriff – which was something Eric and Henry were utterly hopeless at, I smugly discovered!*

...Oh no, Brother, not fallow deer! They were still relatively new to Nottingham. Indeed the first herd had come to the fenced park to the west of the castle about the time that John, Allan, Baldwin and I had left the shire. For myself, I never have seen the attraction of the spotted deer. Oh they are very pretty to look at, but their antlers are too soft to make anything of, and since they depend so much on human help to forage in the depths of our English winters, they are hardly so wild as to provide what I would describe as good sport. And it was in providing good sport for a bunch of nobles with the king's permission to hunt in Sherwood which allowed me to show off my tracking skills to my sheriff in person that winter. That, thankfully, meant that my duties were swayed most vigorously towards the venison and not the villagers during 1187!

Therefore if there was any deeper personal gloom on my part it was largely due to the fact that I had been moved westwards while John remained in Lincolnshire, although Tuck kept me in touch. Yet the Almighty – or more probably one of Tuck's Welsh saints – was keeping a close eye on us all, I feel, for things were not as settled as they seemed.

For John and Tuck the winter of 1186 drifted into 1187 in quite a settled fashion allowing John to recuperate, for Tuck was far more of an active and willing partner in helping to run the large flock than ever Allan had been. It was a good thing that it happened that way. We had anticipated that Tuck would leave in the spring after the lambing had finished, thinking that John would have the summer to find a young lad who would want to learn about shepherding to come and work with him.

However, nature or God had other plans. We had a disastrous summer that year. It rained and it rained in the east midlands, although I cannot say if the awful weather affected all of England, for we were too caught up in our own troubles to worry about elsewhere. Of course, high on the rocky knoll the castle was in no danger of flooding, and neither was John's cottage which lay up on the edge of the wolds, but he and Tuck were worked hard through that summer. Flocks which had been turned out to graze in the lower fields had to be rescued repeatedly from rapidly rising flood waters. With their greater strength, John and Tuck were able to haul sodden sheep into boats or onto makeshift rafts, as the frantic farmers tried every way they knew how to save the precious beasts.

I saw them in passing only a couple of times in all of this chaos, and both times they looked exhausted. It also made ours lives difficult in another way, for John and Tuck often found themselves playing temporary hosts to many of the low-lying farms' flocks and the shepherds who minded them. Therefore, with the cottage overflowing with neighbours, there was no way that I could make unnoticed visits, even when I was officially heading for Gisborne for a week or so, and free from having to account for my movements.

We were still determined to avoid anyone making the connection between John and any sheriff's man, even if it was not the same sheriff who had supposedly demanded Allan. We continued to believe we could not afford any whiff of misdoing after Allan's antics, even if it was only a gossiping neighbour getting totally the wrong idea. At least John's charity and willingness to help his neighbours in distress mended his relationship with the preceptory at Willoughton, who now saw him as something of an asset and not a liability. So during 1187 we began to hope that John's position was at least secure now, and also, having heard nothing of Allan – not even a whisper of wrong doing or of him being caught – we foolishly breathed sighs of relief and thought our lives settled.

The first inclination that something portentous was happening was in late autumn 1187 when I saw Tuck, for he came to visit me in the guise of a wandering monk seeking solitude on the road as he made a pilgrimage supposedly from Easby in Yorkshire to the shrine of Our Lady of Walsingham, over the border in Norfolk. He had adopted the appearance of a White Monk instead of his own Black Monk's garb and, if any stranger asked, he was making for the order's priory beside the Holy House at Walsingham, which, having being a well-known shrine for over a hundred years, was therefore an unremarkable destination for him to be aiming for. He had consequently selected Easby as his fictional starting point, since there had been White Monks there for the last twenty years, and it made his passage down through Nottinghamshire all the more believable. For my part I applauded his care in creating his disguise – it might have seemed excessive to some, but I shared his wariness and desire to remain out of official scrutiny.

He was making himself scarce now on account of an impending inspection visit by John's Templar overlords, for neither of them wanted questions asked about where a monk had appeared from, nor why he should be working for John. His presence during the floods had been covered by a story of Tuck being in transit for somewhere distant, and getting caught out by the roads all around being cut off, but of course that excuse no longer existed. This, he told me, was also why he had begun to appreciate the need to have a much more specific tale to hand, and not to wait until someone caught him out with an unexpected question. John had currently borrowed the son of a neighbour, just to make out that he was not doing all the work single-handed. His position had improved, but he had admitted to Tuck that he was not wholly convinced of the Templar's charity if they thought they no longer had complete and total control of what went on upon their estates.

So Tuck had decided to visit me and then maybe go over and visit Maelgwn and Ianto if the inspection was still impending in a couple of weeks' time, for of course the Templars had not deigned to tell a mere tenant the precise day they were due to be in the vicinity. However, he had more than news of John to give me. He told me that he and John had heard of a great defeat in the Holy Land while visiting Willoughton to deliver shorn fleeces. Back last year in July 1187, Guy de Lusignan had led a great host out to face Saladin, which was utter lunacy, Tuck informed me from his personal knowledge of the Kingdom of Jerusalem. We now know it as the great defeat at the Horns of Hattin, but in that breaking news it had no name. Men had died in their hundreds from heat, thirst and exhaustion, and Saladin and the Saracens had simply wiped out the weakened survivors.

But the most shattering news was that the crusaders' army had lost the True Cross, the beautifully jewelled casket in which that holy relic lay having been taken out on the ill-fated expedition to ensure the Almighty gave them a victory. Tuck was more shaken by this than by anything else I had ever seen him be. ˜This bodes ill for us all˜ he told me, and he was sincere in his fears of what lay ahead, for he believed God was punishing us for our arrogance in carrying such a potent symbol of the Lord's into battle and expecting an easy victory. He saw it as a divine punishment for the presumption of assuming we could know the Lord's will. Or rather, he thought not _us_ in the sense of those of us lesser folk in far off England, but the crusading nobility who saw the conquest of the Saracen territories in the name of God as a way of enriching themselves, and their families back in France, England and elsewhere, in a very material way whilst here on earth.

Do not puff so, Brother Gervase, this is all pertinent to our story, for I am not repeating well-known historical incidents for the sake of it. Take note, Brother, for soon you will see why this was so significant! In the meantime, if you must have a pacifier, this visit established a means of my communicating with John and others via Tuck, which we would use for very different reasons in the coming years. Until he became too well known, Tuck was to use his status as a monk to liaise with me when the others dared not enter Nottingham.

Then in late November, Sheriff Murdac had news that Prince Richard had taken the cross and was intending to go on crusade whether his father liked it or not. We small folk wished him well in this, as any Christian would, but never dreamed it would have such an impact on us. In this instance, though, the initial consequences came upon us more swiftly than expected, for in the new year King Henry announced his intention to collect what we came to call the Saladin Tithe – and this time it really was a tenth on _everything_! It had been little over a year since we had been asked to dig deep into our pockets and pay up for the sake of recapturing Jerusalem, and now the king was demanding more, and for the same far-off cause.

Everywhere I went on my business I was being asked the same things over and over again. How much _more_ does the king want? What does the king think we shall live on when we have paid all we have to him? And, on those occasions when I met someone whom I had established a trusting relationship with, some even said what many more must have been thinking, which was that it was the noblemen and knights who had lost the True Cross, so why must the poor folk pay for it? If God was that displeased with us Christians in the West that he would allow such a sacred object to be taken, then what possible difference would the few pitiful pennies of the poor make? And I had to admit I agreed with them.

But once again, Brother, I am getting ahead of myself. For now all you need to know is that by the time the next events happened we knew that things were looking very desperate in the Holy Land, and you shall not get me to say more on that subject until you have heard this next part of my tale.

Derbyshire/Nottinghamshire
July, the Year of our Lord 1188

Guy sat on his horse and stared back at the angry villagers of Aston. Behind him Bin Hill and Bamford Moor rose green and wooded with purple-shadowed folds, and he wondered how many of the folk who should have been in the villages round here had taken to the hills and gone into hiding for the time being. He couldn't blame them and he had no desire to punish them, for technically if they were in the woods beyond Aston then they were right inside the royal forest of High Peak, and today was the last day of Fence Month when no-one was allowed in the forest while the deer fawned. However, Guy wasn't about to be picky over one day since it would hardly make much difference to the deer, but equally he had come to realise a painful truth during this last year – that being overly lenient with poor villagers when it came to taxes was doing them no favours. If he failed to return with the full quota of goods due, then the sheriff would only send another forester knight with walking foresters or even men-at-arms, and they would be far less restrained than he was. Better that he face their ire and only take the minimum he had to. They might not appreciate it now, but if they ever had dealings with some of the other knights they would soon see and feel the difference, for many of Guy's fellow forester knights were not above making a small profit on their own behalf on the side. Sheriff Murdac's fury at Mahel's profiteering clearly hadn't deterred the more brutal members of their company a jot!

"Just give me the eight sacks of grain," Guy said with weary resignation. "I'll take those in payment for the wood collection and the pannage charges, and the other charges as well as the new tax. Don't worry, I'll sort it out with what's due at the agisters' meeting at Mansfield next week for you. Do that and I won't tell the sheriff about those two new cottages I can see on the edge of the village. I'm guessing that someone here's son is living in one of them? Someone setting up a family home on their own? Especially as I can see that you've cleared that wasteland over on the south side of the village near them, and now have crops on it! That's definitely since this spring! But that makes them a separate household to be taxed, and even if they're not occupied by locals, you know the sheriff ought to have been told about that as well. Whoever they are it would make them obligated to pay just like you, wouldn't it? And that would increase what's due.

"Well I'm just going to pretend that they've been built to replace two old buildings, if anyone asks me. I can even say that you've reused a lot of the timbers, so that you won't have to pay any more for the extra felling I see you've done – for God's sake get your oxen and pull those stumps out I can see in the far field! Even the dimmest forester will notice those! I'll tell the sheriff that there are the same number of families living in Aston as are on his list, shall I? Or are you going to force my hand and make me really act as bad as you're making me out to be? Or worse, let me go empty-handed and have Sir Robert of Crockston come back here in force? I don't want to ruin you, but I can't save you if you force me to report your resistance to Sheriff Murdac."

The head man stared back at him in defiance for a heartbeat, then shook his head in resignation. "Give him the grain, Paul," he told another villager standing nearby. Guy held out the reins of the two packhorses he had brought with him for the purpose to the said Paul, who led them off towards a barn. The rest of the villagers turned their backs on him and went back to their daily routine, grumbling, poorer, but still in one piece.

"I'm sorry Edwin," Guy said to the head man now that they were alone. "You know I'm only doing what I have to do."

The sandy-haired, stocky man pulled a face. "I know, Sir Guy, but it won't stop our bellies grumbling when we go hungry."

"We're all the same," Guy agreed, "and if it helps console your folk, you can tell them that for us ordinary folk in the castle the rations are short this month. You wouldn't believe how much we've sent off to market in the south to raise more money! That bloody Jerusalem Tithe is emptying every barn and coffer in the shires, because the king has demanded it all gets paid by the beginning of next year." He grimaced. "It's all got to be in London by the second of February, which means *we've* got to get it all in before this Christmas, *and* the others taxes besides! God forbid that we should be late with those as a result! We're absolutely scraping the barrel for every last morsel, you know. The pennies, grain and beasts might be going into the castle, but they aren't filling our bellies any more than yours."

"Really?" Edwin's astonishment was almost comical. He clearly thought that anyone living in a great stone castle must be eating until they near burst on a regular basis. Guy fingered his belt and showed Edwin where the worn leather had now had to be pulled in a notch. Edwin's ginger eyebrows went even higher. "Good God! I would never have believed that," he murmured.

"Well believe it now," Guy said solemnly, "and if anyone else official rides through here make sure you call me all the hardhearted bastards under the sun, and tell them that you got on your knees to plead with me but all to no avail, I took the lot!"

"Oh? ...Oh! ...Right, I see!"

"And your oxen for the ploughs only went into the forest tomorrow," he added pointedly, making Edwin cringe. "Don't worry, I'm not going to say anything or fine you, but be more careful the next time! You knew we were coming, so didn't it occur to you that someone would think it a bit odd that there wasn't an ox in sight when you've clearly ploughed your fields?" Now Edwin was looking horror-stricken as Guy hammered the point home. "So even a fool of a forester would start wondering where they were when St Cyril's Day isn't until tomorrow, and therefore not even a bloody chicken should be in the woods! Heavens above, Edwin, be more careful!

"And watch out for a stocky, redheaded knight about a head shorter than me, riding a roan horse with long white socks and a star on its forehead. That's Sir Henry. He tends to ride alone like me, but in his case it's because he doesn't want to share what extra he extorts by his sword from the villagers. He's unlikely to come this far into Derbyshire, I'll admit, because although he's brutal and vicious he's also lazy – and this isn't really in his circuit – but just in case I would find somewhere outside of the village to make a small hoard of essentials.

"And the other one to watch for is Sir Eric – he *does* ride across into Derbyshire, because he sees you over here as easier prey than the villagers of western Nottinghamshire who can make the walk to Nottingham, and the sheriff, to complain more easily than you! He'll be riding a pure black horse which is as black as his heart. You were lucky you got me today because you're a small village and Sir Alan of Leek trusts me to get all the dues in one go. But Eric's riding with the rest of our group to get other forest fines whilst the main party gets the Tithe. You were more lucky than you thought today, because he went to Bamford and Hurst and as they'll tell you, he won't come alone! There are likely to be at least three or four men-at-arms with him because he's after your daughters for sport, and the men he picks to ride with him relish joining in! He knows even the most placid of peasant farmers will risk fighting back over that, so he can have his wench and a fight to cool his blood all in one go. And God have mercy on you should you be successful in fighting him off and saving your women, because then he'll come back with a bigger force and drag you off to the castle for attacking the sheriff's foresters."

"What can we do? How can we avoid these men?" Edwin was obviously torn between disbelief and worry. Why should one of the forester knights warn him against another sheriff's knight? Yet the warnings sounded all too believable, and Guy seemed a fair man who took no pleasure in harrying them.

"Set the youngsters to keeping a daily watch on the rise over there when the due payments are approaching," Guy suggested. "No-one would think anything of seeing a child running around. Have some prearranged places for your folk to hide. Not all of them. If either one of those two knights, or any other, comes in and sees the place close to deserted then they'll make a thorough search, and it'll be all the worse for you. But you can have the time to hide the most vulnerable. Any girl who's comely, and anyone who can't run fast but might take their eye."

"I'll do that," Edwin promised, "and thank you, Sir Guy."

Receiving the reins of the laden packhorses, Guy turned and rode out of the small village. It wasn't much but at least he'd done some good today – if they acted upon it, that was. As he rode south he met up with a party of other knights who had been to the larger village of Hathersage and were similarly burdened. For once Alan of Leek was riding with them with men-at-arms for the collection of the king's extraordinary tithe, while the foresters were led as normal by Sir Walter. The forest of High Peak in Derbyshire had its own hereditary foresters, but they tended to patrol the uninhabited south-western area, leaving the eastern side to the sheriff's men, as today. Now the main party was returning from Hathersage, for the sheriff currently had control of the manor which encompassed the village, and so the unfortunate folk had to pay not only the king's taxes to him, but those on top which elsewhere they would have paid to their landlord.

The dreaded Sir Eric was coming back from Bamford, which with Hurst, Aston where Guy had been, and part of the hamlet of Offerton on the other side of the valley, formed this wealthy manor – or at least wealthy for its lord, Guy thought grimly. The poor souls actually living there were far from wealthy at this point! Eric wore a self-satisfied smirk on his face, and Guy cringed inside when he saw two of his accompanying soldiers cleaning their swords as they walked. That looked worryingly like blood and Guy feared for what had happened to the peasants there. He wasn't about to ask, though, for Eric would only gloat and try to enrol him into his next miserable foray. Several of the other men took in the sight and exchanged worried glances, not wanting to be caught up in the repercussions if Sir Alan noticed the blood and brought it to Sheriff Murdac's notice.

There was therefore little conversation as they rode along in company until Sir Walter happened to say that he'd heard that Archbishop Baldwin had reputedly ridden into Wales recruiting Welsh archers for the crusade.

"I can't imagine why the king would want a bunch of stunted sheep-fucking peasants in his army," Sir Eric said snidely. "It's not as if they're useful swordsmen! They don't even use proper crossbows!"

"Maybe it's because they could skewer you from way beyond your reach with their longbows," Guy answered, rising to the bait for once.

"What? You don't mean you think they're any good?" Eric said in astonishment. Then his face twisted into a sneer. "Oh yes, I forgot, you like using a peasant's bow yourself, don't you! Lived over there, didn't you! How many more of their filthy ways did you pick up? Leave some good friends behind did you?" and he imitated a sheep's noise whilst making an obscene gesture.

"By Our Lady!" Sir Walter snorted in disgust. "You really are uncouth, Eric, aren't you! Keep your perverse thoughts to yourself, and pray to God for forgiveness for thinking them!"

Since Walter was senior enough to be able to speak his mind unchallenged, and Alan of Leek was also looking at him with utter disgust, Eric's mouth snapped shut at the reproof and he heeled his horse hard with his spurs so that it shot forward, charging erratically amongst the packhorses which were being led ahead of them, and causing chaos. As Eric disappeared over the next brow, several of the pack horses broke or pulled free their lead-reins and shied at shadows, scattering in all directions.

"Get hold of the bloody things!" Walter snapped irately at the soldiers, who then caused as much mayhem as they resolved as they pounced at the already spooked horses. One horse made an enterprising bound over a dry-stone wall and began pounding up the hillside away from them, and no-one was near enough to stop its companion following suit.

"Judas' balls!" Sir Alan swore bitterly. "That's the one with the money on it!" Losing the grain was bad enough, but Sir Robert and the sheriff would have a fit if they lost the hard come by coins.

"I'll go," Guy called and set his horse to follow, while Walter and Sir Alan tried to instil some order in both men and beasts down on the road. His own horse was faster than the packhorses and so Guy had no reservations that he would catch both animals, but they had a head start and so had disappeared around a shoulder of high land before he was close to them. He galloped around the rocky knoll and realised thankfully that it formed a dead-end miniature valley up on the moor, which had luckily stopped the laden horses' flight. Vaulting off his own horse, he threw its reins into a gorse bush to signal it to stay put and went up to the first packhorse on foot, all the time murmuring gently to it. Having caught this one with ease, he was surprised to find the second skittering around and refusing to let him come near it.

In the end he took the first captive horse back to his own and tethered both of them securely, well out of the way of the spooked beast so that it wouldn't infect them with its panic. Now empty-handed he walked back very slowly, then was surprised to see the horse shy away from what appeared to be nothing at all. The horse was dancing about like a whole nest of adders were at its feet, which Guy sincerely hoped there wasn't!

"Come on, my lovely," he murmured soothingly, "stop being such a bloody silly beast and let me catch you. ...Oh you awkward mare!" His tone had never changed from gentle and cajoling, although he knew he could call the mare any names he liked for all that she would understand the words. Luckily a swing of her head made the lead-rein fling outwards and Guy seized it with both hands, but she jerked him hard and he stumbled on the uneven ground, unable to save himself whilst having both hands still hanging on to the rein. Head first he was plunged into a large thicket of bracken, and as he came up spitting fronds out of his mouth, found himself staring into a pair of familiar eyes.

"God's teeth!" he exclaimed, then yanked on the rein hard as the mare tried to pull him along the ground. Hauling himself to his feet by the rein, he managed to get hold of the bridle right by the bit and pulled the mare's head down by sheer brute strength. "Now stop it you villainous beast!" he snapped sharply, and having control of the horse at last, turned back to the gorse and bracken from whence a familiar figure was rising.

"Guy?"

"Bilan! What on earth are you doing here?" Guy was astonished, then stepped forward and grasped Bilan's arm with his free hand in a warm gesture of friendship. "By Our Lady, it's good to see you again! Come out of there, man, don't hide! Come down to the castle and I'll find you a room and buy you a beer in the brew-house!"

Yet Bilan flinched away from him.

"Good God, what's wrong?" Guy asked. "You surely aren't afraid of me?"

"Not of you, but of those you were riding with," Bilan told him in a hushed voice. "Please go, Guy! Please don't draw anyone's attention to us! Tell no-one you saw us."

"Us? Who's us? What do you mean? And why are you hiding?"

Bilan looked worriedly about him. "Promise you won't tell anyone, Guy? Promise?"

Guy was about to ask 'tell them what?' when a rustle came from behind him, and he turned to see an older version of Bilan aiming an arrow at him from a very short range.

"He can't tell anyone if he's dead," the older version said.

Before Guy could respond another version of the same family likeness popped up out of the bracken and knocked the arrow away, saying in a broad Welsh accent,

"Don't be bloody stupid, Piers! He's with the sheriff's men! *Dewi Sant!* What do you think will happen if he doesn't go back soon? They're only the other side of that ridge, you sodding idiot! They'll be all over these hills like a biblical plague of locusts, that's what, and we'll be slaughtered like so many hares in the jaws of those greyhounds!" The figure, whom Guy guessed to be the oldest of the three, turned to him. "I wish it wasn't so, but I fear we have to trust you to keep your word, if you give it. Bilan told us you were honourable, so for all our sakes I hope he was right."

"These are my brothers," Bilan said shyly. "Piers and Thomas."

Guy's memory suddenly clicked into place. "Ah yes! The two you said had gone to be archers! ...What went wrong? ...I assume that something did go wrong."

The three Cosham brothers looked from one to another. Finally it was Thomas who spoke.

"We were doing fine except for the fact that neither Piers nor I were happy about bullying poor folk who couldn't fight back when we went out with the sheriff. But then the Archbishop came through with Gerald, the Welsh bishop who's King Henry's man. De Braose couldn't do enough for them! So before we knew it a whole bunch of us Welsh archers were being packed off with them."

He stared defiantly up into Guy's face, for none of the brothers were as tall, although the older two had true archers' massively muscled shoulders and arms. "I'm not a coward, Sir Guy! And nor is my brother! But I tell you, we have no intention of dying for a cause that's been lost before we start fighting!"

Guy was still perplexed. "What cause? What do you mean?"

Bilan took over the story. "We were marched down into Devon and had to wait near Dartmouth for the other men who'd been recruited to assemble there – I was to go as a cook's boy, so I was a bit behind the main group on the road. The thing is, when Sheriff de Braose sent them off he thought, like everyone else, that they'd be forming part of Prince Richard's army. But while we were waiting down by the south coast the word started going round that we were all there was. Just us and a few lowly knights! None of the important leaders were going. Not one! And the prince is apparently already back in France and fighting against his father again over something or other! Well what kind of difference will three thousand Welsh archers make on their own against the Saracen army, eh?"

"We'd be like lambs to the bloody slaughter!" Piers growled, full of Celtic indignation. "And that's only if we made it to the Holy Land! How were we supposed to get through France and beyond without any lord to vouch for us? What would happen if someone took us for a band of marauding mercenaries? I'd have fought to get the True Cross back, by *Dewi Sant* I would! But not that!"

Guy could see their point. He'd heard about the king squashing any ideas of English knights going to fight in the crusade as part of a formal contingent led by his heir – after all, against odds any betting man would have given five years ago, King Henry was starting to run out of heirs! So anyone going on crusade just now would be truly without leadership. Bad enough for a knight, but hopeless for ordinary men-at-arms and archers. Piers was right, they'd be treated like mercenaries in many places.

"So you ran away?" he guessed.

"Aye," Thomas confirmed. "Especially as we had Bilan with us by then. De Braose couldn't wait to get rid of the spare lads he didn't want to train up for his own men-at-arms, especially us Welsh! Sees us as rebels in his own camp, he does! Better far away in his eyes, all of us are. Fewer for the Welsh princes to recruit, someone heard him say, daft bugger! If Bilan had been left behind we would've had to wait at least until we'd crossed to France to run for it, so that word wouldn't get back and him be punished on our behalf. You know what the sheriff is like!"

"Oh I know de Braose!" Guy agreed. "He's a vicious bastard even on a good day, let alone when he's in a temper. But with Bilan with you, you didn't have to worry about that, I can see, and I understand why you ran. I think I might even have done the same in your place. So where were you going?"

The three looked from one to another again until Thomas said, "We just kept running at first. We knew we couldn't go back to Wales. Just getting there would have been signing our own death warrants, and we'd have had to join one of the Welsh princes fighting the English – and I never want to be facing King Henry's army and his wrath! We didn't think any of the border counties would be any safer, either, even if we'd gone up to Shropshire, say. With so many archers taken from either side of the border, we'd have stood out a mile in any town or village for what we are. The trouble was that we weren't any better off where we were, because in the south the villages were just too close together. There was nowhere to hide, and we hadn't realised how much our voices would give us away. Bilan wasn't so bad, but Piers and I only had to open our mouths for someone to ask what Welshies were doing here."

Guy had to smile. Their accents were very strong, but clearly they'd had no idea of how much so until they'd moved out of Wales. "So you've just kept on walking?" he guessed.

"Pretty much," Thomas admitted.

Guy's brain was working furiously. They were right, he had to get back to the other foresters and pretty soon or they'd come looking for him, but where to send the brothers on to where they'd be safe? He hadn't given a moment's hesitation over whether he should help them, that was inherent in his very being where a friend was concerned. Despite the fact that Bilan alone had been his friend, it was good enough reason for him to aid all three. The Gisborne estate was no use, though, because if the Earl of Chester or one of his senior men ever visited the manor which he leased to Guy, they too would spot the older brothers for what they were in a heartbeat. It would have to be John's cottage, although Guy had no idea whether Tuck was still with him at the moment. Tuck had indeed gone on to Gisborne manor after visiting Guy – this time acting the returning priest from Walsingham to Easby for the first leg of his journey at least – but had seemed set on coming back.

"Look," Guy said hurriedly, "you're right, I have to get back, but please, promise me you'll follow us a safe distance behind. You can come into Nottingham…"

"No!" Piers interrupted emphatically. "No way! Not inside the town with the castle so close!"

Thomas was no less emphatic if not as aggressive, "No, not Nottingham!"

Guy sighed, maybe they were right, Welsh archers in Nottingham who weren't already with the sheriff's men would soon find themselves recruited, by force if necessary. "Very well then, go north and east through Sherwood Forest to the Great North Road beyond Nottingham. I'll meet you at the inn at Blyth in four day's time. I have to go there on less unpleasant business than today's. For God's sake don't go too far south or you'll end up by another of the sheriff's castles at Bolsover! Aim for Eckington and Worksop if you have to ask for directions – they're both towns with good weekly markets who have people travelling to them. You won't arouse suspicions that way.

"Just say you're looking for work as shepherds, and if you'll take some advice unstring your bows and keep them that way! Few people over here have seen a longbow, so they'll think they're just some strange Welsh walking stick with a bit of luck, because it'll be all the worse for you if someone thinks you're after the king's deer! I can't protect you from my fellow foresters if they clap eyes on you, and while Sheriff Murdac is no de Braose, he does enforce the laws to the very letter. But if you come to Blyth, I can give you directions to a cottage where you can rest for a while. It's being rented by someone in my family. Someone you can trust. He can't risk keeping you there forever, but it will give you a bit of time to make some kind of plan instead of just running every day."

Piers still looked doubtful, but Thomas was now nodding thoughtfully while Bilan was smiling encouragingly.

"Very well," Thomas confirmed. "The inn at Blyth in four days. But may *Dewi Sant* have mercy on you if you play us false!"

Guy needed no elaboration on what Thomas meant. He knew that if he gave the older brothers reason to fear him then he would end up with an arrow in his back, no matter what Bilan might say in his defence. For now, though, there was nothing more he could do, and he hurriedly mounted up and towed the two errant packhorses down to where Sir Walter and the severely chastened soldiers were waiting.

There was still no sign of Sir Eric on the road, nor at the inn in Mansfield they stopped at that night, and Guy suspected that he had ridden off in high dudgeon and had hammered on back to Nottingham at high speed, now that he didn't have to slow to the packhorses' pace. No wonder his horse was so bad tempered – once again it would have suffered for Eric's foul mood. It gave him some satisfaction to know that Sir Robert would view Eric's early return with less than pleasure, and it was likely that the headstrong knight and the castle's constable would be having harsh words yet again before the rest of them got back. Eric's relationship with their leader was becoming more fraught with every month. With any luck that would also mean that Eric would have already taken himself off to his chamber by the time they got back, and so Guy could leave it to Sir Alan and Sir Walter to tell the tale of today. That way he wouldn't have to cover why he'd taken so long to capture two horses by inventing a tale, and one he would then have to make sure he remembered for future reference.

His luck held, and thanks to Eric's arrogance their return was very much the secondary subject of conversation in the castle come dinnertime. As predicted Sir Robert had been furious, and to Guy's smothered delight, the arrogant Eric had been handed out a whole list of punishment tasks in a chastising which half the castle seemed to have had no trouble in hearing. Certainly most of them couldn't stop talking about it, which suited Guy just fine.

Come the morning he was able to slip out of the castle unnoticed to find Tuck, who had fortuitously returned the previous night, and had left a guarded message at the castle stables to the effect that he'd taken up lodgings at the nearby church with the small band of brothers attending there. Hurriedly explaining the dilemma, he got Tuck to agree to meet him well beyond the city walls at dawn on the morrow and, providing all went well, to take the three brothers up to John's cottage. It would certainly be better than trying to give directions, for Guy himself would have to wait a good while before he could hope to engineer his duties so that he could travel John's way.

Together he and Tuck rode north with all despatch for Blyth, for Tuck had brought with him into the town the two shaggy horses Guy had purchased for Allan's rescue. The horses normally got moved around pasturing with the sheep at John's, but of course they'd had to be moved for now, and Tuck had originally simply decided to ride on this supposed pilgrimage to vary his appearance, in case anyone was curious enough to remember him a second time. Now it was proving unexpectedly useful for Tuck could ride and keep pace with Guy.

At Blyth they hurriedly dealt with Guy's business regarding a licence for more timber for the building of a new south aisle and porch at the Benedictine monastery there, and then made for the inn. In the gloomy, smoke-blackened main room they could see no sign of the three brothers, but as Guy's presence seemed to be inhibiting the merrymaking – having been spotted as a forester by the hunting horn of office hanging from its lanyard across his shoulder – he bought two pints of ale and a large fish pie to share, and went outside with them to where he'd left Tuck watching the horses with Spike and Fletch.

"No sign?" Tuck asked after he'd taken a welcome swallow of ale. The road was dry and dusty and they were both parched in the summer heat.

"Not inside," Guy told him after he too had slaked his thirst. "But it looks like they'd spot a stranger a mile off in there. It's not overly welcoming. If the brothers have come I'd expect them to be waiting outside. That way they can watch us too and see if we brought others with us to make an arrest."

"Not very trusting, are they?" Tuck murmured through a moustache of beer froth.

Guy grinned after he'd wiped his own top lip clean. "Well at least they have some cause to be like it. Not like your less than Christian brethren back at the old monastery, eh!"

"No, suppose not," Tuck chuckled before wondering, "do you really think they'll come?"

"I hope so. It's not as though they've got a lot of choices open to them. Give it another twelve months and they could masquerade as returning men. Maybe as having been ambushed *en route* to the Holy Land in the Holy Roman Empire or somewhere. God knows that's a genuine risk and a misery many have endured. That way no-one would think any the less of them for not going all the way to Jerusalem. But just at the moment the Welsh recruitment's a bit too sharp in everyone's minds, and even if they can satisfy villagers' curious questions, they certainly wouldn't be able to pull the wool over the eyes of any lord they encountered. They're going to have to stay well out of all but the smallest hamlets for a while to avoid anyone official."

"That's what we thought," a voice said behind them. Tuck jumped, startled, but Guy had been watching the way Fletch and Spike had been staring fixedly at a point behind his left shoulder and had guessed that they were being watched. He stood up slowly and turned around to find Thomas Cosham there but no sign of Piers and Bilan. Seeing him looking Thomas said, "They're in the trees by the hedge. Piers won't come out until he's sure you're not going to arrest us."

"What, with one monk? Arrest two archers and a boy who's still probably pretty good with a bow?" Tuck snorted loudly, his own Welsh accent very audible. "For Heaven's sake! You could stick me full of more arrows than the blessed St Sebastian before I could even get near to you!"

Thomas smiled. "Well put like that I suppose it is a bit unlikely! Did you hear that Piers?" he called over his shoulder, and from the nearby greenery the two other brothers emerged, Piers scowling and Bilan grinning sheepishly.

"Come on," Guy said, dumping the two empty wooden beer mugs on the inn's window ledge, "let's get you out of harm's way!"

He saw them off on the road towards the Trent with Tuck, and then rode home on his own with just the dogs for company. Part of him was secretly hoping that Bilan would be willing to stay on for longer with John. That way John would gain a legitimate helper and Bilan would be safe. Guy was pretty sure that the surly Piers wouldn't have been happy with anything less than a royal pardon and a purse filled with gold for his trouble, so he was quite expecting him to move on.

In fact he had suggested that Piers and Thomas could do a deal worse than go to the Templars. Not locally, but up in Yorkshire where there were many preceptories, and where there was always plenty of trade going on which might benefit from having a couple of expert archers amongst the guards. As he'd told Thomas, it would mean them entering the order at the lowest level as lay brothers, but going on John's experience the Templars did look after their own, and if they really did end up going to the Holy Land then it would be as part of something much larger than just a contingent from one country. It was the best he could do, and he was aware that he was being foolish if he thought he could sort every problem out for his friends. Yet the way he had been turned to time and again for help whilst growing up had left its indelible mark on Guy's soul, and he suspected that he would still be trying to sort someone out on the day he died.

It was two weeks later, long before he'd had chance to ride to John's, when the nasty surprise came. He was walking through the outer bailey of the castle when Sir Eric rode in, his favoured men-at-arms clustered around him, and with a smug grin on his face.

"Hello, what's he been up to?" Giles wondered as he and Guy strolled companionably towards the keep from the stables. "What – or should I say who – is that they've got there? We don't have any rebels locally, do we Guy?"

Guy turned on his heels and peered into the press of bodies clustered in the centre of the bailey, and to his horror saw Piers and Thomas Cosham there. As his own shock must have registered on his face he saw Piers and Thomas spot him in return. For a horrible moment he saw Piers start to shout 'traitor!' in his direction before Thomas elbowed him sharply in the gut, driving the air out of him and preventing him being heard. Thomas must have registered Guy's shock, thank God, because Guy then read his lips saying 'it wasn't him, you fool,' before he lost sight of them in the crush once more.

"Are you all right, Guy?" he suddenly realised Giles was saying. "You've gone very pale."

"No, I'm fine," Guy managed to say with more calm than he felt, then realised that he had to come up with some reasonable but unremarkable explanation for his apparent sudden pallor. "By Our Lady, it gave me a funny turn there! Just for a moment I thought it was someone I knew from back when we lived at Alverton when I was a boy. It can't be the same man, of course! I'm remembering him how he was twenty years ago when he used to come after us lads for scrumping apples in his orchards! He'd be a much older man by now, but it's strange how the eye deceives in that momentary glance, isn't it?"

Giles, totally accepting of the story, nodded solemnly. "Oh yes! Once, when I was a boy, I could have sworn I saw my mother come out of my lord of Chester's chamber at night. The next morning I saw how she never even looked his way and realised how silly that was. I must have been half dreaming – I often walked in my sleep as a boy, you see."

"Oh, a dream, no doubt about it," Guy agreed, while thinking that Giles must still be very naive if he hadn't heard about such goings on at court by now. Still, it wasn't his place to destroy Giles' peace of mind, and he had bigger problems to expend his thoughts upon. How on earth was he to get Thomas and Piers out? If he was honest with himself he was far less bothered by Piers' capture than by Thomas', except that if Piers was questioned he was the one who might drop Guy into trouble. Could he pass Thomas off as someone he could vouch for from his time with Sheriff de Braose? Possibly. But would Thomas allow himself to be freed without Piers? Guy had a nasty feeling he wouldn't, not even if it would mean reuniting with Bilan. And where was Bilan? Not here, thank the Lord, and so not in immediate peril – or at least not unless he'd died in some kind of fight when his brothers were taken. That thought gave Guy a nasty jolt. He must try and find some way to talk to them, and soon.

His chance came that night. Eric, full of himself for having apprehended two runaway archers from their lord, was regaling the other knights in the castle with the tale of how he'd come by them. He was making a regular feast of the tale, and since it was after everyone had eaten and they were full of food and beer, most were letting him ramble on, even if they weren't actually taking that much notice. Martin and Walter had already risen and retired to their chambers with backwards glances of distaste at Eric, and the more senior men were entertaining a passing abbot and his retinue in the great hall at which event Guy's presence was not required, so the night was his own. He so rarely sat amongst the coterie of walking foresters, plus the few soldiers, who clustered about Eric and Henry in the forester's hall at night, that his departure wasn't even noted. He hurried out of the ancient works and forced himself to walk with apparent calm down the short, steep motte slope towards the inner bailey and the keep. Now his love of animals served him well, for the one man who passed him close by the great hall assumed he was going to the stables.

"You'll be doing the grooms out of their jobs if you're not careful," the man teased as they passed one another, and Guy smiled at him in return. Then when the shadows had swallowed his outline up from the gaze of anyone outside the great hall, he swung off to his left instead of continuing on through the great inner gate out to the stables. A few more twists and turns brought him to the top of the stairs in the main keep which spiralled down to the dungeons, where he did another quick check to make sure he was alone. He was.

Silent as a ghost he slid down the stairs, keeping to the outer wall in order to see as far ahead round the bends as possible. His luck held, there were no guards immediately outside the prisoners tonight. Not that there was any reason for such close guarding. Anyone trying to break in would have to get through the outer fortifications and into the inner bailey, then find their way into the great keep without being challenged, before they could even start to descend to the dungeons. For the small fry Sheriff Murdac currently had incarcerated no-one in their right minds would risk such a fight, and who would ever think that someone within the castle would try to free a felon?

Hurrying to the grills in the floor, he looked down into the first pit and softly called out "Cosham? Are you there?" He'd thought about using their Christian names and then hurriedly thought the better of it. He didn't know Thomas or Piers' voice well enough to recognise them by sound alone, and there could be several Thomases held there for all he knew. He could end up with more freed prisoners than he could cope with that way.

"This one! Over here!" a voice called quietly but urgently from the grating behind him over the second deep cell.

Guy turned and knelt down to peer into the gloom, then quickly went back and lifted the burning rush torch from off the wall at the bottom of the stairs, holding it out over the grating so that its limited light at least lifted some of the pitch blackness from below him. In its wavering light he saw Thomas' upturned face.

"What happened?" he hissed urgently. "How on earth did you get caught? And where's Bilan?"

"Bilan's with your cousin still, I hope," Thomas told him, immediately calming some of Guy's fears, and he brushed the clammy sweat of worry from his brow with relief. Part of him had been dreading that they'd been taken at John's cottage, and that his cousin might be languishing in a Templar cell somewhere to await his masters' displeasure. "But it was the Templars at Mere who turned us over to the sheriff," Thomas added.

"Mere? What in God's name possessed you to go there?" Guy demanded in exasperation. "I told you to go well over the border into Yorkshire before approaching anyone. Mere's far too close to Lincoln! And the Bishop of Lincoln was sure to have heard of his father's men recruiting in Wales, just as I told you he would. Even his prior would have turned you in! ...Why? ...Why did you go there?"

Thomas looked miserable and jerked his head back towards the darkness of the cell. Guy needed no further telling. It had been Piers. Of course it would have been Piers! Guy had said go one way, and so as soon as his back was turned Piers would have set out in the opposite in sheer pigheaded defiance. Thomas had probably been faced with the choice of leaving Piers to go alone and staying with Bilan, or trusting John and Tuck to watch out for Bilan and go and try to save his pestilent middle brother.

"Can you get us out?" Thomas called up to Guy.

"Not tonight," Guy replied firmly. "Sir Eric's far too full of his deeds. He's been bragging to the whole castle about it. If I get you out it will be blindingly obvious someone inside here let you loose in sympathy, and then it wouldn't take them that long to track you down even if they didn't suspect me. You'd be back in here within the day and then put under heavy guard where even I couldn't get to you. I'm afraid you'll have to put up with it for a day or two. Take heart, though. Sheriff Murdac's due to go off acting as a justice on eyre on a distant circuit tomorrow for the next four weeks at least, so nothing will happen until he gets back – you aren't that much of a priority! We can afford to let the novelty of your capture be overtaken by something else. Trust me, it won't take long for Eric to put his foot in his mouth and offend our constable, Sir Robert, again! He's the one who'll be staying here in charge and he can't stand Eric any more than I can! If I know my master at all he'll find some excuse to send Eric out of here at the first opportunity."

"Then what?"

"Then I'll find a way to get you out and away from here." Guy hoped he sounded surer of that than he felt. "But I'm sorry Thomas, it will have to be the greenwood for you two from now on. You've been marked up here now, as well as in the south-west. Everyone will be on the lookout for two escaped Welsh archers, even over the border in Yorkshire if they send out word that you've fled the king's army and put a price on your heads. And you'll still be taken as runaways if you try to use your own names to rejoin any lord's army up here. You're too easily marked as Welsh to fool many lords as to where you come from, and once that's known there'll always be the danger that someone will put two and two together and work out what you are. I'm sorry, but you'll have to find refuge in Sherwood. I'll be able to guide you away from the parts we regularly patrol, and you should be able to go and see Bilan, if you're cautious, but you won't be able to make a home for yourselves in any town around here. The only place I can think of where you might get a warm welcome and be safe now is Scotland!"

"I thought so," Thomas admitted sourly, with another, more venomous glance over his shoulder at where Piers undoubtedly lay in the darkness. "Will you come and speak to us tomorrow night?"

"I'd better not. Too many visits increases the chances of me being spotted, and if I'm seen then someone's sure to recall my face when questions get asked as to how you got away. When you hear me again, hopefully it will be to tell you we're going, and that could be day or night, so make sure you get some rest while you can. Here..." He dropped a couple of loaves of dog bread down through the grating to Thomas, "that's all I could sneak away, I'm afraid, but it's no doubt better than what you've had so far."

Out of the gloom, blurred shapes shot out and pounced on Thomas, wrestling the food from him in a heartbeat and leaving him with nothing. One of them, Guy was sure, had been Piers – fast enough to appear when he was getting something for free and when the blame was deflected from him. The rest were just anonymous prisoners brought in to await the sheriff's judgement, and Guy felt a sudden burst of shame that he had no idea of their names or why they were there. When they'd grabbed, gone, and begun a scuffle in the corner, Guy whistled softly and the stunned Thomas, who had stayed in the same spot staring at his empty hands, looked up again. Guy held his hand out again and Thomas saw that he'd held back a little bread but also some meat. Without a word Guy dropped both into Thomas' hands, and this time the oldest brother got to keep all of it.

"Watch for me, I won't forget you, I promise," Guy said, and quietly slunk back up out of the dungeons without anyone amongst the garrison being any the wiser.

The next day he made himself busy about the castle, and in the process worked himself into a position where he could look at what the charges there were on the prisoners. He felt his heart sink into his boots when he saw that as far as the sheriff's immediate records were concerned there were only two other prisoners in the cells apart from the brothers. Who were the other poor souls? How long had they been there? He hoped only since the town gaol had got so full in the last year, but a voice inside nagged at him that they might have been there since long before that, and been forgotten about by all except the lowly men who dragged buckets of water and some food to the prisoners on a daily basis.

Since it was raining as though it would never stop outside, he told the sheriff's incurious monastic scribe that he was using the wet day to check up on old records, to make sure he hadn't missed any forestry charges or fines from the outlying villages. The monk just nodded and went on with his copying, and so Guy dug into the old rolls of parchment with a vengeance. Six hours later he had only stopped to briefly go and relieve himself and to get a couple of mugs of small ale and a chunk of bread, yet he had more names than the two shadows he'd seen with Thomas and Piers, so some must be in the other cell.

Three prisoners in the lists were awaiting trial for crimes against the king's venison, having already come before the verderers and charged, but the next of the triennial justices' eyres for the Nottingham circuit wasn't due until the beginning of next year at the earliest. Even so, had they been forgotten about? Were they actually on the scribes' list to come before the justices? He could find no evidence of attempts for their bail being renewed, and one poor sod had been unlucky enough to have been caught only two weeks after the last eyre, so he'd been down there nigh on two years already! Guy felt positively sick at the thought of not seeing daylight in over a year. He knew he might well go mad under the same circumstances, for he'd never liked being cooped up. So what should he do about them?

A fourth man was supposedly a murderer, so he would be hung if the sheriff was reminded of his presence. Yet from the sketchy report from Sir Walkelin who had brought this man in with the men-at-arms, Guy was far from convinced that the man had done anything but be unlucky enough to be in the wrong place at the wrong time. He too had been languishing in one of the pit cells for a good eighteen months. Would anyone in the village even remember the details when they were called in as witnesses? If Guy reminded the sheriff, he could well be doing the man no favour – at least for now he was still alive, but that could rapidly change!

As he crawled into bed, his eyes feeling as though they'd been bathed in sand after squinting at the writing in the abysmal light the dank day had thrown out, he desperately wished he could talk this over with Tuck. However, he had neither the time nor the opportunity to ride over to John's cottage. How long had he got until the sheriff got back? Was there any way he could cause a distraction if they were still here when Murdac returned and brought them up for trial? Could the other prisoners even walk far, given that some had been immured in the tomblike dungeon for so long? No point in creating a cover and then finding they could manage nothing more than a slow crawl instead of a sprint for freedom! The questions rattle round and round in his head, not producing any answers but only more questions for him to fret over.

Nor did the situation improve the following day, despite Sheriff Murdac riding out with a goodly number of the castle's men-at-arms as escort for the abbot going up into Yorkshire, for there were still far too many in and around the place for Guy to even risk a visit to the dungeons to take food again. The next day and the next day came, and still he could find no loophole in the castle's security. With growing horror as a week rolled by and then another, he began to suspect that there wasn't a damned thing he could do for either Thomas or Piers. If they were to avoid the fate of traitors and a hanging it would require an act of divine intervention, and not the hand of a mere mortal like himself.

Oh how that vexed me, Gervase! It brought it home to me how blessed by God, or fate, my last two attempts at rescuing someone had been. Getting someone out of a great royal castle was a world away from de Braose's keep at Abergavenny, and the Templars' defences now looked positively like child's play in comparison! By day I went about my business with my usual efficiency, but by night I found sleep ever harder to come by as the weeks rolled by and Sheriff Murdac's return loomed closer and closer. The dark circles appearing under my eyes would surely have incited comment except for the fact that we were enduring a summer heat-wave and no-one was sleeping well.

Under normal circumstances the castle's thick stone walls ensured that any room not blessed with thick wall hangings would become chilly at night, even in the warmer months. But weeks of baking heat had turned the stones into something of a bread kiln, for they had soaked up so much of the blasting sun that they never fully cooled in the short darkness of the summer nights, and therefore as the days rolled on it got hotter and hotter in the smaller rooms. For once the lesser folk had the best of it, for a few well placed tarpaulins kept the little bit of summer dew off them and they could sleep outside of their wooden homes within the bailey, where there was at least some vestige of a breeze. However, there was nowhere near enough roof space up on the tops of the castle buildings for all of us housed actually inside it, so my nocturnal prowlings were ascribed to trying to find somewhere, <u>anywhere</u>, cool to sleep.

Oh it was wearing! And I prayed, Brother, so I hope you make a note of that! I prayed with a deep and sincere desire for help for someone other than myself, and I confessed every sin I could think I might possibly have committed in those prayers, if not to a priest, then in the desperate hope that my faults might not stand in the way of my prayers being heard. I prayed to Our Lady and to Saint Thomas night after night, but no reply seemed forthcoming, and I began to fear that either there was some divine reason for letting Thomas and Piers swing which I could not see, in my lowly state, or that they were beneath the notice of those divine beings.

...What did you say? ˜Well they were only Welshmen?˜ By Issui Sant, if I could rise more quickly from this bed I would box your sanctimonious ears for that, Gervase! No man is just from here or there, and you can wrinkle your nose in disgust all you like at my being infected with Tuck's morality, for I shall not change that now! Sickbed or not! His Celtic reading of the Christian word was far kinder than yours, and I shall take my chances on the Almighty understanding that when my reckoning comes, even if you cannot! You should hark to Saint David's words a little, as Tuck did, and be the better priest for it, ...Brother!

˜Gwnewch y pethau bychain˜ Dewi Sant said, and since you disdain such a holy man in your false superiority, I shall translate for you, ˜Do the little things˜ it means, and there is much to be said for that! And you should take serious note of the words of that divine bishop of Wales, for in the depths of one night at the end of the third week I belatedly thought that if anyone would have a care for two Welsh archers' fates it would be one of their own saints. And so I began to pray again, but this time to Dewi Sant – and I was respectful to call him by his Welsh name and not the English version of it – and also to the blessed saint's friends, Saint Teilo and Saint Padarn, and to Tuck's favourite saint, Saint Issui.

And did they harken unto my prayers, you ask so sarcastically? Oh yes, Brother Gervase, they harkened all right!

Chapter 11

I had been to see Thomas and Piers once more in those long weeks, blessing the fact that a fellow Welshman of theirs, Ianto, had unwittingly been of great help to me in their cause. This had come about when someone working the great bread oven for the castle kitchens let slip to the kennelmen that I brought in bread of my own recipe to be baked for my dogs. Ever suspicious, Arnold the head kennelman came to find me to demand what I put into my bread if it was so special. At first he clearly thought he would just be confirming what he thought of me, which was that as some high born Norman I could not possibly know anything he did not about the care of hounds. However, by the time I had explained that I put flaxseeds in for the oil to help their coats, and parsley, rosemary and mint for their digestion, and some sage which I had been told was good for stopping their teeth from rotting, he was half way convinced that there might be something in it. So he tentatively asked for all the dog bread to be made to my recipe as a trial.

When four weeks later Sheriff Murdac complimented him on how the hounds coats seemed to be shinier, I found that I had won the unwilling Arnold over. But apart from making my general life easier, it now meant that I daily went into the kennel's general store and helped myself to dog bread for my own two and the stable's ratting terriers, rather than making my own anymore. So having been doing this for over a year now, it was a simple thing to go and help myself to a few more loaves on the night when I stole down to the dungeons once more. Food I was sure my friends would be in dire need of by now! I had chosen this night since the captain of the guard had wed that day, and all the men were down around the castle's brew house outside of the bailey walls – commonly called by the entire garrison The Trip To Jerusalem, since it acted as our own alehouse for such celebrations – getting splendidly drunk.

˜Who else is in there with you?˜ I asked as I dropped the dog bread down to Thomas and Piers, and got a worrying reply, for there were more men down there than even I had anticipated. Oh Brother, what a shock that was! And now they too knew that <u>someone</u> within the castle was sympathetic to their cause, even if not the whole story – and I desperately prayed that in their extremis Thomas and Piers had been circumspect with their comments! What might happen if I could not rescue these other men, and they took their revenge on me later on in front of the sheriff? It was the stuff nightmares are made of and I certainly had plenty of those!

Nottinghamshire
July, the Year of our Lord 1188

"Joseph of Elston?" Guy called softly.

There was a shocked silence then a croaking voice, unused to talking much anymore, called back,

"Aye, I'm here. What's happening? I thought you'd forgotten me."

"The sheriff has!" Guy told him, realising that the man was over in the second cell. "I found your name when I began going through the older records. "Who else is in there? I know of Godric of Headon and Walter of Fiskerton, from the verderer's records."

"They're over here with us," Thomas called back. "And there's another man too, Algar of Costock, who got a broken leg when they threw him in here a few months back. It's nearly healed, but he won't be able to run far!" Guy returned to their grating and looked down into Thomas's upturned face. "We've been making him get up and use it more, but it's hard just going round and round this cramped space and the floor's slippery with ...well you don't want to know!"

Guy felt his gut turn over. So the straw hadn't been changed down there in a while! Possibly not even since the time when the Bishop of Lincoln's woodsmen had been down there! That had been shortly before the last eyre, and since then there'd just have been some new thrown down on top whenever someone thought of it.

"Do the best you can," he said, hoping that the despair he felt at ever getting them out wasn't showing. At least in the gloom they wouldn't be able to see his face too well to see the lie there. "Is that it for those with you in this cell? Just the three of them – Godric, Walter and Algar – and you two?"

"Aye, the five of us," Thomas answered sadly, and Guy could tell that it was only the hope that he would get them out that was keeping Thomas going.

"The five of you. Right." Guy hoped that sounded positive enough, then turned back to the other cell. "So if you're over here, Joseph, who else is in there?"

"I'm Hugh of Barnby," a stronger voice called up. "Another one's an old man. I think he's deaf and a bit blind. There's one young man who's lost his mind completely. He sits in the corner and just rocks."

"And then there's me!" a younger voice called up. "I'm Much, ...Miller White's son!"

Guy reeled back and sat on his heels. No mention of Much was anywhere in the records! "What in God's name are you in there for, lad?" he demanded.

"Don't really know," Much answered, and Guy saw him shrug as he came to look upwards in the faint light. "I was on my way to market in Newark for my pa, 'cause although we live over the border in Yorkshire, Pa had commissioned a new knife from a man in Newark at the last big fair he went to. The next thing I know I'm being smacked over the head and tied up by this big forester on a chestnut horse and got dragged back here."

"Mahel!" Guy spat savagely. Working up by the Yorkshire border it had to be him, especially on a chestnut horse, but there wasn't a thing in the scrolls about Mahel bringing someone in. Was he hoping to win favour with the sheriff by producing Much as some incurable poacher when the eyre came round without anyone else stealing his glory? Mahel had been slipping in favour over the last year or so, and Guy could believe he'd have some cockeyed idea like this.

Sheriff Murdac wouldn't believe this lad would be capable of such things, for he was far too astute for that, but Guy also knew that he wouldn't just let Much go, either. To do that would be undermining one of his foresters too much in public, and however much Murdac might tear Mahel to pieces once in private again, Much would have to suffer some penalty to save face in the court. That could mean having his hand taken off, for once it became clear that Much's family lived in another shire the sheriff could hardly impose a fine in another sheriff's shire. Much's fate was suddenly looking as bleak as the Coshams'!

"What about you, Hugh?"

"I got brought in at the same time as Much," Hugh called back. "Like him, that ugly knight said I was poaching when all I was doing was gathering berries to brew some wine out of! I used to be a soldier. I won't be helpless if we have to fight our way out of here! One thing's for certain, they aren't taking my hand off without a fight!"

That optimism by yet another wrongly imprisoned man only made Guy feel worse, and his prayers to Dewi Sant and Issui Sant became even more fervent that night and the one after. By the third night he'd had virtually no sleep at all, and as the early summer dawn came around Guy was still no surer of what he was going to do.

A thunderstorm was rattling its way across the sky, getting closer and closer, and although it was still far earlier than his normal rising time, Guy went out onto the walls to watch it. As the accompanying deluge arrived he had to retreat inside, and from one of the tower doorways he stood and watched the lightning ripping great jagged lines across the clouds, as the thunder thumped and cracked overhead like so many demonic stonemasons.

"My God, it's a storm and a half!" Giles whispered in his ear, coming from Guy's old room to watch beside him.

Suddenly a huge flash struck the ground not far from the castle, mercifully not amongst the town's wooden buildings, but a tree burst into flames, lighting the countryside despite the cloudburst drenching it. The next flash, though, struck right inside the castle's outer bailey.

"Jesu! It's hit the edge of the stables!" Giles yelped as they both saw a plume of smoke beginning to rise by the light of another close flash, and the two of them dashed back inside calling the alarm. Sleepy men piled out of bed and hurried out to where the thatch over the stables had begun to smoulder and flicker in earnest. Guy pounded down the stairs and tore across the inner bailey and out through the gate, frantic to make sure that Fletch and Spike weren't trapped inside the burning building. Luckily it had hit the very ridge of the stable roof, and it was still possible to get inside as the flames were running along the top of the hayloft and hadn't descended yet. With an old rag drenched in the horse's water trough clamped over his nose and mouth, Guy got through the swirling smoke and opened the door, whereupon Fletch and Spike shot out unharmed. Leaving them to fend for themselves, Guy loosed the horses nearest the door and slapped their rumps to get them moving, then went in to get those tethered deepest within the long wooden building.

Before he'd got the first one out he was aware of other men running in to get the rest of the horses, everyone blessing the fact that at this time of year most of the beasts were out in the fields, and that only those expected to be used early the coming morning were inside for convenience. For a few minutes it was chaos, but then order established itself, at least to the extent of men forming a chain from the water cistern and the well with buckets. The rain was coming down in a steady sheet, drenching the fire fighters, but the thatch was tinder dry through to its heart, and it would take more than just the rain to stop it all from going up in flames, meaning the men hauled buckets with desperate energy. If the stables truly caught then other buildings might follow, for even in a big castle like Nottingham, the wooden buildings were close enough for sparks to easily jump the narrow gaps between. Some bright souls were already hauling buckets up to soak the nearest thatches, and as the smoke lifted for a second Guy saw one of the stable lads astride another other ridge with a blanket, smothering stray sparks.

There, in the half light of the late-summer dawn, Guy suddenly realised that this was the chance he'd prayed for and needed. He looked about him, saw that no-one was taking a blind bit of notice of him now that more senior men were directing things, and walked away with the air of a man with a purpose. Fletch and Spike were fine and had taken themselves off to hide under one of the chicken coops, for neither dog liked thunder, so there was no fear of them following him right now – and that was another bonus since everyone would recognise him even in this gloom if the pair were at his heels. He knew that acting furtively would be the worst thing for drawing attention to himself, so he braced himself mentally and tried to behave as though he had every right to be going towards the dungeons, although the rain was lashing down so heavily it was hard to see even halfway across the bailey.

To his relief all the guards were gone, although a pint of ale on a table in the cellar room beyond that which gave access to the dungeon gratings told of a recent presence. Dice alongside it made him think that maybe there had been a second man too, no doubt down here as one of the cooler places to while away a night rather than having been posted as guards, but would still have given him away if they'd seen him.

Hurrying to the grill over Thomas and Piers' cell, with some effort he withdrew the heavy bolts holding it down. With a heave he managed to lift the massive iron grating up and over on its hinges to lie it on the floor behind.

"Now get down there with them," an icy voice said from behind him.

Guy whirled and saw Eric walking towards him with a superior sneer on his face. Worse, Eric had his sword and the point was aiming at Guy's throat and coming closer.

"Guy? Is that you?" Thomas' voice called up.

"Ah! One of your peasant friends! How endearing," Eric sniggered, still advancing on Guy so that he was being forced towards the gaping drop into blackness.

"Guy?" Thomas sounded more worried now.

"It's all right," Guy called back, despite feeling anything but right. He had no sword or weapon of any kind, and his drenched linen undershirt wouldn't stop a blade half as sharp as a sword. He'd nothing but his wits with which to defend himself. He began to move sideways, crabbing around the edge of the drop.

"No you don't!" Eric snapped, moving faster to try to get again to a point where he could drive Guy directly backwards once more.

However, Guy was now at the other side of the rim from where the grating lay folded back. Spinning on his heels he turned and leapt. He'd had no illusions of making a full leap across the wide hole from a standstill, but he'd been pretty sure that he could reach the grating and he did. As he fell and hit the edge with his hips he threw his arms out and caught hold of the stout iron grilling, scrabbling with his feet and, half climbing half pulling himself out, rolled quickly away from the drop but stayed down. Eric gave a savage snarl and jumped two steps forward then realised that he needed to get to the opposite side and swung around, stumbling in his haste. In the process he had become unbalanced giving Guy the chance he'd sought. Instead of getting to his feet he kicked out with his long legs, entwining them around Eric's as he came at him, then twisted into another roll even as he hung onto the grating.

Guy was prepared for what happened next, Eric wasn't. In a tangle of flailing limbs he wobbled and staggered, then lost his balance and fell. Already disentangled, Guy pounced on him, and shouting, " 'Ware below!" heaved Eric over the edge. The knight went down in a clatter and was silent. Guy had no time to think about consequences. He ran to the wall and hauled the ladder over which was there for the purpose of getting prisoners out for the courts.

"Quick! Hurry, Thomas!" he called, steadying the ladder.

The ladder began to vibrate with a man's weight and then Thomas came into view.

"We have to take the others!" he gasped.

"I know," Guy said, halting any further argument. "And not just from your cell either. There are wrongly accused men in the other cell too!"

As Thomas held the ladder for his brother, Guy hurried to the other cell.

"Hugh? Are you there?"

"Yes, and ready!" the steady voice called back, and eager hands reached out for the second ladder Guy dragged over.

Guy turned back to see Thomas, who was now standing behind him, with a worried frown on his face.

"Piers says that knight is dead. He broke his neck on the way down."

"Strip him!" Guy said with more authority than he felt. "Piers, can you go and make a mess of his face and hack his hair about, like he was a poor man who'd just took a knife to it?"

For the first time Piers smiled at Guy, and without a word disappeared down the ladder. There came the sounds of ripping and thumping, but in short order Piers was back, carrying a fine dagger in his belt and Eric's sword. Guy held his hand out for it but Piers was reluctant to hand it over.

"We have to get out through the bailey," Guy said firmly, "And one look at a supposed peasant carrying a sword will give the whole game away. You can have it afterwards, Piers, but not until we're out of sight."

Thomas nodded firmly and gave Piers a steely glare. This time Piers had enough sense to see that Guy was right, he couldn't be the one seen with a fine sword like Eric's and he shrugged and handed it over without a word.

The next struggle was to get Algar out, for his broken leg wasn't up to negotiating the ladder alone, but between them Thomas and Piers got him up to where Guy and Hugh were keeping guard. Within minutes they had Algar up on the dungeon floor and had fashioned a crutch for him out of an old broom someone had left mouldering in a corner, although they might have to carry him for speed.

It felt like the emptying of the cells had already taken hours, yet it was still only minutes since Guy had come down and fought with Eric. When he and Thomas lowered the gratings back in place and put the bolts back, beside the two of them and Piers in the lowest hall of the keep were the accused poacher, Joseph, and his cell mates Hugh and Much; and from Piers and Thomas' cell they also had Algar and Walter, all men accused by the verderers and awaiting trial. Godric had refused to join them, repeatedly telling them all that it was a trap and that they'd be caught before they got far, and how it would be the worse for them when the sheriff found out. There'd been no reasoning with him, and he'd actually fought against them when they'd tried to push him to the ladder.

So they'd left him behind along with the two whom they couldn't take from the second cell – the old man and the poor mad lad whom Guy had now worked out was the supposed murderer. Whether he would confess or not was doubtful, but since he couldn't seem to recall one day from another the escapees felt they had little to fear from him, or the senile old man who remained with him. However Piers had punched Godric hard on the jaw, cracking it, ensuring that he wouldn't be speaking clearly for many days – they weren't taking any more chances than necessary. At least it didn't look like they'd completely emptied the dungeons, so maybe their escape would go unnoticed for a while.

Guy hurriedly led them out of the dungeon and out into the yard.

"Stay together and follow me!" he hissed. "Try to look as though you know what you're doing! We're going to head for the fire."

The first hurdle was going to be getting through the inner gate out to the bailey, but that stood open and forgotten, for which Guy offered up heartfelt thanks. He strode out into the outer bailey and sodden chaos, and was gratified to see that all of the men-at-arms and forester men were as black and dishevelled from the smoke, ash and rain as any of the lesser men – there was no telling who was who! The thunder storm was also aiding and abetting them by doing the usual summer storm trick when there was little wind, of just rattling round and round the Trent valley going nowhere fast. The rain was still coming down so hard it was bouncing off the cobbled walkways, with plenty more in the thick clouds before it rained itself out, and the soot and ash was instantly turning to a charcoal-like mush which stuck to everything and everyone. The prisoners in their state were hardly going to stand out except for being too clean! And with the horses shitting everywhere in fright, and men slipping in it in their haste, the stench of the dungeon would be less noticed as well.

Therefore Guy swiftly got them to smear more of the black, sooty muck over them to blend in. Thomas now took it upon himself to bring up the rear of their file while Algar, helped by a strong supporting arm around him from Walter plus the crutch, practically stood on Guy's heels they were so close. Piers came in the middle, constantly scanning around him for any signs of danger, and between the two Cosham brothers Hugh was chivvying the frightened and worried Much and Joseph along.

Guy took them around the back of the stables and then deep into the shadows of the high bailey wall.

"We're close to the main gate now," he told them softly. "I'm just going to check if it's open yet. We wouldn't normally unbar it this early, but Sir Robert will want the soaked straw dragged out as quickly as possible, and fresh put down for his horse if for no-one else's! He's due to ride out to Linby today and he's not fond of sitting on a wet horse before he's even got wet himself!"

He was right, the main gates stood open and unattended for once. Hurrying back, Guy left Piers guarding the others while he took Thomas and Hugh to claim one of the handcarts. Wheeling it back to by the stable, they shoved Joseph and Algar in, then covered them with water-soaked hay from drenched feeding nets. With Walter and Piers joining them in pulling the cart they made swift progress out through the gate, no-one looking twice at four men pulling one cart because Guy had seized the biggest he could find. The very reason it wasn't in use already was because it was far larger than most and meant for a pony to pull, and consequently very heavy even unladen. He'd given Much the pitchfork which had been with the hay, partly to make him fit in, but also because he knew Much was unlikely to start a fight with it. Piers might well try and stab the first guard they passed if he had it!

They only had to pause beside the expanding pile of stable detritus for a moment for another cart to go back inside. Then they hurried around behind the great heap and deposited the cart. Free of the cart, they continued following Guy on foot around the castle walls until they came to the road running off towards Lenton Priory, Walter and Hugh carrying Algar slung between them on a sodden hay net for speed. As soon as they were under the eaves of the park woodland, Guy halted. The incurious fallow deer were taking no notice of them, and for once Guy blessed their tameness, for red deer would have been skittering to get away from them and signalling their presence to anyone still up on the castle walls, even if in this weather they themselves weren't so visible.

"I have to go back before I'm missed! Carry on until the trees draw in on the road." He thrust a small handful of coins at Hugh. "These should buy you some food in Ilkeston! Then walk north. You should come to a large clearing where there must have been another big lightning strike years ago. Although there are oaks all around it, the clearing only has young birches growing in it, but in the centre is the trunk of an old oak. You can't mistake it because it got so badly hit it's no longer round but like a big old gravestone, and there's a hole going through it like a church window. Wait by there for me, but back under the trees. I will come, but it'll be much later today or maybe tomorrow. Then I'll guide you part of the way into the forest and show you where to stay clear of."

"God bless you!" Joseph whispered in his cracked voice. "I never thought to see daylight again."

"Hurry, Guy," Thomas interrupted. "We can't have you getting caught after all this. Don't worry about us, we'll be fine now."

And so the escapees made their way off into the forest and Guy went back to the castle, making it back into the outer bailey without anyone ever noticing that he'd been away. He was even commended when Robert of Crockston saw Guy covered in soot and filthy, and assumed he'd been in the thick of the fire and for saving his horses – which was all true, but rattled Guy's nerves something shocking. Then someone said that Giles and Guy had raised the alarm in the first place and he found himself even further in the constable's good books. A stark contrast was the way that no-one seemed remotely aware that Eric wasn't around during the following day. Surely, Guy thought, someone will eventually ask where he was during the fire? So that, for all that Guy had known that the arrogant older knight was pretty useless, it was still highly unnerving to have it proven so forcibly and on such a day! Midday came and went and still no-one said anything about Eric, and by the time everyone fell into their beds on a thankfully altogether cooler night, Guy could only assume that the day had been so abnormal that nothing had been noticed in the chaos.

The following morning Guy was summoned to Alan of Leek and went with a pounding heart, only to be told that he was to go out and find more bedding for the horses. The saints be praised, Alan told Guy, only the last of the old season's bedding had gone up in flames rather than much of the fodder. Much of the new season's crop of hay and straw was blessedly still out in farmers' barns awaiting transport into the castle, for there was only so much which could be kept in the confined space within the walls at any given time. Sir Robert had therefore let it be known that Guy's reward for helping raise the alarm was the easy task for the day of going and arranging for farmers to bring some of the already requisitioned harvest into the castle. Had he known what else Guy intended to do with the day, Guy felt sure he wouldn't have been half so generous! Therefore Guy rode out on a fresh morning of light breezes and fluffy clouds to the farms he had already decided upon, then hurried off on his own mission.

As promised, the others were waiting at the clearing, although well hidden in the lush growth of bushes and bracken around the clearing. Fletch and Spike instantly spotted them, though, making Guy realise that if he was ever to meet someone covertly with a danger of being observed, then the dogs would have to be left behind, even if it was an occasion when he would normally have taken them and therefore would have to concoct some excuse for them not being there. Sadly they were just too good at pointing towards that which human eyes might otherwise miss. On this occasion, however, it mercifully made no difference and Guy was able to meet the men and take his time discussing their options.

Walter appeared to be a steady man in his forties – although Guy was to revise that opinion of him later on – while Hugh was every bit the calm former soldier he had seemed during the escape. With these two to support Thomas, Guy held out the hope that this time Piers might not so easily lead him into trouble, and it was clear that these four would be able to survive in the forest without much trouble. Algar too, would survive in the forest once his leg had improved, for the actual break was well on the way to being fully mended and it was the way the muscles had wasted with the prolonged cramped conditions which inhibited him the most now. Both he and Walter declared that they would rather take their chances in the forest than risk being taken in another sweep of the villages by men as unjust as Mahel and Henry, even if the dreaded Eric was gone.

"If I die it will at least be as a free man!" Algar announced, and got many nods of the head in agreement with that sentiment.

However, Much and Joseph were a different kettle of fish. Poor Joseph's health was the biggest worry, for his long imprisonment, in dreadful conditions and with little food, had left him frail beyond his years. Much, on the other hand, being a lad not yet out of his teens had no woodsman skills to aid his survival, even with the others. Given that he had been taken only recently, though, there seemed to be no good reason why he couldn't be returned to his family as quickly as possible. They were millers at Norton near Campsall and tenants of the Templars, as it transpired, which was excellent news since not only did they come under the jurisdiction of a totally different sheriff, but had the kind of landlords who were well able to stand their ground and protect their tenants against the most aggressive king's officer. This meant that once home Much would be as safe as any low born freeman could ever be, and Guy expressed the hope that the White family might even take Joseph in out of gratitude for their son's return. Guy himself couldn't risk going that far afield even if he could have got the time away from the castle. Campsall was far too closely associated with the Templars at Temple Hirst, Faxfleet and the Lincolnshire preceptory of Willoughton, and therefore to the whole episode with Allan and John, for comfort.

Instead he sent them off towards Tuck and John, trusting Hugh with a quickly scribed letter to Tuck and John asking Tuck to take

Much and Joseph on northwards, to allow the others to make their way back into northern Sherwood where the forest was densest and least populated. He didn't say as much then, but Guy felt that Walter and Algar at least might be able to start a new life somewhere else in a year or so's time, even if Thomas and Piers would always be marked as archers and have to be looking over their shoulders. Few sheriffs sent word of the lesser felons out to other shires, Guy told the older two men, hoping that they would take the hint and gradually make their way north to one side or the other of the Pennines, for by Walter's own admission, his wife had been dead for several years and he had no children in Nottinghamshire left to worry about.

Algar said little of any family, and Guy could only assume that he was in much the same position. Only Hugh expressed a longing to at least say goodbye to the lass he'd hoped to marry, and Guy had faith in him not doing that at any point when it might draw the others into danger. So on a day when the forest steamed while at the same time drenching them with secondary showers coming down from the leafy canopy, Guy believed that the only time he might see these men again might be in the distance when he was out working, and then not in any official capacity.

In the following weeks, Guy often found himself up on the battlements looking north out over Sherwood straining his eyes, as if he might see where the seven might have got to. He still didn't trust Piers, and his nightmares were of going out into the forest one day with other foresters and coming upon them cutting up a deer carcass, or even worse catching them in the act of bringing a deer down. Yet no-one mentioned seeing any new outlaws in the forest, nor did anyone speak up about the prisoners in the castle's dungeons being fewer than there had been.

There was a heart-stopping moment when Sheriff Murdac returned and declared that the eyre would be coming before the year was out. However, Guy now realised something which had not been brought home to him before – only rarely did sheriffs sit as justices in their own counties! Therefore once the prisoners had been brought up from the town gaol or the castle's dungeons, that was the end of Sheriff Murdac's dealings with them until it came to the actual execution of the sentences. Therefore if men weren't in the scrolls of records sent to the coming justices in the first place – as Much, at least, wouldn't be – then no-one was going to be any the wiser if some were missing.

It confirm to Guy just how little attention was paid to the poor, for no-one commented that there were fewer than expected dragged into the light of day, and he had the unpleasant thought that maybe justices were used to the poor expiring in the dreadful conditions of the castle's dungeons even if they didn't in the town gaol. However, it did mean that the senile old man and the lunatic youth were brought out, and Murdac was sufficiently Christian a man to see that they could not stand trial, instead sending them off to the care of a nearby monastic hospital. The sheriff was less than pleased with Sir Henry for bringing the old man in since it was obvious to the meanest intellect that the poor old fellow could hardly walk, much less go off poaching, and lacking his fellow bully Eric for support Henry soon found himself living a very isolated life indeed, since no-one else wanted to attract Sir Ralph's ire.

The dreaded Godric did as Guy had feared and told the whole story of the rescue for all to hear, the only blessing being that he couldn't name the mystery rescuer. For that Guy offered up many prayers of thanks, and also for the fact that the justices having seen two prisoners already who were as mad as March hares, then assumed that Godric was nearly as addled in his wits. Who on earth would break mere peasants out of a stronghold like Nottingham castle, men laughed. Who would risk that for so little? Who indeed, Guy agreed, laughing with them although it verged on the edge of hysteria at his relief.

Without Sir Eric there to tell his version of events the two missing archers were regarded as something of a mystery, for the men-at-arms who had been with him had only come upon him trying to drag them off when they'd heard him calling for their aid. Clearly the ever ambitious Eric had said nothing about the Templars being the ones who had handed Thomas and Piers over to him. He'd no doubt spun some tale about a fight where he'd captured them by his great prowess, which some of the men-at-arms hinted at, but to Guy's intense relief the Templars were never mentioned, let alone sought as witnesses. Now none could say for truth where the men had come from, or where they might have been bound for.

Some said that the pair claimed they had been going on pilgrimage, and given that by now Sir Eric had been missed, it was mooted whether he had changed his ever fickle mind and taken them off on crusade. Someone else then said that Sir Eric had failed to come up with the required Saladin Tithe for his manors, and all knew that the one way out of paying that tax was to take the Cross yourself. Typical of Eric, many sniffed, if he'd gone to save the Holy Land to skip his debts rather than out of any Christian sentiment, and even Ralph Murdac didn't argue with that!

Yet the biggest surprise for Guy was the discovery of Eric's mouldering corpse. Not one person who saw the body recognised him for who he was. Expecting to see a prisoner, that was what they saw and not the remains of a knight. Even his larger stature was re-attributed to him being one of the missing archers. Guy was flabbergasted. Granted, Eric was in something of a state when they pulled him out, but the dungeons were cold even in summer and he wasn't as far gone as he would have been in a normal grave, and Guy for one could have said who it was in an instant. It was a salutary lesson to him, that people would see what they expected to see.

Time moved on, autumn came and went without any of Guy's fears materialising, and gradually he relaxed, believing all was settled once more. It wasn't a happy autumn because of the way that even the foresters were dragged into the collection of the last remaining moneys owed for the Saladin Tithe, but aside from that Guy was gradually able to breathe a bit more easily and he found himself almost looking forward to the coming feast at the turn of the year. Yet the prospect of the coming Christmas festivities was suddenly and unexpectedly marred for Guy from a different quarter by the sudden appearance of Tuck with an urgent message. John was being moved by his Templar masters!

"I feel so guilty!" Tuck fumed to Guy. "Some unchristian soul told them that he had a helper and the Templars have assumed it must be Allan! *Dewi Sant*, I could have understood it while Bilan was still with John – at least he's closer to Allan's age than me – but Bilan went off with his brothers as soon as they came to fetch him and that was months ago. There's not been anyone else who could remotely be mistaken for Allan anywhere near the place! No matter that John and his close neighbours have all sworn that I was a travelling monk and nothing at all like Allan in any respect!"

"So what's to happen to him?" Guy asked anxiously. They were meeting in the *Trip To Jerusalem* brew-house beneath the castle's southern wall, which was mostly the haunt of the castle soldiers, and where Guy's appearance mixed in with those casual visitors to the castle wouldn't be likely to cause comment. Huddled on a couple of upturned half-barrels in a dark corner at the back of the cavern-room, they were even further out of sight than the room's other occupants, most of whom were huddled around a blazing brazier and fending off the winter chill with warmed porter. "Sweet Jesu, John's not to be cast out, is he?"

"Not cast out, praise the Lord!" Tuck replied with feeling. "No, he's not been put out on the road to beg. It's not good, but he's to go to a small farm way over at Hathersage to work as shepherd there."

"Hathersage? Oh that's not so bad then!" Guy sighed with relief. "You know it?"

"It's actually now part of my regular patrol – when the weather allows, unlike now!" A heavy fall of snow had come in during mid-December, and although no more had fallen closer to the festive-tide it had remained cold enough for the snow to still be lying thick on the ground. In towns like Nottingham it had soon turned to muddy slush with the passage of so many feet and carts, but out in the higher countryside it was a different matter. Despite it being hunting season, Guy knew few would set foot out into the wilds of the forest, or the uplands of the Peaks as they rose ever higher towards the Pennines.

"Do you know? I think John might actually be safer there than where he is now," Guy mused after taking a swig of his beer in relief. "The old knight at High Peak Castle rules with a rod of iron but is a law unto himself, and he certainly wouldn't bother reporting something as minor as a new shepherd to the sheriff. It's off the beaten track, despite its tactical importance, and the main thing they have up there is the lead mines. Sir Ivo of ...oh, I can't remember where in Normandy, who's the constable up there, doesn't have a reputation for astuteness, so John should be fine – although that could change if ever the king wants more of a hawk up at High Peak. I know the folk of Hathersage. I've warned them against some of my more unscrupulous fellow foresters in the past, and I've only taken what I absolutely had to in the way of taxes.

"Fredegis apparently stripped them bare when he dealt with the area – according to Osmaer – but I could never bring myself to do that. If I tell them who John is then I don't think there'll be any trouble – especially if they realise that I haven't deliberately sought this messy situation to presume on their kindness. They'd probably be glad to see you too, Tuck! It's only a small hamlet, well on the way to nowhere much, and they don't get much attention from the local priests."

The only major ecclesiastical landholders in Derbyshire were the Abbey of Burton – a decent enough sized place, but certainly not the most influential of institutions – and the Bishop of Chester, who was only too happy to delegate the collection of his tithes to officers more local to the scattered churches. Consequently, in some of the more remote places the Church's grip on its flock was less than total. By contrast, in Nottinghamshire there were four great church landowners and all of them of some standing.

As Guy knew only too well, the Bishop of Lincoln had lands in and around Newark, while the Archbishop of York had land around Southwell and several other manors, like Cropwell Bishop. As if that wasn't enough fingers in the pie, both the Bishop of Bayeux and the massive Peterborough Abbey had claim to many manors in Nottinghamshire too. All of which meant that there was enough vested interest in protecting the Church in the shire that the minor churches and chapels were also kept a keen eye on. The Church's right to claim payment for the burial of villagers, for instance, was a constant source of irritation to the poorer folk. Bad enough that they had to haul the corpse very often for miles to get to the nearest graveyard, instead of having a burial at their local chapel. But to have to then pay for their loved ones to be found a corner of hallowed ground, and usually at the priest's sufferance and disdain, only rubbed salt into the wounds of the bereaved.

Therefore what Guy had not needed to say out loud to Tuck was that in such far-off hamlets, where even their secular lords often had no idea of who had been born or died if they weren't the actual householders, there would most likely be unofficial burials. Some were only temporary, while others might be more permanent if necessity forced the villagers' hands. Often it wasn't a matter of lack of faith, but rather of practicality. When a distant hamlet might be cut off in winter for weeks on end it wasn't possible to leave a corpse mouldering until the weather allowed transportation down to the churchyard, and its frozen earth could be hacked apart for a grave. The villagers would be only too glad of Tuck's presence to say a mass over any who had died in this latest winter, both to save their souls and to ensure that the departed spirit lay quiet in its temporary quarters.

Tuck, like Guy, also knew of instances when more than one body had been put into a grave. The villagers might be doing the right thing by their late relatives, but if it was possible to make only one payment and get more than one soul secured a hallowed grave, then they would do it. Frail old folks seen off by winter chills didn't weigh much newly dead. A few months later and they'd weigh even less! And who would notice the weight of a babe or young child added into the woollen winding sheet as long as the shape looked right? When a corpse was that ripe, few priests wanted to get too close!

"A few masses would no doubt smooth John's entry into their community," he said obliquely with a smile.

"Exactly!" Guy smiled back. "Phew! We've been lucky again! There are many places I would have felt unable to leave John in. Places where the people are just too beaten down and cowed. Where they'd tell the first official who came their way that John had a regular visitor who was a sheriff's man." He grimaced and shook his head in despair. "Not that John would be doing anything wrong. But they'd just assume that any visit by a sheriff's man or forester must mean trouble! You would've had to go back to Gisborne – both of you! Although the Almighty only knows how we would've worked that out with Ianto and Maelgwn. If there wasn't enough to keep you alone going alongside them, it would be even worse with a fourth man in his prime about the place. You'd have been walking the walls like spiders within a month! ...Both of you!"

Tuck grimaced back. "I know!" Then he grinned. "But that won't happen for a while yet, at least. One day maybe, but not now!"

"When does he go?"

"Now! He's just packing his stuff up. He'll stagger off down the road with all his goods on his back to paint the right picture for all to see. I'm taking the horses back to meet him where the old Roman roads cross just north of Lincoln. Then we'll head west and aim to get to John's new cottage for the New Year. We decided that he must be seen to be alone in his leaving, just in case the Templars send someone to make sure he goes without trouble! It would be even worse if they came and then saw two of us leaving. It would confirm John is the liar his masters already think he is."

Guy snorted in disgust. "Not very trusting for men who supposedly live by such high moral codes!"

Tuck shrugged. "I think it's because they set themselves such high standards to live by. And when it comes to abstinence they put most monasteries to shame! As near as we can work it out, they think John has constantly been less than truthful with them, and in their eyes that's no different to out-and-out lying with the worst of intentions. They don't see it as being cruel at all. To them they're protecting their honest tenants from the company of a morally dubious person. Hence them sending him off to what they see as the wilds of Derbyshire away from any towns."

"And because – as far as they're aware – John is of very lowly birth, they'll think he's more prone to falling by the wayside!" Guy sniffed in disgust. "Do you know, Tuck, I never thought twice about how the ordinary people were treated back at home at Alverton while I lived there. But now, having been out amongst them, I look back now and think that it wasn't so very different there either. One time, a wheel of cheese went missing from the dairy, and without so much as a blink of the eye, old fitz Waryn put the dairymaid out onto the road. It had to be her in his eyes. No questions. No wondering who might have had *reason* to take it. Or even if it might just have been the band of mercenaries who'd passed through only a day or so previously going north on the Foss Way."

He shook his head wearily. "Wealthy lords and ladies, and many of them of not so very high a degree, all looking down their noses at the great mass of ordinary English folk. I'm ashamed of my heritage at times like this, Tuck, I really am! They don't see any further than the cut of a man's coat! Do you ever normally see a peasant of John's stature? No! If he'd had to eat a peasant's diet while he was growing up, I bet he wouldn't have been anything like the size he is! We weren't rich by any means, but old fitz Waryn had the hunting rights to neighbouring woodlands and he used those rights to put plenty of meat on our table. *And* we had a series of small fishponds. Nothing on the size of some of the really big manors or monasteries, but enough that we could have fish regularly too. And would they look on John differently if they knew that he came of noble parents, albeit illegitimately?"

He shook his head in disgust and got up and drained his mug. "I must be getting back. I have to ride out as the sheriff's messenger again tomorrow morning."

"Anywhere interesting?"

Guy suddenly grinned as he made the connection. "Yes, actually! I'm being entrusted to go and take the bequest of an old guildsman to the Bishop of Lincoln on account of having dealt with them over there before! This bloody weather means we're hardly hunting much, although no doubt come the thaw we'll have plenty of cases of poaching to investigate, because someone's bound to have got desperate for something to keep their family going in this bitter cold. And I can be spared from the cutting of foliage for those stupid fallow deer! God's wounds, Tuck, but they're nearly as useless as those damned peacocks the king foisted onto us as the latest fashion last year! Pretty to look at but bugger all use except in the pot! And Jesu, don't they make a racket with their screeching! Bloody things!"

Tuck guffawed at Guy's mimicking of a strutting peacock, but glad that at least Guy could laugh at something. Sometimes he worried over what prolonged living as a forester was doing to his younger friend. "Then we can ride in company!" he declared cheerfully, determined to put a brighter slant on things for Guy, and was rewarded by a sudden, real smile.

"Yes we can! Oh that makes me feel even better! I can see John for myself and tell him about the folk at Hathersage too. ...I'll meet you a mile beyond the north gate, then!"

Come the morning, Guy and Tuck had a companionable ride out to meet John, and while Guy went to the bishop's residence, the other two sorted out John's packs in the small inn where Guy had purchased rooms for them. In the early morning they left Lincoln, John now taking one horse with all his baggage decked about it, while Tuck rode the other with some more of John's belongings behind him.

"God bless you, Guy!" John said from the heart as he hugged Guy farewell. "I don't want to think what the last year or so would've been like if you hadn't been here! I certainly couldn't have got Allan out of that mess with the Templars, and you've brought me a friend in Tuck who's worth is beyond measure. And I'm going to be able to ride to my new job and get there on time instead of arriving late and being in bad odour with my new master before I even start. I'd have been walking all the way without these horses you bought us."

"Who is your new master?" Guy asked. "I'm sorry, I thought from what Tuck said that you were just going to some farm where the Templars had heard there was a shepherd wanting."

"Oh it is," John confirmed. "But that in turn belongs to some bigger manor, and they haven't deigned to tell me what that is! I've got a letter for whoever it is, but it's sealed tight and I'm supposed to just hand it to the farmer when I get there."

Guy examined the rolled parchment which John fished out from inside his heavy sheepskin tunic where he'd put it for safe keeping. "Damnation! It's been properly done! Bloody Templars! They would! Most of the sealed rolls which come out of the castle I could guarantee to open and seal back up without anyone ever knowing they'd been tampered with. Well just be careful, John. It might simply be a wealthier farmer, but it could be the sheriff's constable at High Peak, and that's a different matter!

"Ivo of Quettehou, that's his name I remember, Tuck! He's a true Norman and prone to stand on his dignity. Hates it here in England, so why he stays is a mystery to me, but it means he can't stand the local people! Not a problem for me as a recognised officer of the sheriff, although I've not personally had much to do with him, but it means he's anything but easy going as a liege lord. And he's at least middle-aged. So sooner rather than later you could have a new lord. It's not a castle the king will put a major baron in, because it's a good barrier between his great men on the east and those on the west. He might put a youngish man in who wants to prove himself, though. Someone who's a real hawk, or even some hardened forester who's proven himself somewhere else already. And that could make your lives more complicated than if you had some established lordly family, who just went through the motions of holding the place and left the work to a bailiff."

"Well at least the villagers won't be turned against me, thanks to you," John said gratefully, "and they're the folk I'll be rubbing shoulders with day to day."

Guy smiled affectionately at his cousin. "And you know I'd do more if I could. Don't forget, Gisborne is still an option if you need it. Now be on your way! And be careful going through Sherwood! There have been rumours that some outlaws have set up a camp near to the old Norsemen's meeting place north of Edwinstowe. You don't look rich enough to be worth robbing, and Tuck's tonsure and garb might help, but I've no idea how big this gang is or how dangerous they might be. Hurry on and try to get to Ollerton before the light goes. They've got a simple inn there where you can stay – I doubt they'll have many other travellers at this time of year, so you should have no trouble getting a room, even though it's a tiny place as inns go. That will mean you can go on through the heart of Sherwood in daylight. You should make Chesterfield by nightfall even if you aren't out of the royal woods by far!"

"That makes a difference?" John wondered.

Guy nodded sagely. "Unfortunately yes, it does. The folk of the royal forests are more sorely put upon than those outside them. You've been lucky so far, John. You haven't had to live with the burden of forest laws yet, being the other side of the Trent. But when you get to Hathersage you'll be in another royal forest – that of High Peak – and one which also comes under Nottingham's jurisdiction! I shall do my best to make sure I'm the one who comes your way, but be careful! Some of my fellow knights might be legitimate by birth but are bastards by their own design! High Peak isn't one of the king's favourite hunting forests, thank Saint Thomas! We're a bit too far from London for him to be suddenly appearing in our midst, although we do get our orders to supply venison for the court if there's a major feast going on. But at least you won't have the king in person to worry about. Just watch your step, follow the lead of the other villagers, and you should be all right.

"But you've got to travel through Sherwood to get there, and the laws I have to help enforce, however unwillingly, mean that there are a lot of dissatisfied and desperate people out there – especially after this year and that bloody extra tithe! Some of them actually live out in the forest, keeping to the thick woodland and hiding from us – and there's a surprising amount of dense woodland in some places to hide folks in. Others are villagers who take what they can on the side just to help make what they have go a bit further. They aren't dangerous, but they are hard pressed and might grasp at a chance they see as falling into their hands by good fortune. So don't hand yourselves to them on a platter by being out at night, or taking something you think is a short cut. We keep the trees along the edges of the main roads cut back so that robbers don't have any cover close to the track, and your fellow shepherds driving sheep to markets keep those roadside grass verges well cropped too. So stay on them where you can see all around you. The opportunist thieves won't risk attacking you on the main highway when there's so little to gain, and you aren't the stuff the real rogues will go for unless you make it easy for them. Now go! I'm due at Hathersage at the beginning of February, so I'll see you then!"

And that, dear Brother, is how my cousin John came to be associated with Hathersage – a village he had never even clapped eyes on until he was a grown man of twenty-nine. He was sent there by his Templar masters! He was not born there, and he certainly did not foist himself upon those folk with any intent of bringing ill-repute upon them. Little John of Hathersage's heritage cannot be so easily traced back in that village for the blindingly simple reason that he never did have any family there. He, like the others who would soon join with Robin Hood fell into his role more by accident than by design, as so often happens in real life. How many others whom you hear of as great heroes seem to stumble into their allotted places by quirks of Fate? ...Oh very well, Brother, by the unseen movement of the Almighty's hands, if you must! Yet if you say you perceive God's hand in this, then you also have to admit to the possibility that we were not so evil as you have hitherto thought. ...Aaah! Caught in your own net, Brother! You cannot have it both ways! We cannot be guided by the Devil one moment and then be the instrument of Our Lord

the next, for no-one vacillates that fast, or far, back and forth unless he be mad – and you surely do not think Robin Hood and his men a bunch of wandering fools and lunatics? No, I thought not!

Yet before we recommence our tale in full I will throw you a morsel to soothe your pique at being caught out, so that you shall listen all the better to the next unfolding of our tale. I now came to the discovery that I had a deep love for the great forest of Sherwood. Until I had come back to it I had never thought of Nottinghamshire as flat, but in comparison to southern Herefordshire, or the land around Clun, it felt strangely lacking in interesting features. I had to go into Derbyshire to find the truly wild and rocky countryside I had come to love in the west, and I willingly went that way whenever I could. But the heart of the old forest pulled at me in a different way. There was something profoundly soulful in the deep quiet amongst the great old oaks in the groves far from the hamlets and homesteads. No axe coppiced or pollarded these venerable giants, and most folk only glimpsed them at a distance through the lesser trees lining those roads which passed beneath Sherwood's boughs.

I, on the other hand, enjoyed getting off the roads. My horse's hooves would make little noise on the bouncy, soft leaf litter which lay centuries deep across the forest floor. The only sounds which often accompanied my rides through it would be the twitter of birds, a chattering squirrel, the call of a stag, or the grunting and rooting of wild boars. I was the only one of the knightly foresters who did not find the intense solitude disquieting, yet to me the massive oaks almost had personalities of their own. Every one was different, and many a time I thought I could see a face in the knots and twists of the gnarled trunks, and I could see how some men might find something fearfully pagan in them, but for me they were rather a profession of faith. Already hundreds of years old by the time I saw them, I would often muse on the fact that some of them might have been young saplings when the word of God was brought to these shores.

...Oh heavens, Gervase! If you gasp any harder you will make yourself faint! What is wrong in seeing the hand of God in the strength and permanence of a mighty tree? And do not forget that it was upon a tree of the forest made into a cross that Our Lord chose to perform the greatest miracle of all! Should I ever rise from this sick bed, I have a mind to take you out into the great forest and show you just what you are missing!

Ah, that has silenced you! But in the interests of getting along with my tale, I shall simply tell you for now that I took every opportunity to explore the depths of the forest when out on my own, or just with dear Fletch and Spike. For the present I was mainly riding out to where the local foresters lived and worked to inspect the woodland, and to check for any signs of poaching or harvesting. Soon I could have matched the more experienced and local foot foresters for spotting when a major tree had gone missing, for a huntsman's talents can be put to many uses, Brother! That might sound simple to you, but when you get deep into such woodland quite often you cannot see beyond a few yards, for thick scrub and bracken fill the lower levels where the great branches do not hang so low. And in winter the bolls of the great trees themselves still block your *view after a few yards, for they do not grow in neat lines but in wondrous disorder.*

Half the time it was by sound that I would pick up on something amiss first, and only afterwards find evidence or actually see what it was I had been tracking. So in my quest to find grazing damage, or in following a report of a wounded deer, I frequently encountered signs of others' passage through the woods. However, unlike my fellow knights, I could tell the difference between a sapling cut down by a crude axe and one broken off by a blundering boar! Or espy the signs of a deer having been brought down even if there were no remains left at that spot. And there were times when I was out with one of the older men when I noted things they did not and chose to keep my observations to myself. Ah, that intrigues you, Brother! Good! Then we shall continue...

Chapter 12

o we come to the most important of years, that of 1189! Ah, if only I could have looked into the future and seen what was in store for me – but I would not change things in anything but the smallest of details, Gervase. I have many regrets, but none for the overall life I have led, and you shall not get me to confess otherwise. I seek understanding from you and any others who read what is being written down, rather than trying to make pitiful excuses for my wrong doings, whether real or just perceived as such by others.

However, to set the scene for the coming events, the first significant change in our small world at the castle came just before Christmas 1188 with the arrival of a knight to fill the gap left by Eric. My replacement with the Le Clay foresters had been a jovial former soldier called Hermer, but Sir Eric's replacement was to prove a very different sort of man, and it was only the upset of John's move which blinded me to his arrival and the kind of man he was at first. It seemed a small change at the time, but this man was to sorely try me over the coming years and if you know anything of the history of Nottingham then you will know that he was soon destined for higher office! His name was William de Wendenal, a vassal of Earl Ferrers, and he came from a family of foresters who had served the de Ferrers family on other estates for many years already.

We welcomed him as one of us, yet from the start he was marked as a man who took offence where none was intended, gave offence where none should have been given, and whose knowledge of every single piece of forest law was ingrained into his very being. Somewhat older than most of us, he clearly felt the slight of being of fractionally more lowly birth than several of those he served alongside, which manifested itself in a determination to out do us all in bringing miscreants to justice. No dog with a bone could compete with Sir William when he had someone marked out for attention, and he was a cruel man too, who might have been a Christian in name, attending mass when we all did, but who had never had a Christian thought in his head except that it involved smiting. Oh yes, Brother, Sir William so enjoyed his smiting! Yet at the time we welcomed him into our midst, and, if we thought him over zealous, we initially ascribed it to his being older and having been passed over for elevation within his former forester ranks, and therefore wishing to make his mark in this new post.

For now, though, having noted his arrival we shall leave Sir William in the background where he currently belongs, albeit briefly, and focus on events closer to my tale. So once the Michaelmas courts of 1188 were over and John had left for Hathersage with Tuck, we passed an uneventful turn of the fiscal year in Nottingham. I rode through Doncaster once in my capacity as sheriff's messenger during the Christmas season itself, and heard the warming news that Much was safely back with his family *at the mill in Campsall and that Joseph was living with the White family too – just as we had planned.*

Tuck and John were a source of worry, for I had not had chance to ride up into Derbyshire and check on them, and I could only hope that if there was no room for Tuck in the cottage where John would live, that he would return once more to Gisborne. During the Christmas masses I prayed that my two dearest friends would be kept safe, and would hopefully remain together for company, even if I might no longer see much of them. Of the Coshams, Walter, Algar and Hugh there was still no sign, which pleased and relieved me, for I now believed that the most I should have to do with them might be a fleeting glimpse as I passed through some village or other. Or that I would hear of some sighting of outlaws which could only be them, and so feel obliged to lead another forester or maybe a couple of men-at-arms off on some false trail, but without coming face to face with them. How wrong I was in that!

Nottinghamshire
January, the Year of our Lord 1189

Outlaws, however, were suddenly back on the sheriff's agenda in the first week of January, for at least one or maybe two men, possibly part of a larger gang, had attacked some noble travellers going south after the Christmas festivities near to Edwinstowe, and an official complaint had been made to Sheriff Murdac.

"I'm putting you in charge, Guy," Murdac said as he came to send out the troop of a dozen knights and their men-at-arms out along with Guy, William de Wendenal, and two walking foresters who'd been mounted up for the sake of speed today. Then he addressed the troop in general. "Sir Guy is in charge because I don't want to hear of any unnecessary brutality. This crime falls within the royal forest and Edwinstowe is important to the king for the running of *his* forest." He emphasised that 'his' heavily in the hope that it would make an impression on those alongside the regular men-at-arms and foresters. Most of the current knights at the castle were the youngest of their families, and here to do the duty due for the knight's *fee* their fathers held in order to get some experience. Few had ever wielded a sword in anger, and Murdac feared what might result if they got carried away with foolish ideas of power.

"The people of Edwinstowe are *not* under suspicion! Do I make myself clear? They were the ones who *helped* Sir Mascerel and his family. They are not in any way suspect! Sir William?" He turned to de Wendenal. "You will commence searching for signs in the woods while Sir Guy deals with the villagers." Then to a knight recently arrived to fulfil his due forty days' service to the sheriff. "Sir Ralf you will lead the castle men under Sergeant Locre, you're with Sir Guy. The rest under Sergeant Harold go with Sir William, but I repeat, I want no harrying of innocent folk who've paid their dues. We are in the middle of the Winter Haining, so there shouldn't be any farm beasts in the forest and there's no reason for law-abiding folk to be there either. That's why I'm setting a forester in charge in the form of Sir Guy. He along with the other foresters will deal with *any* crimes against the venison or the vert you happen upon. Is that clear? I want no word coming back of knights or men-at-arms taking it upon themselves to punish any locals! They will be dealt with by the normal means in court, not heavy-handed instant punishments! You knights and men-at-arms are out in numbers simply to cover the ground as quickly as possible and bring these bloody thieves to justice!"

He signalled them to ride on, but caught Guy's horse's reins. "Watch Sir William!" he said softly to Guy so that no-one else would hear. "I've already had complaints from the hundred courts of his brutality and he's only been out patrolling once! We can't afford for him to turn the people against us, Guy. Not at the moment when the king's bled them white! At the moment they tolerate the heavy taxes and do nothing more than grumble at us."

He cast about him briefly to ensure that they were still out of earshot of anyone else. "Few lords understand what I'm about to tell you, but if the folk turn against us ...well, let's just say that I wouldn't want to be sheriff then! Oh they can't rise up and defeat us. They don't have the arms or the trained soldiers. But if they start hiding grain and coin, hoarding it where we can't find it, a sheriff could start to look very bad in the eyes of the chancellor and the king. Very bad! And the start down the slippery slope to that place will be if the hundred courts start protesting. King Henry is very protective of their rights because he sees them as a counterbalance to his barons, and he may be an old lion these days, but I still don't want to feel his bite!"

"Me neither, my lord!" Guy said with feeling. "Don't worry, I'll send Sir William off away from folk. In fact, since the first complaint of sighting some new outlaws was from Newstead Abbey, I'll get him to flush through Abbey Woods while we ride through Blidworth Wood first. It should be checked out in case part of some new gang is lurking there, even if not exactly the same men who attacked Sir Mascerel. That should wear William down a bit! Then once we're into the Rufford Woods he can do the same, while we ride on to Edwinstowe and get there first. That way he'll be mostly flushing through the private hunting parks and won't be stopping in the villages."

"Good man!" Murdac said with a look of relief. "I knew I could count on you!"

Guy wasn't so sure of that by the time they were passing through Hucknall. Sir William was as stubborn as a mule, and he'd got it into his head that he would be clearing the woods north of Edwinstowe and that was all.

"Yes we will," Guy repeated for the fifth time, "but not *yet!* You heard the sheriff! We have to sweep the *whole* area. Or do you think they've just been sitting on their arses in front of a nice hot bonfire just waiting for us to find them?"

"If they've cut down trees illegally I shall take the full penalty there and then," retorted Sir William belligerently, his little piggy eyes staring back at Guy in challenge without a trace of humour. "Off with their hands! I shall do it myself!"

"Oh I've no doubt you will," Guy replied dryly. "But my *point* was that they have undoubtedly moved *on* and *away* from where they made the attack on Sir Mascerel. Therefore we *search!*"

As Sir William heeled his horse off onto the smaller road north in high dudgeon, Guy and Ralf rode with the other party towards Blidworth.

"By Our Lady, Sir William is full of spleen!" Ralf commented. "I wonder he doesn't sicken from it, his humours are so out of balance."

Guy smiled. He'd come to know to Ralf on the three previous occasions the young knight had come to serve at the castle, and he was one of the most passive men he'd ever met. No doubt he would never have made a knight had it not been for some serious family negotiating and a brother at court. But Guy liked Ralf. There wasn't a hint of malice in him at all, and the worst Guy could ever level at him was a complete lack of imagination in order to be able to see just how poorly off some of the ordinary people were. If the king said that the people could afford to pay another tithe then that was what Ralf believed, being incapable of thinking anything else for himself. Yet the one person who'd instantly got under Ralf's skin was Sir William, and that, Guy thought, was a pretty significant measure of just how much of a boar William was. And a boar was exactly what William de Wendenal was, going through life tusking and goring people in a blind haze of fury at something life had dealt him, and which Guy had neither the energy nor the inclination to find out about.

"Do you think we'll find them?" Ralf asked, breaking Guy's train of thought.

"I honestly don't know," Guy answered. "Why? Are you keen for a fight?" It seemed pretty unlikely knowing Ralf's nature.

The other knight shrugged. "Well not exactly a fight. It's just that... Well my brother is always telling my father of his exploits, ...you know ...over in France with the king."

"Ah... And when you saw them last you didn't have anything to say which would compare?"

Ralf looked sheepish but nodded. *Well at least he's honest about it,* Guy thought, *and there's nothing bloodthirsty about his longing. He just wants a good chase and he'll be happy.*

"Come on, then!" Guy declared and clapped his heels to his horse. "Let's get ahead of Sir William and see if we can find them!"

"But sir, what of searching Blidworth Woods," the sergeant-at-arms protested.

Guy turned and gave the man a withering look. "Oh come on, Locre! Do you really think any self-respecting outlaw is going to loiter *this* close to Nottingham? Sheriff Murdac only wanted a heavy presence to go towards Newstead Abbey to keep the abbot and the bishop happy."

The man's face registered understanding, as did the other men with them, and all now willingly joined Guy in a short canter through the woods while the ground was soft enough to allow them to without risking damage to their horses. This last week had seen the start of a substantial thaw, and in the sheltered ground amongst the trees the iron-hard frost had melted. With any luck, Guy thought, it would make it fairly easy to track the outlaws as long as he got to the ground before Sir William churned it all to mush in his haste. It was about twenty miles up to Ollerton, where they too would be spending the night at the inn he'd previously directed John and Tuck to, and while it was a goodly ride in the wintery conditions, it wasn't so far that they wouldn't have time to cast about them on the way. Sir William, on the other hand, would have his work cut out to reach Ollerton that night, and Guy was quietly praying that the belligerent knight would find the prospect of Mansfield village's ample alehouses a more attractive prospect than chasing after him. Mansfield would be safe from Sir William's worst inclinations, being a big village with two churches and plenty of men of good repute and wealth about the place capable of standing their ground.

At the northern end of Rufford Woods, Guy found his first clues. These woods were closer to the heart of Sherwood and the trees grew thick on the ground with few tracks between them, let alone roads. Either there were tightly clustered birches with hawthorns and blackthorns, or the undercover flourished in the shade of the great oaks. This was no beech wood, where the thick mat of mast kept the undergrowth down, and the tall straight beech bolls made it easy to see through the trees. Here the forest was thick and gave up few of its secrets. Therefore, what Guy had already taken the time to find out was just where Sir Mascerel had been set upon, and it had been here in Rufford. That certainly cut down the number of spots where it might have taken place, due to a limited choice of roads the nobles might have taken, coupled with where there was the opportunity for an ambush. Heading for the first spot Guy was rewarded with a scattering of footprints in the remaining pockets of snow.

"Heading north," he said decisively.

"Good Lord! How can you tell?" Ralf wondered in bafflement.

"Because this man walks with a limp," Guy showed him. "See? The one foot doesn't go down onto the ground properly? Now here he's going south. But when he's going north again his footprints are deeper. So I'd say he was laden in some way. I know they only took jewels and furs off Sir Mascerel and Lady Godgifu, but I'd bet that they didn't carry any heavy stuff to here only to then abandon it for a few trinkets. More likely they were catching a deer or two and Sir Mascerel was just unfortunate enough to cross their path."

"Sir Guy, you're quite a wonder!" declared Ralf, making Guy cringe and making the men-at-arms snigger quietly behind Ralf's back. A moment later, however, Guy was glad Ralf had made him blush for then no-one took any notice of the fact that he felt his heart begin to race. A man with a limp? Could that be Algar? He could imagine Piers Cosham being the one to think it a good idea to rob Sir Mascerel and dragging the others into this sorry mess with him. There was nothing for it now, though. He'd have to follow them. His reputation as an expert tracker was known to every man with him, and none would believe he could lose a trail so blatantly marked.

Guy's heart was near in his mouth at the thought of being the one to track down the very men he'd risked so much to rescue, and with so many men all armed to the teeth with him as well! This was no couple of walking foresters whom the others might fight off. His worst nightmare was happening right now! Could he make a better fight of it if he turned coat and sided with the outlaws? No, he might deal with the knights for them, but there were still too many men-at-arms for seven to stand a chance against. Yet it would only take Piers to call to him by name for the game to be up anyway, and he would rather fight than be dragged back to Nottingham bound hand and foot and heading for the dungeons. He was mentally fuming. Damn it, was he to be endlessly beset with problems of conflicting loyalties?

He walked his horse steadily along the trail of footprints, easily picking them up in the mud when the patchy ice and snow gave out again. The bloody things were as clear as day now! Even Ralf could follow this trail, especially when they found the remains of two butchered deer! They headed north a short way then turned west. When they turned onto a small but well-used track it became mercifully harder again to follow, and Guy was just casting about to make sure that they hadn't turned off a few yards back when the hammering of hooves was heard. Thundering up to them came Sir

William and the rest of the men, straight over the tracks Guy was trying to follow and obliterating the lot.

"What are you doing down there?" Sir William demanded when he'd sawed on his horses reins and turned the wild-eyed gelding back to come up to Guy.

"I was *trying* to track a band of outlaws we found evidence of here in Rufford," Guy stated with withering sarcasm. "Unfortunately you lot have just wiped them out completely in all directions!"

The men-at-arms and two young knights looked suitably abashed, but Sir William was too wrapped up in his own world to be even listening. "Well stop messing about down there! We heard in Newstead that there are outlaws up by Clipstone! Come on!"

"Wait!" Guy bellowed in barely controlled fury. It was so rare for him to lose his temper that all the men brought their horses to a halt, forcing Sir William to stop to or collide with them. Guy had flung himself back onto his horse and now he rode to sit face to face with Sir William, quivering with anger.

"God's *bollocks*! How do you think the people of *Newstead* would know of what's happening at bastard *Clipstone*?" he demanded, spitting fury. "They don't even go to the same bloody *markets* to talk to one another! Christ on the Cross! It's just petty *gossip* you've heard! What kind of mad outlaw would stop to cook his venison right by the bloody royal hunting lodge, anyway? They won't be at fucking *Clipstone*! And on the basis of that piddling snippet, you give up the proper search you were *supposed* to be making and coming haring up here like a bunch of madmen, and in the process wipe out the evidence we were so carefully following. Evidence which was well on the way to giving us something to *really* work with."

"Like what?" demanded William, all boar-like aggression again, lacking the wit to be able to think of anything approaching an excuse or an answer.

"Like they made camp near here for about two days!" Guy virtually spat into his face. "Stopped to cook the king's *deer*! Based on us finding *these*!" and he grabbed the sack he'd slung behind him and brandished two sets of antlers right under William's nose. "Now they might not be the same outlaws who robbed Sir Mascerel, but don't you think that the sheriff might be *vaguely* interested in such blatant poaching?" William just stared back at him. A sure sign that Guy had won this round. "Get your men back behind mine and bloody well *stay* there!" Guy ordered. "Since there's not a damned thing I can do here any more, we shall continue towards Ollerton."

"Why not Edwinstowe?" grumbled Sir William, making Guy want to throttle him on the spot. Was the man incapable of hearing the simplest of commands without arguing the toss over them?

"Because they don't have a large enough inn or anything like enough fodder for this many horses," Guy snapped at him. "Given that you've ridden your horse so hard he might be lame in the morning, unless you want to *walk* with us for the rest of the foray, I'd suggest you come along and try to see he gets some rest and maybe a poultice on that foreleg. Now *get back in line!*"

Guy heeled his horse to the front of the line and everyone, even Ralf, gave him a full two horse's length space. His fury was only fuelled as they passed a copse the other side of Clipstone, from where they saw the top of the stone walls of the royal hunting lodge up on the rise above the small water meadows. There in the trees above him sat Piers Cosham! Guy gave a terse and furious gesture to him, and at least the archer had the wit to disappear from sight around the other side of the massive oak tree. So it had been them! And right by where the sheriff himself might have come hunting too!

Now Guy was half torn with feeling grateful that Sir William had trampled the trail, and an anger equal to that which he'd felt towards Wendenal was now also directed at the Coshams. It wasn't until they were nearer to Ollerton with the early winter dusk falling that Guy saw another sign of the liberated men. He'd kept his own party moving at a steady walking pace, making much of scouring the landscape even though all behind him were too taken-a-back by this unusual fury in their leader to look much themselves, but recently he'd spied odd glimpses of a man in the distance running across the fields.

As soon as he'd stabled his horse, Guy left Ralf in charge of getting a meal ordered and some ale for the men out of the surly innkeeper, and after berating Sir William over the state of his horse once more, Guy declared he was going for a walk before he killed someone. No-one argued! Even Sir William was dragged muttering darkly into the inn by his right-hand man, who clearly thought he might be bearing Sir William's corpse back if he pushed his luck further.

Just outside the village he found a very breathless Hugh.

"Dear God, Guy, I'm so sorry," the former soldier panted. "I told them, honestly I did! Told them we had to move on faster. The trouble is, Algar and Walter haven't got a clue about how to live this kind of life. They've never had to live off the land before, gleaning as they go, like we had to when we fought in France. And Thomas is a good man, but Piers would make a saint weep!"

Guy felt his anger draining out of him. Poor Hugh. What an unenviable position to be in. "It's not your fault," he told Hugh, and meant it. "Where are they now?"

"Back down the road," Hugh wheezed as his breathing slowly eased. "Thomas was trying to knock his brother's head through a tree the last I saw!"

"Waste of time!" Guy growled. "The tree would see sense before he would!"

That made Hugh smile.

Guy clapped him on the shoulder. "Look, we're heading to Edwinstowe tomorrow, so take them further west. Keep south of Bolsover Castle and then go north again after that. You should be well away from our search then." Hugh nodded gratefully. "Just tell me one thing." Hugh was now standing and looking Guy in the eye. "Was it you lot who robbed Sir Mascerel seven days ago? ...Old white-haired knight, definitely on the portly side. Wife's a skinny old lady with a voice like a rasping iron file – you couldn't mistake it!" To Guy's immense relief Hugh was looking totally blank.

"No Guy, that wasn't us! We took two deer, yes, but not people!"

"Then did you see anyone about? Travellers?"

"There was a party of armed men. I'd say they were Templars heading for one of the northern granges. The only other man was that bullish knight you have riding with you. The one you were haranguing outside the stables. He was on the road, of course."

"Sir William?" Guy was completely taken aback by that, then recalled that Sir William had been sent to Eakring with a letter over an argument between the sheriff and the resident reeve of the de Gaunt family, concerning a rebuilding of the church for which oak trees had been felled. Now that he thought about it, Guy remembered Sir William griping on about having to make the ride, and then taking far longer than Ralph Murdac had thought necessary to complete such a simple task. William had taken the dressing down with a smirk hardly concealed. He hadn't tried to justify his time, and had simply said that he'd only rejoined the main road at Bilsthorpe and so after Sir Mascerel had been set upon.

"By St Thomas!" Guy breathed softly. "The bastard! *He* robbed them! No wonder he loitered! He could hardly risk turning up at the castle and have Sir Mascerel point the finger of blame at him!"

"You believe me?" Hugh sounded surprised.

Guy blinked in surprise of his own. "Yes of course I do!" He smiled at the former soldier. "Of course it helps that you're accusing a thoroughly obnoxious and brutal man! If you'd accused Sir Ralf I'd have thought twice, and then maybe again. But that's because I couldn't imagine Ralf having the brains to even think of such a thing, let alone carry it through! Bless me, Ralf isn't one of life's great thinkers! I sometimes wonder how he'd get into his armour if he didn't have help."

Hugh shared the companionable laughter at the thought of the affable Ralf's unlikely role as a robber.

"I'm glad you don't think so badly of us," he added, which made Guy give him a wry smile.

"Hugh, if I'd thought any of you were as bad as the charges levelled at you, there's no way I'd have set you free to prey on the world once more!"

Hugh grinned more widely. "I suppose you have a point there. It wouldn't make much sense if you had."

"Good! I'm glad we're clear on that!" The more Guy saw of Hugh the more he wished he could get him into the castle, that he could find a way to ingratiate the former soldier into the garrison. Hugh was someone Guy would find it easy to become friends with. And Hugh was probably about Baldwin's age, so a bit younger than Guy, but not much, and the two of them seemed to think alike about a good many things. A real friend living under the same roof was a luxury Guy could only dream of. Not that such a thing would ever happen, he thought regretfully. His life was becoming defined by what was absent once again – not only no wife, but no close friends he could speak openly to on a daily basis.

"You'd better get going," he said instead of speaking his mind. "As I said, go west as fast as you can!" Then a thought came to him. "Listen, I have to ride up Hathersage way in February. I'll be on my own apart from a couple of men who'll be busy checking on the local payments of royal forest taxes. I'm also going to meet meet my cousin John and Brother Tuck, who you should remember took Much back home. I'm not quite sure what to describe Tuck as now, but John's a shepherd there now. If you can get the others up there we'll have time to talk over where you can go, and what you most definitely *shouldn't* do!

"Some things you'll get away with with hardly anyone noticing, and others will bring the force of the sheriff down on you like a fall of rocks before you can even sneeze. I can put you right on those, but we'll need to meet away from inquisitive eyes. Do you think you can move the others? I'm sorry I have to push this onto you, but there's no way I can sneak out of the castle unobserved for something unofficial at this time of year, and I definitely can't leave this bunch without the sheriff knowing it."

"Don't worry," Hugh reassured him. "I think Piers has had the shock of his life. He tore into our camp like the hounds of Hell were snapping at his boots! I don't think he expected to see such a huge troop of soldiers out *hunting* outlaws. The Lord Almighty only knows how he thought outlaws got caught! I didn't hang about to hear his dithering excuses. All I could think about was making sure you knew who you were hunting. I didn't want you to track us down and then give yourself away when you knew who we were."

Guy was touched by Hugh's declaration of concern. So at least one of those he'd rescued truly appreciated what he'd done and what he'd risked to do it. "Thank you," he said warmly and clasped Hugh's hand. "Now go before someone comes to find me and sees you!"

Hugh melted silently into the darkness and Guy realised how cold he'd become standing out in the winter's night. Turning on his heels he strode briskly back to the inn and claimed his share of the stew just in time before Sir William troughed a second helping.

Overnight Guy fretted over what he was going to do about Sir William. It would be nearly impossible to accuse the knight outright. Face to face Guy was sure de Wendenal would simply lie and accuse Guy of blackening his name, and somewhere along the line Guy was sure that de Wendenal had a powerful patron too. He had to have to have risen this far when he had few natural qualities to recommend him! In front of Sheriff Murdac Guy would need proof, and he couldn't get that without searching the knight's possessions to find the stolen jewels.

But what to do about this present search? He couldn't just call it off as the pointless act it was without saying why, and that brought him back round to the need for proof. So he'd have to go through the motions. Was there any way he might trick de Wendenal into betraying himself, Guy wondered? Allow him to take the lead tomorrow in the hope that he became over confident? In the small hours Guy had to concede that de Wendenal was too crafty to fall that easily. The belligerent knight wasn't overly intelligent, but he had a sharp animal cunning which Guy couldn't risk underestimating. No, all he could do was play along as if he knew no better, and watch de Wendenal as closely as he could without alerting him as to what was happening.

In the morning they rode out and spent a fruitless day quartering the forest up to the hamlet of Budby and back, ending the day down at Mansfield with worn out men and horses, and not a sign of outlaws anywhere. Or at least that was what Guy was allowing the others to believe. He'd noticed the signs of another old kill of a deer and the remains of a campfire just emerging from under the snow in one patch, and some threads of a fine garment stuck to a winter-bare thorn bush betraying where the unfortunate Sir Mascerel and Lady Godgifu had been waylaid. At that point Guy stole a covert glance at de Wendenal and was satisfied to see a smirk on the other knight's face. Nothing would have given Guy greater pleasure than wiping that smug look off his face, but he bit his lip and pretended to be scouring the ground for signs to avoid catching Sir William's eye.

Back at the castle Guy had to wait nearly a week before he found a chance to creep into de Wendenal's room, not least because like Guy, William was sharing with another knight and that one was Sir Henry, who would happily pick a fight with Guy if he found him in his quarters. Because of the vast size of Nottingham Castle, the knights had a rare amount of privacy away from the servants all sleeping on the benches in the halls, but it meant that the rooms still received many visits during the day as different men came back for an item, or to leave something behind. Luckily, this day most of the knights temporarily here to fulfil their knight's *fee* had ridden out on a short exercise with Sheriff Murdac with half of the foresters, and Guy, having been out on a similar exercise the day before, was free for a few hours.

At speed he slipped into the tiny room in the thickness of the wall, and had to find which of the two ironbound chests was de Wendenal's. He'd feared that the two might be indistinguishable, but Sir Henry's had his old shirt airing on it, while clearly Sir William wasn't the trusting kind and his chest was the one with a lock. Using a fine old knife which he'd long ago ground down to a slim point, Guy fiddled with the lock and was rewarded by it clicking open after a few minutes. A really good lock would have defeated him, but de Wendenal's was more for the show of warding men off than being a real deterrent.

Opening the chest, Guy was very careful to lift everything out and place it in order on the floor. He wasn't sure how observant de Wendenal was, but it wouldn't do to take chances on him spotting that his baggage had been rifled through. Inside the draw-string pocket matching de Wendenal's best tunic, Guy found a small pouch. In it were a pair of rings, a handful of gold coins, a pretty little clasp which must have come from Lady Godgifu and which was studded with small garnets, and half a dozen gems which looked as though they had been prized out of their settings. Whether these had come from one item or several Guy couldn't tell. What was beyond doubt was that they were of a quality he doubted Sir William could have afforded to buy for himself.

Guy sat back on his heels and rolled the gems about in his hand while he thought. He could take these and hide them somewhere else. That would make de Wendenal sweat! He'd have to be crafty about where, though. The foresters knight was already well aware that Guy disliked him, and Guy would be one of the first to have the accusation of thief thrown at him, even if he couldn't imagine how de Wendenal would twist it so that he still appeared innocent while making Guy the guilty one. Against his desires, but following his head not his heart, Guy put them all back except the little clasp, and carefully arranged de Wendenal's things back in the order they'd been before.

He carefully locked the chest again, then took the delicately worked clasp to where he knew there was a small cleft in the masonry of the oldest tower two floors up. Hardly anyone went up there these days except to hurry past to get to the battlements, and there were magpies nesting at the top to whom Guy could point any finger of blame if the clasp was found. He didn't know what he was going to do with it yet, but his instinct told him to hold onto at least one piece of proof, and the clasp would be the last thing he thought de Wendenal would try to sell since it was so distinctive. With luck, if William was hurrying to retrieve something to take to sell before Sir

Henry's greedy eyes saw anything, he would go for the gems and not miss the clasp. The fact that it had been the most deeply buried was hopefully a hint that Guy had read the knightly thief right.

For a couple of days longer he mulled over and over what he could do. It went against the grain to let de Wendenal get away with his crimes – especially if he then managed to plant some of the evidence on a poor soul brought in for a lesser charge. Guy wouldn't put it past a man like Sir William to find it funny if some unfortunate lad like Much got pulled in for a minor offence, and then ended up swinging from a rope for a greater crime he'd never committed. In that time Guy also found out that de Wendenal was amongst them thanks to being the favoured man of William de Ferrers, Earl of Derby. That really set the cat amongst the pigeons, because it meant that the damned man was being set up for serious promotion, and Guy would need something really cast-iron to be able to bring him down. The word of a lowly knight of Guy's station would count for very little against that of someone with the ear of an earl.

Even though Sheriff Murdac thought highly of Guy, Murdac himself wasn't as high up the social scale as Earl Ferrers, and wouldn't be able to save Guy if the earl took against him. It also explained much to Guy as to why de Wendenal was with them at all – Murdac must have had very little say in the matter despite being sheriff, and Guy belatedly realised that just as he'd been foisted onto Murdac by the whim of the king, so might de Wendenal have been. That was a really sobering thought! Guy had no wish to cross the king, then felt a spark of hope that maybe King Henry would be the one person who might strike fear into the dreadful Sir William. If he let it slip that he too had been promoted here at the *king's* personal request it might at least curb William's worst inclinations, especially if he thought Guy might be daring enough to act upon that connection.

However, regarding the present situation, Guy decided that the best thing to do was to see if he could find further evidence. Sir Mascerel had been very vocal over the loss of fur collars as well as the jewelled items, and Guy realised that as they hadn't been amongst William's things, he must have disposed of them already. Also, he didn't think de Wendenal knew the castle well enough yet to feel confident of having a hidey-hole which no-one else knew of. Nor had William been far enough afield unaccompanied since the robbery to find a merchant of quality goods other than here in Nottingham. There were few merchants in Nottingham who would be able to buy quality jewels, and even fewer who might buy the fur collars which had been cut from the necks of nobles, and so Guy resolved to start with them.

On his next morning off he walked out of the castle and into the town, continuing away from the everyday merchants selling food and utensils, and around to Mount Street. Down at the bottom of the street, a small shop contained a selection of more decorative items. As soon as he ducked in through the stout oak door the wiry little proprietor scuttled out of the house at the back, rubbing his hands as much against the chill as anticipation of a sale.

"It's damnably cold, isn't it?" Guy answered his greeting and giving the man his most winning smile.

"That it is young sir, that it is."

Guy looked about him with studied innocence. "I've come to have a look because I was wondering if you had such a thing as a fur collar I could buy? It's so cold riding out these days! I had a fancy to keep my neck warm with something more than a woollen scarf! Such a thing isn't very knightly, is it?"

"No indeed, sir!" The shop keeper pulled out a wooden box and opened it up. "I'm afraid all I have is some poor quality hare and squirrel skins at the moment. Trade has been brisk, as you might imagine given the weather."

One look at the contents of the box was enough for Guy to see that what he was looking for wasn't there. In fact the few remaining bits of fur had seen better days, and he wouldn't have parted with his coins for any of them. The shop keeper was clearly disappointed when Guy declined to buy anything, but was mollified when Guy told him that he had better furs curing at the kennels from the plentiful hares Fletch and Spike brought in. Hurrying back to the castle, Guy got the bundle of hare pelts he'd cured and then kept tucked away with Harry in the stables, and was negotiating a price with the delighted merchant for the furs, and the making of a collar for himself, as the sheriff rode back in with the men.

"Engaging in trade, Sir Guy?" Sheriff Murdac teased.

Guy smiled back. "Oh you know those dogs of mine, sheriff. It occurred to me that they might be useful to me for once! This good man has been running out of stock so we were helping one another out, you might say."

"Good God!" Murdac leaned out of his saddle to inspect the pelts. "Your dogs caught all of these?"

"And more," Guy admitted, although didn't say that those had been roe deer whose skins were currently being worn as over-tunics by Harry and some of the other stablemen!

The sheriff reached over and lifted a couple of paler than normal and almost honey-coloured pelts out. "Neatly cut too. Is that your work, Guy?"

"Yes it is."

Murdac looked impressed and handled the pelts again. "Make these into a collar for me!" he instructed the merchant, then turned to Guy. "If you can get more of this quality out of those beasts of yours I shall be well pleased."

Guy didn't have to think twice. He went straight to the bottom of the pile and brought out four more hares of a similar honey colour. He couldn't forget them, for he'd caught them at John's cottage – or rather Fletch and Spike had. "Like this, Sheriff?"

Murdac beamed back. "By God, yes! Oh this is excellent! A hat too, then, if you please, Master Felton."

The merchant shot Guy a look of pure gratitude as he hurriedly took the pelts, and made his promises that the work would be done swiftly and with attention to detail. He would benefit from being on the sheriff's good side when it came to collecting taxes, and what he would be paid for a prestigious commission like this would help those same payments nicely. As the sheriff rode on with a glowering de Wendenal behind him, having witnessed the whole exchange and been unable to do anything to tarnish Guy without revealing his own guilty secret, Guy turned back to the merchant.

"I tell you what, Master Felton, I won't ask you to pay me for those pelts the sheriff's just had," he said kindly. "It's our good fortune they're the colour he's been after. I'll get my reward from him for having provided them in the good will he'll show me. Just pay me for the others."

The merchant couldn't quite believe his luck. "Are you sure, Sir Guy?"

Guy nodded. "Quite sure! But can I ask you something? We've had a report of some furs being stolen – not just deer skins either, which I know you'd report if someone offered them to you." He knew full well that the furrier wouldn't, but it didn't hurt to make him feel he was trusted. "We're talking something richer than that. If you should hear of another merchant being offered furs for sale which have been already made up, and which come from what I might call a 'dubious' source, would you let me know? I know you wouldn't deal in stolen goods," he added hurriedly so that the merchant wouldn't think that Guy had him under suspicion. "And I doubt that these items will be brought into Nottingham – or at least not in the first place," he added innocently. "But if they don't turn up then that will at least tell me that the thieves were probably passing through. However, if they do come into Nottingham for sale," he continued in a confidential tone, "then the chances are that they were taken by men who might still be in the area, and we don't want good, honest men like yourselves being set upon, do we?"

The merchant was taken in hook, line and sinker, and was almost falling over himself to tell Guy what he knew. "But we did have something like that! Oh, it was back closer to the beginning of the month, mind you, and it was only a couple of collars and a hat and a pair of gloves. The man who brought them in said they'd been his father's and that the old man had died. Said that his father had been a much smaller man than him and so the gloves wouldn't fit and neither would the other things, and that he needed the money to pay the Church scot to bury the old man. He was a burly man, even muffled up against the cold, so I thought nothing of it."

"What happened to the items?" Guy asked gently. There was no point in losing his temper with the man. He'd done nothing wrong intentionally. It did confirm his suspicions, though. De Wendenal must have come out deliberately on a bad day so that he wouldn't arouse curiosity by being bundled up and unrecognisable.

"Ah, the head of my guild from York was passing through and suggested that I sell them on to him. He thought there was a Jewish moneylender up in York who would pay him handsomely for them, whereas I don't have customers for anything so fine as them."

"Not hare, then?" Guy assumed.

"Oh no! Finest sealskin from the lands of the Norsemen! That's what they were. And the ladies collar was arctic fox if I'm not mistaken. It was old. Must have been handed down through his family..." The merchant stopped and clapped a hand over his mouth. "Oh dear! But they weren't his family, were they?"

"No, and unfortunately the collar is very much wanted back because it was the lady's mother's. But you've been extremely helpful. If you can just tell me the name of your guildsman I can take my enquires from there. Don't worry, I shall not be involving you in any recriminations!"

With a pocket of coins and a name scribbled on a bit of spare parchment, Guy returned to the castle and hurried to Sheriff Murdac. He covered the merchant by telling Murdac that the guildsman from York had simply told Master Felton of his good fortune at being able to buy the fox fur collar from a grieving relative, and of his expectations of having a buyer for it.

"York, you say?" Murdac said leaning forward keenly as he listened to Guy.

"Yes sir, York. Do I have your permission to follow this trail?"

Murdac was quick to assent. "By Saint Thomas, yes! Well done, Guy! A clue at last. Sir Mascerel will be infinitely less disparaging of us if we can at least get his wife's heirloom back for her, and although I know he's not one of our mighty barons, nonetheless it doesn't do for him to be declaring our incompetence to all and sundry. Tomorrow, you may go to York."

Guy made his small bow of deference to the sheriff and then turned to go, but not before catching de Wendenal's eye. The other knight was glowering at him ferociously, and Guy couldn't help but be secretly amused. He must be furious that anyone had tracked him even this far, and because of that Guy kept his expression neutral. He would be away from the castle for some days and he didn't want de Wendenal going all out to blacken his name behind his back. Most accusations he was sure he could counter, but if de Wendenal was grimly determined then there was some damage bound to be done. Better to leave him guessing, and not wanting to rock the boat too much. Hopefully Sir William wouldn't risk appearing inexplicably guilty to the sheriff, but if cornered he still might do something rash. Fletch and Spike would come with him too, Guy decided. He didn't need to take them, but he feared what de Wendenal's spite might lead him to do to the dogs, and the kennels here didn't have a strong kennelman like Ianto to watch over his charges.

On a cold and foggy morning, Guy therefore rode out with his favourite horse and another favourite mount on a lead rein, and the two dogs padding at their heels. He wanted to ride for as long as he could each day, and that would be easier if he could swop horses. Or at least that's what he told the grooms. They weren't fooled though, and one even went as far as to say openly that he was glad Guy was taking the beasts out and away from de Wendenal. The castle whispers had already got word that de Wendenal was in a mighty temper over something, and that Guy was particularly in his sights for revenge. Yet it said much for de Wendenal's unpleasant reputation that already his tempers were being thought of as irrational, and no-one believed that Guy had done anything to incite his ire other than be praised for doing his job well by the sheriff.

For his own part, though, Guy was under no illusions. He'd made a real enemy out of de Wendenal, however much he'd been in the right. Even dropped hints that he had the ear of the earl of Chester, just as William did the earl of Derby, had changed nothing. De Wendenal had sniffed derisively at Guy's comment, and worse, his eyes had told Guy that he viewed this as a challenge to be overcome rather than a deterrent. If Guy couldn't get rid of the damned man then he'd be living in close company with a vicious enemy. It was a grim thought that he might have to start watching his back again as he'd done under de Braose's sheriffdom. What was the matter with these damned second- and third-generation Normans, he thought in frustration? By now he felt so completely at odds with such men as to not think himself as of the same lineage at all.

Three days later he got to York, and on the next spent his time meeting the merchant whom Master Felton had given him the name and address of. Of all of Lady Godgifu's items, only the fox fur collar remained in the merchant's possession, and while he moaned mightily at having to part with an item he'd paid money for, it soon transpired that he'd paid Master Felton very little for it because it was old and of an unfashionable cut. So feeling well pleased with himself for having recovered the most missed item, and gratified that de Wendenal hadn't got the money he must've hoped for from his ill-gotten gains, Guy allowed himself the luxury of a leisurely ride back to give himself time to think of what to do next.

Since he was up this far, he decided to visit Much and his family at Norton. The mill was substantial but hadn't been rebuilt in many a long year, leading Guy to think that Much's father was probably fairly honest, despite the common belief that all millers were corrupt. There was no suspicious sign of wealth here. Tethering his horse to a convenient rail which probably normally held draught horses while their carts were being unloaded, Guy ducked into the mill by a small door. The wider door on the upper floor, where the sacks of harvested grain would be hoisted up, was closed at the moment.

"Hello? Is anyone there?" Guy called out, but received no reply. He ducked back outside and was about to investigate the outside when a burly older man appeared with a pitchfork in his hands. It was a good ploy. The pitchfork was such an everyday tool about a mill that only a fool would try and pretend that the miller had a weapon in his hands, and yet the way the miller held it in his meaty fists was certainly not friendly. The sharp tines were pointing at Guy's midriff and he stopped in his tracks and lifted his hands away from his sides to show he had no intention of going for his sword.

"Are you Much's father?" Guy asked in as friendly a tone as he could manage.

"What of it?" the older man demanded, even though there was no mistaking the family resemblance.

Luckily, before anything turned nasty, a figure began scrambling out of a nearby oak calling out, "Pa, no! He's a friend!"

Much appeared in a flurry of bits of leaves and twigs to grasp Guy's hand and pump it in friendship, all accompanied by a huge grin on the young man's face. "I'm so glad you came!" he declared enthusiastically. "Pa, this is the man who rescued me!"

The older version blinked owlishly in his surprise, but was saved the embarrassment of speaking by the appearance of a comely woman of equally middle years. Much's mother gushed happily over Guy and insisted that he stay for a meal with them. Also hobbling out of a dark corner at the back of the mill came Joseph too. Just being out of the dungeon and being given a decent meal every day had already knocked years off his appearance. He might never regain the bloom of good health, but Guy was gratified to see that he no longer looked at death's door either.

"This last month or so Joseph's been able to start helping Pa out!" Much enthused, confirming Guy's assessment of the man's recovery.

"Aye, he's been a steady worker," the miller agreed. "He'll be worth his keep when harvest time comes around," and the miller shot his bouncy young son a despairing if loving look.

Guy had to smile. It was clear that Much was temperamentally unsuited to working in the mill. Something which was confirmed by Much's excited questioning of Guy as to the campaigns he'd fought in. He was quite disappointed when Guy made it plain that he'd never even been as far as France.

"You see?" the miller said despairingly. "Sir Guy might be a knight, but it's not all about riding into battle and rescuing damsels in distress. Is it?" He turned to Guy with a pleading look in his eyes.

"By Saint Thomas, no!" Guy agreed. "I don't think I've ever even come across a damsel in distress." He resolutely kept the thought of the conniving Rohese firmly out of the conversation – she had turned out to be anything but the innocent damsel! "I tell you, Much, it's a life of being at the beck and call of the sheriff. And it's far from glorious when it's a case of being sent out to enforce the king's forest laws. I hate most of what I have to do, but if I didn't do it then men who are far worse than me would be the ones the villagers have to face, and they're the sort who'd enjoy doing the persecuting! Duty can be a cruel master."

Much looked glum but his parents were silently thanking Guy with their eyes. It didn't take a seer's gift to work out that they'd been scared to death that their romantically inclined son might take off on some harebrained notion one day, and that that thought had been the source of many a lost night's sleep.

"I'm serious, Much," Guy added gently. "You know those other men who came out of the castle with you? Well I've seen them only a few weeks ago. Be very grateful that you had a home to come back to! They're out in Sherwood, watching over their shoulder for any foresters coming their way, or any of the sheriff's soldiers. It might sound fun for a week or so in summertime, but in the winter it's a cold and bitter way to live.

"Someone else robbed a rich merchant and I had to try and track them down. By sheer misfortune your old friends had crossed the tracks. I very nearly ended up tracking them instead, and I had a good many well armed men with me too! There was no way I could have avoided getting into a fight with them if we'd caught them up. And it was simple good luck which got their tracks wiped out, nothing more. They can't count on that a second time and they know it now. They've had to move into the Peaks, and I'm sure you can imagine how rough that can be at this time of year." He looked pointedly at the fire glowing gently in the hearth over which was hung the cauldron of stew from which they'd all partaken.

Much sighed heavily but nodded in understanding. Guy felt sorry for the lad. It must seem like a very dull existence at that age, and he could remember very well how he'd felt. At least he'd been able to get out and about on fitz Waryn's estate and he'd been off to Clun when not much older. Much would have no such escape, and no doubt his parents were now reluctant to let him even go into the nearby towns on errands after he'd been swept up without reason once already. At such a thought Guy couldn't help but relent a little.

"Look, I tell you what. Sometimes I have to go north of here – to the Templars even if not always so far as York. If I'm passing this way I'll try and bring another horse with me and you can join me posing as one of the grooms, or something. This far from Nottingham Castle no-one will know the difference. It won't be often and it won't be for long, and you'll still have to come back here, but at least you'll see something of the rest of the world."

Much's eyes lit up like candles once more, and if anything his parents were regarding Guy with even more gratitude. Clearly they thought him the responsible, steady sort who could be trusted to keep Much out of mischief. *If only you knew the half of it*, Guy thought as he took his leave of them.

Oh if I had only been able to see into the future, Brother Gervase. The next time I was to hear of that mill the circumstance would be far from as happy. And if I could have known just how much of an enemy I had made of de Wendenal, and just how high he would rise in the very near future, I might have thought a ratty old fur collar not worth it. But then I can still remember the delight on the old lady's face when I was sent to take it to her, too, and I should not begrudge her that. De Wendenal would have been a blight on my life without that, and if nothing else it made him regard me as less of a soft target for his venom a couple of years later, for he will soon be stepping more to the fore in my story when he becomes sheriff in his own right. There, that is a teaser for you, is it not?

But you must by now be getting a glimmer of a hint as to how our futures were to become intertwined. I managed to briefly ride over to Hathersage later in January – under false pretences to the sheriff of going straight to Gisborne, I must confess, Brother, although I did briefly visit Ianto and Maelgwn – and found John and Tuck well ensconced within the village community. John's great strength was considered a boon, since he could shift loads most of the men could only move in twos, and Tuck's goodness and kindness were a testimony all of their own without any intervention or introduction from me.

Somewhat more surprising was the discovery that my tiny band of outlaws had already made a camp not far away. They had struck up a kind of agreement with the villagers of Hathersage, Castleton and Hope, amongst others. They went out and poached the meat, thereby taking the risks, and in return for skinned, butchered, and therefore suitably anonymous meat, they received payments in kind of what milled grain the villagers could spare, and small portions of vegetables from the cottage gardens. From one village alone the men would have had poor pickings, but having spread their net widely they had found that they could survive in relative comfort.

They had even found some caves which they could live in. Many in that area were being quarried for lead, of course, and the largest cave in the area, the huge cave called the Devil's Arse, lay almost beneath High Peak Castle itself. Their caves, though, were further afield and much smaller, but they did afford some shelter from the worst of the winter weather, especially once Hugh and Thomas had got everyone to build a good sized wooden shelter in front of the mouth of their primary cave. They had decked it about with dead foliage to disguise the marks of their regular passage, and had planted a few young gorse bushes in front of the dead stuff. Come the spring, Hugh and Thomas hoped, the bushes would thrive and fully mask their hideaway.

I have to say, though, that I was glad that Piers made himself scarce when I was there. I still felt some ire towards him, believing him to have been the instigator of the little band hunting so close to Nottingham, even if the others loyally never said so. Young Bilan was delighted as ever to see me, and it now struck me that it was a pity that he and Much had not met for long enough to really get to know one another. The two were of an age and would, I thought, have been sufficiently alike to become friends. But Bilan had remained with John while the others took Much home with Joseph, and it had only been after that that Bilan had rejoined his brothers.

What a prescient thought that was, though, Brother! Looking back on that time from where I am now, I am struck time and again by the way God, the saints or fate, were manipulating us. In the end, I now see that it was inevitable that we should all become so entwined. You may think it near blasphemous for me to say this, but I feel that the Lord intended us to come together.

Yes, I thought that would crease your brow! Have you never thought of it in that way, Brother? That maybe God was moving in mysterious ways? That maybe he looked down on our small patch of his earth and was disheartened by the way that his ordinary folk were treated? ...No? ...Well then I may have to ask Dewi Sant or Saint Issui to intervene on my behalf for such thoughts when I reach my Maker, Brother, even if your own preferred saints turn their noses up at me, because I believe I have felt the heavy hand of destiny on my shoulder, and it was not so easy to shake off.

Chapter 13

Now we come on apace, Brother Gervase. I had barely got to Hathersage early in 1189 – fully officially, for the coming half-yearly forest rents were due at Easter – when it seemed as though a divine hand was pushing me off in yet another direction and this time at high speed. John and Tuck were both well, as were my outlaw friends, but the resident knight at High Peak was not. I can still remember that ride up into the higher land towards Castleton. It was bitterly cold up there and High Peak Castle perched on the rocky knoll as a dark, forbidding presence in the enclosed valley. I was looking forward to a hot meal and a decent bed, and so I think was my horse.

Have you ever seen High Peak, Brother? Ah, then I must describe it for you, for it is not like any other castle I have seen. It perches on a triangle of flat land atop a rocky outcrop. The route up to it is formidable even in good weather, for you must zigzag up a narrow and very steep path if you are to enter by the main East Gate. There is another way in, but to get to that you must either scale the surrounding hills to the west to come at the additional outer bailey from behind. Or you must ride through Castleton and beyond, to make a great sweep around up towards the head of the valley in order to come back to it. Having done that you come to the outer bailey, but to get into the castle itself you must cross a bridge over a deep and dangerous drop to reach the lesser West Gate.

On that day, Brother, I looked up at the route to the East Gate, and at the good coating of ice which encrusted it, and decided that I would risk neither my horse's legs and neck, nor mine by going that way. The other route was hardly a grand entrance, coming into the main bailey after the bridge by a small picket gate in the wall beside the keep, but foregoing the grand entrance was hardly worrying me at that stage. My horse would be stabled in the outer bailey across the bridge anyway, so I heeled her on and we plodded wearily through the village.

It was only then that a gruff man, grubby as only a miner can be, accosted me and asked if I had managed to find the priest. Startled, I asked him why he should ask and received an unsettling reply. Sir Ivo of Quettehou, the knight holding this distant fastness, had taken a chill during the Christmas festivities and not only had he not recovered, but was now sinking fast. The senior sergeant-at-arms had come down to the village demanding that a priest be sent for from Hope or Hathersage, yet so far none had come.

When I told him that I had come through both villages and that there had been no sign of a priest in either place, and that I had been told that the priest at Hope had himself died just before Christmas, the man's face fell. He feared the retribution which would fall upon them if Sir Ivo died without being shriven, he told me, not least because Sir Ivo was notorious for being a hard master, and no-one living in the castle wanted to stay there if his ghost was likely to be prowling restlessly about the place.

Of course my thoughts turned immediately to Tuck. It would take very little time for me to ride back and get him if I had fresh horses, and I said something to that effect. The effect was astonishing. A young lad tore off and I saw him scrambling up the eastern icy slope to the castle with the sure-footed gait of a mountain goat. His high voice echoed across the snow-muffled valley and I realised that he was calling for fresh horses to be brought out to meet me. The villagers meanwhile ushered me into their tiny alehouse and gave me the seat closest to the fire while I waited.

Never had I had such an enthusiastic welcome, Brother! Nor did I have to wait long. I had barely had chance to eat the bowl of hot broth which was offered me before a harassed man ducked into the low-beamed room, introducing himself as Sir Ivo's steward. His face fell even further when I told him that I had come from the sheriff to enquire whether Sir Ivo and his men had begun to hunt for the requisitioned meat the king had ordered sent south for the Easter court. In this kind of weather the meat was hardly likely to go bad, and venison needed to be hung anyway, but with Lent already looming, there were not so many weeks left before the meat would have to be bundled onto wagons and taken on the road if it was to reach the court in time – and that was if the court was in London. If the king chose to venture further afield, such as to Winchester, then there was even less time left. The poor man hardly seemed to know which way to turn first, and I felt it my Christian duty to help him as best I could – not to mention my thoughts on what Sheriff Murdac would say if he was let down in the king's eyes!

Derbyshire
February, the Year of our Lord 1189

"So how many men do you have?" Guy asked the harassed steward. "Are there any who can go out hunting straight away?"

"There's the rub, sire," the steward moaned desperately. "There are normally only a dozen men permanently here unless the sheriff plans something, as you know. We'd normally leave the forest law matters to one of you men from Nottingham anyway, but if Sir Ivo received any such message of hunting then he never mentioned it to anyone else, and I've certainly not seen any such missive. I swear to you that nobody in the castle had any idea that we were expected to provide any meat for the king.

"But it wouldn't have done any good if we had! A full six of the men are sick as can be with the same aches and shivers which afflict Sir Ivo. They haven't taken so badly as him, for they took sick after him and are getting better, but they're still a very long way from being able to sit in a saddle and hunt for a day. Nor could they take over guard duties yet and let the others go out instead. And Sir Ivo has insisted that the security of the castle must take priority over everything else – especially since with all the snow we've had, many of the knights and men who were due to come to do service haven't made it through the valleys."

Guy thought furiously. What was his best option? To ride with all despatch back to Nottingham and inform Sheriff Murdac of the disaster brewing over here in Derbyshire? That would certainly result in several of the foresters, and heaven alone knew how many knights, descending on these quiet valleys with a promise of a legal hunt, and possibly the sheriff in person. If John and Tuck weren't hiding out here that might have been an option, but not now, and particularly not with the outlaws camped virtually on the doorstep too. They were well enough away from High Peak Castle in the normal run of things to remain hidden. But if a mass hunt were to take place – and by the time Guy had gone all the way to Nottingham and then brought men back here again, it would need to be a very big hunt to catch up with the meat requisition – what chance was there of a panicked deer taking to the higher slopes and stumbling into the hiding place?

Yet if he didn't do that, then what? Doing nothing was not an option. However, he might just possibly co-opt the outlaws into doing the killing. They were all competent hunters, and if he did the tracking and led them to good hunting sites then the cull of deer might, with some much needed luck and the good will of the Almighty, meet the deadline. All he would then need would be the folk of the three nearest villages to each send their carts filled with the meat with him back to Nottingham. Could he bring it off? Could he spin a good enough yarn to the sheriff to convince him that he, Guy, had led a bunch of miners and villagers in a successful hunt? He scratched the stubble of his two-day beard and gazed into the fire while the steward stood over him wringing his hands.

Yes, the latter was the only viable option, if only because it gave the outlaws a chance to move on before they too were hunted, for Guy was sure he could account for some kind of men having been travellers stranded in the area by the weather. Maybe men whom he could say had already been moving on into Lancashire even as he had left High Peak himself? That should satisfy some questions ...hopefully!

"I shall ride with all haste back to Hathersage," he told the steward, standing and shrugging his heavy woollen cloak back on. "There's no priest in the vacant living, but a monk is there. I believe he said he was coming from the north to visit Walsingham." Thank Jesu they had used that excuse before, and so he had it to hand without having to cook a new one up out of nowhere! "Now Steward...?"

"...Edwin, sire..."

"...Steward Edwin, ...we come to a pretty pickle! There isn't time to send back to Nottingham for more hunters I fear, so I shall personally take charge of the hunt. I was a huntsman over on the borders, so I know my trade. However, I cannot hope to bring in that much venison alone, and you're saying that there aren't the men to help within the castle either."

"No sire," the wretched steward said miserably, clearly thinking that Guy was about to threaten him with the sheriff's wrath.

"Now, now, man, bear up!" Guy chided him. "I am merely warning you that we shall have to take some ...extraordinary ...measures under the circumstance!"

The steward blinked and looked up at the tall, dark knight who now loomed over him. "Extraordinary measures?" he said wonderingly, looking even more worried if that was possible.

"I mean," Guy said gently, as he took Edwin by the arm and steered him towards the door, "that we shall have to get our hunters where we can. I shall grant a dispensation to those local men from the nearby villages who can help us."

"They won't take kindly to hunting for the king when their families are starving, and sick from eating mouldy turnips and the like!" the burly miner who had first met him told Guy with a growl.

Guy turned back to him and nodded, somewhat confusing the miner who had been bracing himself for an argument. "I totally understand that. But we don't need the whole deer for the king! Think on it! We need the main carcasses. Most of what will go to the court kitchens won't appear at the tables as whole beasts! It will be in haunches for the lords, and the lesser cuts to go into pies and other dishes for the lowly."

He grasped the miner and Edwin both by an arm and gave them a small shake. "Think on it! We send the best stags with their heads and antlers as full carcasses except for the guts. But we can't possibly send all of them like that – they'd never all go into the carts, for a start! And most will need to be salted and put into barrels, or at least wrapped up. So all the innards can go to the villagers for a start, as can nearly all the forelegs which traditionally go to the huntsmen, and the tails, and any heads other than the stags'. The hooves can be boiled down too! We can only send two or three beasts uncut and we're charged with finding fifty deer – that's a lot of offal and poor cuts for a few small villages! And for once they can do it legally! That's surely going to tempt them to help?"

There was a murmuring of surprise and interest from the few men left behind Guy, and the other two who now stood in the doorway.

"Are you willing to go along with this?" Guy asked. "Because I can't do this alone. I can find some men from down in the valley whom I passed on the way here. I'm sure I can talk them into helping. But we shall need your wives and the older men to join in helping gutting and jointing the beasts too. If we bring the deer in, then can you find people to do those jobs? People who will divide up the spoils fairly amongst the villagers?"

"Aye, I can!" the miner said decisively. "Many of the older folk can remember jointing deer when we used to have the right to take them on the other side of the Derwent, if not this side. If you hold to your word for us to have food out of it as well, we can do the job."

Edwin dithered, then nodded, adding,

"But you will get the priest for Sir Ivo first? He raves so terribly, we're sure he must be afflicted by some dreadful demons. He speaks to something only he can see!" and he shuddered.

"I'll get your priest here by the morning!" Guy promised. "You just get the villagers organised for when I get back!"

It was a bitterly cold ride back in the dark to Hathersage, and one which Guy didn't dare take at anything more than a walk for the sake of the horses. The icy ruts were bad enough in the day, and the last thing Guy wanted was for them to fall and break a leg. He found Tuck and John snugly wrapped within the shepherd's tiny cottage and poured out his news.

"Of course I'll come," Tuck said with characteristic decisiveness. "Although I doubt the poor soul is possessed! He most likely has a dreadful fever and is raving from nothing more than sickness. But I won't let him die with his sins upon him, however badly he may have lived his life." He shook his head resignedly as he wrapped himself in several layers to fend off the winter night. "*Duw Hollalluog!* Why is it that such men only think of their immortal soul when it's about to be weighed in the Lord's balance? It's not for want of the Church's preaching! I'm sure your Sir Ivo would not be so afraid of leaving this world if he'd paid more attention to what comes afterwards while he lived!"

"No doubt!" Guy smiled. "And had you been his priest then I'm sure you would've pointed it out to him."

"Aye, and have got transferred back to the monastery for not telling him what he wanted to hear," John added dryly. "If your Sir Ivo is as much of a tyrant as this steward makes out, then I doubt that anyone but the sheriff or the king has been able to tell him anything in a very long while!"

Tuck turned back and quirked an amused eyebrow at him. "Then he'd better listen to me now, hadn't he?"

Guy led the way back again to Castleton, leaving John with instructions to find the outlaws in the morning and get them to meet Guy in Hope village. That was far enough from the castle for them not to feel threatened. John was also going to round up those Hathersage villagers who might help, which was something Guy didn't need to give him detailed instructions on – the memory of hunts back at Alverton in their youth were still clear enough in John's mind, and he knew how much help they were going to need for the laying down of the meat, since it would be no small job. With a mature stag weighing up to seven hundred pounds each, and even most hinds at least half of that, everyone would be kept very busy.

As the tired horses clattered back through Castleton there was no sign of life except a light in one small window peeping through cracks in the wooden slats, and at the sound of their hooves Guy saw the miner's face ease back the simple shutter and peer out. So he was watching, was he? Sir Ivo must have given them a very poor impression of what a knight was like if they had so little trust in one's word, Guy thought. However, that wasn't his first priority, and he led Tuck onwards and round to the less treacherous slope up to the outer bailey.

"You say you never met this Sir Ivo?" Tuck said softly to Guy as they neared the gate.

"Oddly, no, not to talk to although I have seen him. The few times I've come up here I've been dealing with the forest legalities in the villages. One of the other knights usually went and paid the sheriff's respects to him. It suited us both – whichever one of my companions I was with. You know I've never been one to fawn over men to win favour. For him to have been left in charge of a place this far from the sheriff's guiding hand he has to be a trusted man if nothing else, and the others always seemed to think that he could put in a good word for them somehow. I doubt he ever did, which was why I was content to let my fellow knights waste their breath on him. Sir Thorsten said that he was an utter bore, rattling on endlessly about his hunts and the amount of lead he could get the miners to dig up. Personally I'd rather listen to the peasants' moans – at least they had some justification for wanting to force me to hear their complaints."

Edwin was waiting for them at the picket gate in the west wall, and hurried them past the stone keep to a hall built against the south curtain wall.

"It's more commodious," he explained as he bustled along. "The king's never spent money on making the keep anything but functional. Not like Nottingham! No fancy drapes or furniture in there, I'm afraid. So we try to make the hall a little more ...bearable!"

Bearable just about described it. The knight himself was swathed in blankets in a simple wooden bed located behind a curtain at the end of the hall, and they could hear his tortuous coughing, moaning and wheezing even as they came in through the main door. Huddled around the fire were the men whom Edwin had said were ill too, most coughing occasionally in their sleep, but it didn't take Tuck's medicinal skills for Guy to see that they were a long way from being in the same state as Sir Ivo. When the three of them slipped behind the heavy wool hanging, the single candle by the bed illuminated a man racked with fever. A serving woman sat nervously on a stool as far from him as possible in the confined space, huddled beneath a heavy blanket.

"You can go now, Janet," Edwin said quietly. "Has he been quiet?"

The woman shook her head fearfully, shot Tuck a glance of almost pathetic gratitude as she saw his tonsured head appear from beneath the scarf he was unwinding, and scurried away in undisguised relief. Guy winced. He knew that look. He wished he didn't but he did, and it always went with women who had been raped. No wonder she'd bundled the thick blanket about her for protection. Even in his dying hours she clearly didn't trust Sir Ivo. What had this knight done to these people?

Guy caught Tuck's arm and held him back for a moment. "This is an evil man," he whispered softly to his friend. "Even when I was in the company of de Braose I've not seen a household as cowed as this! Maybe back then we used to spread the pain around more thinly because there were more of us, but these folk are terrified of him!"

Tuck nodded. "Don't worry, I'd already noticed that. He has much to confess, I'm thinking!" and freeing himself from Guy's grasp with a pat on his friend's hand, he went and sat on the bed. "Are you ready to confess your sins, my son?" he asked the hacking man, whose red nose was just about visible above blankets.

A pair of hard grey eyes opened blearily, then focused on Tuck's simple cross held in his hands.

"I want a proper priest!" he wheezed barely audibly, but even as sick as he was there was no doubting the expectation of being obeyed.

"I am a proper priest," Tuck answered calmly, "and if I'm not as fancily dressed as whoever you normally confess to, that makes me no less in God's eyes. And unfortunately I am the only priest within reach of here in this dreadful weather. If you wish to go to meet your Maker with your sins still burdening you, then I can go...?"

The knight shuddered and gave an awful retching cough which brought up as much blood as it did phlegm. His eyes were now filled with fear and he feebly reached out to clutch at Tuck.

"Very well," Tuck said. "Then we shall begin." He turned and looked over his shoulder pointedly at Guy.

The last confession of Sir Ivo would be kept secret by Tuck by his own sacred oaths, but Guy was bound by no such oath and really he should not be present. For the sake of appearances, Guy therefore gave Tuck a nod and slipped back out of the room. However he didn't go far. The steward was coming forward with a tankard of heated porter which Guy took thankfully, but he sent Edwin back down the hall to the hearth while he remained as close to the heavy hanging as he could without disturbing it and betraying his presence.

Sir Ivo had done something truly dreadful here, if Guy wasn't mistaken, and just what it was he really needed to know. For the sake of everyone in these cut off and lonely valleys he had to ensure that the sheriff's wrath would not fall on them, but to do that he had to know what would bring them to his side, and what would alienate them to the point where they would see no reason. There was no time to go around questioning everyone to find out, and anyway, if Guy had assessed the situation accurately, they probably wouldn't tell him outright. So much trust had been eroded here that if he went at them heavy-handed and throwing his authority about, all he would get would be silence and non co-operation. The fear of the moment would outweigh any fear of what might come in the future, whatever Guy said.

He dared to lean a little closer and felt the coarse wool of the hanging brushing his face. Luckily the bed-head was against the side wall so that there was room for a fire to be kept going in the chimney in the end wall without the risk of sparks igniting the bedclothes. That put Guy only feet away from Sir Ivo, but the danger was that Tuck was sat facing him across the bed and would see any swaying of the hanging. So to keep his balance better Guy moved to the wall, right into the corner where the heavy wool brushed against it. Now he could lean on the wall, and he was by the tiny gaps close to it which the wool hanging afforded him. Tuck was still going through the litany with Sir Ivo, praying for the forgiveness of his soul in the hereafter, allowing Guy to have a goodly draught of the warm ale which gave a welcome glow deep inside him after the chill of the ride here.

Then he heard Sir Ivo's dry and rasping voice beginning to croak his sins out to Tuck, and Guy all but held his breath in order to hear better. At first it was the usual catalogue of misery the son of any affluent knight might inflict on an unfortunate manor. Guy disliked the fact that such things happened, but knew from his experience of watching Fulk, Philip and Audulph, that most villagers would take the petty viciousness in their stride, and that once he'd come to England from his family's other home in Normandy, during Ivo's youth the voice of the hundred court would have made itself felt for the greater of his excesses. It had taken coming to this more remote spot for Sir Ivo to really get the bit between his teeth and start his reign of terror.

By the time he got to his arrival at High Peak, Guy already loathed Sir Ivo, the man condemned by his own mouth. It was therefore little surprise that things had only got worse.

By now Tuck was also having to prompt Sir Ivo more. Maybe it was having, at the very last, to so extensively catalogue his sins which was making Sir Ivo reticent. Guy thought he himself would have been quaking his bed if his list was that long! But, as Tuck kept reminding the sinking soul, no deeds would stay unseen before Saint Peter, Christ and God. Just because Sir Ivo didn't confess them would not mean that he wouldn't be held to account for them. Already Guy was hoping that the Almighty, or at least St Peter, was someone after his own heart, for he could have thrown Sir Ivo into the fires of Hell without much hesitation. By the time Sir Ivo reluctantly admitted that there was hardly a woman in the village whom he had not taken by force, Guy was having to resist the impulse to march in and despatch the miserable knight to his judgement with the rest of his sins hung about him to weight him straight down into the fiery pit.

Yet still there was more. A fall of stones in one of the lead mines had left men trapped, but Sir Ivo had refused to send his soldiers to help dig them out. Good miners had died, yet Sir Ivo had later whipped the rest for not fulfilling their quota of lead, regardless of the fact that he could have helped – although that wasn't quite how he phrased it to Tuck, and the monk had to work hard to get the truth out. On another occasion he'd had the hands chopped off a man for purportedly poaching, knowing the man couldn't have done it, but punishing him just the same so that his comely wife would be forced to come and work in the castle to support their children, and therefore into Sir Ivo's grasp. Guy made a mental note to ask after the fate of that woman.

By the time Sir Ivo got to the end of his confession, Guy had a sizeable list of people to ask after, and he left Tuck to the rest of his work to go in search of a quill and piece of parchment to write all the names down on before he forgot them. As a ragged dawn of gusting winds and blustery rain finally arrived, Guy woke to find that he'd nodded off over the table he'd been sitting at writing. Someone was coming to the fire with a bucket of water, and it was only when they swung it backwards that Guy realised that the woman was about to douse the fire.

"Stop!" he commanded, struggling to his feet and hurrying to her side. "What on earth are you doing?"

"Sir Ivo insists that all the fires are doused come morning except for the kitchens and the one in his room," the woman answered fearfully.

Guy put a hand on her shoulder and both felt her flinch, and how thin she was beneath the wool shawl wrapped around her. "Well

Sir Ivo won't be giving any orders here any more," he said gently, taking the bucket out of her hands and setting it down on the floor. By Saint Peter and Saint Paul, no wonder the men were sick and not improving! What kind of idiotic parsimony was that? To leave the sick freezing cold and with a damp wind running through the place? It was amazing that more hadn't actually died. He must check with Robert of Crockston and find out if High Peak had received a higher than normal number of replacements, and what excuse had been given! For now, though, he told the woman to get the men to bring more logs in instead and get the fire going properly for the day. Already the sick men were regarding him with something like awe.

"I shall be taking charge of this castle for the next few weeks," Guy told them. "We have hunting to do on the king's behalf which won't wait for a new castellan to arrive." He turned to Edwin. "I want these men and all of the castle's folk to be fed a good breakfast."

"We only have oats for porridge," Edwin replied worriedly.

"Really? Sir Ivo had just porridge like any peasant?"

Edwin looked confused. "No sire, of course not. Sir Ivo had bacon and sausages and often an egg cooked in the meat fat too."

"Then there's a store of this bacon and sausages?"

"Yes sire, in the cellar in the base of the keep, but it's not for the likes of me to go in there."

"Why not? You're the bloody steward!"

Edwin winced and Guy mentally chastised himself for being so forthright. These folk weren't used to being spoken to normally. He tried again. "Edwin, why weren't you allowed in there? And how did you get the meat to cook for him if you didn't go in?"

The terrified steward rallied a little at Guy's gentler tone. "Sir Ivo himself used to go and bring a week's worth out at a time for the cook to keep with the other food in the kitchen store. He has a small meat store which is right in the rock of the hill, so it stays cold even in summer. Sir Ivo's weekly meat was kept there."

And not one of you dared to even think of touching it either, Guy thought in disgust. Ivo's hand had been heavy indeed if folk could be so very hungry and still leave prime meat within their grasp untouched. "So where is the key?" he asked carefully.

Edwin just pointed to the woollen hanging.

"Hmmm. And has he had any meat since he's been ill?"

"Sergeant Ingulf went down a couple of times," Edwin admitted, pointing to one of the sick men, who nodded feebly. "But Sir Ivo only let him have the key while he was awake. And even then he was calling for the sergeant before he'd even had chance to get in and get the meat."

Guy went and crouched down in front of the sick sergeant. "Where does he have the key?" he asked firmly but keeping any edge out of his voice.

The sergeant seemed to respond to the authority. With a sigh which sounded very like one of relief, he said,

"It's under his pillow. Right where he can touch it at all times." He paused, looking up at Guy with an appraising eye. "Are you really taking charge here, sire?"

"Yes I am. My name is Sir Guy of Gisborne. I'm one of the sheriff's forester knights. Normally I deal with royal forest affairs, but I have every authority to take command of this place until the sheriff decides who should take over properly. And that, as far as I'm concerned means that I have a duty to get you and your men back and on your feet to be able to do your duties."

He straightened up, massaged his back where it ached from falling asleep in such a strange position. "And that means getting that bloody key and getting you all fed properly!" He marched up to the wall hanging, swept the loose edge aside and strode into the chamber. Tuck was kneeling on a folded blanket beside the bed, praying softly, although Guy noted that he'd stoked the fire at least once overnight despite whatever Sir Ivo might have said. Without preamble Guy strode to the bed and groped beneath the pillows.

"What are you...?" Tuck began as Guy suddenly lifted a heavy iron key triumphantly out of the bed.

"The bastard's been starving these folk!" Guy fumed. "This is the key to get them some decent bloody food!"

Yet the sight of his key in the hands of a stranger galvanised Sir Ivo to one last effort.

"Noooo!" he wailed, stretching his claw-like hand out to try and snatch it back.

"For God's sake, your miserable old miser!" Guy snapped, jerking the key well out of reach and turning on his heels. "Can you not spare a bit of bacon in one last attempt at a Christian act?"

Sir Ivo was turning a very odd colour, a gargling half cough issuing from his mouth as his lips became blood flecked. Again he almost tried to fling himself in Guy's direction, giving Guy a nasty thought. As a parting shot before he went back out through the hanging, he demanded of the dying man,

"Are you sure you've confessed all? Since when did a piece of pig weigh so heavily on your soul?"

The death rattle which came after Guy's words was loud enough to be heard beyond the woollen hanging, but Guy didn't bother turning back.

"He's dead," he declared to the assembled cluster around the now glowing fire. "So don't worry about what he's going to say ever again. Edwin? Go and tell the cook to prepare a *goodly* portion of porridge for everyone, and then to get his skillet warming – we're *all* going to have bacon today!"

He grabbed his cloak from off the bench where he'd left it that night, and wrapped it around him against the sudden flurry of wind and rain outside. It was only a short walk to the keep, and his first act was to instruct the three half-frozen men on watch to go and get more fuel for the small brazier they had to keep them warm. When he told them he was going for bacon for everyone, they forgot to be suspicious or even to question him.

"I'll get the lads well fed who are coming to relieve you," Guy told them, "and then you can come and have a good meal yourselves before you get some rest. ...Oh, and the fire's been topped up in the hall as well, so you'll be warm while you sleep too!"

The spontaneous grins which accompanied his announcement told Guy that he'd won these men over already. He wouldn't have any trouble with them.

Going down the internal stairway to the basement of the keep, Guy turned the key in the stout oak door and let himself into the secure area. As he would have expected in a castle of this type, there were supplies of arrows and other bits and pieces necessary for repairs and replacements of armour and weaponry. Hanging from stout hooks in the beams of the floor above were several whole hams, well smoked and salted and filling the air with a mouth-watering aroma, even uncooked, and also sides of pig well-cured. That accounted for the bacon, for one had already been cut into, and Guy hauled a chest across to stand on it in order to lift this one down.

Yet Edwin had said sausages too. Where were they? Possibly packed in salt in a barrel somewhere? That would be the most likely place if they weren't also smoked for keeping. There were a good many barrels stacked against the far wall and Guy went to investigate. Several sloshed wetly when moved, and Guy guessed that some would contain wine for entertaining official visitors. Nothing odd about that. Four others, though, were so incredibly heavy that even a man as strong as Guy couldn't even begin to move them, let alone rock them. Definitely no wine in those!

The last two he went to told him by his nose that he'd found more meat. One had a loose top and upon opening revealed the missing sausages. The barrel was already half empty and he had to scoop some salt out of the way to get down to what seemed to be another layer of preserving. Someone around here was good at making them, though. They were good and plump and to Guy's eye had been properly prepared. Today they would be a bit salty, for Guy didn't want to waste too much time soaking the salt off them before cooking, but he made sure that he took enough for the next day. The cook would have time to do a proper job on those.

Locking the door behind him, Guy lugged the heavy ham and the long links of sausages over to the kitchen building. Already there was quite a little gathering, all eagerly waiting with bowls as they watched the cook stirring a large cast iron pot full of porridge. Guy dumped the meat onto a well scrubbed table and took his sharp hunting knife out of its holder on his belt. Without preamble he swiftly sliced several dozen thin strips off the bacon joint, and then cut the long links into individual sausages. Looking up he saw the castle's inhabitants staring at him slack-jawed.

"I was the head wolf-hunter for Sheriff de Braose over on the Welsh border," Guy declared, matter of factly. "I've had to butcher deer and boar out on the hunt too."

There were some silent "oh"s and a few blinks, but they all seemed to accept that a knight in such a far off place as nearly into Wales might know such things, even if those closer to home wouldn't sully their hands so. If they hadn't been so hungry Guy guessed that he would have had to answer a good many more questions. However, he'd taken the cook's skillet and had already put some of the bacon on to cook. The smell of that alone was making several stomachs rumble audibly! As people gradually filed out clutching brimming bowls of hot porridge, Guy also made sure that a good dollop of honey went into each bowl too. Many faces said that they couldn't quite believe that this was true, but they weren't going to turn such a gift away, even if it was only for one day and they had to pay later.

Finding a tray, Guy got a bowl of porridge each for him and Tuck, and carved a thick slice of bread each off a newly baked loaf onto which he put their share of the bacon. With a tankard each of small beer to wash it down with, he carried it across the bailey to the hall and up to the end of the long table.

"Breakfast, Tuck!" he called out, and almost instantly Tuck's massive head and shoulders appeared around the wool hanging.

"Excellent!" his friend declared, appearing fully, drying his hands on a cloth which he dumped on the bench as he settled down at the table.

"You're laying him out?" Guy asked as they both blew on the spoonfuls of scalding hot porridge to cool it a little.

Tuck nodded and took his first mouthful before answering. "Yes. A grim job, but better that I do it than one of these folk." He puffed mightily on another spoonful and ate that before adding. "Most of them would be too terrified to do it, and the rest might decide to take revenge upon his corpse in a way that they dared not do when he was alive."

"Well there's a definite mystery surrounding him waiting in the keep's basement," Guy added softly. At least they were alone at this end of the table, for all the servants not involved in preparing meals had joined the six ailing soldiers around the glowing blaze of the hearth and an almost festive air had infused itself into the little gathering. There was even a little laughter percolating out occasionally. "There's something in some of those barrels in the keep,

Tuck, and whatever it is, it isn't food. I can't begin to shift them! We'll leave well alone for today, but tomorrow I'd like you to come into the keep with me and help me get into one of them. I'd say they were once used for large joints of meat because they're bigger than wine casks, but I don't think they've got meat in them now!"

Tuck's eyebrows went up. "Hmmm? Is there, now?"

They both knew one another well enough to not need to say more – that they were thinking that Sir Ivo had been feathering his own nest on the quiet. Tuck was nodding sagely now.

"Mmmm ...and while you can be seen to be generous in handing out the food supplies..."

"Exactly! ...Wouldn't go down very well if the sheriff heard that instead of collecting taxes...!"

"Quite!" A twinkle came into Tuck's eyes. "Much better if the hand of the Lord was seen to move in mysterious ways, eh? I've been looking at the late priest's breviary and it occurs to me that Lent begins next Wednesday – just time for folk to have a good feast before the fast! And then have something to buy plenty of bread with, if nothing else in the holy weeks," and he grinned broadly.

Guy smiled back and nodded. No doubt some poor souls were barely keeping the most basic foods on the family table if Sir Ivo had been thieving off them unofficially as well as officially. A quiet gift left at a few doors could do a lot of good, but Guy couldn't hope to do that just at the moment. A wandering monk, however, would not have the soldiers watching his every move. It was a happy thought that once again he would be able to do some of the more quietly rebellious things he had done over at Grosmont for the few days he was away from the watchful eyes at Nottingham. In the meantime, though, there were Sir Ivo's remains to be considered.

"You'll be taking him down to the church soon?" Guy asked with a flick of the eyes towards where the corpse lay.

"As soon as everyone's been fed," Tuck said firmly. "Straight down to the church!"

"Will you bury him today?"

"I don't think we'd get a spade into the ground, it's too cold," Tuck replied regretfully. "But he can certainly be nailed into a wooden coffin and left on holy ground! I've asked Edwin to send word to the village carpenter to make a rough box up quickly – no winding sheet will do for him, or them! His wicked body needs a more secure holding place than that! I've wrapped him in plenty of vinegar soaked cloth to preserve him a bit, and the cold does have its advantages!"

"Would you do ...whatever it is that you do when there's an unquiet spirit about?" Guy asked thoughtfully.

Tuck was surprised. "What, straight away?"

But Guy nodded. "It might be for the best. They're so frightened even now, Tuck. I don't want my work disrupted because some of them start having nightmares that the bloody man's come back and started haunting the place! And they could, you know. Let's get him down to the church and safely out of here, and then you go around and very visibly do your cleansing or blessing or whatever. Let them see that even his miserable spirit has gone for good."

For a moment Guy thought Tuck would declare such actions unnecessary, bolstered by his firm faith as he was. Then he realised that the silence was only because Tuck was watching how certain of the servants and two of the guards were still glancing nervously at the shadows in the hall.

"Yes, I think you're right, Guy. These people must not be left in any doubt that he's gone."

"Especially the women!" Guy added and got a disapproving look from Tuck.

"You listened?"

Guy could tell that Tuck was disappointed in him for that. "I'm sorry, Tuck. But look at it this way. You had the care of one man's immortal soul to minister to. I have to act in the sheriff's name to many. I had to know what had gone on before we got here. You know I can keep a secret! I'm not going to go around blackening Sir Ivo's name to the sheriff or anyone else – or at least not with what I learned listening in. Whatever we find in that keep is a simple matter of something I discovered without ever resorting to keyholes or the like, and if there is something which needs reporting then I can do it without reference to his miserable confession.

"But that's something very different to what we're talking of here. From what I overheard, I now know that if I ask the women to all work together in the castle yard or down in the village, then I'm likely to get co-operation. Yet if I try to separate them out into small groups or even singly then it just won't happen. I'm still a knight in their eyes, and it will take a lot more than one breakfast to repair the damage Sir Ivo's done.

"And the men won't be any different. If I say that the old men who aren't able to go hunting can work alongside the women, then all the villagers will be even happier. It'll mean that the castle bailey will look like a slaughterhouse for a week or so, but better that than me bringing in deer and the odd boar and the meat not getting properly laid down and rotting by the time it reaches court. That would be disastrous for everyone."

Tuck sighed. "Yes, I suppose the king's wrath might take some appeasing if roused."

"It's not just that, though. What if he actually came up here in high dudgeon? What if he called the hundred court to account? You know King Henry sets high store by them! How would he react if he found out by the testimony of dozens of good men that the sheriff's man was on the fiddle from the crown? And Sheriff Murdac in turn would be called to account for that."

Tuck gulped on his beer and coughed. "Good grief! I hadn't thought of that! Yes, that could well be disastrous – for us in particular!" He didn't have to mention John and the outlaws for Guy to be nodding as vigorously as he dared in unknown company.

"Could mean a new sheriff, you see? One who wouldn't give me such a free rein, maybe? One who would feel that he had to come in and personally inspect his whole holding...?" Guy left his words hanging knowing that Tuck was capable of finishing them for himself.

The big monk shuddered. "You're forgiven, Guy. But please don't make this a habit."

"Not on your life! I have enough on my conscience without listening in to everyone else's sins! Eugh! It's like washing some else's dirty underwear! I don't know how you can do it, Tuck. Not even for the rewards in the afterlife!"

Tuck's face creased into a more normal smile. "Practice my boy, practice! Now then, let's get this miserable old miscreant down to the church!"

With Sir Ivo safely ensconced in Castleton's humble church, Tuck spent the rest of the day walking about the castle, very visibly and audibly praying, singing and sprinkling holy water. By the time he sat down to share an evening meal with Guy, he was actually saying that it hadn't just been a gesture just for the servants and guards.

"May the Lord forgive him, Guy, but there was evil lurking in some parts of this castle. What happened there I cannot say, but there was some kind of lingering presence of evil deeds which made the hairs on the back of my neck stand on end! Christ was guiding us with your words, I feel, for now I'm sure that these folk would have been afflicted with the shades of the dead sooner or later."

"Well let's see if we can lay a few more nasty shades to rest tomorrow," Guy responded cheerfully.

Come the morning they went to the keep under the pretext of checking the food. The cook had come and said that the sausages were uneatable, declaring that they had to have been from last year's laying down and early too.

"I told him!" the cook declared stoutly. "I said one man would never get through that lot before they went bad! But would he listen? No! Fit for the fire, that's all that barrel's good for now! What a waste! Even my dog won't touch them!"

"Jesu, I hope you didn't try to feed them to him or her?" Guy asked in a sudden fit of panic. He only ever fed his dogs pig's blood and entrails, and then only of wild boar and very well cooked at that, knowing that pig was not good for dogs.

"Oh my Bessie's a good little girl, and shrewd!" the cook said proudly. "She earns her keep keeping the kitchens and stores free of rats and mice, but she knows off meat when she smells it. I use her to test stuff. One whiff of it being less than good and she won't go near it."

Guy breathed a sigh of relief. Clearly Bessie was a clever little terrier. Some of the big dogs he'd known wouldn't have been half so discerning and he was very glad that he'd left Fletch and Spike behind because of the weather – those two would probably have stolen sausages straight off the skillet if they'd had the chance! Of course, it helped that she was the cook's dog and was undoubtedly fed all the scraps, and if she was small then she probably never went hungry. That would make a difference too.

So he and Tuck had gone into the basement, walked the other barrels of meat and the hams to the door and then summoned the cook. Having been the one to lay the meat down he was quick to sort out what was still usable and what needed to be destroyed before it poisoned someone. It went against the grain with everyone to burn what looked like good meat, but the cook was insistent and luckily all but one of the hams were still good. Even the barrels of the condemned meat had to go on the fire, for once contaminated, Guy and the cook agreed that they would only turn any good meat which was subsequently put into them. With the meat having been taken out, it then gave Guy and Tuck time to investigate the mystery barrels without being disturbed, under the pretext of sorting out what was wine and what mead – something which the cook couldn't help them with since these had all been brought in from outside. When they prised the top off the first heavy barrel they were astonished. It was full to the brim with silver pennies.

"This is good!" Guy exclaimed.

"Yes it is," Tuck agreed, but somewhat unsure of why Guy was quite so pleased.

"They're pennies!"

"Yes?"

"So that means the people can spend them!" And then Tuck caught on. Had they been gold it would have been so very much harder for any peasant to account for why he had such a high value coin in his possession.

"But how will we get so many coins out to the people?" he wondered to Guy. "We can barely move one barrel between us!"

"It'll have to be done carefully," Guy agreed. "Do you know, I think we might ask the lads to bring a wagon up to the bailey. If John helps us we can probably lift these on to a cart. We'll say that the big barrels are needed for the meat down in Hathersage, although we'll have to come up with some distraction. No-one will believe an empty barrel weighs so much. Hmmm ...I think we'll shift it when the first lot of butchery and salting is going on. Everyone should be too busy to notice much by then. But we can certainly make a start before that. Can you ride down to Hope this afternoon and find John? We can fill a couple of saddlebags with coins if you ride. Maybe drape your cloak over them so that they don't seem so obviously full. If I give you that big hairy fetlocked beast from the stable it should carry quite a load, even with you riding – no offence intended!"

Tuck chuckled. "None taken!" He knew his size was an issue with villagers' ponies. "How much shall I take?"

"I don't know. But I'll have a look at the castle records. They should tell us how many families live in Hope and what they pay per year. If we give them this year's tithe back and say openly that Sir Ivo held it back for himself, I think we'll be believed. By Our Lady, Tuck, how ever did these poor souls find the bloody Saladin Tithe as well? They must have been living hand to mouth for over a year now! I'll have to check with Edwin that the full dues from High Peak were really paid at Michaelmas, but I don't remember the sheriff complaining of them not arriving and he surely would have, because he would've had to find the money himself or risk the king's men's wrath when they came to collect it. Bless these poor souls! No wonder they're all so thin!"

With Hope only being a mile away, Tuck didn't have to set out until the winter sun had well passed its zenith, although the sun itself never showed its face and the time was only betrayed by the lowering light. He and Guy chivvied people into different jobs, and were able to load two very heavy bags onto the big horse unobserved. Then Tuck mounted up, and with a comment about fetching some hunters back with him tomorrow, set off. Guy in the meantime was giving the men a master-class in butchering deer, after setting out for a short hunt and almost falling over a winter-weakened hind which he brought back to demonstrate on. Any fool could hack a carcass to pieces, but if they were going to fool the king's cooks into thinking all had been done by foresters then it would have to be done right.

Two men in particular were surprisingly skilled at skinning, making Guy sure that the desperate families had secretly used the forest's resources when they thought they could get away with it. And a neat skinning was the biggest hurdle to perpetrating this deception. Sheep weren't so very different when it came to muscles and bone, and most families would have butchered their own old beasts if nothing else. However folk in villages nearer the big castles never got chance to properly skin anything much bigger than a rabbit or a sheep, and for the slaughter of old plough oxen in late autumn, or the new bullocks in spring, one man would most often come and do the job for all the families in the villages thereabouts, then take the skins to the nearest tanner. In this instance, once the soft, supple deerskin was off, it was a simpler matter to joint the beast, but it still had to be done right.

"I'm sorry I can't leave you the skins," Guy apologised to the villagers, "but I have to take them to the tanners at Nottingham. If I don't the sheriff will start asking questions, and once he's started being suspicious then I can't guarantee to hide what we're about to do. Better for you to have the meat and no fancy gloves or jerkins! Just clean the skins and salt them so that they'll keep until I can get them to Nottingham. If you put them bloody-side to bloody-side they won't stain one another and we should be able to make a bundle of them."

No-one argued. They were far too grateful for the sudden influx of food after Sir Ivo's heavy-handed parsimony.

At Hope, Tuck found John and the outlaws camped just up the River Noe on the north side of the cluster of houses and just out of sight of the Castleton road. They'd already made a good start on the hunt and three good sized hinds had been gutted and jointed, with the villagers enjoying the best stew they'd had in weeks in their respective cottages. Consequently the humble streets were deserted, although the sounds of cheerful voices echoing out of the cottages said everything about the inhabitants' thoughts on their change of fortune. With that in mind John had an idea of his own.

"These folk are already happier at having some good food," he said thoughtfully. "I can see what Guy's trying to do, but do you know, I think it might be better to wait a little longer before we hand them their coins too. Because, heaven forbid, if the sheriff *does* come through here in a week or so and they're practically holding a festival, he'd have to be a fool not to ask what's going on."

"...And then someone will surely tell him everything without thinking!" Hugh concluded.

"Exactly!" John said emphatically. "No disrespect to Guy. He's had to do a lot of quick thinking and it's a good idea as far as it goes. I certainly think he's right about us getting those barrels away from the castle and up to our cave, or some other secure place."

"And that doesn't mean us dipping our fingers in either!" Hugh said firmly with a pointed glance to Piers Cosham. The middle brother gave a cursory shrug, although Bilan and Thomas blushed at the implied shame brought on their family. However, for once Algar of Costock and Walter of Fiskerton were nodding their agreement with Hugh and that was enough to convince Piers that he would risk a serious beating if he overstepped the line this time, and it wouldn't just be from Thomas either.

"What about this lot, then?" Tuck asked. "I can hardly leave it lying around, and you lot are going to be running here, there and everywhere with this hunt."

John creased his brow in thought. "Can't be Hathersage for the same reason. Anyone coming to Castleton from Nottingham will pass through there too."

"Ashford-in-the Water!" Hugh declared. "It's one of the king's manors, so the hand of Sir Ivo will have fallen heavily there too! Rowland, Hassop and Longstone are all hamlets this way which answer to Ashford, and Tuck can easily get to them by taking the Tideswell road out of Hope. The difference with them is that a good Samaritan could have arrived by one of many roads."

Algar and Walter were nodding again, Walter adding,

"They were sorely pressed when we went through there a couple of weeks ago. If they could go down to Bakewell and buy some grain at the market it would make all the difference to them. The bloody sheriff's bled them white!"

Tuck looked around at the collective nods. "The Tideswell road it is, then. You lot take those beasts up to Guy tomorrow morning and I'll ride on."

"Bilan can stay here and keep watch," Thomas added.

"Why?" his youngest brother exclaimed indignantly. "I can shoot nearly as well as you two!"

"Yes, boyo, but you can run a damned site faster!" Thomas said firmly. "We've got to have someone on lookout, just in case the sheriff thinks Guy's taking far too long and sends someone out to check on him. That someone will have to run like the very Devil were at his heels, and over rough ground, to warn us so that we can get out of that castle in time!"

Placated, Bilan demurred, but Thomas' words later on prompted Tuck to suggest quietly to Hugh and John that they persuade Guy to send one or two of the soldiers with an official message to the sheriff. Pre-empting a visit was infinitely better than exercising damage control once he was in sight.

On an altogether brighter morning Tuck rode off and made good time down through Bradwell and Hucklow. Hugh's directions had been clear, and Tuck was glad he'd listened to the former soldier instead of Walter and Algar, both of whom had been quick to offer encouragement and directions, but whose instructions would easily have set Tuck off in the wrong directions when he came to the main crossroad. He attracted some attention when he got into each of the little hamlets since they rarely saw visitors, being somewhat away from the main roads. It took little persuasion on Tuck's part, though, to convince them that they should say nothing of their sudden good fortune, and he made a point of telling them that he'd given coin to other villages too – so hopefully they wouldn't feel tempted to brag of their good luck to their neighbours knowing that they too had been gifted. He'd had to use a little discretion over the amounts, for one of the saddlebags had been intended for the Hope households, which like Hathersage was a much larger settlement than Castleton.

He had plenty of money to spare, therefore, but he was careful not to overload the desperate families with good fortune. John and Hugh's common sense approach had made him think again while on the road, and he believed it would be better to hand out the money in small amounts. It would be too much to ask a family on the brink of starvation to not go out and spend it all at once out of nothing more than relief.

Nonetheless, he felt a bit ashamed that it was him and not Guy who was getting all the pleasure and the thanks. It made it all the harder not say, when questioned where the money had come from, that there were still some honest knights left in the world. Had it not potentially endangered Guy to say so he would have found it even harder to stay silent. Instead he wove a tale of a generous old knight with no family who had made a bequest, and that he, Tuck, as the old knight's confessor, was fulfilling the old man's dying wish. The worldly side of Tuck gained substantial satisfaction at the thought of how that description would have riled Sir Ivo in this life, and his spiritual side hoped that the miserable old miser was being forced by a few muscular saints up on high to watch this distribution of alms.

It was a happy thought, and he allowed his horse to take a drink at the river when he returned to the riverside on the way back. He'd gone through Longstone, to Rowland and then to Hassop and had decided to see if he could find a room for the night down at Ashford. He'd paused just outside of the village to watch the sun setting on the fast running little River Wye, and was offering up a few prayers of thanks for the lovely sight, when he heard hooves on the road. Before he could pull his horse off into the cover of a small copse, he heard a martial voice calling,

"Hey traveller! Is this the right road to Ashford?"

He sighed, crossed himself with a quick prayer to the Lord to not allow everything to go wrong at this late stage, and stepped out into view from behind his horse. His heart sank into his boots. Templars by the look of them!

"Good day, brothers!" he called cheerfully, although far from feeling it inside. "Yes, you're on the right road. I don't know the area well, but I'm assured that Ashford is only just around that bend."

"Ah! The mystery monk!" a rough-looking soldier said, and the party all pulled up in front of Tuck. There were six of them, all browned from years under blistering suns, all scarred, and all wearing the kind of battered gambesons and scabbards which spoke of years of hard use. There was no way Tuck would be able to fight his way free of all of them. He didn't like the sound of that 'mystery monk' comment either, and belatedly realised that they must have been almost on his heels by the time he'd turned onto the Ashford road from Hassop. He hoped he could find some kind of bond with them – it would be the only way out without someone getting hurt.

"Are you long back from the Holy Land?" he asked pleasantly.

"A long and *hard* journey," the roughest looking one answered bleakly, "but then here no-one seems to have heard of the disaster happening in the east."

"Disaster?" Tuck was surprised. "No brothers, but news gets to these parts very slowly. Please tell me, though. I was in the east myself once – albeit many years ago when I was a younger man!"

"And thinner!" a flame-haired knight quipped in a voice heavy with a Irish brogue.

Tuck didn't take the bait. All the better if they thought his bulk was fat and not muscle. He'd rather they underestimated him at this stage. Then he saw a movement out of the corner of his eye and realised too late that the darkest knight had moved his horse softly forwards and had just reached out to the saddlebags.

"Some weight there," he said with careful pronunciation, and Tuck realised that he was probably a Saracen, the genuine article rather than a sunburned English knight.

"Where does a humble monk get so much silver?" the leader asked in a dangerously soft voice. "What of your vows of poverty?"

""It doesn't belong to me," Tuck said bluntly, "But it certainly isn't stolen, if that's what you're thinking ...or rather it wasn't stolen by me! I'm returning it to those it was taken from."

"Are you now!" the rough soldier said with grim humour. Tuck was having some trouble working out who was a knight and who a lay brother or man-at-arms with the order, for none of them wore their surcoats. He'd only known them for Templars by his own experience, their distinctive sword pommels, and the glimpses of white and red surcoats strapped to the back of their saddles over their packed ringmail. This one, however, looked as though he could be real trouble, and Tuck guessed he was a sergeant, and one who'd probably seen his fair share of tavern brawls on the journeys to and from the Holy Land.

"On whose authority?" demanded another dark-haired man whose skin didn't look like it was naturally so dark as to be native to the Holy Land.

"A representative of the sheriff of Nottingham," Tuck answered firmly. He was determined not to show an inch of being flustered or lack of confidence. That, he was sure, would be the worst thing he could do. They would take it as a sign of weakness or of guilt.

"Phfaa!" the same young man snorted. "When did Giendara develop a conscience?"

"Giendara?" Tuck was taken aback. "Who's Giendara?"

"Why, the sheriff of Nottingham!" the young knight said with sickly sarcasm. "Did you not know that? And you being a representative of his and all!"

"No he isn't!" Tuck retorted, then remembered the name from talking to Guy. "Oh, ...he was the sheriff years ago! I've never even seen him! But the current sheriff's Sir Ralph Murdac, and has been for a good few years – eight at least, I think."

That now wrong-footed the newcomers. Tuck watched as the young dark knight looked to the one who seemed to be the leader. He couldn't quite see them well enough to lip read what they were saying, but clearly they were the two who knew the area and were conferring on whether they thought he spoke the truth.

"I swear to you," Tuck said calmly, holding up his simple wooden cross in his hand as he spoke, "that the sheriff really is Murdac."

Of all the moves he could have made it shocked him that this would be the wrong one. The rough soldier gave a snarl and launched himself off his horse straight at Tuck.

"Don't you dare swear on the Cross, you bloated old hypocrite!" he screamed as he cannoned into Tuck, taking a swing at him with his fist as he did so. "Don't you dare!"

The assumption of being fat was what saved Tuck. The other man hadn't expected to hit solid muscle, and he certain hadn't expected to be flipped to the ground and punched hard in return without having his own blow land as intended. Tuck had enjoyed the wrestling contests at the village fairs over on the border, and when there'd been no-one but the villagers watching he'd joined in with good humoured gusto. Since then he and John had practised together, finding it fun for each to come up against someone who was a match for their own size and strength. So when the soldier had collided with Tuck it had been instinctive to turn and heave him over his shoulder and use the man's own momentum to bring him down. Even as Tuck heard someone shout "Will, no!" he'd laid the man out cold, then rolled himself and come to his feet several paces away from where he'd started.

The leader had vaulted from his horse and was advancing grimly towards Tuck with a dagger drawn.

"That was a little too good for a man of the cloister," he said suspiciously.

"Don't do it, son!" Tuck warned. "I've been out of monastery for many a year serving the poor, but I'm a priest good and proper! Think of your immortal soul!"

The young leader quirked his head on one side, then flipped the knife back to plant it in the ground back by his horse, where one of the two very dark men leapt nimbly down and retrieved it.

"Still, rather handy with your fists for a priest, aren't you?" the young leader said, still advancing.

"As I said, I was in the Holy Land too," Tuck repeated calmly. "And I spent many years ministering to my fellow Welshmen on the borders after that. It might not be plagued by wild Saracens out there, but there are plenty of lawless men all the same. Some of them don't respect priests or men of the cloth."

"Probably with good cause!" the flame-haired Irishman spat back fast.

With someone else it would have been the distraction the leader was waiting for, and foolishly he pounced before realising that Tuck's eyes had never left him. The two of them went down in a tangle of limbs.

"Get him Robin!" someone called, and the young knight was certainly intent on bringing Tuck down. But for all the younger man's keener battle experience, whenever Tuck rolled on top of him the greater weight of the monk nearly squashed the breath out of him. Tuck also had a plan, and so he kept rolling, then suddenly came to his feet, seized the knight by his gambeson and hefted him out into the river. It was the young knight's good fortune that here the river banks had lessened from the almost cliff-like banks of a few hundred yards upstream. Nonetheless the shock of going into an icy English river for one more used to being too hot was an abrupt shock, even with the gambeson affording some cushioning, and he yelled out.

Mistaking his shout and thinking he was really hurt the other Templars leapt off their horses and surged forwards. Seeing the roughest man blink as he came round, Tuck picked him up and threw him into the river into the arms of the young knight, who'd just got close enough to the bank to get his feet down again. The two of them disappeared in another giant splash. The river was running fast at this time of year, so Tuck hoped they would go several yards downstream and away from him before they sorted themselves out again.

The redheaded Irishman and the dark Englishman were the two at the fore, and Tuck regarded these two as the more dangerous. The two Saracens seemed to be unsure of just how far to take this skirmish, and so far were holding back a little – praise the Lord, Tuck thought!

"Your friends aren't hurt and I'm no thief!" Tuck told the advancing pair. "In the name of the Lord I command you to stop this nonsense! I have no wish to harm any of you, but if you force me to to defend myself then I will. That is not *my* money! If it was, you could have it, if silver will salve your twisted souls! But I have a sworn duty to do and you're stopping me from doing it!"

"Wait, Gilbert!" the Saracen who'd inspected Tuck's saddlebags said, running forward to grab the redhead's arm. "What if he tells the truth?"

"Fucking lying priests!" the one called Gilbert snarled, spitting in contempt on the ground. "It's twisted Churchmen like him that made God stay his hand and let Jerusalem fall."

"What?" Tuck was so taken aback that he dropped his guard. "Jerusalem fallen? The last we heard it was besieged but likely to hold!"

Something in his shocked face must have registered with those facing him for they halted, but then the world turned black as someone whacked him over the head with a substantial branch from behind.

So there you have it, Brother Gervase. That was the legendary meeting between Robin Hood and Brother Tuck. They did fight, and by a river at that, but not for some fish to feed Tuck's gluttony. Nor for some trifling matter of who had the right to be there. It was a matter of principle, which both of them had strong opinions on, and there were to be many more such disagreements between them in the coming years. But of course at this point in time I knew nothing of these happenings. I was busy hunting deer with the outlaws and chivvying the castle servants into activity. However, I shall not bore you with the dull details when we have reached such a crux! More parchment, Brother! We must keep writing it all down!

Chapter 14

*A*h, you are ready? And we have a new quill too! Then let us lose no more time, Brother. But just one tiny point before we plunge once more into my younger days. You ask me to repent for my deeds, but as I said earlier, sometimes I have felt the divine hand at my shoulder, working in mysterious ways, and that fateful day was another one of those times. While Tuck had been handing out our fortune-gained alms to the poor, John and I had led a successful hunt into the Derwent valley, going north from the road between Hope and Hathersage.

I therefore decided that the following day we should go south. The others thought we should go north once more, but I believed strongly that leaving the deer to settle for a day or two without being hunted again would make our job easier later on, not to mention the fact that I did not want to deplete whole herds of deer, for the healthiest should be left to breed in the coming season to provide for future hunts – such management was, after all, my job. So against their clamouring, I threw my weight in as official leader and declared the hunt would go south that day, and you shall now hear why I feel that the Lord was pushing me into my future fate.

Derbyshire
February, the Year of our Lord 1189

It was another dry day, and if not as sunny as the one before, still a good day for being out in the saddle. Guy had commandeered the garrison mounts for the outlaws, and the guards – still revelling in the new pleasure of being warm and having enough to eat – had happily handed over the hunt to this energetic young forester and the odd assortment of huntsmen he'd collected. They were still too busy coming to terms with the massive changes in their enclosed world to worry about the outside for now.

During the morning they had such a good hunt that at midday Guy sent Algar and Walter back to get carts to carry the two big old stags they had brought down, and taking back two culled hinds slung across the spare horses they'd brought for the purpose. John, Hugh, Thomas, Piers, himself and a very excited Bilan would carry on, he decided – Bilan having been excused his watch duties by the expediency of Guy sending the senior sergeant, and one other man, off to Nottingham to let the sheriff know what was happening.

With ten deer already being butchered and preserved in the castle's kitchens and yard, the sheriff should be satisfied that matters would be dealt with speedily, and Murdac wasn't a man to fuss unnecessarily. There was something to be said, Guy thought to himself, for High Peak being such a distant Royal Forest so that it had been hunted less, and the red deer were far less wary than in the parts of Sherwood closer to castles and towns. It was certainly making his job easier given that he didn't have the dogs to help him scent herds out, or to flush beats towards the hunters. The lack of hunting also showed in the number of elderly beasts and runts Guy had spotted in the glimpses of the large wild herds on the distant hillsides through the leafless winter woods, and he had no qualms about whether they could fulfil the rest of the quota.

The six of them were therefore clattering along the road through Middleton Dale when John spotted another small herd through the trees. One hind seemed to be trailing a back leg and would be easy to catch, and if she wasn't quite good enough to grace the king's table, Guy saw no reason why they shouldn't put her out of her misery and give the folk who were working so hard something extra for their pains, especially when this was a wholly legal hunt.

"John, you take Thomas and Bilan and get that one, and that lagging young buck too, if you can," Guy decided. "Hugh, Piers and I will cut across country and see what we can find in the upper Wye valley." Some of the locals had said that the small wooded vale was prime deer country, even if it was far smaller than that of the western River Wye Guy had known on the Marches. "We'll meet you at the cross-roads by Tideswell. You never know, you might find Tuck, too, if you stay close to the road!"

Guy's words were to prove prophetic, but at the start of this day Tuck had woken to find himself locked in a stout storeroom. He thought about banging on the door, then despite his pounding headache, decided that a show of more monastic patience might convince his captors better. He therefore found a box of something to sit on and began to try to focus on his morning observances. Out in the real world keeping full monastic hours simply wasn't practical, but Tuck still remembered many of the prayers and tried to say something of them morning, noon and night. It didn't always work, and on this day he found it extraordinarily hard to stop his mind from fluttering all over the place, and to settle to a calm contemplation of the divine office.

It was even harder to praise God when he knew he was, to all intents and purposes, a prisoner. He got through the invitatory and tried to recall which might be the proper antiphon for the day, but without a breviary he was totally lost as to where he was in the four week cycle – and had to admit that he had been for a very long time. Sighing, he moved on to Psalm 95, and tried to cudgel his mind towards the appropriate thoughts of praise.

He was glad he'd tried, though, when the door opened and caught him in mid chant. With the kind of happy coincidence in which Tuck thought he saw the hand of at least an angelic guide or lesser saint, he had just reached the end and was singing in Latin,

"It is a people that do err in their heart, and they have
not known my ways.
Unto whom I swear in my wrath that they should not
enter into my rest."

It clearly took the Saracen by surprise even if he had no idea of the meaning of Tuck's words. It was the more bulky of the two darker men, as Tuck could see once he came in and was no longer silhouetted in the doorway. Tuck was glad about that. He'd been the calm one who'd tried to stop the mayhem the day before. Now he stood and let Tuck finish before he spoke. That endeared him to Tuck even more. A man who was respectful of another's prayers, even if they weren't his own, might be a man who could be reasoned with.

"You say your prayers at this hour?" the man said in carefully enunciated English, although his words weren't that heavily accented.

"I try to," Tuck said civilly. "It's much harder outside of the cloister, but despite what some may think I still hold to my vows as best I can. Although I'm not sure whether I'm closer to Prime or Terce right now."

He looked at the plate the man had balanced on a mug in his left hand. The right one was out of sight and Tuck guessed that it might hold a knife. "Is that food for me?" he asked instead of challenging the man. It looked like fairly fresh bread and a slightly wrinkly but sound apple and a pear.

"Indeed," the Saracen said with a half smile.

"Thank you. I wasn't sure whether I'd be fed given what your companion said yesterday."

Now a real twinkle appeared in the Saracen's eyes. "I believe Gilbert changed his mind when he had to help get you onto your horse."

Tuck couldn't resist grinning back at the thought of the Templars heaving and sweating to get his bulk up onto the horse when he was a dead weight. "How many of you?" he asked with what innocence he could muster.

"Four," the Saracen answered with a hidden laugh in his voice even if it never quite came out fully. "Robin insisted we take you with us." He paused, then some good humour within him couldn't refrain from adding, "it was not a popular choice with Will and Gilbert!"

This time Tuck laughed out loud. "No I'm sure it wasn't! If I had just been fat it would have been a bit lighter load, I'm sure. My mother always said I had heavy bones!" and the two of them laughed briefly together. It broke the ice so completely that Tuck felt he could ask,

"Are we in Ashford?"

The man gave a single nod.

"Then may I beg you to relay this to your young leader? The castle I came from is only a short ride north of here. Sir Guy, who commands there at the moment will be able to vouch for me. The castle is called High Peak. Ask any of the local folk, they'll tell you where it is. We were there because the old lord has just died. He was Sir Ivo. They'll know him, believe me!"

"Sir Eudo?"

"No, ...Ivo," Tuck corrected him gently.

"Ivo. ...Very well, I shall tell Robin."

"What's your name?" Tuck asked quickly as the man moved to go. He wanted to know who this man was, if only to vouch later that he at least had not harmed a man of God when this matter got sorted out. "I'm Brother Tuck."

"I am Malik ibn Balian," the Saracen said with a small bow of the head.

"Then, shukran jazilan, Malik ibn Balian," Tuck said and saw the Saracen jump in shock at being thanked in his own language.

He was left in the dark once more, but the bread and fruit were good, and Tuck couldn't help wondering whether he was being treated more to Arab courtesy than Templar charity – he couldn't see the fiery Gilbert wanting to give him anything other than a kick in the teeth! Malik must have passed on the message and said something more on his own account, though, for Tuck had barely washed the dry bread down with the small beer from the tankard when the door opened again. This time it was the leader, Robin, flanked by the other dark English knight and Gilbert.

"Well you've done something few other men have done," the young leader said with somewhat ill grace, "you've impressed Malik! And he doesn't impress easily! So I have to consider what you have told him. Also the locals tell me that a villainous old knight called Sir Ivo commands on Sheriff *Murdac's* behalf at this castle of High Peak. They also say that a dreadful fever has passed through these villages this winter, and that it might be true that Sir Ivo took ill and died, just as many others did. Since you've been right about all of that, and you've actually asked to be taken there, I have to conclude that either you were telling the truth – however unlikely that might be – or that you are totally mad!"

"Thank you," Tuck said with as much gratitude as he could summon, which wasn't a lot. "Am I free to go?"

"Not quite," Robin replied. "We shall escort you back to High Peak Castle and I shall speak to whoever this Sir Guy is."

Tuck managed to control his exasperation by focusing on the thought of the coming confrontation between Guy and this Robin. Guy was turning into quite a force to be reckoned with, all the more potent because he didn't throw his weight around wantonly. Yet Tuck had seen him with the men at Nottingham, and knew that his young friend was treated with well-earned respect by the soldiers and foresters there, and for reasons which went beyond Guy's acute sense of fairness. Quite what Guy would make of this rather pompous Templar would be nothing if not amusing to watch. And so Tuck allowed himself to be led out under armed escort. However, once on his horse he turned in the saddle and had removed one of the bundles of pennies from his saddlebag before his captors had realised what he was doing.

"Here, brother," Tuck called to the innkeeper, holding out the coins. "A blessing from Saint Govan! Share it amongst the villagers." There was no chance the innkeeper would get a chance to pocket the money since most of the village seemed to have come out to see this exotic party departing. Nor could the Templars really object when their rules positively insisted on charitable donations.

Robin's eyebrows went up at this, as did Will's.

"Saint Govan? Ain't ever heard of him!" Will growled suspiciously.

"He's a Welsh and Irish saint, you bloody sassenach!" Gilbert sniped back, forcing Tuck to duck his head to hide his smile. Trust the Irishman to know that! Tuck had spent a lot of time in his youth in the monastery finding out about how things had once been done in the Celtic Church, but he hadn't expected to find someone here who knew of the old Celtic saints.

Yet after that Gilbert seemed to regard him with rather less distaste, making Tuck wonder what kind of experience had so soured him against most of the clergy. He also desperately wanted to know more about what they'd said about Jerusalem the day before, but it didn't seem politic to ask right now, just when they were starting to believe him. He had the feeling that it was such an emotional subject that even mentioning it would set Will and Gilbert off again, and he wanted that unpredictable pair to remain stable if at all possible.

It was as they came into view of the cross-roads at Tideswell that the unexpected happened. There, waiting dismounted at the roadside was John, with Thomas and Bilan and three deer slung across their horses.

"By Our Lady!" Robin swore. "First an errant priest and now poachers? What has England come to that such things are commonplace and attract no attention?"

"They aren't poachers!" Tuck called out hurriedly, hoping he'd made it loud enough for John to hear.

He needn't have worried. John was already saying something to Bilan and the lad took off like a hare. Gilbert made to go after him and Tuck risked another beating by reaching across and grabbing him in his saddle. With his feet still in his stirrups Gilbert was yanked backwards, thereby hauling on his horse's reins and stopping the beast in its tracks.

"Do that again priest and I'll slit your throat!" the Irishman snarled.

"And you'll burn in Hell for it too!" Tuck shot back. "That boy is not a poacher! Don't you dare touch him!" *And run like the wind, Bilan, and find Guy,* he prayed under his breath.

Moments later he heard the lad's clear high voice carrying on the wind calling Guy's name.

"Lord, carry his words on your wind," Tuck prayed out loud, earning him another sideways glance from Gilbert. However, Gilbert was not the one causing concern this time.

"Who are you?" Robin was demanding haughtily.

"I'm John ...of Hathersage," John answered. He, Guy and Tuck had debated whether the Peverel family he'd been born into, albeit on the wrong side of the blanket, and the castle of High Peak were still connected. But current knowledge of the family who had founded the castle was something none of them had, and anyway, it had been in the king's hands for most of King Henry's long reign, which was longer than any of them had been alive. John therefore felt that claiming any association was hardly going to help his cause, and so he used the village now instead merely adding, "once I was part of the Peverel family."

"A peasant attached to a Norman family? I don't think so!" the other dark English knight scoffed.

"I'm a freeborn man," John said firmly, "and if my family has fallen lower due to not being able to pay King Henry in order to retain our lands, then that makes me no less freely born."

Yet once again, to Tuck's surprise, this seemed to hit a very raw nerve with some of the Templars – far more than such a statement would normally warrant.

"Pay King Henry?" spat Robin. "To pay the king you would've had to be of noble birth!"

"A big ruffian like you, *noble?*" the other knight sniffed, looking down his nose at John.

John drew himself up to his considerable full height and took a couple of steps towards the young mounted knight, emphasising just how tall he was by being able to look the man in the eye without much craning of his neck.

"And you, young sir, don't look exactly the picture of knightly elegance either!" John challenged him. "You carry ragged ring-mail and wear much-patched gambesons, yet you expect me to take your word for the fact that you're a knight! Who are you, then to challenge my birthright? Apart from being a *Templar.*"

Tuck winced. Of course John would have spotted that, and his shabby treatment back in Yorkshire was undoubtedly the reason why he wasn't going to back down in front of this group now. John had had a belly full of Templars and their stiff necks!

The young knight flushed somewhat under his tan, and Tuck guessed that he might not be so very highly born himself. Yet it was Robin who was galvanised into action by John's words.

"How dare you!" he exploded, vaulting off his horse. "We've fought for the Cross at a terrible cost! The True Cross! And for Jerusalem!" His voice cracked with emotion at the last two statements, and again Tuck wished fervently that he knew what that was all about. It was a raw, suppurating wound in the soul of all these Templars, that was clear. But Robin was now standing with his sword drawn and pointing at John. "Kneel and pray to God to forgive you for slandering one who's fought valiantly in His name!"

John stepped back but made no move to kneel. "Quite the big man with that sword in your hand, aren't you," he sniffed in disgust, "especially against someone unarmed!"

"You shit!" Will snarled and stood in his stirrups to dismount, clearly intending to force John to his knees, or worse.

But before he could kick a foot free a thick Welsh voice rang out across the valley. "Move from your horse and I'll drop you! By *Dewi Sant*, I will!"

They'd all forgotten Thomas, dismissing him as some simple peasant, but now he was stood a little apart on a small hillock, huge Welsh bow drawn and nocked and looking every bit the lethal soldier he'd been officially not a year before. One look at the muscles flexing beneath the woollen shirt (for Thomas had shrugged off his thick outer tunic for ease of movement) and none of the Templars doubted he could do what he said. Will dropped back into the saddle, furious but trapped, and not so stupid as to take such a poor chance.

Tuck found himself flanked by the two Saracens and said softly, "Don't make me fight you, boys. These two are my friends." Malik's head whipped round to look Tuck squarely in the eye. "Don't interfere," Tuck said softly and calmly. "If God is guiding your leader then let Him sort out the rights and wrongs of this one. John can stand his ground against one man."

He heard Malik give a sigh which might have been of regret or confusion, but out of the corner of his eye Tuck saw him give a small shake of his head to the other man who had one hand up to his lips in a gesture of devotion which Tuck recognised from his time in the East. That hand had a small tremor in it, though, and Tuck guessed that this hitherto silent man was suffering some kind of terrible internal conflict. Please God, then, that nothing triggered him into some self-sacrificing act. If he decided to draw Thomas' first arrow it would be the spark which ignited an explosive fire. Someone might end up dead, and Tuck desperately didn't want it to be John.

"Give this rogue your sword, Siward!" Robin commanded the dark English knight.

"Robin?" The now named Siward looked aghast.

"Give it him!" Robin snapped authoritatively, and even though Siward clearly didn't want to, he pulled his sword out of the scabbard and threw it onto the ground towards John.

"Which end do I hold?" John asked sarcastically, stepping carefully to pick the sword up, watching his opponent all the time. The moment his hand closed around the hilt Robin lunged at him, but it was Robin, not John who was surprised. Expecting to get an easy cut in, Robin was caught out when John not only anticipated him, but instead of doing the expected other option of running backwards, parried Robin's cut with muscular ease. The force of John's parry sent a shiver down the blade into Robin's arm and the point was knocked far off target, making a parry of his own against John's counterattack impossible. Robin was the one who ended up doing a fast retreat, and Tuck felt some un-priestly glee at the sight.

Robin was clearly a very experienced fighter, though, for he recovered quickly and it became a proper sword fight. Robin was by far the better and more experienced swordsman, but John's greater muscles meant that whenever he made contact with Robin's blade the force behind it was more than Robin was used to encountering. Time after time his blade was battered away by a parry so fierce it nearly knocked the sword from Robin's hand. If John wasn't landing any hits on Robin, he was certainly fighting such a blinding defensive action that Robin couldn't get a cut in on him either, despite instigating most of the attacks. Robin only once tried getting in close, for that was disastrous too. He only just escaped being grabbed, for John's massive left arm came at him like a snake as the hilts clashed, reaching out to pull Robin into one of his bear-hugs from which the younger knight knew he wouldn't escape.

Even worse, John wasn't tiring. The big man knew that the worse thing he could do was to let the lighter man run him ragged. So he stood his ground and let Robin do all the running, allowing the young knight to expend his energy while he conserved his own. When a panting Robin wasn't quite so quick to retreat, a lightning quick punch from John's left sent him reeling backwards. It enraged Robin and he came on again snarling. Yet as he tried an unusual feint John actually laughed!

"Oh you won't get me with that one, boy!" he chortled. "My young cousin's favourite trick, that one was!"

"Shit!" Tuck heard Will say over on his right. "You don't think he *is* a bloody nobleman, do you?" The remark was addressed to Siward, whom Tuck now registered was positively twitching in his saddle. The young knight's head kept turning from the fight to Thomas and back, and Tuck could see that Thomas had singled Siward out as the one most likely to do something stupid, and the big bow was trained on him, even if Thomas wasn't daft enough to ignore the others altogether.

Robin suddenly went flat on his back as he tripped on something unseen. John stepped in with a roar of triumph and put his sword point to Robin's neck. Of all of the Templars it was the silent Saracen who vaulted from his horse, sword and dagger drawn, and launching himself towards his fallen leader. The hiss of arrow flights gave only a heartbeat's warning and then a yard-long arrow thudded into the ground between the Saracen's legs. Tuck grabbed Malik's arm.

"No! Please don't! This is all wrong!" he yelled at the man who of all the Templars he didn't want to fight, stopping him in the act of dismounting.

Another hiss and a thump announced that Thomas had fired again.

"The next one kills!" his voice rang out, and Tuck saw that Will was also dismounted now, but was looking in shock at the arrow which had gone through his cloak and taken him backwards to pin him to the ground. The force of an arrow fired from the big wyche-elm bow at such close range was enormous. And Thomas was already ready to loose another.

John and Robin were rolling on the ground, and Tuck could only guess that the young Templar had tripped John too in some way. The difference was that although John had got one punch in, going by the split skin over Robin's cheekbone, Robin had a knife in his hand whereas John was now unarmed again. Gilbert launched himself off his horse in a falling roll and Thomas' arrow only just missed, cutting the Irishman's face and making his horse cry out in pain as it nicked its leg as it embedded itself into the ground at the horse's rear hoof.

"Stop! In the name of God, I command you, stop!" Tuck bellowed as loudly as he could, then to his intense relief heard a familiar voice echo his command.

"Stop in the name of the sheriff of Nottingham!"

Guy had arrived!

Another arrow thudded into the ground missing Will's nose by a whisker as he lurched to his feet, but this one hadn't come from

Thomas. Piers was standing on a hillock to one side, big bow drawn and mirroring his brother's lethal appearance. Beside him Bilan was standing with his lighter hunting bow also drawn, and over such a short distance that wasn't going to be much less effective.

"Halt, this instant!" and Guy and Hugh cantered into the fray, both the epitome of sheriff's men.

Everyone stopped.

"Insh'allah," Malik breathed and Tuck agreed,

"Yes, God wills it, my friend!"

The other Saracen turned a surprised glance up at Tuck from where he stood frozen by the arrow.

"Oh I understand what your companion said," Tuck said gently. "You may be in the service of the Templars, but sometimes what we've been brought up with stays with us, doesn't it?" That seemed to startle the young man even more, but he closed his eyes tight as if trying to prevent even more emotion leaking out when Tuck said very softly to him, "God is Great! That's what's said in your homeland, is it not? It's not the words but the intent which we carry in our hearts which matter to him. Only men kill for words they don't understand, spoken in a language not their own."

It diffused whatever was going through the young man's mind, but Tuck had no time to find out more, for Guy had ridden straight up to the leader, Robin. John had immediately let Robin go, and had got to his feet and begun brushing the loose dirt and vegetation off himself, although not before stepping well back from his adversary.

"How dare you attack my men!" Guy snapped. "Is this Templar land? ...No! ...Do you have any authority here? ...No!"

"And you are?" Robin counter-demanded, although it was blatantly to try and save some face.

"I am *Sir* Guy of Gisborne," Guy answered without any hint of the braggart. It was a flat statement of authority, and from one who believed he had every right to be obeyed. "I am the Sheriff of Nottingham's representative in this area. The *king's* forester! As such, I want to know what you lot are doing riding armed and prepared to fight through these peaceful villages?"

"We found this thieving monk!" Will answered for Robin, only to find himself on the receiving end of Guy's piercing glance – and Tuck knew how cold those green eyes could look when Guy was truly angry!

"Brother Tuck is no *thief!*" Guy riposted. "Furthermore he was acting upon *my* explicit instructions! Shall I march you back across to Nottingham and get you to explain to Sheriff Murdac, in person, how you think you have the right to challenge that?"

Only Tuck had a glimmer of understanding the reason for the full extent of that fury. Guy couldn't believe their bad luck. Of all the random interference he could have dreamt up, a wandering band of

Templars was one of the least likely. Yet he had to deal with this here and now. He wanted them gone, but gone north to Yorkshire or off to some obscure preceptory in the west, not lurking close to Nottingham where they might betray the others. That mixture of anger and worry lent him power.

"Where are you bound to?" he demanded. "There are no preceptories in Derbyshire, nor do I even know of any manors your order farms hereabouts. You can have no official business in this shire."

No-one answered and Guy edged his horse closer to Robin so that he was now looking straight down at the young Templar.

"I repeat. ...Where are you bound? ...I will not tolerate you marauding your way through this shire!"

"And what would you do about it if we don't tell you, *knight?*" Will asked with sullen sarcasm.

Guy whipped round and fixed Will with a look which had got even colder. "If I have to I will get my archers to incapacitate every one of you!" he said in a tone which left no doubt that he would carry out his threat. "After that I would get Brother Tuck to bind your wounds, tie you on your horses, take you back to High Peak tonight, and then in the morning I would get the rest of my men and escort you to the Master at Temple Hirst preceptory. Quite what Frère Pirou will say, I can't imagine!"

Keeping his face stern and his voice droll, Guy enjoyed the moment of seeing the surprise on the Templars' faces. They were clearly taken aback by him knowing the preceptor at Temple Hirst by name, and even more by the implication that he knew him personally. Which Guy really did, because he'd belatedly realised that he couldn't keep avoiding the whole order just because of the episode with Allan. One petty thief wasn't that memorable, as he now knew from the bitter experience of being on the other side when he'd explored Nottingham's dungeons! Consequently he'd made it a point in this last year to get to know the important Templars of all the preceptories which ran along the River Aire and the Humber.

So much so that Ralph Murdac had wanted to know why Guy would want to act as messenger all the time to the Templars. Therefore Guy had told him about Baldwin and used him as an excuse, but really he had little hope of finding any more clues as to his lost cousin. Instead, his thinking was that he would've built enough of a relationship with them that if John had got charged with any crime by them, even with John as one of their tenants, he could demand John's release to him on the claim of a previous or more serious crime, and be believed. Now, though, his tactic had the advantage that he knew beyond doubt that his word would be taken seriously, even against these errant knights from the Holy Land – men whom Frère Pirou had never set eyes on, let alone knew and trusted.

He gave this unknown man called Robin just long enough to sweat, but not long enough to start thinking of ways to evade the question, then asked again,

"So, ...for the last time, ...where were you heading?"

"To my father's house on the Welsh Borders," Robin answered bleakly, knowing he'd been outmanoeuvred. "He's an old man now. I haven't seen him in over ten years. We've come back to find that all the Temple in London wants is to ship men back out to the East to retake Jerusalem." His voice caught with suppressed emotion, and Guy's heart too skipped a beat. Jerusalem fallen? That had to be a very bad thing!

"They don't know what they're asking of men. It can't be done," he continued. Now Guy and Tuck could see his eyes beginning to fill. "We left so many of our friends dead on the walls of that city." He swallowed hard. "We only got out because Saladin is a chivalrous man, if nothing else. Balian of Ibelin negotiated a hard truce, and the women and children, along with those few of us left who'd fought to hold Jerusalem, were allowed to leave unharmed. ...*Unharmed*," he choked out. "I'd defy any man who fought there to say he walked away 'unharmed'!"

"I'm sorry to hear of your losses," Guy said with genuine sympathy. "We get to hear very little of what's happened out in the Holy Land here. The last we heard, Jerusalem was besieged but nothing more. I suppose if you're at court it's different, but not up here." Then he braced himself to say, "But if the men at your headquarters in London are indifferent to what you've suffered, that still doesn't give you the right to come up here to the north and start taking the law into your own hands."

He saw the Templars blink again in surprise at his words, and wondered to himself whether they'd even thought of what they were doing in that way. Trying to keep the sympathy in his voice he asked Robin directly, "So I have to ask *again*, where is your father's house? I presume you thought to stay there until King Henry has decided how many men he might send to the East?"

Once again the king was under pressure to lead a crusade, that much Guy did know. If Jerusalem had fallen then that would explain why, and also why these veterans would be under immense pressure from a different source to go back again. For his own part Guy had enough imagination to be able to visualise why they couldn't face the idea. He didn't doubt for a moment that in their boots he would feel just the same. What he didn't expect was Robin's answer.

"It's at Hodenet. That's near Shrews..."

"I know where it is!" Guy interrupted in shock. "Hodenet? *Your* father's?"

He looked to John in astonishment then back to the tall man facing him.

"Baldwin? ...Is that you, Baldwin?"

Now Robin jumped as though someone had poked him with a sharp stick.

John stepped around him to peer hard at him again. "Can't be him, surely?" He took a step closer and fixed Robin with a hard stare. "Baldwin was a short-arsed little squirt! You're a good head and more taller!"

"John!" Guy cautioned him, even as he leapt of his horse, throwing the reins to Hugh, and striding up to Robin too. "Baldwin was only just sixteen when we last saw him. He would've grown a lot since then, whatever happened. God knows I have!"

He went to stand face to face with this stranger who might just be his lost cousin. "I hate to have to tell you this, but word came to me via the Earl of Chester. If you are our Baldwin, then your father died last winter of a chill. Your oldest half-brother holds the castle now. I'm so sorry to have to tell you this and now of all times." He was watching the man's eyes like a hawk for any telltale signs. If he stayed blank then Guy would know that it was all lies. Instead he saw his words hit like a knife in the gut.

"Oh Baldwin!" he gasped and swept his cousin into a tight hug. Holding him tight he found himself saying, "Thank God you're alive! We were so worried! So, so worried!" He released him and held him back at arms' length so that he could look at him again.

The tall man who could look him in the eye was utterly confounded. "Who? ...You? ...*You* worried about me?"

Guy gasped. "Did you think we wouldn't?" Please God this wouldn't turn into a repeat of his reunion with Allan! All bitterness and reproaches. "When I was over on the borders I asked at every possible Templar preceptory I could get to. No-one had heard a thing of you. Not even your name!"

"We thought you'd died," John said thickly, taking his turn at hugging the stunned Baldwin. "So long and no word at all." Guy hear Baldwin's hiss of breath as John forgot his strength and squeezed tight in affection.

With a wheezing intake of breath, Baldwin got free and stood back to look in perplexed shock at these two men who were total strangers to him.

"Don't you recognise us?" Guy asked gently, suddenly taking in the lost expression in Baldwin's eyes. "Surely you know cousin John? I know he's half hidden beneath all those whiskers, but even so..."

"But he was..." Robin began, then faltered. "But we were all little then."

"Little?" Will guffawed. "*Little* John? Not much! I'd hate to meet big John! That beard's bigger than me!"

John's beard was rather luxuriant, grown as a defence against the bitter winter whilst out with his flock. He now smoothed it down as best he could, his grin still shining through, and Baldwin suddenly cocked his head on one side and screwed his eyes up to look harder at the man who managed to tower over even his above-normal height. They saw him swallow hard again, then recognition come into his eyes. "Sweet Jesu, is it you? John? ...God in Heaven!" His face broke into a tremulous, hardly believing smile. Then he turned back to Guy. "But you said you were Guy of Gisborne. I know of no-one of that name."

"He's our Guy! He got knighted, you cloth-head!" John growled affectionately and cuffed Baldwin's ear playfully. It was akin to being patted by a large bear and Baldwin staggered from the effect, yet that familiar boyhood gesture finally convinced him.

"Guy?" he gulped, hardly able to believe the sudden transition. Then a thought occurred to him. If they were who they said they were then there was someone missing. "There were four of us when we left Alverton. Where's ...?"

"Allan?" Guy was the one who answered. His expression fell. "Allan isn't with us any more, Baldwin."

"We had to let him go," a choked John added. "He became ...difficult. Nothing satisfied him. He wanted..."

"...more than John or anyone could give him," Guy chipped in to save John having to explain. "He never got over not having the status he'd grown up with. Couldn't come to terms with not being the young lord at Alverton, you see. He acted as though it was John's fault. You've no idea what John's been through with him, Baldwin. When we've got more time we'll tell you all about it. For now, though, come with us! You can have a roof over your heads for as long as I have control of High Peak. It might not be for long, but if nothing else it will give you time to think of where you can go and what you'll do."

He gestured to Tuck. "You've already met my good friend Brother Tuck. He's been staying with John of late, helping him with all manner of things. The three archers are the Cosham brothers – Thomas, Piers and Bilan – and this is Hugh of Barnby," he gestured back to Hugh who'd not let his guard drop, just in case Guy's new cousin's friends were less inclined to be friendly. "Who are your friends?"

Robin shook his head, still reeling from shock. "My...? Oh ...err, ...this is Siward of Thorpe – so he's sort of local to this area, or was." He gestured first to the dark English knight, then to the redhead. "And this is Gilbert of the White Hand. He came east with one of the de Lacy's from Ireland." He turned to Will. "This is William Scathlock. His family are in the wool trade up in Yorkshire, but he's become a smith. We call him Will 'Scarlet' on account of the burns he gets when he's working steel. Best sword-smith I've ever met!"

"A pleasure to meet you, Will," Guy said pleasantly. "We could really do with someone who knows his craft at Nottingham. If you ever wanted to enter the sheriff's service, I'm sure he'd be delighted to have you."

"Not a chance!" Will growled. "I'm staying with this lot. And if not them then I'm not grovelling to another Norman lord! I'll find my own way in the world, but I'm being no Norman's liegeman again!"

Guy and the others bit back retorts. Will had been unnecessarily rude, but now wasn't the time to object.

"And your two other friends?" Guy prompted.

"James of Tyre," Robin said gesturing to the silent Saracen on Tuck's left.

"You're not a Saracen, then?" Tuck asked in surprise. He'd thought the young man's silence was due to a difficulty in speaking English.

"Part Saracen," Robin answered for him. "After we left Jerusalem there was no way he could have stayed in the Holy Land. Not now. Not with men like Guy de Lusignan still around ...they got Reynauld de Châtillon, Lord be praised, but still too many men like Lusignan left. Too many, and too few like Balian of Ibelin." He took a deep breath and turned to the final man. "And this is Malik ibn Balian."

"Balian? That doesn't sound like a Saracen name to me?" Tuck queried carefully.

"Of course it isn't!" Will snorted.

Baldwin shot Will a weary glance, revealing to Guy that, while the burly smith might have been a close companion of Baldwin's for some time, he also grated on his cousin's nerves at times as well.

"He's named after Balian of Ibelin," Baldwin continued as the man in question stood impassive and silent. "He's that Balian's much younger bastard half-brother. The great man himself ordered me to bring him west." He turned and gave Malik a sympathetic smile. "He had to *order* Malik to come, too, to make him leave his side." He turned back to Guy and John. "So these are my friends and companions. Every one of them knighted by my lord of Ibelin in the siege. Saladin challenged him, you see. Asked how he would defend Jerusalem with only a handful of knights. So my lord Balian knighted every man who could fight!"

Robin's admiration for this Outremer lord shone from his eyes. Clearly he'd been a force to be reckoned with. For his part, though, Guy was appalled at the naivety of bringing two men who would be regarded as Saracens into the heart of England. What in the name of all that was holy had they thought would happen when the news of the fall of Jerusalem reached these shores? Had it never occurred to them that these two men might be seen as prime targets for revenge? Or that their less than enthusiastic welcome by the English Templars might have something to do with these two members of their company?

Come to that, if Will, Gilbert and Siward were simple lay soldiers with the order who'd been knighted in the field under somewhat dubious circumstances, then Guy could imagine that they might have been looked at somewhat sideways too. And where had the rest of the Templar order been at this siege? Their story raised more questions than they'd answered. For now, though, the late-winter sun was getting very low and it was more important to get back to High Peak before dark.

"Come on! Time to get back to the castle!" Guy said decisively. "Mount up and follow us. You'll have a warm place by the fire tonight and a hot meal in your bellies, at least."

He gestured Thomas, Piers and Bilan to bring up the rear, then led the strange party off with Hugh. He left John to accompany Baldwin for now. Why 'Robin', he wondered? When had that name stuck to his cousin? He glanced back over his shoulder and was surprised, but pleased, to see that Tuck was right behind him riding with Malik and James. Unless he was very mistaken, Tuck had just found two new people whom he felt needed looking after. Behind them, John was riding with Baldwin, while Gilbert, Siward and Will were behind them in turn, twitchily alert to the three archers riding in the rear. Piers looked ready for a fight but Bilan was calm enough, and Thomas saw Guy looking back and gave him a reassuring nod. Hopefully they would get back without incident, then.

"An odd assortment of knights," Hugh said softly to him. "Not really knights at all, are they? ...And what about those two who are of mixed blood? Did it not occur to the others that it was asking for trouble to bring them to England?"

"I know," Guy sighed. "Poor bastards – literally! Why on earth did the others not help them find somewhere to live sooner, ...say Cyprus? The Templar brothers I've spoken to all say that there's a big Templar presence on that island. At least it would've been closer to their homes. There must have been other refugees, surely?"

Hugh breathed out heavily. "Humph! You'd think so, wouldn't you. ...Do you know, Guy, I wonder whether the regular Templar knights over here – who must be high born to a man – might not condescend to recognise them as fellow knights? You said your cousin went out nearly penniless, so he would have had to work his way up to being a knight, wouldn't he? Maybe he never got as far as having a higher rank until this siege they've talked about?"

"By God, Hugh, I'm glad you said that, because I've been thinking that too!"

"And there's something else too. They've been through some kind of terrible experience – probably the siege, but maybe something else, something *more*. Have you noticed the way they twitch and jump at every shadow? I've seen men like that back when I was fighting in France. Men who'd seen far too much death, and blood, and violence. Men who look like they no longer know what a restful night's sleep is. If I were you, I'd give them Sir Ivo's old sleeping quarters, then move the rest of us a bit away from them. If I'm right they'll be calling out in their sleep even on a quiet night!"

Arriving back at High Peak they had a busy time of it before the evening meal was served. The cook was mollified from having to find so many more meals by the present of the lame hind John had brought down. Having added six hungry men to the castle's rota, Guy felt that the deer would have to help feed them first. He could purposely catch the odd deer and boar for the villagers at the end of the hunt if no more scrawny deer fell into their path. No-one minded the new men having Sir Ivo's old bedroom, though. Even Guy had decided he didn't fancy the idea of sleeping in that bed quite so soon after it's last malevolent occupant. So some more straw mattresses were hurriedly cobbled together, and the covers from Sir Ivo's bed were shared out with the Templars' own blankets to give each man a good deal more warmth than they could have had since coming back to England.

Therefore it was only after dinner, when the servants and guards naturally dispersed to their own friendship groups, that Guy and John had much chance to talk properly to Baldwin again. With a good fire roaring in the hearth, people could spread out more in the hall – indeed standing very close to the fire now risked singeing, so the groups weren't so close to one another that anything over the general hum of conversation could be heard easily.

"Why 'Robin'?" Guy asked, coming to top all the Templar's mugs up with some porter warmed with a hot poker from the blaze. "When did you stop being Baldwin?"

Will and Gilbert laughed and Baldwin looked faintly embarrassed. "There's sort of two reasons," he began. "For a start there were so many Baldwins out there, there had to be a way of distinguishing us. There were ten of us just travelling out there together!" He flushed a little deeper. "And I was foolish when I first got to Palestine, I…"

"He was daft enough to take his shirt off!" Will interrupted, chuckling.

Malik laughed too. "Told Will he thought he would be able to get cooler!"

"Turned into a little Robin redbreast!" Will added with a guffaw. "By Saint Thomas, I'd never seen anyone so red before!"

Guy mouthed 'ouch' while Tuck frowned.

"Did your skin peel?" he asked solicitously. "That sounds as if you were really badly burnt."

Baldwin nodded ruefully. "Oh yes! I was shedding white bits for weeks! They even wondered whether I'd caught leprosy, I peeled so badly."

"But surely you would've had to have come into contact with a leper for that to happen?" Tuck quizzed him. "When I was out there, the western soldiers were all really careful to try and steer clear of the leper colonies. Has that changed? Was everyone forced together in the fighting?"

Baldwin shook his head. "No, just one leper in particular."

Will took up the tale, and for the first time Guy and John could see some of his pride in his young leader in his face. "A royal leper! The Temple in Jerusalem is right at the heart of the city and the Palace is in the same set of buildings. We'd not been in the Holy Land for more than a few weeks and we were tending to the horses in the Templar stables – I was shoeing some, and Robin was helping me – and the king came out and we kept our heads down. As you probably know, King Baldwin was already sick. Well he stopped his horse just as we were walking a mare up and down outside. Next thing I know the king is slipping out of his saddle and Robin here runs and catches him. Poor bastard had passed out. He wasn't as rotten as he was by the end, but he was still in a bad way. Robin just pulls the stopper out of his own water bottle and gives the king some water, propping him up in his arms. And all the bloody leeches and crows following him from the court just sat on their horses staring at them like he'd gone mad. All too bloody scared of catching the disease to help the poor sod – gutless bastards!

"Then the king's servants rush up with a litter to carry him back in, but before he goes the king grabs Robin's hand and asks him what his name is. Robin says 'Baldwin'. That tickled the king so he asks how old Robin is. When he finds out they're more or less the same age he's even more pleased. Well we thought nothing of it, but the next day we get summoned to the Master. He's as pleased as can be with Robin. Says he's shown the right attitude for one of the order. There'd been quite a bit of bad feeling between the Templars and King Baldwin in the last few years, you see.

"First off, in '79 the king led his army out against Saladin, but the Templars were in front, and the previous Master led them in a daft charge into Saladin's army. They got chased back – or those who didn't get caught did – and as a result the whole army had to retreat. Then the Templars backed Guy de Lusignan to marry the king's sister, Sybilla, against the king's wishes. All that had happened before we got there, of course, because we didn't land until late '80. So by the time we appeared the Master was well pleased to have something make the king think better of the Templars. Didn't last, of course, because that mad bastard Châtillon went and deliberately broke the truce six months later on, and his cronies in the order made sure he got plenty of support."

"Poor King Baldwin," Robin sighed, staring off into a distance he alone could see. "All he wanted was peace in the Holy Land. He was such a good man, and yet he suffered so much."

"Well at least you made his last days a bit better," Will said consolingly, totally ignoring the others, his attention now focused solely on Robin. The rest of Guy's friends had clustered around them by now and they all exchanged glances. That sounded like Robin had had more than a passing association with the king.

"I'd like to hear more about him," Guy said gently, reaching across to clasp Robin's arm. "When you're ready to tell me," he added as Robin's head whipped up with a disorientated daze in his eyes. "He sounds like an extraordinary person."

Robin took a deep breath and rubbed his eyes with the heel of his hand. "Yes he was. Most extraordinary. He deserved to be served better than he was."

"Then I really would like to hear about the man you knew," Guy confirmed.

"Not tonight, though," Robin said with a wince.

"No, not tonight, but when you've settled a bit more, maybe?"

They didn't get much more out of any of the newcomers after that, but as Hugh predicted, the rest of the household were woken repeatedly during the night by their nightmares. Given that, the newcomers couldn't have had much sleep, so Guy declared that he would take only his own men out hunting the next day. However, he did ask Baldwin and the others to do what they could to sort the castle out and make it less of a shambles. Guy was very aware that the constant running of the place on a pittance, while Sir Ivo had filled his own pockets, had left it in a parlous state. He couldn't do much about anything which required large amounts of cash, but he did entrust Baldwin with the secret of the barrels in the keep's basement, and told him to spend what he needed but to be careful.

Most of what was needed, though, was simply someone with a good eye for fighting to sort out what repairs were urgent, and others to put the tiny garrison through their paces. Guy was sure most of them hadn't done anything more than chase a few miserable peasants in years! He still left Tuck with them, though – just in case there was any friction.

With another good day's hunt behind them the outlaws and Guy rode back to High Peak to find Tuck in pensive mood. As soon as he could he got Guy on one side.

"I'm going to ask you for something," he began tentatively.

Guy looked at him quizzically. "That sounds as though I might not like it?"

Tuck wrinkled his nose. "Mmmm... Can you not go out hunting tomorrow? Stay here?"

Guy jumped. "God's bones, Tuck, there hasn't been a falling out between our guests already, has there?"

"Oh Lord, no, nothing like that! No, it's rather that I want to perform a long service tomorrow. ...In the castle's chapel."

"A service? You mean more than your normal observances?"

"Yes, and not for me." Tuck sighed and tugged Guy a bit further into a corner of the hall. "It's the Templars. They're in a real state, Guy! Oh they did what you asked of them. Indeed they've worked hard all day. But every so often one of them will just stop and stare off into space. When that happens their eyes fill up, and when they start working again I couldn't help but notice that several of them have the shakes."

Guy nodded. "Hugh picked up on that too. He said they'd seen too much fighting."

"Did he now? Young Hugh keeps going up in my estimation! Well I want to offer to do the full Office of the Dead for them. I doubt they've had chance to stop and properly grieve for those they lost, you know. But it will be a long day of prayer. A very long day! And at the end of it I doubt they'll be in any fit state to do anything but fall into bed. So as you've had remarkably good hunting so far, I'm taking it as a good sign from Above that you won't need to hunt on a Sunday? That you can afford to have a day spent here in the castle? I'd feel a lot more comfortable doing it with steady men like you, John and Hugh around, you see."

"You think there'll be trouble?"

"Not trouble in the way you're thinking, but rather maybe someone having an outburst of rage in their grief. I've seen it happen before. Someone keeps the lid firmly shut on these terrible memories, and then when they take it off it's like everything has to come pouring out. Everything! You can't ask them to stop. That's not an option. Think of it like the dams on a row of fishponds bursting – you can't do anything until the backlog of water has gone before you can rebuild and restock again. So I want you to be prepared to have to watch over a man while he rants and rages just to make sure he doesn't seriously hurt himself, or even worse. I'm expecting the chapel's walls to get a few punches, but I'm concerned about ...well something beyond that."

Guy didn't need any elaboration – he had a good enough imagination to fill in the gaps. Tuck was worried that one of them might try to take his own life in the extremes of grief, in a wave of guilt at surviving when so many others had died. Yet he knew Tuck was right. They needed to grieve for their lost comrades, and better to do it here amongst friends than somewhere where there wasn't a sympathetic soul in sight.

"Come on," he said, grasping Tuck's elbow, "let's go and speak to Baldwin ...no Robin ...oh Lord, what am I supposed to call him? I presume you haven't approached them yet?"

"Well I did think it best to ask you first."

Guy snorted in wry amusement. "As though I'd say 'no' under the circumstances!"

Tuck looked a little sheepish. "Well you are in charge! And they are used to military order! Might have looked worse for you than me if they think I can just do what I like without you saying a word."

"Humph, you're forgiven, then! But the only thing which would have stopped me saying 'yes' would have been the sheriff arriving in our midst – and I don't think that's very likely!"

They found Robin sitting amongst a singularly silent bunch of Templars.

"Tuck is offering to conduct a service for you," Guy said without preamble.

Six heads came up and fixed their eyes on Guy and Tuck.

"If you would like me to," Tuck hastily added, "I was thinking of a full Office for the Dead for your fallen comrades. I'm guessing that since you left Jerusalem you've been constantly on the move. And I was wondering if in any of the preceptories you might have stayed in, has anyone bothered to ask you if you would like someone to officiate over such a service?"

Will's eyes became hard. "Offer? The bastards have shoved us out as fast as they can! We don't do much to promote the spirit of crusade in our state, and in France, at least, they're quivering like hounds at the leash to be let at the Saracens. Bloody fools! And we're not proper knights in their eyes, or none of us except for possibly Robin. He, at least, was a squire, so his knighting by Ibelin they see as a natural progression. The rest of us?" he sniffed derisively. "We're just a bunch of sergeants and turcopoles who've got ideas above our stations! Never mind that we've died in our hundreds!"

"Which is as good a reason as I've ever heard to honour them properly," Tuck said firmly.

"What's a turcopole?" young Bilan asked, having followed hard on Guy's heels, intuitively guessing that once again things were going to get interesting around Guy.

Will's sigh was almost a groan, but Tuck spoke quickly to save Bilan from a waspish answer given more in despair than anger. "Not all Saracens are Muslims, Bilan. Many around Jerusalem and some of the other towns have been Christians for centuries – descendants of Christ's first converts, no less! They fight with us. With men like Robin and Will and their friends. Some are simply freemen in the east, just as Will no doubt was here in England before he took the Cross?" Will nodded, the tension having diffused with Tuck's calm explanation. "They're fully Saracen in their bloodline but not in their faith.

"Others might be the sons of western soldiers who've taken local wives. And a good number are the illegitimate sons of French or English noblemen. Sons whom their fathers can't fully acknowledge but who, had they been born in England, might have been given a manor or some other means of living at or above freeman status. In the Holy Land the turcopoles are an essential part of our army, making up a huge proportion of it, and they come somewhere in the hierarchy between the ordinary sergeants and the noble knights – whether fighting with the forces of one of the great nobles, or in an order like the Templars or Hospitallers."

Bilan was all agog. Such exotic people weren't part of his normal world, and yet he was also a kind lad and his first thought after the initial wonder was,

"And after all that fighting the knights here won't say a prayer for them? That's not fair!"

His innocent indignation unexpectedly brought a real smile to Will's face and surprise to James and Malik's.

Tuck beamed back at the Templars. "You see? Not everyone is uncaring of your loss! So... will you let me say the office for you?"

"What are you going to do?" Robin asked softly, almost as if he couldn't believe that this was really happening.

"We'll all go across to the chapel at dawn," Tuck said with assurance, now very much on ground he was sure of. "I'd love to say we'll do Matins at the proper hour, but working out what's the proper hour to begin at outside of a monastery is nearly impossible. But we shall start at dawn with the Matins for the Dead and go straight into Lauds. I know you don't normally celebrate Lauds in your order, but since this is an office for the dead it seems appropriate to do it. I've been thinking long and hard all day. Most of the time I'm lost without a breviary to say the offices of the day, with all their special seasonal antiphons and collects. I'd need the mind of a saint to remember the hundreds of variations. But for this service I've done it often and it never changes, so I'm sure I can remember all the psalms and lessons.

"After Lauds we'll say Mass instead of Prime – which is perfectly acceptable. There'll be a point in the Mass before Communion when you will have the chance to speak the names of your fallen comrades. Think on that tonight. I shall let you take as long as you want over that act of commemoration. There's no hurry.

"We shall break then until midday. I can't say Terce and Sext properly without a breviary anyway – they're too variable – but I would like to say Sext in a form I think I can make up out of the bits I can remember. Then you can take a break, or pray individually until Vespers in the afternoon. Then we'll do the full Vespers for the Dead, then take a break again until Compline. It will be a long day, make no mistake about that, and if some of you feel that you need to step outside during an office – that it's all got a bit overwhelming – then that's perfectly acceptable too."

Tuck could imagine several abbots, priors and monks he had known being appalled and shocked at such a statement. Leave mid office? Acceptable was the thing it absolutely wasn't! But Tuck trusted that the Almighty would be more understanding and forgiving of these men's suffering. "This isn't meant to be a penance for you! It's meant to heal, not make matters worse, so don't feel you have to stick out every step of every service. Now, ...I suggest you get to bed and get as much sleep as you can. Tomorrow is going to be very long!'"

Oh Brother Gervase, you are so easily shocked! What bothers you so much? That full monastic discipline would not be maintained come what may? That Tuck should presume to say the offices of the Church even when he knew he could not possibly hope to say them perfectly? ...Yes? Well then you are less of a Christian soul than you aspire to be! My dear friend Tuck was always moved to be compassionate when he saw someone suffering. His belief positively forced him to do as much as he could, and to trust to God to understand when a man's best could not quite manage to reach the heights of perfection. I sincerely hope that if you ever have the misfortune to meet good men who are in such torment as my cousin and his friends were, that such compassion would be your first thought, and not whether it would demean you to try to offer some religious balm to their wounds and possibly fail in the minor details.

And this offer of a service was to have an importance beyond applying a salve to their souls. I tell you this now so that you will pay attention to what I'm saying next, and not sit there in high dudgeon, so listen, Brother! Our behaviour over this offer of Tuck's was to act as the most unlikely of cements to our collective friendship. Without it there would have been a distance between our men who were already outlaws, and these men who had fought together in the east. No sooner had Tuck made the offer, and I had explained why Tuck wanted us to stay behind to my outlaw friends, then some surprising initial bonding took place between the two groups. Thomas announced that he had fought in France at least, even if the cost in his comrades' lives had been substantially less than in the East, and went to talk to Will. More unexpectedly, Will actually listened to his approach and then sat talking to him for a while – I knew not what about, but it was a far cry from the brusque rejection I had expected Will to make.

Hugh, with characteristic tact, slipped over to Siward and Gilbert, and Tuck had some words to say to Malik and James, whom we now knew were Christians by virtue of their fathers, but had members of their families who worshipped in the Muslim faith of our enemies. For them I felt a particular sympathy. It must, I felt, be dreadful to have different parts of your family on opposite sides in a war, regardless of the rights and wrongs of what we were fighting over. Meanwhile Will's nickname for John stuck and went down into legend simply because from then on they were in one another's company for almost the rest of their lives, and it all started that night. So you see John became Little John on the very day he met the man who would be Robin Hood!

For my part I went to Baldwin, as I still thought of him then. Within the year I would be calling him Robin without a second thought, for the more I got to know this person whom I had last seen as a youth, the less I could find of the boy in the man. His experiences in the Holy Land had changed him irrevocably, and although his sense of honour was still there, his spirit had been tempered in fires far hotter than England could ever have provided. I will not pretend to you, Brother, that I always agreed with him. Some of the legend of our opposition came from a grain of truth! But he was always my cousin and I loved him for that, even if for nothing else, during those times when we saw things in opposing lights.

Chapter 15

N ow you may judge how well Brother Tuck managed that day of offices, given that he had no breviary to aid him. And before you are too harsh, think on this, Brother. Could you do so well? If you were called upon to say the Office for the Dead in such circumstances, you might find it reflecting just how much attention you pay to those observances you make day in and day out! Do you really know those psalms, antiphons and responses well enough to tell someone not versed in Latin exactly what they mean, rather than repeating them like some pet raven? Or even speak with all the words there and in the right order, but with no understanding? Think on that, Gervase.

Ah, you are blushing! Is your own conscience quite so clear now, eh? How often have you said ˜mea culpa˜ but not from the heart, because you secretly believed that you have very little to confess? Perhaps you think that sins committed within such sacred walls as these are not of the same magnitude as the greater span of wickedness out in the world? But tell me this, who is the worse of the two? The humble man who falls by the wayside in genuine error and repents from the heart? Or the priest who knows what he should do and does not? Who performs the sacred mass before humble folk, and secretly looks down on them so much as to not care if he performs it correctly, or with a pure intent?

Well the next time you sit before a fellow priest you might want to confess to saying the words of your offices by rote without taking even enough notice of them to be able to repeat them without prompting. And what does that say of your holiness? Yes, well may you look disconcerted! Say it the next time you are at confession, Gervase, ˜mea culpa, mea culpa, mea maxima culpa˜ and _mean_ it!

Even now, at the twilight of my life, you will not get me to say a word against Tuck and his good intentions. And before you sigh too heavily in response while we continue, remember this: without Tuck's actions on that day there might not have been a core of faithful outlaws who would follow Robin Hood through thick and thin! I, for one, have that day ingrained on my mind in a way that all the routine details of the forest judiciary have never stayed with me, nor have any of the services which I attended in Nottingham churches. I cannot tell you exactly what fine we were forced to charge for a certain infringement down to the last halfpenny in any particular year, but I only have to close my eyes and I can still hear and see Tuck before that altar in the castle chapel on that chill March day.

High Peak Castle, Derbyshire, Sunday 25th February, the Year of Our Lord 1189

John, Thomas and Guy between them agreed to sit watch in turn through the night, so that someone could wake Tuck the instant that the deep night sky began to turn a faint shade paler. Before going to bed, the four of them walked to the castle's little chapel which nestled against High Peak's south wall, north-east of the hall and closer to the East Gate. Inside it was very stark, but it was clear that Tuck had worked on the place while they'd been out hunting. It was scrubbed out and smelled of fresh herbs, and the altar was bare. Now Tuck draped it with Robin, Gilbert and Siward's white Templar surplices. It took a bit of adjusting, but he managed to get them to drape properly across the front so that the crosses showed, then he placed the simple wooden crucifix in the centre and the two heavy oak candlesticks to either side to weight them down. Guy raided the castle stores and found some good beeswax pillar candles, which he declared would be put to better use on the morrow than they would have been if kept in reserve for the next of Sir Ivo's cronies who might come to visit.

"I can't imagine that the sheriff has a clue about the number and quantity of candles, or cares" he said witheringly. "Sir Ivo really was the most dreadful old miser!"

Before the rest of the household bedded down, Guy made a point of going and speaking to all of them to let them know what was going on. He didn't say what Tuck had told him, which was that the original office said for Sir Ivo had been the shortest Tuck had felt he could possibly justify doing, and had said what he remembered made into only one nocturne in Matins instead of three. Tuck had been sure of the old miser's soul being contained and restrained within the village church, and had focused far more on the cleansing of the castle, but Guy wasn't about to complicate matters by telling the castle's folk that.

Instead he said that it was a simple service of remembrance for their new guests, and that performing a second rite so soon after the last could only seal the bane of their lives even more securely in the afterlife. As he predicted this was greeted with some warmth, and it dispelled any questions of why the service was being held here and not at a Templar preceptory before they'd been thought of.

Yet Guy had had another reason for telling everyone. He'd been thinking about how he would feel about performing such a long office for people he had known, and maybe loved, and what an intense experience that would be. And being ever the practical soul, he'd also realised that by noon the Templars would likely be weary and drained. But they would still have Vespers to get through in the mid afternoon. And so Guy had made a point of saying that if any of the servants wanted to come into the chapel to hear Vespers, and maybe think of someone of their own they would want to have the office said for, then he and Tuck would welcome them. That was covered by him saying that he suspected that there must have been times when Sir Ivo had prevented them from attending such services at the time of a loved one's death.

However, for the crusaders he couldn't imagine anything worse than someone being the last of the six still on his knees, when his distraught friends had staggered away to weep or sleep depending on their state, and being alone in his grief with just Tuck officiating. That would be so lonely and cold, and Tuck had said he wanted it to be a good thing, something to ease the Templars, not add to their suffering. No, much better to have company! Company and light – so plenty of candles too!

With the castle still wrapped in darkness, and only the faintest hint of a line of paler blue on the eastern horizon, Tuck led the procession of Templars across the castle bailey. Guy had taken the last watch, although John had sat up with him, and so once Tuck was awake and while John woke the others, Guy slipped across to the chapel and lit all the candles. His efforts were rewarded by the expression of amazement on the six faces when they came in and saw the chapel fully lit. The two big pillar candles on the altar had been scented with lavender and sage and their fresh scent was gradually beginning to percolate around the room, but a dozen more flickered cheerfully in sconces and on stands around the small room dispelling all shadows. Hugh and Thomas, with the surprisingly committed and willing Walter and Algar – for all that they'd never seen conflict – had brought across two of the oldest bracken-stuffed mattresses from the hall the previous evening, and had folded each in two lengthways to make a thick layer for the Templars to kneel on. The six were going to be spending a long time on their knees, and it had been John who'd realised that kneeling on the cold flagstones would soon become excruciatingly painful. Two benches were also placed in front of the folded mattresses for the Templars to lean on while in prayer – and to help them get up again after so long in one position!

"Shame it's not the feast of *Dewi Sant*," Tuck thought aloud. "Still half a week to go for that if my dates are correct, although last Wednesday was Ash Wednesday, if I'm not mistaken." That thought cheered him. "So we're already into a sacred time, which must be good. And we can ask Saint Issui to intervene on our behalf!"

"Who in Heaven's name is Saint *Issui*?" Gilbert couldn't help himself asking. This really was a Celtic saint he'd never heard of.

"A holy man from the Black Mountains, and one of King Brychan's many saintly children," Tuck declared, his accent suddenly broadening in patriotic fervour. "A beautiful well there is at his shrine! Oh I'm very fond of Issui Sant! Local to me, see? But then I like the small, local saints. I always think they have a bit more time for ordinary people. Not so caught up in the great events of the world. And today we need a saint who's got his eye fixed on us, don't we?"

He went to kneel at the altar.

"I think a prayer to him before we start wouldn't hurt!"

Once he'd said his silent prayer, though, he was keen to begin the proper office. As Tuck began going through the Pater Noster, the Ave Maria and the Credo, most of the others slipped out leaving just Guy and John at the back, and the six Templars kneeling before Tuck. Slowly the voices warmed up until they were reciting the familiar words with Tuck. Psalm 94 and its responses gave way to Psalm 5, and Guy was once more struck by the depth of Tuck's memory. The big Welshman was standing squarely before the altar in a position Guy suspected he could hold for hours, and his rich voice was lending the words a power and warmth which filled the small space of the chapel without a hint of hesitation. John stayed for long enough to see that any help wouldn't be needed just yet, and then squeezed Guy's shoulder in farewell and slipped silently out, unnoticed by anyone but Guy, and leaving him to sit on a small stool propped up in a rear corner of the chapel to watch.

By the second nocturne and the twenty-second psalm the office began to have some effect, possibly because Tuck took the time to repeat each verse of this psalm in English after he had said the Latin. It was something Guy had never known anyone else do, but he knew that Tuck had often made an effort to translate certain passages of the Bible for his rural flock in order to enhance their understanding. He couldn't abide standing aloof and lording it over simple folk with such knowledge, however against the Church's rules it was. Instead Tuck fervently believed that the words of the Bible should be allowed to bring blessing and relief to the simplest of souls – and how could that happen when they hadn't the first idea of what the words meant? Tuck had had a vituperative argument with his last abbot on that score, Guy knew, yet now he could see why Tuck wanted people to be able to understand the words.

"*Sed et si ambulavero in valle mortis non timebo malum quoniam*," Tuck intoned. "Though I should walk in the valley of death I will fear no evils," and Guy saw James, Siward, Gilbert and Robin all shudder. Yes, they had seen valleys of death, and probably too many of them, Guy thought. Even in the name of God there ought to be a limit to what any man should be expected to endure.

"*In loco páscuæ ibi me collocávit*," Tuck intoned the closing antiphon. "In green pastures he will feed me," coming as the immediate translation after it.

Certainly the previously acerbic Gilbert was now furtively wiping tears from his eyes at the words of green pastures. Out in the Holy Land it must have seemed at times as though they would never see a lush green field again, Guy supposed, and even though they'd come back only in time for winter, it must still be a good deal greener than anything in the East. When Tuck got to a verse in the next psalm which he translated as 'look upon me, and have mercy upon me for I am alone and poor,' Gilbert began openly weeping. It was also a passage which Guy would have bet good money on Tuck having translated many a time for the poor folk of the Welsh borders. You didn't need to be a Templar to find solace in those words!

The third psalm of the nocturne certainly had something pertinent and particular to the Templars, though. And as Tuck translated "*si steterint adversus me castra non timebit cor meum si surrexerit contra me bellum*," as "though an army in its camp should stand against me, my heart shall not fear, though war should rise up against me," a collective ripple ran through the six men again, leaving Guy even more admiring of Tuck's understanding. No hedge priest, Tuck clearly knew his Latin not just well but fluently, and had understood just what he would be translating for the Templars and the effects his words would have. As did the words of a later verse, "do not deliver me over to the will of my enemies," – another collective shudder coming as the six's own antiphon to the psalm.

Each psalm Tuck recited clearly and steadily. Each lesson in a measured delivery, so that even in the Latin without translation, he imparted a measure of understanding. Guy dug deep into his own memory, wondering why Tuck wasn't translating the three lessons for each of the Nocturnes, then remembered that Tuck had said they would be from the Book of Job, and that was hardly cheerful stuff if he remembered correctly his days of being instructed in the faith with his cousins by the elderly neighbourhood priest. That had to be it. Too much fire and judgement for men such as these to be bludgeoned with. Psalm 40 seemed more of the stuff Tuck thought appropriate to untangle the Latin of, though, and at the words "for even the man of my peace in whom I trusted, who ate my bread, has supplanted me," Guy heard several sniffs from in front. And slowly the sky outside lightened, although no beams of light found their way into the chapel yet.

Matins came to an end, and Tuck invited the men to stand for a moment and ease their limbs a little before they went straight into Lauds. He had been making them stand for the three lessons in each nocturne, if only to keep some blood flowing in their joints, but it was still a long time to remain unmoving in an old stone chapel on a chilly

March dawn. John popped his head around the door and asked Guy to let Tuck know that he would bring a hot drink over at the end of Lauds, and before they said the Mass, which Tuck heartily agreed to.

"It's going to get harder for them from now onwards, I suspect," he softly added to Guy, as they were about to return to their respective places to continue.

Wrapping his cloak a bit more firmly around himself, Guy settled back on his stool and braced himself. The first outburst came in the third psalm during Lauds. Tuck had just begun Psalm 62 and translated,

"In a dry and thirsty land, where there is no water, so in the sanctuary I have come before you to see your power and glory," when Will staggered to his feet.

"Power and glory?" he howled. "Where was the power and glory at Hattin? We died like bloody flies in that Godforsaken valley! ...Why?" he ranted, shaking his fists heavenwards, as if expecting God to give him an answer. "What had Oswald and Eadgar done to offend you so much that you should want such a sacrifice of them?"

Will seemed to crumple, then spun on his heels and like a raging bull, head down and eyes red with grief, he stormed to the door, then stopped and threw an almighty punch at the stout oak as he once more realised where he was, why he was here, and why he shouldn't just storm out. Guy winced as Will's knuckles struck. That had to have hurt! He certainly left a bloody imprint on the wood, and as Will spun back again, swaying like a pole-axed ox, Guy could see the blood drip from the smashed skin on his hand.

Tuck's eyes gestured Guy to see to Will, while the big Welshman simply took a deep breath and continued with the next verse, virtually forcing the other Templars back to their knees from their half-risen states. All Guy could think of to do was to step up to Will's side and say softly, "walk with me." Like a caged bear, Will prowled back and forth across the width of the chapel behind the kneelers, Guy keeping pace with him but saying nothing. Yet even the steady rhythm of such pacing seemed to slowly calm Will. By the time Tuck had got through the Song of Zacharias and on to a repeat of the Pater Noster, the big man had stopped shaking so badly, and so when Tuck announced the Collects for the Dead, Will patted Guy on the arm, nodded silently to him in thanks and went to kneel beside Malik once more.

Their chosen groupings intrigued Guy. Viewed on his left, Will knelt at the far side by the wall. Malik knelt in the middle of the three and Robin on their right, yet it was Malik who leaned across and put a consoling hand on Will's shoulder, while Robin, despite being their leader and Will's longest standing friend amongst the men, didn't even acknowledged his return. There was definitely some close bond between Malik and Will, Guy thought, and it wasn't just because they happened to be next to one another. Possibly it was because they were the oldest two in the company, for they seemed to be John's age or a year or two older – mature men around thirty, and that bit more worldly-wise.

Of the other three Guy would have expected Gilbert and Siward to be close, yet it was the silent and seemingly brittle James that Siward seemed to have attached himself to. James currently knelt at the inward end of their right-hand trio, just across the gap from Robin, with Siward in the middle, and Gilbert on the outer edge by the other wall. And it was a clearly distressed Siward who nonetheless had a comforting hand on James' forearm as the former turcopole was so bowed in prayer as to be in danger of toppling forwards. Yet no sooner had Tuck's final "Amen" rung out, than it was Gilbert who slipped forwards to put his head on his arms on the bench and to sob in wrenching gulps.

"Let's have another short break before we say Mass," Tuck said firmly, having seen Guy hurry to the door and step outside to signal to John. Tuck himself went and ushered Siward and James to their feet, then went and knelt in front of Gilbert, speaking to him softly in words none but Gilbert could hear. Feeling that Tuck had his hands full enough, Guy went and half-helped half-pulled Robin to his feet.

"Come on, cousin," he said affectionately. "Up you get! Plenty of day left to pray in! You don't need to punish yourself by excess this early on," and he went to hug Robin. The look in his cousin's eyes stopped him, though. It was a haunted, hunted gaze, and once again Guy had the feeling that just for an instant his cousin was seeing someone else – and it was a someone else he was in half a mind to kill! Or at least one of those people was, for he had a suspicion that there was a veritable host of ghosts held back in the tears swimming unshed behind the dark lashes.

"A warm drink!" Guy added encouragingly, feeling that he should leave the delicate stuff to Tuck's more experienced hand. Robin might still have held back more, but Malik looked Guy in the face with no hesitation and declared in his quiet, measured voice,

"That would a sensible and welcome thing to do," and gave his restrained flicker of a smile.

Guy was warming to this member of the company by the day. A thoroughly sensible man, Malik clearly understood that these new friends were doing their best at trying to help, and also that there would be nothing gained by making themselves ill in the process of commemorating the dead. He was already steering Will to the back of the chapel and the door, and Robin reluctantly allowed himself to be guided outside by Guy in their wake. The hall adjoined the chapel, and between them there was something of a wooden lean-to covering a walkway in the lee of the south walls, and here John had set up the largest brazier he could find. Walter and Algar were handing out mugs brim-full of a warm liquid and chunks of plain bread which had come out of the castle's oven only moments before.

"What is this?" Siward asked, taking another swig from his mug just as Gilbert came out with Tuck to join them. "It's unusual but I like it," he added, as if surprised.

John chuckled. "It's Guy's secret recipe, actually!" Everyone turned to look at Guy in amazement, especially Robin.

"I got it off an old Welsh woman," Guy explained, although not bothering to add that it had been Bethan's mother. This wasn't the day for such another sad tale. "It has dandelion and burdock roots in it and a few other things. Warms you up on a cold day, doesn't it? She always used to brew some up on Sundays, saying that it was better than drinking beer on the Lord's day, even if it was weak beer." Guy had a feeling that her antipathy to beer on the Sabbath had to do with the way many of de Braose's garrison had regularly got thoroughly soused on that day, when their lords were otherwise occupied at the instigation of the Church, and they were just hanging around and bored. He'd had to drag many a drunkard back to the castle, at the plea of the villagers, when the men got it into their heads to flex their beer-fuelled muscles in what they called fun, and the villagers, persecution.

The memory of Bethan's mother triggered another thought, and Guy dug deep into the pocket of his tunic and pulled out a small bundle. Inside was a wooden pot of salve and a couple of clean bandages. He now walked over to Will with it.

"Show me your hand," he said neutrally but pointing to the blood-encrusted knuckles.

"It's all right," Will brushed off the incident.

"That old door's full of splinters!" Guy remonstrated softly, then took Will's hand and dobbed a liberal amount of the honey-based salve onto the knuckles. "Honey. A wonderful thing for stopping wounds from going bad," he said calmly as he bound the knuckles.

"Didn't have you down as the castle apothecary!" Will muttered in surprise.

"I'm not."

"Then how...?"

"The hounds," Guy answered with a twinkle in his eye. "I'd have been a lousy kennelman and huntsman if I hadn't known how to treat cuts and scrapes!"

There was a flickering range of emotions running across Will's face and then the bulky Templar gave a guffaw. It came out more as a half sob than a laugh, but Guy saw some more of the tension disappear in the process.

"You're treating me with *dog* medicine?" It clearly amused Will, and obviously removed any suspicions in him that Guy was in some way creeping around them with ulterior motives.

"Well, just in case you decide to lick your paw, I thought I'd better not risk poisoning you!" Guy joked back, but was glad that Will and Malik at least were now taking the help in the spirit in which it was intended. Tuck gave Guy a minute nod of encouragement too, making him feel that he was making the right kind of moves, even if he himself felt he was groping in the dark to find the way.

As soon as the mugs were emptied and the bread eaten, Tuck ushered the Templars back inside. This time John and Thomas came in, too, and stood with Guy at the back, making Guy think that it was now that Tuck was anticipating the worst outpouring. Gilbert's eyes were as red as his hair, and yet Guy thought that the young Irishman had probably finished with his burst of uncontrollable grief. There was something to be said for the passionate, Celtic temperament at times like this, he believed. The more he saw of Gilbert the more he could imagine him as being the wild warrior, but also as a man who could openly grieve for his friends regardless of social constraints and niceties. If that was so, then Gilbert was probably coming to the end of his grieving, not starting it.

Will, too, had potentially vented a fair amount of his emotions during the time they'd been travelling, even if they'd come out as anger. As for Malik, Guy suspected that he was a man who, like Tuck, could be sustained through the most horrific times by his faith. He would mourn the loss of friends, and deeply too, but would also be able to console himself with the thought that they were no longer suffering.

That left Robin, Siward and James – three men who, even to Guy's less war-experienced eye, were walking a very precarious path through life at the moment. While Tuck was preparing for the Mass and Communion, Guy observed those three closely. It was then that he caught Robin casting furtive glances to his right. Was that Gilbert he was looking at? Guy shifted his stance to move sideways to the other side of the chapel. Yes, Robin's glances were a strange mixture of emotions, almost loving at times and pained at others. Another step to his right, though, and Guy realised that it wasn't Gilbert whom his cousin was favouring with those strange looks. That would account for why Gilbert was acting with complete indifference to them, despite having looked almost straight into Robin's face at one point. No, the object of those tortured gazes was James.

What was going on there, Guy wondered? Siward was speaking sporadically to James, more out of nerves Guy suspected than of really needing to say something. And James was turning to him to listen even if he wasn't responding much. No, James wasn't returning Robin's looks, and that brought to mind of one of the young soldiers who currently had a terrible crush on one of the town's girls back in Nottingham. That sent shivers down Guy's spine! Did Robin have more than brotherly feelings towards James? Guy had to admit it wasn't something he was overly comfortable with, but, in a military world where men usually outnumbered any female company many times over, he was worldly enough to know that such things would happen, and that no amount of lawmaking or threatening could change how someone felt inside. Now his heart did a lurch of its own, for he could foresee only too well how such behaviour might be seen in a parochial preceptory. Tuck had talked to him often about how life in the east was far more liberal. So did Robin have any idea of what he might incite if he didn't guard himself better? Guy thought not and it worried him deeply.

However Tuck was now going through the opening antiphon of the Mass and then moving smoothly into reciting Psalm 42. He'd barely got into it when his words began to take effect.

"*Tu enim Deus fortitudo mea quare proiecisti me quare tristis incedo adfligente inimico,*" he intoned. "For thou are God, my strength. Why have you cast me off? Why do I mourn because of enemy afflictions?"

At that last sentence, Guy saw Robin's right hand come up to his face and heard a deep sob. As one, Guy, John and Thomas took a step forwards but were halted by a fractional shake of the head from Tuck. The psalm was short, and then came a sequence where Tuck spoke and the Templars responded. It wasn't at all recognisable to the three at the back, but clearly to the Templars – who were used to almost monastic offices – this was all very familiar, and that familiarity seemed to steady Robin for now. Even more surprising to Guy was that the Templars joined in with the Kyrie. He'd heard monks singing the Kyrie when he'd been at one or other of the monasteries on sheriff's business, but it hadn't occurred to him that the Templars would say it too. His visits to Garway hadn't included attending Mass with them, and it brought it home to him that although he knew quite a lot about the Templar way of life, there were also huge gaps where he knew nothing of what his cousin's life had been like these latter years.

Tuck moved surely onwards, and it was clear that in some ways the Templars were at last feeling more on recognisable ground. So much so that Guy wondered if for once Tuck had got it wrong. They all seemed to so much steadier now. Was that all that had been needed? To find a way back into the routine which must have sustained them through all manner of trials?

However, when Tuck came to the consecration of the bread and wine, even the most unimaginative of men would have felt the sudden shift in mood. The big Welsh priest had lifted the bread first to bless it – only humble bread from the castle kitchen's early morning bake, but the best they could do in the circumstances. Then the chalice of wine – Sir Ivo's best silver and filled with wine from a particularly good hogshead Guy had found in the keep's basement.

Tuck's rich voice was filling the chapel with his fervour, and Guy was just thinking that this had been almost as good for Tuck as for his small congregation, when the major crack appeared.

"*Memento etiam, Domine, famulorum famularumque tuarum*," he said and paused and turned back to his tiny congregation. "That means, 'remember also, Lord, Your servants and handmaids.' I want you to say out loud the names of your lost comrades."

It was as though someone had thrown a bucket of icy water over the six. They froze, but Tuck stood before them patiently waiting with no signs of wanting to hurry them on if they didn't respond immediately. The tension built to almost unbearable levels and still no-one spoke, not because they didn't want to, but rather as though they didn't dare to because once they started they might not stop. All of them were making as if to speak and then stopping as if in pain. Guy took a deep breath, hoped this would help, then stepped over to go down on one knee beside Will.

"Oswald and Eadgar," he said carefully, praying like mad that Will wouldn't turn and punch him for his daring to speak those names. Even bandaged, the smith's meaty fist would deliver a mighty blow. A tremor ran through Will but he shot Guy a grateful glance.

"Yes," he said gruffly, cleared his throat and then said more clearly, "Remember, Lord, Oswald and my brother smith Eadgar." He coughed again, took a deep breath and added, "and Robert the smith, Guillaume the smith and Tancred." He looked up to Tuck who nodded encouragingly. "And James from Trier and James from Canterbury."

"Abraham of Acre, and Saul, Asahel, Joab, Nabal, Telem and Caleb, all also of Acre," Malik's voice rose from the other side of Will, for once struggling to remain level.

Like a dam breaking, suddenly the Templars were tripping over their tongues to speak names. Many were not only distinguished by their place of origin but also where they fell.

"Benjamin of Haifa who fell at Hattin," might be followed by "Odo of Caen who fell in Jerusalem," but those two places time and again were the ones where most of the dead had met their end. As the role-call went on and on, Guy found himself with John and Thomas at the back looking to one another in growing horror. How many men had died in these places? It was one thing to hear that the True Cross had been lost to the enemy at the Horns of Hattin, but to hear of so many dead whom just this small band knew of spoke of a major disaster on a scale none of them had dreamed of.

Gilbert once again was only held up by the bench in front of him and was repeating a long list of names, each one punctuated by wet sobs and several "oh God"'s, or "Jesu preserve him"'s. Siward was shaking like a leaf with his hands clasped so tightly before him that Guy wondered if he would get them apart again, yet still managing to stutter out his own list of names. James, on the other hand, was measuring out each name carefully, a long pause between each until, that was, he came to one in particular.

"Remember Lord," he gagged, swallowed and positively spat out, "my beloved brother, David," with such a retch that Guy thought for a second he might have vomited too. The howl of grief which came on the heels of the name made Guy realise that he hadn't, but James was now really in trouble. He slumped to one side as he threw out, "and my other brother Daniel. ...*Wayn inta Daniel?* ...*Oh limadha?* ...*Esther habibti!*" He slipped a little further and Guy saw Robin reaching out to him, and registered the tears pouring down Robin's face too as James wailed, "*Esther, ana aftaqyuduki! Mowlud Elihu wa Joshua. ...Oh Joshua uhibuk!*" reverting to his native language in his distress. Then gagged again and couldn't seem to get another word out of a throat too thick with emotion.

Luckily John was moving as fast as Guy. In a couple of strides he was beside James, dropped to his knees and swept him into his arms, cradling him like a child as he rocked him soothingly, murmuring, "There, there, lad." He held James tight, letting the younger man howl out his grief with his head buried in the massive shoulder. Guy dropped to his knees beside Robin and wrapped an arm around his shoulders.

"Lean on me, cousin." He could think of nothing else to say which wouldn't sound trite, and for the first time felt this strange person, who was half the old Baldwin and half this new person called Robin, relax into his embrace. It had always been like this when they were boys he recalled – John being almost fatherly to Allan, and Guy being the one who went to Baldwin when they were upset, and only afterwards Guy and John comforting one another as best they could. Guy had begun to wonder whether this new Robin's trust in anyone, other than the band of men he'd arrived with, had been so destroyed that there would never again be the sense of them having been in the same family and so close.

Vaguely they were aware of Will stumbling to his feet and crashing out again, and when Guy managed to cast a glance over his shoulder he saw that Thomas was gone and that Hugh had come in to stand in his stead, and was hovering closely behind Siward and Gilbert. And bless him, Bilan had come in, looking very scared at all this tempest of emotions, but with the look of one who was determined to help if he could. Guy had a sudden idea. He had both arms around Robin now, supporting him, but he managed to catch Bilan's eye and to gesture him to come and kneel at Malik's side. It worked, for Malik, whose voice had begun to really waver, suddenly spotted Bilan kneeling anxiously by him. He gave a small sob but then turned to smile at Bilan.

"We lose dear friends ...so many friends ...but others can be found in the strangest of circumstances," he said softly, with his eyes clearing and the hint of a smile breaking through.

Thank you, God, for Bilan's endearing smile, Guy offered up the silent prayer of his own. Malik had an apparently fatherly arm around Bilan now, but Guy was sure that it was Bilan who was doing the supporting. As for Robin, he was chanting a long list of names in an emotionless drone – emotionless only in tone though, for Guy could feel the dreadful shivering which was running through his cousin's lean and muscular frame. It was a terribly long list, and yet every so often Robin would add, "and Baldwin," who seemed to be the same man time and again. Was that the young king, Guy wondered? He wasn't going to ask now, but later he really wanted to know.

As the frenzied mourning began to ease, Tuck calmly turned back to the altar and completed his preparations for Communion. Very deliberately he began the Pater Noster again, waiting at the end of each line for the Templars to join in. At first it was Guy, John and Hugh who were the only ones speaking, but by the last line all of the others were joining in, if very quietly and in choked voices. When Tuck came to them with the bread and the chalice he took his time too, allowing each man to collect himself before offering either of the sacred items to him. He began with Gilbert. The redhead rallied surprisingly well at this offering, as though something had been completed for him, and he shuffled aside and gestured Hugh to come and kneel between him and Siward.

"You're a soldier. You should partake of this Mass too," he said kindly.

Hugh's thanks were very quiet and short, and he took the sacrament with simple, calm dignity, allowing Tuck to move swiftly on to Siward. From where he knelt Guy could clearly see Siward, for James was still hanging on to John for dear life and therefore leaning back from where the others were kneeling. The former squire was worrying Guy badly now. Only he of all of the Templars seemed to be unable to let go and grieve. It took him several goes to be able to unclasp his hands, and in the end it was Hugh leaning across and massaging them to relax them which enabled Siward to prise his fingers apart, so that he could lean towards Tuck without pitching on his nose onto the bench.

Yet after taking the sacrament, Siward sat back on his heels and continued the inaudible litany he'd been carrying on since they began saying the names. If his hands weren't clasped as they had been, he was now unable to keep them still, and the right hand constantly crossed himself, while the left clenched and unclenched spasmodically over a fold at the side of his tunic. His breathing was shallow and ragged too, and Hugh was watching him like a hawk, ready to catch him should he pass out.

John virtually lifted James up towards Tuck for the next offering, refusing Tuck's quizzical look of an offering for himself with a single shake, as he once more took James into his arms and began rocking him again. At least the former turcopole ceased his sobbing now, which they could all only hope was a signal that he in some small measure felt better. Tuck so far had been very astute in his reading of these men, and he'd suggested that the Mass might be a turning point and it seemed to be working. He offered Guy the host and he took it, easing his cousin up with him to a more upright kneel so that Robin was in a position to take both when Tuck moved on to him. Like Gilbert, the receipt of the sacraments seemed to steady Robin in a way that nothing else had, and Guy felt able to loose him a few moments later, even if he did keep a gentle grip on his shoulder just in case. Like Hugh, Malik then took the offering with quiet dignity, then with a quirk of an eyebrow invited Bilan forward.

"Me?" the young lad said aloud in stunned shock. "Oh this isn't for the likes of me!"

"You've never partaken?" Malik was clearly as surprised.

"Villagers normally only witness the priest and any monks around the place taking Communion," Tuck explained softly. "Our noble, Norman," that word came out with very Welsh venom, "bishops decree that the peasants must confess their considerable sins, yet never think to offer them the means of redemption!"

Guy felt his lips twitch in a suppressed smile. So very like Tuck to be outraged at that! However, he did lean forwards to catch Bilan's eye, and mouth, "Go on! Take it!" and give an encouraging nod. Nonetheless Bilan looked worriedly to Robin, clearly wondering if this strange warrior would take exception to him butting in on their remembrance service. Yet Robin, too, nodded.

"Take it," he said flatly. "Don't forego such a blessing if it comes your way. You never know if you might get the chance again, so don't waste it – it's too precious!"

And so Bilan very nervously took the bread and then the wine from Tuck. Will still hadn't appeared, and Tuck made no point of looking or waiting for him. With short prayers which at least Malik, Robin and Gilbert joined in with, Tuck concluded the Mass.

"Come!" Tuck said with fatherly authority. "Time to eat and rest now!"

He led the way to the chapel door and held it open for them. Malik left first with a rather stunned Bilan, and was closely followed by Gilbert, now walking steadily and looking a good deal calmer than he had since Guy had met him. Hugh and Siward walked out side by side, silent, but Siward still giving occasional grateful glances Hugh's way. It left John with James and Guy with Robin.

"Go on Tuck! Go and get some food!" Guy said firmly. "You've worked hard this morning. We'll be along shortly."

He eased himself up onto the bench so that he could sit and look the still kneeling Robin in the face.

"Has this helped?" he asked carefully.

Robin took a deep, ragged breath. "Yes, ...I think so, yes." He sighed, but this time it was more of relief than in sorrow. "It's been such a long time since we did this. Oh, we participated at preceptories along the way through Cyprus, by Rome and in France. But the further west we got, the less anyone was interested in what we'd been through. Sometimes..." he paused and shook his head. "Sometimes it was as though these so-called brothers of ours – who'd never seen a day's fighting in the east – somehow blamed us for the loss of the True Cross and of Jerusalem. As if in surviving we somehow demonstrated that we'd not fought hard enough, or with enough belief. ...As if they thought, ...how dare we still be here to tell the tale?"

Guy could hear the anger beneath those words. How awful to have survived such horrors only to be made to feel guilty for simply being alive!

"Well John and I are *very* glad that you lived!" Guy declared warmly.

"Oh Lord, that we are!" John concurred with equal sincerity.

Robin smiled, for the first time showing an echo of the smile John and Guy had once been so familiar with. "I never thought to see you again," he said, as if it was a wonder to him to suddenly realise that he was back in England and with his cousins once more.

"We feared we'd lost you, too!" Guy responded swiftly. "By Our Lady, Baldw... What do you want us to call you now? I fear I'm totally at a loss. Baldwin is the memory I have of the lad I said farewell to on the borders twelve years ago." He refrained from saying he felt he didn't really know the man.

"I've been Robin since I landed in the Holy Land," his cousin said in a voice as distant as the look in his eyes. "I don't think I can go back to being Baldwin. He seems like someone totally different to me now. All those years at Alverton... They're like a dream. Like someone else's life I've stood by and watched happen."

A silence filled the chapel, then John's pragmatic voice said,

"Better get used to calling you Robin then, hadn't we?"

Somehow that hit the right spot with Robin because he actually laughed softly.

"God Almighty, I've forgotten in this last year or so how much I've missed you two," he said with a shake of his head. "I walk in here with five other soldiers you've never met from Adam, and within two days you've found us a place to stay, provided us with food, and found a priest who cares more about God than the bishops. Oh that our supposed brethren had done as much!"

"That," Guy said firmly getting to his feet and hoisting Robin up to join him, "is because we're family, you daft sod! Now let's go and get something to eat. I'm ravenous!"

But Robin walked his first few stiff-jointed steps over to James and bent over him.

"James?" he called gently, brushing the hair back from his friend's face so that he could see him better. It was another of those gestures which worried Guy. So open to misinterpretation! For now, though, the other knight was sitting up, and although he said nothing he let Robin and John help him to his feet.

"Thank you, John," Robin said gratefully, wrapping an arm around James' other side. "You were always so good at comforting everyone."

James blinked and looked up into John's face. Again, no words, but his weak smile said what he couldn't in the way of thanks.

Together he and Robin walked out of the door leaving Guy and John to bring up the rear.

"Robin and James..." John murmured thoughtfully.

"Ah, so you noticed too," Guy sighed. "Do you think there's anything more than closeness there?"

"Depends on what you mean by closeness," John said dubiously.

Guy raised his eyebrows. "Hmmm! I was thinking of the kind of bond you must get when you've been in such a fight as they have. To have to depend on someone for months on end for your very life... must make you close in a way nothing else can."

"But it's more than that with those two, isn't it?" John sounded as though he was almost begging Guy to tell him he'd been wrong.

Guy scrubbed his hands through his hair in confusion. "Oh Lord, John, I don't know! In James' case, possibly not. He doesn't seem to act any differently towards Baldw... Robin than anyone else. If that's the case then it might be a case of unrequited love. That doesn't make me happy for the anguish it must cause ...Robin. He could hardly be happy under those circumstances. But for myself I think I'd rather it was that, because that would mean that nothing's ...happened. If you see what I mean?"

"Oh I do! And Heaven help me, but I feel the same." They'd come out of the chapel and were greeted by a grey but rather warmer morning than of late, and John stretched mightily and drew in a deep breath of the suddenly spring-like air. "Who on earth could we ask, though? To find out for sure? We can hardly ask ...Robin!" Like Guy, John was stumbling over this new name. "And we do need to know, because if it's the worst we fear, we're going to have to do something to protect him, aren't we? I mean, we can't just escort them off to one of the Yorkshire preceptories and leave them to it, can we? And I don't imagine we could be so lucky as for you to be able to find a place for them. The sheriff isn't going to hand over even a remote castle to a bunch of Templars who barely qualify as knights in his eyes, even if they've fought more battles than he's had banquets!"

By the time the pair of them had reached the hall neither had come any closer to resolving their problem. The Templars were clustered around the big hearth getting warm, all except Will that was. Tuck came up to Guy with a purposeful amble.

"I know, I spotted!" Guy said softly before Tuck spoke. "I'll go and find him. Thomas isn't here either, so I wouldn't worry too much."

It didn't take Guy long to spot them. The burly smith was walking along the walls accompanied by Thomas and Piers, and Guy intercepted them at the turret before the East Gate.

"There's a good cooked breakfast waiting in the hall," he said as a good, non-judgemental opener.

"Oh we've eaten already," Thomas said cheerfully. "We got first pickings of the bacon when it came off the griddle!"

Will waved what was in his right hand to confirm that. He had two thick slices of bread in between which were several rashers of crispy bacon.

"Ahh, ...I can't tell you how much I've missed bacon!" he said with relish, taking another mouthful and chewing it with every sign of enjoyment. "They won't eat pig out there, you know. Say that they're 'unclean'!" He savoured another mouthful. "Do you know, I've *dreamed* about eating bacon!"

Guy couldn't help but laugh. "If I'd know that I'd have got bacon out of the store and not sausages for yesterday's breakfast! We're only eating sausages so much because the last castellan was hoarding the bloody things for himself, and the cook's said that if they don't get eaten soon we'll have to burn them. Apparently once they go off we'd be daft to even feed them to the village pigs – something about not feeding them their own, which is something I've heard pig men say before so I believe it. The bacon's much better preserved so we've been saving that for later, but we don't need to hang onto it that much if it would be so welcome."

Just one look at Will's face told Guy the answer to that, and he made a mental note to ensure bacon stayed on the breakfast list while their guests were with them. It was hardly a hardship for him either. Normal breakfasts in Nottingham castle were hot porridge and some bread. There wasn't enough meat for it to be handed out at every meal when there were so many mouths to feed, and pig in particular was reserved for the more highborn folk. So Guy was relishing the change of diet too. However, the bacon had broken the conversational ice, and so he ventured to ask the dreaded questions he needed answers to. Will was looking quite his old self, so Guy hoped he wasn't risking his life asking such a thing when up on a very tall castle wall with a sheer drop over the edge!

"Will, ...I need to ask you something," he began tentatively. "It's rather ...delicate. I don't want to know just for the sake of it. It's rather that John and I are more than a bit worried that Bald... Robin has forgotten what life is like back here in England." Will was looking at him with a perplexed frown now. "Robin and James...?" Guy left the names hanging in the air, but looked desperately to Will.

"Ahhh... You've noticed," Will said flatly. He turned and leaned on the stonework to look across the narrow valley.

"He's... They're going to have to be very careful," Guy said despairingly. "I know what some of these Churchmen are like, Will, and forgiveness isn't a word they know the meaning of!"

"It's just Robin," Will said gruffly, coughed and then tried again. "James isn't ...that way. Poor lad, he's a terrible mess, but not like that. He had a young wife, you see. And two children. That's who Elihu and Joshua were ...his little sons. Esther was his wife. Or at least she was until the Mamelukes who are allied to Saladin came to their village. James thought that by being one of the turcopoles that he would be protecting them. That his troop would be around when any fighting came their way. He wasn't, and he can't forgive himself for that. After they died he came into the order. He said he couldn't even think about serving his time and then settling down with another woman."

"Do you think that was misunderstood?" Piers asked with unusual perception. "About another woman, I mean?"

It made Will blink in surprise. "I don't know. I'd never thought of it like that, ...but maybe, yes, maybe you could be right there. ...All I know is that there's been no hint of those two ever being together in the way you fear. And we've travelled together for long enough for me to notice if they had been sneaking off at night." He gave Guy a strange look. "He talked about you, you know, ...Robin did. When we were sat around a campfire in the early days out in Acre and Jerusalem he used to tell me about his family. He missed you all terribly. He used to tell me and the others how you lot were never apart."

He gave a wry laugh. "I didn't believe him entirely. I didn't think that cousins would be so close. I fought like cat and dog even with my brothers – although Robin did say he had much older half-brothers he hardly knew. I couldn't bloody stand my cousins!" He laughed again. "But you two? You're just like he said you were! And maybe that will help him not think so much about James – because I'm not entirely convinced that lust comes into his feelings. I think he was just looking for someone to be close with like he was with you two and the others. 'John's like a big bear' he used to say. 'When he's around you feel totally safe.' ...I saw John with James through the chapel window. He's a good man."

"He's the best," came without hesitation from Guy's heart. "He's as honest as the day is long. He'd never cheat you or desert you, and, with the possible exception of Tuck, he's the kindest person I've ever met too."

Will nodded thoughtfully. "A rare man."

Guy leaned back against the stones. "Go on then, tell me what he said about me! I'm sure there were a few choice memories!"

Now Will grinned. "He said you were the clever one!"

"Me?"

"Yeah! He said if ever there was a tricky situation you were the one to find a way out of it." Will's grin faded. "I think he was a bit shocked to find you as the sheriff's man, to be honest. It wasn't how he thought you'd be living."

Now Guy really was surprised. "Really? How did he think I would get along? I had no money, no patron and both parents gone – even though as far as I know Mother is still alive in the nunnery – it wasn't as though I was going to have all that many choices!"

"And you didn't exactly ask to come to Nottingham either," Thomas added loyally. "All sorted out between the king, de Braose and the earl of Chester, see?" he informed Will.

"Then you'd be doing yourself a favour if you told Robin that," Will said firmly.

"Thank you, I'll do that," Guy told him. "For now, though, do you feel like coming and joining the others yet?"

"I'll walk a bit longer with these two," Will decided. "Don't worry, I'll be down in time to go in for the next service. I just need to clear my head a bit." He paused and then seemed to decide to trust Guy with another confidence. "Sometimes it gets a bit too repressive being just the six of us," he said carefully. "Not like when there was a whole troop of us. Robin I've known since we landed in the Holy Land together. Malik I've known a long time too. But the other three we've really only known since the retreat from Hattin."

Understanding came to Guy. "So you don't really have any history to talk about with them except for the last months in the Holy Land."

Will nodded. "And so that tends to be what we keep going over and *over*. It's not healthy, you know, ...keeping dwelling on the past. Nothing's going to change it. And although it was bad, very bad, it wasn't all there was to life for me. It's nice to have someone different to talk to," he said with a nod to Thomas and Piers. "Men who've seen some of the other places I've fought in too. It helps. Having that breathing space helps a lot!"

"Glad to be of service," Thomas said with a very wry Welsh sniff, making them all laugh.

Will caught Guy's sleeve as he was about to turn and go back down to the hall. "It doesn't do Robin any good being shut up with those three either," he said urgently. "They drag him down, James and Siward especially. They brood too much! Gilbert's not so bad. He's a bit of a cracked-pot, but he only wallows in his Celtic twilight for so long. Then he pulls himself together and goes and thumps someone! It isn't doing him any good, either, being with Robin and the other two when they get all morose. If you want to do something really helpful then split those four up! Take Robin off somewhere and talk about the old days with him, and get that Hugh to do the same with Gilbert – he seems like a steady man."

"I will," Guy promised.

However there was the rest of the day to get through first, and at noon Tuck summoned the Templars back to the chapel.

"As I said before," he began, "I can't say the full Sext office for the day, since even my memory won't run to all the variations without recourse to a breviary. So we'll start with the three standard prayers and then say together Psalm 78. That's the Templar's psalm," he added for the benefit of the cluster of others standing at the back, for Walter and Algar had come to join John, the Coshams and Guy. Most of the Templars gave the appearance, so far, of being calmer. Yet Siward seemed to have got a terrible fit of the shivers as soon as Tuck mentioned the psalm. Guy could see the sweat starting to stand out on his brow, and he and Hugh sidled closer to the young knight, while John padded softly to behind James, ready to support him if Siward triggered another outburst. Robin turned briefly, saw where John and Guy were, and mouthed 'thank you' to them. So there was still some of the old caring Baldwin hidden inside, Guy was relieved to see.

The opening prayers went without a hitch with their appropriate responses, and then Tuck began the psalm, doing as he had done before and translating the verses as he went. Guy and the others at the back were on tenterhooks as he spoke, and at only the second verse they realised why Siward had reacted so strongly.

"They have given the bodies of your servants to be meat for the fowls of the air, and the flesh of your saints for the beasts of the earth," Tuck intoned, the words barely out of his mouth before a dreadful howl went up from Siward. His arms were clasped about him as if they were the only things holding him together and his head thrown back, eyes clenched shut as if trying not to see something before him.

"*Naaoow!*" he yelled, the tendons on his neck standing out and the shaking getting worse. "Nooo! No more! For the love of God, no more!"

For an instant those at the back thought he was begging Tuck to stop, but then he lurched to his feet, arms waving in front of him. "Blessed Virgin, take them away!" he pleaded. "No more! Please, no more!" and now there was a frisson of fear that he might be possessed. Were these visions only he could see, just memories, or something more? Only Tuck's complete calm stopped the observers from having a panic of their own.

Then Siward lurched to his feet, spun, and cannoned so unexpectedly into Hugh that he sent the former soldier reeling into Gilbert, who had half risen to his feet to reach out to Siward. The two of them entangled giving Siward the space to stumble over them and make it to the door, which lay in the chapel's north-side wall, and was therefore closer to him than to Guy and the outlaws. He flung it open and ricocheted out into the bailey, then began running towards the keep. Guy had no doubts about what he intended to do if he got to the top of the tower and sprinted after him.

The distraught Templar put on a surprising burst of speed and Guy found himself hard pressed to make any gains on him, then a flash of brown cloth went past him. Bilan, with the speed of youth caught up with Siward and launched himself at him, bringing him to his knees. The knight threw Bilan off easily enough, but it had slowed him enough for Guy to catch up with them. Guy's greater weight was not so easily shaken away, and after a wild scuffle of thrown punches and kicks, Guy got Siward on the ground and pinned him down by the simple expediency of sitting on him.

"Guy's got him!" he heard Walter call from somewhere behind them, but he was too busy dealing with the writhing Siward to be able to look around.

"For God's sake, stop fighting me, I'm not your enemy!" Guy panted.

"Let me go! Let me finish this!" Siward wept and suddenly went limp. He was dry-eyed but a series of wracking sobs still shook his body.

"No," Guy said softly, gradually easing his grip but not letting go altogether. "No, I won't let you do that." He managed to sit Siward up as he became aware of Bilan sitting up rubbing an already growing egg-sized lump on his head. "Are you all right, Bilan?"

"*Ngnnfff!*" the lad responded, screwing his eyes up and then blinking hard. "Ouch! That stone was hard!"

"Oh God! Oh, I'm so *sorry!*" Siward gulped, horrified that he'd hurt Bilan.

"I'll mend!" Bilan answered with his normal cheeky grin returning. "You still didn't hit me as hard as Piers used to when we played together as lads!"

However the shaking had returned to Siward even stronger than ever. Guy saw him swallow reflexively and got out of the way just in time before Siward was violently sick. The poor man continued to retch violently long after he had anything to bring up, and Guy found himself holding Siward and trying to support his head as he knelt on all fours in the bailey like a sick dog. Bilan sat on his heels looking worriedly at the sight until he said to Guy,

"He's starting to bring up blood!"

Guy looked down in horror. Siward was in some kind of spasm and he couldn't seem to stop, nor did Guy know what the proper treatment ought to be. The only thing he could think of to do was to knock Siward out.

"Hold him up!" he commanded Bilan, virtually throwing Siward upright into Bilan's arms, then drew back his fist and hit the knight hard on the jaw. Siward's head whipped back with the blow, then his eyes rolled up and he went limp as he and Bilan sat down hard on the flagstones at the base of the keep. The violent retching stopped, but Siward continued to shake uncontrollably even in his unconscious state.

"Poor lad," Walter said, coming over with Algar at his heels.

"Help me to carry him into the hall," Guy ordered them, and the three of them picked the twitching Siward up between them and carried him inside.

"Straight to the big bed!" Guy told them once through the door, and they went up to the far end and through the curtain to Sir Ivo's grand oak tester-bed. Throwing back the covers, Guy got Walter and Algar to help him get Siward's outer clothes and boots off.

"I saw something like this once," Algar confided. "A woman. She saw her husband fall from the scaffolding at Nottingham Castle. Right from the top to land at her feet. She went like this, and as cold."

"By Saint Thomas he is cold!" Guy realised. "Get all the blankets you can! Pile them up on top of him! Let's see if we can get him warmer!"

Walter disappeared, and Algar began scooping up the blankets the other Templars had been using, and which were rolled up and set aside for now. A strange clanking sound materialised into Bilan coming in carrying a small brazier, and Walter behind him with some coals and wood to light it.

"Good idea!" Guy praised and saw Bilan turn a little pinker. So it had been his quick thinking to bring the brazier! He must remember to thank Bilan properly later on. Slowly Siward's violent shaking eased, although he was still terribly cold to the touch. It was only when Robin's voice came at his side that Guy realised how long they'd been trying to chaff some warmth into Siward's hands.

"What's happened to him?"

Guy thought Robin sounded very much on edge himself. Very brittle, that was the word, he realised, as though at one more thing going wrong Robin would shatter into pieces.

"His grief is coming out in a different way to you," Tuck's reassuring voice answered before Guy could, and the big man eased himself into the room, which by now was filled with Siward's friends and the outlaws. "You've done the right thing, Guy, by trying to keep him warm." Tuck went and placed an expert hand on Siward's forehead. "Let him rest," he said firmly. "He's becoming fevered but don't let him throw the covers off, keep him warm. Everyone but two of you come out. There's nothing else you can do for him. The Lord and St Issui will watch over him."

"We'll sit with him," Walter offered, as Algar moved to the other side of the bed and nodded his agreement. "You go, Guy. Get something to drink and talk to your cousin. He needs you, any one of us can sit with this poor soul."

"Thank you," Guy said gratefully to them.

He went out into the hall and realised with a shock that it was still only just after noon and the castle's household had just finished their midday meal. Only noon? It felt as though he'd done three days in the saddle already! John pressed a warmed ale into his hands and he drank it thirstily, welcoming the feeling of the heat of the drink reaching into his innards. He inhaled the strong malty aroma and found comfort in that too. Thank God for beer! Then saw John waving him over to the long table. A cauldron of thick stew was keeping warm by the fire, and John ladled Guy a generous couple of spoonfuls of the steaming mixture into a bowl, then came to sit down with a thump beside Guy.

"I don't know about you but I feel like I've done all the wrestling fights at a summer fair in one day!" John groaned. Guy nodded vigorously although his mouth was too full of stew to reply. The big man propped his head up on one arm and slumped across the table. "I don't begrudge helping these poor souls, ...but how long is this going to keep on for?" he wondered with a certain hint of despair in his voice.

Guy paused in his eating. "I think..." he began tentatively, "that Malik, Will and Gilbert will be fine from now on. For them, I think Tuck doing this day of prayer was just what was needed – an official chance to mourn and draw a curtain behind what they saw in the east. Hugh says they'll still get nightmares every now and then, but I think mostly they'll be fine. But the others...?" He sighed. "I hope and pray that the sheriff doesn't summon me back in the next few days, because I think it will take at least that long before James or Siward will be fit to travel anywhere, and I'm not so sure about Robin either!"

"Can they withstand Tuck finishing these prayers, do you think?" John wondered.

"I suspect Tuck will carry on even if there's no-one left watching him," was Guy's response. "It would be like him to believe that completing the cycle of offices would help the dead, as well as the living, through some kind of divine intervention. I wish I could believe as devoutly as him!"

"So do I!" John agreed.

Yet when Tuck called them to Vespers, the five remaining knights still went, and now Guy was infinitely glad that he had opened the afternoon service to the castle folk too. This time the little chapel was crammed full, and the Templars had to be shuffled forwards until they were right close to Tuck and the altar. Vespers was not as short a service as Sext, but Tuck instructed his congregation of mixed novices in the correct responses, and everyone joined in with a will. At the end Tuck moved among them and many of the servants talked about a lost loved one. In the midst of this Robin appeared at Guy's side.

"I understand that this is your doing," he said.

Guy didn't quite know how to take this. Was Robin angry at him for including the lesser folk? So he was more than a little surprised when Robin threw his arms around him and hugged him.

"Thank you, Guy! It was getting unbearable with just the six of us, and now Siward isn't with us...," he paused and shook his head as he held Guy back at arms' length again. "It would have been horrible with that empty space and nothing to fill it!"

"I thought it might be a bit much for you," Guy admitted. "In fact, I'm surprised that only one of you hasn't made it this far. You're all so strained! I thought all those hours of prayer might take more of a toll than they have."

Robin bowed his head. "It has been a strain. But your monk friend was right to do this. We desperately needed it – all of us did!" Then he hugged Guy again. "But this is the you I remembered for years! The one who'd come up with something no-one else had thought of!" And he hugged Guy tight again. "I've missed you so much! All of you!"

Guy hugged him back, then held him back so that he could look him in the face. "We've missed you badly too! And that's why I want to hear all about what happened to you." He held up a silencing finger as Robin went to shake his head and protest. "All of it! Not just the bad stuff of the last few months you were out there! There must have been some good times? And I want to hear about King Baldwin too!"

Robin sighed, but now with a weak smile. "Very well. But only if you in turn explain how on earth you came to be a sheriff's man! It's so unlike the Guy I knew to hold an office like that. You despised the sheriff's bully-boys who used to come round to the villages when we were boys. What happened?"

Guy shrugged. "It was all very simple in the end, and I had no choice in the matter. Believe me, that bit won't take long to tell, although the rest of it might!"

He took the Templars off to the end of the hall as the afternoon drew into evening and told his story.

"So you met Prince John?" Robin was quite amazed. He was even more surprised when Guy told him of his unexpected knighting. However, Robin was soon laughing and telling the others that this was more like the cousin he knew when Guy got to the part about turning the tables on sheriff de Braose, and taking Ianto with him.

"They might have given you the knighthood and the job," Robin said as they staggered off to Compline for the last round of prayers for the day, "but you're still the same rebellious old Guy underneath, aren't you!"

"You have no idea!" Guy told him, and thought that he hadn't even told Robin the half of it. Only Tuck had any idea of all of Guy's schemes and plots, for he hadn't mentioned Maelgwn yet. He couldn't risk one of the Templars mentioning that name later on in a preceptory by accident. Secrets weren't the half of it, Guy thought dryly, later on as he gratefully rolled into his blankets and wriggled into the straw mattress a little deeper. He had more secrets than some priests in their confessionals!

That was the strangest and most traumatic set of Church services I have ever attended in my life. I confess to you now, Brother Gervase, that having seen the cost to such men's lives, I began to doubt the wisdom of trying to hold on to the Holy Land. That was not from a lack of belief in the sanctity of the place, nor from idleness or a lack of caring if that most holy of places was desecrated. Instead, it had much to do with the kind of men who went out there with only their personal gain in mind. Both on that day and the next I heard so much of men like Reynauld de Châtillon, murderous adventurers for whom religion was simply a tiresome observance, and it made me wonder whether God had allowed the True Cross to be taken as a warning or a punishment? What were we holding onto the holy sites for if men like them profited most from them? I was deeply bothered, Brother, for it seemed wrong to me that decent and honest men like my cousin and his friends were subject to such trials as to leave them in danger of losing their sanity, and to carry such a burden through the rest of their lives. Men whose faith nonetheless never failed, and yet who were looked down upon by men of the Church and others.

It certainly eroded what little trust I had left in the senior men of the Church. I thought hard upon why a man like Geoffrey Plantagenet should be made not only a bishop, but be in the line for the archbishopric too, with no other attribute than being the bastard son of a wilful king who wanted him in the Church and out of the way of the line of succession. Can you then see why I fell more and more under Tuck's Celtic philosophy? As we stumbled into our makeshift beds that night my good friend declared that he believed his Saint Issui had indeed watched over us. I was too tired to question him that night, but I thought on it more in the following days and I could see what he meant.

If Siward really had intended to take his life that day, then maybe some guiding hand had been behind Bilan and me getting in the way and stopping him. Siward had certainly not been spared any consequence of his life so far. Yet it was less harm than he might have taken. And, for all of Will's rage, he had hurt no-one but himself and that only minimally, while Gilbert was restored to something like his old self, and even James and Robin were substantially better once they had got over the weariness of such a draining day. No great miracles had taken place, and yet there was a sense that of all the outcomes possible, we had come away with the best. Maybe, I thought, Tuck was right and the small local saints should be paid more heed to, and not left to just a few poor peasants to continue holding faith in them.

Who do I pray to? You sound suspicious, Brother! Very well, I must confess a fondness for Saint David. You surely cannot object to him, for Gerald of Wales was one of his bishops and he was a good servant to the English crown, even if King Henry and King Richard dealt less kindly with him in return. Your revered William of Malmesbury wrote much on Saint David too, I understand, so he must be considered reputable by the English Church. It might surprise you to know that I made a pilgrimage to Wales to Saint David's shrine. Ah, you are impressed! I am not all you presupposed you see! Yes, for all that I am no Welshman, Dewi Sant is a saint I am very fond of.

You might be less impressed with my choice of Saint Cadoc the Wise, though, but if what Tuck taught me was right then Cadoc had a special relationship with stags. As a forester and someone who spent an awful lot of his time in the woods that was something which struck a chord in my heart. You can never have seen such sights, Brother, cloistered here within these walls. To be in the forest at dusk or dawn and have one of God's magnificent creatures step out of nowhere in front of you, and then just as mystically disappear again moments later, is a breathtaking and humbling sight. If you cannot see the hand of God there, then you must have very little heart in you to be moved by anything. I also liked Cadoc because his church is built above the Roman fort of Caerleon upon Usk, very close to where the Roman soldiers Julius and Aaron were martyred for not praying to their emperor. That sits well with me too, for as a soldier I saw very little in the kings I served to warrant worshipping.

Saint Melangell was another local saint from mid-Wales whom Tuck introduced me to, and like Cadoc she had an affinity with the animals of the field and forest. She was known to be a protector of hares, and I had one or two incidents with hares which made me think she was not entirely blind to my predicaments at the time – but you must wait for those to appear in their own time in my story!

Very well, since you continue to press me harder, I harbour a fondness for Tuck's other local Welsh saints. Saint Meilig was another of King Brychan's holy children, Saint Arfan was a wandering Welsh bishop who sometimes seemed to hear our pleas quite clearly, and Saint

Cenau was a confessor who seemed to answer Tuck's prayers if not mine. But Saint Issui seemed to have a way of answering all our prayers or giving some protection on a less majestic scale, and though you may sniff in derision, Brother, such interventions were most welcome at the time. Oh yes, I still pray to Saint Issui, and I visited his shrine as well on my way to and from St David's. Is that not supposed to count as almost as good as going to Rome? Ah, two visits to St David's to every one to Rome. A good thing that I made it twice then, even if one was hardly a regular pilgrimage!

There, does that satisfy you for now? That I have not imperilled my soul, even if my choice of saints is not yours? May we continue with our tale now?

Chapter 16

We woke the morning after our epic offices to a dark and stormy day. Rain thundered on the roofs unrelentingly and the sky remained as dark as evening, even at noon. There was no point in going out hunting on such a day. Any animal tracks would have been obliterated by the big heavy raindrops before the beast had passed on a few yards, and I had no inclination to lead tired men out to get cold and soaked to the skin when there was no hope of coming back with anything. Instead, we stoked the fires and John and I pressed Robin to tell us his tale when he woke, for we allowed them all to sleep late and Siward had not woken from his stupor.

Robin was still a little reticent when we assembled around the table in the hall after midday, and John had to tell him the whole sorry tale of how we had lost Allan before he relented. However he and the others were much amused by our pulling the wool over the eyes of their fellow Templars to effect Allan's release, which I had not expected. The Templars still in England had clearly not endeared themselves to the travellers, and Will went so far as to say that such supposed fighting monks would not have lasted an afternoon in the Holy Land if they were so unobservant of strangers.

When we finally got Robin to speak he still needed some cajoling from Will, but he gradually warmed to his subject. We learned that he and Will had met when they had left France in a great company of Templars to march eastwards. With the two of them being good with horses they had found themselves working together often. Robin was quick to say that he would not have survived the journey had it not been for Will. He had been, he said, still far too naive and trusting back then, not only of those who would have waylaid the stragglers of the massive and well-armed party, but also of the less scrupulous of those travelling amongst them – such as merchants and their men, who took advantage for their own safety of travelling with a heavily armed company, but who saw nothing duplicitous in increasing their fortune at their guards' expense.

I could believe all of that. Baldwin had always been one to believe what he was told and trust folk, until John or I made him stop and think otherwise. I could also begin to see that even now Will sometimes treated Robin as if he was still the young lad he had first met. That was where the irritation between them sometimes erupted. Robin's idealism was still there, yet Will often had trouble distinguishing between the high aspirations of a grown man and the naivety of youth. For his part Robin could struggle at times to comprehend Will's cynicism, mistaking it for brutality or uncaring indifference. Yet I could see Will's earthier point of view too, and that was to create a different kind of friendship between him and me. But I digress again!

Along their way east there were tales of horseplay between the young men, the odd fight, and at least one escape from a whorehouse just in time before they were apprehended by either the owner, or their stern Templar knights. It all sounded reassuringly normal, and I could see that John was thinking much the same as me – that this, at least, sounded like the Baldwin we had previously known, who was as interested in the village girls as the rest of us. Baldwin's knight, to whom he should have remained in service, had died on the way before they had hardly got a handful of miles from the French border. So Baldwin spent his time with the sergeants, barely getting any acknowledgement of being a squire, of which there were very few amongst the travelling Templars anyway, and certainly none in the regular mixture of men who he was to spend most of his time with.

Most squires, it seemed, were back at the preceptories and granges in France and England training, not going on crusade until they were elevated to full knighthood. Why his knight had decided to take him along when he went east was a mystery to Baldwin, for the knight had never deigned to explain why to Robin, or any of the other knights in their company either. That had left Baldwin very much adrift when the knight died, and it had been Will who had scooped him up and found him a place in the rapidly shrinking company as they got to the point of embarking on ships – and again it revealed to me why Will could at times be quite parental towards Robin, as we were coming to think of him, in much the same way John had been to Allan.

For Robin and Will, Cyprus had seemed exotic enough, but nothing had prepared them for landing at Acre, an eastern fortress with its medina and souks, all filled with a strange mix of people from all over the known world, which was quite overwhelming. The more they talked of this world, the more our castle faded and we could almost smell the teeming cities – the spices and incense mixed with the sweat of animals and men. Friends made on the journey dispersed to their different destinations, and Malik appeared in their lives when they finally got to Jerusalem early in 1181.

High Peak Castle, Derbyshire, Monday 26th February, the Year of Our Lord 1189

"You should have seen the Templar quarters!" Robin said with real enthusiasm. "Heavens, Guy, it made my father's little castle look like a pigpen! There's a large square, walled area on the east side of the city which abuts up to the main city walls – that's the Temple Mount. The Dome of the Rock is in the centre, while on the southern side and facing inwards with its back to the city wall, is what was originally the Temple of Solomon. Then it became the Al-Aqsa mosque when Jerusalem was first lost, and by the time we got there it was the royal palace, with our Templars' headquarters in its corner adjoining the western wall, which was on the city side.

"There we were, ordinary soldiers like Will and me, quartered in a place with beautiful tiled floors and tall ceilings! And even the humblest of houses had brightly coloured carpets, and the furniture was carved or inlaid with patterns, let alone in a great palace like that. We had so much that seemed exotic at first. Everything which could be decorated was decorated. We felt we were living like kings! It seemed all the more amazing because to get to it you had to ride or walk through the cramped and crowded streets of the city – and most of the time walking was quicker!"

"Sounds like Nottingham!" Guy jested. "Half the time you can't move for carts and people!"

"Ah, but we had camels!" Robin quipped back, "and you've no idea what a bane they can be! ...So then suddenly you came through the Mount's gate out into this wonderful open space. Open of buildings that was. You were never far from another person in Jerusalem! The outside was grand enough, but inside the buildings were the most breathtaking sights. We just don't have plaster-work like that here in the west. It was like lace! All white and delicate! Even the archways had cut-work in the stones too. At night you could draw shutters against the winter chills, but in the summer you were grateful to leave them open for the cool night air to bring some relief from the heat of the day. But what you had to do then was burn incense all the time to keep the insects at bay – especially at night when they'd be drawn in to the candlelight. So there was this constant slightly perfumed scent about the place, which took some getting used to at first. I think we all felt it was rather decadent when we got there!"

Will chuckled. "I remember saying to Robin that it wasn't very manly! You know, for all these fighters to be living in rooms smelling like a lady's chamber! Soon changed my mind the first time we all got bitten to pieces by the bugs!"

Robin and the others all smiled at the memory and their little audience smiled too, glad that there were at least some happy memoires for these men. "By the time the next lot of recruits came in we'd got so used to it we'd ceased noticing it," he recalled, "and we had to stop and think when they asked us what the smell was! Of course we only got the regular blends of incense which were on sale in dozens of stalls in the souks, but high class myrrh and frankincense are just lovely fragrances. They surrounded the king with them, you know. The first time I was summoned to his chambers it was the first thing I noticed. Every room, all the time, had frankincense burning in it. Apparently it has medicinal effects. Sadly it couldn't cure poor King Baldwin's leprosy, but everyone was scared stiff that one of his damaged patches of skin would become infected with something else, and that a second infection might kill him before the leprosy did."

Robin stared off into the distance. "When I was with him more – when he was dying – he told me they used to get him to chew the purest frankincense too. He thought it helped for a while. He said it eased his digestion at first, but in the end he was struggling to eat sufficient food, let alone chew something as sticky as that."

"Yes, but we've got a way to go in our story before then," Will gently reminded him.

Robin blinked and refocused. "Yes, ...of course, ...I'm getting ahead of myself. ...By Our Lady! In peacetime Jerusalem was an incredible place to be! You felt as though you were at the centre of the world! The great nobles would amused themselves going out to hunt, just like they do here, and the rest of us had to train to fight, of course. But our days were completely upside down to what we were used to. You can't do a thing during the hottest hours of the day for half the year, and we all dressed like the locals when we weren't in armour, because to wear our type of woollen clothes was just unbearable!"

The sad frown disappeared into a smile again. "Even the ladies of the court wore a long under-robe and then a short tunic over it in the eastern fashion – our haughty ladies would be scandalised if they saw them! And the courtesans! Sweet Mother of God, they were beautiful! We would catch glimpses of them, decked in shimmering silks and jewels. They took your breath away!"

"And a good few of the others were lovely too!" Gilbert said appreciatively, giving Bilan a knowing wink which made the lad grin at the implications.

"Oh in peacetime it was a grand place to be!" agreed Will with a lascivious grin. "Not so much fun when we had to ride out to one of the castles, mind you. They were just as bloody uncomfortable as this place!" And he looked around him resignedly. "Great for fending off your enemies, but when you've lived in the east you begin to realise just how rough life here is."

"It got rough enough there, though, when the truce was broken," Gilbert added. "Riding out in that terrain was a trial all of its own, and once the Saracens were at your heels it was tough just staying alive, let alone fighting back. The newcomers always wondered why we would agree to peace with Saladin. Later they learned that only a fool would want to break the peace. But of course some idiot always did!"

"It was all Reynauld de Châtillon's fault," Robin said resignedly. "Always him! In the summer of '81 he attacked a caravan which was on the road from Damascus to Mecca. He should never have attacked a peaceful party of pilgrims and merchants – especially not the pilgrims. He knew it would incite Saladin to anger and retribution, but then all Châtillon ever wanted was another chance for a battle. I swear that man would have fought his own grandmother if there was no-one else to fight! King Baldwin did his best to make peace again, but he was so isolated at court. He was hardly to blame when in revenge Saladin imprisoned a party of Christian pilgrims, blown ashore in Egypt.

"So then the king was pushed by Châtillon and his friends, who sadly included our Templar leaders, to march our massed army around the Dead Sea to Oultrejourdain to intercept Saladin in a supposed response – although the fault was all on our side, thanks to Châtillon." He shook his head. "Saladin never came near us! It was contemptuous, the ease with which he simply disdained to fight – as though we weren't worth bothering with yet! He came out of Egypt via Aqaba, went further east, spent some time in the north in Damascus, and then started marching south to come round the far side of the Sea of Galilee towards our northern castles. So there *we* were trailing in his wake! We had to turn round and march north to meet him. All the long way up the west bank of the River Jordan. It was our first taste of a campaign in the Holy Land, and Lord that was a long, dusty march!

"Aye it was!" Will agreed. "Everything tasted of sand! You couldn't get rid of the bloody stuff no matter how careful you were. It was in your food, in your clothes, your hair, everywhere! And the worst is, half the time you can't see into the distance much. The air's so full of fine dust, you see. Some arrogant arse-hole of a sergeant in France whom we met on the way back said we should've been able to see for miles since it never rained out there. I thumped him, then told him that the rain at least clears the air of muck. Out there, if you're lucky, you get a bit of dew in the dawn, but even with that the mountains look hazy. And there we were, with the highlands which are on either side of the Jordan valley towering above us, and never knowing whether Saladin's army was sitting up there watching us and laughing at the stupid Franks – as they called us all, regardless of where we came from – cooking like so many crabs in our armour."

Robin nodded at his words then carried on. "We finally fought Saladin beside the Hospitallers' castle of Belvoir – it's close to Mount Tabor and just south of the Sea of Galilee, so it was a long way north from Jerusalem. We seemed fated to always meet Saladin in that area. They brought the True Cross with us that time, too, but unlike at Hattin, that time it was never in danger. What a spectacle it was! The reliquary must have been seen for miles! It was an amazing thing to see, Tuck. All gold and jewels! And never a bishop far from it either," he added rather more waspishly. "God forbid that any of the ordinary soldiers touch it! Not that it made any difference that day. Oh, many claimed a victory, but any man with eyes in his head could see that we just wore one another down and then gave up. We'd marched all that way for nothing but a lot of sword waving!

"We were so disappointed, those of us who'd been anticipating our first proper set battle instead of just the odd skirmish. The old hands said we should be grateful! That Saladin's army was not to be underestimated. That we were a pathetically small army when it came to this vast collection of desert kingdoms. Now I know they were right. The force Saladin could call upon was immense in comparison to ours, and they knew their own land in a way our leaders never bothered to even try to. In their arrogance they believed that they could continue to fight as they'd done in France or the Holy Roman Empire or Sicily or Spain. Instead, many men just died in their armour from nothing more than the heat before they'd struck more than a few blows."

He stopped and blinked, realising that he'd got ahead of himself again and came back to his tale.

"Saladin didn't give up the whole fight, though. He craftily moved back northwards, knowing we'd follow and that our resources would be more stretched than his. So the next thing we knew, we were marching like mad even farther north to relieve Beirut. God's bones, I got some magnificent blisters on that march! Not on my feet – for we rode and our poor horses bore the brunt of the heat – but on my legs from being in the saddle for so long when we sweated like pigs! By Saint Lazarus, that hurt!"

"God's teeth, it didn't half!" Will agreed, wincing at the memory. "I was sore in places I didn't know could be so sore!" The subconscious hand to his groin made all the others wince in sympathy. Sores *and* blisters there?

"Apparently Saladin's ships had come to join in the fighting there. We never came to battle, though. Once he saw us, and then our ships which had come from Acre and Tyre, he must have realised he'd never be able to break into Beirut any time soon, so he retreated.

At the time no-one was sure where he'd gone – or if they did they never told the likes of us – so on we went, supposedly to raid Damascus. We never got into the city itself, but we'd already got a lot of booty by then from the places we passed through on the way, so we were marched over to Tyre for the Christmas. People back here, including our brother Templars, think it's all hot and sunny out there like a permanent good summer here, but in the winter it can be desperately cold. They get snow, you know! Especially in the highlands. And just like here, fighting in winter isn't much of an option because what rain they get comes then, and the roads turn to mud just as ours do."

He shivered at the memory. "It's a hard place to fight in. The spring and autumn are just about bearable, but fighting in armour in the summer is a hell all of its own. You wouldn't believe how hot it gets! If the flames of Hell are hotter than that, then I'll do any penance I have to to avoid going there!"

"It was after that Christmas that you started spending more time with the king," Will prompted, understanding that what Guy and the others wanted was the personal touches, and not a report back on the army. For that he got a nod of appreciation from Guy, Tuck, Hugh and Thomas, who'd been thinking that for all that it was fascinating to hear of these far off lands, they weren't getting any closer to Robin himself. The others were swept up in all the exotic details, but Tuck had been there, and Hugh and Thomas knew enough of what fighting could be like not to need much of a picture drawn for them. Guy, meanwhile, was straining to catch any hint of what had turned his beloved cousin Baldwin, who'd always worn his heart on his sleeve, into this distant man who revealed almost nothing of what he was thinking.

"The king? Yes." Robin's face softened. "Poor man, he fell terribly ill on our way back south from Tyre. We weren't even a third of the way back to Jerusalem before we had to halt for him. At Nazareth of all places. You would think that resting at such a holy place he might have been cured. Instead he was prostrate for weeks. He had a terrible fever. I think so much exertion told on him badly and his disease got worse the moment he over-tired himself. He should never have gone, and may Châtillon be cursed for creating such a situation where he felt he had no choice but to act the warrior king."

He looked at Will and then smiled faintly at a new memory. "We were amongst those who remained with him to guard him. The whole army could hardly camp around one small town for weeks on end. There wasn't enough food or fodder there for that. Three times a day we went to help his physician turn him. So many wouldn't go that near to him out of fear. Strangely enough I never feared catching his disease. I don't know why, but now I thank St Lazarus for being spared. Often, when our duties were done I used to go and read to him. His sister and that madman of a husband of hers, Lusignan, didn't like any of the court getting too close to him, you see. They wanted to control him. I was no danger to them, being a humble Templar squire with few prospects of rising even to make knight, let alone anything else. So I was allowed into the most private areas, and they thought I soothed Baldwin. Kept him distracted and quiet," and he sniffed in disgust at such machinations.

"You reminded him of what it was to be young, I think," Will said gently. "Of the life a young man of his age *ought* to have had. Hearing you talking of the horses, and mucking out and cleaning bridles, showed him what life was like in a real world he never saw."

Robin brightened a little. "You're probably right. He loved to hear me talking of you lot," he looked directly at Guy and John. "He said he would have loved to have cousins like you. He'd never had anyone but Sybilla, and to be frank she could be a selfish bitch. He couldn't imagine what it would be like to have a big family. It made him laugh to hear of things like us fighting mock battles in the barn in winter when we were little. I think it was like a fairy tale to him. So when he was ill, if I wasn't reading to him, I would tell him every last thing I could remember of home. I didn't know at the time if he heard a single word, but later on, just before he died, he once told me he could recall quite a few things. I think he was fading in and out, as you do with a fever. The tragedy of it was that once he fully came around from the fever his leprosy had got worse. The poor soul had lost the use of his arms and legs and he was almost blind."

He winced at the memory. "He was only twenty-one! Only twenty-one and crippled worse than any old man I'd ever seen. How could God let that happen? Some said that his father's marriage to his mother was closer than the Church permits. That it was incestuous and that it was a punishment to the kingdom to have a sick and weak king."

Robin's face darkened. "I hated them for saying that! He was the one who suffered most, and what had he ever done? Nothing! He never had the chance to sin before he was struck down! Nine years old he was when the first signs were noticed by his tutor, he told me! What possible sins could you have on your conscience at nine? And even then it was already too late for anything other than a miracle to save him. He grew up knowing he would never live to grow old. What a terrible thing for a child to live with!"

"He bore it with the most remarkable fortitude too. I think he was the bravest man I've ever met. It's one thing to stand your ground in battle, with what feels sometimes like the gates of Hell opening before you, but it's over and done with in a day or so." Guy thought he was wrong there but said nothing. "Baldwin's torment went on for over a decade. A decade! All the time he should have been out enjoying life was spent with bits of him going numb and then rotting. And he still managed to think of his kingdom even when he couldn't even turn himself in bed or feed himself! How many other men could you say that sort of thing of?"

Guy reached across and squeezed his cousin's hand. "None! He was surely one of a kind." He was rewarded with Robin covering his hand in a gesture of thanks.

"I'm glad you can see it. So few could."

"And if he suffered so much in this world then God and the saints will have rewarded him in the next life," Tuck declared with certainty. "Rome may not recognise such saintliness – look how long it took them to recognise Dewi Sant! And despite all my pleas to my bishop, getting Saint Issui recognised by Rome is proving uphill work." He rolled his eyes despairingly over the myopia of the senior clerics. "But that doesn't mean a higher authority than the all-too-human men of the Church is so disregarding!

"God doesn't always work the way we as mere mortals expect, Robin. You say your poor young king didn't complain, but does it help you if you think that at least – if he had to be afflicted with something – then it was a disease which deadens all feeling? Not something which wracked him with excruciating pain day and night? Maybe there was a strange kindness involved? One where a young man with burdens beyond his years and experience to ever have normally hoped to cope with, was given the grace to manage them?

"Your Baldwin might not appear in any breviary amongst the saints any time soon – for Rome would want witnesses to miracles and other deeds, and who is there left to watch over his tomb and the places he lived in to tell if anything happens? But he sounds to me as good a candidate for elevation as any I have heard. A young man who spent his whole life struggling to bring peace to the Holy Land must surely be revered in Heaven if not on Earth. *Duw bodlon!*"

"Do you think so?" Robin asked hopefully.

"Definitely!" John agreed, while Guy added,

"And you had a rare opportunity – you saw a great king for the man he was! God knows, *I* know how people can get the wrong ideas about such men! Talk to our sheriff, Ralph Murdac, about Prince John and you soon see that! Murdac thinks that John has it in him to be a great king. That King Henry is right to favour his youngest son because he understands England better than Prince Richard ever will. But I've met John face to face, and he's nothing but a spoilt, obnoxious little shit! And one day, God willing, those powerful men who think like Ralph Murdac will get to see it. But you've seen a king of a wholly different kind. You can speak of the evidence you saw with your own eyes of his bravery. You can tell people that you know he worried about his kingdom because you heard the words from his own lips.

"By Our Lady, Bal... Robin, there are many at court in England who've said fewer words to King Henry than you did with the king of Jerusalem! You and I owe it to the ordinary people who will never get within yards of such men to tell them the truth. Of how they are men who eat and sleep and bleed like the rest of us, and who *choose* to behave well or badly. Your Baldwin must have had so many chances to just give up, and as a man – not some strange semi-divine being who's barely human – he made the right choices, just as I would lay bets on Prince John making the wrong ones every time! So the more men like you tell others about Baldwin and how good he was, then the more you're guaranteeing that he, the man – not just some king by name – won't be forgotten." Then he had an unexpected thought. "You said Baldwin was taken very ill in early '82? Did he continue to rule then? To hold his courts? Even as sick as that?"

Robin shook his head. "We stopped with him in a house where there was a large roof room. The simple houses just have flat roofs which people sleep out on in the summer, but his was a grander affair and it had a light roof over the flat rooftop of the house itself. So once he'd regained consciousness, we used to carry his bed up there for him to get some fresh air, making sure we had plenty of braziers burning around his litter to keep him warm, because the air was still chilly at times. It was still a while before he was strong enough to withstand the journey. We brought him home in a litter in the spring. He couldn't hope to ride anymore.

"Will and I led his horses by his request, and even our Templar master, de Toroga, wasn't so miserable as to deny him that small favour – one insignificant squire and a smith were a small price for what they gained by having King Baldwin out of the way, as they saw it. I kept the pace steady all the way back to Jerusalem, and I thought that was the end of Baldwin ever leaving the city again at the head of an army, even in a litter, especially to somewhere as far as Galilee. He still kept control of Jerusalem for himself, although he told me once that it was more for the irreparable damage he feared Lusignan and Châtillon would do to that holy city and its people than for anything he would need now for himself."

Tuck was nodding sagely. "A good man, as you said."

"Yes, but it was clear he couldn't hold the rest of the land. Lusignan, as Sybilla's husband, took control of the kingdom – and that pleased the senior Templars no end! After that it seems now, looking back, that our fate was already sealed. No sooner had Saladin moved his army again, than Châtillon took ships into the Red Sea to attack Mecca. Madness, utter madness! How on earth did he think we could hold that belt of land along the coast with all the peoples around us now hating us even more than they did already? Did you know that Saladin swore that Châtillon, above all other Christians, must be punished for the outrages he performed against those pilgrims to Mecca?

"Well revenge eventually came – Saladin not being a hasty or reckless man. It was in the autumn of '83. We'd sweltered our way through the summer in Jerusalem, holding our breath and waiting for some sign of what Saladin would do next, and then news came that he'd crossed the Jordan and was besieging Tiberius on the Sea of Galilee. Lusignan summoned all of his forces, including us in the Templars because our leaders were endlessly at his heels. I could never understand them. Lusignan was never going to be the man to drive the Saracens from the holy places, and what were we Templars formed for by the pope if not for that? Oh the ordinary knights weren't so bad, but the Lord knows there were never that many of us!

"It served men like our master, Arnold de Toroga, right! In the end, when faced with an enemy army and the need to act like a king, Lusignan dithered and prevaricated! The advance-guard nearly came to grief, and it was only the lords Balian and Baldwin of Ibelin who saved the day for them, riding in with their own knights and men to rescue those poor bastards left out in front. Lusignan just sat with his main army opposite Saladin's and let our supplies run out. Saladin was the one who turned and moved away, but he'd made Lusignan look like a fool, and in some ways that was as big a victory than any beating we could have taken in arms. It broke the barons faith in their regent, you see, and many of the soldiers went from admiring him to thinking him a coward. I never thought him anything else!

"When we got back to Jerusalem I was horrified at how far King Baldwin had deteriorated while we were away. I swear he was held together by sheer willpower by then! His bandages were drenched in essence of frankincense and myrrh to keep infections at bay, but you could see it did nothing else. His fingers had long gone – there were just stumps at the end of the bandages – and I used to wonder how much of his poor arms were bandages, not flesh. Yet he still managed to think like a king!

"At first he never said a word against Lusignan in public. Instead he asked Lusignan to let him move to Lusignan's territory of Tyre in the hope that the sea air would help his health. The exchange would mean that Lusignan as ruler would then have Jerusalem, and the king, Tyre, but the arrogant fool refused and rudely too – I think the king half expected that and wanted Lusignan to condemn himself with his own words. Baldwin told me late one night when we were all alone that he knew what Lusignan was thinking, that he wouldn't have long to wait and then he could have it all.

"Baldwin was furious! Such kingly anger from such a sick man! I wouldn't have believed it possible if I hadn't seen it. He summoned all his chief vassals, had himself carried into their presence and deposed Lusignan from the regency, then took back control himself.

It was something to see! Such a frail body by now, swathed in bandages and robes for protection and to prevent everyone from seeing just how sick he was, and every one of the nobles present sweating in fear in case he demanded that they kiss his hand! And as king he could have demanded that as a demonstration of fealty! A demonstration no-one could have refused without looking as if they were taking against the king. It would have served them right if he had asked them to, and then thrown the ringleaders against him into a dungeon for refusing!

"The next thing we knew, Lusignan took himself off to his county of Ascalon on the coast in high dudgeon, and King Baldwin was demanding a litter be made ready for him to go in pursuit! Such courage! He knew it might be the end of him, but he felt he had to maintain the image of kingship. I feared for him, by Our Lady I did! And do you know, even from his litter he managed to order his troops well enough to take control of Jaffa, although Lusignan sat secure behind the walls of Ascalon. What a hero, to be too cowardly to face a poor leper!" Robin's sarcasm dripped with disgust for the would-be king of the holy kingdom.

"I wasn't allowed to go with the king on that trip. Master Toroga was in too much of a temper with King Baldwin to let me go this time. Then when everyone but Lusignan was back in Jerusalem, the two grand masters decided to intervene on Lusignan's behalf along with the Patriarch. Do you know, Baldwin banished the lot of them! So there we were, a whole preceptory of Templar knights, squires and sergeants, living in the same huge building as the king, and no leader!"

"Ah, that would be when the Patriarch came to London?" Guy suddenly realised.

"Yes, and how I wish King Henry had come to Jerusalem," Robin sighed.

"He wouldn't have been any better," Will said cynically.

Robin shot him a look of reproof but Guy quickly spoke again.

"Will's probably right, as it happens, Robin. King Henry only fights battles he knows he has a chance of winning. Out there he would have been faced with the choice of fighting Saladin, where the land itself must have made predicting outcomes difficult if nothing else did, or withdrawing to the sea and just defending what he could hold. He would've pulled back to the sea and Jerusalem would have fallen anyway."

Robin and the other Templars looked to him in surprise.

"He's right," Tuck said sorrowfully. "The one you needed was Prince Richard. He's tried to take the Cross already once, but his father prevented him from raising an army."

"Aye, that's how we come to be here," Thomas chipped in. "All ready to go we were, and then King Henry put his foot down and that was the end of that! Left hanging in mid air we were, so to speak, so we ran before we got dragged off to fight in some squabble in Normandy – I'd already had a taste of that! Not something I want to repeat!"

"We'd have come to fight for Jerusalem," Piers added, "but without Prince Richard it was never going to happen."

Tuck was nodding in agreement. "He might yet go on crusade when he gets the chance, but that won't be while King Henry lives, I'm sure."

The Templars all looked a bit more hopeful at the prospect of an English king in the Holy Land.

"Then I wish Prince Richard had been allowed to come to Jerusalem while King Baldwin still lived," Robin said wistfully. "With the dogs of war away, Jerusalem was as near peaceful as it ever gets. Except for Châtillon, of course! He didn't even have the decency to leave with Lusignan. And he was at his games again! His heir was marrying King Baldwin and Sybilla's half-sister through their father's connection – that was the daughter of the dead king's second wife, Maria. The dowager queen Maria and her current husband, Balian of Ibelin, went for the girl's sake, even though they were Châtillon's sworn enemies – she was only eleven, poor child! It was her misfortune that Saladin chose that moment to try to exact revenge upon the worst of his enemies. So while the wedding feast went on, the walls were being bombarded with rocks from Saladin's trebuchets. A message came for help to the king, and so we marched again! This time I was at the king's side once more, for the army was under the command of Count Raymond of Tripoli – an altogether fairer man and one whom the king could trust.

"My poor king! There was nothing I could do to make that journey better for him. The only thing I could do was describe in detail everything I saw, to be this eyes for him now that everything was growing dark. I walked beside him the whole way while Will led the horses, with the native servants all around us. This time it was a march north only far enough to get around the Dead Sea, and by the time we'd passed Jericho and approached Mount Nebo, Saladin was packing up his army and moving off. To this day I wonder whether he heard that Baldwin was travelling with the army and wished to spare him further pain. He thought very highly of King Baldwin did Saladin. He was heard to call him a great king, and from him that was an enormous compliment. It would have been very much like him to be so courteous. To put his own desire for revenge aside to spare a man he regarded.

"So back we marched to Jerusalem once more and not an arrow shot. The trouble was, the dogs of war came back to the East. It could have been better because Master Toroga died on the way back, but for some unfathomable reason our knights elected Gerard of Ridfort in his place – another warmonger and a sworn enemy of

Count Raymond, so there was always going to be conflict there." He shook his head in despair. "The king had no control over either of the orders, you see. They answer only to the pope, and that far from Rome they're a law unto themselves. I know I should feel more loyalty to my own master, but I don't. Poor Baldwin barely had time to get them to swear an oath to honour and uphold his will before he went into his final decline." He bowed his head. "I shall be saying a good many more prayers for his soul. He was just twenty-four."

He stumbled over the next words. "I...I've never told anyone this before ...but I ...I went into his bedchamber in the middle of the night after he died. I'd heard they were laying his body out ready to wrap in his shroud, so I hid outside his room until the servants left with the last of the old bandages to burn them. ...I just wanted to see his face. ...To see him again without all the coverings." He covered his eyes with his hand. "It wasn't a face anymore, it was more of a skull with tatters of flesh. His eyes ...I realised why they had been closed for him while he lived ...they were ...sunken. I don't know if there were even any eyes left behind those shredded lids ...and once they'd been the thing you noticed first! Oh how he could fix you with that kingly glance once upon a time. I can't ...I can't imagine how he found the strength to carry on. How he actually spoke *anything* in those last weeks...? And his arms and legs..." He was lost for words, sitting shaking his head slowly in disbelief with his hand still over his eyes.

"Where was he buried?" Guy asked fearing the worst. That some warmongers had treated the poor young king's body with less respect than they should have because of his disease.

"In the Holy Sepulchre," answered Robin.

"And as appropriate a place as anyone could wish for such a soul!" Tuck declared stoutly. Robin's head shot up. "Well it is, isn't it!" Tuck insisted. "The place of Our Lord's resting, however temporary. The most holy place in all the world! You're not telling me that the Saracens desecrate the burials there?"

Malik answered for the Templars. "No, Saladin would not allow something like that – although some of the other graves were desecrated. Whatever some might think, as Robin said, Saladin is an honourable man. More honourable than most of the highborn men he fought, God curse them."

"Then your young friend lies in a very sacred space," Tuck said consolingly.

"Tell me something, though," Guy said gently. "What was it about this particular man that struck such a chord with you? You must have met a good many young men of much the same age as you – indeed you've mentioned several whom you seem to have had brief friendships with – yet you come back to King Baldwin time after time. Clearly he was far more than just your lord. There must have been dozens of others who you had contact with every day. Why him?"

Robin paused and stared off into the fire as though he had never thought of it in quite that way before. "I think," he began tentatively, "that I remembered how you and John always stood up for me and Allan. You set quite an example to live up to, you know. The older I got, the more I realised that so many times you two could have gone off on your own and left me and Allan to the mercies of Fulk and Philip, but you never did. I know I was closer to your ages than Allan, but nonetheless you still acted as though you were responsible for me. As if you couldn't imagine not caring for me, or saying that you didn't want the little cousin tagging along.

"And then when I saw King Baldwin fall off his horse that first time, and no-one jumped to help him without stopping to think of themselves first, ...that was when I couldn't help it. I had to help him. ...Then I got to talk to him, and I liked him. He was so much wiser than me about politics and court intrigues, but when I talked to him about the ordinary world it was like talking to Allan, to ...to someone much younger than me, because that was something he knew nothing about. I suppose I tried to be a cousin to him to try and fill the gap you all left inside me, and he let me because he trusted me to never take advantage of him."

Suddenly John guffawed. "Are you telling me that you played big brother to the *King of Jerusalem* because of *us*? ...Baldwin, you're bloody priceless!" He came around behind his cousin to get to the fire and riddled it back into life with a long iron poker, then hugged him on the way back. "Only you would think of it like that! ...And some arse-backwards compliment it is too!" he chuckled again, making the others laugh with him. It broke the tension which had been building unnoticed, Guy realised.

"I wish I'd been able to meet your royal friend," he said consolingly. "But it sounds to me as though you were a great comfort to him. It must have reassured him that all men aren't as bad as those leaders you've spoken of. If the poor lad had to be stuck in that dreadful situation, bedridden and with the vultures circling, I bet he looked forward to the nights when you would come and talk to him about stuff that had nothing to do with the cares of a kingdom."

"Do you think so?" Robin asked earnestly.

"Well even you rattling on about how much horse shit you'd helped shovel must have been *something* of a change for him!" John teased, making them laugh again.

By now some of the servants were starting to filter into the hall for the evening meal, and so Robin's tale was halted. However, once everyone settled down again afterwards, Guy had every intention of getting Robin to start up again.

"Are you going to push him any harder?" Hugh asked Guy softly as they let the others go ahead of them to where the cook was carving up the first of two great pies, and his assistant was ladling out a good thick soup into bowls.

"Harder?"

Hugh grimaced as he tried to find the right words. "Look Guy, I'm not saying that your cousin is lying or anything. But can you tell me that you know anything more of the man he's become than you did this morning? We're hearing a lot about the Holy Land and the leper king, and I'm sure that's all perfectly true. And if your cousin was as close to King Baldwin as he's making out – and none of the others are batting an eyelid about that, so I assume it's true – then I suppose it is part of his story. But as someone who didn't know your Baldwin before, I certainly don't feel as though I'm any closer to knowing Robin, if you see what I mean."

Guy had stopped in his tracks and was looking at Hugh with a furrowed brow, making the young former soldier ask, "I haven't offended you by saying that, have I?"

"No." Guy shook his head and blinked. "Good lord, Hugh, no, but you have hit the nail on the head. Something was niggling away at me while we were sitting there and I couldn't put my finger on it, but you've gone straight to the heart of it. I was hoping to hear of some special girl he fancied, even if he didn't get the chance to live with her. Or maybe more about the men he shared the fighting with."

Hugh nodded. "That's just what I meant. I was waiting to hear whether there were more local men like Malik who were in their group of mates. Your cousin very clearly wasn't with the king for most of the days, even if he went to the royal apartments at night. Who *was* he with then? What did he do – apart from mucking out horses? He must have done *something*! So who with? And what did he think about the ordinary, everyday stuff? What annoys him, makes him laugh? When I was soldiering I had a good friend, like Will is to him, but there were about eight of us who all hung around together."

He suddenly grinned at a memory. "This one time we were besieging a castle – God knows whose, some arsey Norman baron I guessed! Well this bloody cockerel was driving us mad every morning, because although it was in a farm over the hill, once it got going all the other damned cocks would start up, even though it was still pitch black outside. So we launched our own raid on the quiet to wring its neck! We thought we were doing fine until suddenly we heard this pounding of hooves behind us, and then Harold went past me like the Devil's hounds were at his heels shouting 'bull!' Well we took off like greyhounds, except that our Will slipped on a cow pat and went arse over tit! Then Edwin fell in the ditch with Ralf on top of him. The rest of us cleared that hurdle gate like ancient Greek athletes – even fat Hubert! By this time the farmers dogs were making a right racket and we ended up having to creep back into camp by going the long way round – after we'd got the shit off Will, that was!"

Guy was chuckling merrily at the imagined scene when Thomas spoke up behind him. "Aye, that's the kind of things I remember from being an ordinary soldier too! One of my mates got into the wine store of some monastery in Normandy and got pissed on some weird stuff they brewed up. It was bloody *yellow*, for God's sake! And syrupy! Out of his head he was! Danced around the camp stark-bollock naked shouting that if the local ladies wanted to see an exotic elephant he had something better for them!" And he waved his hand around in front of his groin. "Big lad he was, but not *that* big! And it was the depths of winter, so he had some spectacular frostbite!" Hugh and Guy guffawed. "Bloody awful hangover he had, though! God alone knows what they put in it, but he didn't half suffer for it afterwards!"

"That's the kind of thing I meant," Hugh said as he wiped the tears of mirth from his eyes. "But listening to Robin it's as though he wasn't ever a normal soldier at all."

"Oh he was!" Will's voice said firmly as he appeared from behind Thomas. "Don't you believe him?" he added suspiciously.

Yet before anyone could begin explaining the door to the hall crashed open and the kitchen boy tore in shouting,

"The sheriff's here! The sheriff's just below! Sheriff Murdac's here!"

Panic erupted, voices all calling out in consternation and everyone milling about but without purpose.

"Be quiet!" Guy's bellow rode over the top of the general hullabaloo, as he leapt up onto one of the benches so that he could see across everybody. "Be quiet, I say!" and silence descended on the hall to the surprise of the crusaders. Yet Guy allowed no gap for anyone to start talking again.

"Edwin!" He pointed to a young lad. "Run to the stables and tell Alfred to get the six new horses out and saddled up. No tack to be left behind! ...Cook! Get rid of that second pie to the kitchens now! ...You lot!" He gestured to the servants. "While you're getting yourselves out of the way, take anything which betrays that we've had extra visitors! Start getting the hall ready to receive the sheriff as you would any highborn guest!"

He spun round to the others. "You lot will go over the bridge to the stables as fast as possible. You've got time to get out through the west gate of the bailey before Murdac's horses get taken up there. He'll come in through the East Gate. He won't be making a quiet entrance through a mere picket gate into the castle!"

He gestured to the back wall of the hall. "Go out of the gate and then turn off the road to your left. Take it steady once you're off the road, but carry on going round to the south and come back along

Cave Dale. You can't use any torches, so watch your footing! But at least you can't get lost. It's a straightforward valley to follow down until you're right back down here below the castle, and by then there'll be torches burning all over the place, so you'll see enough not to wander into the gorge below the stable bridge."

"Murdac's soldiers will see us!" snapped Piers.

"No they won't!" Guy all but snarled. "I'll be getting them fed! Christ Almighty, this isn't exactly outlaw country to be setting guards against! And anyway, I'll get so many torches lit it'll destroy any watcher's night vision to see that far down into the gloom!"

"Where...?" Robin was about to ask, but overtaken by Guy saying,

"You're going to the Devil's Arse cave beneath the castle! It's huge and it'll take all of you and the horses without any problem, so you can go deep inside, well out of view. It's not perfect, but Murdac won't be going down there tonight, and that gives me time to find out what the bloody hell he wants! Now *move*!" And he gestured furiously for them to get started before calling, "Tuck! You'll stay! I can pass you off as a temporary replacement for the dead priest." And before the others could protest turned to two of the castle's burlier servants. "Joseph, Harry, go and pick up poor Siward! Carry him and his bedding into the servants' hall! We'll say he was a passing traveller taken ill and you've got him there so that someone can look after him, and you, Tuck, can be ministering to him tonight to explain why you're up here and not in the village. Now for Christ's sake will you all *bloody move*!"

Everyone sprang to their tasks with more purpose now, and Guy was quickly hustling some of the slower servants to do the right things.

"He's pretty impressive when he's like that," Will muttered to Thomas as they scooped up their belongings. "I'd begun to wonder how on earth he could function as a sheriff's man, and that maybe what we saw when we first met was more bluster and show than substance."

Thomas chuckled as he slung a bag over his shoulder and grabbed his longbow and quiver. "Oh Guy's quite the natural leader when he wants. I think that's the difference between him and a lot of the other knights and foresters. They're fine while they're lording it over lesser men and have convention on their side, but to really command they have to try almost too hard. Whereas Guy doesn't even have to think about it when it matters, so he carries that authority very lightly. But Tuck tells me that the men at Nottingham castle say that you only have to have a bollocking off him once to ensure you won't make the mistake of thinking him soft ever again!"

"That was some kind of fast thinking!" Gilbert agreed as they pounded out of the hall and round the keep to the west picket gate.

Will nodded as he paused to push Walter and Algar on faster in Thomas and Piers' wake, and then shut the picket gate behind him as the last man out. "Quick thinking about what to do with Siward, too," he said with approval as he met Thomas again on the other side of the bridge, and they hurried to bring up the rear.

"Oh that's Guy all right!" John added as he ran with them out of the stables in the wake of the horses. "Always could think on his feet better than anyone!"

With Robin and Hugh leading them, the party scrambled down the side of the road while Alfred and three of his fellow grooms held torches aloft for them to see by, then waited under the pretext of lighting the way for those men of the sheriff's bringing the horses round to the stables.

In the hall a kind of order had established itself, and with a last sweeping glance around to make sure that nothing had been left to betray the fact that the castle had been harbouring outlaws, Guy went to meet his lord.

By Heaven, Brother, that was such a shock to the system! If the sheriff could have seen me properly in the dark of the castle bailey that night he would have spied my pulse racing and heard my gut churning! I could scarce believe our bad luck! What on earth had possessed him to come all this way in person? Surely the sergeant had conveyed my message without embellishing it and telling just who I had got to do the hunting? Then I saw Sergeant Ingulf himself amongst the other soldiers and also saw the slight shake of his head which he gave me when he caught my eye. So it had not been him, and if not due to betrayal then I could not fathom why the visit, but I did not have long to wait for an answer. No sooner had the sheriff dismounted, for his horse alone had been led up the now slightly less frozen eastern approach to save him the breath-stealing climb on foot, than he took me by the arm and marched me towards the hall.

˜God's bones, Gisborne, this is a mess˜ he said as I handed him a goblet of mulled wine brought by a shaking servant. Oh Brother, I still recall the frantic turning of my mind as to what mess he could be alluding to, such are my moments of guilt at my wrong doings made of! And if my pain at potential disclosure was not very long lived it was certainly acutely painful!

˜God rot that fool Ivo!˜ were Murdac's next words, and the feeling of relief which washed over me is as memorable as the panic before it! For it transpired that Ivo of Quettehou had been derelict in his duties for many months. The ill-tempered knight had made the mistake of not sending the money for the Saladin Tithe to the sheriff in time, and Murdac had been

forced into the dreadful position of paying the shortfall himself in order not to seem incompetent before the king. Now he was on his way out of Nottingham to head for the Easter court himself, where he would have to present the Easter accounts for the shire. Never as weighty as the Michaelmas accounting, the Easter moneys nonetheless still had to be paid, and without this money due from northern Derbyshire the sheriff would have to request more time to pay. Not that that was an unheard of thing, for many a sheriff had to ask for more time to pay their shire's dues, even in King Henry's reign, let alone later on when King Richard's demands were greater. However, Ralph Murdac did his utmost to never ask for such delays unless there was absolutely no alternative, and so he had descended upon us, all set to extract the owing payments by whatever means necessary.

"I do not hold you responsible" he told me, "for you have done well in getting the hunt in hand and saving me the embarrassment of failing to supply the king in that respect too" To which I offered up a heartfelt prayer of thanks, I do admit Brother. I dared to believe that the good Lord could not be so very displeased with the deception I had perpetrated if all had not been uncovered, for it would have been so easy for every one of my plans to fall apart in ruins that night.

However, before you start chastising me for that belief, let us hurry onwards, for there were further revelations coming that very night!

Chapter 17

Why did Robin not take the lead when danger struck? you ask, Gervase. "He was against the sheriff after all!"

Heavens, man! He did not return from the Holy Land all afire with venom against every sheriff without reason, and even you must allow him that breathing space. He had to see for himself the agony of the people, for he was no warmonger. Surely you can see already that he had had enough of men like that in the East, and knew full well what chaos such men brought to wherever they were? My dear cousin could and did fight with a passion for a good cause, but not without provocation.

You think it sounds little like the great man of legend? By Saint Issui and Saint Cadoc, that is a foolish comment! No, Brother, you deserve that chastisement if that is all the attention you have been paying! So open your mind as well as your ears! My dear cousin was capable of being a very good leader and everything else the legend said of him at times, but on that particular night he was still recovering from the effects of Tuck's cathartic service. You also have to allow that he was not so very long back in England as to know what to expect at every turn.

In the coming years he would be very alert to what the appearance of a sheriff in person could mean – but not yet, Brother, not yet! Also, unlike our other cousins and me, he had not yet felt the full effects of falling away from the state of privilege which came with our being Norman born and bred. If his life in Outremer had been harsh beyond belief in many ways, at least he had still kept some illusion of being of noble blood with aspirations of being a true knight, and only now was that to be stripped away.

Yet we must move on, for what happened next was as much a revelation to him as it will be to you, since it was to open his eyes dramatically to the fate of the ordinary folk of England, and you shall see the change.

High Peak Castle, Derbyshire, February, the Year of Our Lord 1189

"How much is owing, my lord?" Guy asked Murdac, as a servant scuttled forward bearing a heavy wooden chair which he placed before the fire, and another hurried up with cushions which were piled on the seat for the sheriff to sit upon.

Easing himself gratefully into the soft seat, Murdac told Guy the sum due, but was too busy stretching his cold feet out towards the warming blaze to notice Guy's reaction. It gave Guy time to do some quick calculations, and to breathe a sigh of relief that he, John and Tuck had already counted out what they believed had come from round here this year from the coins in the barrels, and there was plenty to spare. Therefore this dread surprise wasn't such an impossible amount to find as he'd feared. Far too much for the poor folk to find if the sheriff went out in force and began taking it all over again, of course, but if they'd reckoned right then it was about what was held in one of the barrels of silver pennies. The trick was going to be hiding the other barrel before it was found! Guy was determined that he wasn't going to hand over Sir Ivo's personal stash as well. That was a reserve he intended the outlaws to use for the benefit of those who had been drained of everything.

"May I give you some good news, my lord?" he said with all due deference, making Murdac look up at him with irritated puzzlement.

"Good news? What possible good news could you have for me? I have to find the bloody parish priest, who seems to be missing, for a start! Then somewhere in this tree-infested wilderness I have to find a Templar and a Hospitaller to witness the collection, as the king demands, and then pray to God that none of the damned villagers start protesting over what is due. Although that's the least of those problems, because if they moan and then are proven wrong we can take the amount due on top of what they've said they'll pay." The sheriff grunted with satisfaction. "That should mean I come away with something extra for all the inconvenience this is putting me to! By St Thomas, our reserve of coin is wiped out at the castle, and little left to fed my men with, all because of this wretched part of the shire!

"At least that boring old fart, the dean, has declined to come this far out with us, and has said he will accept and sign to whatever I and the three others decide. We'd have been here until next Christmas if he'd been involved! Thanks be to God that he's the worst of those men I have to deal with and there's only one of him, although I'd hoped Ivo would've stirred himself and already shaken the old goat into some kind of action! And if that's not enough I've got a bloody woman vagabond we found on the road coming up here making wild presumptions, and had to take her prisoner!"

Guy's head was spinning at all this information, then began mentally kicking himself for not remembering the details of the collection of the Saladin Tithe. Unlike other tithes, it wasn't just the sheriff involved. Whether King Henry thought to make sure that his sheriffs didn't give up too easily when told there was no more money for yet another tithe, or whether he actually thought some of them would swindle him, no-one knew; but Guy knew it was right that the sheriff had to go and get the Saladin Tithe in person, or delegate to a very senior representative and not the usual lesser men. Sir Ivo would have done as a constable of a royal castle and a head forester to boot, but no-one else over this way qualified.

And it was also true that a Hospitaller and a Templar had to do the rounds with whoever did the collecting. Also, for each area's collection its rural dean had to be involved on the Church's behalf – all to emphasise the holy cause, Guy thought bitterly – and on top of all that, in each parish the priest had to swear to the honesty of the amounts demanded. If he hadn't been so thrown by the events of the last week or so, Guy knew he would have recalled more swiftly that it had been to avoid this very tax that people in Nottingham had said that Sir Eric had taken the Cross, thus allowing Guy to quite literally get away with murder. The poor folk of the Hope Valley and round about wouldn't have the option of packing up and going east, though.

He was so lost in these thoughts that Guy didn't register someone being dragged into the hall, hissing and struggling like a caught wildcat. Only when a voice spat out,

"Let me go, you bastards!" did he come to his senses, and what he saw took his breath away.

"Sister Marianne! What on earth are you doing here?" he gasped.

"Sister?" Ralph Murdac spun to fix him with a steely gaze. "This harridan thinks we're so foolish as to believe she's a sister of the Hospitallers! As if there was such a thing!"

"But she is!" Guy protested. "I thought as you do, my lord, but I met her when I was in London! When I was knighted! She was there. Right there in the Hospitallers' headquarters! And not just some random servant! I saw her with keys to the Patriarch's very own quarters. She was one of them. She was trusted, my lord!"

Murdac looked at Guy as though he'd sprouted horns and a devil's tail.

"I am utterly serious, my lord," Guy said, realising that he'd been close to babbling, and that he must sound more measured if he was to be believed. "Sister Marianne came from Jerusalem itself where she was serving in the great hospital there – with many other Hospitaller sisters, my lord! She travelled with the Patriarch's company as a nurse to some pregnant noble ladies who were returning west, and needed someone who knew what to do if anything happened on the way. My lord of Chester will be able to vouch for her too." That was stretching it a bit, since Ranulph de Blundeville had not been that close by when Guy had spoken to Marianne, but it was another of those lies slipped in on the back of the greater truth, and which Guy therefore hoped would be believed. His own word might not be enough alone, but throw in an earl's to back it up and he knew it would carry much more weight.

"The earl of Chester?" Murdac took the bait. Then with a sudden wave of inspiration, Guy realised he could hook the sheriff on a scheme of his own making and began working to land his prize fish.

"Errr, ...didn't you say you had no idea of where you would find a Hospitaller out here?" he asked with studied innocence, then for a horrible moment thought he'd been too clever for his own good as Murdac went a shade paler. "Sister Marianne has said her vows to the order," Guy persisted in somewhat less forceful tones, winking at Marianne and hoping she would play along with him.

"That's what I've been trying to tell you all along," she said with asperity, but at least struggling less and making an effort to look a little more dignified. "I did *not* steal the Hospitaller's robes you found me in! They were my own! Didn't you think they were a bit small for a man?"

Before her waspish tongue could dig her back into a hole, Guy leapt into the conversation again.

"I saw you back in '85 in London. Where have you been since then, *Sister* Marianne? Not back to the East?"

Marianne pursed her lips and sniffed in disgust. "No, the Patriarch and the Grand Master thought I could do some good by going to one of the order's houses, and teaching some of the sisters there the new healing skills I'd learned in the Holy Land. I went to Carbrook, in Norfolk, which is part of our order. It's only a small place," she added witheringly to Murdac, "which is no doubt why you've not heard of it, ...my lord!" Murdac didn't rise to the insult, but was looking somewhat disconcerted at the realisation that the fighting orders might really have women amongst them.

"...That was a pretty good place to be," Marianne was continuing, "because Sister Basilia who ran the place was as interested in healing as any of the sisters I'd known back in Jerusalem. But the next year the king decreed that all of us female Hospitallers had to be brought into one place, and we all got moved to Buckland in Devon. And women like Sister Basilia who'd been in charge of their own places, were now just ordinary sisters, and only Sister Fina kept her rank as the one in charge of the new place. I don't think many other of us were happy at the move either, because we were expected to be just a contemplative order of women after that. That's not what I joined the order for!"

"No I'm sure you weren't pleased," Guy agreed quickly, "not after all the *training* you'd done." He emphasised the training for Murdac's benefit in the hope of pushing the fact that Marianne wasn't just some cracked-pot wise-woman with delusions of grandeur. "So you've been in Devon since then?"

Marianne grimaced again. "Well I stood it for the rest of '86 and most of the next year, but by the time that next Christmas came round I was nearly climbing the walls! I begged and begged to be allowed to go on to somewhere else where there was a hospital. Somewhere where I could do some real good. The problem wasn't with the senior sisters. They would have let me go. It was the king's rotten imposition on the order against having active female Hospitallers, and us having to be contained. Did he think we'd become some kind of army for Queen Eleanor, or something?"

King Henry and his wife had notoriously been at loggerheads for many years, but it wasn't the most tactful thing Marianne could have said! "In the end I decided to..." She caught Guy's frantic eye signals of warning, for he'd guessed she was about to say that she'd walked out. "...I decided to go on pilgrimage," she said with strained humility, but luckily Murdac was still too surprised to find that there were such things as female Hospitallers to pick up the subtleties and nuances. "To look for guidance," Marianne added for good measure, in case further explanation was needed.

"You undoubtedly need much contemplation at *each* of your places of worship," Guy said rather pointedly, hoping that she would take the hint that she would still have to fill the best part of two years in order not to look the vagabond and a troublemaker, but rather a woman of faith.

"Oh indeed!" Marianne agreed, warming to her tale now that she could guess what Guy was trying to do. "My first place wasn't that far away." She looked at Guy and said more to him than Murdac, "It really wasn't! ...We heard that after the big fire at Glastonbury Abbey in '85 they'd discovered the tomb of King Arthur and that they were getting more and more pilgrims there. Well that's what I was used to doing – looking after pilgrims who got sick along the way, or arrived footsore and weary. So I went there first and stayed quite a while." Her fleeting smile towards Guy made him think that she had probably left there under a cloud, having spoken her mind to some imperious prior or the like, but now wasn't the time to inquire as to the details.

"So when you did move on, where was your next site of pilgrimage?" he asked innocently, and catching the slight hint of panic in her eyes, mouthed 'Canterbury' silently to her while his head was turned away from Murdac.

"Oh to Canterbury," she said firmly and looking away from Guy so that she wouldn't be tempted to laugh at this charade. "St Thomas' tomb. ...Who could go on pilgrimage and not go there?" she added with a slight roll of her eyes. Guy nearly lost his own composure at the irony of that statement, especially with Marianne's expression as she said it, and had to cover his laugh with a quick bout of coughing.

"So many pilgrims," Marianne was saying with enthusiasm as she got into her story telling. "So, *so* many pilgrims. And so many sweaty feet all covered with blisters and weeping and festering, and needing poultices and powders to soothe them."

Murdac's face was a picture, and when Guy noticed that the sheriff had swiftly drawn his own no doubt sweaty and blistered feet back under his chair, instead of leaving them by the fire, he had to turn away for a moment to cover his amusement. Why the sheriff should be so disconcerted by the idea of a female Hospitaller treating his blisters was beyond him, but clearly Murdac's own idea of hell was to be treated for even such a minor ailment by a woman.

"But there's only so many sweaty feet a woman can cope with," Marianne was saying with blithe dismissal, "and what I'm really good at is difficult childbirths, so I thought I should go to Our Lady of Walsingham, because I thought 'there's bound to be lots of pregnant mothers going into labour there'. A good few complicated breech births and tangled cords that would require my skills!"

Poor Murdac went another shade paler. Clearly the thought of multiple screaming women, all in the throes of childbirth, was more than he could stomach, and for his sake Guy felt he'd better pull this tale to a close before Marianne got too carried away and reduced the sheriff to nausea, or painted herself into a corner from which he couldn't extract her.

"So you were on you way from Walsingham to...?" he prompted her, once more mouthing silently to her, this time 'Wales'.

"Yes, to Wales," Marianne said, this time keeping it short for want of inspiration and thus allowing Guy to finish for her,

"Ah to St Winifrid's at Holywell! The blessed *virgin* martyr. That will give you much chance to *contemplate* on, especially on the matter of *obedience*." He was mentally thanking Tuck for that one! A nice Welsh saint in the far north was a good explanation for someone to be travelling north and west from Walsingham in Norfolk, and therefore through Nottinghamshire – regardless of where Marianne had really been coming from – and allowed him to say, "but you may have trouble getting to her shrine," to give Marianne a chance to not be too tied down to that particular journey.

Being mentally alert Marianne was quick to agree. "Yes, I fear that may be difficult and I might have to go back to Buckland without going there." She endeavoured to look suitably downcast at the prospect, although Guy alone knew that it wasn't the disappointment of not seeing St Winifrid's shrine she was gloomy about, but the thought of re-incarceration with the sisters at Buckland.

Guy turned back to Murdac. "I assume we can release Sister Marianne, my lord?"

Murdac's "Yes, yes," was swift enough for Guy to be sure that he'd been convinced by their performance, and he nodded to the two men-at-arms who were behind Marianne and who now thankfully stepped away and went in search of hot food and drink. Marianne herself stepped as quickly as she could to beside Guy, relying on him for her protection, as he continued.

"Good, my lord, because the good news I was about to tell you, was that I found some money which Sir Ivo had already set aside in the basement of the keep. I didn't know that the Saladin Tithe from here hadn't been sent, or I would have made that my first priority and escorted it back to you. I did think it must be some kind of tax collection, but as the hunt for the king's venison requisition seemed more pressing, I left it, believing it was safe where it was and that there would be time afterwards to sort out just what it was for."

Murdac lurched to his feet. "Good God, man! You have it? Here? Already?"

"I believe so, my lord," Guy replied with greater calm than he felt. "If not all of it than very nearly all, for there's a barrel of silver pennies locked away in the keep."

"A barrel of pennies? How big a barrel?" Clearly Murdac was thinking of something like a small pin-barrel used for mead or lesser quantities of beer.

Guy measured out the barrel with his hands and saw Murdac breath a huge sigh of relief at the realisation that Guy meant a really big barrel, and that in turn meant a lot of money, which made it pretty certainly to be the tithe.

"God be praised!" Murdac sighed and flopped back in his chair in relief. "Thank you, Gisborne!"

"Well before I let you go to your bed for the night," Guy added pointedly, "let me give you my final piece of good news. There is no parish priest, because he died before Sir Ivo did, but there's a monk who's acting as a temporary priest until the new one arrives, and the reason he's here in the castle and not in the village is because there's a sick Templar being looked after in the servants hall. He fell ill on his way up to one of the Yorkshire preceptories, not having been used to an English winter for many a long year. He's only just back from the Holy Land, and you might have to give him another day to recover because he has a bad fever at the moment.

"But if you acknowledge Sister Marianne as your Hospitaller, then you have your Templar and priest here within the castle with the money too! All we need do is find Sir Ivo's records and confirm that it's all there, and then the four of you can sign to say it's correct, and you can leave for the Easter court without delay – and taking a good half of the meat with you for the requisition too!"

Murdac was stunned. "A Templar here?"

"Yes, my lord. Very sick, but the genuine thing. He's returned home after being wounded at the siege of Jerusalem, no less." Which to Guy's mind was right. Siward had been wounded, in mind if not body.

"And a monk acting as the priest for now?"

"Yes."

"And how much of the venison...?"

"Ah... Fifteen of the thirty deer the king wanted are already killed and have been salted and put into barrels. I've had the villagers helping with that. ...I didn't catch them all by myself, of course," Guy added hurriedly to cover all angles. "I had to commandeer the help of some travellers and a couple of local men. The travellers went yesterday and the men from Hathersage went home for a night or two. I said I'd go back that way when I needed them again. I had to pause in the hunting to make sure the skinning was being done properly, you see."

"Miraculous!" Murdac breathed as if to himself. "Bloody miraculous!" Then to the company at large, "I'm off to my bed!" He turned to Guy who had just begun to lead him towards the curtained-off bedroom. "I shall look forward to seeing your mysterious hoard in the morning, Gisborne, and this lost Templar! But I do believe I shall have the best night's sleep in some weeks tonight thanks to you!"

"My pleasure, my lord," Guy said obediently, as Murdac turned and clumped off to the end of the hall.

Moments later they heard him give a groan of pleasure and the words "Aah, a warm bed!" in deep appreciation, although he might have been less appreciative if he'd realised it was warm because Siward had only just vacated it!

The soldiers who'd come with him took this as a sign that they too could take their ease, and so as soon as they'd been sorted out with space to bed down in inside the hall, Guy was free to take Marianne across the bailey to the servant's smaller hall by the kitchen.

Tuck greeted him with a face almost grey with worry.

"How bad is it?" he enquired before the door had even closed behind Guy.

Guy came and clapped him warmly on the arm. "Not so bad at all, my friend! ...This is Marianne, the Hospitaller sister I told you about!" Tuck's astonishment forced a lengthy explanation and introductions all round. However, Marianne immediately endeared herself to Tuck by going to Siward's side and examining him.

"Hmm... Crusader's malaise," she said with professional detachment. "What's happened to him recently?"

Guy and Tuck told her of the service for the dead and Marianne's brow furrowed in thought.

"I think at the very least you did no harm to him, and possibly much good," she told Tuck reassuringly. "So many of the men I've seen won't let themselves grieve, and that really does do damage!"

"I know," Tuck replied. "I saw it for myself when I was in the Holy Land. Too much bottled up inside and only coming out in dreadful nightmares. Some do it purposely because they don't want to seem weak in front of other men they see as stronger. With others it's their minds instinctively shutting out what's too painful to contemplate."

Instantly Marianne and Tuck began a rapid conversation exchanging patients they had known, effective cures and some sad outcomes. When Guy felt that they'd had chance enough to bond with one another he interrupted.

"I'm sorry to stop you when you're exchanging ideas for cures for Siward, but we have a rather more pressing problem here. Tuck, can you and Marianne get Siward up and talking enough for him to pass with Sheriff Murdac? I really, really don't want him to send away for what he'll see as a proper Hospitaller and Templar, who could be the kind of serious, sanctimonious men who feel they have the right to demand more and more in the name of a holy war we all know we can't win. If they then say what we have isn't enough, then Murdac will have to start scouring the shire, and who knows who they might find in the process! So the only way to prevent that is to have Siward awake and acting halfway normally. I wouldn't ask if it wasn't important, but if we don't do this then it gives the sheriff time to poke about here, and I've no idea where that will leave us with Robin, John and the others."

The two looked contrite at having forgotten the immediate circumstances, and began talking about what herbs might be effective for Siward. However, the young knight surprised them all by levering himself shakily up onto one elbow and speaking.

"What do you need me to do?" he croaked hoarsely after all the sobbing, and having had very little to drink in the best part of a day.

"Siward, thank God!" Guy exclaimed and sat down to tell him what had happened.

By the time Guy fell onto his own bracken-filled mattress in the early hours they had a plan. Siward would speak to the sheriff and agree to try to get up to at least sit in the hall with Marianne. Guy would have to appear to carry on with the hunt, for as a forester the Saladin Tithe really wasn't his concern, but at least in the process he could get the others out of the Devil's Arse cave and out into the woods, under the pretext of getting men to help him hunt the remaining deer. Tuck would have to carry the main burden of deflecting the sheriff from the villagers, though, and it was lucky he'd taken an interest in the miners and farmers of this enclosed valley, so he would be able to speak with some conviction. Their biggest worry was what Sir Ivo might have had written down, for none of them had gone that closely into the tax collection records, thinking that they weren't of immediate importance. Now it was too late, and Guy could hardly go rummaging through them without raising suspicion as to why he was bothered with something outside the remit of his job.

Come the morning both Tuck and Guy felt that someone divine was looking out for them when they got up to another day of torrential rain. There could be no question now of Guy going out to hunt in such dreadful conditions, and so he was able to be around when Sheriff Murdac got down to the business of sorting out what was owing. Bilan had managed to creep into the bailey in the mass of extra people milling around first thing, and passed a message to Tuck that Piers had been sent off on Siward's horse with the other five mounted crusaders to show them the way to the outlaws' main hideout.

They'd gone just before dawn, and in the filthy weather it was clear they'd not been noticed. That relieved Guy greatly, for how to get the horses away without being seen had been worrying him stiff. Men on foot were far less distinctive up here in the steep-sided valleys, where most people travelled on foot unless they were going any distance. He was also glad that the ones left were those who could blend in with the ordinary folk, and no Piers to do something daft! Men like Algar and Walter instinctively ducked their heads when someone in authority rode by, whereas the crusaders' blunt stares back would reveal their sun-darkened skins if nothing else.

Ralph Murdac immediately set his monastic clerk to read out to him Sir Ivo's records, themselves written down in a poor, crabbed hand which spoke of the recorder possibly being the deceased parish priest. To Guy and Tuck's relief, most of the families who had been helpful to them had already paid what Sir Ivo had thought they should, however unjust that might be. These included the miner who had first organised things for Guy, Earnwine.

When the clerk read out how much Earnwine's family had been stung for, it was all Guy and Tuck could do to not gasp out loud. No wonder folk had been so hostile to them until they'd found they could be trusted. And Earnwine, as the leading miner, had been recorded close to the beginning of the list which just went on and on. The man himself had come into the hall to appear before the sheriff for the accounting, and only now did Guy discover that with the mining interests in the area there should have been another official involved.

"We ain't had a proper beremaster since Sir Godfrey Foljamb went," Earnwine grumbled disgustedly to Murdac. "We bin waiting for someone to come with the king's letter to replace old Cedric who went with him, but nobody's come. If we could've sold all the lead we mined we could've paid up faster! T'ain't our fault it's bin slow coming!"

Guy suddenly spotted a letter in the box which the clerk had retrieved from under Sir Ivo's bed.

"Would this be it?" he asked, pulling out the roll of parchment with what looked suspiciously like a royal seal on it, but a seal which had been broken and then resealed.

"God blast the man!" Ralph Murdac snapped, snatching it off Guy and ripping it open, then thrusting it at his long suffering scribe to read.

"It says that Earnwine, the miner of Castleton, is to act as beremaster for Hope Dale," the scribe read tremulously, obviously well attuned to when things might erupt into violence when his master's patience was too sorely tried.

"That's me," Earnwine said flatly, but with clear sourness at having been so blatantly side-tracked.

"When is it dated?" Guy asked quickly.

"Two years ago, in the March," the scribe answered with a wince.

"God's teeth!" Murdac swore. "Two bloody years, damned near to the month! What was Ivo thinking?" Although he was clearly more concerned with the implications if word got out about one of his knights cheating, than the effect it had had on the surrounding communities.

"He acted as beremaster himself," Earnwine told him sullenly. "He wasn't going to give us the chance to pay up fairly, the bastard! He said he had to act as beremaster since he was constable and master forester of these parts. He provided the dish for weighing the ore, as the beremaster should, but it wasn't a proper sized one, and he certainly demanded more than we thought fair for his share."

"The king and the Church take what's due to them," Murdac said dismissively, still not thinking of the Vale.

"No, I said, what *he* took!" Earnwine insisted belligerently. "We ain't such fools as to not know what tithes go to the king and which to the Church! We all bloody know that it's four-pence a load of raw ore, and every thirteenth dish of refined lead to the king! We've been doing it for long enough! We're in the old royal forest up here, not the new lands, and have been for generations. And even the daftest lad knows a tenth of what we mine goes to the Church. It's what comes out of what's *left* I'm talking about. What the beremaster takes for *his* services!"

Ralph Murdac's head had come up and he was staring aggressively back at the burly miner, irate at being challenged.

"Is there anything in those scrolls which looks like Sir Ivo kept a private record?" Guy asked hurriedly to diffuse things, but the scribe only looked blank, shrugged, and pointed his quill pen to a large handful of rolled scrolls off to the side of the long table.

"I think those might be records of sales," he said cautiously.

"Ah!" Guy pounced on them. "Then we can compare what was mined against what went to market!" and he began unrolling the scrolls.

"Gisborne?" Murdac snapped gruffly. "What the hell are you on about?"

Guy looked up, realising that he'd thought quicker than the sheriff. "Oh! ...Well we have the weights of the raw ore, don't we sire? They have to be calculable even if they're not written down, because all we have to do is multiply what was sent in value to the Church by ten and we have the amount the miners brought in. If we then take away the Church's tenth, whether in money or weight, and what was due to the king, it should give us what went to market in the ordinary way. That has to be what the sales are on these scrolls, or ought to be, because they make up the miners' individual incomes, and that's what the extra Saladin Tithe as well as the miners' dues are calculated on! If there's a noticeable difference, then that's what Sir Ivo took for himself." It was all Guy could do not to say the word 'stole'. "Here, Earnwine," he had a scroll unravelled, "this seems to be regarding your family," and he began reading aloud.

Murdac and the scribe sat back and watched as Guy rapidly did a rough calculation of what had gone missing between the two accounts. When that came up as a surprising amount, Guy more hurriedly began calculating more and more families records.

"It looks as if he was taking the equivalent of the king's share again for himself," Guy told the assembly, not needing to bother to hide his emotions this time, for it really was extortion on a grand scale.

"Where the bloody hell is it, then?" Murdac demanded. "Where did all this money go?"

"I have no idea, my lord," Guy replied. "There's not that amount of money lying around in the castle!" And there wasn't! The sum contained in the second barrel – which he and Tuck had manhandled in the depths of the previous night into the darkest corner of the keep's basement, and had bedecked with all the old spiders' webs they could find to make it look like a forgotten empty cask – certainly didn't contain anything like as much as the sum Sir Ivo had extorted. Again the truth that the main sum was missing concealed the lie that Guy knew where some of the money was. The only plus was that if the counting of the money in the known barrel – which was being done by a second Nottingham scribe under the watchful eye of Murdac's captain of the guard now that it had been brought up to the ground floor of the keep – was in excess of the Saladin Tithe, then now there was a reasonable explanation for the difference without

Murdac having to go digging for it. That at least gave Guy and Tuck one less thing to worry about. The big monk had been sitting in uncharacteristic silence down at the far end of the hall with Marianne, trying to look suitably humble and unremarkable, but Guy knew that nothing had gone unnoticed by his friend any more than by himself.

"You won't be needing to go in search of the lost tithe, then, my lord," Guy said, trying to not to sound too relieved that Murdac would soon be on his way.

However, Murdac was shaking his head. "Only when we're sure everyone has paid, Gisborne. I can't have the people of this valley going to the hundred court and complaining that they've paid up when some other village has got away with paying nothing."

Guy found himself clenching his jaw in frustration. Trust Murdac to see it like that! And to be fair, he was right in a way. It would be bloody unjust if the next time the folk from villages hereabout got together for a large market, or met up at some abbey fair, someone declared with glee that they'd not had to pay the Saladin Tithe because the sheriff had never bothered to come and get it. Few would let such a thing go without raising some kind of complaint in the local courts.

"Is there anywhere that hasn't paid?" he growled to the scribe, who picked up on the menace in Guy's voice even if the sheriff didn't.

"K... K... Kinder, Sir Guy," the poor man answered tremulously, glancing fearfully from Guy to the sheriff and back. "They don't s...s...seem to have paid anything yet."

"*Where?*" Murdac demanded. "Never heard of it!"

"Kinder," Guy and Earnwine answered together.

"It's the tiny hamlet right up beneath the big peak with a couple of small manors close by," Guy explained. "There's not even a church or a mill up there, it's too small. It's just a few wooden cottages for some miners, and one farmer who has some sheep up on the slopes of Kinder Scout in season. I usually ride up there because it's right in the heart of the forest, and Sir Ivo didn't like going up there, so I'd go whenever I came this way to check on the venison and the vert."

"Didn't *like* to?" Murdac exploded, pounding the table with his fist in his fury, and making the poor scribe turn white with fear. "Why did no-one tell me this? He was *paid* to be the master forester, not some mincing milkmaid! Why didn't *you* tell me, Gisborne?" and he got up and began prowling behind the scribe, unable to sit still any longer.

Guy felt a cold sweat breaking out down his back. If it had been de Braose here someone would already have been bleeding, and he wasn't sure how much further Murdac would be pushed before he too acted the Norman lord and began pounding someone to a pulp. Please *Dewi Sant* it wouldn't be himself or his friends!

"I thought you were aware of it, my lord! It was going on long before you moved me over to this side of Sherwood, and although it's no excuse I admit, I personally never spoke to Sir Ivo. My normal patrol was to ride on up to Edale from here, then make the scramble up to Edale Cross where there's a nearby farmhouse where I'd stay the night. The next day I'd make my way up onto Kinder Scout itself and check for deer signs up there, then make my way down onto Black Ashop Moor.

"Then depending on where I'd been the previous time, I'd either go out onto Shelf Moor and check the herds up there and then come back along the valley of the River Ashop, or I'd swing eastwards and then south through the upper Derwent Valley and return that way. Either way, sire, it would take me over a week, and sometimes longer if I went right up to the border with Yorkshire, in which case I'd return directly to Nottingham without ever coming back here."

"Aye, he's right, my lord," Earnwine came in unexpectedly in Guy's defence. "I knew Sir Guy by sight, but I'd never spoke to him until he came this time 'cause he always rode off first thing in the morning after the foresters arrived."

Murdac was looking more furious with every statement, and yet for all that his face was getting darker with anger, Guy suddenly got the feeling that he was no longer the object of that anger.

"So who came with you most of the time?" Murdac demanded in a growl.

"It was sometimes Walkelin or Fredegis," Guy admitted, "but mostly it was Sir Henry."

"And while you were riding the distant parts of this forest what did they do?" snapped Murdac, to which Guy had to answer,

"In truth, my lord, I don't know. If I thought about it, I suppose I assumed that when they left here that they checked around this valley, and maybe south of here. I always made my report to Sir Alan or Sir Walter, and I presumed the others must have made some report of a similar kind to them or there would have been questions asked long ago."

Murdac grunted but took in Guy's words. "Damned scoundrels! They must have been covering their tracks well." He fixed Guy with his grim stare until it was all Guy could do not to break away or squirm. However, it was the sheriff who broke off first with a heavy sigh.

"Aach, I should not chastise you, Gisborne! You've been all honesty and hard work, as is proven by the way you've rescued this situation out of the jaws of disaster. And if you made reports to Sir Alan then you'd have known I could check up on you at any time. ...Well we have the Easter court coming up here too! I want you to take charge of that for me. Sort this bloody mess out for me! I make no promises for the future, for the gift of this castle isn't wholly in my hands, but I shall make my recommendations when I see the king later in the month."

"Yes, my lord!" Guy gulped at this unexpected compliment.

"However, we must get the Saladin Tithe sorted before then, so help Brother Benedict here sort out who's paid in full and who hasn't!" the sheriff commanded, and with a wave of his hand got up and walked off to the fire while calling for a mug of small beer to quench his thirst.

For the rest of the afternoon Guy and Tuck laboured with the scribe Benedict. It was a miserable task because in a hurried conference over a bowl of soup at midday Guy and Tuck had regretfully agreed that Murdac was right, there could be no question of one village getting away with not paying because that would win them no friends with the other villages – and they both knew that they and the outlaws needed the villagers along this valley to be on their side if their own secret wasn't to be given away. Mercifully, in the end only Kinder hadn't paid anything, but there were three miners' families in Edale who had argued over what was due, and another two just down in Hope.

"Can we warn them the sheriff's wrath is about to descend on them?" Tuck wondered, as he and Guy met secretively in the depths of the kitchen once everyone else was fast asleep.

"No, not a chance," Guy sighed. "It'd be risking too much. What if they took off into the woods to hide from him? The sheriff would be bound to ask me to track them, and God knows I hate hunting people, Tuck! But what if we then happen to cross our friends' tracks? How could I explain them away to Murdac? They'd be far more plentiful than those of a small family, so it'd look pretty suspect if I just dismissed them as being of no consequence! There's no legitimate way I could know such a thing, and Murdac's not stupid! And anyway, if the miners run, then Murdac will be convinced they're guilty of something. If they stay put I might just be able to convince him that they've paid enough."

He wasn't wholly sure he could pull such a thing off, but he had to trail in Murdac's wake into Hope the next day. Both of the families in question swore that they'd paid all they could, and Guy believed them, but by now Murdac was in no mood to be lenient.

"I have written testimony that you pay four pounds a year to lease this mine," he said sternly, looking down his nose at the head man of the family from the height of his horse. "My records show that you are getting over a hundred tons of ore a year out of it."

"Yes, my lord," the poor man spluttered, "But that's raw ore! Not pure lead! Not profit!"

However, Murdac just stared back coldly. "You claim you can only pay three shillings for each man, yet my knight Sir Ivo claims you can pay five."

Guy winced at this. The ordinary miners were paid a penny a day in wages but rarely saw much of the profits, and even the head miner was hardly living in luxury. Three shillings was enough to ask, and even that would be hard to find on top of every other tax and rent they had to dig deep to find on such wages.

"Five, my lord?" The miner had gone white and there were rumblings of discontent from the men clustered around him.

"If you protest, I shall get my men to seize chattels to the value of the full five shillings on top of the three you've paid," Murdac declared, at which a wailing and sobbing broke out amongst the women who were clustered behind their men.

Guy could stand it no longer. "My lord, have pity!" he said heeling his horse to beside the sheriff. "Look at them! What could they possibly have in hovels like this which would fetch even close to five shillings? How on earth could you sell chests or platters and pots begrimed with lead spoil as they are? Do you really want to set off to London clattering along like some itinerant tinker?" He was seriously pushing his luck and he knew it.

For one horrible moment Murdac's furious gaze turned upon him, and Guy feared he would be out on his ear and living in the forest with his cousins.

Then Murdac snorted like a furious bull and shook his head. "God curse you, Gisborne! ...You have a point."

"I shall make it my business to have these folk properly assessed come Easter," Guy said with more firmness than he felt inside. "But at the moment we cannot say for certain that Sir Ivo's records are ...up to date." It was the most politic way he could think of to remind Murdac that Sir Ivo had been fiddling the accounts without saying it openly in front of those Ivo had fleeced, but Murdac took the hint.

"What say you, sir Templar?" he asked Siward, who had ridden out with them swathed in two thick cloaks and looking very pale, but upright. "Should we allow these folk to get away with the lesser payment? You who have seen the fight for the Holy City for himself?"

Siward had been doing his best not to say anything in his horror at this forcing of cash out of folk already barely making a living, while Marianne had been biting her glove to prevent her screaming in anger at the sheriff, and Guy saw suppressed tears of fury in her eyes when he turned to face them.

"I don't think the chattels of these poor folk will do much to stop the march of Saladin's army," was the best Siward could think of to say, but it was a show of support for Guy and it allowed Murdac a way to retreat without being the one to have the last say on what happened here. The sheriff wheeled his horse so sharply that its nose swiped one of the miners hard and sent him flying into the slush with blood pouring from his nose, but at least the families in Hope got away with paying no more.

In Edale they got an initially more frosty reception but less argument, and the head miner concerned there brought out a purse with several shillings more in pennies for the sheriff. However, as he handed it over the miner made a point of saying to Murdac,

"I knew that twisted old hypocrite Ivo would bend the accounts! Thieving bastard! Here have the bloody money, and I hope the king chokes on it! It's robbed us of every penny we had to replace our tools with when they break, never mind eat! Don't come complaining to us when the production is down this year!"

"I shall investigate this further, too!" Guy leapt in hastily before Murdac could take offence, but the sheriff gave the miners some very dark looks as they rode away.

Once they were back in the castle that night Siward had to sit with Guy, Marianne and Tuck at the long table in the hall to eat with the sheriff rather than going to lie down, as he desperately wanted to do, but at least the racket from all the men-at-arms crammed in with them meant that they could speak without Murdac overhearing them.

"You took some chance back there in Hope," Siward said to Guy with admiration. "I thought for a moment he'd take your head off with that sword he carries at his hip."

"He was seriously pissed off with you for challenging him in front of the peasants," Marianne agreed, her ripe language earning her a surprised glance from Siward. Clearly the Templars didn't have sisters amongst their ranks in the East, or if they did, then they weren't so fiery as Marianne.

"I couldn't not try," Guy admitted. "Lord, but it wears at my soul sometimes, doing this job!"

"Well be careful!" Tuck cautioned him. "Tomorrow come and ride further back behind us. That way if the sheriff starts on someone you won't be the one they look to first for help. If you contradict him again in front of the miners, I doubt he'll forgive or forget a second time."

"It won't make me feel any better," Guy sighed.

"No, it won't," Tuck agreed, "But it might keep you your job!"

When they rode into Kinder the next day Guy was behind his three friends, and believing that here at least the folk had got off lightly so far. Yet it didn't save him from a very different nasty shock. As he rode in the rear towards the tiny cluster of houses which made up the hamlet of Kinder he saw signs of movement up on the hillside above them. To his horror he then realised that it was Robin and several of the others keeping pace with them. He couldn't believe that they were taking such a risk! When he'd said to Robin and the others that most of the sheriff's men couldn't find their own arses with both hands, he hadn't meant them to take it to mean that the soldiers were stupid and blind!

It took him a few deep breaths to calm himself before he could look again. Actually the outlaws were doing a pretty good job of keeping a low profile on the hill, and now that he was thinking a bit straighter, Guy admitted to himself that he was a lot sharper at spotting such movement than even most of his fellow foresters. And it wasn't as though any of the men riding with the sheriff had ever seen much real fighting. They were just the heavy-handed ones from the garrison at Nottingham who enjoyed beating up the lesser folk of the towns and villages. If they ever came up against any real fighters, Guy knew they would fold like so much rain-soaked parchment. The Welsh raiders would have made mincemeat of them! And in that case, Robin's experience of avoiding the Saracens might well give him a serious edge, especially if he listened to men like Thomas and Hugh.

While seeming to be gazing idly around him, Guy scrutinised the area where he'd seen the outlaws, and in darting glances worked out that as best he could tell it was just Robin, Will and Malik with Thomas and Hugh. Thank God for that! No Walter or Algar, both of whom might be prompted to rash actions in defence of the peasants if the sheriff got rough with them, and no hot-headed Piers either, praise be!

Suddenly Guy had an idea. "My lord," he called ahead, trotting his horse up to the head of the column. "I've just seen a young hind with a wound, I think. I'm just going up the hill to investigate. I'll be back with you by the time you reach Kinder."

Murdac was a bit taken a back but could hardly protest at Guy doing what he was employed to do. Kicking his mare into a slow canter, Guy un-slung the small hunting bow he used when in the presence of men like the sheriff from around his shoulders. He didn't want someone like Murdac to know that he was a good shot with a full-sized Welsh bow! He loosed an arrow into the bushes just in front of where the outlaws were to make it look good, then slowed his horse to a walk and began taking her on a zigzagged course up the steep hillside. By the time he was at the bushes most of the party below had rounded the next shoulder of the hills, and he was able to vault off his horse without anyone looking back at him.

"What the hell is going on?" a furious Robin demanded.

"The bloody Saladin Tithe!" Guy riposted. "Don't blame me! I can't work miracles!" He scrubbed a hand across his weary eyes, and Will and Malik both put restraining hands on Robin's arms.

"What is wrong?" Malik asked in his measured English.

Guy exhaled heavily. "That old bastard Ivo has been doing some very creative record keeping," he sighed. "Yesterday I managed to stop it from being too bad in Hope and Edale, but I fear if I step in today the sheriff will have my head!"

"But why's Siward riding with you? And who's the girl?" Will wanted to know.

In hurried words Guy brought them up to date. "It was the best I could do with what I had," he apologised, and was relieved to see Robin calming with understanding.

"I have to get back," he said, "but please promise me you won't interfere at Kinder. It won't help the folk there if you do. The sheriff will just come back with more men and take even more. He has the king's authority to take what he deems due on top of what the people think they should pay if they protest too hard."

"The *king*?" Robin gasped in disbelief.

"That's plain wicked!" Will growled.

Thomas nodded. "Yes it is, but it's not just here. Guy's not making it up. It's the same everywhere. The Saladin Tithe doesn't hit the royal forests any harder than anywhere else, it just seems worse to these folk because of all the extra taxes and fines they have to pay for the privilege of competing with the king's deer for space."

Robin looked from Thomas to Guy and back again. "This is going on *everywhere*?"

Guy sniffed, "You wait until you see it actually happening. It turns my stomach every time. I've never got used to it, and I don't want to! If I do then I would really begin to fear for my immortal soul. The only consolation is that it's harsh, but in these shires I've not seen the violence against folk as I did in my previous place." He turned and remounted. As he turned his horse back down the valley he reminded them, "Remember, don't interfere! For their sakes not yours!"

Back on the level he cantered in pursuit of the others, and covered himself with Murdac by saying he was going to have to track the wounded hind much further than he had time for just now, but would return soon to find her.

By now they were entering the loose collection of buildings which made up Kinder. A modest wooden-built manor very like his own stood off to one side, but there wasn't even a side road going off the main track into the huddle of small houses. From the manor an old man came hobbling out on rheumatic legs.

"Yes, stranger, what can we do for you? Oh it's you Sir Guy!"

"This is Sheriff Murdac," Guy introduced his lord miserably. The old man must have picked up by the way Guy was unable to meet his eyes and his slumped shoulders that something was wrong, for he began to back off.

"You haven't paid the Saladin Tithe!" Murdac declared as if he was pronouncing a sentence.

"Yes we have!" the old man protested. "That ugly big foreign knight of yours came in just after the last time Sir Guy was here. Said he was from Sir Ivo!"

"Oh God, no!" Guy groaned without thinking, earning himself the sharp reproof of,

"Gisborne! Fall back into line!" snapped Murdac, clearly not wanting to have his actions questioned again.

Guy turned his horse and let her plod back at her own pace, unable to look back as he heard the crashing and thumping of the men-at-arms plunging into the humble houses, and the distressed screams of the women and children from within. The thug-like men-at-arms must have realised they were on a very loose leash with Murdac in his current mood, and were being rougher than usual. *Please Our Lady and Dewi Sant there'll be only broken furniture*, Guy prayed, *and the houses stay sound given this bitter weather!* He saw rather than heard Marianne scream, and Tuck reach out to grab her and her horse's reins before she could join in, although he was muttering darkly in Welsh what sounded suspiciously like curses. Siward looked like he might be sick at any moment.

"Is this what we were fighting for?" Guy heard him whisper in despair as he brought his horse alongside him, and reached over to put what he hoped was a comforting hand on the Templar's shoulder.

Looking back over his shoulder, to his horror Guy saw a man being dragged forcibly out of a hut by two of the men-at-arms.

"He struck me, my lord!" the bully following them called to the sheriff. "Hit me with a hammer and broke my arm!" His arm was hanging at a strange angle and his face was pasty white with pain, but Guy was sure he had provoked the miner, and the man clearly was a miner and the hammer one of the tools of his trade.

"Take his hand off!" Murdac snapped. "The right one! See how he fights then!"

Guy felt his stomach lurch. This was worse than Hope, much worse! Ten burly men-at-arms against a bunch of unarmed peasant miners and their families. Now he saw another man being beaten to a pulp by three other soldiers and his wife lying on the ground unconscious. It was wrong! It was completely and utterly wrong! Without thinking Guy found himself reaching for his bow regardless of Tuck's hissed warning of "Guy, no!"

Then out of the blue there was a whistling, and five long arrows planted themselves in a cluster in front of the soldiers, who were just dragging the miner forward to a fallen tree trunk which they intended to use as a chopping block. Five more followed before anyone had hardly had a chance to blink, and another flight, and another! The soldiers suddenly loosed their captive and began diving for cover. The bemused miners stood in stunned shock as yard-long arrows shrieked past them, harrying their oppressors until they began backing out of the village. Siward recovered quickest of Tuck, Marianne and him, and began chivvying them to ride back.

"What are you laughing for?" Marianne whispered at him frantically, catching him biting his lip in mirth as they urged their horses to a trot.

"Malik's fletching," Siward replied so that only the pair of them could hear.

"Ma...!" Tuck gasped, then casting about him ever more urgently, "Where's Guy?"

The forester had disappeared!

Then there was the sound of another bowstring closer and above them than the others, and another arrow shot out of the tree cover higher up the hill towards the village. Two more arrows came out of the copse, and by the sudden screams coming from the village some must have been finding their mark. A pounding of hooves spoke of the sheriff coming back their way and in a hurry.

"Quick! Ride on!" Siward cried. "We have to get round that bend so that he doesn't see Guy isn't with us," and the three of them heeled their horses into a gallop around the shoulder of the next tiny valley coming down off Kinder Scout. Luckily, although the trees weren't that dense, there were enough to obscure the view, and by the time they rounded the next bend they saw Guy jumping his horse down off the hillside to join them just in time for Murdac to coming thundering up with three dead men across their horses and with a face black with fury. Two more men were clutching wounds with arrows protruding from an arm and a thigh, and one of those arrows looked suspiciously like the fletching on the two remaining ones in Guy's quiver. Luckily Murdac wasn't even looking at Guy.

"Judas' balls! Where did those arrows come from!" he demanded of no-one in particular.

"Not from the village," Tuck dared to answer, wanting to get in before Guy brought the sheriff's wrath down on himself, making the sheriff take note.

"The villagers were as shocked as you were," Siward confirmed, making Murdac blink in surprise. "I've seen enough action in villages in the East to know when an attack is a surprise to them and not an ambush they've helped set up. These peasants were more shocked than you!"

"They weren't in league with whoever that was, you think?"

"No, my lord!" Tuck said firmly. "There have been no outlaws in this area for years! They must have come over the hills from Lancashire or Cheshire."

"Gisborne?" Murdac roared, for Guy was sitting a little way off behind his friends to give his horse time for its breathing to ease so that it wouldn't be clear that she'd been ridden hard. "Outlaws here?"

Guy shook his head. "None I've ever heard of, my lord. Brother Tuck is right, they must have come from the west."

"I don't have time for this!" Murdac snapped furiously. "I have to be in Winchester in under four weeks! And I have other things to do before then without having to weed out a nest of outlaws in some Godforsaken valley in the arse end of Derbyshire!"

"I'll go back tomorrow with the castle garrison," Guy offered. "I know the hiding places up on the hillside. If they're up there we'll soon flush them out."

Murdac brightened a little at that. "Yes, you will! Go up there with half a dozen men and flush them this way and we'll be waiting down here. You'll go with him, captain! I will not *tolerate* this!"

"It's not as though the payment from Kinder was that much," Tuck added consolingly, but hoping to plant another idea into the mind of the irate sheriff. "So few houses couldn't have owed more than a few shillings, and you have that in the extra the captain found in what he and your clerk counted yesterday. They may even have paid just as they said, and you wouldn't want that to come out in a local court before another sheriff, would you?"

Murdac just grunted at that, but the possibility of another sheriff coming as a justice on eyre and hearing of such goings on certainly threw cold water on any plans for revenge. He was in a foul mood for the rest of the day, retiring to bed early in the evening to everyone's relief, but with no further outbursts.

When they returned to the valley the following morning, Guy led the captain of the guard and six of his men, plus six from the castle, in a scouring of the top of Kinder Scout. As Guy had hoped, there was no sign that Robin and the others had ever been there, except for a few bent twigs which he was sure only he had noticed. Sheriff Murdac therefore had a very cold day hanging around at the bottom of the slope doing nothing, and once the captain had told him that Guy was right and there was no-one up there, Murdac announced his intention of departing the next day to take the silver back to Nottingham to be added to the other money heading for the court.

It was with intense relief that Guy stood watching the sheriff's party depart in the mid morning of an altogether brighter day, as if even the weather was glad to see the back of them. Murdac had confirmed him as the temporary constable and forester of High Peak, and had his memory of Guy's outburst in Kinder overwritten by the sight of the wagons being filled with the barrels of prepared venison.

"I'll get the other fifteen deer caught and butchered as fast as possible," Guy promised him, and was sure that it was the reassurance that Murdac wouldn't be left looking a fool at court which had finally secured him the keys of the castle. Sergeant Ingulf was once again making the ride to Nottingham with the main party, with the soldier Guy had come to know as Stenulf, in order to bring the carts back and also Fletch and Spike, for Guy had never anticipated being away for so long.

No sooner had the sheriff's party disappeared down the valley than the outlaws skirmished in through the west gate, let in by the stablemen who much preferred them to the bullying soldiers.

"I thought you said there'd be no violence?" were Robin's accusatory first words when he got to Guy.

Guy could only shake his head in sorrow. "That's the first I've seen of such things in this shire, believe me."

"Why didn't you do more to stop them?" Robin badgered, still standing nose to nose with Guy. "There were women and children getting hurt down there! I saw mere boys show more spirit in Jerusalem than you did back there! Did you finally join in thinking I wouldn't notice that you'd waited until we'd softened them up a bit?"

"Robin stop!" a husky voice called, and Siward came staggering out leaning on Marianne for support.

"Why? I never thought to be calling my cousin a coward, but you are!" he near spat at Guy, earning a growl of disapproval from John coming up behind him.

"Baldwin that's enough!" John said firmly, yet when Robin whipped round and glowered at him, Guy was surprised to see John drop his eyes and back away. That was a real shift in their relationship, for John had never backed down from Allan in such a way. Yet when Robin turned back to Guy he could see the almost murderous anger in those eyes which had so squashed John.

It didn't halt Siward, though. "Robin! Stop it! Guy's not a coward!" the young Templar insisted, coming to stand between Guy and his leader. "You might not have heard it, but Guy did try to stop them! And what did you want him to do? He was only one man against all those others! I couldn't even use a knife at the moment, much less string a bow or use a sword! What did you expect him to do? Go up against Murdac and his men alone with just Tuck and Marianne to help?"

Will tapped Robin on the arm. "He's got a point. Use your head, Robin! We had the advantage of surprise, and we were attacking from under cover. Guy was out in the open! At best he'd have brought one down before they ganged up on him."

"And they would have," Malik added, "because if he had done anything they would have seen him as the greater threat. The one they had to take down first!"

Robin's anger was wavering in the face of this unexpected support for Guy from his old friends.

Siward was nodding his agreement, adding, "And you didn't see what Guy did the day before. The people of Hope have much to thank him for for stopping it getting bad there. We all told him that night he was risking a lot to face up to the sheriff like that."

Robin turned and looked Guy in the eye, dark brown eyes

searching for the truth in the clear green ones. "Did you really? Did you put yourself at risk the day before for the ordinary folk."

Guy found himself blushing. He hated trumpeting his own deeds. He did what he did because it was the right thing to do, not because he wanted someone to fuss over him afterwards. But he wasn't about to take being called a coward either! "Yes, I did," he said bluntly. "And not because I wanted your approval or anyone else's!"

Suddenly Robin's face creased in a smile. "Oh that takes me back! That look on your face! By Our Lady, it's good to know you haven't changed that much!"

"That 'look'?" Guy growled.

Only John's softer smile joining in stopped him from smacking this strange man before him, whose moods seemed to shift like quicksand, with his fist.

Robin actually laughed to Guy's confusion. "That belligerent scowl you get when someone accused you and you knew you hadn't done anything! Like when Audulph rode Fulk's pony and strained its leg and then swore it was you! I can still remember you squaring up to him even though at that stage he towered over us. You were red with temper and that look in your eyes! You punched him in the guts before he landed one on you, and I'll never forget the surprise on his face when you ended up on top of him, grinding his face into the mud, and still swearing at him that you'd never touched his bloody pony as you did it! He never forgot that, you know. Of all of us you were the one he was just a little bit afraid of if he pushed you too hard."

John was chuckling now at the memory, making Guy take a deep breath and step back, yet somehow he couldn't quite laugh it all away. It wasn't the offence to his honour. Strange to say, he was far less affronted by that coming from someone whom he felt he hardly knew anymore than he would have been if it had been Tuck who'd made the accusation – because Tuck knew him for who he really was now, as a man and not the boy of more than ten years ago. No, Robin's opinion of him was of no great consequence. But he was shaken by that dangerous look in Robin's eyes which seemed to come unbidden and then disappear in a blink. That spoke of something frighteningly unpredictable and dangerous, and where it might lead Robin and those who followed him was anyone's guess.

And the first example came straight away.

"So who is this *woman*?" demanded Robin, looking Marianne up and down in a less than friendly manner.

Merifully it was Siward who spoke up for her, thereby provoking Robin less than if it had been Guy, given the current tension.

"This is Sister Marianne. A Hospitaller sister from the Holy Land."

"Is she?" Robin said with a sniff of doubt. "A Hospitaller? On whose word? Hers?"

"No, mine!" snapped Guy, now throughly fed up with his cousin's high and mighty attitude. "And if you don't trust me, that's your problem! I met Marianne years ago *inside* the Hospitallers headquarters in London. In uniform! Or do you think women just randomly wander in and out of the place on a regular basis? Do you think them so debased? Is *no-one* up to your exacting standards?"

For the first time Robin seemed to realise the very real offence he'd caused, and also that even his friends from the east were looking at him somewhat askance, as well as the others.

"She's done much to help the local people," Siward said with as much firmness as he could summon, "and she's helped Tuck nurse me back to health. She is what she says she is, Robin. Don't you remember the sisters at the great hospital in Jerusalem?"

"Of course I do!" snapped Robin. "I just find it strange that one of them should be here!"

"What? Stranger than *us* being here?" Will demanded with no small measure of sarcasm. "For God's sake, Robin, go and kick some bales of hay or something to vent your spleen on! Not those helping us! And certainly not these two in particular – don't single them out for blame where none should be given!"

Robin glowered at Will for a moment, then turned and stomped off to the table where a pitcher of ale and some mugs waited, muttering as he went, "Well don't expect me to be looking after her when we have to leave the castle for good!"

Quick as a flash Marianne riposted, "I wouldn't dream of asking a *Templar* to anyway!" Then, feeling Siward stiffen as he was still leaning on her, added softly, "Sorry. Didn't mean all of you – just him!"

"That's all right," Siward said with a weak smile. "No offence taken – he started it, not you."

"I never knew there was such acrimony between Templars and Hospitallers," Thomas commented to no-one in particular.

Yet even as Siward and Gilbert were shaking their heads and Will began saying, "There isn't..." Robin snapped,

"How many other monastic orders do you know of that have women along side men, hmm?"

"There are many nunneries alongside monasteries!" Tuck protested, but was dismissed with a vehement wave of Robin's hand.

"No! Not in separate houses! Together! They had women working in the same hospital as the brothers!"

"And a damned good job too!" Marianne riposted. "I wouldn't trust a *man* to care for female pilgrims and children! Or do you think that women and children don't deserve to visit such holy places? Are we all corrupt by our courses in your eyes?" At which Robin went red in the face and turned on his heels to storm out, yet harried by

Marianne shouting after him, "Because there'd be no bloody men without *women* bearing them! And no Christ either! Even *God* needed a mother for his son!"

"Oh dear!" sighed Tuck, coming to pat Marianne's hand sympathetically. "I think we might have a problem there!"

Oh, so you are all ears now, Brother! Yes, that was Robin Hood's first clash with a sheriff of Nottingham, although it would be a little longer before he decided that it was his calling to fight injustice in quite such a vigorous way. I tried hard over the coming days to explain just how hard it was for men like Murdac – who by and large did their best to be fair – to cope with the new and heavy demands from the king. Murdac knew that there was little money going spare, Brother. He was not such a fool as to think the peasants could simply conjure up extra shillings out of thin air just because the king wished it. And the other crusaders, if not my cousin, had a little more sympathy when I pointed out that Murdac had a family of his own to consider, even if they did not live at the castle with him. Fall out with the king and he too would be without income, I told them, and was grudgingly believed.

Yet Robin and the other crusaders felt it was an insult to them that they had fought so hard in the Holy Land for a Christian way of life, to then come home and find that the people who were funding the fight for Jerusalem were being treated so shockingly. Nor could I offer any balm to soothe their souls on this matter, for I too felt that there was something very wrong in bleeding the ordinary folk white for a war which could not be won – as I was hearing now from more than just Tuck.

However, if nothing else, we now had some breathing space. The sheriff had been and gone, and could now not be expected to return for probably two months, given the need for him to travel south to the Easter court and then make his way back – since his captain had told me it must be easily a three hundred mile round trip from Nottingham to Winchester. That relieved a lot of pressure on me, and I now began to enjoy having my cousin and his friends, as well as my own friends, around me on a daily basis. I had not had such companionship for a very, very long time, and if it did the others some good it also cheered me mightily. We completed the hunt in plenty of time, and I sent the good Sergeant Ingulf off once more with cart loads of venison to Nottingham, while the villagers of Hope and Castleton were treated to a feast provided by me, and the other hunters, of venison plus two magnificent wild boar I managed to bring down. In our little corner of Derbyshire we celebrated Easter in fine style that year!

My relationship with the folk of Hope had also become much warmer following my outburst in front of the sheriff, and at least it was easy to then distribute the money they were due back from Sir Ivo's exploits, knowing that they would not betray me the next time the sheriff came through. For all of the villages I was also able to set the records straight as to what they should be paying, and for once I was able to be a little generous because I suspected that the sheriff would think I had been a bit of a soft touch, and would expect anyone new to increase the payments by a small percentage if nothing else.

I was not so naive as to think that I would hold the position of constable of High Peak permanently. I am not, and was not, so vain as to not be realistic about where I stood in the pecking order of knightly foresters in Nottingham. And do not forget, Brother, that I was a forester, and for all that the constable of High Peak was also the master forester there, the man in charge was never likely to be a forester first and foremost. King Henry, I was sure, would want someone with more military experience in charge in this tactically important castle, even if in terms of size it was nothing much at all. And so we began to make plans against the day when we would have to move on.

Chapter 18

e did our best to plan for an uncertain future, Gervase, and yet our short-lived happiness was not terminated by the king objecting to me, but by him dying! In mid-July we heard the king was dead, and our new king, Richard, was still very much an unknown quantity. Yet amongst Robin and the others from the East there was an outbreak of unrestrained joy, and all the more so because Richard did not turn from Tours, where he had been fighting his father, and come directly to England. Robin, Siward and Gilbert, in particular, saw this as King Richard possibly preparing to go to relieve the Holy Land straight from France. For our part, though, Thomas, Hugh, Tuck and myself feared that it was a sign that he would always favour his French territories, and in particular his beloved Aquitaine, over a country he had hardly ever set foot in – and how we were to be proven right in that, Brother, although it is only with much hindsight that I can say that now.

Then in the third week of August, word came in a flurry that our new king had landed with much pomp and ceremony at Portsmouth on the thirteenth, and I dared to believe that my cynicism had got the better of me, and that Richard would be the king we all hoped for. There was much promise in those first weeks, as you may recall, for although the king took his time getting here, he sent his mother on ahead of him, and upon her arrival those imprisoned in the country's gaols were set free. I had to admit that, whilst I was glad that some of the poor souls had been released who had been incarcerated for minor offences simply because they had become too impoverished to pay any sort of fine, I was less enthusiastic about the hardened criminals who had been released alongside them. I could foresee a spate of cutpurses and thieves afflicting the country if not worse.

Why did I care so much, you wonder? Ah Brother, at every turn you show that you have never had to wonder where the money for your next meal will come from! How was I supposed to collect money from folk for grazing their animals in the royal forest? Or chase them to pay fines for having collected wood, when some scoundrel had broken in and taken what few pennies they had tucked away for such things? Already barely holding body and soul together, the last thing most folk needed was to have a lightning-strike of petty crime going on around them. So to me, you see, it seemed like an act of sweeping generosity, but one which had been poorly thought out, and therefore one done more for the immediate effect than any real sign of care for the ordinary people. And I instinctively knew that it would be men like me who would have to deal with the repercussions. Like you, Robin could not understand why I was not celebrating as if the Second Coming was nigh, yet to Tuck, Hugh and myself it seemed more like the gates of Hell were to be opened without any waiting angels to do the sorting of souls!

Then a month on, on the thirteenth of September, Richard was crowned. We knew when it was happening, and Robin insisted we toasted the king's health with one of the better casks of wine from the cellar at High Peak, but what took place outside the great abbey and palace of Westminster took a few more days to reach us. I had had to go over to Nottingham as part of my regular duties, taking a persistent and blatant poacher, who was also a braggart, for imprisonment before he caused more grief for the villagers and us, and so I was there when the news came in. I tell you, Brother, it chilled my blood, and I felt compelled to rush back to High Peak as fast as was seemly and without raising questions, for I feared it might have repercussions for Malik and James if no-one else.

Our king had gone humbly enough to his anointing in just his breeches and with his shirt open baring his chest, and had promised to administer fair justice to the people committed to his care. Maybe that was what prompted the Jews of London to go to see him afterwards, despite being told beforehand they would not be admitted to the king's presence. I do not know. I was not there.

What I do know is that in the midst of the revelry, Jews bearing gifts for this much praised prince and now king arrived outside the palace of Westminster. The crowd outside the great hall, no doubt in a froth waiting for a glimpse of King Richard, fell upon them and beat them. It was claimed that this was in a spate of crusading fervour, and certainly that was how it was told when I first heard it, although later some murmured that many folk were heavily in debt to the moneylenders after the last years of Henry's reign, and saw a way to wipe those debts clear.

Some of the Jews died there and then, others – according to the reports – staggered away half dead, and many of those died later. The trouble then spread through London like wildfire, with Jewish houses being plundered and burned during the course of that night. The king was reportedly furious at this desecration of his celebration, not least because all Jews were under his protection and he would need their goodwill to act as bankers for his coming crusade. For my part I prayed that he would take strong action as I rode like the wind back across to Derbyshire, giving thanks that I had left Fletch and Spike behind so that I could keep changing horses and pound on with the news.

High Peak Castle, Derbyshire, Winter, the year of Our Lord 1189

Guy burst in on the still jovial gathering in the wooden hall at High Peak, dumping his cloak on a bench without regard, and barely sparing time to ruffle Fletch and Spike's ears as they bounded up to greet him.

"Guy? What's wrong?" Tuck asked, perceptive as ever.

"The Jews in London have been set upon after the coronation and many murdered," Guy reported grimly. There was a collective intake of breath, but Guy wasn't going to allow anyone to deflect him from his warning. "Malik, you're going to have to be very careful," he said urgently. "Most people up here in the north don't know a Saracen from a Jew, and they'll know even less about native Christians from the Holy Land! If they can attack the Jews who've had no part in the war in the east by mistake, I'm fearful that they might pick on anyone who looks different. The others are less at risk these days now that they aren't so sunburned, but you and James are naturally much darker, and this late spate of summer sun hasn't helped matters, because you're no paler now than when you arrived."

The two looked worriedly to one another.

"What do you expect them to do?" Will demanded with a touch of irritation.

Guy threw his hands up in frustration. "God's teeth, Will! We could hear at any moment that I'm to leave here, and that will mean all of you leaving too! I know Malik and James can't change what they are, but I'm trying to warn you not to take them into towns with you. Most villages won't want any trouble, and with six of you all well-armed and looking like you know how to handle your weapons, they won't push their luck beyond a few black looks and some insults. But what I'm desperate to get through to you is that you can't bite back! Let it go and get out of there if something like that happens!"

"Why should we? We've done nothing wrong?" Gilbert demanded.

"Surely the law will be on our side?" Siward added, nodding his agreement with Gilbert's sentiments.

Guy flopped onto the bench as Thomas brought him a flagon of ale, and it was Thomas who asked the vital question. "Did no-one try to stop it? The attack on the Jews. What's happened to the attackers?"

Raising baleful eyes up again Guy just shook his head. There was a sharp intake of breath from the locals.

"What? ...Nothing?" Walter gasped in disbelief,

Algar adding, "No arrests?"

"None I know of," Guy sighed. "There was some word, according to the rider who brought the news to Nottingham, that it was too hard to identify the perpetrators of the worst crimes, and that they could hardly put the whole of London on trial."

"Sweet Jesu!" Walter and Algar breathed in shock.

Hugh, Thomas and Piers just exchanged weary glances, but Will picked up on it.

"What?" the big smith demanded.

Hugh sighed. "I don't want to sound like the voice of gloom, Will, but I don't see anything getting any better under Richard's rule."

Robin was instantly on his feet. "It *will* get better," he declared vehemently. "King Richard will take the Cross. He'll make the right decisions! He *will*! He's another like King Baldwin. A proper king! Not like Prince John – and you don't have to worry about him, because King Richard will surely have sons to carry on his work. Maybe even becoming kings of Jerusalem in time!"

No-one had the heart to argue against him, but as time passed and there was no word of any trials in London, even Siward and Gilbert began to think the local men had been right.

A couple of weeks later Guy and Robin nearly came to blows over the matter, when Robin declared that King Richard would be fighting for the people of England when he went on crusade.

"I don't think the king gives a fig about 'his country' or the people," Guy responded witheringly, making Robin snap back at him,

"He fights for us all to regain Jerusalem. For us in England, for his people in France, and for those who have made their homes in the Holy Land!"

Guy shook his head. "Including the Jews? I don't think so! Wake up, Robin! He did nothing when those poor souls were massacred at his coronation – and them he needs more than us and our paltry taxes."

"He condemned the murders! The king made his displeasure known!" Robin riposted.

"And what happened? ...I mean it. What actually *happened*? ...In practice? ...Oh the king *said* he was furious, but if King Richard was really angry then we all know what should have happened then! He would've taken to arms! And please don't tell me that he was too preoccupied with preparing for the crusade. Men like him aren't the ones who run around like madmen trying to get everything together. They're the ones who make the announcement and then sit back and watch the rest of us scurrying like mice around them. It's one of the things which makes them feel powerful!

"So if he'd been *really* angry at how the Jews of London were set upon and massacred, then he could have ridden out of that big white castle by the Thames and dealt with the offenders within the day. It's not as though he had far to go, or that they had run too far already! No! King Richard sees England as the pay chest for his next glorious burst of chivalry! Look at the way he excluded all but his men from his coronation feast. Not even his mother was there!"

"There were no women there ...at all! I'm sure Queen Eleanor understood!"

"Are you?" Guy hooted with sarcastic laughter. "Good luck with telling her that if you ever see her, because I reckon she was spitting blood at that one! Shut up for years by her husband, and then when her favourite son finally gets the throne he shuts her out of the most important event of his new kingship. Her? ...Understand? I don't think so!"

Robin glowered back at Guy. "She understands chivalry! It's fundamental to the court in Aquitaine! The queen has fostered culture and the jongleurs who tell the tales of the great heroes. She's groomed Richard to be another such as them. A hero! And she knows that it's men who fight the wars. *She* knows what it takes to be a glorious king! ...She *knows*!"

Guy snorted derisively. "Heroic tales, hmmph! And 'glorious king'? What use is that to us here, eh? We can't eat glory! Will glory or tales help us when the king demands more taxes? Are they going to increase the farmers' harvest for them, so that in the name of the sheriff I can go and take more off them? In Jesu's name Robin, can you not see it? If you had ever had to look into the faces of so many starving villagers, as I have in this last two years, and tell them you need more than they had altogether you wouldn't be so sure of the right of it all."

"The king cannot take the Holy Land alone!" Robin insisted doggedly, completely missing Guy's point, although Guy wondered if the reason he was being so forceful was to convince himself in the face of his faith wavering over the rightness of even trying to retake Jerusalem. "If the saving of Jerusalem for all Christians is to be accomplished, then the part those who cannot fight must play is to pay for those who can fight."

Guy was incredulous. "And what do they get out of it? These simple farmers and townsfolk who may well starve in the process of all these righteous endeavours?"

Without so much as a blink Robin came back with, "That their actions are weighed against their sins in Heaven. Their immortal souls will reap the benefit." That still sounded a bit too well rehearsed, and Guy felt sure that he'd made another dent in Robin's convictions by the way he was falling back on what he'd no doubt been told at Templar preceptories, rather than arguing his own views.

Guy gave a choked cough of a laugh, with no humour, only disbelief. "I don't think *they* see it that way, Robin!" He recalled the utter misery on the face of a couple he'd been to only weeks ago. The two youngest children dead for want of good food, and the babe in arms sickening because his mother had so little milk. He couldn't imagine any words he could say which would make them see Robin's view of the world. The saving of them had been some of the silver pennies from Ivo's hoard, which he had willingly handed out instead of taking money off them, not fine words.

"You still haven't seen much of what it's like here these days," he said as the only way out of what was becoming a shouting match between them. "While you've been here, I've been able to be kind and generous thanks to Ivo's miserly actions. What you saw at Kinder wasn't the end, I fear, it was only the start! And unless I join Hugh and Thomas and the others in the wilds, I'm going to have to bear the brunt of it more than you ever will. And I can't do that, because what will become of Ianto and Maelgwn then?"

He had taken Robin with him on his last two visits to Gisborne, and knew his cousin had seen for himself how frail Ianto was these days. "*I* don't have the choice!" he declared angrily. "You only have *yourself* to consider, but I have responsibilities to others who I *will not* let down! I can only hope that you'll come to see reality sooner rather than later," and turned on his heels.

However, of much more pressing concern was the next news to come to High Peak in the form a rider direct from Ralph Murdac himself. The king had done as expected and announced he would be leaving on crusade with all despatch, and in the light of that he needed all the funds he could get. He therefore proclaimed it abroad that all his sheriffs would have to pay him handsomely in order to retain their offices.

Sheriff Murdac, as honest a man as any could be in that office, had no great reserves of money, and certainly not enough to pay King Richard's princely demand of two thousand marks to keep his post. That was a fortune by anyone's standards. Especially as the king charged those leaving their office an outgoing fine of a thousand marks for one of three failings, all of which were a total nonsense. Ralph Murdac was charged with nonfeasance – failure to perform his duties. King Richard could hardly charge a man like that with malfeasance (illegal acts within his duties) which was the other favoured excuse, or misfeasance (trespass), since Murdac had been in office for so long during his father's reign. As Guy insisted to the others, it was to Murdac's credit that he took the time to send a warning to them as fast as he could, or at least he had signed a message coming from Robert of Crockston to that effect.

"He didn't have to do that," Guy pointed out to the sceptical others. "He could have just left for his own manor without a second thought, and I bet Robert is running round like a mad man trying to keep things together. He and Alan of Leek are staying as constable and assistant constable, but they must be worried sick over how long they'll hold onto those posts."

For all that they had been making plans for weeks now, it still came as a blow to know that their companionable assembly would soon be broken up. All knew that they had little to fear from the folk of Castleton and Hope. Guy had been true to his word and had looked into all of the tax returns at Easter, and with Tuck acting as his scribe to make it look all above board, he had set down what each family should pay – not the old records of what Sir Ivo had thought he could extort! When the others had helped Guy distribute more of the hidden hoard after that, many of the villages round about could scarcely believe their good fortune. They could send the mined lead and harvested crops off to market this year as always, but for once it didn't matter what it all fetched, for all of it could go in taxes this time and they would still have money to buy new tools, and seeds, above and beyond putting food on the table and clothes on their backs. Folk who had been weak and sickening in their poverty rallied and grew well again in the sunshine and warmth. The summer of 1189 was one of great bounty in the eastern dales of Derbyshire!

There was therefore no danger that anyone beyond the castle walls would say a word about whom Sir Guy had had living up at the castle with him. Especially since, during the drier spells, he had provided additional employment for some of the local men in putting High Peak to rights by repairing the stonework and mortar, and some of the woodwork too, and had paid well for the work done – some out of funds the sheriff had already granted, and the rest topped up from their hidden reserve.

The people who were in a potentially more compromised position were the twelve men of the permanent garrison. In all of the chaos of the change of king, there had been a blessed halt in knights and men coming to do service during the summer, as noblemen negotiated which sons would go on crusade and which would stay, and on the odd occasion when someone had turned up unexpectedly they'd been got rid of swiftly but without comment. However, these twelve would now be under the same roof as whoever the king appointed, and there would be a real danger of someone letting something slip when they were tired, albeit never intentionally. Guy, Hugh and Thomas therefore had a long talk with them and persuaded them that the best thing would be for them to return to Nottingham with Guy and leave the castle to a wholly new garrison. Much would depend on their new lord and master, of course, but what clinched it for them was Marianne's observation that they surely didn't want to stay and be tarred by a new lord with the same brush of corruption as Sir Ivo, given that they'd served under him too.

Marianne herself was another problem which was proving harder for Guy to find a solution to than he would ever have believed. It took most of the summer to drag the information out of everyone in dribs and drabs, and then several discussions with Tuck to check whether he had the right of it, but finally he thought he understood the Templars – or rather Robin's – antipathy to having Marianne go with them to wherever they could find a new home, for it certainly wasn't that most of them disliked her personally. The Templars as an order followed the monastic rule set down earlier in the century by the great Abbot Bernard of Clairvaux, with all of its austerity and reforming zeal, and that meant a very definite prohibition on having women anywhere around them! Robin in particular was quite vehement on the matter, and Guy did wonder whether he was trying to be the proper knight he'd so wanted to be, yet because of fate not misconduct had not officially had the chance to become.

Guy had by now seen enough of the White Monks himself, to know that they were a very different kettle of fish to the Black Monks, to whom Tuck belonged. The White Monks, with their reformed Cistercian rule of Saint Bernard, looked upon the much older order of Black Monks as decadent, and as having fallen very far from the rules set down long ago by Saint Benedict. However, the Hospitallers joined the Black Canons in following yet another form of monastic rule as set down by Saint Augustine. And if the Black Canons placed greater emphasis on moderation in the practicalities of life, they also felt that the Black Monks of Saint Benedict were somewhat decadent. Yet they also thought the White Monks too zealous and austere to a fault.

Where the more moderate rule of Saint Augustine made a difference to the Hospitallers, was in the degree to which women were allowed to interact with the brothers. Consequently, while there were no women associated with the Templars in any way, shape or form, the Hospitallers had happily had many sisters working with them in the great hospital in the East. And elsewhere, whole preceptories of sisters, in particular beyond the Pyrenean Mountains in Castile and Aragon, but also here in England. A handful of sisters lived in each of the separate cells attached to male preceptories, or had until Henry's move had swept them all together.

"Bloody old lecher!" had been Marianne's verdict when she'd told the others of what she'd really been doing. "He's got more mistresses that he knows what to do with! Yet he can't resist interfering with women who are trying to do some real good!"

She really had gone to Glastonbury after leaving Buckland, and had spent the best part of the year there. However, as one of the greatest and richest of the Black Monks' abbeys in England, the Glastonbury monks had not wanted a woman wandering around the place, even if she was behaving in accordance with Saint Augustine's rule, was staying around the hospital not the cloisters, and was skilled with the sick.

"Honestly," Marianne fumed, "you'd think I was planning on seducing the lot of them! I was shut out of the monastic enclosure every night! I managed to find a place to stay with a kindly farmer, but in the end I could see that they were never going to let me have any real position in the hospital, even though they were struggling like mad to cope with the increasing number of pilgrims coming in."

"Did you argue with the abbot?" Guy asked with an amused quirk of the eyebrow.

Marianne did her best to look surprised but couldn't pull it off as the others laughed, everyone having swiftly realised that diplomacy was not Marianne's forte. Of course Marianne had argued with someone in charge, but it turned out to have been the prior, yet the upshot was as Guy had guessed, and she had been thrown out with instructions not to come back. Since then, it transpired, she had been drifting from monastic guest house to monastic guesthouse, each time offering help with the sick and needy, but ultimately realising that she was outstaying her welcome. And therein lay the problem. Marianne just wasn't cut out for the contemplative life of a nun, and the atmosphere of a religious house absolutely stifled her. Even the nunneries of the Black Canons were too enclosed for her free spirit.

Therefore at first, Guy had rather hoped that she would stay with John in the cottage he still had up towards Edale, and which they had kept going by taking turns looking after the sheep, just in case of emergencies. After the encounter when John had backed down in front of Robin, Guy had belatedly realised that John would probably have been much happier settling down with a wife and a family, for he was certainly no natural leader or rebel. The outlaw life would be harder on him mentally more than physically, for John could cope with living outdoors better than many of the others. It made Guy feel very guilty that John had carried the burden of Allan for so long, meaning that he'd had little chance to find a girl he could create his own family with, and for once Robin joined him in that guilt when he was told the full story. Both wished there had been another way for the cousins to stay together right from the start.

For once Guy therefore had an ally other than Tuck in trying to persuade John to look to his own happiness. He half hoped that if he left John and Marianne together that she might turn out to be the woman John had been waiting for. Sadly, it became apparent as the summer moved along that fiery Marianne was never going to attract John, or he her, and with that the question arose again as to where Marianne should go.

For the six former Templars, Guy and Tuck hoped there was still the possibility of them going to a preceptory rather than taking to the forest, not least because even months on from their return, Robin, Siward and James were still not sleeping properly, and Gilbert was also prone to nights of terrible dreams, even if they weren't as frequent as those which afflicted the other three when they could get rest. Tuck and Marianne agreed that it might take years before those four gained any sort of lasting peace, and along with Guy felt it might be better if they were somewhere where they could be taken proper care of if they fell into a state of malaise again. The thought of Will being confined to a strict rule, however, worried everyone, and Hugh and Thomas had already said that they would be more than happy for Will to come with them when the time came for a move to be made. And if all else failed then Marianne would have to come with them too, although the worldly Thomas and Hugh joined Guy in worrying what the reality of having one woman with so many men would turn out to be like. At that point having Robin not involved with her seemed best for everyone concerned!

Yet what defeated them most in making their plans was not knowing what decisions King Richard might make. Would he empty the Templar granges to take them with him on crusade? Would he scour the land for such soldiers? If so then all of the six would be in greater danger back inside the order, and a preceptory no place of safety at all. Therefore, with the weather closing in for winter again, and no-one wanting to go out and start living in the forest until they absolutely had to, they stayed put. While Guy still had nominal control of High Peak they would build their reserves and keep planning as news came to them.

Consequently, they were still there come Christmas and living on their nerves, and so Guy broke all the forest rules by declaring that they would hunt enough meat to have a damned good feast this year, if never again. In near festive mood they all rode out to bring down a couple of deer, and succeeded in bringing down a big old stag trailing a herd led by a younger one who had clearly replaced him. Guy had then surprised all of them except Tuck by picking up wild boar tracks, and then using Fletch and Spike to drive the beast towards him before bringing it down with a spear by himself. That had shocked Robin in particular, for when he, John and Guy had left home they had still been regarded as too young to go looking for wild boar, and anyway, in the tamer fields by the Trent there had been almost none around. Consequently they had never seen a big brute of a boar such as came thundering out of the oaks and bracken that day up in the Peaks, and the way Guy had come alongside it and then thrust the spear down to make a clean kill, despite the boar's tough hide, had earned him great respect.

As the huge carcass of the boar was then turning on the spit in the hall, and with everyone in jovial mood, Bilan finally summoned up the courage to ask the six Templars,

"What *did* happen to you in the Holy Land, then? At the end? You've never really told us."

"Aye," Walter agreed, "you said that King Baldwin's heir was only a lad who didn't last the year, and that Sybilla seized power with Lusignan, but not much more. How did you get to be at the great siege and then that battle at ...where was it? ...The Horns of somewhere?"

"And how *did* you get home?" John wanted to know. "It's a long way. You've only spoken of France, but by then you were almost here. What happened before then?"

Siward and James immediately looked glum, and Robin was about to protest the rawness of the wounds yet again – as they'd always done when asked before – when Malik spoke.

"We have to tell them sometime," he said patiently. "You cannot expect them to understand if you never tell them. See? Walter has the battle in the wrong place." He turned to Walter and Algar who were sitting side by side on a bench at right-angles to where he himself sat, with Hugh and Thomas between him and them as part of a rough circle. "The battle at the Horns of Hattin came *before* the siege of Jerusalem. ...Where did we get to in the telling?"

"King Baldwin's death," John prompted him.

"Ah yes. ...We had a whole year of peace after King Baldwin died and while his nephew lived."

"The writ of his will had cut the claws of Châtillon and Lusignan," Gilbert added, clearly bracing himself, but now as determined as Malik to explain to their friends, realising that this lay like an invisible barrier between them still. "Saladin was struggling with some rebels of his own for once, so that got him off our backs for a while, but then when little Baldwin V died, in under a year everything got thrown up in the air again. His mother Sybilla's uncle – and so uncle of our King Baldwin too – seized power behind Count Raymond of Tripoli's back, and proclaimed Sybilla queen now that there was no need for a regent – which is what Count Raymond had been."

"The only one with the balls to oppose them was the Hospitaller master, Roger de les Moulins," Will added, explaining at least his lack of anitpathy to the other order. "Our bloody leader, de Ridfort, and that twisted bastard of a Patriarch, had to deceive and twist him to get his key for the coronation regalia chest! Master Moulins said he wouldn't break his sacred oath to King Baldwin and he didn't, even though they went around him. I think we all wished we'd been in Moulins' service then. He, at least, was a man of honour you could respect!"

Robin agreed. "He was. Whereas our master's main motive was to get back at Count Raymond, who years before had denied him the chance of marrying a rich heiress. The selfish bastard was so sure of his position, now that Lusignan's wife was in control, that he yelled it out at the coronation! Confessed his vengeance right there in the church porch for God and all to hear."

"How wonderfully Christian!" John commented wryly. "The more I hear, the more I can imagine the Almighty being thoroughly disgusted with the lot of them! I know I would be!"

"At least Balian of Ibelin was one more of the few honourable men left," Robin said in defence of another man whom he clearly had admired. "His brother, Baldwin of Ibelin, quit the kingdom for good in '86 when Sybilla was crowned. That Baldwin went to Antioch and so we lost an even finer knight than Balian. But thank God my lord Balian of Ibelin stayed! When the peace was broken at the end of '86 I hardly need to tell you who it was..."

"Châtillon?" Thomas said before anyone else, although that name was on everyone's lips. They'd all heard him cursed so often by now that it didn't take much guessing.

Now Siward picked up the story. "That was when it got really messy. Châtillon attacked yet another caravan of innocent pilgrims! Well, Count Raymond did his best to try and renegotiate a truce with Saladin, but only managed to get it for his own county of Tripoli. Lusignan had the cheek to call him a traitor! If it hadn't been for Balian of Ibelin making Lusignan and de Ridefort – our new Templar leader – see sense, God knows what might have happened. The fools were actually talking about acting against Count Raymond, and I don't think there was a man amongst us who was happy about the thought of fighting against others of our own. Men we'd fought alongside only weeks before!"

Gilbert nodded. "Count Raymond then had to let Saladin's nephew cross his lands with an army as part of the peace agreement, but he also sent word that it was happening to King Guy, as we now had to call that pompous arsehole de Lusignan! Our 'king' had already got as far as Galilee, and so he loitered and sent Balian of Ibelin on to negotiate with Count Raymond, along with the two grand masters. So they and their knights were well ahead of the royal army.

"For some reason, though, Ibelin wasn't still with the two masters when the news came of the army coming towards them – we think he might have been the one sent on by them to do the actual talking to Count Raymond, and so was even further ahead. That meant that although there was still a kind of peace, without the restraining hand of Ibelin the two warmongers chose to pick a fight with Saladin's nephew and his army."

Robin agreed with Gilbert's sniff of disgust at the confusion. "Bloody de Ridfort must have been fairly champing at the bit at the thought of our order going up against some of Saladin's men! Again, according to a sergeant we spoke to later, Master Moulins of the Hospitallers warned them that a confrontation would break the truce and they would be breaking their oaths. He might as well have been talking to the desert sands for all the good it did!

"De Ridefort thought it was a God-sent opportunity – literally!" Robin shivered. "What a day! There weren't that many of our lesser ranks there – and thank God none of us were amongst them! By the time de Ridefort had called upon our Marshal of the Temple, whose castle wasn't far away, there was a grand total of about a hundred Templar knights, plus a few Hospitallers and some local ones."

"A *hundred?*" Bilan, who'd been on the edge of his seat with excitement at these tales of far off places, was stunned. "I thought there were *thousands* of you?"

Will shook his head. "Not of Templar *knights*. Oh we could summon a *mixed* army of thousands when we had the infantry made up of mercenaries, turcopoles and anyone we could pull from the towns. But not knights. They were only ever numbered in hundreds. What Robin's talking about now was a fight which was really made up of mostly the Templar elite, because apart from the knights there were only about three hundred mounted sergeants. Men like Gilbert and me. And against them were seven *thousand* under Saladin's nephew!"

"Seven thousand?" Thomas gasped. "Sweet Jesu! More than ten to one? You couldn't have fought that many successfully with a few companies of good Welsh archers to even the score for you!"

"But de Ridefort did," Robin told them sadly. "We lost our Marshal, James de Mailly that day, and apparently that damned de Ridfort had had the effrontery to accuse him beforehand of being too much the coward to fight! How dare he! De Mailly was as good a leader as you could hope to find anywhere, and a good Christian too."

"Built like a big, blonde Roman gladiator, like in the tales, he was," Will reflected. "But even he couldn't countermand an order from the master, and so he died with all the rest."

"They went ahead and fought?" Piers asked in astonishment.

"Near Nazareth. Apparently against the advice of both de Mailly and Master Moulins," Gilbert confirmed, "but yes, they went into battle, and both those good men died and yet de Ridefort lived. The only one of those three who made it out of there alive! He had the luck of the Devil!"

"And the Devil looks after his own!" Will added bitterly. "We had a few in his service, I reckon. It wasn't the Muslims and Saladin who really did for those two good men, and so many besides. It was those demon-spawn de Ridefort and Lusignan! They just fed all those poor souls into the hands of our enemies without so much as a backwards glance. I'd believe anything of them!"

Guy looked around him to those who had never been outside of England, and then back at the six. It was no wonder they were so scarred! The odd skirmish he'd experienced with the Welsh still wouldn't have prepared him for a battle with those sort of odds. And he could see that even Hugh and Thomas, who'd fought in bigger battles in Normandy, were nonetheless shaking their heads in dismay at the thought. No wonder Siward, James and Robin had trouble sleeping. It was all the more remarkable that Malik and Will didn't!

"We heard afterwards," Robin continued, "that Count Raymond saw the Muslim army go past his castle, but thought nothing of it since it was what the truce allowed for. It was only when he saw them going back, with the heads of the Templars, and the few Hospitaller and local knights, impaled on their spears, that he realised something had gone badly wrong. After that, although the massacre of the Templars was all de Ridefort's fault not the Saracens', Count Raymond and Balian of Ibelin courageously went out with their men to join forces with King Guy. What else could they do? All the money which came from England was spent in preparations for war then."

"So glad our hard earned taxes were put to good use," Walter muttered darkly."

"Bloody Jerusalem Tithe!" Algar agreed. "Should never have sent it! And can we expect the Saladin Tithe to do any more good?"

Guy winced, waiting for someone to take offence – this was something very personal to these six, after all – but Gilbert surprisingly agreed with them.

"Yes it might have been better if the money hadn't been there. Without it, King Guy could never have assembled all the fighting men he had left, and the battle at the Horns of Hattin couldn't have happened."

However, Robin didn't fully agree. "I think they would have fought regardless of what support they had. By Saint Lazarus, they'd had no need to fight before with so few, what makes you think they wouldn't have fought again against even more impossible numbers? But by then I can't believe that Lusignan and de Ridefort were actually sane anymore. Mad or possessed, it made little difference in the end! ...Well this was when we marched out. Oh we'd seen action in many skirmishes by then, but what came next was like nothing we could ever have anticipated. We mustered at a place called Sephorie which is near Nazareth, on the road from Acre to the Sea of Galilee.

"Saladin must have known we were coming because he launched an attack on the town of Tiberius now that Count Raymond had been forced to side with King Guy. Count Raymond's wife was trapped in the castle after the town fell, and, brave lady that she is, she took charge in her husband's absence. Yet despite that, it was Count Raymond himself who pointed out that in the July heat, Saladin would have to fall back sooner or later for want of water. He advocated waiting, even though his own home was being besieged, and then for us attacking when they gave up – when they were retreating weak and worn down with thirst. We could wait within our fortresses where we had wells and grazing, he said. At places like Ibelin's castle of La Feve, and come out fresh to meet them. That would redress the balance their numbers gave them, he told them – according to James, here."

James nodded. "He did. He said that. I was there. They should have listened to the count!" That made Guy think. Why had James been with Count Raymond and not with Robin and the Templars, if Robin hadn't been there to hear it for himself? Damn it, it was always like this when you tried to get something out of them about the Holy Land. It inevitably raised more questions. If the answer didn't come out he'd have to ask, but for the moment he didn't want to stop Robin.

"Instead we marched! God Almighty, the heat! We set out from Sephorie heading for a known spring at Turan, which would have been about a third of the way to Count Raymond's Tiberius, but we struggled to even get that far. It was just too hot to march fast. And Saladin had stolen a march on us! He was already at Hattin, right in our path and in the village with plenty of water and shade. And his men were harrying our flanks even as we staggered on under that infernal sun. At the time we cursed the fact that we were in the rear, for there were so few Templars left by now that we were put with Balian of Ibelin along with other remnants of forces. Instead, Raymond of Tripoli was in the van, and Lusignan and his knights in the centre."

"How many of you were there this time?" Bilan asked breathlessly.

Will exhaled heavily. "Oh, about twelve hundred knights in total, but with the rest of us we must have come close to twenty thousand, because this time it wasn't just the orders fighting. The king had pulled every man he could get out in the field for this one."

Bilan grinned broadly, this was more like what he'd expected, but Will saw his expression and shook his head sadly.

"No, didn't do us any good, Bilan. Saladin had easily half as many again, and twelve thousand of that must have been cavalry. Not that we were sitting there counting them! We learned the true extent of his numbers later on from bits and pieces of information we got while we were retreating and then back at Jerusalem. All we thought when we saw them back then was, 'fucking hell, how many?' 'Cause they were like bleedin' flocks of rooks all around us, just waiting to start pecking at our bones – except they weren't all in black, of course."

"And the cursed vultures knew too!" Malik added, joining in for the first time. "They can smell a battle from miles off. All day we kept gaining more of those damned birds circling above us! They just sat there, riding the hot air, looking down on us and waiting for us to die."

"We got to the rise above Hattin by the afternoon," Robin continued. "Being in the rear, our lot had suffered most from Saladin's skirmishers. We had to keep all our armour on because they'd ride in, loose arrows at us, and then gallop off on their local small horses. Meanwhile we'd been told we couldn't break ranks even to defend ourselves, so we sweated in the heat. Men like us had been walking from the start, but by then even many of the knights had to dismount and go on foot as the horses began to give up too.

"By the end of the day we just couldn't go any farther. Some wanted to fight Saladin for Hattin there and then, but most men were incapable of putting one foot in front of the other. Some of our men broke out that night and went in search of water. We never saw them again. The Saracens had men all around us and they must have been killed."

"And we didn't get any sleep either," James' soft voice startled the listeners by coming in unexpectedly. "He knew we were weak, Saladin did, so he decided to deprive us even of our sleep. All night! All night they banged drums, or wailed in prayers or their singing. All night!" He had his eyes fixed on some distant point and in his mind was back in the east. "And if that wasn't enough, they set fire to the brush so that we choked on smoke too."

"So we woke up to find ourselves surrounded," Gilbert continued, dropping a hand onto James' shoulder and giving him a little shake to bring him back into the present. "We could see the waters of the Sea of Galilee when dawn came. It drove some men mad! They ran forward despite all of the Saracens in the way. Most of us, though, closed ranks and stayed up on the Horns of Hattin. Up on the high ground. It wasn't much of a hope, but it was the only one we had."

"Count Raymond led the first charge up in the front," Robin picked up the relay. "Saladin let him and his immediate knights through, then slaughtered the rest. Maybe he thought Raymond more honourable than the others, I don't know, but then Saladin was like that. He would respect a man who showed some decency, and Raymond had always been one of the voices of reason.

"Lord help me, I shall never forget what I saw that day, though. We made charge after charge out of our ranks to try and break through. In a battle like that you soon forget who you're supposed to be with. You just close ranks with anyone who's left standing! That's how we all got together. Will and I were with the Templars. Malik was a turcopole with the king's men, and Gilbert a sergeant in the same army. James was a turcopole with Balian of Ibelin, and Siward had become a squire to one of Ibelin's knights after his lord died out there on pilgrimage."

Guy was shocked to register that these six had therefore not even all been Templars, yet he glanced about him and saw that the others were too caught up in the story to have picked that up. At first he'd thought that they'd just got together over the months and years of being out there, but then he'd recalled Will had said their friendship was relatively new back when they'd first come here. Yet somehow Guy had still thought that they'd all been Templars *somewhere* out there, even if not together. This changed everything, not least the prospect of finding them all homes at a preceptory in the coming year!

"James was the one who kept us by his lord – by Lord Balian," Robin was saying with clear gratitude. "He said Lord Balian would find a way out, and he did. Without him I doubt we should be here to tell the tale. At the last we managed to break out with Lord Balian's force and the men of Reynald of Sidon. There was no chance to go back to try and break any more men out. ...So few of us, so few!"

He sighed. "And the True Cross was right in the heart of our force, by the king. I hear the bishop of Acre died defending it. Serve him right for his arrogance in thinking he could decide what God wanted! ...And would you believe it? Reynauld de Châtillon was still alive! He and King Guy were taken prisoner. We heard later that the few ordinary Templar and Hospitaller knights surviving had their heads taken off by some Egyptian priests. No ransom for them!" He looked sick and said shakily, "We heard sometimes it took seven or eight strokes to get the heads off..."

"Mind you, I'd shake Saladin's hand for lopping off the head of Reynauld de Châtillon – mad, bloodthirsty bastard!" Will interrupted darkly and got nods of agreement.

"Saladin did that with his own hand," Robin admitted approvingly.

"A pity he didn't get the chance years earlier!" John said, sympathetic to their feelings.

"Yes, a great pity," Gilbert agreed. "And pity the poor bastards from the infantry. They got marched off to slave markets all over Saladin's territory. Few of them will ever go back to their homes. That we're here is something to be *very* grateful for."

Tuck was shaking his head in disbelief. "We heard of the news of the losing of the True Cross. That reached here quite quickly. But we had no idea that so many men had died! The word was that it had been a great defeat, but even great defeats don't normally lose that many men! What a terrible, terrible thing to happen. All those lost souls!" And yet the way he looked around him made Guy think that it wasn't just the dead whose souls Tuck was trouble by, but those who had to live with the memory too.

Nor was Robin as easily cheered as Gilbert. "It took Saladin just three days after Hattin to reach Acre and for it to surrender. What else could those left in the city do? There weren't enough of them left to withstand a siege. Most of the soldiers had come with us and perished at Hattin. There wasn't a single garrison left in the Holy Land with a full compliment of men. Even our impregnable Templar fortress of Gaza surrendered with not a blow struck.

"Would you believe that bastard Master de Ridefort actually managed to survive Hattin somehow, too? He was the one who surrendered Gaza to Saladin on the condition that he be allowed to go free. He ruined what was left of our good Templar name that day! The only castles not to fall that I know of were Montreal, Kerak and Belvoir, and that was largely because they were more distant and off Saladin's marching route. Most of the survivors from Hattin went to Tyre with Ibelin, but our little band had been trailing in the rear because we were all wounded in some way.

"We fell farther and farther behind. It wasn't anyone's fault. Those with the main army were just about dragging themselves along, let alone the wounded. We hid when we heard Saladin's army coming up behind us on the way to Acre. Those valleys are wooded, you know. Not like our English woods, by any means. Nothing like so thick and dense. But there are cyprus trees, and whole woods of pistachio and almond trees there, and we managed to hide amongst a couple of trees which had fallen down the previous winter. We were already the colour of the soil by now from the dust, so we hunched down between the dead wood, pulled our cloaks over our heads and prayed for all we were worth!

"After they'd passed, and we knew they were between us and the main force, it seemed that all we could do now was make for Jerusalem. There was no way we were going to catch up with Ibelin's troops let alone get to Acre. In the end we got to Jerusalem later on in July – we'd fought at Hattin on the fourth, it turned out. The worst thing was that we could hardly ask the ordinary citizens to let any of us soldiers lead them in the defence of their city, because the hatred towards any Templar by now was substantial to say the least – especially when news of de Ridefort's surrender of Gaza arrived. Well you couldn't blame them, could you? They must have thought the moment Saladin turned up, we'd open the gates and let him in!

"Thank God Balian of Ibelin arrived. His wife, the dowager queen Maria, was still in the city, as was his young nephew and other members of the Ibelin family. So Saladin had allowed Lord Balian to come to Jerusalem to fetch them to be taken to the safety of Tyre, which by some miracle still held out against the Saracens. But when he arrived the people of Jerusalem wouldn't let him leave. It says a lot for Ibelin's character and standing that Saladin understood why he felt compelled to stay."

He rubbed a hand across his eyes. "It was like watching a house of sand fall into dust after that. In Jerusalem the only news we got was of the ports falling to Saladin. The great coastal castles held out, but they were so far away. We had no chance of reaching them, and even they succumbed in the end. Then we were besieged in the September."

Robin's expression became pained again. "Saladin's army arrived on the twentieth. Thousands and thousands of them! They made a great semicircle around the north of the city. They'd completely cut off every gate from David's Gate for the road to Jaffa, going round past the Gate of St Stephen and the Gate of Flowers to the Gate of Jehosaphat. The only two gates you might have got out of were the Sion Gate and the gate of Siloam, and even then you wouldn't have got far before being cut down by riders. We were well and truly stuck!

"We had the Patriarch with us – much use he was! But what we desperately needed was a leader and we got it in the form of Lord Balian. We had refugees from all manner of places, fifty women to every man, and the grand total of two knights! Even in the Templar and Hospitaller precincts we only had a few squires like me, some sergeants and a lot of servants who'd never had to fight before – well there weren't any of the knights left by now in that part of Outremer! What kind of army was that to hold the most holy city with?

"They brought up their ballisters and bombarded us. There were fires within the city and the piles of dead mounting. And the only advantage we had was that we had water in our wells! It was then that my lord of Ibelin made a controversial decision. He knighted sixty of us. Men who could fight, yes. But of such noble birth as knights are normally made of? No. Just squires, sergeants, turcopoles, and some freemen of the city who could just about wield a sword in anger. That's why we call him our lord. We owe him so much!

"I take, ...we all take, ...great pride in the fact that we held Saladin off for a whole week. We burned the bodies of the dead each night, and by day we fought with whatever missiles we could load into our own ballisters. We fought with bows and arrows, even though we weren't archers of the calibre of Thomas and Piers here. And we fought hand to hand with those who tried to breach our wall, and tried to take our gates. The dust and smoke choked us, the sun cooked us, and we died like flies, but no-one gave up."

"Then you truly deserved your honour," Guy said warmly, in an effort to lift Robin's bleak mood. "Better to be raised up like that than like some of the useless pups who gain honour prancing about in tournaments, as I've seen here!"

"Absolutely!" Hugh agreed heartily. "I know I'd have felt very differently about fighting if I'd had someone leading me who'd actually done some real fighting. The idiot knight whom I had to serve under in Normandy was just the younger son of a vassal of King Henry's. When the fighting started he had to get soused in wine just to face them. It was a miracle he ever managed to stay on his horse! You've all earned your knighthoods the hard way."

The six managed to summons smiles at their friends pride in them, making Robin say,

"Maybe we should have told you this much earlier on."

"Then you could have been calling me *Sir* Will!" Will joked, earning him an apple thrown at him by Thomas which he caught deftly and began eating.

It broke the tension and Robin's voice was somewhat less strained as he continued. "By the time a week had gone by, Saladin had begun to mine his way in on the walls facing the Mount of Olives. By the twenty-ninth, there was a huge breach in the wall and precious few of us to hold back the tide. The next day my lord of Ibelin did the only thing he could do, he went to Saladin to discuss the surrender. We'd fought for a whole day trying to stem the unending tide of enemies pouring through that hole. It couldn't be done.

"So many gave their lives and does anyone remember their names? No, because they were, to most eyes, only servants or workers. No great knights died on the walls of Jerusalem in those dark days. No chronicler wrote it all down for kings and courts to preen themselves over in pride at what their families had done. But poor women mourned the loss of husbands, brothers and sons, and many of them had lost so many men from their families already." He grimaced. "It's a small miracle that all six of us survived. We were certainly in the thick of the fighting and have the scars to prove it," and he subconsciously massaged his forearm where one of the worst of his physical wounds lay.

You wonder why we need the details of the defeat at Hattin and the siege of Jerusalem when they are known events, Brother? Why I am so intent on speaking of the scars those places left on all of the six? Because I feel, in my age now, looking back, that it was the terrible shock of those events which turned my affable cousin into the man, tempered like Damascus steel, who became hero of legend. And also because it was becoming increasingly clear to me that for the man Baldwin had become – this stranger called Robin – the world had separated out into good and bad. Into black or white. Into the bleakest winter, or the balmiest summer of glorious days and nights of gentle showers. Spring and autumn, or shades of grey, were things he no longer saw.

You were either with Robin or against him, and that you will agree is very much the Robin Hood of legend. Having had his eyes opened to the misery of the ordinary people of England, in his eyes it would soon be

the case that <u>no</u> sheriff could ever be good. And all of that started, I do solemnly believe, in the life-changing experience of living through those two horrendous defeats in the Holy Land. Ask yourself, Brother, who could <u>not</u> be affect by such sights? By such events?

I, on the other hand, could all too easily see someone else's point of view, and that was both my strength and my weakness. I confess to you, Brother, that sometimes, in retrospect, I can see that I gave some people too many chances. That I seemed, in others' eyes, to lack conviction because I would not commit myself wholly to one side or the other – such is the fate of men like me! Yet because I could understand the workings of the minds of the men who would become our sheriffs over the years, I often saw consequences or openings which others did not, and in that respect I aided my cousin in ways no-one else could.

I may be the infamous Guy of Gisborne, and yet I am not fully the villain of the story any more than I am the hero. Ah you begin to see it now, do you not? That things were not so altogether simple as you once supposed! And it is so easy to sit in judgement when you have only a portion of the facts, rather than when you know the full story with all its complexities. Robin Hood the legend begins in the fires of Jerusalem, but we must return to those fires now, Gervase, because you – like I and the others – have forgotten that it closely affected someone else who will be part of this greater story.

Chapter 19

Yes, Gervase, we must linger just a short while longer on the matters in the East, for they were vital to the forging of Robin Hood's band of outlaws, and if you know this then you will understand much of why they were so very loyal to one another – not just to Robin. Oh yes, it is most important for you to appreciate that the bonds were not just those of a bunch of lesser men to their sworn liege. Many a man has sworn to do his duty to his lord, while caring little for the well-being of that person. A soldier may fight, and fight well, without giving a damn for the man who gives the orders! But what welds a band together, as a smith does the rods of steel into a damascened blade, is shared experiences. The knowing that, come what may, the man beside you will always watch your back for you, and you his. That, dear Brother, was what made Robin Hood's band special, and this was how the first beating of that most magical of blades was done!

High Peak Castle, Derbyshire,
Winter, the year of Our Lord 1189

Somewhere in the background a servant added more logs to the fire in the hall at High Peak, but those grouped around the six returned crusaders at the far end of the hall took little notice as Robin continued.

"Thank God for my lord Ibelin then! He still had a reputation as a good man with Saladin and they negotiated an honourable surrender. I don't think there was anyone in the Holy City who wasn't scared witless of what would happen to us during those days. Saladin had little reason to be merciful. When the crusaders took Jerusalem from the Saracens the previous time it had been besieged, the horrors that were committed against the local people were indescribable! So we all feared, I can tell you, that he would feel justified in doing the same back to us, even though not one of us within those walls had been amongst the devils who'd harmed his folk.

"Yet Lord Balian managed to negotiate a bulk ransom for all the Christians in Jerusalem – thirty thousand dinars for seven thousand people to be freed. Not very dignified by some folk's reckoning, I'm sure, to be haggled over as less than camels in a market, but we opened the gates on the second of October and walked out with our lives if not much else. That's better than the poor bastards who are currently trapped in Acre have got a chance of!"

Now Robin's tone became bitter. "That old goat the Patriarch paid his dinars to Saladin and then went out with a cart-load of gold which would have freed many thousands more! Saladin was more merciful to us then than our own! First his nephew was moved by the long column of people who had nothing and were going into slavery, acquired a thousand of them from his uncle as his reward for his services, and then promptly set them free! There was *genuine* kindness and charity! But not from *our* Church! Only then did the Patriarch dip into his funds and purchase seven hundred more, but another five hundred were *given* to Balian – which I think says everything about how Saladin saw the difference between the two men. Our great enemy himself freed all the aged amongst the poor, and made provision for the widows. You can't hate a man like that – or at least I can't." Even unimaginative men like Walter and Algar were nodding their agreement at that statement.

"He held true to his word to leave us in peace, and we all made our slow march across to the coast to leave the Holy Land for good. We got to Tyre escorting my lord's wife, the dowager Queen Maria – whose presence must've been a part of why Saladin was so gracious. We had to go into Tyre with Lord Balian. They were only admitting fighting men, stretched to bursting as they were, but by Saint Lazarus they wanted us in there, and you could understand why. Count Conrad of Montferrat had come and secured Tyre ahead of us, but although it's almost surrounded by sea, we were still in danger of Saladin's ships cutting us off from the supplies our own ships brought in. And, sweet Jesu, did we need supplies with so many crammed into the city!

"Montferrat had sent word, upon our arrival, back to the pope with the bishop of Tyre. The leaders of the two orders at Tyre – de Ridfort had weaselled his way to freedom, God curse him! – also sent pleas westwards for more men and more funds, and all the time we sat there holding our breath and licking our wounds. Then in November, Saladin appeared outside the city. Thanks to Montferrat's courage and tenacity, Saladin realised it could take all of the winter before he even got close to bringing Tyre to the point of surrender, and decided not to attack, just keep us holed up there."

"And of course Pope Urban had already died of the shock of hearing of the loss of the True Cross," Tuck added thoughtfully. "And then his successor died within two months! *Duw*! If He wanted to gain our attention over what had gone wrong in the Holy Land He could hardly have shouted any harder! Not that it helped you folk still stuck over there, of course. But it's no wonder you failed to hear much word in return, looking back on the events."

"No, the call for a crusade was all too slow in coming from our point of view," Gilbert agreed. "Malik was barely hanging on to life from his wounds at that point, while Robin had taken a blow to the head and kept seeing double off and on, and like the rest of us, was cut to ribbons in different places. We were all incapable of raising so much as a finger to fight! So our saving grace at that time was that men like de Ridfort had so few of their own there, they couldn't dislodge Conrad of Montferrat as leader within the city, and the ordinary people thought him a hero and wouldn't have stood for it anyway. When King Guy was ransomed – Christ knows by which misguided idiot! – even he couldn't shake Montferrat out of ruling Tyre, and for once we had a bit of sanity about the place."

"We left as escorts to one of the messages going to Cyprus," Will continued. "We weren't in a fit state to do much else, and all we were doing was eating food and taking up room. So they shipped us out."

Robin nodded. "Two nights before we left, my lord of Ibelin called me to him and asked me to take Malik and James with me back to England, or at least as far as a major preceptory in France. We were all so sunburnt by then it wasn't so obvious that they would be seen as different, and anyway, Balian of Ibelin had been born in the East. He had no idea of what England's really like. Malik's safety was something he cared very much about, though."

"Why you in particular?" John asked Malik curiously, feeling by now that he could ask such a blunt question of someone he'd come to regard as a friend.

"I am his half-brother," Malik said simply. "The old lord of Ibelin's son by a local woman. She died when I was small and I was raised among the servants in his household. Baldwin and Balian used to practice at being knights, and I was always fascinated by the moves. They couldn't keep me from trailing round after them! Balian and I were always close even though I'm a lot younger than him. He kept me with him wherever he went when we were both older. He was so glad to see me when he got to Jerusalem and found that I had not died on the way back from Hattin, as he had feared."

"But he knew he could only protect so many of his family," Robin added. "I suspect that he foresaw a very bloody time ahead. He said he feared too many knew who Malik was, and that in the event of the whole crusader state falling, that he'd be marked out for retribution. My lord of Ibelin was a realist, and I think he could see that while that madman Lusignan was still king, things would only get worse. If he could, he wanted to find a way to save at least some of the men like Malik and James."

"God knows why he bloody chose us, though!" Will muttered wryly. "Not that Malik isn't our mate," he added hurriedly, "and James too, but we were hardly in good shape ourselves, and there must've been others of higher rank Ibelin would've known and could've asked."

However Robin was looking straight into Guy's eyes. He didn't need to say any more. Guy suddenly knew why the old lord from Jerusalem had chosen Robin. He'd clearly known of Robin's past, at least as far as his kindness to the dying king, but maybe with some enquiries he'd known just as Guy did, of those memories of John and Allan. Had Lord Ibelin maybe even known that Robin still carried the emotional scars of the betrayal of his two cousins for the circumstances of their birth? If so, then of any man, Robin would be the one to watch out for an illegitimate brother.

Guy's face slowly dissolved into an affectionate smile. "Of course he chose you! Why wouldn't he?"

As Robin's face relaxed and began to smile back, Malik quirked an eyebrow at Will in question, who responded more bluntly,

"What? Well aren't you going to tell us then? Eh? ...What's that all about?"

"It's me," John said equally bluntly. "I'm a bastard too, sired onto my lord Peverel's wife by old Fulk fitz Waryn, who raped her in revenge for Peverel having had an affair with Lady fitz Waryn. Robin and Guy and Allan are all related through their separate mothers. Allan's mother, Lady fitz Waryn, had one sister who was married to one of fitz Waryn's knights – those were Guy's parents. Robin's mother was the third sister and married to the lord of Hodenet. Old Sir Fulk has two legitimate sons, young Fulk and Philip, and I'm their half-brother via the old man, and through them I supposed I can claim the kinship of cousin by marriage to Guy and Robin."

"So you're not actually related to Guy or Robin by blood?" wondered Gilbert.

John said, "no," just as Robin said,

"I'd totally forgotten that," and Guy looked askance to say,

"As if that would've mattered to us?" earning them some amused looks and smiles.

John continued, "The youngest of us, Allan, was supposedly legitimate – a full fitz Waryn – but when old Fulk died it all came out that Lady fitz Waryn's affair hadn't died off that much, despite her husband's rage, and that her youngest child, Allan, wasn't really fitz Waryn's after all but Peverel's! Allan and I were opposite sides of the same coin, if you like. I'm fitz Waryn's bastard by Lady Peverel, he's my lord Peverel's bastard by Lady fitz Waryn. Then, when the old man died and young Fulk inherited, he was willing to leave me and Allan to our fates when he couldn't hold onto the manor."

"He was willing to send them as mere bondsmen to the sheriff of Nottingham," Robin recalled.

"And we weren't having that!" Guy concluded firmly.

Malik's face creased into a smile of understanding, and comprehension slowly registered on the faces of the others too.

"Of course your lord Balian chose you!" Guy said again with a teasing rolling of the eyes to Robin. "If he'd heard even a whisper of your background – and why wouldn't he if he'd ever had private words with the king? – then he would have known how you felt about John and Allan's betrayal. Especially as you said that the king was fascinated by your talk of your large family, and that this Balian of Ibelin is married to your King Baldwin's stepmother – those two were hardly strangers, were they? Of anyone in that place, he must have realised that you would understand his wanting to protect a brother the law might not recognise, but whom he cared deeply for."

Robin's face was a picture as he blushed at the praise from his cousin, especially as Guy now looked to James and said pointedly, "You found not just one replacement cousin in the king but two more, didn't you?" and was relieved to see the confirmation in Robin's eyes.

"And now you've got the lot of us!" John chuckled, then turned to Malik. "Oh well, greetings cousin! Looks like you're part of the family now, whether you want to be or not!"

Malik blinked in surprise then grinned back.

"And we're all here in Guy's castle," Robin added, if somewhat in bemusement. "Do you remember I said I would fetch you all to Hodenet when I inherited? Looks like you beat me to it Guy!"

"Although for how much longer I don't know," Guy sighed regretfully. "But listen, I hadn't realised that James and Siward were Ibelin's men, and Malik and Gilbert were with the king of Jerusalem's men. That makes a massive difference over where you can go now! I mean, do you really *all* want to go to a Templar preceptory? Because what will happen if they find out that only Robin and Will have any claim on the order?"

Marianne came and brought another pitcher of ale over, but adding, "And with all those prohibitions! Do you really fancy taking vows of chastity for life?"

"That's not a problem," Robin said blithely. "We already took the vow of chastity when we were knighted."

"We did?" Gilbert turned a shocked face to Robin, as did the other crusaders.

"Of course you did," Robin was oblivious to the depth of surprise on his friends' faces as he stared off into a lost distant past.

"We took the vows in front of Balian of Ibelin, but we're all Templars now and that means chastity too."

Siward's face was a picture, and even Will wore an expression of sardonic amusement as if to say 'you must be joking!' Meanwhile, the local outlaws were just laughing the matter off without seeing that there were implications here for them too.

"You're all going to have to be careful," Guy said pointedly, looking at all of them pointedly. "Even if you aren't in a preceptory, you can't go around chasing the local village girls when the fancy takes you, you know."

This wasn't just a case of being let off from the worst of the Templar's prohibitions, there were very practical reasons why all these healthy young men should be careful of the local women. He braced himself, then said firmly, "The last three outlaws I had to help catch were all taken easily. And do you know why? It wasn't because the sheriff's men and I did anything clever. It was because the villages in the forest around where they'd made their camps told us where they were. They were sick of them coming into the villages and acting like they were the lords, demanding food and drink and with nothing to pay for it. But worse, after a while they started chatting up the young women, and you can imagine how those girls' fathers felt about that!"

"Yeah, but we're more good looking!" Bilan quipped back with a cheeky grin.

Guy couldn't help but smile, but then forced himself to look stern again. "That won't help you, lads. Two weeks after we caught the last one, Hubert of Beaumanoir – who has a manor over Mansfield Woodhouse way – and I rode into Mansfield on market day. Normally with him beside me we'd just about escape being pelted with rotten fruit and eggs, because he's hated with a passion! But for once we were treated like heroes. Us!" He paused for emphasis to make sure they were really listening.

"And Hubert is a fat pig of an old man, too fond of strong ale and even stronger wine, and with a foul temper as a result most of the time. That outlaw was a fine figure of a young man, as fair as Hubert is foul, and yet the villagers had had enough of him. The final straw was that he took a fancy to one of the young girls, and when she was out collecting fruit from the hedgerows he thought he'd do a bit of harvesting of his own. Luckily her father and some of the other men were working in a field not far off and heard her start screaming. We didn't have to catch him, Bilan. They had him trussed up like a chicken for the pot ready and waiting for us, and when Hubert gave him a good kicking they bloody cheered!" Even the ebullient youngsters were looking a bit more sober now.

"That lad swore he never tried to rape her. All he wanted was a kiss or two. And he also swore she'd been winking at him every time he'd come into the village to get food, and that she'd helped him steal some of it." Guy sighed. "For what it was worth I believed him. I think it was all so exciting for the girl to help an outlaw steal a pie and some bread at night behind her parents' back. But not such fun when the morning came, and she realised that the pie was intended for market to help buy repairs to the plough's blade, and the bread going missing meant that she would have to have short measures herself for a few days to spread their remaining flour out again. He's rotting in Nottingham town gaol now awaiting the justices and not such a fine chap anymore."

They were all listening intently now, Guy was relieved to see. Yet he was so focused on what needed to be done that he hadn't realised that Robin had stepped back from the group and was watching him intently, and that Tuck had gone to stand beside Robin.

"He does that so easily, doesn't he," Tuck said softly to Robin, who jumped at the sound of a voice so close, but then nodded.

"I envy him that," Robin admitted. "He always could think on his feet, even as a little boy."

Tuck gave a soft laugh. "That doesn't surprise me! But it's more than that Robin. You assumed that your fellow crusaders were fully aware of the implications of taking those vows when you were in Jerusalem, but I think you missed something too. Your friends didn't take vows to become *Templar* knights – they just became *knights*!"

Robin spun to give Tuck a horrified stare as the implications sunk in, but Tuck hadn't finished yet. "You've made a lot of assumptions, but if you carry on doing that you'll lose these men. Look at them! They're hanging on Guy's every word! Watch him and learn. You have every bit as much potential as him to be a good leader, but what Guy knows from experience of dealing with simple folk from villages, is that you can't just give them an order and expect them to work the rest out for themselves."

Robin sighed. "It's not going to be like becoming the Templar knight I expected to be, is it?"

Tuck shook his head. "I'm afraid not. Even those five you came from the East with aren't tied to you by orders come what may. There'll be no senior officer with you in Sherwood to issue punishments if someone doesn't do as they're told, or be there to back you up with carrying it out. ...Listen! ...You see? Guy's standing there in front of them, and his tone of voice is making them listen and realising that they can't argue with him, but what he's actually saying is also making sense to them. He's taking the time to explain to them what it means to them personally."

"But he knows the area. He knows the forest!" Robin protested in an urgent whisper to Tuck. "I don't! I can't possibly know even half of what he does when I've not even been in England for years!"

"No you don't," agreed Tuck calmly, "and that's why you need to learn a different style of leading from what you were in training for.

You have men like Hugh and Thomas with you. Good sensible men who know all that local stuff. So never be afraid to ask them what they think. You'll get far more respect from them if they think that they can trust you not to go rushing headlong into something they know to be all wrong, and that you in turn respect their knowledge and skill. And you know Guy cares deeply for you. He's not trying to take the leadership away from you, he's trying to help you!"

They turned back to the group just as Guy was saying, "So do you now see why I'm saying you mustn't start chasing the village girls? By St Thomas I know that's going to be hard! I'm not being gloomy just to make your lives even worse than they are already. But you have to get the villagers on your side if you're going to survive for long in the forest. And don't think that if you upset one village it'll be all right because there are more. Remember that most of them will go to market in the largest one around – whether at the next big village or a small town – and there they'll tell all their neighbours what has happened. Upset one and within a week – or even less depending on when each market day is – you'll have seven, eight, or even ten places, all turned against you!"

"Sweet Jesu, you're right," Gilbert said mournfully, clearly not impressed with the thought of an enforced life of chastity, then brightened. "But going it alone will still be better than being told what to do at every turn in some bloody preceptory."

Tuck whispered in Robin's ear, "Told you so!"

Thomas had been thinking similar thoughts. "We'll have the same restrictions you know, it won't just be you who can't go into the villages. But at least we'll all be in exile together, so you'll be with us, who understand what you went through. Do you think you could've coped with being cooped up in a preceptory with men who've never seen a battle of any sort, let alone a massacre such as you went through?"

Will and Malik by now were emphatically shaking their heads, and Gilbert wasn't far behind, with even Siward and James looking less than certain.

"I'm sorry," Guy said. "I still think the forest is the safer choice, even if it won't be a bed of roses all the way. If I'd have known just how bad it was for you out there, I don't think I would ever have suggested that you could fit in with men in the order like those I've known. They all come from a time when the fight for the Holy Land was fierce, but not so mad. Not so ...without honour! Not on your part – your leaders'! They always talked of their leaders as men to be looked up to. I hadn't realised the ones you had the terrible misfortune to serve under were such utter madmen! So totally disregarding of life."

Hugh, too, was looking at the six with an expression of deep sympathy on his face. "When I fought in Normandy we saw some vicious battles, and some of the men I served with had nightmares. In their case, I think it was because the people we were fighting were sometimes fellow English men, hauled into the petty squabbles of barons who had land on both sides of the sea. I said to Tuck and Guy right when we met you that I thought you'd seen too much fighting, but I thought it was due to the length of time you'd been out there. Now I can see it's the legacy of just those last few months, and only you can tell me which was the worst for you each."

"Jerusalem," James said immediately with a shake in his voice, but with no sense of holding back now. "It was seeing the women and children dying that finished me."

"Too close to your own family?" Hugh asked gently, and got a small, sad nod in reply.

Malik was nodding too. "I had no family to remind me, but they were still my people. It still haunts me – the sight of women lying dead and unburied, or going into a burned out house and seeing blackened corpses, or sometimes only ash covered skeletons, and knowing that they must be of women because they were too small to be men. ...And of children too. Families who had done nothing to bring that hell upon themselves...."

"...but in some ways Jerusalem was easier," Will chipped in, "or at least it was for me, because it was never-ending once the bombardments started. You didn't have time to think! It was just ...keep fighting! And then when you weren't fighting it was a case of catch a few winks of sleep where you were. We didn't have time to go anywhere and lie down properly, 'cause you never knew when the next lot was going to start coming. It was run to the next breach in the walls and start again."

"I hated the bombardments, though," Gilbert said firmly. "That's what I see in my dreams! The heads of those from outside the walls coming flying back over at us along with the stones. Or of the poor devils they captured. You'd duck out of the way of something you'd think was a rock from their siege engines, and then it would hit and sound all wrong and you'd look," he gulped convulsively even after all this time, "and it would be several heads." Another gulp. "And they'd be all strange shapes from hitting the flagstones. ...Some had even burst op..." He stopped, repeatedly swallowing hard and unable to carry on.

"Here, drink this." Of all of them it was surprisingly Piers who appeared by Gilbert's side with a small leather mug of strong mead, and then wrapped a brotherly arm around Gilbert's shaking shoulders.

"That's what haunts me too," admitted Siward, his face pale. "That's the worst bit. I still see hundreds of blank staring eyes in my dreams. Men's dead faces just lying there with flies crawling over them as we all but trampled on them to get away from Hattin. That horrible sound as something crunched beneath your feet. You felt it more than heard it, because you couldn't hear anything above the din of battle, and then if you glanced down you'd find you'd stamped on some dead man's hand or foot. It was just..." He couldn't go on, raising his hands in despair at trying to find the words to express such horrors.

This time it was Bilan who brought across the mead and filled his tankard with a hefty measure.

"I wish I'd never asked," the kindly lad said guiltily. "I shouldn't have asked you to tell it all again if I'd had any idea what it was like."

Malik reached across and squeezed Bilan's arm. "It is all right," he said reassuringly. "You did not make those dreams, ...those memories. They come back whether we speak of them or not. Tuck and Marianne say it is better to talk of them, so do not feel badly that you did not understand. How could you? And I hope you never see anything like that yourself to be able to."

Bilan's relief was plain to see, and he gratefully came and sat beside Malik, who seemed to have become a third older brother to the young Welsh lad despite all the cultural differences between them.

"What about you, Robin?" John asked cautiously, very aware that of all the crusaders he hadn't spoken yet.

His cousin took a deep breath. "Both I think. The difference for me at Hattin was that apart from Will, there were virtually none of the Templar sergeants left whom I'd come to know as friends. They were all gone already! All cut down in the madness of de Ridefort's zeal and Lusignan's incompetence! I knew Malik because he'd been around in the Temple complex as one of the king's turcopoles."

He turned and smiled weakly at Malik. "As one of their most senior men he was in and out getting orders, even though he wasn't quartered there. And I'd spoken to Gilbert on various occasions, but not to get to know him well. So when we marched out into the desert it was as though I was marching to my own death. I didn't see how I could be the one to survive when so many others had already died."

Thomas was looking at him in consternation. "How on earth did you survive then? Every man I've known who went into battle thinking he would die, did! You have to find some way of thinking you'll get through it or you're done for!"

Robin nodded. "I know. And at first, on the way to Hattin, when Saladin's riders kept swooping in on us and loosing arrows at us at every turn I think I was close to giving up. Will kept on at me then."

"Bloody right I did!" the big smith agreed. "I wasn't having you lying down and leaving me on my own with a thousand screaming Saracens in my face!"

Laughing weakly at his friend's indignation, which had obviously been voiced before, Robin continued, "But what did it for me... What shook me up, ...was seeing James trying to pull his brother to his feet even though he was dead."

"Your brother died *there?*" Thomas was aghast, turning to the younger man. "Oh James!" And he went and wrapped his arms around the knight in a fierce hug, clearly thinking of how he would have felt had it been him and Piers or Bilan.

"His brother Daniel," Will supplied since James couldn't find the words. "Cut down in front of him. We saw him trying to lift the body onto his shoulders to carry him back through the lines."

"Daniel was already past helping," Robin agreed, "but it made me remember that I had a family back here too, if only I could get to them. And it made me think that at least if I'd lost friends, that I hadn't lost anyone so very dear to me as James had."

Suddenly it was all making much more sense to Guy. "So you thought that someone from James' family should make it out of there?" he guessed and was rewarded with a nod. That, at last, explained why Robin had been so protective of James when they'd first met him, and why the relationship seemed to have shifted now that there were others to share the burden, and Robin confirmed it.

"Yes, although it was only later that we found out that James' other brother David had died only months before, and that there was no-one for him to go home to. I just focused on getting him out, ...but I kept thinking of you all, too – or at least as much as anyone can think in that kind of mayhem. It's more little flashes of memory in between trying to keep your sword arm moving, even though your muscles are cramped and aching, while dodging out of the way of any cuts you can't deflect with your knife or parry."

"No shields?" Hugh wondered.

Will sniffed. "Had 'em at the start, but the bloody things were so heavy! With the heat of being in our ring-mail in that killing sun, there was only so much you could lug about with you. Swords and knives which hung on your belt you could sort of forget about, but when just taking another step is taking all your will power, carrying a damned great piece of wood is beyond you."

"We'd dumped them long before the battle really began," Siward agreed. "They weren't much use anyway when the arrows were coming from all sides. Fine if you're facing a line, but not when you're being harried on all sides."

In the silence which followed as everyone tried to take in the horrors of such conditions, they suddenly became aware of someone sobbing. Looking about him Guy realised that Marianne was crying her heart out as Tuck held her in his arms. Robin too now looked worried.

"I didn't mean to upset you with such talk," he said guiltily. "I forgot that such things aren't for women to hear!"

Marianne's head shot up and her misery turned to anger.

"*Women?* I'm not some pathetic little flower to be cosseted!" she snarled, leaping to her feet and striding to stand within a few feet of Robin. "You bloody *Templar!* All you've talked about is the fighting men! Well I had *sisters* in Jerusalem!" Guy felt his gut lurch in dismay. How could they have missed that! "Everyone I grew up with was in that hospital up on the Rock! They stayed because they couldn't march out before Saladin got there, and anyway they wouldn't have left the women and children and wounded! They said their *vows!* They promised they would do their *duty!*"

She took a few steps forward and thumped Robin hard on the chest with her fist. "*You* lot weren't the only ones to hold to what you promised before God! ...To *God!* ...And you aren't the only ones to have lost people you cared about!" By now the other fist was coming into play and Robin was making no move to defend himself, as she all but screamed between hiccupping sobs,

"Where's Adeliz? Where's my best friend? I've heard nothing! *Nothing* of her! Or Gila! Gila was the best there was at comforting the dying. At making them less afraid at the end. She would have stay even if there was only *one* last patient in that hospital, and now she's dead too! ...She *is* dead isn't she? Because no-one's heard any more of her or Ermensend! Ermensend was the *mother* I had back there. She took me over when my father left me. She cleaned my cut knees when I fell over as a child," she took a gulping sob, "she told me what to expect as a woman when I was frightened by the changes which came, and she held me in her arms when I had bad dreams! And now the bad dreams I have are of her and Gila and Adeliz and Mariotta and Arsen and Raimonda and Bona and Galburga ...and they're all lying dead and unshriven, and with no-one to lay them out properly ...and they didn't *deserve* that!" That last was such a howl from the heart that Robin swept her into his arms and held her tight until her sobs gradually subsided.

"I'm so sorry, Marianne," he finally said gently as he stroked her hair. "We forgot you'd been out there."

Will's voice was gruff with emotion as he added, "We did see some of the sisters marching out of Jerusalem with the other women and children, but not many."

Strangely, her raw emotion seemed to bridge some kind of gap with James, as if he finally saw something which linked these people he was with back to his homeland, and he added calmly, "We left no-one behind, Marianne. Everyone who was not dead came out with us. You need not fear that your sisters were made prisoners – they were not."

Marianne raised red eyes to him, but managed a watery smile. "Thank you for that, James. It was something I've worried over." She released herself from Robin's embrace and rummaged for a cloth to blow her nose on. With a couple of sniffs afterwards, she was able to explain, "It's been the not knowing which has been driving me mad. That's why I had to leave Buckland! Sister Fina who was in charge was a good woman, but it felt like we were just shoved off there and then forgotten about. As though all of what *we'd* done in the Holy Land not only didn't *matter*, but had in some way offended all these bloody high-and-mighty *men*! As though the deaths of Hospitaller sisters was a trifling thing in comparison to the men's sacrifices. I left because I wanted news. I wanted to hear what happened in those last days in Jerusalem!"

She smoothed the front of Robin's crumpled and damp tunic with an apologetic hand. "You shouldn't feel badly about talking in front of me. I *needed* to hear that. To understand at last what it was like for my friends ...my sisters. I think, at least, I won't be having those nightmares again where I see them being marched off into the desert never to be seen."

Siward got up and came and gave her a hug. "Good! I'm glad about that! I wouldn't want anyone to have nightmares like that!"

And then, all of a sudden and without any prompting from Guy or Tuck, Robin was saying, "You'll come with us, then, when we leave. If nothing else we can keep on asking if there's any news from the East, and maybe someone will take more notice if a man asks than you just as a woman on your own. You deserve to know what happened to your comrades too."

Guy looked to Tuck and saw the relief in his eyes too. Thank God for that! Finally something had got through the wall in Robin's mind put there by the haughty leaders of the Templars, and no doubt a few sanctimonious priests too. And once Robin had seen sense, it was clear that there'd never been much opposition in the first place to Marianne joining from the other five, who were all taking turns to hug her now.

Hugh came and stood by Guy who'd risen to stand in front of everyone and they waited until everyone else had sat down again.

"There's no way you lot are going to fit into some closeted little preceptory," Hugh observed out loud. "You won't fit in any more than Marianne did in the nunneries! You'll be taking the head off the first man who makes some stupid remark about the Holy Land!" His words were said kindly and no-one took offence.

"I agree," Guy said. "I think the only thing now is for you six to take to the forest with Thomas and Hugh and the rest. And thank heavens you've seen that Marianne is going to have to go with you, too. You can't ask her to do what you can't do yourselves and remain shut up somewhere. She's seen her share of the outcomes of battles out in the East, even if she hasn't fought in them like you have, and she's certainly felt the consequences! And I think that given what you've told us before and now, you need someone with you who has some idea of how to look after you if one of you falls ill when the memories get too much for you again. She's the obvious choice for that."

Tuck was nodding. "And for that reason I'll be coming with you too." He turned to Guy. "It's the right thing to do! I'm going to stand out like a sore thumb in this valley if I stay, and I can do more good going, because such strains on the mind have a habit of sneaking back up on you just when you thought you were all fine again."

Marianne's smile lit up her face and she came and hugged Tuck tightly, emphasising how closely they'd become friends over the summer. That at least quelled some of Guy's fears over her being the lone woman if she was going to be spending her time at Tuck's side.

Robin sighed. "I know. And you've been right all along, Guy. If Jerusalem is going to be retaken then it won't be achieved by bleeding the poor folk of the shires of everything they have. I've been trying to tell myself that our friends didn't die for nothing. That the Holy Land isn't lost forever. I've tried so hard to keep faith with that idea. But these last months have forced me to see a different sort of cost of that war. ...You're right, Hugh, I would punch the first Templar lay brother who said that the Holy City shouldn't have been lost and should be retaken, but not just because of the price we paid! It's only taken us a few months of being back here to see that the king can demand all he likes, but if there's nothing more to give then how can you justify such a war? I pray at nights for the king to win Jerusalem again, truly I do and with all my heart, ...but not at the price of killing off half of England! And I'd argue that with any Templar, even the Grand Master!"

Everyone was nodding their agreement with that, which meant that with no-one now excluded, Guy felt he could bring up another of the practicalities of living in the forest.

"What do you eat most of?" he asked firmly, looking round all of them.

"Meat! Lots and lots of meat!" Bilan chirped, obviously relishing the thought of how much venison was going to be coming his way. "Big juicy chunks of it!"

Even Guy couldn't refrain from a chuckle, but was reassured to see that at least Thomas and John had caught on to what he was thinking.

"You'll need bread," he said firmly. "Bread and vegetables! And you can hardly go around creating your own fields within the forest without exciting some sort of notice and comment. *I* can turn a blind eye, but my fellow foresters won't. And if I keep on doing it, then sooner or later someone is going to wonder how on earth I haven't noticed too." Will had now joined Thomas and John in nodding sagely as he spoke. "So you're going to need the villagers to be on your side for that too! You'll be depending on them to give you those essentials if nothing else, and you'd better start thinking about what you're going to trade with them in return, because they can't do it for nothing! They don't have enough going spare."

Tuck's thoughts were firstly of food they could trade. "We could gather fruit and nuts from deeper in the forest than the villagers normally go," he said thoughtfully. "There must be whole woods which hardly get harvested, especially up in the north of Sherwood."

"Oh joy, the life of a wild outlaw – picking nuts," Piers sighed with withering contempt and clearly feeling the affront to his soldiering skills.

"Yes, but we could bring down a good few deer," his brother Thomas reminded him with a nudge. "If we skin them and take the meat off the bone so that there's no proof of what it came from, there'd be no evidence in the village midden from bones and stuff. We could trade meat easily! We've got more time and expertise to hunt than any of the villagers!"

Guy was quick to praise, earning a sideways glance from Tuck to Robin, who was clearly taking note. "That's more the idea! And you're absolutely right, Thomas. Get the meat off the bones and skin so there's no evidence. Take the villagers cuts, not whole haunches or sides! They'll certainly welcome that, because they rarely get meat unless a cow or a sheep has died."

"I could make charcoal," Will added thoughtfully. "I know how. If we're careful and use only the wood that's fallen rather than actually cutting down trees, I reckon I could still get a few charcoal kilns going deep in the forest. Especially if they're a long way from any village in case they do get discovered. I bet the local smiths would be glad to get some of that for free."

"By God they would!" Guy agreed enthusiastically, immensely relieved that some of the men at least were already starting to think creatively about how they would survive. "Charcoal's a brilliant idea, Will! It means they can trade, or fulfil orders from the sheriff, without spending huge amounts of cash they can scarce afford on the raw materials. Anything like that would be very welcome, and pretty much every village will have a smith, even if he's only part-time. And those are the very men who can't compete with the professional smiths in Nottingham to pay for materials, so the villagers will be delighted if they can get their ironwork done without paying a fortune out."

Will was now deep in thought. "If I can get my hands on some tools I could even make some stuff," he said with a far off look in his eyes. "I bet most of the villagers make blades which shatter sooner rather than later. Well I know how to make a proper damascened blade! Not that the villagers would know what to do with one of those, but I bet I can make a better plough share than them, given what I know."

"And we'll need new arrow heads fairly quickly if we're hunting for more than just ourselves," Piers observed, surprising Guy by thinking ahead rather than doing his usual job of complaining when things didn't go his way. "Thomas and I can fletch arrows, and so can Malik, but heads sharp enough to bring down a big deer can't just be fire-hardened wood, they'll have to be steel. I think we need to get Will those tools sooner than you thought."

"I bet the smith down in the village would help," Bilan said helpfully. "You helped him with that order from the sheriff, Will – or rather from Robert of Crockston – for all those arrow heads for the castle. If we paid him for his new tools I bet he'd be happy to go and get some more from another market to the one he went to before."

"Either that or he'd put in a good word for you with the man who made them," agreed Thomas.

Hugh was looking relieved. "Yes, going into the forest with something to trade for food and arms is a much better prospect."

"Very well, then," Guy declared. "It's off to the green-wood for you lot!"

"Sir Robin and his men!" quipped Siward, making it clear that to the crusaders, at least, there was no doubt about who the leader would be.

"There's something else you're going to have to be careful of," Guy said when the friendly banter had calmed down again. "I don't mean to nag, but it's better you think of this now, before you get into trouble. For most of you this isn't going to be much of a problem – certainly not for Malik and James. Your families are too far away to be in danger from any English sheriff. And you Coshams are all here together anyway. Hugh and Siward, you need to be very careful not to give away where you came from, but it's you, John, and Robin I'm thinking of most. Especially you, Robin!

"If you're going to lead this band then you'll be the target for any sheriff, whether it's mine here in Nottinghamshire and Derbyshire, or the sheriff of Yorkshire, or the one of Lincolnshire, or wherever else you might go. I know, I've seen it! They go for the one they see as the ringleader first, and they'll question anyone you might have spoken to as to who you might be. If you say nothing, then stupidly enough that wouldn't be believed, and those who hunt you will only press the poor folk harder. So you'll have to have *some* kind of name, and it can't be associated with Alverton!"

"Why ever not?" Robin demanded, perplexed. "It's not as though we owe the new owner anything. He'll just have been the highest bidder to King Henry. Why should we worry about him?"

Guy shook his head in frustration at Robin's slowness to catch on. "It's not the lord I'm thinking of, you idiot! He can say in all truth and honesty that he never knew you, or John, or any of the others of us, and be believed because he took over after we left. But do you think that will stop the sheriff questioning all the people who *did* know us? Do you want poor Henry the steward and his wife Martha to fall foul of a brutal sheriff in his dungeon? Or Simon the carpenter who made us those little spears to play with when we were seven or eight? Or Edwina the cook? Do you want her to suffer when the sheriff gets wind of your gang in the forest?"

"He's right, Robin," John said firmly. "I saw that happen at our first grange. One of the lads from the nearby village came back from the wars in the east a bit strange, and the priest swore he was a warlock and had a witch somewhere. An utterly stupid thing to accuse a mere village man of who'd only ever been a foot soldier, you'd think. But the bishop got involved, and before we knew it the whole village had been questioned until they hardly knew what day it was.

"In the end the simple daughter of an elderly couple was singled out as the supposed witch. I don't know if anyone in particular gave her up in order to save everyone else more grief, or whether she was just someone who couldn't account for her movements on the night of the next full moon. Neither she nor the man would have know where to start with being familiars of the Devil, but there was no stopping the bishop and his men until they found what they believed was there – and they were about to bring the sheriff into the mixture, because they were even talking about racking some folk to get them to 'confess'! So don't roll your eyes at Guy like that. He's absolutely right. We mustn't mention Alverton!

"In fact, I think I shall become John of Hathersage. Your nickname is already sticking to me in those parts, Will, so I can be Little John, and just turn it to be John Little of Hathersage, if necessary. Then if questioned, the poor folk up there can say the truth – that I was an itinerant shepherd who came alone to their village. There's no other family with the surname Little in the area. So I'm not bringing misery down on some poor unconnected souls. And if pressed they can say the truth, that I came from over eastwards as a shepherd thrown out of a Templar grange on the wolds. The Templars are strong enough to look out for themselves, and to take a bit of criticism for turning me out on an unsuspecting world as a villain!"

"That's exactly the right kind of thinking," Guy praised John. "That fits you perfectly. But to come back to you Robin, it wouldn't hurt if you hid you face a little too. Made it harder for someone to give a full description of you."

"I am not sneaking around like some coward!" Robin snapped immediately. "Let the others take the risks while I hide away? No!"

"I don't think he meant that," Will said hurriedly. "You mean smear some dark streaks of charcoal across your face like we did when we hunted at night to break up the outline. That's the sort of thing you meant, Guy, isn't it?"

Guy nodded vigorously before his tense cousin could take further affront. "Yes, exactly. Or wear a hood or a hat so that some shadow falls over you face. Not all the time, for Heaven's sake! Just when you confront anyone who might think to court favour with the sheriff to give a really good description of you! I didn't mean you had to hide in the woods!"

"Aaaah," teased Will in his familiar way, ruffling Robin's hair. "Our little Robin redbreast hiding in the wood. Poor little birdy! Can't have you missing out on a fight!"

Robin fended him off but couldn't help laughing too, and Guy mentally thanked the Virgin and his favoured saints that Will had come with Robin. Those years of him watching Robin's back had given him a familiarity which none of the others had, and Guy himself would have been at a loss as to how to handle Robin's often unexpected taking of offence when none had been intended. It had certainly not been part of the young Baldwin's personality, and Guy could only assume it had come with the strain of living every day expecting it to be the last. That or from the agony of never getting a full night's sleep – that would make even a saint brittle. He breathed a sigh of relief as everyone laughed as Will now fended off Robin, who was swatting him with a handful of rushes off the floor.

When calm had descended once more, Guy tried again. "I've been doing a bit of thinking about where you could say you came from, Robin, as it happens and I think you could say you are Robin of Loxley."

"Loxley?" Hugh spoke up. "There's no such place anymore!"

"No there isn't!" Guy said triumphantly. "And that's why it's safe to use the name!"

"Hang on," John chipped in. "I've heard the villagers round High Peak talking of Loxley."

Guy nodded. "It's sort of famous up here in the Forest of the Peak, even if nowhere else. It was only ever a little hamlet. Nothing much in particular. But it got burned when the Conqueror harried the north as being one of the places he thought was a hotbed of rebels. Of men hiding out in the forest and being supported by the village. Saxon men who stood up to the new Norman lords!"

Robin perked up as he listened to this. Clearly this was far more appealing! "Go on," he prompted.

"Well there's absolutely nothing there anymore except the few standing stones of old chimneys and the odd sheep pen," Guy added. "And it's all deep in the valley of the Loxley river, hidden amongst the trees. Almost no-one goes there, except maybe the odd forester, or very rarely the king's hunters might come up to stock up on venison – but as you've seen, that more often gets delegated to us men already up here. But it would make a good base when you come this way, because it's right on the boundary between Derbyshire and Yorkshire, so neither sheriff takes a lot of notice of it in wild country like that. There aren't any folk to tax for several miles in any direction for them to bother about either.

"And being an old haunt of rebels that's already been wiped out it wouldn't incite retribution," Tuck added with a grin. "Oh that's very nice, Guy!"

John had been staring off into space with an air of concentration on his face and now suddenly exclaimed, "That's it! I remember at last! One of the shepherd's told me that the leader in Loxley in the old days was Robert Hode, a fletcher! Apparently he was an incredible archer. The best shot in the county! Well if you call yourself Robin Hode, it sounds like a diminutive of the family names, because that Robert's son was another Robert who went on the run after the Conqueror killed his father. So you'd be believable as the next generation of a lawless family of no fixed abode, who still bear the name of your last home."

"Our Robin is a brilliant shot!" Siward said loyally. "The best there is ...apart from Malik, of course." The turcopole gave a wry smile at this, and Guy guessed that this was an old rivalry.

Thomas rubbed his hands together with gleeful anticipation. "Right then! We'll be getting you two started with longbows, then! You're both strapping lads, so you won't have a problem with the weight. No offence, Malik, but those recurve bows you've talked about having in the east, and of making again, can't be made here. The glue to hold the sinew and bone laminates together can't cope with our English rain. That's why our hunting bows are all self-wood bows made of one piece, but even they won't have much more range than the soldiers' crossbows do. If we're going to get the better of armed men without getting hurt or caught ourselves, then we need the advantage the Welsh bows will give us. Robin Hode, the outlaw with the Welsh bow!"

Malik just gave his calm smile, accepting Thomas' judgement, although Robin looked a bit startled. It was Will who once again nudged Robin into acceptance – this time quite literally with an elbow in the ribs!

"There you go, then! Robin Hode! The man from Loxley with a hood!" He gave his deep guffawing laugh and a wink. "Quite suit you that would! One of those nice big hoods with the cowl like the foresters wear. You could flip it up when you need it, just as Guy suggested, and it'd be out of the way the rest of the time. And a Welsh longbow over your shoulder's not the weapon of choice of someone born of Norman blood. That should blur the matter nicely too!"

"If you take that as your guise right from the start you'll carry it off, no question," Tuck agreed, adding his weight to the plan, and Guy knew that in Robin's eyes Tuck's opinion was already valued for his piety if nothing else.

"Very well," Robin said, squaring his shoulders as the dark spiritual cloud passed over, and he returned to a more cheerful demeanour. "No mention of Alverton except between ourselves. I shall become Robin Hode of Loxley. The great grandson of a rebel Saxon archer." The Baldwin grin Guy remembered from boyhood suddenly spread across his face. "I rather like that idea, the more I think about it! But we shall definitely be more successful than my newly adopted ancestor, I think! By the time I've done with the name it won't just be a few folk up in the wilds of the Peaks who remember it this time!"

And that was how we saw it, Gervase. Not of a band of outlaws luking to the wild woods to wreak havoc on all and sundry, but as a bunch of friends trying to make a new life for themselves away from the nightmares of their pasts. We all talked about if they got into a fight, never of it as a certainty. Robin Hood and his men thought, as of at that Christmas of 1189, that they were going to move clear of the established territories of sheriffs, not pick fights with them. And that once the dust had settled on King Richard's new reign, that they would be able to decide where there might be a place to settle for them to make their own. For now, it was sufficient that they would all be heading off in company, and would be strong enough together to feel sure that they would not fall prey to any marauding gangs of cut-throats and thieves also haunting the forest. Such was the way we all thought of them – as honest men forced to flee, and not at all like the villains who gaily broke the law, nor of them setting up in competition with the lawless bands already there.

So, we have reached another watershed in our tale. The first members of Robin Hood's outlaw gang are all but fully assembled, and the reason for them taking to a life in the forest has been laid out before you. Is it what you expected? A little more mundane, perhaps? Ah, Brother, but does it not make it all the more poignant for you to realise that the men who would undertake such heroic deeds were not careless rogues? Nor men who had never a care in the world, and could indulge themselves in such pastimes as if they were going out for the day on a jolly hunting party? Does it not impress upon you that, had they been given half a chance, they would have happily remained law-abiding citizens?

I see that you are thinking on that. Good! And so you should! The ˜outlaws˜ were men who deeply cared about the fate of others, Gervase, and I very much wanted you to see that they were not careless of the lives they sometimes had to take, any more than I was indifferent to the suffering of the people upon whom I had to invoke the cruel laws imposed upon every one of us by the king.

Therefore we shall move on now to 1190, and an escalating rate of change taking place within the country, which would finally push Robin Hood and those who followed him into wholehearted opposition of those who would have ruled us. An opposition which I could not be outwardly seen to endorse, but which at every possible turn I would support in invisible ways. Sharpen the point of your quill, Brother! We move on!

Chapter 20

I n January 1190 the news we had dreaded arrived with a true winter chill. The new sheriff was to be Roger fitz John, as spoilt a Norman youth as ever sat in a saddle, and connected to the de Lacys. Later he was to be known as Roger de Lacy of Pontefract, but at this stage he had no such claim, since it would come eventually to him through his paternal grandmother. No, Gervase, the dreadful Sir Roger was not a de Lacy in the sense of inheriting from father to son! To find a male de Lacy in that miserable line you have to go back to Ilbert de Lacy who came over with the Conqueror. He it was who first got Pontefract, and this was handed down via a son and then a daughter before getting to Roger fitz John's grandmother – now there is a tortuous family tree for you! Suffice it to say, therefore, that I saw little sign of the honourable de Lacys I had known on the border in the youth I found myself serving.

All of twenty years old, he had supposedly been Constable of Cheshire for the last ten years while his father, John fitz Richard had been away fighting in the Holy Land. Of course he could not possibly have held that post without substantial help from key men within his absent father's household, not initially as a child of ten or twelve. And he had remained there because the role of constable of Chester was a hereditary post, and was therefore his family's to hold, not like ours at Nottingham.

However, for all that I did not know him from being with the de Lacys who had come through Grosmont in company, I had encountered young men like him all too often when they had come hunting with de Braose. Young men who had no idea of their own limitations, especially living in the wilder lands of the borders, and who had been able to buy their way out of any trouble they got themselves into. Spoilt, protected by their positions, and totally self-centred, they were the stuff of nightmares, and young Roger was to prove to be the epitome of the breed!

Even worse, from my point of view, we learned that King Richard in some misguided fit of brotherly generosity, had given Nottinghamshire and Derbyshire, along with Dorset, Somerset, Devon and Cornwall, to his younger brother John – as if that would ever have consoled the youngest Plantagenet for not inheriting a kingdom of his own! So even before he came, we realised that this undoubtedly ghastly young lord fitz John would not even have the restraining hand of the king's men to curb his excesses. Prince John was made count of Mortain by his brother too, and the only minor blessing for us was that although he no doubt had plenty of castles over in that distant part of France, here at least the castles were to remain under the firm hand of the constables, even though the sheriffs would be reaping the incomes of the shires for the prince's benefit.

I tell you, Brother Gervase, I was in total despair! I now know the dreams I had in those nights of waiting for my direct orders were *premonitions of the dangers to come. Warnings I could not ignore. And I spent hours on my knees in the chapel once the others had left the castle, praying with a desperate fervour for whatever help God and his saints could give us. And yes, Saint Issui came in for a fair number of those pleas, along with Saint David and Saint Lazarus, whom I petitioned in particular on Robin's behalf in the hope that, having kept him safe so far, he might be inclined to continue to help.*

Yet the dreaded day finally came around when I heard of my fate, and that of High Peak, and it was not auspicious!

Derbyshire, Nottinghamshire, & Yorkshire, January-February, the year of Our Lord 1190

"It's *who?*" Guy could hardly believe his ears.

The messenger, one of the more bearable soldiers from Nottingham, grimaced and repeated himself. "The new sheriff – or maybe it's one of the king's men – thinks that a 'more experienced' forester is needed here and he's sending de Wendenal."

"God help us and save us!" Tuck moaned and sank onto a bench, having come in on behalf of the others hiding not far off when the messenger was spied, and for the present having been introduced as the priest from nearby Hope for the benefit of the messenger.

"I fear so," the messenger said sympathetically, then looked to Guy. "I know it's not much consolation, but we're all glad you're coming back and he's going!" Then he winced as he continued, "And de Wendenal said that you're to bring all the men-at-arms back with you because he'll be bringing his own, and to get rid of all the castle servants because he's bring his own of them too." The young man couldn't resist a faint smile then as he added, "Apparently he thinks that the cook might poison him and the others stab him while he's in bed! Or at least that what Sir Giles has told me to tell you he heard him saying to one of his cronies!"

Guy thought that de Wendenal's fears were probably all too justified. He knew how isolated High Peak Castle was, and that if he couldn't count on his own household then he would be lost. And he didn't know just how cowed they'd been under Sir Ivo, because one of the few good things Guy could ever have said about de Wendenal was that he'd never been one to creep around his betters, so he'd not bothered with visiting Sir Ivo in person any more than Guy had. It still didn't make Guy's life any easier when it came to breaking the news to the servants, though. The cook in particular took it as a personal insult.

"All the years I served that swivel-eyed old miser, Ivo, and still I never poisoned the bastard! By St Thomas I wish I had now! I'll not leave this new by-Our-Lady swine a single sausage more than what's on the inventory, that's for certain!"

"We could move the hams to one of the caves," Guy said before thinking, then realised all eyes had turned to him and mentally cursed. Too late to take back the words now, though. He'd shown himself for the rebel he was at heart once again, and this one he couldn't blame on the company he'd kept of late! Oh well, he was potentially in trouble so deep now that a few shovels further down into the hole weren't going to make much difference to his fate.

He took a deep breath. "Do you think the hams would keep if we hang them well up away from animals and where it's not too damp? One of the higher caves perhaps? That way the villagers could make use of them, and if de Wendenal searches the houses then he won't find anything."

"Is he likely to? Search?" Earnwine the miner asked. "I mean, what would he think we have to make it worth a search? Surely he's not that suspicious?"

Guy had to answer honestly. "I think that there isn't much de Wendenal isn't capable of doing, to be frank. I would definitely expect him to search your houses, and sooner rather than later, just to satisfy himself that you don't have something you shouldn't have."

"God help us!" muttered Earnwine, and Guy had to agree.

"Oh he's an absolute bastard! And he's crafty too! About the only good thing I can tell you is that he'll leave your women alone. He's not a great one for the women, and the few times he seems to have felt the urge, he's gone into Nottingham, found a whore, paid his coins, used her and come home again. We've not heard of him beating the whores either, although he's free enough with his fists on almost any other occasion you could name. Strip your houses down to make the stores cupboards look as poor as you can and still be believable. Find some hideaways up in the hills in caves but away from the mines – Robin and the others can show you a few before they go if you need help – and store what you can up there. When you need stuff send some of the older children to bring it down on the quiet.

"Don't try doing anything like that at night! De Wendenal's got night-time already marked as the time worth watching for underhand dealings. He's the only knight in Nottingham who'll go out in the town at the depths of night just to see if he can catch some poor sod out! If I were you, Earnwine, I'd also check the houses yourself again as soon as he comes. I'll go round beforehand to help you make it all look right, but you'll need to go again just in case someone hasn't believed our warnings. I wish I could protect you all, but my own position is precarious enough with this new sheriff, and Sir Ralph Murdac can hardly help himself just at the moment, let alone me."

"Don't worry, Sir Guy, we'll survive," Earnwine told him wryly. "We managed before, we'll manage again. Thanks to you at least this time we're ahead of the mining quota. We'll hide as much as possible of the refined stock we have for the taxes deep in one of the old workings, and carry on working hard to make it look like we're just about scratching the quotas together. It might be better if this year we only just scrape the full amount together for him and grumble a lot. Then if he gets heavy-handed with us at least we'll know we have something to fall back on."

"It pains me to agree with you, but that sounds like a good plan, knowing him as I do," Guy admitted.

It was still with a heavy heart that he assembled the men in the bailey a week later, Bilan having brought the news that a band of heavily armed men were coming up the valley before taking himself off again in a hurry. De Wendenal rode in looking more like some border warlord than a royal forester, a coarse sheep-fleece over-jerkin covering his leather one against the winter chill, bull-headed belligerence written on his wind-chapped face, and armed to the teeth.

"Gisborne!" he bellowed coarsely. "Still here?"

"Just waiting for the last of your men to get in through the gate," Guy answered frostily. "You didn't think I would walk out and leave one of the king's castles defenceless, did you?"

It was a small victory but one which he was pleased to see hit home. Clearly de Wendenal had forgotten that he would have to man this castle as well as patrol the royal forest there about, and Guy felt the stirrings of a small hope that de Wendenal would make less of a castellan than he was a forester. It was very different to be the man solely in charge of a castle, instead of being able to focus on infringements of the forest laws alone. He'd got enough men, though, and Guy wondered how he'd got the new sheriff to agree to letting so many of the soldiers go. There must have been a good two dozen men-at-arms at de Wendenal's heels, plus half a dozen who looked as though they might be recently recruited walking foresters.

To Guy, though, they looked more like the dregs of mercenary gangs! Those foresters would have very little to do up here in the higher lands where there were fewer trees to mask unlicensed felling, pasturing or hunting. Somehow he didn't think they would have the woodsmen's skills to patrol the deeper wooded valleys to the north without getting lost, either. And that made Guy fret over what they might do in their boredom – the villagers and miners might be in for a rougher time than even he'd feared.

Sheriff Murdac would never have let so many soldiers leave Nottingham, for sure, and it made Guy wonder just how inexperienced the new man was. He still had the small clasp he knew de Wendenal had stolen from Sir Mascerel's wife, for he was holding on to that against the day when he might have to use it as leverage against the knight. But that would depend very much on the character of whoever was in office as sheriff at the time, for Guy had only ever thought in terms of exposing de Wendenal's crime to Sheriff Murdac's honesty, not some easily lead youth or someone as twisted as de Wendenal himself – one who might make his own hoard as Sir Ivo had done.

At least they had long since got the last bags of silver pennies out of High Peak, and hidden where only they knew of them. There had also been the unexpected discovery of more silver coins, buried under the altar of the village church in Hope when Tuck had gone to put it to rights in preparation for the arrival of a new priest. It confirmed that the old priest had either been in cahoots with Sir Ivo, or had been too terrified of the man to protest – which seemed more likely. Therefore the majority of Sir Ivo's ill-gotten hoard had now been found and was still hidden away against a time of greater need. And if this fitz John was a real inexperienced and sadistic fool then they might have desperate need of that reserve before too long; leaving Guy with only the problem of how he would know when that might be if he wasn't here that much. Clearly Robin might have to bring the others round this way every so often just to check on things.

"What did my lord fitz John say as to my orders?" Guy demanded frostily. "Am I to return straight away, or does he wish me to patrol any of the forest on the way back?"

"The young milord hasn't got here yet!" de Wendenal said nastily. "I got my orders from Prince John's household in advance of him getting here."

"What? Prince John is coming to Nottingham?" Guy couldn't help himself showing his dismay. Luckily de Wendenal was too puffed up with anticipation at his elevation to High Peak to notice Guy's reaction properly.

"No, you dolt, the new sheriff! Due here next Monday. So if you get a move on you can greet him and start licking his boots."

That's the last thing I shall be doing, Guy thought. *I have every intention of keeping well out of the way until I can see what kind of man he is!*

Unfortunately that was easier said than done. On the appointed Monday, young Roger fitz John rode into the inner bailey with much clattering of hooves, and flourishing of banners and expensive robes, just as Guy was walking across the outer bailey towards the stables with Fletch and Spike.

"You there!" he found himself being hailed as.

Guy turned, desperately trying not to let his displeasure show on his face.

"My lord, welcome to Nottingham Castle," he said as pleasantly as he could, instantly guessing who the anonymous young lord must be. Gesturing Fletch and Spike to sit, he went to take the reins of the fine horse for its rider.

"And who are you?" the imperious youth demanded.

"I'm Sir Guy of Gisborne, one of your senior foresters, sire," Guy answered politely. He found himself looking up into the face of a blue-eyed, blonde young man who was the epitome of Norman aristocracy, right down to the sneer which marred what might otherwise have been quite a good-looking face.

"Really? Then, Sir Guy, what are those curs doing in my castle bailey?" Fitz John's face was a mask of revulsion as he took in Fletch and Spike's rather shaggy grey coats and big bones.

"Those curs, sire, are the best trackers in the county – as you will discover when it pleases you to go hunting. They came with me from my previous appointment on the Welsh borders where they were very successful at tracking wolves too!" *There you arrogant bastard*, Guy thought, *that might give you something to think about!*

Fitz John sniffed. "Wolves eh? Well there aren't any wolves around here! Get rid of them! Knock them on the head with a warhammer. I don't want to hear of them running about killing my deer! Or covering one of my prize greyhounds! I want them dead ...*today.* ..Now!" he snapped at Guy's apparent paralysis.

He swung a leg over the pommel and leapt to the floor, ignoring Guy's face which had gone white at the thought of killing his beloved dogs. "See to my horse!" And fitz John was gone, snapping at a poor man who seemed to be in charge of the considerable household which had streamed into the castle in the young lord's wake.

"Good God, Guy," a voice came at his elbow. "Are you all right? You look like you've seen a ghost!"

Guy turned and looked into the face of the amiable Sir Giles. "Not a ghost Giles," he said heavily. "The Devil! And he's our new master!"

"Oh no!" Giles groaned. "As bad as that?"

"He's just told me to knock Fletch and Spike on the head with a hammer."

"*What?*" Giles was appalled. "But ...but...?"

"He thinks they're curs who might kill his deer," Guy answered sadly. Then a flash of anger replaced the shock. "Damn him to Hell if he thinks I shall do it, though!"

"Oh Guy, I know you love them dearly, but you can't defy the sheriff!"

"No Giles, I suppose I can't," Guy replied, struggling mightily with his emotions and allowing his anger to be apparently squashed, and to look just suitably miserable again. Clearly he would have few allies here amongst the knights and foresters if they were all going to be so in awe of the prancing young fool as Giles was. "I'll take them away and do it, though. I'm not sacrificing my dogs for his entertainment in public."

Then a shout came from the south side of the bailey where the new Great Hall doorway was standing open. Sir Roger fitz John was summoning his vassals!

"Shit!" Guy swore. "Go Giles! ...Tell him I'm carrying out his orders!" he added bitterly, as he ran with Spike and Fletch at his heels to the stables. "Harry!" he called urgently and saw the head stableman turn to him. "The new bastard wants Fletch and Spike dead and now!"

"*What?*" the stableman was as appalled as Guy.

"Has Tinker caught any rats this morning? I need blood! Plenty of it!"

Harry was much quicker on the uptake than Giles, and more understanding of what Guy was intending to do. "Tom! Put Fletch and Spike into the farthest stall of the old stables and don't let anyone except Sir Guy or me in there!" he ordered, then pulled Guy over to a sweating mare. "Over here! I was about to bleed her anyway!" He pulled a metal blade with a triangular wedge on it out of his jerkin pocket and a small hammer. Guy, used to helping with the horses, knew what to do and got her down onto the ground and then held her head steady. With a swift and skilled tap, Harry had the bloodletting blade in and a spurt of hot, red blood shot out of the vein and all over Guy.

"There! Now *go!*" Harry said, giving him an approving check over. "You look as though you've just killed something! Don't worry about Fletch and Spike. I can hide them until tomorrow morning without any trouble, and I doubt you'll leave it that long before you get them away?"

"Tonight!" Guy answered firmly. "I'll be taking them out as soon as everyone in the household is asleep."

"I'll wait for you then," Harry promised. "I'll personally keep an eye on those two, just in case!"

Guy was already at the run and hurtling back towards the great hall. He skidded in on the heels of the last of the foresters and the temporary knights here to do service, and made his way to the front to where they all stood uncomfortably watching the young fitz John. Their new sheriff was walking up and down gazing about him.

"It'll do, I suppose," Guy heard him murmur in a disgruntled tone, then he turned and saw the blood-soaked Guy.

"By St Thomas! What do you mean appearing before me like that?" fitz John exploded.

"I carry out my orders promptly, sire," Guy said in a flat, cold voice. "You ordered me to kill Fletch and Spike with a hammer and that's what I've done."

The sharp intake of breath from everyone there could almost have moved the heavy wall-hangings.

"But they were the best trackers we had..."

"Now how will we find those poachers in Derwent Vale?..."

"We'll never catch those outlaws up in the north now..." were just the more audible of the horrified comments which rippled through the assembled men. Fitz John looked at Guy and knew he'd got off on totally the wrong foot in his new post, and Guy knew he would never be forgiven for that. This young lord was too conscious of maintaining the best appearance at all times for such a *faux-par* to ever be forgotten.

"Then you'll all just have to work harder!" fitz John snapped at the assembled men. That wasn't the right thing to say either! It was as though an invisible barrier had been drawn across the hall between the sheriff and his new men. Without bothering to find out who was who in the castle, fitz John hadn't comprehended that Guy was very popular amongst a large number of the men and knights, and even those who didn't like him much at least understood that Guy's tracking abilities made their collective jobs that bit easier. The few who would have instantly taken fitz John's part were all now absent at High Peak, and unlikely to be seen again for many a long month. And it was hunting season!

"You!" Fitz John pointed to young Sir Simon, a nice enough youth although hardly the most astute of the knights, who was the best dressed of all those present simply because he'd been in his chamber changing out of rain-soaked clothes at the time of the call. "You will take charge of the castle for now until the constable returns!"

Poor Simon looked as though the world had fallen on him. He was going to be utterly out of his depth and he and everyone but fitz John knew it. "And arrange for a hunt tomorrow! I shall go and investigate my chambers now. I shall expect you all to attend me at dinner tonight!" And he swept out with what he no doubt thought of as a dignified flourish. It would have been a good deal more impressive if all the household hadn't known that the only place beyond the room into which he'd flounced was a privy!

"Shit calling unto shit," Guy commented softly, but in the silence everyone heard and the smothered chuckles acted as a relief to the tension which had gripped the men.

"Blessed St Thomas, Sir Guy," one of the sergeant whom Guy normally was at loggerheads with, came to him and said. "I know we've had our differences in the past, but to order you to do that to your dogs! Totally uncalled for! And before the stupid boy had even got into the castle!" The man walked away shaking his head in despair at the thought of what the coming months were likely to bring.

"What am I going to *do*?" Sir Simon's panic-stricken cry was heard from behind Guy.

Sir Martin and Sir Walter were the two most senior knights remaining in the castle at the moment, given that Robert of Crockston had left to desperately try and maintain some continuity of order by going out to collect the taxes due for the Easter court, and Alan of Leek was currently with the bishop of Lincoln's men arguing over further illegal felling. Either Martin or Walter would have been the sensible choice to temporarily promote. Unfortunately, the first impression that fitz John had created, especially with the incident with Guy, meant that now those two had already left the hall, clearly intending to keep as low a profile as possible. Guy could understand their actions but felt they were missing the point. This young lord would punish them all, and indiscriminately, if Sir Simon fell flat on his face within the first couple of days, and it wasn't likely to get any better.

Guy turned wearily back to Simon, already sick to his stomach at how quickly his world had fallen apart again. "Send people over to the royal hunting lodge at Clipstone!" he said firmly. "Tell them to get the place ready as if the bloody king himself was coming!"

"Clipstone?" Sir Simon said faintly. "But the king hasn't consented to any hunts!"

Guy gritted his teeth and wandered over to the trembling man. "Listen!" he said with as much patience as he could summon. "He's the bloody sheriff and he can do as he likes! Clipstone is a *royal* hunting lodge. Never mind what the king will say if he finds fitz John's been as good as poaching his deer – we'll cross that bridge if we ever come to it! You tell his lordship's seneschal, or whatever that poor man's proper title is, that Clipstone's where the best hunting is and fit for the king, and suggest that his lordly young master might wish to spend tomorrow night there since it's a good sixteen miles from here. So if he wants to have *good* hunting he's not going to have time to ride out, hunt and get back here again, ...*is he*?" he said pointedly so that Simon began nodding frantically. "In the meantime I'll have a word with Sir Walter and Sir Martin for you. See if I can persuade them to lend you a hand."

The gratitude on Simon's face was genuine, but in his current mood Guy couldn't find it in him to be graceful in accepting it. He turned and stormed out and up to the room the two oldest knights shared in the buildings surrounding the inner ward. He knocked on the door, forcing himself to be at least that civil, and was rewarded by Walter coming to open it.

"Guy?" he said in surprise. "What are you...?"

"...Here for?" Guy finished and brushed his way in, forcing Walter to jump back to avoid getting smeared with blood. "You two are going to have to help young Simon," he said without preamble and held up a bloody hand to halt any interruptions. "I know it's not fair, and either Sir Robert or Sir Alan should have been here to greet the obnoxious little shit. Simon couldn't organise a piss-up in the brew-house – you know it, I know it and so does everyone else here *but* that stupid spoilt pup in his fancy clothes, and all because he wanted to make the grand entrance!"

He sighed. "And I know his sort, God help me! I saw enough of them when I worked for de Braose. If you don't help Simon, then that young lord is just as likely to throw us all out and tell Prince John that we rebelled against him."

"No!" Martin spluttered. "He wouldn't dare!"

"He bloody would!" Guy contradicted him. "He would and worse! You'll find out fast enough that he'll hand out punishments to the first poor sod whom he lays eyes on, guilty or not! And we'll be very lucky indeed if either Sir Robert or Sir Alan can stop him. They may hold the castle, but the power is with the sheriff. With Ralph Murdac the three worked together, so you didn't see what it's like when a sheriff really gets the bit between his teeth, but if this damned lord pushes his luck, you'll find that Sir Robert's control only extends as far as the perimeter of the bailey walls – outside of that fitz John can do as he likes! And Sir Alan will be lucky if he can hold onto that whenever Sir Robert is away!

"So the trick is not to let fitz John have anything major to complain about. He'll never be satisfied, don't ever be foolish enough to think that! But what we all knew at my last post, and which I also saw at de Braose's other castles, was that the places which suffered least were the ones where all the castle folk pulled together to limit the effects of having such an unreasonable lord. However idiotic his demands might be, we all have to work to put them into effect. It's the only way!

"Now I've told young Simon that he needs to get Clipstone ready for his lordship to arrive tomorrow night. We're going to get the bastard out of our hair for one night, at least, while we think what else can be done. I'm going to check now that he's done it and sent a rider out. Then tomorrow morning I shall lead the hunt out."

"Oh Guy, that's harsh on you!" Sir Walter gasped sympathetically, believing that Guy had just had to kill Fletch and Spike.

"Yes, bloody harsh!" Guy agreed bitterly. "But I'm the best huntsman we've got and this one's like de Braose. He needs blood to vent his spleen on! If he just goes out locally tomorrow and gets nothing but a few scruffy hares, he'll be ten times worse! So for all our sakes he's got to get something big, ...and would you trust Mahel or Jocelin to lead him to that, for all that they should know the area?"

The two senior knights shuddered and shook their heads.

"However, I will take those two with me, and Fredegis and Walkelin," he continued, "because in the two days' grace you'll get with him and them being away, you'll need to rally the other knights, and together you'll need to spend some serious time with his household and find out some really important stuff. Like what makes him fly into an uncontrollable rage? A man like him isn't going to have much control, and we'll just have to get used to him having regular tantrums. But what I'm talking about is the stuff which will make him do something truly awful. What has him absolutely apoplectic? So enraged that he won't stop to think of what the king in London or Winchester might say if he..."

"The king's not here," Martin interrupted heavily.

"No," Guy agreed, "but he's..."

"...Already in France and heading for the Holy Land on crusade," Sir Martin finished. "That's the bit you missed in the hall. King Richard sailed on the eleventh of December. You know he left the bishop of Durham and the earl of Essex as joint justices in charge of the country, with William Longchamp put in as chancellor to help them? Well the earl's already dead! Died in December before he could even get back to England from France. Apparently the king was in such a rush to be gone, when he got that news he just appointed Longchamp as justiciar too. So the bloody man's not only chancellor but one of the two chief justices in the land, as well! And to cap it all, all the king did to try to balance things out was to make two of his high servants, Hugh Bardulf and William Briewer, their aides."

"God help us!" Guy gasped. "Hugh de Puiset might be highborn, but he's no kindly bishop, or experienced in government at that level. And Longchamp was Richard's man in Aquitaine, wasn't he? What does he know of England? Nothing! What's worse, not one of those four will be a steadying hand on Prince John. Has the king not even waited to see if they can hold the country while he's away?"

They both shook their heads and Walter added,

"Prince John's been made Count of Mortain. That might have helped things except that Richard's married him off to Isabelle of Gloucester – so that now makes him John, Earl of Gloucester, to boot. And he got the honour of Lancaster too! The bloody prince owns nigh on half of England!"

Guy felt his whole world sliding into a hellish abyss once more. He'd hoped and prayed that he would never serve under a sheriff like de Braose again, but with Prince John as good as ruler it seemed like his prayers were destined not to be answered.

"Very well," Martin sighed after a moment's silence as all three had let the implications sink in. "You've convinced us. I've never served under a man like fitz John before but my brother has. He used to speak like you've just done."

"So you believe me?"

"We believe you," Walter said sadly. "Go on. Go and get your dogs' blood off you. We'll go and find young Simon, and we'll tell Fredegis and Walkelin for you that they're to lead his lordship out on the hunt, but that you will find the game. Meanwhile we'll send riders to tell Sir Robert and Sir Alan to get back here with all despatch. The taxes will have to wait a bit longer. This is a crisis, the taxes aren't!"

It was a tortuous evening for Guy. He sat mute while others tried to make some kind of conversation with the new sheriff, but even the ebullient Sir Henry eventually floundered into silence. It was with great relief that everyone fell into their beds early, although Guy had told Osmaer, with whom he once again shared his room, that he would go out overnight to find some good tracks, pleading an inability to sleep on the thought of what had happened that day. Once down in the stable, he found several of the hands still up and waiting for him. Fletch and Spike had always been popular with them, and had clearly been made much of in the intervening hours.

"Take Tinker with you too," pleaded young Sam, holding up the squirming terrier to Guy once he'd mounted up. "We'll make do with the stable cats. I'd rather that than see Tinker come to harm."

Guy took Tinker and tucked him into the folds of his cloak. "I'll make sure he's looked after," he promised.

"What are you going to do with them?" asked Wilf, another of the young grooms.

"Best we don't know, lad," Harry warned. "A man like this sheriff will trip you up over your own tongue. If we don't know we can't be forced to tell. The main thing is, we trust Sir Guy, and we don't trust this new sheriff. Leave it at that, eh?"

Guy had been surprised to find that there were three horses waiting for him too. One was the gelding he would ride back on, but the other two were a pair of elderly brood mares, much loved by everyone for their good natures but not the kind of fine looking animals the young sheriff would like. Now Harry said that he feared they would be slaughtered the first time the sheriff inspected the stables, especially the roan Maisy who had a sway back and the tattiest mane, but who produced beautiful foals. Harry guessed that fitz John wouldn't even bother to check that the splendid gelding Sir Alan rode was one of hers, but would just see her as cluttering up the stables. Clearly he suspected Guy had somewhere specific in mind as a hideaway for the dogs and that the mares could be accommodated too, but he had no intention of asking where that might be. It suited Guy's purpose too, because he could ride the two mares through most of the night, then change to the gelding later and not tire him unduly.

So with his extended animal companions, Guy rode out of the castle, the two lone sentries at the outer bailey gate pointedly turning their backs as he rode through, so that they could honestly say they hadn't seen him leave – or with what! Guy detected Harry's hand in that and silently blessed him. He had already arranged to meet with the outlaws in the denser woodland just south of Blidworth within a few days, asking them to keep well hidden, but to be there as soon after the Monday as possible. Now he was hoping and praying that they would be there early. His luck held, and as he got close to the distinctive lightning-blasted oak which he'd described to them, he saw them melting out of the deep night shadows into the small clearing. Keeping it short he told them of what had happened.

"Don't worry Guy, we'll keep them safe with us," Bilan promised, hugging Fletch and reaching out to ruffle Spike's ears. In the months at High Peak, Bilan had become as attached to the two big dogs as Guy was. Now, though, Guy spoke more roughly than he'd intended.

"No! You must *not* keep them here!" He saw Bilan's shocked face in the light of the fire they had got going and fought some moderation into his voice. "No, Bilan," he said more gently. "What would happen if they saw me out riding one day? Do you think they wouldn't come to me? And two big hounds loose in a royal forest? At best they'd be lawed."

"What's 'lawed'?" Bilan was worried now.

"They cut off their toes so that they can't run," Guy said bleakly. "Not just cut off their claws, the whole toes and pads! The dogs can never run after that. Poor things can barely walk for weeks. That's if they don't die of shock from the pain of having it done."

"That's barbaric!" Bilan exclaimed.

"Yes it is. And it's a law I've thankfully never had to enforce ...yet! But if I ever have to do that to a dog I never *ever* want it to be one of my own! So Tuck, will you take all three dogs and these two mares over to Gisborne for me, please? I'm sure Ianto and Maelgwn will find something for them to do!"

"Gladly!" Tuck agreed. "In fact we'll all go! Best if we're out of the two shires for a while if this dreadful sheriff gets it into his head to take a look at his new holding."

Robin had said nothing as yet about the way Guy had so forcefully handed out instructions. Now, though, he came to his cousin and clasped him to him.

"Dear God, Guy, I'm so sorry," he said with genuine sympathy. "I had no idea that things could change for the worse so quickly. Are you sure you don't want to pack up and come with us? I'm sure we can find service with one of the Scottish lords!"

"But what to do about Ianto and Maelgwn?" Guy asked regretfully. "This sheriff will soon have it out of someone what the terms of my service were, and then the message will go to Chester and that will be the end of that! We've a lot of bad weather to get through yet before spring comes, and you might have a very long road to travel before you find a lord who will take so many in at one go – and if you do, it'll be because he's got a fight in mind!"

"Aye, that's a fair assessment," Will agreed sagely. "We said no more big battles, Robin. We all agreed on that! I don't want to be fighting English men for a foreign lord – Norman-Scottish or Celtic."

"Guy is right," Malik also agreed. "We may have a long, long march to find someone. Not something you can take a very old man and a blind one on."

Marianne added her own voice of reason too. "And there might be a time when we're very grateful for Guy's manor," she pointed out. "What if someone falls and breaks a leg like Algar did? It doesn't have to be a full battle wound. We'll have to take them somewhere! You can't leave someone out in the winter weather when they can't move about much." She looked at Guy with deep sympathy in her eyes. "I'll go with Tuck and take your dogs to safety, Guy. And I'll check on Ianto, and make sure that we have things set up at Gisborne in case we have to use it as a hospital. If you can stomach facing this horrid sheriff to keep the manor, then we won't squander your gift."

"Thank you, Marianne," he said with gratitude, if not much enthusiasm, then pulled Robin to one side. "Look, Robin, I don't want to undermine your leadership before you've hardly started, so I'm saying this to you alone and not everyone together. You can't all descend on Gisborne. Just at the moment every villager across the whole country has eyes in the back of their heads trying to second-guess what will happen now. Of all people, the king's made William Longchamp his chancellor, and no-one has said a good word about him yet. And worse, I fear Longchamp and Prince John may well clash, and some poor soul will undoubtedly end up caught in the middle. Once upon a time I would have said the prince didn't have the power to challenge a chancellor's authority, but with him now having been given so many shires, I wouldn't discount the possibility! That scares people like me, and the way the king's just buggered off without a backwards glance scares the ordinary folk, because they knew King Henry listened to the hundred courts and stopped the worst of the barons' excesses, but if Richard's far away in the Holy Land then anything could happen."

Robin put a consoling hand on Guy's shoulder. "No, it's alright, Guy. I realise that. I'll send Tuck, Marianne, Walter and Algar over to Gisborne with the horses and your dogs. The rest of us, though, need to go somewhere out of sight for a few weeks. Where can we go where the hunting will be good but where we won't be in danger of falling over foresters or villages?"

Guy didn't have to think hard. "I'd go north well beyond Edwinstowe, for a start, because Clipstone is too near that village, and I've no idea how often this boy-sheriff will want to hunt. And the most northerly of the verderers courts meets at Edwinstowe as well, and the next one of those is due in only two weeks. You need to watch your step by Budby and Carburton because there are private parks around both of those manors, and they have a woodward each.

"One woodward alone won't trouble you personally, but if he sees signs of you being there he'll come screaming for help to Nottingham, and I don't know how this new sheriff will react yet. He could come out mob-handed to throw his weight around, and then you'll be in real trouble. But if you get north of Budby there's only a scattering of isolated villages in the forest. Right up to Blyth, then, you'll be fine. The trees are good and dense and there's loads of cover. The official keeper of the old forest – before King Henry expanded it and made Sherwood – only has a few men up in the north, and if you're careful you'll be able to avoid them on their patrols. Don't leave clear signs of your hunting and you won't get noticed."

"Should we go over the border into Yorkshire?" Robin wondered.

"If you do then I can't tell you much of what you'll find," Guy confessed.

"Safer to stay in northern Nottinghamshire, then," Robin thought aloud.

"I'd say so. Get deep into the forest and you're as safe as anywhere. I'll try to meet you at Blyth at Easter. With any luck fitz John will have cleared off to court by then and we'll have a chance to get back to normal for a bit."

I told my collected friends of the safe spots that night before I rode back. About the way they could follow the valley of the River Rother, which formed the western boundary between Nottinghamshire and Derbyshire, in relative safety as long as they stayed on the eastern, Nottinghamshire side. This side of the river was still heavily forested and had nothing but a scattering of tiny hamlets either side north and south of Worksop. North-eastern Derbyshire, on the other hand had many villages before the land rose to the Peaks and our old haunt of High Peak forest. Scarsdale Hundred, which encompassed that area of Derbyshire, was much more heavily populated than the adjoining Bassetlaw Hundred of Nottinghamshire, maybe because folk were making the most of the

cultivatable land in the lee of the highlands. Such was the kind of information my friends and family would need now.

And it was now that I thought long and hard about those villages in northern Nottinghamshire up towards Yorkshire, Brother, for the folk there were not so cowed by persistent visits by the sheriff and his men as those closer to Nottingham. Robin had the makings of a fine leader, but I knew my area far better than he could possibly do simply because I had personal knowledge of so much of it from having ridden around it, and I knew that I had to help him by sharing as much as I possibly could.

Ah you wonder why I speak again of that? Have you ever thought how much bread we eat, Gervase? That we eat so many meals on trenchers of crusty bread even when we do not really think about it, let alone those times when we consciously eat chunks of bread during the day? I see that you are realising it now that I mention it, though. And where were the outlaws to get such bread? In the heart of the forest they could hardly build themselves a good brick oven, and thin dough cooked on a griddle only goes so far towards satisfying a grown man's appetite – especially in the winter! This was what we had talked about back at High Peak, but without knowing back then where we would be starting and with which area. Therefore the best I could do now was to direct Robin and those he led northwards towards those villages which might prove sympathetic.

However, for the present in our tale it was me who was in the greatest danger from this new sheriff, and it was my cousins and friends who feared for me rather than the other way round. Unless they were uncommonly unlucky they would all be a good deal safer than I was with my mercurial sheriff. And so I had to go and check up on the route I would take this new bane of my existence on come the morrow, for at this early stage I could not afford to allow him to form an opinion of me which might result in my movements being curtailed. I had to smile to his face and curse his miserable soul only once his back was turned.

Now do you see why my time spent under the awful William de Braose was so vital to my story, Brother? That was the training ground on which my skills at such actions were developed and honed. The Guy of Gisborne you know of from the stories could not have survived if sheriff fitz John had come as a totally new experience to me. Just as Robin was made into the leader who was ripe for playing his part in the circumstances of King Richard's reign and beyond by the Holy Land, I was prepared by those early years for taking the part of the man on the inside. The covert presence who passed on vital information to the outlaws and enabled them to defeat sheriffs who might otherwise have had them swinging from the gallows before the first year was out. No, Gervase, that is not bragging, it is the truth!

Chapter 21

So now we come to that first hunt with fitz John. A hunt in which I made an error of judgement which mercifully was not fatal, and for that once again I thanked my favoured Welsh saints, in particular St Cadoc, for his guidance and care. I have mentioned that fallow deer had already come to the parks around Nottinghamshire, yet they were not yet so plentiful that they abounded out in the woodlands as well. I had so far taken very little notice of them, dismissing them as hardly worth the bother except for the fact that their softer flesh meant that they could be eaten on the same day of killing if necessary. Personally I would still rather they were hung for a short while, but a skilled cook, with the aid of a good sauce to marinade the venison in for few hours beforehand, could make fallow deer palatable on the day of a hunt. In my ignorance I saw that merely as a useful attribute in moments of food shortages – such as when important dignitaries arrived at short notice. In my eyes the herd in the castle's park was therefore nothing more than a rather decorative walking larder, and meant no more than spare cattle to me.

It had never occurred to me that they would be valued as sporting beasts in their own right, and therein lay my folly. For I had forgotten that young fitz John was not of the same generation as myself, and had not grown up thinking that a day's hunt necessarily involved the danger of bringing down a beast which might weigh as much as an ox bull, and which was armed not with just two horns but a set of twelve-point horned antlers, and could move as fast as many a horse. Some indulgent guardian of the young lord, I was later to presume, had never allowed him to be exposed to such wild and variable dangers, and then I went and led him into the jaws of death by offering not just the much larger and wilder red deer, but the even more randomly vicious wild boar. Mea culpa, Brother, truly mea maxima culpa! And my only excuse is that I was thinking so hard about reviving the survival skills I had learned under de Braose, that on that day I was half believing that it was a young de Braose I was leading out on the hunt, and not fitz John.

However, if you wish to know whether the young lord survived the experience you will have to listen on.

Nottinghamshire, February-March, the year of Our Lord 1190.

Guy got back to the castle in the early morning with a fair idea of where he would lead the young lord. Mercifully young fitz John played into his hands by not starting until over half of the short winter morning had already passed, making it impossible to go any decent distance out and back in the one day. And so, with Fredegis and Walkelin riding just a horse's head back from Sir Roger, and Guy way out in front, they set off for Clipstone.

Once they got to the royal park it was an odd sort of hunt, for it was already into the afternoon and there were no dogs accompanying them. Apparently the young lord had a pack of hounds of his own, but they hadn't caught up with him yet, and Sheriff Murdac had taken his hounds away with him. So not only no trackers except Guy, and no beaters of any experience, but no pack either. It made for a strange outing without the baying. However, no-one could have said that the hunt was quiet!

The foresters and knights Guy had managed to contrive to come with them on this hunt were all those who talked a lot but weren't particularly good hunters. Only the three walking foresters, currently mounted on ponies to get them to the site swiftly, had anything like the skills needed. These three were Richard Lene and Richard Cooper, and John of Rufford – all of them known by their family names or location for ease of distinction from the multiple Johns and Richards in the castle – and once the party got near to the parkland around Clipstone they began to give Guy some very odd looks. With the rest of the party chattering away like a flock of starlings there was no chance of catching any deer.

"Aren't you going to ask them to be quiet now?" Rufford finally asked Guy deferentially in hushed tones.

"We're never going to catch a deer at this rate," agreed Lene.

Guy grinned at them but without humour. "The bastard said he wanted a hunt. He didn't specify what sort! And you're right, we'll never even get close to a herd of red deer with all this racket going on. So how do you think he'll react if we don't catch anything?" Understanding dawned on the faces of the three lesser foresters and they began to look truly worried. Guy confirmed their suspicions. "It'll be our fault, won't it! So I'm going to give him something that won't frighten quite so easily. We're going after boar!"

"Boar!" Cooper looked horrified. "I've never hunted boar, before!"

"Are there any round here?" Lene wondered worriedly, because, Guy suspected, he was both scared stiff of meeting one and because he'd not seen any.

"Oh there are boar round here," Guy assured them. "Very few these days in the royal preserve, but they're there if you know what you're looking for. And if you three have never taken part in a hunt for one then keep well to the back of the group, and when I call the warning keep to the sides of the tracks too, so that you don't get tangled up in the chaos. If you keep still then the boar won't see you as much of a target, especially if some idiot is harrying its rear!"

Guy had got some odd glances from others in the party too when he'd set out with two horses, but within Clipstone park, by the time they had witnessed him riding ahead, vaulting off his horse to check on tracks and then cantering back to tell them where to go, it was obvious to all of them that he was covering double the ground they were and needed the change of mount. Each time he came back to direct them, and the longer they went on without sight of any game, Guy could see Walkelin and Fredegis beginning to sweat more and more, despite the sharp winter air. Apart from Cooper, Lene and Rufford, who had at least spied signs of deer herds twice already, no-one knew that Guy was playing with all of them.

He wanted to see their young lord really wound up out here, where there were fewer potential casualties. And he also wanted the two most brutal knights in the castle to know what it felt like to be scared for once too. The two former mercenaries were no courtiers or hunters. They could fight men and brutalise peasants, but when every ploy they tried to distract or amuse the young lord fell flat, they were utterly at sea. And finally Guy wanted to see the reaction of the fitz John household men when their lord began to get tetchy – men whom he'd not laid eyes on until the day before, of course, and could therefore not ask in confidence for fear of them reporting his words back to fitz John. How they responded to their lord now would tell him a lot, and he was in an ideal position to observe them with his riding back and forth.

He was gratified to discover that he'd judged the sheriff's temper just about right – bless de Braose, he thought for the first time ever! He'd learned something back then even if it hadn't been anything good. Fitz John seemed on the verge of exploding with petulant temper by the time they got to the third set of boar wallows Guy had spotted along the way, although he pretended that these were the first. He'd been hoping this would be the point when he let fitz John loose, because from memory he thought there was a big male boar and at least two good sized sows in this extended wild pig family. On several occasions the boars had broken through the park fencing, he knew, and they'd done so again, so that Guy led the party through the wrecked pale fence and hedging to outside of the more managed woodland, and into a tangle of old forest. It was pretty clear to the experienced eye which coppice they would be lurking in at the moment too, and Guy called the warning of boar ahead, made sure the three foresters pulled up and stayed back, and then disappeared off to drive them out the party's way.

The big boar came out of the undergrowth like a charging bull, and he was big, really big! Making an unearthly squealing, the massive male came straight into the clearing with his powerful short legs propelling him along at a furious speed, making the ground vibrate with his weight. Fitz John stood in his stirrups trying not to look panicked and wildly launched a spear, which did nothing but skitter along the boar's humped shoulders and enrage him further. The boar turned with remarkable speed and went straight for fitz John, who suddenly looked very much his age and downright terrified as he attempted to turn his horse on the tight woodland track and flee. As the boar set off in pursuit of fitz John – instead of the other way around – there was a sudden crashing in the undergrowth, an ear-piercing squeal, and one of the big sows with a younger sow at her side came thundering into the fray. In a heartbeat the hunt descended into chaos.

Seated on his favourite hunting horse on a small knoll within a coppice of birches, Guy could see out through the gap between the top of the undergrowth and the bottom of the browse-line of the foliage, and found himself chuckling. Fredegis, for all his bravado at attacking defenceless villagers, was clearly no master of the hunt. He was frantically pulling his horse one way then the other to try to avoid the advancing wild boars. Meanwhile Walkelin had got his horse to one side from the main party so that he could at least manoeuvre, but then made the error of dismounting to try and use his spear. It might have worked with smaller boar, but the male was a monster and the older sow as big or bigger than many young males. They were old and wily, and Walkelin was suddenly forced to the ignominious expediency of leaping up and grabbing hold of a low oak tree branch to pull himself out of the boar's way, while his horse took off back towards Nottingham and safety. And best of all, Sheriff fitz John was shrieking like a girl, first running away and then thundering through the undergrowth to try to come behind the boars, making wild stabs with his sword, and getting precisely nowhere.

Before there was any damage done to the horses, Guy decided to intervene. He rode his own horse down on the male, avoiding the others, and drove his spear with both hands down into it behind its shoulders just as it was in danger of goring fitz John's mount. The big pig went down on its knees, screaming, as Guy called,

"Finish it, my lord!" and turned his horse with a fresh spear in his hand to deal with the young female. The big sow could escape, he thought, as she turned and battled her way deep into the undergrowth. She would provide much good game for the next season. He then let Walkelin finish the young sow after his first strike incapacitated her, and turned to see fitz John, one foot on the dead boar's neck, posing with a grin like a child at a feast-day fair.

"What a kill! Did you see that?" the young sheriff crowed, oblivious in his triumph to the telltale damp streak down one leg of his fancy hosen showing beneath his long tunic, which told of his earlier panic.

Guy was glad to see the discomfort of the rest of the hunting party. What was there to say when it was blindingly obvious that the boar had all but been handed to fitz John on a platter? And they were all fully aware of his fear beforehand. Most stood mute, unable to work out what on earth they should say, a few even deeply pink with embarrassment as they looked from Guy to fitz John and back. Surely the day was Guy's, not his, after that display of superb huntsman-ship?

"An excellent kill, my lord," Guy said, giving the spoiled youth what he wanted to hear. The expressions on the faces of the Nottingham men when fitz John took the compliment, and delightedly elaborated on it until it sounded as though he'd killed the boar single-handed, were something to behold. Yet Guy was glad. He'd played a risky game but it had paid off, and now no-one at the castle would be in any doubt about just how dangerous this new sheriff could be. He knew he could have told them until he was blue in the face, but that it wouldn't have had half the effect of seeing it for themselves, and now a good number of men had born witness to just how changeable and egotistic this man was.

Guy watched him like a hawk at the hunting lodge too. He'd had his suspicions ever since he'd seen fitz John in the castle hall, but the man's behaviour here confirmed Guy's guess. For Guy knew a couple of royal hunting lodges along the Welsh border, and Clipstone was vastly superior to any of them, having a gatehouse and a grand, stone-built hall with an undercroft, apart from the wooden buildings around it. Yet fitz John made out that he thought it barely adequate.

"He's playing games with us," Guy told the others when their master had retired to bed. "I know one of the de Lacy hunting lodges over on the Marches – and he's apparently related to them and so might just know those – and while it's big and well appointed, it's a hovel compared to this place. And he certainly isn't part of the main de Lacy family, or why would he be serving as constable to my lord of Chester instead of being over in Ireland where there's much to be gained?"

"Why's he being so sniffy about it then?" the forester based at Clipstone, called Angold, grumbled.

"Because he doesn't know how to behave towards us or this place which is grander than his home," Guy told them. "Don't forget that up until now he's relied very heavily upon his father's name. He was constable of Chester because he was holding it for his father by hereditary right, not because he earned it from King Henry. For all his bravado and confidence, he's never had to stand alone on his own two feet until now. So he's trying to fool us that he comes from something so much better, because he's scared to death that we might realise that he doesn't know what he's doing.

"But be warned! That makes him dangerous! Very dangerous! He'll order us to do things which we know are wrong or illegal and he won't, but he'll still expect us to go through the motions of acting upon his order. So whatever he says, at least say 'yes, my lord sheriff' in his presence and then work out what you're actually going to do when you've got away from him."

Walkelin had already fallen into his bed in drunken dismay, but Fredegis, previously disdainful of Guy, was now listening intently along with the other foresters.

"He's fond of whipping men," a timid voice came from beside them and they realised that the knight who'd come with fitz John to replace William de Wendenal had spoken. He was a tall, thin young man, who hadn't said a word to anyone until now. "You're right," he told Guy, "he's terrible when he's in a temper. I'm stuck with him because my family hold a manor of him, but I wish I wasn't. He terrifies me and I'm not ashamed to say so. I saw him beat his one groom to a bloody mess in the castle bailey. Beat him with a thick stick about the head until the man was dead and then some. And just for bringing the wrong horse!"

The Nottingham men looked from one to another. If Sir Roger tried that with some of the Nottingham stablemen there might be murder done and it wouldn't be to one of them! Even Guy, who was recalling the poor lad who'd died at Grosmont, would have put his money on the stablemen at this castle, for fitz John wasn't de Braose when it came to hand to hand combat.

"Sir Payne," Guy addressed him, having found out his name if little else, "I don't doubt you for a moment, but the worst thing you can do to men like them is let them see that you're afraid of them. It only makes them worse."

"Then you have more courage than me," Payne said dolefully. "It's all I can do not to piss myself when he's like that. It's as if the very Devil himself inhabits him!"

Dark mutterings followed that. A possessed sheriff was a very threatening prospect indeed. However Guy wanted them focused on the very human possibilities of keeping the two shires in one piece for as long as this man was with them, not fretting about things beyond their control.

"Listen!" he said sternly. "Lent begins soon. That's the time to call upon the saints to save us from any malevolent spirits. But we have to get there first!" He fixed the Nottingham men with a steely gaze. "So you tell *everyone* you meet what a madman the new sheriff is! Don't think you can sit back and wait for Robert of Crockston to deal with him, because Sir Robert can't, and neither can Alan of Leek. He can overrule them whenever he likes. We have to look out for ourselves and pass on the warnings whenever we can. People who are scared of him are at least forewarned, and they're less likely to put themselves in harm's way."

If they didn't wholly believe him that night, they certainly did after the following day. For some reason only known to himself, nothing anyone did pleased fitz John from the moment he got up, to the moment he left everyone for his chamber that night back in the castle. Young lord Roger was now covering his confusion from the day before by demanding that this time he wanted deer, and even went so far as to say that he was sure he would bring one down by himself if he could despatch such a mighty boar!

Guy tracked for all he was worth and found two good sized stags, but he could hardly be blamed for the fact that his lord and master couldn't manage to bring them down, even when the second was flushed straight at him. The others in the party then came in for a vitriolic diatribe for having failed to bring the pair down, despite the fact that fitz John had ordered them so far back that they couldn't possibly have got to the beasts after he'd failed. When he went into a full tantrum over the fact that he wouldn't be having haunch of venison that night, Guy was utterly at a loss as to what to do. Did the fool not know that game needed hanging to tenderise it? Boar you might cut into chunks to stew up on the same day, or to roast, but it was a shocking way to treat a good haunch of venison. And did the fool not know that the forequarters – which were only good for stewing anyway – went to the lesser huntsmen and their families? Or at the very least to the servants' hall?

At which point, while considering the conventions attached to a hunt, he suddenly had the revelation that what fitz John had wanted was one of the newfangled stylised hunts after fallow deer – where only a total idiot could fail to make a kill. Where a deer was flushed in a preset line to go past where a young lord's audience might sit and watch while he acted the big man and made his kill with much flourishing and little skill. Fitz John had never expected Guy to lead him out on a proper hunt for the much bigger and more dangerous red deer! No doubt when young Lord Roger had been told that he was going to Clipstone park he'd expected that there would be fallow deer roaming around just waiting for the killing, similar to the park by the castle. Praise be to Saint Melengall, Saint Cadoc and Saint Issui, Guy thought, that the sheriff couldn't have seen the deer-park right by the castle yet, or he'd have wondered what had got into Guy to be leading him so far off just for an afternoon's mild entertainment.

However the royal park here held only red deer, and only such of them as the recently installed pale fencing could restrain – and many of the larger deer could jump that without trouble. Belatedly realising his mistake, and given that there were no fallow deer anywhere near Clipstone, towards the end of the day in desperation Guy brought down a straggling young buck, then hoped like mad that the castle kitchens had some venison salted away which could be presented tonight. In the end, though, the young lord dragged his feet so long there was no time to ask anything of the kitchen, and they had to make do with what was presented to them when they got back.

After that hunt, though, everyone walked around fitz John as though they were on thin ice. Guy did find the chance to point out to fitz John that, like him, he was enfeoffed to the Earl of Chester – a small victory in that it let the bombastic youth know that Guy knew exactly where they both stood in the grand scheme of things and that it wasn't so very high. Especially as Guy took a gamble and let fitz John know that it had been the Earl of Chester himself who had knighted him on the king's behalf. Fitz John had looked as though someone had slapped him with a rotten fish at that news, but Guy had been canny enough to do the telling in front of Alan of Leek, Sir Martin and a visitor from the sheriff of Lincoln, so trying to claim he'd known nothing of Guy's association with his family's own overlord later on wasn't going to be an option.

Guy could only hope that it might act as a some kind of muzzle if fitz John now feared Guy going behind his back to the earl. If fitz John then took revenge upon Guy, the earl, at least, would want an explanation as to why his constable's son had killed or maimed another of his vassals – although it was to be hoped things wouldn't get that far! However, Guy knew that the threat of telling the earl was one he would have to use only when there was a real chance of carrying it through. Fitz John wouldn't be bullied easily, and if he wasn't from amongst the first tier of barons, then at least his family must have plenty of money to have bought him this sheriffdom, and Guy knew how money could sway men's opinions.

With Robert of Crockston back at the castle within the next two days, some sort of order reformed within the castle's walls, although it was blindingly obvious the strain which Sir Robert and Alan of Leek were now working under with such a vacillating and ill-tempered sheriff. Poor Sir Robert suddenly seemed to have an awful lot more grey hairs than he'd had when Guy had been last working out of the castle. Guy took himself off away from there as often as he could, as did everyone else who could find the slightest pretext for spending a night away in some shabby inn, or at a manor or farm – anywhere, in fact, but in the precinct of the castle. The only place they collectively made any headway in impressing him was in getting him to recognise the daily tasks they had to get on with. And Guy had a suspicion that they won by simply boring him stiff with the minute details.

It was therefore cause for a very hushed celebration in the foresters' hall in the oldest part of the castle, during the last week of February, that the monies due at Easter were coming in. A small pin-barrel of wine was smuggled out of the stores, and they quietly congratulated themselves on having got him to listen just a week before a very frosty message from King Richard's new chancellor, Longchamp, demanded to know where the fines from the last lot of forest courts were. William Longchamp was becoming the most hated man in England at lightning speed!

With Longchamp having managed, against expectations, to virtually remove Bishop Hugh du Puiset of Durham only months after Bishop Hugh had bought the secular office of sheriff of Northumberland, no-one wanted to cross the chancellor. Especially as Longchamp had already recently contrived to put his brother Osbert into place as sheriff of Suffolk and Norfolk. Guy hadn't had to work hard at convincing young Sir Roger that his position had suddenly become very precarious when they got that news! Having just doled out his two thousand marks to King Richard for this position, Roger fitz John was potentially in no position to then try to bribe the chancellor in order to keep a lesser post of sub-sheriff under the dreadful Osbert Longchamp, if he got on the wrong side of William Longchamp!

Therefore a hurried court had been set up for the cases in and around Nottingham, and all the knights for once pulled together to ensure that the proceedings were so unutterably dull that fitz John fell asleep and left the workings to Guy and Sir Alan. It was ironic, Guy thought, that it was the misery of having to work under such a sheriff which had brought the sixteen knights together, rather than the amicable atmosphere which had existed under Ralph Murdac.

Yet Sir Hermer and Sir Thurstan, who took the collected fines and taxes south with a suitably large armed guard, came back with disturbing news.

"A week into Lent the Jews in King's Lynn and Norwich were set upon," Thurstan told them before they and the soldiers had even got inside the hall. Standing in the inner ward, they had a large audience from those who had remained in Nottingham. "The rumour is that in Norwich, at least, some of the Jewish families have disappeared and are presumed dead."

"Why in Heaven's name?" Sir Walter wondered. "We need their good will! There must be many a man who's indebted to them after these last years and the heavy taxes we've had to find, by Saint

Thomas — especially with the way Longchamp has been bleeding us white this last few months! We'll need their services again soon!"

Hermer shrugged in incomprehension. "The word is that it's because everyone is distraught about the loss of Jerusalem and the True Cross, and because wandering monks have been preaching the virtue of going on crusade with our new king."

"But we're not fighting the Jews," a perplexed Giles commented.

"No we're not," Guy said sadly, "but to many ignorant folk it's hard to see the difference between Jews and Saracens — and I'd include some of our nobles amongst those who are too stupid to see that they aren't the same." His warnings to James and Malik now felt more like understatements than overreactions. "There are Saracens who are Christians too," he tried to tell them, but that was just completely ignored as the foresters and knights debated their own problems, and whether the Jews would increase the interest on the many loans they had made to men of noble birth. These often large amounts of money had been borrowed to maintain their arms, armour and standards of living, when other income was being gobbled up by the government.

The only other considerations which penetrated their minds were those of the king and the Church, both of whom would also want their coin soon enough. The Church in latter years had, after letters of instruction had appeared from the pope, preached that Jews were to be protected; but would that carry any weight at the moment, Guy wondered privately? Bishop du Puiset had been the one communicating with Pope Alexander against such protection and on the dangers of too much toleration, as Guy had heard from several sources. Therefore if that same anti-Semitic bishop was now seen as the moderate voice, and a voice which had been heavily squashed since the start of the year by Longchamp, then the future was suddenly looking very bleak indeed.

"Blessed Saint Issui, it's Palm Sunday in three days' time," Guy forgot himself by speaking out loud. "If Lent incites such feelings what on earth will the advent of Holy Week bring?"

"You think there'll be trouble?" Giles asked dimly.

Guy despaired of his fellow knight's intelligence at times, and for once he could see the others rolling their eyes in frustration. "Let me put it this way," Guy told Giles patiently. "We have the kingdom still all of a jitter with a new king crowned, and him straight off and out of the country to go on crusade. The Church has been doing all it can to *stir up* passions in order to get men to go east with the king. And we've had the example of the Londoners beating and threatening the Jews at the king's very coronation, with no-one brought to justice for the murders which happened then.

"Against that, if what we're hearing is right, we have only three experienced sheriffs left in office in the whole of England.

Everywhere else there are men like our sheriff here, who have no local knowledge and aren't known locally – and that's in the sheriffdoms which haven't been swept up by Longchamp's family and which, for all practical purposes, are therefore in the hands of under-sheriffs with even less authority!

"And to top it off we have Prince John – or the Count of Mortain as we seem to have to call him now – as the final word of royal power. A man who's always been trouble, and now is left behind without anyone to restrain him. Can you see anyone being afraid that he'll be the one to punish them? I know John's not supposed to set foot in England for the next three years, *if* he honours his recent oath to King Richard, but I wouldn't bet money on that happening! He'd be more likely to see it as good for him if he can make the troubles worse, not better. So when we're now hearing of terrible acts of violence against the moneylenders of Norfolk, surely you can see that there's nothing left to stop such ideas from spreading and being acted upon?"

"I pray you're wrong," Giles said fearfully, but Guy had a nasty feeling that all the prayers in the world wouldn't prevent some sort of catastrophe from happening, and he was proved horribly right.

Little more than a week later, they had just come from the chapel after the Good Friday Mass when a rider hammered into the outer bailey bearing news. To Guy's annoyance fitz John hadn't been required to go to court this Easter because his acquisition of the sheriff's office was so recent. The accounting for the past six months would be made by Ralph Murdac, even though he wouldn't be the one actually bringing the money now, and only at Michaelmas would fitz John have to answer personally to Longchamp.

Robert of Crockston had therefore gone south with an armed escort and the money, leaving Alan of Leek to suffer their master's ire over everything from the state of his feather pillows to the uncooperative spring weather. Consequently, with fitz John being in residence in the Great Hall, the messenger had to present the news to him first, but that didn't stop everyone in the household, and a few others besides, trying to cram into the hall on the messenger's heels to hear the news being delivered.

"There's been a riot in Lincoln, sire," the messenger said deferentially to fitz John, holding out a scrolled message. "For you from my lord Gerard of Camville, the sheriff of Lincoln."

"Well what does he expect *me* to do about it?" fitz John demanded petulantly. "It's his riot, not mine!"

"The message isn't just about the Lincoln riot, sire," the messenger relayed with as much tact as he could muster. "Something terrible happened at York before that on the sixteenth of this month. Messages have gone south to the chancellor, to Longchamp! My lord sheriff is warning you that the might of the chancellor's court is likely to descend upon the north, and in such a mood as to not tolerate anything being out of place."

Fitz John muttered something under his breath and snatched the proffered message out of the gloved hand, then marched off to get it read to him in private by his scribe. It gave the knights a chance to quietly question the rider from Lincoln.

"What happened at York?" Sir Martin asked. "What was so bad?"

"It started with an attack on the home of Benedict of York – he was the leading Jew from there who was killed on his way back from London after King Richard's coronation. Now all his family have been killed as well, their house ransacked and then set alight. The next day after that, many of the York Jews took refuge in the castle, but that night their new leader's house was set upon too. This time, though, the rioting and looting went on into the next day. The Jews were so frightened that they refused to open the castle gates to the constable of York after he went out on business that day. The rioting continued off and on for days! The Jews were in the castle and the sheriff was outside with the mob and armed men! But the worst is that there were no experienced men left in charge. Even Archbishop Geoffrey Plantagenet is in Normandy arguing with the king, as only a brother would dare! So there's not even a senior churchman there to calm things down."

The messenger looked furtively over his shoulder to make sure fitz John was nowhere near and listening before he went on. "Sir John Marshal, the sheriff of Yorkshire, made a terrible misjudgement! He decided to force the Jews out! Someone, maybe even him, told all the young men who were still rioting that an attack upon the Jews would endear them to their new king."

"Oh dear God above," Guy swore, foreseeing what was coming as the man continued,

"Well the Jews held out for several days more until the sheriff brought up siege engines to be used against his own castle."

"And York's still only got a timber keep," Sir Walter groaned, like Guy already anticipating the worst. "A few decent stone shots from a good trebuchet would soon make a dent in those walls. That or the threat of fire."

"That must be what the Jews thought," the messenger said in hushed awe. "They must have been utterly terrified after days with that mob still baying for their blood all around the walls. From what little we've heard from folk who brought the news south, quite aside from the official messages, the local young lords were all in on the act. You can't blame a few hot-headed apprentices from the town for trouble this time. There were proper men-at-arms involved."

He faltered at the enormity of the news, then found the words to continue. "It was last Friday when the siege engines turned up. I'm told it was the Jews great Sabbath that Saturday before their feast of

Passover. Apparently, our own bishop says, they must have thought it prophetic of disaster or something. The Jews ...the rabbi and the men ...they killed their wives and children, and then themselves, believing it would be better than the fate awaiting them when the sheriff's men got in."

"By Our Lady, no," someone gasped.

"How many?" Guy found himself asking yet dreading the answer.

"More than a hundred in the castle. But ...but the tiny few who survived that and came out of the castle begging for mercy, and willing to submit to the besiegers' demand that they submit to baptism, they ...they were butchered to the least one. No... not one Jew survives in York."

"Jesu save us!" Thorsten gasped.

"And it gets worse," the messenger added shakily. "Then the mob went to the Minster, forced the canons there to give them all the documents which were copies of the agreements with the Jews, which were held there. The signed deeds for debts to the Jews. They built a fire of them in the crossing of the church, ...right by the high *altar*!"

"Sacrilege on top of murder!" Sir Walter was appalled. "No wonder word has been sent to the chancellor. Exactly when did all this happen, did you say?"

"The deaths were a week ago today, on the night of Friday the sixteenth. The fire in the cathedral on the Saturday – a week ago come tomorrow. The very day before Palm Sunday when everyone was preparing for Holy Week."

Guy felt his blood running cold. This was the kind of religious savagery Robin and the others had talked of happening in the Holy Land. He'd never thought it would happen here too.

The messenger had taken a draught of the beer which someone had brought in for him while he waited, for fitz John had a scribe penning a reply to the sheriff of Lincoln. "Well you can imagine our thoughts when we got the news. Thankfully we'd put a stop to the riots in Lincoln! *Our* Bishop Hugh – as good a Christian man as ever held that office – and our sheriff, have been very vigilant and quick to act, praise be. But it makes the blood run cold, doesn't it! My master is very concerned for us *all* in the north to have everything under control when the king's men do arrive. We have to make sure that York is seen to be a temporary aberration. That the rest of the north isn't seen as rising against royal authority again."

In the long century since the arrival of William the Conqueror in England there had been several brutal suppressions of any hint of disloyalty in the north – none in anyone's time who was present today, but the tales still told made everyone seriously worried over the prospect of an irate king's army turning up again. And that would have been enough on its own had this happened in the last few years, but with Longchamp now having the bit well between his teeth, just about anything might happen.

Once upon a time, Hugh du Puiset (a very different Bishop Hugh at Durham from the devout Hugh of Lincoln) might have been able to temper Longchamp's actions. He might just possibly have stepped in to stop the riotous excesses too, out of self-preservation if not Christian charity. But he was currently in Normandy with King Richard, no doubt still trying to get his own offices and lands back from the king if not his chancellor, and to all intents and purposes he was now as powerless as any of them. About the only good thing Guy could think of was that, despite his appointment as archbishop of York, Geoffrey Plantagenet was under the same oath as Prince John to not set foot in England for three years following Richard's coronation. So the great warmonger was safely distant in Normandy and under Richard's eye, not in York making matters even worse, because Guy didn't share the messenger's faith in Geoffrey, even if the bastard Plantagenet son had been made archbishop.

When the messenger had been allowed to leave and get some food before setting off back on a fresh horse, fitz John turned to his men.

"I have decided to act," he said pompously, completely oblivious to the worried exchange of glances this caused amongst his knights and the foresters. "The sheriff of Lincoln has given me cause to think that the perpetrators from York may now be realising the depths of their ...mistake. It would not look well if someone carrying loot which has very obviously come from York should be detained by the king's men while in *this* shire. I therefore want all of you to begin searching for any suspicious travellers."

Guy thought frantically. How to get the sheriff to let him do what he wanted, which was to go towards York and find out for himself what had happened? And to get to Blyth for that rendezvous with his friends! He knew fitz John loathed him, so he must play on that.

"The attack was over a week ago, sire," Guy pointed out. "Even if the perpetrators were held up for days because of the week long Easter festivities, they're likely to be well on the roads away from York by now." If they were well-born men, Guy guessed that the chances were that they would be forced to stay at monasteries along the way, or risk roughing it in inns little better than cottages. "Nottingham to York, ...about eighty miles as the crow flies. That means they could already be hereabouts or nearly so, or maybe even south of here. Maybe at Tickhill? No, we'd have heard of that. ...We could try eastwards! In case they try to get to a port!"

"That's the sheriff of Lincoln's territory, you idiot!" fitz John snapped. "And Tickhill? Are you mad? That's another of Prince John's castles! Why would they go to a *royal* castle, you dolt, if they fear the chancellor? Just for that, *you* can be the one who trails off all the way north to the Don! Then you can go and gaze at bloody Tickhill if you want! And you can go and speak to the Templar preceptories on the Ouse. I have no wish to be kept in the dark over events on my border! See if those cursed Templars have heard anything. Or at least you can try! I doubt they'll give answers to the likes of you!"

Got you, you bastard! Guy thought triumphantly, although forcing himself to look suitably disgruntled. He still listened hard to the knights presently doing their annual military service being given their search areas, though. He didn't want to be saddled with one of them at his heels for what he was proposing.

Yet Saint Issui seemed to have answered his prayers in every respect today. Given the extra men de Wendenal had siphoned off for High Peak, and then those who had gone with Sir Robert, there weren't enough men to go in force with everyone and still secure the castle. Even better, it fell to Guy to sort out who of the ordinary men went with whom. Allan of Leek was busy trying to moderate fitz John's responses, and to get the fool to realise that he could not go tramping into the territories of the sheriffs of Leicestershire, Lincolnshire and Yorkshire just make himself look good.

Meanwhile Sir Walter and Sir Martin were frantically trying to keep the everyday business going, and these two knew that, despite having been away for months, Guy still knew the individual soldiers better than they did. He therefore managed to leave six of the men he'd brought from High Peak at the castle – to keep them out of the worst of what might happen – and to take the other six with him, while ensuring that the likes of Sir Henry got the really keen men and those bullies who hadn't gone with de Wendenal.

Henry was becoming almost as much of a pain in the neck to him as de Wendenal had been, endlessly fawning around fitz John in a frantic attempt to ingratiate himself. It wasn't working, but Henry was turning into a regular telltale. So Guy had been secretly delighted that the knight had been given the road down to the crossroad with the Fosse Way to patrol. With any luck, with that crossroad being close to the Nottinghamshire-Leicestershire border, the bullish Sir Henry would pay scant regard to the political niceties and make a nuisance of himself in Loughborough or Melton Mowbray, or at least in one of the bigger villages whose voices the sheriff of Leicester would heed.

Yet even fitz John didn't dare to not observe Easter properly, for fear of what that might mean to his immortal soul. It was therefore only on the Monday, the day after that fateful Easter Sunday, with March blowing itself out like a lion, that the knights rode out with their men-at-arms, and various foresters added in to make up the numbers. In consequence, it wasn't quite the trip to Blyth which Guy had envisaged, but at least everyone now rode out of Nottingham as though the hounds of Hell were on their tails, allowing him to do the same. Everyone was keen to get away from their pestilent sheriff and to do something which might enhance their prestige for once. Guy was just glad that he was heading north with men he could trust, and as he rode Guy also reflected that at least the outlaws weren't in danger of being captured in this immediate hunt, for they wouldn't match the descriptions of young noble men being circulating as having done the worst deeds at York.

Most of his concern was instead over the thought of them being swept up in some greater catastrophe. In the past, King Henry had come north in person to quell uprisings of his barons and those in league with the king of Scotland, therefore King Richard didn't need to look back as far as the Conqueror for a precedent for being heavy-handed with the folk of the northern shires. Moreover, the new king might feel a deep urge to flex his muscles here and now, simply to show that he was every bit as formidable as his illustrious father. To have such a blatant flouting of his wishes so early on in his reign could very well rouse the infamous Plantagenet temper into dramatic action, Guy feared. And if that happened then what size of force might King Richard bring with him? If it was simply a small one to escort him to York, and be sufficient to deal with any remaining troublemakers, that was one thing. If he really wanted to make an example of York, though, Guy had the nastiest of suspicions that the warrior king might bring a sizable portion of those mercenaries and French fighters whom he had already assembled for the crusade.

Such men in great numbers would do a very thorough scouring of the whole of Yorkshire, and maybe those shires connecting to it, and if that happened, and there were hundreds of armed men riding through northern Sherwood, then the best place for Robin, John and the others was going to be back in the rugged hills of Derbyshire. And if he thought of Derbyshire in any other way, it was only with relief that not only was de Wendenal not here to enjoy such a hunt, but that the rocky shire was probably the most unlikely refuge for the perpetrators from York to flee to, and therefore their villager friends were free from this particular danger. No reprobate from York was likely to head that way, but then in Guy's eyes the chances of him encountering any of the troublemakers from York anywhere in that shire or this had to be beyond slim, unless they were exceedingly stupid – who would stay where they were expected to be once the chancellor's displeasure became known?

Ah Brother, looking back I can see that I was being far too optimistic. You see I was not worried about my friends and family in any other way than that the <u>king's</u> actions might impact upon them. What I really wanted at that point was to get news of them and from Gisborne manor, because my deepest concern was still this new sheriff. What if he would not honour my need to go to Gisborne as Sheriff Murdac had done? In theory he had to, given that the manor was given to me subject to my working in Nottinghamshire, and was hardly going to run itself. Only I and those close to me knew that I hardly needed to do a thing when I went there, since my friends ran it so well for me in my absence. Yet I feared that young fitz John might refuse me that leave out of petulant spite, and I therefore wanted to know that all was well there for the time being, since it might well be a long time before I could ride that way myself again.

I was consequently most anxious on my own behalf to find Tuck and Marianne at Blyth with Walter and Algar, and to hear that none of the current unrest had disturbed the peace of my little manor. I also wanted to know that they had made it to Gisborne and back without incident, for that would tell me much of the state of fear in other shires. But better still would be the news that they had met up with Robin and the others once more. Nothing would please me more, I believed, than to wander out of Blyth and find the whole lot of them camped not far off and ready to move on. If royal retribution was to descend upon us I wanted Robin and the others well away from here as fast as possible.

Not having left Nottingham until well into the morning, and with the daylight not at its best, we arrived in Blyth at noon on the second day having ridden with speed, but no undue urgency once the castle was out of sight. King Richard's force, or whatever other punishment he might visit upon York, still had to be at the very least a week away, and probably more than that. Any other problems would come from either our own sheriff, or the disgraced sheriff of Yorkshire, and I sincerely hoped that the awful realisation of the mess that man had made of things would not extend to harrying some miscreant across the shire boundaries. Therefore I left the soldiers enjoying an ale by the fire of the local inn while I went to search for my friends.

Dear me, Brother Gervase, you do fidget so! I am not digressing in telling you of all the goings on at Nottingham to taunt you, now that you have met Robin Hood and want to hear of him. That massacre has a very important role to play, and so does the first sheriff of Nottingham I learned to really deceive! Just let me catch my breath and we shall continue.

Chapter 22

The first of my shocks came when I wandered out of the inn's yard and found Tuck and John waiting for me, but no sign of Robin. They quickly hustled me off to a quiet lane and explained that things had gone wrong in ways we could never have expected. Tuck and the party who had gone to Gisborne had had an uneventful journey, praise be to God, and had delivered my dear hounds into Elyas and Ianto's enthusiastic care – so I knew that they at least would be well cared for. Marianne had been good to her word too, and had left full instructions for the gathering of medicinal herbs, and the acquiring of good clean linen which might be made into bandages. That was not where the trouble lay!

That, Gervase, had come in the most unexpected form of another crusader from the east determined to return to his Templar preceptory. While all of my friends had still been together, they had come upon him and his two men, who had been set upon by foot-pads not far from where we stood now. I tell you, I felt my heart sink then, Brother, for I knew that if anything would make Robin and the others disregard my warnings it would be the prospect of helping a fellow fighter from the Holy Land. The three were a Templar knight and two sergeants, who were returning to the preceptory of Penhill, which lay up on the edge of the Yorkshire moors.

That Robin knew of where it was there was no doubt, for I myself had mentioned it to them on several occasions, before the idea of them going back into the order had been rejected. Even worse, I realised guiltily, I had portrayed it as one of the safer order holdings, since Penhill's chief claim to fame was for breeding horses not fighters. With one sergeant nursing a terrible head wound, John now told me, Robin had decided that he and the five others who knew what to expect from a Templar holding, would take them on and see them safely to the preceptory. He had asked John, the Coshams and Hugh to stay local to Blyth, so that if they were not back in time for our meeting that someone would be here to meet both myself, and also Tuck, Marianne, Walter and Algar when they returned. It was little consolation that Robin had also thought enough ahead to ask the remaining five to start surveying the area to find hideouts, and that Hugh had been deliberately left behind because, as a native of nearby Barnby, he knew the area well already.

My heart sank even further when I heard that nothing since had been heard of Robin and the five. However, my friends now gathered around me had heard enough of the troubles in York as to be very worried on their own account for them.

˜Robin was going to take them straight up to York˜ Hugh told me. ˜Then they were going to follow the old Roman Deer Street north and west towards the moors.˜

That certainly made sense as far as it went. Under normal circumstances it was even a halfway safe plan, although I was more than a little worried that they had planned to go into York itself, and not just because of the recent trouble. A shire town with a sheriff in residence was not the safest place to go as a renegade crusader – especially when that sheriff was the warlike John Marshal! My fear, therefore, was that six men acting as Templars and bringing three more with them would stand out like a sore thumb, even in a busy place like York, and Sheriff Marshal was just the sort of man to notice and start asking questions Robin would not have the answers for.

Why, I asked the others, had they planned to do that? And was told that it was the state of the sergeant with the head wound which had forced Robin's hand. Apparently, knowing of such things from their own experience, they feared that they would have to leave him at a monastic hospice somewhere if he struggled to cope with the journey, and therefore, if they might need such a place, then they had little choice but to stick to the main roads and towns. All I could pray, then, was that hopefully on their way north they would have been well past the city before it had gone up in riot and flames.

Oh how I feared for them, Brother! As did the others, and we were all resolved to go looking for them. Therefore when my friends heard that I had the six men-at-arms with me from High Peak, and not some of the sheriff's henchmen, their relief was plain to see – it being somewhat hard to distinguish men's face beneath the ring-mail coifs we had all ridden into Blyth wearing as protection against unexpected trouble. These six – Sergeant Ingulf, Ruald, Alfred, Big Ulf, Osmund and Leofric, along with the other six from High Peak – will appear again as my secret allies within the castle, Gervase, so mark them well!

For now, though, I – as designated leader under the circumstances – had to make a decision as to which road to take north, and chose to go the slightly less direct route through the woods. If Robin and the others had been any closer, I felt they would have made their presence known in some way, and anyway, once back in Nottinghamshire they would not stick to the roads for safety's sake. Therefore there was little chance of us missing them by likewise avoiding the main road.

I definitely wanted to avoid Tickhill, too. The big, stone, royal castle there was the first over the border into Yorkshire, but with its constable having something of a free hand in the royal lands immediately across on our side of that shire boundary, and I had no intention of getting embroiled in cross-shire arguments. However, to veer much further east from Blyth would mean going a bit too close to Harworth and Scrooby villages, and I wanted no-one from there commenting on the number of men I had with me, should they be put to the question. So instead we went west for a while, and then steered a middle course to the west of Tickhill and east of Maltby in a very narrow corridor of safe land, where we almost crept along the hedgerows in order to remain out of view from the massive square keep up on its motte at Tickhill.

We all felt that we should at least go as far as Doncaster to check for signs of Robin and the others, and since we were heading that way, Walter and Algar were vocal in wanting to go that bit further and see Much if we could. The lad had not been forgotten by any of us, you see, and in this time of unrest we felt a strong compulsion to make sure all of our friends were well and unharmed. Oh, Brother Gervase, what a prescient thought that was! Ah, you frown again. Would you rather I ascribe it to Fate? ...No? I thought you would not! Then do not sigh so, and let me draw you into our chase after your hero, Robin. Ah, I thought that would please you!

However, I will also tell you now that I was most disturbed to hear that my cousin had taken on two young peasant lads before they left. My friends had come upon them poaching, and had found out that they were on the run from their village, having been caught there setting traps by the forester for the north of the old forest. I was touched by Robin's new-found compassion for the ordinary folk, but what worried me most at this news was whether we could wholly trust them.

Again, I confess most humbly, Gervase, that my fears were for my own position at that moment, for I was the one most in danger of being exposed as having what would be seen as traitorous leanings. Lads like that might not see me in the same light as those I had had time to develop a bond with! And now the final blow fell, for Robin had taken Bilan along with him to act as his squire, and the two lads to act as their ~lay brothers~ to make their appearance all the more believable as full Templar knights of some standing. Poor Thomas and Piers were near frantic with worry for their youngest brother, as you might well imagine!

However, you must follow our band of men into Yorkshire for what happened next.

Yorkshire
March, the year of Our Lord 1190

Tickhill was easily avoided by the small armed band, but they still had to cross the River Don and that meant going into Doncaster. However, Guy had high hopes that with so much armed traffic using the bridge due to the riots, the good folk of Doncaster would be unable to remember the details of one specific group, and as a place it was a good bit bigger than the villages they had avoided, making such confusion more likely. Doncaster Castle had been destroyed years ago at King Henry's command and had never been a particularly grand affair anyway, so at least they wouldn't have a garrison in the town to contend with. Mercifully there was plenty of bustling trade going on at the warehouses along the river front, and so Guy rode through with his legitimate party of six, and the others came across the bridge in a pair and two threes in the general throng on foot.

It was as Guy waited with John and the others for the last three of Tuck, Algar and Hugh that they heard John's name being called, or at least someone named John. Furtively Guy and John looked about them, trying not to make it obvious that one of them answered to that name.

Suddenly the crowd parted and Allan appeared in front of them, but it was a very different Allan to the sulky, petulant youth they'd put on the road to York. Now a grown man of twenty-five he was still slightly built, but in contrast to his former self he currently looked positively ill-fed. The rounded face of youth had become one of fine bones showing too prominently through pale skin, and he walked with a slight limp, although whether that was permanent or not wasn't clear.

"John!" he gasped, "I thought it was you!" Then he turned and caught Guy's frosty stare and blushed. "Cousin Guy, hello." There was a substantially more humble tone in his voice than any he'd used to Guy when they'd re-met the last time, and Guy decided to give him the benefit of the doubt before thumping him and getting the men-at-arms to drag him north with them.

"Allan," he said smoothly, "what brings you here?"

"York," Allan gulped, his eyes darting towards the north road more than a little fearfully. "The riots. By God and Saint Thomas, they were awful! That castle burning was horrible! We could hear some of the screams of the women and children as they died too." He blinked. "Those noble thugs actually laughed! Can you imagine that? Laughing at someone dying?" He shivered, and Guy and John belatedly recalled that whatever he might have become, the child-Allan they had known had always been a sensitive soul.

"What were you doing in York?" Guy asked calmly. A lot would depend on the answer to this question – whether he thought Allan was answering honestly, for a start, and whether there was a legitimate reason for him being there, as opposed to stealing in one form or another. If Allan had changed, then with John already going into the forest there would be no reason not to take Allan – unless, of course, Allan had got himself a lawful occupation. Somehow, though, Guy doubted that, if only because Allan looked so ill-fed.

"I've been working as a minstrel," Allan told them without hesitation, then smile ruefully. "Not exactly regular work, but then there's not much I *am* fit to do." He even had the grace to look shamefaced as he added, "I'm no good at farming – even despite your best efforts, John! Jesu, I was a horrible lad, wasn't I! I didn't realise what you did for me, or why, until I was on my own."

"Did you get caught?" Guy asked, seeing that John was struggling with his own feelings and not trusting himself to speak just yet. He didn't need to elaborate over getting caught at what.

Now Allan couldn't meet his eye. "Yes, ...a few times." He flicked a glance up at Guy who simply quirked an eyebrow at him, and realised he would have to be a bit more specific than that if he was to redeem himself with his cousins. He sighed and looked down again. "I broke into a couple of merchants' houses ...and the second time got beaten badly, but managed to escape before the sheriff's men got there. Then I went north again. Went to Carlisle, ..." He paused and winced. "That was when I decided that the dice weren't a good idea anymore. ...Or at least not to go from tavern to tavern with."

"The stocks, the town gaol, or the dungeons?" Guy wondered, putting as much insouciance into his voice as he could manage. He didn't want Allan to think it was too much of a foregone conclusion that he was welcome amongst them again, even if Guy knew John was unlikely to let him go a second time.

Allan wrinkled his nose. "Err ...all ...not all in Carlisle, though."

That made Guy blink in surprise. No wonder Allan looked rough! Well at least he'd made it out of the dungeon in one piece. "Which castle? Whose dungeon?"

"Oh ...luckily only a place called Harbottle up by the Scottish border, where I got out because they had trouble with the Scots and wanted the room for really dangerous men." Suddenly his face broke into the old cheeky grin. "All I'd done was sneak a kiss off the daughter of a visiting lord!"

"The girls like him, they do!" a voice came from behind Allan.

Popping up beside him came the most disreputable looking character any of them had seen for a long time. Positively scrawny, with tatty, mousy hair and missing part of one ear, the young man nonetheless was matching Allan's grin and Guy sighed inwardly. If he was any judge of character these days he would bet on these two egging one another on something shocking, and it would always be into mischief if not downright trouble.

"This is Red Roger," Allan said by way of introduction. "We've been travelling together now for quite a while."

Roger beamed a mischievous smile at them but it was lost on Guy and John.

"So what have you been calling yourself, then, Allan?" Guy asked dryly. "Should I be prepared for enquiries about disgraces to the fitz Waryn name from the sheriffs in the north?"

Allan shook his head while trying to nudge Roger into fidgeting less. "No, I left that name behind in Carlisle very early on," he admitted. "Back then I thought that since Fulk and Philip had abandoned me, I would abandon them," he added with a bit more humour. "After that it was ...politic ...not to be associated too closely with one place, if you see what I mean. So I've been calling myself Allan of the Dales. Nice and general, you see. Especially up north."

"Hmmm," Guy agreed with an attempt at a stern frown, although by this stage he was struggling not to show his amusement. "Rather a lot of dales in Yorkshire, eh? So rather depends on how bright the sheriff's men are, and if they actually think to ask which one they should put you on record as coming from, ...or have I got that wrong?"

Allan ducked his head and his wince told Guy that he'd hit the truth full on, and that Allan and Roger had probably had run-ins with a good many law-keepers in the last few years.

An idea which John picked up on and frowned, fixing Roger with a stern look. "And what's your brand of trouble, then?"

The air of assumed innocence which both he and Allan immediately took on yet again made Guy groan out loud. "Oh for Heaven's sake, stop it! Just answer the question! John and I weren't born yesterday, you know."

Allan and Roger shuffled guiltily, then Allan gave Roger an elbow in the ribs. "Go on then, tell him!"

"What?" Roger didn't seem all that convinced. "How do you know he ain't goin' to tell someone?"

Guy pounced, and with his greater height and strength had grasped Roger by the scruff and nearly lifted him off his feet before the young rogue had realised what was happening. "I happen to be one of the sheriff of Nottingham's senior forester knights," he said drolly. "If I wanted you in custody you'd be under arrest by my men already."

"Bleedin' 'Ell!" Roger squeaked to Allan. "You di'n't tell me 'e was one o' *them!*"

Roger's perturbation was so comical that Guy dropped him in laughing, and none of the other soldiers made to step in since Guy seemed unworried. If nothing else this convinced Allan, and now he took hold of Roger's arm to stop him running off.

"Roger comes from London," he told them, "But he's been up here a long time."

"Could've fooled me with that accent," Guy interrupted wryly.

"Can't 'elp it. Ain't never lost it," Roger muttered huffily, forcing Guy to smother a grin at the indignation. "Got brung up 'ere on account of bein' apprenticed to a dyer, see? I got knowed as Red Roger as a lad on account of always bein' stuck with doin' the red dyes, and me hands was permanently stained."

Guy managed to keep from smiling enough to ask innocently, "Not that you were ever caught red-handed then?"

"I ain't never *killed* no-one, if that's what you mean!" Roger protested vigorously.

"Roger's the best thief I've ever met," Allan was forced to confess. "But he only takes from the rich and what they carry out into the streets with them. Purses and trinkets. Light stuff like that."

"I don't do houses," Roger added with a vehement shake of the head. "Too dangerous! Too much risk of there bein' servants in the way. Gotta have room to run, see?"

Guy looked to John and rolled his eyes in good-humoured despair. Clearly Allan was destined to live on the edge of the law whatever they did.

"So what are you two doing *here*?" Guy asked again. "In Doncaster specifically, I mean, apart from fleeing York."

Allan became serious again, which at least convinced Guy and John that it was something even this irrepressible pair couldn't joke away.

"We came down here because Roger was apprenticed here in Doncaster. He knows the place like the back of his hand, and we wanted somewhere we could find hiding places, either in the town or out in the country. It started out with us just running from York. That mob was getting bloody dangerous! We were scared that if they didn't get their fill of blood from the Jews, then it would be the likes of us they started hunting for sport."

By now Tuck had appeared and was standing behind Allan with an expression of surprise on his face, but didn't interrupted him.

"We reckoned it was still too early in the year to try and hide up on the moors or over in the Pennines, so we came south. Still snow up in the higher valleys, you see. We went west of Selby because of all the Templar granges and preceptories round there. The trouble was, too many of the troublemakers from York had the same idea a day or so later. We'd slowed down thinking that we'd look less suspicious if we were travelling at a normal pace, like anyone would if we were just going to market or something."

Then he shivered. "We'd got as far as Ferry, on the Aire, and were crossing the river when they caught up with us. We would've run for all we were worth at the first sight if we hadn't been in mid-river when they turned up. Well we got off that ferry and ran like hares! I doubt the ferryman knew what he was taking across but we recognised one of the faces. Only they were mounted and we weren't. We hoped we'd lose them, bearing east as we did, but they were on our tails all the rest of the day. Finally we hid out in a copse of beeches, but they went to find refuge at a place Roger says is called Norton."

"Norton?" Walter gasped. "But that's where Much's folk are!"

"Not now they ain't!" Roger said grimly. "Half of 'em fled, the others who weren't fast enough are dead. They burned the mill and the cottages around it."

"Who's Much?" Allan asked. "We took three kids to Campsall after those burning, murdering bastards had gone. Is he a grown-up? Will he have a wife and children there?" He'd taken in Guy and the others' despairing expressions and realised the connection must be important.

"Much was one of us when Guy got us out of the sheriff's prison," Walter said sadly. "Poor lad had only gone into Newark to get some special tools for his father, because the blacksmith there was more of a craftsman than most, and some stuff for his mother as well. The sheriff's thugs just swept him up for poaching without him ever having done a thing. He got dragged to Nottingham for the court then never got taken out of the dungeon. He'd still have been there, and us too, if Guy hadn't found us."

Allan looked at Guy askance. Clearly this was a side of his cousin which he'd not expected.

"We shall have to go and look for Much," Guy said before any of the others could plead him to do so. "If his parents are dead and possibly poor Joseph too, then he'd be better off joining you lot in Sherwood."

"Sherwood?" Now Allan was really shocked, and Roger too.

"You ain't goin' into *Sherwood*?" Roger gulped. "There's ...there's wild beasts and monsters in there! Them old trees are alive! It's haunted!"

"Oh don't be daft," John growled. "Anyway, it's not like we have much choice. There's nowhere else left for us to go."

"What does Much look like?" Allan suddenly asked.

"Smallish chap of about ..." Guy had to stop and think, "oh coming up twenty I suppose. But like you, Allan, he looks young for his age. ...A shock of dark, curly hair that never lies down, and quite well muscled even though he's slim, because his folks ran the mill and he was used to lugging sacks of flour and grain around. Why? Do you think you've seen him?"

Allan had suddenly brightened. "Yes, and if it's the same lad he's here!" He grabbed Guy's arm and began pulling him over one way. "We saw him running out of the mill when they set it alight. We tried to get him to come with us back then, but he wouldn't. Wanted to see if anyone was alive when he could get close enough. Said something about a place under the floor, so we guessed he hoped his folks might have hidden themselves there. We didn't dare say that they'd have suffocated with the smoke even if they didn't burn.

"Well we walked on here once we'd taken the little ones to Campsall. Slowly this time, to let the horsemen get ahead of us, and we've been camped out here in Marsh Gate." He gestured to the ramshackle cluster of huts on this side of the Don, which seemed to be filled with the poorest of folk, of the kind who probably couldn't afford a place in the town proper. "He wandered in all blackened and singed last night..."

"...Show me!" Guy interrupted fiercely, and Allan took off at a jog with Guy and the other outlaws at his heels, leaving the bemused men-at-arms to bring up the rear.

Under a rotten-thatched lean-to they found Much lying shivering and crying. Walter and Algar surged forward but it was Guy who got to him first.

"There, there, Much, we've got you," he said gently as he put his hands under Much's arms and bodily lifted him out.

Much looked up, realised who it was who was in front of him and collapsed into Guy's arms with a sob of relief.

"They're dead!" he choked out. "All of them! Ma and Pa and Joseph! I found them..." and he wept, unable to say more.

"You're safe, at least," Guy told him with substantial relief in his voice. "And we were coming to look for you anyway."

"Were you?" Much sounded surprised.

"We all heard about York," Walter said, coming to hug Much. "I don't know why but both Algar and I had worrying dreams about it and you. We convinced the others that whatever else we did now, that first we had to come and check on you first." Guy thought that was stretching reality a bit given how everyone had thought of Much, but he wasn't going to argue with Much so shaken.

"And you were right to follow your instincts," Tuck agreed. "Do you think anyone else from Norton got away?"

However, Much shook his head.

"They'll pay for this," Guy assured him. "Maybe not for your mother and father and Joseph, but things in York are already being brought to the chancellor's attention. The king won't like his main moneylenders being abused again. Someone will have to pay a price other than with coin for this disaster."

"But how will they know who?" Allan asked sadly. "The sheriff of York was involved, so he and maybe one or two others will be fined or something. But who knows who the other men were? There were so many and an awful lot of them have already fled. By the time the king's men get there they'll all be long gone."

"Cuckney," Much said in a wobbly voice.

"Is that a name or a place?" Allan asked.

Much sniffed and wiped his nose on his sleeve. "That's what one of the two noblemen called the other when they were in Norton. 'Hey, Cuckney, come over here'. I heard it quite clearly."

Allan and Roger were about to say that that still didn't mean a lot until they saw the expression on Guy and the soldier's faces.

"Cuckney is a wealthy manor with a village, five or six miles north of Mansfield," Guy said positively, "and I'm pretty sure that one of the sons is, or was, a squire to someone in Yorkshire." He grinned wolfishly. "What would you bet on it being him, and him running back to his home if he came south? I've never been there on account of it being in the old Forest of Nottingham part of the forest, and therefore it's under the keeper's authority not the sheriff's, but I know where it is." He gave them a moment for this to sink in then added, "We shall be virtually passing the door on the way back. What do you say, lads? Shall we give that new sheriff of ours a present?"

The six men-at-arms all grinned back. That would be a much more palatable kind of justice to be handing out for once.

"But that's for me and these lads to deal with," Guy added firmly to the others. "I want you lot well out of the way when we do, too! Just in case the sheriff gets some harebrained idea of there being more trophies in the area, and he rides back with a whole bunch of us to search the area more thoroughly. I'm sorry, Much, but you won't be able to see these men getting what's coming to them, but I promise you they won't get away from us."

However, of more immediate concern was which way they were going to go now. Neither Allan and Roger, nor Much, had seen or heard of a band of Templars riding through the area prior to the disaster, or after it. Yet none of them wanted to leave without at least trying to find Robin and the others. Camping just north of the poor cots and huts of Marsh Gate for the night, John and Guy brought Allan up to date on their reunion with Baldwin, that he was now called Robin, and why they would be searching for him and the other five. For the first time in a very long time John saw Allan being genuinely impressed, for his cousin's desperate fight in the Holy Land seemed to hit a nerve with him in a way that nothing Guy or John had done did, and by the time they rolled into their blankets he was as determined to find the soldiers as the rest of them.

However, the choice moment of the evening came when Allan, Roger and Much met Marianne. Once they'd all made camp she insisted on taking a look at Much's burns. He had several which had come up in great swollen blisters, and was wincing with pain at almost every movement. His hands in particular were terribly burned from where he'd tried to move timbers to get into the mill.

"Sit down here!" she told Much in the kind of voice which wasn't to be disobeyed, while pointing to where the fire was burning brightly and she had some light to work by. "Let me look at those hands!"

" 'Oo the 'ell's she?" Roger asked in hushed awe, his eyes running up and down Marianne's figure as he took in the long blonde hair in a tousled, curly knot, and the way she was attired like a lad in hosen and a long tunic, with what had remained of her Hospitaller black tunic after the sheriff's men had torn it, made into a tabard which she wore over the top.

Even John couldn't resist the chance to tease Allan back for once. "She's a fighting Hospitaller sister from Jerusalem," he said with deadly seriousness, "and she's one of us now."

"Bleedin' 'Ell!" Roger gulped, eyes opening like an owl's in shock.

Allan gasped too. "A Hospitaller? A woman?"

"Yes," Guy replied firmly. "A Hospitaller and a woman, and you will treat her with respect! She's not some village lass to be sneaking kisses off – although I think you'd be in more danger than her if you try that."

He said it as a statement of fact, deliberately not making too much of the issue so that it wouldn't be seen as a challenge for the mischievous Allan and Roger. Marianne didn't deserve to be hounded by the irrepressible pair every time there wasn't someone more responsible around to stop them. However Allan's face was a picture just at the thought, making Guy struggle to keep his amusement hidden. As for Roger, Guy had never seen a hare come face to face with a fox, but if he ever did he would bet the expression on the hare's face would be much the same as the one currently on Roger's.

"We need egg-white for these burns," Marianne was saying to Tuck. "Do you think you could get any eggs in Doncaster?"

Guy pulled out his purse and handed some coins over to Tuck. "Get as many as Marianne needs."

Tuck nodded and disappeared into the gloom while Marianne began carefully cleaning the soot off Much's hands. Strangely, it was Allan and Roger who were most fascinated by what she was doing.

"Why egg-whites?" Allan asked her with as near respectful awe as Guy had ever known him have.

Marianne replied without looking up from her task. "The egg-white dries without going brittle and cracking, so it makes a kind of second skin over the burn. That's really good for a start because it stops dirt getting into the raw bits. But there's something in the egg-whites themselves that helps the skin heal quicker. I suppose it's because it's got all the goodness in it to help the tiny chicks grow. I can't explain it better than that, I'm afraid, but we saw a lot of burns out in Jerusalem – especially amongst people who'd only just come out there.

"They didn't realise how hot any metal would get in the sun out there. It was mainly soldiers we treated for that. Men who grabbed a sword handle and had the pommel or the guard burn them. Or the ones who thought that in the heat they would try to do without wearing something thick under the ring-mail hauberks." She stopped working on Much's hands and began turning her attention to the lesser burns, then noticed how Allan and Roger were hanging on her every word.

"Ring-mail's incredibly heavy," she explained, "so no-one puts it on until they're right up to where they're going to fight."

"Too true!" Guy agreed. "If you can, you load it into carts and get it brought up alongside the marching men. If you've got to be faster you can load it onto pack horses to ride with you. That was one of the nightmares of fighting the Welsh raiders. You had to move fast, and that meant sometimes you didn't have the chance to put a hauberk on. You just had to trust the gambeson had enough padding to stop the worst of any cuts. And that's bad enough to march wearing even here in England. God alone knows how they managed in the Holy Land!"

Marianne nodded. "So there was always some clot-head who thought to try putting the hauberk on over just a linen shirt, thinking that it would be cooler with all that weight if they didn't have all the thick padding of the gambeson on as well. But they didn't realise that the mail had been getting hotter and hotter in the sun. So they'd grab it to put it on in a hurry, then if they were lucky they'd drop it quickly and suffer a few burns on their hands, but one or two I saw had gloves on and so they didn't realise how hot the metal was until they were dropping it on over their heads."

"Sweet Jesu!" Guy swore. "That would be horrible!"

Allan turned to Roger to explain, realising that his friend would never have handled such a thing as he'd grown up. "Ring-mail is a nightmare to get out of quickly. I remember when cousin Fulk got his first proper hauberk and was putting it on to show-off to us. Once you've lifted it up and got it positioned to go on over your head and arms, when you let it go there's so much weight in it it just drops like a stone. It flows like heavy cloth, being all inter-linked rings. We laughed back then, because Fulk hadn't got it right and ended up with it all collapsed around his shoulders."

Guy and John were already chuckling at the memory of the imperious Fulk being red with exertion and embarrassment as he tried to extract himself from the unruly tangle of rings.

"The only way we got it off him was to get him to bend over from the waist, so that he looked like he was trying to touch his toes, and then Guy and Philip had to pull it off him," John chortled. "He was utterly stuck by himself!"

"But if it was red-hot...!" Allan added as an awful afterthought.

Marianne nodded. "Terrible! The worst one I saw, they brought the lad in screaming, and when we tried to get the hauberk off, the linen shirt came off with it and so did most of the skin off his back."

"Blessed Saint Thomas!" Walter gasped, as Piers and Thomas breathed,

"*Dewi Sant!*"

"What happened to him?" John asked, fearing the answer, and was right to do so when Marianne shook her head and said,

"He died. The shock and the pain were too much for him." Then she turned and smiled at Much. "But you don't need to worry about that! Your burns are nowhere near that bad! They'll be really painful for several days yet, I'm afraid, and you'll have to use your hands as little as possible to not burst the blisters, but Tuck and I have plenty of willow bark for the pain. I've bathed your hands in water which I'd put some of the bark into to infuse, and now I want you to drink this infusion." She handed Much the small wooden cup carefully so that he could take it without knocking the blisters. He pulled a face at the bitter taste, but Marianne was standing over him to make sure he drank it all. "If you really can't stand the taste," she said with little sympathy, "hold your nose and knock it back in one go."

"How does that help?" Roger challenged her, then wilted under Marianne's stern gaze.

"You sound like our ma," Piers grumbled too, then immediately cringed as he saw Much's face fall at the mention of mothers. For once his older brother digging him in the ribs already came after he realised his mistake.

Marianne neatly deflected the awkward moment by demanding of Roger, "Did no-one ever make you hold your nose to take medicine?"

Roger shook his head. "Don't remember anyone givin' me much of anythin'," he answered with uncharacteristic honesty, making Marianne blink in surprise,

"It's amazing you've survived then!"

"Roger pretty much brought himself up," Allan leapt in before Marianne said something which would unwittingly upset his friend. "He didn't have anyone to watch out for him until he met me."

Marianne blinked, then demanded of him, "Was there something weird in the water where you grew up?" before looking to John and Guy. "There's Robin going around adopting kings and stray soldiers. Guy feeling that he has to keep on rescuing people. John's been acting like he's everyone's father ever since I've met him and fretting about you all, and now even Allan – who I thought would be the one expecting everyone to cosset *him* – turns out to have been rescuing scruffy thieves as a sideline! You can't help yourselves can you? You just have to do it!"

Her words were clearly not meant as censure, but Guy, John and Allan all looked guiltily at one another. By now Tuck had returned and had heard this last as he brought the eggs over to Marianne.

"Put like that it is obvious that something happened to you four," the big Welsh monk said thoughtfully, "and yet from what Guy's told me of your three older brothers or cousins, it definitely passed them by. So who had such an influence on you four and yet not on the others? Clearly not old fitz Waryn, given the description Guy's given me of him!"

Guy and John were too busy trying to absorb and assess the implications of this observation, but Allan answered without hesitation.

"It was Lady Alice, Guy's mother. Oh my mother was very loving, but looking back on it now I can see that although she doted on me while I was little, she wanted to keep me tied to her as a remembrance of her affair with Edmund Peverel. I was this little flesh and blood mirror of her lover. It wasn't wanting me for my sake, and as I got older it got harder to cope with her suddenly getting all weepy over me for no reason I could see, or smothering me with hugs and kisses when all I'd done was maybe get out of bed! It was Lady Alice who came and marched me off to where she was schooling Guy and John and Baldwin. In her case, I now think, the determination to make us four into a proper family was because she was sure that Audulph – her older son – never wanted to be a brother to Guy. He'd come under the influence of the old man and Fulk and Philip too early on, and he looked down his nose at Guy because his father wasn't a well connected as his own had been."

"Aye, Lady Alice was always the kind one to me," John recalled. "Lady Hawyse – Allan's mother – couldn't stand the sight of me! But when I arrived as a lost little lad, Lady Alice just took over and did all the things a mother should have done for me. And your father did too, Guy, while he lived. Both of them were so kind."

"Clearly they set a very strong example," Tuck observed.

Guy smiled. "Yes they did! And you're right, Allan. I never thought of it until you just said, but your mother was either smothering you or completely indifferent. She might have been the lady of the house, but I'm sure that the reason why old Fulk let us live on at the manor after my father died was because he knew that the woman running the household was my mother, not his wife. And I couldn't begin to count the number of times mother said to me, 'go and rescue Allan. Hawyse's having one of her bad days again!' And I know that the reason why she was so insistent that we all learn to read was that she thought that, if all else failed, it would help any one of us secure a place in a monastery, so that we'd have a roof over our heads if old Fulk turned us out for some reason. It didn't quite turn out that way, but I've been very glad of her teaching over the years."

"And what about Baldwin?" Hugh wanted to know. "How old was he when he came to live with you?"

"Oh surprisingly young," John answered. "Only about six or seven."

Allan nodded. "I can hardly remember a time when Baldwin wasn't there with us! It was because when they were young, Fulk and Philip needed to go back to the borders to train, and Brian de Hodenet was the only one old Fulk could ask to take them on. So in return we got Baldwin, but he stayed with us all year even though Fulk and Philip only went in the summer. I can't wait to see him again! He was closest to me in age and very much my playmate. I missed him so much when we got thrown out. John was so serious all the time in those days, and Guy was gone too. I just wanted to go back to those days when we had such fun." He turned to John with a half apology. "I know you were doing your best for me, really I do, now. But you hardly ever even smiled! You trudged through life with such grim determination! And I just didn't understand!

"I can see it now. You always knew right from the start that you wouldn't get much favour once you grew up. That you'd be a man-at-arms, or at best a manor reeve or something. But my mother filled my head with such nonsense despite Lady Alice's best efforts. She kept telling me I'd be a wonderful knight, and that all the young ladies would love me because I could play the lute and sing so beautifully. And worst of all, that one day when old Fulk was gone, that I'd have a manor of my own! God alone knows where she thought that would come from! But she said Fulk would get Alverton, and the old man would set Philip and me up in manors of our own! Bloody ridiculous!"

He turned a watery smile back to John. "And that's what made it so terribly hard once you kept telling me that I had to muck out sheep pens, and make up that horrible concoction to dip them in to stop the bugs biting, or whatever it was for! It just never let up, not for even an hour in the evenings. You were always mending something or making something. It's taken me years to see that that's how most of the peasant families live."

He got up and walked to where John was sitting and wrapped his arms affectionately around his cousin's neck. "But I've also now seen how they laugh together at the same time, ...and we never did! It was only when I found Roger, and a boy called Henry with him who had rickets and needed looking after, and started to help them, that I understood what a strain you must have been under, being on your own with me." He hugged John a bit tighter. "And I'm so sorry that I made things worse. Because I thought you just didn't care that Guy and Baldwin weren't there anymore. You gritted your teeth and never let me see *your* pain! Oh I wish you had, John! I might have understood you better then. But you have to allow that you never talked to me, either, even just about the old days, about the things we had happy memories of."

John sighed and patted Allan's arms where they still lay around him. "I know. But I feared reminding you too much of what we'd lost. You were so unsettled as it was, without keeping going back over what we couldn't have anymore."

Allan sighed and released John, but squatted down on his heels in front of him so that he could look him in the eye. "Yes, I was unsettled! But, by Saint Thomas, John! People talk about folk who've *died* more than we talked about Baldwin or Guy! I'm happy beyond belief to see you and Guy again, and to know that Baldwin's been found, but I won't apologise for wanting to live my life with a smile and a laugh. I've learned the hard way that I can't go through life just taking what I want, and when I can I earn money."

Now he grasped John's hands tighter. "But when I see people with more money than they know what to do with. When the only way the bloody monks would take poor Henry in to be looked after was if we'd give them a big bag of coins...!" He threw his hands in the air. "I'm not going to apologise for taking matters into my own hands and redressing the balance a bit!"

"What happened to Henry?" a fascinated Algar wanted to know. Guy's family was turning into the most exciting thing to cross his path in many a long year!

"We done a job or two," Roger said inscrutably. "Know what I mean?"

Guy quirked an amused eyebrow. "A job or two?"

Allan's grin was full of the old mischief. "Well we tried to leave Henry with the Black Monks at Wetheral Priory, but the bastards said that he was too old to be given. What they meant was that he was clearly poor and would need care in the infirmary, and that they weren't going to give him that unless we paid! Carlisle's not that far away, so we went off and Roger lifted a few purses on market day. Only rich men's mind! We didn't rob any poor folk! I couldn't show my face actually in Carlisle on account of what happened the last time I was there." Clearly Allan wasn't about to elaborate on that, and it had been a painful enough experience to make him wince involuntarily just at the thought, but he swiftly moved on.

"I looked after Henry while Roger worked Carlisle market." Guy thought 'worked' was probably not the best word to describe what had been done! "Then Roger stayed with Henry while I passed myself off as a minstrel and played for a fancy wedding taking place at a manor a few miles away – I picked up a few trinkets while I was doing it too! Nothing big that would set the hue and cry after us. Just little bits. Then we moved on quick to Hexham, and I sold the bits of jewellery there. So that meant that we couldn't really leave Henry at the abbey there just in case someone got wind of where the money with Henry came from, you see? We didn't want to leave him and then have him put out on the road again."

"We didn't like them monks at Hexham, anyhow," Roger sniffed. "Not nice men, even for bleedin' monks!"

"You don't like the brethren?" Tuck asked neutrally.

Roger frowned. "They ain't all like you, Brother! Most of 'em are swivel-eyed old hypocrites! Full o' God when it suits 'em, then as cruel as any knight the moment there's somethin' they want or don't like. And the brotherly love some o' them hand out ain't so brotherly! Harm can come to a young lad in a place like that if he ain't careful, or can't run fast, if you get my meanin'!"

Tuck beamed beatifically at him. "I won't argue with you on that. That's English monasteries for you! Just so long as you don't tar us all with the same brush!"

Allan grinned back at him. "We finally got Henry into St Mary's in York, ...or rather we took him down to the river, scrubbed him up to look halfway respectable, dressed him in some clothes we picked up in Durham, and then left him at the gatehouse of the abbey with a purse and a note for the abbot. ...You see Guy? Your mother's teaching did come in useful! I wrote that he was 'my son' by another woman, and that following my 'wife's' death I was going on pilgrimage to the Holy Land and might well join the crusade, but that my conscience had pricked me to do right by the poor lad on account of him being crippled."

"Wasn't there a danger Henry would give the game away?" Hugh wondered. "Surely he would be bound to say something sooner or later?"

Allan shook his head. "The poor lad's got a hare lip. He can talk, but not well. We got to understand him pretty well, but you have to work at it, and most people just dismissed him as mad because he's crippled as well. Even the oh-so-Christian monks had to be seriously persuaded with gold to see him as not cursed by the Devil, remember! Crooked on the outside means crooked on the inside to most of them, and that's what they preach as well! That's why we were so glad to get Henry inside a godly place – so that he wouldn't get persecuted by the ignorant!"

Guy suddenly put two and two together. "Oh, so that's why you were in York!"

Allan nodded. "Yes, but we'd left Henry there, oh, three years ago now. But we try to go by there once a year to make sure he's still being looked after. We usually break into the abbey after dark and between offices."

"Break into the abbey!" John was scandalised.

"Well we could hardly stroll into the precinct and say, 'oh, we've just come to visit our mate Henry,' could we?" Allan retorted with a laugh at John's naivety. "Lads like him don't go near the guesthouse in case they get ideas – like getting a glimpse of a woman, God forbid! And do you think the likes of us would even get in through the gate?"

Guy smiled back. "No. I can see that if you wanted to see Henry you'd have to do it that way. Did you, though? Get to see him?"

"Oh he's doing fine!" Allan replied cheerfully. "They've got him helping out in the herb garden. Crippled and disfigured like he is they won't have him too close to the holiest places – very Christian of them, eh? But it means he's not too cooped up, and he'll only ever be a lay brother, which is the best thing as far as Roger and I could see. He's grown and put some weight on, and he seems happy."

The others just looked to one another. What could they say in censure when the fate of this poor boy was so clearly at the heart of Allan and Roger's exploits?

"So were you leaving York, then, when the trouble started?" Tuck asked.

Roger nodded. "We was just up on top of the wall what gives down onto the river, on account of the brothers don't think anyone will come or go that way."

"It gets very slippery at this time of the year," Allan clarified. "With the river levels going up and down it's often downright treacherous in the mud unless you're sure of foot like Roger and me. That's one of the reasons we were there just now. In summer, when the banks of the Ouse are drier and firmer the brothers are a bit more watchful, so it's paid us to come earlier."

"Thing is," Roger said more soberly, "once we was up on the wall we could see down the river a ways. With the castle being up on its mound we could see that real well, 'cept for where St Martin's church blocked our view a bit."

"Henry had told us about the riots at the beginning of March," Allan sighed regretfully. "That some Jewish houses had been set alight, and that the Jewish people in York had sought refuge in the castle. We'd even seen the sheriff coming up with armed men – or rather we'd seen a lot of soldiers outside of York and thought we'd better get in quick and see Henry, then get out of there fast, before we got caught up in something. You could hear the shouting up by the castle, and the odd thing being broken, even that far away. Any fool could see that there was going to be trouble before long, but we thought it would be the sheriff going in to break up the rioters, not to side with them!

"We got down to the river and then back up to the streets as fast as possible. Then we had a quick think and decided that we'd get over to the other side of the river from the castle, if nothing else. We reckoned it was a bit risky, because we'd have to get closer to the castle to get to the bridge – and that was where the worst of the rioting was going on – but we knew enough of the layout of the city by now to know that the turn for the bridge was still a couple of streets before the area around the castle itself. We thought we'd be all right!"

"It was 'orrible!" said Roger. "We was goin' down Coney Street, and all these nice houses we'd seen the last time we was there was all smashed in and broken up! No wonder the Jews was scared shitless! I was! It was like wild animals had been through the place! ...Well we got over the bridge all right, but then just as we was about to go down Micklegate there was this almighty bangin' and crashin'!"

"We didn't stop to look," admitted Allan, "but we're pretty sure it was some of the mob looting more of the Jewish houses on that side of the river. So we turned and ran down Skeldergate that runs alongside the river on that side, because we knew that it would turn just opposite the castle and head away from the city on a proper road. If we'd turned right immediately at the bridge it wouldn't have got us anywhere but into the surrounding fields, and by then we wanted to get as far away as possible! We knew Henry would be safe inside the precinct, but with there being just the two of us, we knew we'd be easy prey if we got tangled up in anything, so the road was the fastest way to leave. ...But that was when we saw the worst of it."

"Aye, we could see straight across to the castle," Roger shivered. "It was like you imagine 'Ell to be – all dark and smoky with red fire, and souls callin' out in torment!"

Everyone shuddered at that. If it could move a thorough rascal like Roger to such thoughts it must have been dreadful indeed.

Allan could only add, "And if it looked bad, Heaven alone knows what it must have been like for the people right there. Some of the ordinary folk of York were themselves trapped in their houses, too frightened to go out and yet not wanting to join in the rioting and looting. Imagine living with your family, all peaceful, and then having that arrive on your doorstep!"

"You'd feel God had forsaken you," Tuck breathed softly, but his words carried in the stunned silence.

"And our little brother might just be there," was Thomas' horrified rejoinder, bringing the others sharply back to the thought that it had been in search of Robin and the five other crusaders, plus Bilan, which had set them travelling this way in the first place.

Guy said what they were all thinking, "We're going to have to go to York," and no-one argued, not even Roger or Allan.

Oh Gervase, how I fretted that night! I was glad beyond measure that once again young Much had escaped a frightful death, and to discover that Allan had come back to us and in a more recognisable guise than the last time I had seen him. But oh how I worried over Robin and the others! Not that there was a single thing which I alone could have done to prevent events from working out the way they had. I had had little choice but to return to working at Nottingham Castle, and therefore I had not been there when Robin had made his fateful decision. And I forced myself to admit, in my calmer moments, that if two such sensible men as Thomas and Hugh had seen little wrong in Robin taking the lost Templars north – especially as Thomas had commended his beloved youngest brother to their care – then at the time there would probably

have been no reason to my mind to protest at Robin's actions either. It was only looking back, and with the foreknowledge of the riots, that it seemed such a rash move.

Now, though, we were all filled with a sense of desperate urgency – even the six men-at-arms – to find Robin and make sure that none of them had come to grief. Therefore we were all up at the crack of dawn and hurried to break camp so that we might set off as swiftly as possible. Marianne and Tuck made another infusion of the willow bark for Much so that he could take a swig of it when needed, in order to dull his pain and allow him to keep up with us. The men-at-arms happily left what protective ware we had brought with us packed on the back of the horses now, and allowed Much to ride, along with Marianne, while everyone else took it in turns to ride for a while to allow for the fastest march possible. And so with March gales blowing the forest in stormy waves about around us, we packed up and set off northwards, wishing that we too could be blown into Robin's path with all speed.

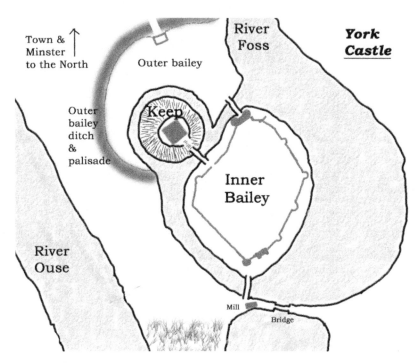

Plan of York Castle c.1190

Chapter 23

N ow Brother, I shall give you a surprise. For the next bit of our story I shall tell you of what happened to Robin and those who went to York with him, not as we were to hear it later, but as it actually unfolded, for you have born with my story patiently enough over the details of such things as the new sheriff arriving, and I am hardly involved here until we come to deal with the consequences of York. I can relate it all as if I had been there, you know, because I have heard it many times from every one of my friends who were there themselves. I have heard one side of how things happened, and then another, and then another, and between all these slightly different versions I think by now I have a good enough sense of what actually happened. And I know you are desperate to hear of Robin making a grand gesture before I have to stop and rest a while!

Therefore, although this is hardly part of my confession, you may hear the story and enjoy it for what it is, rather than having to wrestle with your conscience over the state of my soul for once. Ah, you do know how to smile! That is good, Brother, for my dear cousin Allan was right in that respect – too much solemnity in the end becomes unbearable. Even the most saintly inclined souls should able to feel some joy in their hearts once in a while, and should revel in a good tale. Therefore enjoy this, Brother, for in doing so you are not offending God, even if your prior is such a sour soul as to think so!

Yorkshire,
March, the year of Our Lord 1190

Robin reined in his horse and breathed a sigh of relief. The great trading town of York rose ahead of the riders beyond the hedges and trees of the open farmland, and Robin couldn't wait to get there. This expedition had been getting worse by the day. It had seemed the natural thing to do to help the three fellow Templars from the East, when he and the others had all but fallen over them lying on the ground amongst the trees. All three had been trussed up like chickens for the pot, and there was no reason not to believe that they had been set upon in an attempted robbery, which had gone wrong once the attackers had discovered that there was nothing of value to take. Granted it had seemed odd that their horses were found wandering not far off, but not something worth fretting over.

Now, though, Robin was having his doubts about almost everything they'd told him about the event. The one sergeant was certainly badly wounded, and Robin and those who were with him had soon been grateful to leave him at the priory at Pontefract for fear of his dying on them. At that point everyone had still been praying that he would gradually recover and be able to join his brothers at the preceptory at Penhill. It was only after they had set out again that they began to suspect that the threesome were not quite the innocent victims they claimed to be, and that maybe they had been tied up after a fight which *they* had instigated, against a sufficiently large party as to overwhelm the three experienced fighters.

Not half a day north of Pontefract, Robin's men with the two remaining Templars had met a party of travellers coming the other way on the Great North Road, innocent merchants minding their own business with laden packhorses. It had therefore shocked them to the core when the knight had called to them to draw arms and prepare to fight.

"Fight? We don't need to fight!" Robin had gasped, slapping a hand over the knight's as he began to draw his sword.

"Are you a coward?" the knight had sneered back, his blank expression suddenly gone in a heartbeat to be replace with one of fierce anger.

"No!" Robin declared hotly. "But these are ordinary people, not our enemies!"

The knight snorted his disbelief. "Who knows what their sort hide beneath those flowing robes and in those bags."

"It's wool!" a perplexed Bilan had told him in amazement. "You can see it's wool!"

The knight's fist came back to strike at Bilan for challenging him, and only Bilan's being just that bit too far behind, and Will's hefty paw blocking the punch, saved him from a blow meant to cause serious harm.

"Don't you *ever* raise your fist to him!" Will growled ferociously, clasping the knight's wrist in a vicelike clamp, which in turn prompted the Templar sergeant to draw his knife in his knight's defence. He was close behind Will and closing quickly, but already Malik and Gilbert had heeled their horses up to his, and the pair held onto him as Gilbert removed the knife from his resisting grasp.

"If my lord de Châtillon was here it would be different," the knight snarled, "or Master Ridefort. You'd have to follow orders and deal with those spies in our midst then!"

Robin looked to his own five who'd come west with him, all of them registering shock. Was this knight utterly mad that he didn't know he was in England? Or was he so corrupted by what he'd seen and gone through in the East that he saw everyone who wasn't a Templar as an enemy? Struggling to keep his voice level and non-confrontational, in the hope of not provoking these madmen further, Robin responded,

"Maybe, but our Master is hundreds of miles away, and we're in England now where there are *no* Saracen spies." He saw the open disbelief in the two men's eyes, although over which part of his statement it was impossible to guess at. Robin hardened his tone. "While you travel with us there will be no violence, do you understand?" The blank expressions had returned to the two faces once more. "Do you understand me?" he repeated with even more emphasis. "We will help you get to the preceptory as we promised, but *not* to go on a killing spree in our homeland!"

Yet he felt that his words had meant nothing to the two. That night, while Gilbert, James and Siward, with Bilan and the two lads – Peter and Tumi – kept an eye on things, Will, Malik and Robin had a covert conference back in amongst the trees.

"We can't take them to the preceptory," Will said before Robin could.

"No," Malik agreed. "Guy said that the men at Penhill were just horse men. He said there would be no fighters amongst them."

"I know, I've been thinking that too," Robin admitted. "And now I think of it, they never mentioned Penhill by name until we did. I'm no longer sure that was ever their destination. I think I put that thought into their heads, God forgive me! And you're right, those brothers will be no match for this pair! Either they'll end up with their throats being cut in the night, when these lunatics take it into their heads that they aren't 'proper' Templars, or they won't be able to stop them going off and causing mayhem the minute their backs are turned. No physician the brothers will have in such a rural preceptory would know how to cure what ails this pair, if anyone could anyway!"

"No, we can't risk them running amok amongst a bunch of ordinary villagers!" Will added determinedly, although neither Malik nor Robin were arguing with him. "It'd be a massacre!"

"And who did they actually serve?" Malik wondered aloud. "They seem unable to give us any sort of account as to how they come to be here, and I agree that Penhill was not their destination and that they did not originally come from there, nor any other of the preceptories in the north you have told us of. They are not taking a message to any of those preceptories either, so why are they in the north of England?"

At least we could tell Guy we were going to the house of your father when we first met him. They seem to have even less direction than that! So are they true Templars who served de Ridefort? Or are they like us four? Men who happened to fall in with Templars like you and Will during the chaos in Outremer? That might make them Châtillon's men in every way!"

Will groaned, "That would explain how they come to have the uniform – if like us they were re-clothed from the Templar stores in somewhere like Cyprus. It's still chaos out there and they could say with genuine truth that they were at Hattin, or any of the other battles Châtillon got us dragged into."

Robin grimaced. "That's a nasty thought, isn't it!" He'd already been thinking that, but it helped to have the others confirm that he wasn't just making something dramatic out of a chance comment. It helped him decide what to do, though. "Listen, we've already said we're taking them through York, so they won't think it's odd that we go there. But once there I think we should hand them over to the sheriff.

"It's drastic, I know, but the sheriff is the only person I can think of who will have somewhere strong enough to lock these two up safely out of the way. Guy said most places have a gaol these days, or at least the castle will have a cellar which will do, if not dungeons. Then the sheriff can get in touch with one of the bigger preceptories and the master there can sort out the truth of the matter. We can't keep them with us for the same reasons we can't take them to Penhill. It would mean at least two of us standing guard over them night and day so that they don't slip away into the forest, and we can't keep doing that for long with only six of us who're able to stand up to them."

Will clapped him on the shoulder. "That's a good plan! It's the right thing to do. I'll tell Gilbert when I get chance. Malik, if you tell James and Bilan on the quiet, then Robin can have a word with Siward, too, when the chance comes."

Robin agreed, "We must keep the pretence of normality going for now. We daren't let them think we're turning on them or who knows what they'll do!"

It was a tense night, with the six of them sitting watch in pairs, while Bilan was under instruction to keep the lads Peter and Tumi, as well as himself, well away from the pair at all times. It was a good thing they did. The encounter with the merchants seemed to have jarred something loose in the heads of the knight, Eudo, and his sergeant, Waldein, for neither of them slept a wink as far as anyone could tell, and they were as twitchy as cats with bells on their tails. It was only another day to York, but it wore them all to tatters as time and again they had to pull off the road to let other travellers go by. Twice it was only by dint of someone riding in front of each of the manic pair's horses, while two others blocked either side, which stopped them from launching into an attack on total strangers. Bilan then had to scout ahead, and also check that all the travellers had disappeared from behind, before they dared move on.

So it was with huge relief that they saw the mighty York Minster rising up on the horizon as the chilly March day drew to a close. Yet tempting though it was to ride in at speed and deposit the dreadful pair at the sheriff's door and be done with them, Robin felt that it would be better if they went into the town in the morning. That way they could catch the sheriff before the day's business took him over, and with luck he might see the dangers. If they went to him at night he might be too tired to take notice, or worse, in his cups and too soused to listen properly.

Guy had told them that the new sheriff of Yorkshire was John Marshal, the older brother of the famed knight William Marshal, but had advised caution. John, he'd told Robin, was not the man his brother was. Already since September and King Richard's coronation, John Marshal had been made the chief receiver for the whole of England on the king's behalf for lands where the holder had died without adult heirs, or heirs of any sort. Yet he'd also already been swiftly removed from that office for reasons Guy hadn't known, and had been given the sheriffdom of Yorkshire as compensation. Holding such a high office for mere months did not speak well of the man!

King Richard might well have intended to elevate the whole Marshal family, since the youngest brother, Henry, had been raised to the deanery of York, but the post of sheriff in that same shire was still rather tainted with implications of disgrace attached to the former sheriff, Ranulf de Glanville – King Henry's chief justiciar. Therefore, Guy had warned Robin, this new sheriff might not see the holding of this office as much of a boon, despite it having come from King Richard's hand rather than having had to pay for it, and might be aggressively officiating over his dubious territorial gift. If William Marshal had served all of the royal family well, John Marshal was very much Prince John's man, and prior to King Henry's death had been serving Prince John as his seneschal – and that association worried Guy too. Therefore Robin had serious qualms about approaching this current incumbent, and if he'd had any other option he would have steered well clear of York. That in turn made him want to go in when the horses at least, if not the men, were well rested – just in case they had to make a very hurried exit!

Come the morning, with Gilbert, Siward, James and Malik hanging on to Eudo and Waldein, Robin risked riding ahead to the town edge to ask after the sheriff, for during the night they had heard some very strange noises drifting over the frosty fields. It didn't sound good to the experienced ears of the crusaders, and although they all remained huddled close around the two camp fires they had lit against the bitter cold of the night, the drifting sounds made the six trained men glad they hadn't just ridden in under the false assumption that normality reigned within the walls. What Robin now heard at the roadside shook him to the core. The sheriff was out of the town bringing up siege engines to be used against his own castle! For of all the unlikely people to be holding it, the city's Jewish population had taken refuge inside the castle following violent rioting against them, and had closed the gates and would not come out. The worried merchant whom he spoke to was clearly fearful of where this might all end, and Robin now shared his fear for very different reasons.

He rode back to where the others waited on the Selby road, wondering how on earth he was going to handle this new development.

"What's wrong?" Will demanded the minute he was close enough to hear, being the one of all of them who could read Robin like a book. Robin grimaced. Much as he was fond of Will and would be eternally in his debt, now as so often before he wished the big smith would think before speaking. Without Will's question, Eudo and Waldein would never have known anything was amiss, whereas with them now alert he was going to have to think rapidly about how to phrase his answer. Jews holding the castle against the sheriff was precisely the kind of thing which would send them off into violent rages.

"The sheriff has a bit of tr..."

He got no further as Peter exclaimed, "What's *that*?"

From around the western curve of the back walls of the town's outermost rows of houses, and heading for the point where the outer bailey wall curved in towards the moated arm of the Foss, and therefore the castle's keep too, appeared a lumbering siege engine hauled by a team of oxen, and with it came a troop of armed men. Knights rode beside it and men-at-arms marched in their wake.

"To war!" Eudo roared and attempted to batter his way free of Gilbert and Siward, who both grappled with him manfully, just about managing to hang on to him even though all three of them came off their horses and crashed to the ground in a tangle. Nonetheless, Waldein would have remained well restrained by Will and Malik, had Peter not urged his horse too close in the excitement of seeing the siege engine and soldiers. The manic sergeant's arm shot out like a striking snake and pulled Peter off the horse he was sharing with Tumi. The two boys had been riding together alongside Bilan on one of the big horses Tuck had used in the past, and until now had been at the rear of the party, but Bilan had dismounted to relieve himself behind a nearby tree and the boys were free to be distracted. Peter now dangled by his neck, feet swinging, and his back arched over the sergeant's thigh, as the sergeant trapped the boy's head in the crook of his arm, whilst holding the reins of his horse with the same hand, and brandishing the knife he'd pulled from Peter's belt with the other. The blade's point swung from his adversaries back to Peter's throat and away again with erratic speed.

"Put him down!" Robin commanded with all the authority he could muster, but Waldein just laughed and urged his horse sideways, causing the horse Tumi was on to skitter in the way of Will's and Malik's, and gaining the sergeant more space between them.

It was just the distraction Eudo needed. Throwing a mighty punch at Siward, which knocked him flying, Eudo clapped his spurs to his horse's sides and broke free. It caused Waldein to begin laughing with manic glee at the six men's indecision, as he sawed on the horse's reins to make it back up further.

"Drop it!" he snapped at James, who had drawn his bow, and to prove his point poked Peter hard with the point of the knife, drawing blood at the lad's throat.

James lowered the bow, pointing the arrow at the floor, as did Robin who had also instinctively grabbed his own bow. But just as Waldein was saying, "No drop it!" another bow sang out and the sergeant's eyes glazed. Peter dropped from a suddenly slack arm, and as he did so the others saw an arrow tip protruding out from Waldein's chest. As he keeled over out of the saddle, the others saw Bilan standing behind with his Welsh bow drawn and another arrow nocked and ready to fly. The months of practise at High Peak had built muscle on the youngest of the Coshams, and these days, if he couldn't quite pull the bows his brothers could manage, he could still handle a full-sized bow. Now the punch from his powerful wych-elm bow had hammered the yard-long arrow straight through Waldein at such close range.

"Bilan! Get Eudo! Get him!" Robin yelled and the young archer swung his bow and loosed the arrow in a fluid movement. It was his bad luck that Eudo swerved around a bush at the critical moment, and then after that had made it to the mêlée at the town's edge before Bilan could shoot again.

"Up lad!" Malik was already saying to Peter, as he leapt to the ground and shoved the boy up onto the horse behind Tumi. Bilan ran and caught the reins of his horse which Siward held out to him, and swung up on it as all the horses were urged into pursuit, James grabbing the reins of Peter and Tumi's horse and hauling it with him, as Malik remounted and galloped to join them with Waldein's empty horse in tow.

In a stream the horses raced the short distance to York and crossed the river, but even before reaching the houses they were forced to dismount. There was no way that they could ride in the surging mass of people milling around.

"Go right!" Robin called back over his shoulder once they were into the streets, waving them to a road which swung off along around the town's perimeter formed by the River Foss and away from the castle.

When they were free of the worst of the press of people, he turned to his men. "We're going to have to find somewhere to leave the horses and hunt Eudo on foot," he told them. "We daren't leave him be! In this madness he'll commit murder after murder and no-one will be able to stop him."

"It looks quieter up by the Minster," Gilbert said, catching on to what Robin was thinking. "We can leave the horses up there and come up on the back of this mob from that direction."

Robin nodded and they remounted to clattered through the back streets to the Minster complex. Leaving Peter and Tumi in charge of the horses under Bilan's watchful eye, the six grabbed their bows and quivers from behind their saddles, tightened their scabbard belts and took off at speed. They ran down Stonegate and turned into Coney Street becoming aware that, although it was still short of noon, all of the shops were boarded up and no-one was on the streets. Clearly here there were some of the richer houses, with many showing signs of looting having gone on, and they slowed to see if there were any signs of life within. Not that they expected any of the inhabitants to still be there, but the last thing they needed now was to have some drunken looters coming up behind them.

As it was, they could see and hear the main mob surging and howling for blood at the end of the street where it joined Bridge Street at the crossroad. Beyond that was the ditch and the palisade fence of the castle's outer bailey – a pile of stout oak timbers around which there was a seething mass of people at every point where the buildings and ditch allowed. But neither the outer bailey, which contained the various buildings to house and cater for its garrison, nor the inner bailey which was reached via a bridge to another island in the River Foss, was the object of the siege engine or the mob. They were aiming at the water-surrounded motte forming its own island, on which sat the wooden keep where the terrified Jews were barricaded in. Had it been possible, the sheriff would have been best to get the engine within the outer bailey to give it a direct line of attack on the keep, but the gatehouse was built to keep such great engines out, not in, and the engine was being dragged around the bailey's perimeter to a spot where the palisade ceased at the diverted river, which effectively created a moat.

The mob lurched and swayed all along the moated river bank where they could find a space to get close, or surged around the outer bailey walls which were closest to the town's streets. They bayed for blood in a swirling, crushing river of humanity, crammed in between the houses, gardens and the banks. Periodically they flowed into the side streets like flood water escaping, or staggered backwards as some at the front got too near to falling into the Foss. Some were actually impeding the progress of the siege engine rather than helping matters.

So far the six hadn't really got close enough to be able to see the full layout of the castle, but they didn't need to to know that the chances of finding one man in amongst that mob was nigh on impossible.

"We're never going to get through that lot," Siward groaned, "and if we do we'll never see Eudo!"

Yet as if by divine providence Gilbert suddenly let out a yelp and pointed. "Look! There! By the house with the tailor's sign!"

In a brief flash of colour they saw the distinctive mustard coloured trews Eudo wore amongst the milling crowd, and he seemed to be coming back through it. Without a word the six shrank back against the walls of the houses to make themselves less visible, their travel-stained clothes blending in with the stone and wood. The deranged Templar staggered out of the crowd hauling a thrashing youth with him and proceeded to lay into him with considerable violence, although mercifully without any sort of weapon. Robin led the dash down the road and was just about to dive at Eudo when some sixth sense alerted him to their presence.

Dropping the youth instead of delivering the killing blow, Eudo lurched off towards the bridge over the River Ouse. A cluster of chanting men surged back in his pursuers' way, and they had to punch their way clear before they could give chase again. Their pounding boots echoed hollowly as they crossed the bridge and into Micklegate, but were drowned out to any others by the mob. Some of these houses must also have belonged to Jewish families going by the devastation, and the Star of David someone had scrawled in what looked worryingly like blood on a door which hung drunkenly on twisted hinges. Of Eudo there was no sign.

Robin held up his hand for silence as Will swore loudly and profanely. Signalling for them to slip just round the corner into Skeldergate, which ran from the bridge-foot along the riverside, Robin strained his ears to hear above the din on the other bank. Yes, after a pause he was sure he heard someone laugh again, as a crash sounded from within the third house on the right. In a quick dash they crossed the main road once more and then advanced in line, hugging the walls of the houses. The first two doors they passed gave views in onto sickening sights of wreckage and filth, but were obviously deserted. However, they could all now hear someone smashing things about upstairs in the next house.

Siward and James nimbly slipped to the other side of the main door, and then with Siward and Robin in the lead, the six skirmished into the house. The first room was a modest chamber which must have served as a trading area, since there were no signs of domestic occupation, although what had once been a desk had been hacked to bits, and ink was splattered up the walls and across the floor. Piles of ash on the floor and in the grate spoke of records burned, but of what type it was no longer possible to tell.

Robin waved Will forward, and with Malik on the other side, the smith went through the next door and signalled back that the stairs went up from this room. Robin had his bow at the ready as he followed Will and Malik through, and ventured to look up the oak staircase. Whoever this house had belonged to had been doing well by the looks of things, or at least they had until Hell had broken loose a few days ago. Robin took a few steps up the stairs, and was just about to signal the others to follow, when a telltale shadow falling across the head of the stairs forewarned him of Eudo coming his way. The knight stepped out into view, eyes unnaturally bright and staring, with a bloodstained knife in his hands and a manic smile on his face.

Robin's bow sang and the arrow pinned him against the doorjamb of an upstairs room. As Robin sprinted up the remaining steps drawing his knife, prepared to defend himself should the knight pull free, Eudo coughed and a spurt of blood appeared from his mouth.

"You had no choice," Malik said softly, as Robin bowed his head and crossed himself at the sign of life leaving Eudo's eyes. "He would have killed and killed again if you had not. Whose is the blood on that knife, hmm? Not the boy's he was beating when we gave chase. He had no knife then. So he's killed or wounded already in just such a short time."

"I know," Robin sighed, "but we said no more killing when we came home. I didn't think it would be so hard not to do."

"Not our choice," Will told him sagely, pulling him away from the body. "I'll get him free, then we should throw him in the river. That way there'll be no repercussions on anyone local. There'll be no way of knowing who or what finished him off once the fish have had their fill. His gambeson will weight him to the bottom until he's at least unrecognisable."

Robin took a deep ragged breath. "Yes. Do it, Will." He looked about him. "Search this place and see if you can find any clue as to who once lived here, or what's happened to them. I'm assuming they were Jews and are among the poor souls trapped in the castle. But this could just be the home of a wealthy Christian who's got caught up in the violence, and who may want to come back when it calms down. If so then they may be close by, and we can fetch them and secure the place for them."

He himself found nothing, while Siward found the body of another looter in a bedroom who must have lost his fight with Eudo just moments before, but James came downstairs when they assembled back there with some tattered pieces of parchment in his hand.

"They are Jews," he said sadly, "but this seems to imply that there are, or were, more of the same family in a street called Hungate. Where's that?"

Robin screwed his face up in concentration as he said, "It's been such a long time since I was here as a boy." He thought for a moment longer then opened his eyes. "I think Hungate is back over the Ouse in the main part of the town." He looked at Will and Malik who were stood over Eudo's body which was now swathed in an old blanket. "Are you ready?" They nodded, and so as he led them stealthily out of the house, Will hoisted the body up onto his shoulders with Malik's help.

Like skulking thieves, they clung to the shadows up to Skeldergate, then took the first alleyway down to the river itself. As the two strongest, Will and Malik lowered Eudo's body into the fast running water and shoved it out into mid stream with a broken boat-hook someone had discarded at the waterline.

"God be praised it's not summer, and the water's still high!" Siward intoned with relief as they saw the body being swept away downstream, sinking as it went.

"What now?" Gilbert asked. "Shouldn't we get out of here?"

At that moment there was a loud crunch echoing down the river from the castle. The siege engine was operational and the first stone had been hurled at the castle's wooden walls. The screams they heard were something new too, for these came from people up on the walls of the castle. If John Marshal shared his brother's military ability, he clearly had none of the chivalrous nature which might have made him think twice before launching such a mighty machine against misguided civilians.

"We have to try and do something for them!" James said despairingly. "This is as bad as Jerusalem all over again!"

"Not quite," Robin told him with firm reassurance in his voice if not his heart, "and we will try, James, but six of us against that mob isn't going to achieve anything. There's a Templar grange just outside the city to the north, I seem to remember. Let's get back to Bilan and the boys, get the horses, and go and get reinforcements!"

They ran back over the bridge, but no sooner had they got back onto the same side of the river as the Minster and the castle than they realised that the violence was escalating. Egged on by the sheriff's new show of strength, bands of young men were now marauding about the place, some of them well on the way to being too drunk to do much, but others making threatening moves to anyone who got in their way. The six saw several men who looked like locals now running fearfully for their own homes.

No doubt it had seemed like high-spirited fun when they were attacking empty houses, but now that there were men amongst the crowd who were armed with knives, swords and spears, the mood had turned uglier. Twice the six had to stand their ground against one of these packs of armed men, but the fact that they too were armed and clearly knew how to handle themselves, soon made their attackers back off with only a short exchange of blades. With growing worry they picked up their pace and were soon running back for where they'd left the boys and horses.

To their horror, when they got to the walls of the Minster precinct they couldn't see any sign of anyone. Calling out they split up, Will, Malik and Gilbert going the one way, and Robin, Siward and James the other. Will, Malik and Gilbert were soon running back to the others, Malik having spotted hoof-marks which spoke of several horses being taken at a pace out of the town close by the Minster during the short time they'd been gone, yet they'd seen no sign of the boys. Together they hurried eastwards around the precinct with fear mounting.

On a small open area close by the east side of the Minster they came upon a sickening sight. Peter and Tumi lay sprawled lifelessly together. As James and Gilbert gently lifted them up they saw that the two had had their throats cut.

"Sweet Mary, Mother of God! And what are we going to tell Thomas and Piers?" Gilbert asked as he scanned anxiously around him and tears of despair glittered in his eyes.

"Yes, where *is* Bilan?" fretted Siward.

"Over here!" Malik called out, and they realised that he had gone into the shadows cast by the great stone church. As Robin and Will sprinted to him they saw him help Bilan to his feet.

"My oath, lad! I'm glad to see you living!" Will gasped as he grabbed hold of their staggering friend from the other side. There was a nasty gash down Bilan's side, but it ran down his ribs and not through them, and he'd also received a blow to the head going by the lump already rising, and the broken skin which was still oozing a trickle of blood.

"What happened?" Robin asked gently, as they guided Bilan to where he could sit down without looking at Peter and Tumi's bodies.

"Some of the sheriff's men," Bilan croaked, then gratefully took a swallow from the water skin James held to his mouth. "They came in demanding we hand over the horses." He looked up at Robin with eyes swimming with tears. "They were all armed men. I think two at least were probably local young knights. I told Peter and Tumi to just let them have the horses. There were ten of them! How could we possibly fight them off?" He had to halt to sob some of his grief out before he could continue. "But they were so determined to prove to you that they could fight too."

"Oh God in Heaven forgive me!" Robin moaned as that sank in. He'd taken two lads fresh off a farm and now they were dead because of him. It had never occurred to him how little they would know of fighting, nor had he realised that there was an inevitability that at some point he and his troop would have to fight, if only other outlaws.

Belatedly he realised this was what Guy had been trying to tell him the last time they had met. That most people put up with living under such dreadful repression because they just didn't know how to fight back. That unlike Guy, John, Allan and himself, these ordinary people had not been routinely put through their paces with weapons as children, even if at that point the four of them hadn't expected to fight in earnest.

Yet he'd not translated that into the logical conclusion that such folk were not the sort of men he could recruit willy-nilly. Guy had said that once they were living rough in Sherwood then they'd needed fighters not farmers, and would have to constantly watch out for and help untrained men like Walter and Algar, but Robin hadn't comprehended the full depth of Guy's words. Too late he realised that it would have been better never to have swept Peter and Tumi up and filled their heads with wild dreams of fighting for freedom. Bilan was right, the boys should have just let the horses go, and the fact that even Bilan had the experience to know when to fight and when to flee – whereas Peter and Tumi hadn't – was born home to him with painful clarity. The horses the six of them and Waldein had been riding still had the Templars' marks on them – in both cases purchased with their dwindling funds back when they'd first landed, from a grange serving the London preceptories. So they wouldn't do their thieves much good in the long run. And the other two were the shaggy work horses Guy had bought for Tuck and John – not exactly prize mounts by any standard, and certainly not worth losing a life over, let alone two.

"How did you get hurt?" Malik was asking Bilan, as he gently bandaged the lad's head with a makeshift bandage made out of a scarf, and a small pad of linen daubed with some honey – both of the last two being amongst the things he carried in a small leather pouch for such emergencies.

Bilan managed a watery smile. "I couldn't let them fight alone, could I? I didn't get close, mind you. But I wounded three with my bow before two of them got to me. I didn't get a clean shot at any of them because Peter and Tumi kept getting in the way. I got away because when they came at me they went for my bow first, so when they grabbed that I let them have it and managed to wriggle free."

Robin was sure it hadn't been quite as simple that and that Bilan had put up more of a fight. And by the way that Malik and Will were fussing over him, they too thought that their young friend had been in the thick of things.

"Well that puts paid to us going to the grange at Skelton, though, doesn't it?" Gilbert said morosely. "We can't get there by foot and back in time to do any good, and if there are gangs of that size marauding about the place, it would be daft to split up into two smaller groups to leave someone here with Bilan. He can't go anywhere in a hurry now."

Robin felt his head spinning and walked away a pace to rest his head against the cool of the great stone building. He'd never expected to be leading his band in circumstances like this. This was England. *His* England! War was something that happened somewhere else. Even out at Hodenet with the Welsh on the doorstep, this kind of mass, random violence was rare, and as a lad he'd certainly never been involved in it. It was wrong, all wrong!

It felt utterly alien to be here beside a big Norman Minster with several lesser churches beyond it, homely houses all about them, the birds singing in the trees with the coming spring and the first hints of fresh green beginning to peak through, and to have so much bloodshed going on at the same time. He was developing a blinding headache, and he half expected to blink and open his eyes to find white houses, sand and scrubby trees about him instead, and the chill wind turned to baking heat.

He struggled to focus on the matter at hand. This wasn't what he'd fought for. This wasn't what he'd ever dreamed coming home would be like. The dreams which had kept him going through the carnage of Hattin and then Jerusalem had been of a quiet, green and peaceful England, where he would be free from suffering and the memories of such deeds. Granted, he now recognised that they were the memories of a young lad born to privilege, and with no responsibilities as yet – that wasn't the point. Through thick and thin they'd remained the anchor for his sanity. And with those thoughts came a growing anger at the petty men who were now destroying his dreams when they'd been cherished for so long. So they wanted to fight did they? Well he'd give them a taste of what it was to fight the way he and the others had done in the East. That would teach them a thing or two!

He turned to face the others decisively. "Right! We're going to go and see if we can find any of the Jews. If we can help any of them we will." He shivered despite the fact that the sun had warmed the March day considerably from its frosty start. "We can't do anything for the poor souls in the castle. Even if we could fight our way to the front of that crowd and then get into the bailey, there's no way that the folk barricaded in the castle would risk lowering the drawbridge to the motte to us, let alone opening the gates, the way things are now."

Siward agreed. "And if we could find a way to scale the keep's walls, we'd just be showing that bunch of thugs a way in to the poor wretches."

"Poor souls," James grieved, and none doubted that he was thinking of the women and children, whom they now realised had to be in the castle with the men of their families.

"What about Peter and Tumi?" Gilbert asked. "We can't just leave them here."

"Go round and see if there's any door open into the Minster," Robin told him, and the Irishman jogged off willingly.

He returned shortly. "The monks have barred the gates, and who can blame them! But there's one of the gateways into the monastic precinct round the corner. If we leave them there someone will find them, and sooner rather than later."

With great care they took the two limp bodies to the gate in the wall and laid them reverently out beside it. After a heartfelt prayer to commend the two boy's souls into the Virgin's everlasting care, the seven of them set off again. This time they kept well to the north of the town and began to look for the better built houses. As the English amongst them, the best Robin, Will and Siward could inform James and Malik, any Jews in an English town were likely to be merchants at least, and many would be money-lenders or maybe gold- or silversmiths. So the chances were that they wouldn't be finding them down in the poorest housing, even if not all of the richer houses were Jewish either. It was a soul destroying search, and they soon got a feeling for where the Jewish families had lived going by the patches of disruption they found.

"This has to be the work of local men," Siward commented. "A stranger would never know that those two houses belonged to Jews and the ones next to them don't."

"Why, though?" a mystified James asked of no-one in particular. "Does the Jewish faith so offend people in this country?"

"It's not faith, it's money," Will answered him cynically. "Only Jews are allowed to lend. It's that thing about usury and the danger it poses to a Christian soul! Pretty two-faced of the Church, though, given that they think it's all right to borrow from them themselves! But that means that a lot of powerful men are in debt to the Jews. Remember what Guy said? The old king was taxing everyone to the hilt.

"But the knightly families have to keep up appearances, don't they? Can't have the mistress going out in worn, old clothes! Can't let the peasants think you aren't much better off than them anymore!" He sniffed derisively. "I reckon you were right, Bilan. There's more than one knight using this as an excuse to pay back the men whom they're in debt to. This isn't about the poor folk but the rich! No wonder the sheriff's involved, it's his own sort doing the rioting!"

They found more houses wrecked and reeking of urine, but with no signs of life, and were beginning to despair of ever finding anyone when their luck changed. They'd paused beside a small church close to the River Foss to allow Bilan to rest, when the door to the church opened and a timid priest peered out.

"Is your young friend hurt?" he asked in a hushed whisper.

"Yes he is," Robin answered, struggling to force some respect into his voice in his angered state, but was rewarded for his efforts.

"Bring him inside," the priest said, beckoning them to hurry as he cast about, as if terrified that others would appear at any moment.

Inside, the church was like many other small country churches, with three tiny windows deeply recessed high up on either side of the narrow nave, and an apsidal east end beyond the round chancel arch, again with narrow windows. They helped Bilan to the altar and let him sit down on the stone ledge to the south of it beside the piscina.

"Here! I have herbs and salves and a needle and some thread!" the priest said scurrying back to them with a hand-sized, carefully-bound, leather roll.

"Unusual things for a priest to be having," Will commented wryly, recognising the Hospitaller insignia on the roll, and realising that it clearly didn't belong to the man offering it to him.

"My late dear brother's," the priest explained with a sad smile. "He came back from the east but not for long." He suddenly seemed to see Malik and James. "Are you Saracens?" he asked in awe.

"By birth but not by faith," Siward answered quickly. "They're Christians who fought alongside us to help defend Jerusalem."

Before the priest could ask any more, though, a feral human baying noise interrupted them.

"Oh Blessed Saint John, protect your house and your servant!" the priest intoned, dropping to his knees before the altar, hands clasped so tightly in prayer that his knuckles showed white.

"Who are they?" demanded Siward, scandalised that Englishmen should threaten a church.

"Some of the local young knights and their men," the priest replied, looking up at him balefully. "They've been before. They say they'll protect me from the mob if I give them all the gold and silver I have here."

They all looked at the altar with its simple wooden cross and realised that this was a very plain church indeed. If this priest had as much as a silver chalice for the communion wine, that's all he would have of value.

"Fucking English!" muttered Gilbert witheringly, his Irish accent very pronounced in his contempt for those who would threaten a priest in church. "Bleeding heathens in disguise!"

A loud hammering sounded on the stout oak door, accompanied

by the sounds of spears being rattled along the stonework and much shouting.

"Let us in Father Cedric and we'll stop these men from hurting you!" a voice called through the door.

"We'll handle this!" Robin said to the priest firmly, placing a restraining hand on his shoulder to prevent him from rising off his knees.

All six loosened their swords in their belts but didn't draw them. Will stood by the latch end of the door, Gilbert opposite him at the hinge side but back a bit to allow the door to open, while Robin, Malik, James and Siward all drew their bows and stood opposite the door with arrows pointing straight at it. As the next knocks came, Will flipped the latch and flung the door back towards Gilbert, who caught it and pulled it wide open. The gap was barely open before Will had grabbed the man doing the knocking, yanked him in, punched him hard, and threw him inside on the stone floor, senseless. The rest of the would be attackers lurched forwards and then stopped, stunned. Whatever they had expected to see it wasn't six ferocious, armed men.

However, Robin wasn't going to give them chance to recover from their shock. As Will and Gilbert pounced on the next nearest two and thumped them, he bellowed,

"Drop your weapons! *Now!*"

As James' bow covered the two men nursing sore jaws along with their still unconscious friend, Will and Gilbert stepped out of the door with swords now drawn, and Robin, Malik, and Siward skirmished forwards with their bows. Outside they found another seven men, all young and all looking terrified at what they'd unwittingly unleashed. Realising that these dire strangers would fell them within a few paces if they ran, they now dropped the various weapons they'd been carrying and allowed themselves to be herded into the church. Using whatever came to hand, including the belts and some rope belonging to the imprisoned thugs, Will, Malik and Gilbert tied them up, while James and Siward remained on guard with their arrows covering the group. Robin stood before them, his eyes alight with suppressed anger and arms folded severely, although only he knew that it was to stop him from throwing a few good punches himself.

"You miserable, scrofulous rats!" he growled through clenched teeth, dark brown eyes glinting dangerously and very visible to his prisoners despite the dim light in the church. "How *dare* you profane this holy space! We didn't fight our way through hoards of heathen Saracens to come home and stand by while boys like you, who haven't earned the right to wear a man's beard, do the Devil's work by creating mayhem in your mindless folly. Coxcombs! *Fools!*"

The reference to beards was due to several of them struggling to grow facial hair in the misguided belief that it hid their faces, and made them look more like the lesser working men of the town. No doubt they'd thought that way they would escape any hint of blame for what they did. Robin now disabused them of that expectation.

"Did you think this some kind of sport? A hunt of folk too below you to be worth the consideration?" The blushes on some of the faces signalled that he'd hit the centre of the target. "Well that's real blood on your friends' faces!" He signalled Bilan to come forward and held his tunic out for them to see. "And this is Bilan's blood! Only because he was well-trained did he survive this attack. And for what? A couple of cart-horses!"

Unable to keep his anger in check any longer he lunged in and hauled the youth who was the leader to his feet. With his fists bunching the front of the young man's tunic, he all but took him off his feet as he snarled into his face, "Two good lads who followed me died this day! Died with their throats cut by *filth* like you!" And he shook the youth like a terrier shaking a rat, making his teeth rattle and his eyes near pop out of his head.

Throwing his 'rat' back onto the floor in disgust, Robin stepped back and addressed them all again, in his fury not seeing how all of their faces were now white with fear. All of them might have been well-nourished young men of breeding, but Robin had grown into an even bigger man, with muscles built from long years of fighting not leisure, and the ease with which he'd picked up his victim shook them to the core. None were used to being overwhelmed and it was an unpleasant surprise to say the least.

"You have two choices. If you give your word that you will remain where we leave you, you can stay here until someone in authority comes for you." There was an uncomfortable squirming at this. "Or if we cannot trust you, we shall put you outside, still tied up, and leave you to the mercy of the rest of your mob. If you can't trust them to recognise you, that's your problem." Several jaws dropped at this, and suddenly everyone was falling over themselves to promise to sit still. Not one of them doubted that this fierce crusader would do as he threatened, especially as Will had opened the door again and was looking to Robin, just waiting for the word to start throwing them out.

"You are worse than Salah-al-Din's men," Malik said with contempt as he prowled, catlike, past them. "At least they treated the Jews with mercy." His use of the Saracen leader's native name, with its full inflections, further rattled these boys who had hardly ever been beyond the shire before. It was another eye-opener. Going on crusade would mean fighting men like this terrifying foreign spectre. One of him was bad enough!

Gilbert picked up on it, and with glee added, "We fought thousands like him at Hattin and Jerusalem. Good job he was on our side, eh?"

Several eyes got even wider and followed Malik, and then James, with open awe as they walked to where Robin now waited by the altar.

"I don't think you'll have any trouble with this lot," he was just saying to Father Cedric when one lad panicked and made a bolt for the door. Without a word from Robin, his five friends began hauling their prisoners outside and flinging them against the outer wall of the church, despite the screams of protest that they would behave. When they were lined up once more, each pinned through their bonds to the ground by an arrow or one of their own spears where they sat, Robin stood before them again.

"You fight together, you fall together," he said in a flat voice. "No excuses. You take responsibility for one another. Learn that lesson and one day, maybe, you'll become men worth fighting beside."

"Who *are* you?" a shivering lad asked in despair, wondering at this stage whether he'd ever live to see another morning.

Robin paused from walking back into the church, and with a tight-lipped, lupine smile replied, "Robin of Loxley. I'd remember that name if I were you, because you don't want to cross my path again!"

Inside, Malik and Gilbert were having an animated conversation with Father Cedric, with Gilbert telling Robin the instant he was close enough, "There are some Jews in a house just on the other side of the church's bounds!"

Father Cedric nodded. "I've seen them at the windows! Not many. Only women and possibly some children. They're in the house right by the river. The poor souls are terrified!"

The crusaders all looked from one to another with growing smiles. Saint Thomas be praised, they might yet save someone in this almighty mess.

"We'll need more rope!" Siward said hurrying to the door and scanning the backs of the row of houses. "We may have to climb to the upper windows if they won't let us in."

"There's a rope-maker back on Aldwark," Father Cedric said. "Tell him I sent you! I'm sure he'll help. He's a good man with a family of his own. Leave Bilan here with me. I'll bolt the door after you've gone. He'll be safe here with me now."

Fired with enthusiasm for the rescue, the six hurried out and retraced their steps to the street they now knew to be Aldwark. As Father Cedric had promised, his name got the door of the shop opened to Robin while the others stood guard outside. With barely an hour passed, they were back down by the bank of the River Foss and making their way over the fences of the burgage plots behind the houses. It was too early in the season for there to be many crops growing in the garden patches except the last of the winter cabbages, and so their passage was uninterrupted except by the naked bean and pea sticks sitting waiting for their summer clothing.

Reaching the house they saw that the ground floor windows were small and barred, with heavy shutters across them. Clearly the owner had feared thieves in the night, but his caution had saved his family now. At first Robin tried calling up to those inside but got no answer, however when Malik and James tried in their native language, a curtain upstairs was cautiously pulled open a way, and the drawn and weary face of a young woman appeared. It still took some long negotiating by Malik and James while the others kept watch, but finally the family within were convinced that rescue had finally arrived. With great trepidation the same young woman came down and opened the back door and the six slipped inside.

Once there they found three young women, and an elderly matron who looked far from well, plus eight small children. The older lady gave all of them serious concern as it was clear that she would be struggling to walk, let alone run, and yet they couldn't leave her – although Malik told Robin when he got him alone that the old lady was telling the younger women to go and take the children, not to jeopardise them escaping by waiting for her.

"She is being very brave," Malik told him.

"Then reassure her that we shall make sure every last one of them reaches safety," Robin told him. "No-one is getting left behind!"

Leaving Malik and James with the family, the others left, for Robin had a plan and it meant getting hold of a boat. As the spring dusk fell they finally found a suitable craft. Going by the grains in the bottom it was used for shipping corn. Big enough to navigate the river further downstream, it was nonetheless shallow enough to cope with the lower water levels in the smaller Foss, whose bank it was tied up at. Even better, it still had a pile of sacks folded up under the bench by the rudder, which could be used to cover their passengers with.

As darkness fell, they retrieved Bilan from the church, checked on the shivering young men, and took pity on them enough to bring them back inside – now that Father Cedric was going to his tiny cottage for the night with the cross and chalice from the church for safe keeping – and then set off in the boat. Pulling in to the bank just yards from the bottom of the house's garden, they kept an armed watch as the family crept out to them. Malik and James had to carry the old lady between them to get her to the boat, but at least at this stage they weren't overlooked.

That was about to change, though, because now the only way they would get free of the town was to follow the Foss down to where it joined the Ouse just below the castle. Upstream simply wasn't an option, since they would soon run aground as the Foss narrowed to its source. Taking up the oars, they propelled the boat out into midstream. There was a single large sail, but it wouldn't be of any use to them until they were clear of the town, being far too easy to see even in the failing light, and so they rowed as silently as they could and allowed the current to take them where possible. They became a silent floating shape on the dark water, hopefully not visible given that everyone's attention was focused in the opposite direction.

What they weren't prepared for was the sudden appearance of flames within the castle. Already Bilan and Siward said they could smell smoke, but in the deep dusk it wasn't possible to tell where it was coming from. Now, though, as an eerie orange glow rose from the keep, by its meagre light it was possible to see the great thick billows of smoke rolling around it, and for the first time they saw the full layout of the castle.

The Foss had been diverted over a century ago to form a kind of figure-of-eight, with the centres being two man-made islands. The southern one contained the well-fortified inner bailey whose palisade followed its banks, and echoed the northern curved wall of the outer bailey on the town's dry land – that having only a palisade fence and dry ditch to defend it where it came up against the town streets, and no defence but the river on its exposed eastern third of its circuit. In the smaller, northern loop of the river, and sandwiched between the land-bound outer bailey and the river-moated inner bailey, stood the tall motte, capped with the keep.

As they drifted downstream, too stunned by what they saw to row, they found themselves looking over a bridge leading from the outer bailey across to the inner bailey, and able to see along the curve of the western loop of the diverted river to the motte. Anyone in the keep was utterly beyond the reach of any but those inside the two baileys.

"God help them!" Siward gasped in horror, as James began to pray quietly even as he rowed.

"Saint Lazarus forgive me. How can I help them now?" Robin sighed, making Malik raise a questioning eyebrow to Will, whom he was alongside at the oars.

"He was trying to think of a way in from the river," Will confessed softly to his turcopole friend. "I told him that we'd never make it."

Malik looked up at the inner bailey wall which they were now sliding closer to and shook his head, then looked to Robin and noted that nonetheless he had his bow in his hand and an arrow nocked. A fine line was attached to the arrow, and Malik knew from experience that it in turn would be linked to the thicker rope which was coiled beside Robin.

"It looks as though he may still try, though," he said sadly. "I fear Jerusalem scarred his soul more than he knows."

Will sniffed. "I know, but he's not Balian of Ibelin and we're only six men! And I don't think this Sheriff Marshal is the kind to negotiate like Saladin did!"

The trailing branches of some old willows brushed against them, making them jump as they realised they'd been taken by the current closer to the opposite bank than they'd realised in the deep darkness.

Then Bilan called out urgently, "Robin!"

Following his outstretched finger they realised what his keener youthful eyes had spotted. There on the keep's south-west section of wall, outlined by the fire's glow, was at least one figure, maybe more!

"We're going in!" Robin instantly announced, despite Will and Malik's exchanged glances of despair, but Robin didn't give them chance to argue. "Get the women and children out onto the bank." he ordered them. "We can't have them put at risk."

"Robin, what are you doing?" Malik asked worriedly.

Their leader pointed across to the narrow channel. "We're going to row under that first bridge between the two baileys. With any luck anyone seeing us will think we're just being enterprising and trying to get into the keep for the sheriff. We'll run the boat aground against the motte at its southernmost point and use the rope to get up onto the walls."

"That's good as far as it goes," Gilbert said warily, "but how on earth are we going to get out?" He pointed to the milling crowd within the outer bailey, which, if not as substantial as that on the town's side of its walls, was still big enough to give six men an awful lot of trouble. "That lot aren't going to let us row back past them once they've realised what we're doing!"

"We won't come back this way," Robin declared resolutely. "We'll row like mad on round the rest of the loop of that inner bailey. Round where the only people who can get to us will be those up on the walls of the inner bailey. Look up there! There are hardly any people up there!"

"But we'll have to go right past the siege engine!" protested Siward.

"Yes we will," Robin agreed, "but if we do our rescuing in the shadow of the motte, out of their line of sight, then they'll be unprepared for us. With luck we'll be able to get up to that point where the palisade of the outer bailey is in everyone's way on the landward side, and we'll just have to hope the bridge to the keep does the same for anyone on the inner bailey walls. And when we row on, think of how wet it's been of late. With the way the Foss has been taken out of its natural course, what's the betting that the land between it and the Ouse is now even marshier than a normal river meeting? I'm gambling on it being too wet underfoot for anyone to follow us down that way."

"Those are odds even an Irishman taken with the mead wouldn't go for!" Gilbert objected in disbelief at what they were about to attempt.

"Better hope most of those men on the walls are drunk," Will agreed with him. "That or near blind!"

However, Robin had already got Bilan out of the boat and was instructing him to lead the women on foot as fast as they could down the eastern bank of the Foss. The old lady would have to stay in the boat, lying low on the bed of sacks and blankets they'd made for her, for she would only hold the others up – a risk even Robin wouldn't take. When they'd all disembarked, the six left took up the oars and swung the boat into the current, and rowed as close to the island of the inner bailey as they could. Miraculously no-one called out to them or cried out anything to give them away, and they made it under the bridge connecting the two baileys before anyone was heard. Then the voices above egged them on in the mistaken belief that they were attempting an assault on the keep from the river in concert with the siege engine, which was still lobbing the occasional rock at the keep's walls.

Insanely, the engine was their best cover because they were assumed to be keeping well clear of those shots which hit and then bounced at high speed back down the motte's steep slope to splash noisily into the moat area. The waves these rocks caused was a serious danger to even a middling-sized boat such as they were rowing, and twice they got an icy drenching of river water.

"Fuck, that's cold!" Will snapped after he'd spat a frond of weed out, and flicked another from off his brow from where it had been splattered by the huge splash.

Siward shook his head like a dog as he rose from where he'd dived down to protect the old lady from the worst of the incoming water. "We'll catch our deaths if we can't get dry tonight!" he hissed acerbically at Robin, but their leader wasn't listening.

With frantic hauling on the simple tiller, Robin plunged them into the shadow of the motte and into its side.

"Robin, we'll never make it up that," Will remonstrated softly as he looked up at the motte. The man-made hillock on which the keep had been built was not only high but incredibly steep, and Siward agreed. Looking at the spring grass covering the slope he voiced his concern, knowing that Malik and James had had no experience of trying to climb on slippery grass, and therefore had no idea of what was being asked of them.

"Even if it was dry we'd be on our hands and knees to get up that slope," he said to Robin, grabbing his sleeve and giving it a shake to try and get him to take notice. "Jesu, would you look at the height of the damned thing! Robin! Whoever goes up there won't be able to have *any* weapon in their hands! It's suicide!"

"Brace the boat!" Robin hissed vehemently as he grabbed his bow and got to his feet.

"What are you *doing*?" Siward was appalled and fearing Robin had lost all reason.

"I'm going to give us a line to get up the motte with," Robin told him with some irritation at being distracted and having to explain what he saw as obvious. "Now brace the boat!"

The others exchanged worriedly glances and shrugs but did as he said.

The boat was big enough not to be too wobbly, and with the others shoving the oars into the soft mud as a further bracer, it was steady enough, but the problem was the extreme angle he was going to have to fire at.

"You'll never make it!" Gilbert hissed, even as the muscles on his neck stood out with the effort of digging his oar in deeper.

Robin took a deep, steadying breath and willed himself to calm. He could hear in his head Bilan saying to him, 'Thomas says to feel the feel the flight', from when they'd last practised together. Back then the young lad had made a shot Robin wouldn't even have attempted, yet now he was trying for something even more improbable. 'Don't just aim! Be one with the bow!' Bilan's voice in his head told him, and he took a steadying breath. *Saint Lazarus and King Baldwin guide my aim*, he prayed fervently and, managing to pull another inch back on the bowstring, let fly. Like a returning lightning strike, the arrow flashed upwards towards the wall and imbedded itself deeply into the oak of the castle's palisade wall.

"Who's going up?" Will asked. He knew it wouldn't be him or Malik, they were the heaviest of the six men, and it would be touch and go whether the arrow would take the strain anyway.

"I will," James said. It made sense. If he appeared over the wall he was someone one of the panicked folk inside would trust. Anyone English stood little chance of reassuring them by now.

Robin nodded and took a bracing arm around the rope which had snaked back down from the loop.

"Who made the arrow?" Malik asked, still more worried than he was trying to show. He was by far the best fletcher of the six, but he hadn't been present at its preparation having been with the Jewish family.

"Bilan did, with some help from me with tightening the lashing," Siward answered.

Malik smiled his relief at that, at least. The lad knew what he was doing better than the others, and that reassured him that James was less likely to get halfway up and then crash to his doom as the loop came away from the arrow shaft. Yet the problem proved not to be Bilan's work, but the steep angle at which Robin had had to fire the arrow into the palisade. The arrow head was taking all the weight, not the shaft as would have happened if the arrow had been able to follow an arc and strike downwards. James had got barely six feet up the slope when, in a fast slither, he was coming back down the slope to land at their feet, already smeared with mud all up his front.

"The arrow's coming out!" he hissed at Robin. "I felt it give!" Of all of them James had been the one who was as determined as Robin to effect this rescue, and yet now even he could see that it simply wasn't possible.

"Robin, let it go," Will told him gently. "If the rope won't even get James up the motte, there's no chance of it taking his full weight to get up the wall."

Robin was standing with one leg out of the boat propped on the bank, straining to see up.

"Can you call out to them?" he asked Malik and James. "Ask them if they can use something to get down off the wall. A rope. Some sheets knotted together. Anything! Ask them!"

Malik looked dubious, as did Will, Siward and Gilbert, but James was already calling out, and after several goes a timid head peeped over the wooden rim to reveal a young woman who answered their calls. The brief exchange brought even more horrifying news. Within the castle such terror had been rife that the rabbi had told his people that death at their own hands would be better than surrendering to those outside the gate. The men of each house had cut the throats of their wives and children, then had taken their own lives, with only a few souls still living. The rabbi himself had set the fire now raging within the castle's walls.

"Tell them to hurry!" Will snapped, now as desperate to get whoever they could out before they burned to death. Cynical enough to know that the Jews fate at the hands of the sheriff would not be a good one, nonetheless Will had believed until now that they would survive, albeit probably in prison, until the mess was sorted out. But now it was clear that there were very few left, and those who were faced a horrific death in the flames if they didn't act soon.

James and Malik were negotiating for all they were worth but nothing was happening, and Siward and Gilbert were giving worried glances along the bank in either direction, knowing that they were horribly exposed out here. If anyone heard them and came looking they were sitting ducks!

"She will not leave her friend," Malik reported regretfully, "and her friend cannot climb down for she is heavily with child."

"Oh Blessed Virgin save her!" Gilbert prayed at the thought of the two of them burning to death.

507

"Can't you pursued her to try?" Siward pleaded. "She might not make it, but surely that's better than the certain death of remaining?"

But then a small figure appeared at the top of the wall.

"Her son!" James yelped, even as the little one was swung outwards.

James, Siward and Gilbert immediately began trying to climb the motte, digging their fingers into what turf there was, and scrabbling with their feet for any tiny purchase. The child slid down the walls the walls so far and then a knot must have parted, for he dropped and then began rolling down the slope.

"Get him!" Siward yelped as the boy shot past him just beyond reach.

Up to their thighs in the freezing water, Robin, Will and Malik scrambled frantically across the bottom of the slope to where the boy was rolling, all caution over making a noise forgotten in their haste. Making a dive, Robin caught the child just as he was about to hit the freezing river, Will and Malik grabbing him in turn and hauling him to his feet as he clutched the small child to him. James, Gilbert and Siward had already used the incline to slide at speed back down to the boat, and all piled into it. Of the women up on the keep's walls there was no sign any more.

Then a whistling broke the air and an arrow embedded itself into the side of the boat from their right. Finally they'd been seen! Thrusting the child into the bottom of the boat with the old lady, the six grabbed their bows and exchanged shots with their attackers – a few men at the water's edge within the outer bailey. Mercifully, whoever their attackers were, they weren't experienced fighters, and once they realised that the six loosing arrows back at them were hitting their marks when theirs didn't, they soon ceased and backed off. There was no time for rejoicing, though, despite the fact the light had truly gone now and their shapes were harder to distinguish on such a clouded and moon-less night, and as soon as they could, Will and Gilbert dropped their bows, grabbed the oars, and began rowing the boat.

Briefly, being in such a confined place worked to their advantage, for the alerted men within the inner bailey had no better an angle to loose their arrows at than Robin had had. Soon, though, they were swinging round the western end of the inner bailey walls and it was now that the fire aided them, for those men on the thin strip of land between the Ouse and the Foss had their night-vision impaired by the rising glow of the raging fire, whereas those in the boat were too low down to be affected and could see where they were going.

Digging the oars into the water they rowed for all they were worth, grateful that the siege engine had at last ceased its bombardment as the extent of the fire was realised. With more speed and success than they could have ever have expected, they shot past the crowd on the banks around the siege engine who were watching the flames licking up out of the roof of the keep. Only as they came to a straight stretch of the inner bailey's wall did they start draw some response from the wall, although only a few random arrows, but it did alert some of those on the bank around the siege engine that something was wrong. However Robin's saints must have been watching over them, because to their right there now rose great clumps of bull-rushes, telling of treacherous muddy land over which pursuit wasn't possible, and cloaking them once again from sight.

Where the second bridge around the circuit of the inner bailey came out to join the Selby road brought their next problem. Some men-at-arms had sallied out of that south gate in the bailey wall, and were waiting for them on the bridge. Four arrows whistled in, two splashing into the water right close to the boat, one clunking ineffectively off a metal rowlock, but the fourth imbedding itself in the boat's prow.

"Back!" Robin snapped, although the others had needed no telling and were pulling them back into the lee of the rushes. Paddling very cautiously they crept forward again, this time with Will prodding the ground until he hissed,

"Solid!"

"Siward, you and James wait until we've engaged them, then get the bloody boat under this bridge, and then turn it under the mill bridge to get back onto the Foss!" Robin ordered as he leapt ashore with the other three in his wake.

Once on the bank the four could see that it had been reinforced to be firmer under foot on purpose to give better access to the mill which loomed ahead of them. Now, though, the mill was dark and silent, and they ignored it as they ran to clash with the men from the castle. Again surprise was on their side, for whatever the castle men had been expecting it clearly wasn't experienced fighters.

Like a human bull, Will went in hard and fast. Laying about him on all sides he had felled three men before they knew what had happened. Robin, too, was using his fists when he wasn't striking with his sword. He had no desire to kill these men, he just wanted them out of the way, but he was finding it incredibly hard to restrain the old familiar battle-rage which was welling up inside him. Luckily Malik and Gilbert were fighting with much more detachment, deliberately seeking to disarm and disable rather than kill, and even Will wasn't following up his initial impact blows with lethal ones. Had they lost control, Robin knew he would have been unable to stop himself. "They know not what they do," he kept repeating to himself under his breath, in a desperate attempt to remind himself that these were Englishmen who were misguided, not his sworn enemies.

A sharp whistle from the river pierced the air telling of Siward and James being clear, and the four began to retreat along the bank, grateful that no more men had come from the inner bailey's gate to challenge them. With all their attackers on the ground, out cold or groaning in pain and not moving much, they turned and ran over the second bridge at right angles to the bailey's which connected the mill and castle to the Selby road. As they plunged off the road down towards the eastern bank of the Foss they saw Bilan had brought the refugees down to meet them, and moments later Siward and James appeared out of the black night with the boat, and swung towards the side. Already soaked to the skin it made no difference to the four to wade into the river and help bring the boat close in for the others to embark again.

As soon as everyone was back on board the men grabbed the oars and all six began rowing again – not only to get them away as fast as possible, but glad of the exercise to keep them from freezing in their dripping clothes. As they finally slipped out into the broader waters of the Ouse and began to speed away from York, the view backwards was grim sight. The whole of the wooden keep was a pillar of flame within, and it was only the dense oak of the outer building works, which was taking longer to ignite, that was keeping the building standing. There was no possibility of anyone inside surviving, and they couldn't imagine the state of mind of the people who had decided that cremation at their own hands was better than surrendering to a sheriff like Sir John Marshal. As the beacon of flame receded, they all leant into the paddles with a will and put as much water between them and York as possible, until exhaustion forced them to ease up and drift into the bank to rest.

Siward was the first to speak. "We couldn't have saved any more," he said in a voice filled with regret.

"I know," Robin sighed mournfully, although his friends knew he was still thinking of what else he could have done, even if he wouldn't admit it.

"If we'd been passing by on the river earlier in the day we'd never have made it past ourselves, let alone have helped someone inside the castle," Siward reminded him. "So if we'd tried earlier we still wouldn't have done any better. We had to wait for dark, and you couldn't possibly have guessed the rabbi would do something so desperate. And if you must curse someone, curse Eudo and Waldein for holding us up on the way here!"

"And you said yourself right at the start, we'd never be able to storm the place with that mob around it," Will added, knowing Robin too well, and that despite everything he'd be blaming himself for not having rescued more of the terrorised Jews of York.

Robin smile weakly at his oldest friend. "I hear what you're saying, Will. It just doesn't sit well with me, this thing that's happened in York."

"With me neither," Will admitted, "but look on the bright side. We've rescued at least a few of them, and if we can get them to more of their own people, then at least they'll know the truth of what happened in York."

Ah, Gervase, you should not look so cheerful. Yes that was the Robin Hood you so wanted to hear about, was it not? Yet the whole event at York was a sad stain upon our country's reputation, and so it should remain. You need not look so superior, and do not dare say to me that those people were <u>only</u> Jews. There are great scholars of the Christian faith who would remind you that such a thing is to be deplored. No-one should go in such terror of their neighbours that the taking of their own life seems preferable to facing them.

However, I will let you in on a family secret to soften my chastisement. Robin told me himself that taking that shot at the castle walls at York was the first time he ever tried to make such an impossible shot. Until that time he had not had sufficient faith in his natural ability with the bow, I think, for in the east, whilst he could loose an arrow with deadly accuracy, he confessed he was always a touch surprised when it hit where he wished it to. Remembering Bilan's repeating of Thomas' words of wisdom did something for him that day. He told me it was like a lock turning inside his head. Bilan's words were the key and suddenly a door swung open inside him allowing him to realise his potential, and I believe they resonated with him for the very reason that Bilan was <u>not</u> the experienced archer his brothers were as yet, and was therefore closer to Robin in ability.

˜Ah, that is why Bilan was important to the story˜ you say?

Yes, and for many other reasons, Brother. I did not bring him in merely for decoration. That he survived the taking of the horses in York, and Peter and Tumi did not, also had a profound impact. Given that they were with Robin for such a short time, you might be forgiven for wondering how any one of us even remembered their names. That we – indeed I, who never actually met them – did, is a testimony to the fact that they did not die wholly in vain. It certainly made Robin wake up to the reality of just what he was asking of those who followed him, and never again would he sweep up farm workers, and the small folk of the towns who had been ejected from home or workshop, without first making sure that they could truly look after themselves. For it is a fact, Brother, that you cannot look after others if you cannot even look after yourself.

However, to return to what Robin told me – for my dear cousin was always harder on himself than anyone else could ever have been – it ate away at his heart that for all that he had hit the castle walls at York, it was not good enough to achieve his purpose, and he vowed to never be in that position again. Therefore night after night he would practice with the bow. Even many years later, while others of the famous band were wrapped in their cloaks asleep, he would still slip away and set himself impossible shots to make, practising over and over again until he could do what no other could. If practice makes perfect, then Robin was a perfect shot with that enormous wyche-elm bow by dint of a prodigious talent, but also by the hours of practice he put in above and beyond what any other man would have done. That, Gervase, was a legendary undertaking all of its own, even if you find it less glamorous than the thought of a man who could aim an arrow at any target and hit it as if by magic. Even the most passionate of knights practising for the tournament would pale in comparison with the hours Robin put in at his endless variety of butts, and I can say with all honesty and without invoking anything pagan or magical, that I have never seen the like of him for handling a bow within a year of that night at York.

Yet we still have some wrapping up of this tale to do before night falls, so let us press on.

Chapter 24

So now, Gervase, we return to my own story. As you will recall I was hurrying north with the rest of the men who would become Robin Hood's loyal band. Worried as we were, everyone was keeping as fast a pace as possible, while still scouring the countryside for any sign which might lead us to our friends. I was fairly certain that they would know from travelling north, that Selby was the best place for them to cross the Ouse before it got so wide as to force them into using one of the Templar-run ferries on the estuary, but that in turn would mean that they would have to cross the Aire somewhere. Hirst was out of the question for that crossing because of the Templar preceptory there, and so I made the decision to head for Ferry following the line of the Great North Road.

It was a risk, for it took us perilously close to the de Lacy's stronghold of Pontefract – a great castle which one day my miserable specimen of a current sheriff would inherit, but not yet, Brother, thankfully not yet! Sir Robert de Lacy held it for now, and so we prayed as we marched that he would not be at home with his knights and men-at-arms, and that we should pass unseen. Yet we did not get as far as the ferry itself, as you shall now hear.

Yorkshire & Nottinghamshire, March, the year of our Lord 1190

As they forked off the old Roman road, and made to cross the River Went further along its wooded valley than under the watchful eyes of Pontefract Castle, they were stopped by an arrow zipping across their path and embedding itself into a tree. Thomas ran forward and looked at the arrow.

"That's Malik's fletching!" he called back in surprise. "I'd know that anywhere!"

They all halted and began looking around them.

"Take your helms off," Guy told the six from High Peak. "Maybe they're worried that you're just any old soldiers from Nottingham."

But that wasn't the problem. A few moments later Malik himself dropped onto the trail in front of them.

"God has been merciful in sending you!" he declared as he puffed for breath. "We saw you but could not catch you. ...I have run after you..."

"Where are the others?" John asked him urgently, fearing that something had happened to at least one of them, and that that one might be Robin.

Malik gestured further along the heavily wooded ridge which swung around towards the north. "Up there," he wheezed, "...with those we protect. ...Come!" And he set off at a purposeful if panting walk, forcing the others to follow him.

Where a track began to climb the steep escarpment on a simple lane, Malik started upwards, and then headed off into the trees along the slope to their right, where the gradient began to ease a little as they got deeper into the Went valley. Far inside the trees they found a small camp. All of their friends were there, plus some nine children and three women, all young, and one elderly matron who was lying on the ground and looked far from well. The way these people almost took to their heels in terror took the band with Guy aback. Some fear was to be expected when confronted by so many men, but not the way they all went so white and at least two of the children wet themselves.

"No, no! They're our friends!" Robin and James were saying urgently to the women, as the others made a grab for the children before they could run off.

"York Jews," Malik said still rather breathlessly as he hung on to two boys who were wriggling like fish on a line in his grasp.

"Oh you poor souls!" Tuck exclaimed, and bustled forward to relieve Will of a young girl he was trying to hold, along with a woman who Tuck guessed might be her mother.

John, Walter and Algar were also quick to hurry to the children, while Much, Bilan, Allan and Roger formed a small embarrassed group on one side, and the six men-at-arms mirrored them on the other. However Marianne was suddenly very much back in her element, and her appearance alongside these formidable looking men did much to calm the shocked survivors. For some time she and Tuck went round every one of the group checking them over, and consulting with each other as to what needed to be done. In the meantime Guy took Robin to one side to find out what had happened, although only after John had nearly broken Robin in two with his fierce hug at the relief of finding him still in one piece. Even after all these years apart, Guy still knew his younger cousin well enough to guess what an effect the sights at York had had upon him.

"We saw enough of that sort of thing in the East to know that it wasn't boisterous good fun we could hear," Robin told him bitterly. "I've rarely been so shocked as when we saw that the sheriff had brought armed men into the city, and was talking about moving the Jews out of his castle by force."

By now everyone else was sitting more calmly on the soft leaf litter as Marianne was expertly bandaging one of the young women's leg, and a kind of hush lay on the place as those who had come with Guy strained to hear, bringing Guy and Robin into the centre of the group again. However, he wasn't the first to speak to the group as a whole.

"They'd only gone there because they were so frightened," James said softly and the others saw that he had his arm around a young woman who was nursing a tiny baby. Guy flicked a look to Tuck and John, and knew that they too were thinking of James' lost loved ones, and what this must have felt like for him seeing such violence towards young families. "The constable of the castle let them in because he knew his duty was to protect them. They are under King Richard's protection and he acted on that! They never stormed the castle, or tried to take it by force. They were *invited* in! Only when the constable left for the day did they become so terrified that they barred the keep gate. And who could blame them with that mob outside?"

"It wasn't the ordinary people of York," Will sighed regretfully. "Oh there were more than a few of the local lads in the mob who were rampaging around the castle, but the instigators were higher born than that. And most of the ordinary citizens were boarding up their shops and praying that it wouldn't all spill back into the streets away from the castle. There weren't enough of them to stop the mob, though. Not when the sheriff's men were at the forefront!"

Guy was horrified at the implications, and his friends all seemed dreadfully sure. "The sheriff's men? Actually *in* the riot? Not just ineffectively trying to stop it? Are you absolutely positive?"

"Oh we're sure," Will answered dryly. "Might have had something to do with the way we saw them in front of the castle, and Sheriff Marshal at their head, bellowing at the poor sods inside that he'd be sending his men in if they didn't come out!"

"In God's Name what was he thinking of?" Guy gasped in incomprehension. "You're right James, of any people the Jews are protected by the king – Marshal *knows* that! And the sheriff's *supposed* to be the king's man! Dear God, Marshal's been treated with more than enough clemency by King Richard. Surely he must know how much he, of all people, owes our new king for the favour he's been shown? Has he gone mad? I'd hoped this was all a distortion when the messenger from Lincoln told us. That in the confusion the truth had got twisted. Even with men like Longchamp running the country on the king's behalf, this shouldn't have happened!"

"Then they brought up the siege engine," Siward added in exasperation. "I mean, what did they think they were fighting? Certainly not frightened traders and their families! You'd have thought they were surrounding Saladin himself by the carry-on!"

Robin nodded. "That's when we thought it best to leave Bilan and with Peter and Tumi up by the Minster, out of the way with the horses."

"Where are the boys?" John asked urgently, suddenly realising that in his relief at finding Robin he'd missed the fact that the two boys weren't with them.

"Dead," Gilbert said sadly, putting a hand on Robin's shoulder as a soft restraint. "Robin will no doubt try and make you believe it was his fault, but it wasn't."

"No it wasn't," Bilan added firmly from where he was sitting between his two brothers, both of whom wore expressions flickering between anger, worry and relief. "You'd never have left us if you'd had any idea of what would happen." He looked to both of his brothers, and then to the others, with all of the sternness his youth could command. "Would any of you have thought that three of us just standing holding horses safely inside an English town would be set upon by the sheriff's men of all people?"

Thomas and Piers grudgingly shook their heads. Even under the dreaded de Braose they knew that the lads might have been roughed up a bit if they'd been cheeky, but given that they clearly couldn't have stolen that many horses, they wouldn't have died under any but the most bizarre circumstances. Bilan turned and gave the closest he could manage to his normal cheeky grin to Piers.

"Gilbert was worried stiff you'd kill him when they came back and couldn't find us at first."

"Oh thank you very much! Such gratitude you young rascal! Casting aspersions on my courage!" Gilbert sniffed with mock offended dignity, but there was no hiding the fact that he was still struggling internally with the thought that they might have lost Bilan too. It did much to ease Thomas and Piers' minds, though, to realise the depths to which the six had been worried for Bilan's safety.

"Everything just happened so fast in York," Siward added. "It never eased for a moment! No sooner had we stopped that murderer Eudo, then we were back in the thick of the fighting again." He shivered. "It brought back some horrid memories," and he didn't need to elaborate for the others to know what of.

Robin nodded. "We all knew Jewish folk back in Jerusalem – made friends of some of them – and I can recall King Baldwin saying that the one thing he feared was people turning on their neighbours because of religion. Armies you can control, but not the civilians if they decide to start taking things into their own hands. Thank God men like Châtillon never thought to look down as far as the ordinary people, or Heaven knows what sort of Hell they could have created by inciting them to violence. And so we couldn't walk away, here any more than there, when there were women and children trapped by that mob."

He didn't say anything about James, but his eyes strayed to the former turcopole every so often, and the others knew that James would have stayed even it had been alone – and the other five would never have allowed that.

"So the next thing was to see if the Jewish houses were all in one spot. I was dreading them being all together in a ghetto, like in some of the towns in France and the Kingdom of the Two Sicilies." Robin sighed. "In some ways it might have been simpler if they had been, instead of looking in a house here and another house five doors away. When we got into the houses it was like a bunch of wild pigs had gone through! Sickening! The dirty bastards had pissed and shit everywhere, and what hadn't been stolen was wrecked. By Saint Lazarus, we didn't see the likes of that from Saladin's men! Not against the Jews, nor against us for that matter. These folk would've been safer in Jerusalem or Acre than York!"

He looked sadly at the frightened bunch of refugees. "We found them in the last house by the river, thanks to a truly Christian priest, all huddled together. I think they thought they were going to die there and then! Their men must have gone to try and find out what was happening and then got trapped somewhere. Whoever they were they're dead now, God bless them."

"We heard about what happened at the castle," Guy told them. "Everyone I've spoken to has been shocked at what happened. It's appalling that people should think that the only choice they have left in life is between taking their own lives or being murdered. That's sickening. It's terrible!"

"I never thought to see such a thing in England," Robin said bitterly.

"None of us here did either," Guy sympathised, but knowing that for the six coming from the East this was all the more shocking. "But that was on the sixteenth and it's the twenty-seventh today, what happened in between?"

"The old lady wasn't well when we got to them," Will admitted. "I think her heart couldn't stand the strain. We had to carry her into the boat, she couldn't even walk that far back then. We decided to hang onto the boat and we paddled for all we were worth downstream to get away from the castle as fast as we could. By Saint Thomas, that was a hair-raising time! We'd had to get past under the very walls of the castle, you see, and with men right close on the banks on either side of it baying for blood!

"After that the current on the Ouse took us downstream pretty quick, and away from York. We pulled over before we got to Selby and waited to go past there the following night. We've travelled more for caution than speed since then. By this time we weren't taking any chances! Once we got to close by Hirst and the Templar preceptory there, Malik, James and Gilbert stayed with these folk, and Robin, Siward and me went to the preceptory to try and get them some proper help." He stopped and spat in fury. "Call themselves bloody Templars? Ha! God help the poor pilgrim who looks to them for help!"

Robin reached across and squeezed Will's shoulder, making the big smith snort but relax when he realised the little lad beside him was looking up fearfully.

"It's all right, little-one," Will said affectionately and ruffling the child's hair. "It's not you I'm wild at! But if I get my hands on the men who hurt your ma and sisters there'll be trouble!"

With a grunt of agreement, Robin continued. "I asked to see the master at the preceptory. They took that as though I was some kind of leper asking for a bed instead of one of their own, but they begrudgingly fetched him. That was just about accepted until I said who we had with us, and that we wanted to bring them into the preceptory for sanctuary. Well, we'd have had more of a welcome if we'd said we were bringing the plague in!" He looked ruefully into Guy's eyes. "I think I shot down with flaming arrows our chances of ever being admitted into an English preceptory when the word of us gets out – not that I'd ever want to be associated with men like that!"

"What did you say?" Allan asked breathlessly.

Robin looked at him with a puzzled air, for there hadn't been time to tell him who this was, but of course Allan knew who he was. Yet it was Will who answered with a laugh.

"He started off with telling the preceptor that if the Grand Master of his order could live side by side with Jews in Jerusalem, then it was bloody good enough for some old man in a soggy backwater!" Allan and Much were hanging on his every word now. "He then told him that it was his Christian duty to help, or had he forgotten about the parable of the good Samaritan? Or that the pope's message is to convert Jews, not kill them?"

"I bet that didn't carry much weight," Tuck interrupted.

"Why?"

"Because Pope Alexander III wrote to du Puiset, bishop of Durham, oh, about ten years ago warning him to be on his guard against the Jewish 'contagion'. I know because my old abbot was all for it – forced conversion and the like! It was another thing he and I argued fiercely about! I don't particularly approve of du Puiset, but I suppose he's better than that bloodthirsty bastard we have as archbishop of York now. At least du Puiset defends the Church and could loosely be called a man of faith, but he wouldn't have defended these poor souls, I'm sorry to say, and I bet most of the senior churchmen in Yorkshire know that for certain and are of the same mind."

Gilbert gave a mirthless laugh. "Aach well, this du Puiset won't be any too pleased when he hears about the so called Christians in York Minster, then."

"No," Siward agreed. "It was while we were by Selby that the word got passed by the ordinary folk of the mob going into the Minster and terrorising the monks there too. Turns out it had to do with the debts all those men had. Not the poor apprentices or farmers. The Jews don't lend enough to them for it to have been a problem, I suppose. No, it was the ones who've been signing away their manors bit by bit, to afford to play with the great nobles in the hopes of getting preferment and being raised up, or whatever it is that they do."

He sniffed derisively, while Will spat into the fire in disgust again, then spoke.

"Hmmph! Twisted bloody noblemen! Even the Godforsaken Church is infested with them like bleedin' rats! And given who the archbishop is – as you said Tuck – we didn't see any of Plantagenet's men trying to put a stop to the mob, either. So I doubt he's left them much in the way of instructions to do anything but feather their own nests while he's away – as long as it's not at his expense, of course. Not that them at Temple Hirst seemed to give a shit one way or the other, anyway!

"Well when that two-faced swiving coward of a preceptor started to object, Robin told him he wasn't fit to wear the white and red. That he was a bloody disgrace to the name – a name we'd fought so hard to try and honour – and that we'd had a belly full of pompous shit-heads like him! Like de Ridefort! ...Told him that Saladin had behaved with more kindness and charity to his enemies in distress than they were doing. I think it was calling him a gutless, shrivelled old scrotum not fit to fuck Saladin's goats that got us chucked out, though,"

"*Woo-hoo*, Baldwin!" Allan whooped, making Robin look at him in astonishment.

"Who *are* you?" he demanded getting to his feet.

"It's Allan, you clot-head!" John chuckled as Allan launched himself at Robin and threw his arms around his taller cousin's neck.

"Baldwin!" the youngest of the fitz Waryns chortled, hugging him hard. "Oh God, it's so *good* to see you again!"

"Allan?" Robin managed to disentangle himself from the embrace and held his youngest cousin out at arms' length. He turned his glance to Guy and John. "I thought you said he was lost in the north somewhere?"

"He was," Guy replied dryly. "We found him ...whilst coming to look for you! ...He was in York too."

While Allan and Robin exchanged stories, and Guy chivvied the rest into making a cooking fire to get some warm food into the refugees, Tuck hurried off in search of early willow shoots down by the river. As soon as he returned, Marianne used one of the small pots they had amongst the soldiers' baggage to brew up an infusion of the leaves, then spent a long time gently spooning the tea into the old lady's mouth little by little.

"The leaves should really be better prepared than this to get the best out of them," Tuck admitted to Guy on the side, "but at least if she gets some inside her it might help. What she really needs, though, is to be somewhere safe and warm in a proper bed. It's her heart, you see. She might not make it even with what help we can give her."

Robin and the others had already paused on successive days to see if she would revive, hence the delay in getting even this far, but without success. The old lady had become so weak they'd been camped here for the last four days, just trying to build her up again, before making the attempt to get to Blyth and the others.

"Then we'll put them on the horses and make straight for Lincoln," Guy decided.

When they told Robin, at first Guy thought he was going to argue – even though Guy assured him that there was a substantial number of Jews there, and that they had avoided the dreadful consequences of the riots, thanks to a firmer hand from their sheriff. Robin's trust in sheriffs had gone completely! However, when they mentioned Lincoln to the bedraggle women, the reaction of relief was so great that Robin instantly gave in. For the next three days they took the most direct route towards Lincoln. It was slow but it was progress now that they had the horses, and they didn't dare go any faster for the old lady's sake.

Luckily they had time to take it in turns to hunt, with Thomas, Piers and Malik expertly bringing down ducks and geese, which were easily cooked over the camp fires at night and were palatable to all. Guy could have tracked boar, but remembering what Will had said about the prohibition on pigs in the east, he didn't want to cause offence to add to the refugees' suffering, and a whole red deer was far too big to cart around with them, even as joints. At least they were safe now, and with a party which numbered twenty-four armed men all marching together, trouble wasn't something Guy expected to have to deal with.

The women all rode the soldiers' horses and so did the children, but the old lady had to be held in the saddle, being too weak to stay on by herself. At first Bilan and Much (as the two lightest men for the horses' sake) willingly tried to ride behind her to support her, but she was very much a dead weight. So she was soon being helped by the stronger Will or Malik, along with Thomas and Big Ulf from High Peak, all of whom had the arm strength to hold her for long periods. By the time they got to Lincoln she was unconscious and hardly breathing, so it was with great relief that the band found a house to take them in. By the next morning she had died, yet all of them were glad that at least they'd brought her to a place where she could be attended to respectfully by her kinfolk, in death if not in life.

Having rapidly found the Lincoln Jews' homes, the three young women were swept into the care of the women, as were the children, and the armed men found themselves on the end of some puzzled questioning by the leading Jewish men. Having only recently escaped from being mobbed themselves, they were understandably suspicious of inviting so many soldiers into their homes, and also of the band's motives. In the end Guy sent the men-at-arms off to find an inn to stop in, while he took himself to the sheriff to explain his presence in the city – something which the Lincolnshire sheriff appreciated, and would save Guy from any trouble with his own lord. Tuck took the outlaws out to find other accommodation on the edge of the city, trying to spread their number out so as to not excite comment, leaving Robin and James to do the talking to the rabbi. When they met up the next morning on the road going west from Lincoln, Robin was able to tell them more of what had transpired.

With there being such a small Jewish community in the north of England, the families were at least all known to one another, he told them, and there was no chance that the orphaned children would be rejected. How soon any of them would get back to York was a totally different question, and Robin suspected that even if the leading men of Lincoln sent men to try and recover what was left of the businesses in York, none of the women would want to accompany them.

"Will they try and set up lending in York again, do you think?" Thomas asked. "It sounds to me as though that was the root of the problem, more than anything religious. Their faith and King Richard's crusade seem to have just been a smoke screen, something to wind the mob up with."

Robin sighed. "Oh I don't doubt you're right. The debts of those noblemen were at the heart of it, and they were the bloodiest attackers, but yes, I think the Jews will go back to York eventually."

However, Guy had his sights set on something more quickly attainable – the capture of the men who had subsequently burned Much's home and the village of Norton. But first he had to move the others out of harm's way. This was a job he intended to do with the six men-at-arms he'd brought from Nottingham, all of whom legally were in the clear if things got bloody, on account of having been sent out by the sheriff himself.

"What were you planning to do next?" he asked Robin, half fearful of the answer but determined to quell any ideas of them riding off to wreak vengeance in their own style.

"I've had enough!" Robin said bluntly, making Guy's stomach turn with dread. "I'm sick of the way we've been treated since we've been back in England – except by all of you that is. I don't want to skulk about in the forest lying low as if we'd committed some dreadful crime. We've done nothing wrong! Not even in stopping Eudo. Not morally wrong, even if some corrupt sheriff wouldn't see it that way. And what we've just seen in York has convinced me that we can keep our vows we made in the Holy Land without being part of the Templars in England. There are poor, innocent people here who need protecting just as much as any pilgrim in the Holy Land."

He looked directly at Guy now. "It's taken a while for it to sink in, but I've come to realise that you've been doing the best you can to protect the most vulnerable. The trouble is, you're hobbled at every turn by your duties. If the sheriff sends you in one direction you can't be keeping an eye on folks in another. Well if we're our own masters in Sherwood, we can go where we please. We'll have to think up some way you can send messages to us. Ways so that you can alert us to places and people who might be in danger, even though you can't get there yourself. In fact, you not being able to get to the places where you might give yourself away would be a very good thing. If anyone catches on to you always being in villages or on roads where the sheriff doesn't get his own way, then you'd be in danger of being thrown in the dungeons for a traitor yourself."

"That's a good point," John agreed. "You've been lucky so far, Guy, even clever as you are."

Tuck was nodding. "And you can no more stand by and do nothing than I can! I must admit it's worried me the number of times we alone have come to you for help, let alone anyone else. You can't be everywhere, Guy, and if you try then the shorter time it will be before you do something which will betray you. Oh this sheriff might not be too bright, but what if someone like de Wendenal got a whiff of you being not all you seem? He's crafty enough to work things out, and so is that Sir Henry you complain about.

"If they shove your actions right under the sheriff's nose he couldn't ignore it even if he liked you, and by your own admission this new fitz John can't stand you. You're too close to the earl of Chester for him to give you any kind of benefit of the doubt. For him, you in the dungeons for a reason which has nothing to do with him personally would be the answer to his prayers. This way you can let us have the information and we can do the acting instead of you, and that would let you still feel as though you're helping, but with far less danger to you directly. And that's important not just because we care about you, but because the longer you can keep going with your secret spying, then the more people we stand a chance of saving or protecting."

Will sniffed thoughtfully and came to look Guy straight in the eye. "Can you do that?" he wondered. "Can you keep up the pretence for months or years at a time?" His tone said that it wasn't Guy's stamina he was worried about, nor whether Guy might betray him and the others, but Guy's innate honesty coupled with the strain of living a double life.

Guy met the gaze straight on. "I wouldn't be here if I couldn't, Will. Living under de Braose's heavy hand for years taught me a lot about masking my feelings in someone's presence. It's not me you should be concerned for." He turned to the six soldiers. "Ruald? Ingulf? Alfred? Can you pretend that you know nothing of some of the things you've seen me do? And what about you other three? Osmund? Leofric and Big Ulf? You'll be living in the soldiers' halls in the outer bailey with all the others who *are* the sheriff's men, along with Ricard, Stenulf, Ketil, Claron, Skuli and Frani from High Peak. You've had a chance to see what your life will be like back in Nottingham.

"Do you think you twelve can keep my secret? If not, should I be asking for transfers for some of you to another sheriff's patch, or at least to another castle? I could find a few excuses, but if more than two or three of you think I'm asking too much then I can't carry on doing what I do. I should have to pretend to be the sheriff's man through and through, and keep all my actions matching that pose."

The six all exchanged glances before Ingulf spoke up, as he often seemed to do when there was a spokesman needed. "I reckon we'll be all right," he assured the others. "We've been a bit of a group on our own anyway, but that's not abnormal amongst the men-at-arms. In a castle as big as Nottingham the soldiers always tend to cluster into natural groups when off duty, anyway – you can't know everyone well, like we did at High Peak, when there's that many of you – so there's nothing odd in us twelve keeping together. And we don't mix much with the men who come in for their forty days' service with their knights. That lot aren't with us for long enough to make friends of, and even when a knight turns up again, it's not always the same men with him every year. To be honest, we don't trust them much, because they're as likely to run as fight if we meet any resistance, so that doesn't make us close either. We'll just have to watch Skuli when he's been on the beer!" and the others laughed, for Skuli notoriously had his Viking ancestor's thirst for strong ale.

It had been what Guy had been hoping for, not least because the soldiers had been at High Peak for a long time under Sir Ivo, and had girlfriends and wives amongst the villagers now. Women whom Guy and the outlaws would be helping to protect, and for which service it would be poor repayment if they were to be hobbled in their actions for fear of exposure. Meanwhile, for now the subject of what would happen next was dropped since they had a goodly march to make before any division of their force need happen. Yet the subject arose again as they all settled down for the evening's camp.

Robin plonked himself down beside Guy, who was expertly jointing a couple of hares by the fire, and scratched at his chin where he had several days' worth of growth which was starting to itch. "Guy?"

"Yes?"

"About the future. I've been thinking."

"Oh?"

"I think we need to help them – Ingulf and his men." He looked over his shoulder to make sure that the six soldiers from High Peak were still clustered around the second fire, then dropped his voice so that only those closest to him could hear. "If nothing else, we have to make sure that those twelve are never put in a position whereby their families are at risk. Loyal though they are, that would be the one thing which might lead them to betray you, and us – but mostly you, since you have the highest risk. So that means that those families must always have most, if not all of whatever money the sheriff demands of them. And we can't do it for them and not the others of their villages, because that will create such bad feeling their neighbours might betray them in a moment of crisis!"

Guy winced inwardly as he said carefully, "I'm not going to like this, am I? What are you going to do?"

"Levy a few tithes of our own," Robin told him firmly. "And before you object, think on this – how long is your fund hidden up in the Peaks going to last? And who do you *refuse* on the grounds of others needing it more? How can we help the people up in High Peak and not the poor souls down here?"

Hugh saw Guy's face fall and came to sit beside him. "Robin has a point, Guy. John, Tuck and I have been talking of the same thing, as it happens. It's almost crueller to offer the people some respite for a few years and then withdraw that help, than not have offered it in the first place. Tuck in particular is worried about how much worse things might get with Longchamp running things." Then as the others around their fire voiced their agreement, whispered to Guy, "actually Tuck said King Richard, not Longchamp," then looked meaningfully at Robin to signal that he hadn't wanted to say that outright.

Robin still had a definite blind-spot where the king was concerned, even after York, declaring that things would have been very different if the king had been in England. Only Siward, James and Gilbert agreed with him on that, though. The rest were coming to the dread conclusion that however much of the heroic fighter King Richard was, he could prove disastrous for the ordinary people if he chose to tax them even more heavily than his father had done. "Tuck was saying we need to be thinking now about how we can be replenishing our reserve of pennies," he added more loudly to cover the aside.

"We should start sooner rather than later," Malik added calmly. "That way we do not have to rush things. We can choose to rob those who have much money, and let others pass by."

Guy couldn't argue with that logic, but let the others raise the objections this time.

"Oh lovely," Thomas said from where he sat beside Guy, and to whom he rolled his eyes in despair, clearly worried that he was going to be living with someone as hard to keep out of trouble as Piers. "So where are we getting this extra money from, then?"

"That's hardly in the same class as hunting some deer for meat, or the wood for Will's charcoal," Hugh pointed out, looking nearly as worried as Thomas.

Robin gave his big smile, the one Guy remembered as heralding some boyhood mischief, except the consequences these days would be far more serious.

"Think about it," he then said more soberly. "How many rich travellers pass through Sherwood, Guy? The Great North Road runs right through it and there's no easy way round unless you want to add a couple of days onto your journey. Not ordinary people. This is a matter of principle not greed. I'm talking about the seriously wealthy. How many of *them*, cousin?"

Guy didn't have to think hard about that. "Quite a few, going by the chiminage charges we collect," he admitted, "and of course that's only from the traders who have to pay the tax. Travellers on other kinds of business? Probably as many again, but Robin, they're usually travelling with guards! Everyone knows that those who become outlawed make for the forest. Only a fool would risk being waylaid by foot-pads, and whatever else you think of the rich, when it comes to their purses they aren't normally that stupid. They'll hire guards even if it's only for a short stretch, and that sort of man will be a professional, not just some hefty groom who's a bit useful at the wrestling at the local fairs."

"Yes, and we're soldiers!" Robin said firmly. "We'll base ourselves well away from the villages, so no-one will be able to say exactly where we are most of the time."

Hugh interrupted him. "That's all very well, Robin, and I hear what you're saying, but we'd be going up against well-trained soldiers as well as professional guards, especially if – as Guy has said before – the sheriff gets word of us and decides to act. They'll have ring-mail hauberks and coifs to protect them. What will we have?"

"Could we not get armour from somewhere?" James asked tentatively.

Siward nodded, "Is there no store of armour we could raid?"

"Not a chance!" Guy scoffed. "You'd have to get into Nottingham Castle itself for that! And think about it! How would you creep out with that much weight even if I could get you in unseen? And where would you keep it? There's not much point in getting a load of mail hauberks when you've got nowhere to keep them where they won't go rusty. You can stuff a barrel of silver pennies into a cave up in the Peaks, but armour would rust away in there. And there's no way you could lug it about with you on the off-chance of needing it. To do that you'd need a horse and cart, and they'd be far too easy to track. The sheriff wouldn't need my skills for that."

Hugh was nodding his agreement with Guy. "And I know a man who might be able to make us a few gambesons on the quiet, but there's no chance of him making enough for all of us. We'd wait years for everyone to get kitted out. So who would get the protection and who not? Do we draw straws?" The last was said with substantial cynicism, expecting some glib remark from Robin, but it was Piers who spoke in favour of Robin's plan.

"I reckon a better bet would be for everyone to get truly proficient with our Welsh bows," the archer said with conviction. "With those we've got a far better range than any crossbows the guards or soldiers will be carrying. Let's get you all able to use a big bow and accurately. With the power of one of those we can penetrate mail at a goodly range and still stay out of harm's way ourselves."

Robin looked Guy in the eye. "And I meant what I've said more than once. I've had enough of killing for one lifetime. I don't want to harm the rich. I just want to levy a tax of our own for them passing through our territory. Come on, cousin, what nobleman will be carrying all of his wealth with him? They won't be reduced to poverty by us lifting their purses on a single journey. So we can tax the rich and then pass the money we collect onto the villagers to pay their taxes with. Don't tell me the villagers won't like that, Guy!"

Guy sighed. Robin's enthusiasm was already spreading to the others and he felt he couldn't squash too many ideas or they would stop listening to him at all. With a glance to Tuck, who was regarding him sympathetically, he answered, "Oh yes, they'll love you all right! But in Jesu's name, give them only silver, Robin! Gold coin is something no ordinary villager could hope to earn legally. Take silver off the rich by all means if that's what you want to do, but if you hand gold onto the poor folk you'll be setting them up as targets for the sheriff, and they can't disappear into the green-wood as you can. The sheriff knows where to find them!"

"How many are likely to be carrying gold, anyway?" Siward wondered aloud.

"You might be surprised," Tuck replied with a cautionary wag of the finger. "I've seen the most unlikely people put gold coin into the hands of a prior if they think it will buy them prayers for their souls.

Gold is the coin you use to impress! You might rob a rich merchant and all he'll have on him is silver, because that's how his takings have come in to his hands. But a rich pilgrim might have less in value, but it could all be in gold. You won't be able to tell just by looking at someone, and if you're lifting purses you won't have time to sort coin at the roadside. You'll have to take what they have and worry about what denominations it's in once you're away and safe."

"Tuck's right," Guy added with all of the patience he could muster for this wild scheme, "and you *cannot* give some poor peasant farmer gold coin! That would really set the cat in the dovecote! By all means start harvesting your tithe if that's what you feel is right, but remember what you're doing it *for*. Jewellery may look awfully tempting, but remember that I tracked de Wendenal's wrong doing by goods he stole, then had to find a buyer for. How often do you think you can go into one of the major towns with riches like that, and have a trader want to buy it off you, before they get scared of the attention it brings from the sheriff's men?"

"Shit! I hadn't thought of that!" Will grunted.

Robin didn't look any too pleased at the thought either. "So you're saying we shall have to take only coin? That may well mean we stop people and then have to let them go without taking much of anything. I'm sorry Guy but that just isn't realistic."

Hugh sighed. "Now that's a point in Robin's favour, Guy. We'll be marked out in weeks if we become the strange bunch of outlaws who pick and chose what we take. I think you have to admit we'll have to stop them, take the stuff, and then worry about what to do with later."

Guy ground his teeth. "Yes, unfortunately you will, but what *I'm* saying is that you can't try to turn it into *money* round here! Bloody hell, you lot! In the whole of Nottinghamshire you've only got Newark, Nottingham and at a push Mansfield which are big enough to have merchants who'll pay for jewels and furs! That makes it far too easy for the sheriff to set a trap for you!"

Malik nodded with sudden understanding, "And so we must store such things if we take them! But then we must hide them somewhere safe too..."

"...because if the sheriff finds the hoard he can trap us there when we come to add more to it," Hugh finished for Malik with the same realisation.

"So it would be better to have that a very long way from any camp of ours," Gilbert agreed. "And it should be somewhere where we can see the approaches to it."

"Maybe a valley we can look down into and see who's there before we go down," Siward wondered.

"Which really means the Peaks," John sighed.

"No!" Guy insisted, "not if you're going to use Loxley as your camp! And that's the best place for you to weather out winters." He turned to Much, Allan and Roger who were the ones who knew nothing of the greater plan. "Once upon a time there was a Saxon village on the edge of Yorkshire and Derbyshire called Loxley, but it got burned to the ground over a century ago by the Conqueror back in 1068, or it might have been in '69. No-one ever rebuilt it, but there are still the stones there of some of the sheep pens, and although the houses are gone, there's plenty of good timber there for you to make shelters from. And it's right on the border between Derbyshire and Yorkshire and close to Nottinghamshire, so you can make good your escape if you have to from just about anywhere. It'll be safe for you there."

"Over the border in Yorkshire!" Allan suddenly said with a bright smile. "Put the hoard in another sheriff's territory! What about up by the Went where we met you with the Jews? That's not far off the Great North Road and if we hide the stuff down in the little valley, we can walk along that ridge under the trees and see who's there before we go to it."

Robin immediately brightened. "Now that's a plan! Brilliant, Allan!" and Allan positively glowed at the praise from his much admired cousin.

"And then you're going to need someone like a moneylender on your side," Guy said, reluctantly conceding that they were going to do this anyway, with or without his help. "You need someone who can act as a moneychanger for you. Someone who won't be questioned if they have large quantities of gold coin. Someone, who in return for a share of your takings, will give you back the value of the useless gold in silver which you can use.

"An abbey! Somewhere with a good relic or two," Tuck added thoughtfully, "that's what you need. Not too big, but somewhere which gets its share of pilgrims. The big places will have some rich-man's son in charge, so you don't want those, but somewhere smaller. Like my old church of St Issui. Tiny place up in the hills, but very popular with pilgrims!"

"And with a priest who's as much of a rebel as you?" Guy teased fondly, and everyone laughed, breaking the tension.

Yet as the laughter subsided, Guy realised Robin was looking pointedly at Allan, and the youngest cousin suddenly spotted him.

"What?" he demanded with a smile.

"We need a friendly abbot or *abbess*," Robin said pointedly.

"Lady Hawyse," John said immediately, making Allan groan. However, to his credit, Allan didn't refuse outright, as Guy half expected him to.

"If I have to, I'll let her sniff and pet me," he told them with mock resignation, "but as a gambling man I don't think it's my mother you need to be looking to, for all that she would have gone to Kirklees with a goodly endowment to ensure her advancement among the sisters."

"Aunt Alice!" Robin chortled. "Of course!"

Allan nodded. "If my mother went with the money to buy her way to the abbesses role, my bet would be on it being Guy's mother who's actually running the place after all these years. She'll have risen by ability, no two ways about it. I'd bet she's at least prioress by now!"

Guy sighed. "Yes, I suppose she will. Very well, I shall make my way to Kirklees on some official pretext as soon as I can." Privately he thought his own mother far too moral to want to get involved in such a scheme, but for now he dared not say so. The only good thing was that it would take a while before the outlaws would have need of such a person, and he offered up silent prayers for silver coins not gold to be amongst the first takings.

For now he changed the subject. "Now, though, we need to focus on the coming days. You lot who are going into Sherwood ...I would suggest you make yourselves scarce from Nottinghamshire for a month or so. I mean it! No starting this scheme just yet! For God's sake, go to Loxley! At least until we know whether Longchamp is coming north with an army at his back!"

That sobered the more mature men instantly, but not the younger ones.

"*Woo-hoo*! We're all going into Sherwood together!" Allan whooped with delight, and Much also wore a huge grin. Only Roger seemed daunted by the idea of living deep in the ancient forest and even he looked halfway excited. However, no-one else seemed set to openly object until Robin himself said,

"But not just yet!"

They all turned to him. "We're coming with you to Cuckney," he said firmly. "We'll stand back when you arrest these men, but we're coming with you in case they have friends there with them."

Guy looked dubiously back. "I'd rather you didn't. We can manage, you know, and what if someone spots you? We'll be worryingly close to Nottingham by then. It's hardly more than six miles north of the royal hunting lodge at Clipstone, and I have no idea after so many days away whether Sheriff fitz John has sent others into the area. Heaven preserve us, but the wretched boy might even be at the lodge himself if he's of a mind to play the part of active sheriff for once!"

"But Cuckney's still well within Sherwood," Piers pointed out to Guy's disgust. "The trees are pretty dense there. Plenty of cover for us to disappear into if any more of the sheriff's men turn up unexpectedly. You said yourself you've not been there even though you've hunted at Clipstone several times with the sheriff. If you could pass by the place without seeing it, surely your idiot sheriff will do no better?"

Unable to dissuade them, and swayed by Much's determination to see the murderers of his parents brought to justice, eventually Guy relented.

In the morning they now marched at speed south, taking it in turns to ride to allow everyone a chance to rest every so often, Guy directing them with assurance straight for the tiny village where the manor lay. Ever since he'd been a child Guy had had a natural instinct for directions and it had developed with age – something which had Allan keeping the others amused with, telling them stories of Guy and Baldwin rescuing him time and again when he got lost, for Allan had been notorious for being able to get lost in the manor's own yard. Guy was grateful for the laughter as it stopped Much from brooding over what was coming, although he was less relieved to see that Much was already being drawn into the irrepressible company of Allan and Roger.

They travelled through the heart of Sherwood, might oaks rising around them still bare of leaves this early in the year.

"For God's sake be careful of chopping down any large branches or removing whole trees," Guy cautioned the would-be outlaws. "This is all part of the old Forest of Nottingham. It's the keepership of High Forest, and the men who patrol this area have learned the forest from their fathers and grandfathers. They know the forest well, far better than the men who ride out in the newer areas King Henry brought into the royal forest. If you need large timber for anything, get to the other side of the River Erewash."

"How many men are there?" Malik asked him as he struggled to understand this complex system of guarding the habitat of the prized deer.

Guy grinned. "Ah! Well that's the good bit! There are just two riding foresters with their pages – although be warned, those pages are grown men, not boys! – and two walking foresters. And they have to cover all of the territory from Birkland Hay by Edwinstowe down to Blidworth, and across from Mansfield Woodhouse almost to Rufford Abbey."

Robin whistled. "By Our Lady! That must be easily eight miles in each direction, and dense forest over great chunks of it!" He grinned. "They must be struggling to keep a watch on all of that!"

"Exactly!" Guy smiled back at him. "So if you don't do anything obvious – like felling one of the great oaks – the chances are that they'll never know you're there. But I wouldn't advise setting up a camp in any part of this bit of the old forest for the same reason. It'll be hard to remove traces if you're there for anything more than overnight, and if the foresters are alert to the fact that someone's actually living deep in the forest, then the head forester may call on the sheriff for help in finding you."

"You always find some gloomy side to everything," Robin said to Guy bitterly, and with a definite hint of disappointment in his cousin.

"It's not that," Guy objected desperately. "Please Robin, can't you see? I'm telling you all this because I have the miserable experience of knowing what it's like on the other side. I could just shut up and let you get on with your schemes and dreams of saving the poor of England. But I care about what happens to *all* of you. I never, ever want to be in the position of watching some of you being brought into Nottingham Castle to face the sheriff, as I was when Thomas and Piers got taken. We were lucky, nothing more, that the thunderstorm gave us the means of getting them out.

"Even with Tuck on our side, we can't count on divine intervention to that extent a second time! My worst nightmare is of having to stand by and watch you or John or Allan be brought out for execution. I would die beside you fighting impossible odds to try and save you, even knowing as I did it that I stood no chance of getting you free and would die in the attempt."

That made Robin blink. "Oh! ...Yes, I can see that would be your worst dream." Then added with the impossible certainty which would drive Guy to distraction time and again in the future, "But God will not allow us to fail! I'm sure of that. We failed in the Holy Land because the motives of those who led us were all wrong. I've thought so much about that since we've been back here, and now I see that Tuck was right – men like de Ridefort committed dreadful blasphemy in thinking they could feather their own nests at God's expense.

"We shall take nothing for ourselves. I swear that by all that I hold dear and holy! We shall never become rich men ourselves. I shall honour my vow to Him to protect and to serve, and who better to care for than those too lowly to protect themselves? It's *right*, Guy. It's more than a cause, it's our Christian duty."

So there you have it, Brother, the high moral code by which Robin Hood lived by, and I see you wholeheartedly approve – a good deal more than you do of my objections, I could see by your changing expressions. And in principle did I too, do not think that I did not. Yet that almost dreamlike quality to my dear cousin was the source of much argument and no little amount of anguish on my part. Once Robin had set himself a target, he aimed for it with a singularity of purpose I could never match. Yet in doing so he often failed to see the chasm opening in the ground at his feet. And my fear was always not only for him, for where he led,

others followed, blind in their belief in him and swayed by the charisma he exuded.

You think that we have seen little of that charisma as yet? Ah, Brother, this was only the beginning! And can you not see that already even men of great sense like Tuck and John could be swayed by Robin when he invoked the Lord? Think back to what I have just told you of Robin's plans to aid the poor. Did Tuck object? Did John? No, already they had been drawn to him, and Allan adored and looked up to him right from the start. Yet even men like Thomas and Piers could be captivated when Robin set them one of his higher targets. And it was all the more potent since he did so with fervent belief and no desire for <u>material</u> reward.

Ah, you picked up on that! Yes, Brother, I shall confess to you that I had many qualms over that, for you see it was easy for Robin to pass over material gains. His time in the Holy Land had turned my gentle cousin Baldwin into the hardened man Robin, who wanted for little beside food in his stomach, and a shelter for his bed at night. But do you not think that there is what I shall call a touch of presumption, in order not to offend you, in believing yourself to be in the right <u>all</u> of the time? Robin acted with the highest of intentions, and yet at the same time could be verging on the callous when it came to the suffering of others as a consequence. And some of those who suffered were not the rich and overbearing. Some were ordinary men and women who, like me, had to bear the yoke of working for the sheriff and other royal officials simply to put a roof over the heads of their families. Did they too not deserve some consideration? I thought so, for they never instigated actions and could rarely turn the tide of events by any form of resistance or failure to act, they were mere threads in the weave of a greater cloth.

You are still not convinced, I can see that, so I shall ask you this – am I so very much worse than Robin because I, and not he, cared about the wider outcomes? Will God be so very disappointed in me because I took steps to help ensure the success of some of Robin Hood's exploits, rather than just believing in Him, and expecting Him to turn his divine attention to our small patch of England whenever Robin invoked His name?

Oh, you bridle so at that! No, Brother, I am not blaspheming or taking the Lord's name in vain. I have every faith and respect in my Maker, and because of that I felt it arrogant to bother him with small things which I could sort out for myself.

~Who should men turn to if not the Lord?~

Have you not been paying attention, Gervase? When I felt the desperate need of higher help it was to the lesser saints to whom I prayed, trusting in their divine status that if they felt my cause to be true and needing more help than they could give, that they in turn would petition a higher authority on my behalf. But come, we shall not argue theology at this late hour! We have one more adventure to conclude before we rest for the night!

Chapter 25

So, Gervase, we left our band of warriors marching on Cuckney through Sherwood, and now we shall rejoin them, and if it pleases you so much to see my failings you shall hear of one straight away.

As I have recounted, I had not been to Cuckney itself, and in my folly I had presumed, going by the taxes it paid, that the village was no great place, and so the lord of it would live in a manor house very similar to my own humble place at Gisborne. I was consequently anticipating forcing our way into a longhouse, maybe made of stone, but more likely a timber frame with wattle and daub infill. You may therefore imagine the shock we got as we crept along the bank of the little River Poulter and found ourselves coming up on a proper motte and bailey castle!

Yes, Brother, another castle for Robin Hood! Let's us continue!

Cuckney, Nottinghamshire
late March, the year of Our Lord 1190

"God in Heaven!" Hugh sighed in despair as he and Guy stood side by side staring up at the wooden keep emerging through the bare tree tops. "Who'd have thought the de Cuckneys had such aspirations!"

"Bastards!" Guy ground out savagely. "It's not a big castle, but it's big enough for us to have to assault!" Now he had little choice. They were going to have to use all of their force if they were to get in and arrest the lord of this damned place. He waved them all back a way to a clearing, only to find himself being immediately confronted by Robin.

"If you're giving up, we're not!" he declared with barely suppressed anger.

Guy's patience was wearing thin. "No, I'm not bloody giving up!" he snapped back, "but we can't go charging in like we could to a manor house, can we? Now get off your high horse and stop acting as though *I'm* your enemy!"

"Steady, you two," John said as he came and stood between them. "We're all frayed after the last couple of weeks. And don't forget, Robin, that Guy has had his share of the stress even if he wasn't with you at York. Now, unless you have a plan of how to get into the castle already, let Guy think and do some thinking of your own."

John's words calmed Guy instantly, but although Robin sniffed and backed off a couple of paces, it was clear that he was still as taut as a drawn bowstring.

"Ingulf?" Guy called softly, summoning the leader of the six men-at-arms to him. "Can you and the other lads go back to that track which seems to lead into the village, and make an official entrance to the village on my signal?"

"How will that help?" Robin snapped, now having Will standing belligerently beside him and seemingly in agreement given that he snarled,

"You're *warning* them?"

Guy scrubbed his hands through his hair in frustration. "*No!* Ingulf and the others are going to mill about in the village asking about sightings of ordinary men from York. They're not going to go near the castle itself! Christ on the Cross, Will, I have to think of what may happen if these villagers get called upon to testify as to *how* we arrested Cuckney and his friends! And they may well do! What do you think will happen to them if they stand up in court, quaking with fear at just being there, and say that Cuckney was taken by a bunch of renegades? A manor we could have entered with ease, but this bloody castle...! Aach, we have to give the villagers something ...*plausible*! You talk with such fury of the corruption of nobles! So why give them the opening to declare the arrest as nothing more than a bunch of rogues taking the law into their own hands against a lord in his own castle?"

"They could do that?" Malik wondered.

Thomas nodded. "Oh yes! God rot them! The bastards stick together! They wouldn't get off altogether, but they might just get a light fine or some other punishment which hardly warrants the name. All depends on how long it takes to bring about a trial, see? If they get to wait for the next eyre it could be years, and in that time they'll have paid to stay out of the gaol, and that might count as fine enough if the right sheriffs are sitting in judgement."

"In that sense it would be better if Longchamp does come north to take charge himself," Tuck said sagely. "A quicker result, you see? Better for it to be done while there's still outrage at what's happened. Leave it too long and who knows what might have happened in the time in between?"

"*Duw*, Tuck! You aren't saying there might be more riots like York, are you?" a shocked Bilan asked.

Tuck put a comforting hand on the youngest Cosham's shoulder. "Not quite like York, no lad, but what if there's something like a riot in London over taxes? We care about what's happened up here in the north because it's personal to us, but it's a long way from London or Winchester, and they're places which, on a grander scale, are seen as being more important. See what I mean? York might become the lesser of two or more evils."

Guy cleared his throat purposefully, having had a moment to think more clearly. "So what we're going to do is give those villagers the presence of very real sheriff's men to testify to. But the men in the castle will just see a bunch of lesser sergeants and dismiss their presence."

"Ah!" Will said with a feral grin of understanding, although Robin still didn't look convinced.

Guy nodded. "Yes, Will. So Ingulf and the other five are going into Cuckney village, but before they get there, Walter, Algar and John will go on along the river and watch the bridge. Marianne can go with you too. The road from the village goes up to Worksop that way. I don't think these fine young men will run that way, but I don't want to leave the route unguarded just in case. Marianne will have to come back and warn us if they do.

"Tuck, will you take Much, Roger and Allan, and Bilan too, and go and watch the other road going out of Cuckney to the west? That's much more of a danger, because the devils might think to run that way and seek sanctuary at Bolsover Castle. It's only a few miles away. I'm sending you younger men that way, because if they come out that way I have a suspicion they'll ride out armed, and one of you will have to run back fast and fetch the rest of us to help take them. Remember, though, we can't just get Thomas or Piers to shoot them as they run! They have to be alive to stand trial!"

"And what of us?" Robin asked grudgingly, finally accepting that Guy really was working out how to take prisoners.

Guy managed to dredge up a smile for his cousin. "You lot are coming to take the castle!"

"How?" Siward wondered with cautious optimism.

"Like this," Guy said, and outlined his plan.

There was still much argument over who would go in, since unexpected resistance came from those who had been imprisoned with Much, and felt his loss very personally. In the end it was James who overcame Thomas, Piers, Algar and Walter's wishes. The slender young turcopole never raised his voice but argued with a heartfelt passion,

"You wish to avenge the family of your friend. I understand that. But what we saw in York went beyond one family. Over a hundred innocent people lost their lives in that castle, people whose bodies must now lie in the ashes within the castle. Some of them may never even be named if they were not living in York and were not known to have been there. Some family somewhere may spend the rest of their lives wondering what happened to a father, son or brother, never knowing for sure whether they died at York or somewhere else. We lost so many friends and family like that in my homeland it burns in my very soul to see it happening again! Please, let us carry your sole cry for vengeance along with our many."

"If the bastards escape us you can nail 'em to the trees with as many arrows as you like!" Will growled with relish, already itching to be at these miserable lordlings who could be so cruel.

And Guy had another trick up his sleeve.

"Give them your hoods," Guy instructed Sergeant Ingulf and his men before they went, for all six had the distinctive foresters' cowled hoods tucked in their belts, ready to be used if proof were needed that they were on legitimate business. Only Guy had the official forester's horn slung over his shoulder, but the six had the hoods for the times when they rode out supporting him on forest business.

"Put them on and pull them up," he told Robin and the others. "If they shade your faces then all the better."

Robin pulled his up, then gave a broad grin. "What say you we have some sport?"

Guy wasn't quite sure what his cousin had in mind until Robin pointed at the horn. "Leave that behind and pull your hood up too! If they ask who's leading us it will be Robin Hode of Loxley, ...no! No mention of Loxley! ...Robin Hood! Let the sheriff sort that one out if he can!"

John was shaking his head in despair at such youthful mischief at such a serious time, but Allan was practically dancing on the spot with glee, and even Guy couldn't resist the chance to partake in such misdirection when it made little difference. He'd just handed the forester's horn to John and was about to go, when Allan halted them,

"No wait!" The youngest of the cousins hurried over. "Stand together all of you!" In the next half hour he, with Marianne's aid, got them to swap tunics and belts with one another and the others, until all seven bore an uncanny resemblance to one another once the hoods were up.

"There!" Allan declared, standing back and admiring his handiwork. "If Malik, Gilbert and James don't say much you'll all be indistinguishable in the chaos. And Guy and Baldw... Robin could be twins! If you both say you're Robin Hood at some point you'll confuse the living daylights out of them!"

"And Siward!" Much added enthusiastically. "You're not far off the same height and build. Three Robin Hoods!"

"Then I think it's time 'Robin Hood' went to work!" Robin said with relish.

As the spring afternoon sank into the evening everyone moved to their allotted positions, Ingulf and the castle men lurking just out of sight of the village until they got the signal to move into the village. Two arrows sailed up into the dusky sky from the river side and dropped neatly behind the palisaded walls of the tiny bailey, and on sighting them, Ingulf and the men tramped purposefully out of the trees talking loudly amongst themselves. On the opposite side of the bailey, two shadowy figures began scaling the palisade on ropes, hidden in the evening shadows until they were at the very top of the wall. Then like cats, they dropped onto the ground which was already higher on the inside, and therefore less of a fall, and were soon followed by others.

Once the arrows carrying the ropes up to the top of the palisade had been fired, Thomas, Piers and Hugh skirmished around the base of the palisade, and waited with bows drawn in line with the castle gate, just in case the young lords came out in a hurry. Guy hadn't arrange this, though, until Tuck and John's parties were out of the way – he had tricked them into thinking they would be playing their part, while moving them to places of safety. There was no way he was risking the lives of the less experienced members of the band against trained knights, even if they were fairly sure there weren't more than three or four inside Cuckney Castle. Mercifully Robin only realised what was being done as the three archers disappeared into the twilight, and for once approved of Guy's actions, although he was soon preoccupied with scaling the palisade.

With Malik and James by his side, Guy now tore up the small mound of the motte and as silently as possible flipped the latch on the keep door. Clearly the young men within had thought themselves safe if the gate on the palisade was barred from within, because the door wasn't locked. That had been Guy's big fear. If the keep door had been locked then they were going to have to shoot another line in through one of the windows and scale the keep's timber walls, and the danger was that they would shoot into the very room where the young de Cuckney was hiding.

"By St Thomas, they're confidant bastards!" Will growled as he and the others all but stood on Guy's heels at the door. "You'd think they'd at least have a watcher on the roof for men approaching!"

"It's as I guessed," Guy whispered back as they eased their way into the ground floor room. "Having got back to their home they think they've got away with it. I'd bet good money on them believing that they can bully the locals into saying they never left the castle, and so couldn't have been at York."

"Surely de Cuckney can't be the lord of all this, though, if he's only a squire?" Siward wondered softly, as they split into two groups and slid around the walls, all the time with one eye on the stairs leading upwards. "Allan did say they were only squires by the look of them, didn't he?"

"No, his father will be the owner, or at least the tenant-in-chief of this manor," Guy answered in a whisper. "But my guess is that he's in Normandy, working on keeping in the new king's favour, and praying that he isn't asked to pay for the privilege of keeping the family home!"

"Are you sure of that?" Gilbert asked with Irish cynicism. "I'd like a bit more warning if we're going up that stair one by one and find the next two floors stuffed with men-at-arms!"

"You'd have heard them by now!" Robin hissed from the far side of the stairs, which he'd reached from taking the other route around the room with Will, Malik and James.

"Even if they were asleep you could count on someone being a snorer!" Will added with a wicked grin and a wink, at which Gilbert rolled his eyes but still grinned back.

With swords drawn and hoods up, the seven of them pounded up the stairs in what was hardly a silent entry onto the first floor. Three young noblemen sat by the large fire in the far wall and all leapt up in shock. The wine goblets in their hands gave away their state. In drunken panic one lurched for the stairs and was thumped by Guy. A second tried to swing a punch at James and was easily subdued without anyone else getting involved, while the third was deprived of his dagger by Will as Malik restrained him.

"Who're you? How dare you!" spluttered the coarse-featured young man whom they soon established was de Cuckney.

"We're your reward for what you did at York," Robin said acidly. "Remember that?"

The three were shaking their heads in drunken bravado.

"You can't get away with it," Gilbert said from de Cuckney's other side. "You were seen. You were heard! *Your* name was heard! English *pig!*"

"No! Not us!" de Cuckney said bullishly, even as his one friend looked furiously at the other and tried to kick him, saying,

"Told you!"

Yet when questioned further, all of them denied any knowledge of York, or of having being there, although there was no mistaking the panic in their eyes, whatever they were saying.

Now the seven dragged them to their chairs and tied them to them. The stout oak chairs easily withstood the struggles which ensued.

"I think we need to refresh your memories," Robin said with silky venom, and kicked the fire into more life before sticking one of the captured swords into it, and then another. What he intended to do with it he never said, but clearly the young men's imaginations were filling in the gap without further help as they began to wriggle at their restraints.

"You can't fool us," Guy added, pitching his voice to sound as close to Robin's as he could. "We have witnesses who swear you were there. And there's still the small matter of the mill at Norton!"

The three looked aghast.

"Norton?" gulped one of them. "Where the bloody hell is *Norton*?"

"It's the hamlet you had your sick sport burning to the ground just north of here, you rat-brained turd," snarled Siward, making all three near wrench their necks with the speed with which they turned to this third incarnation of the same demon persecuting them. They had never expected for one moment that their actions would be tracked back to them, and so speedily at that. All they'd done, by their lights, was get rid of the irritating problems of the loans they'd taken out and now could not repay, then had a little sport on the way home. There were always more peasants about the place, so a few less wouldn't make much difference, and anyway mills were notorious for having fires, so who was to say that this one hadn't been another accident? Or at least that was what they'd thought.

"They must remain fit to stand trial," Guy reminded Robin, as Will removed the now red-hot sword-blade from the fire and spat experimentally on it, his spittle immediately vaporising.

"Now," Robin said conversationally, "which finger would you like to lose first? Or is your memory returning yet?"

"Who *are* you?" whimpered Richard de Cuckney, no longer the cock-sure and arrogant squire so sure of his status.

"Robin Hood." Robin, Guy and Siward said in unison, making the three captives gape in terrified incomprehension.

"Now I'll ask you again," Robin continued, as Will stepped closer with the hot sword. "What did you do in York and Norton? Let's get your story clear for the sheriff, shall we?"

Yet before they went any further, Gilbert appeared from the chambers up on the top floor with a silver menorah in his hand.

"Now *this* was a mistake," the Irishman said with deceptive softness, wagging a finger at the three and being rewarded with blank expressions. "Don't you know what this is, you thick fuckers?" he demanded in a more dangerous tone.

"Maybe they were thinking of converting," Malik said coming in behind him holding something reverently in his hands.

"Were they?" Robin queried sarcastically.

Malik nodded, replying equally witheringly, "Must have been. They have a copy of the Torah here," and he pulled back the sack covering on his bundle to reveal a large book with a beautifully decorated hard cover on it.

"The Jewish version of the Bible?" Guy checked with Malik and Robin, and got nods.

"And the menorah is a *sacred* candlestick!" Gilbert all but spat in the face of de Cuckney. "Not just some bit of silver you could stick in your mother's bedroom, you ignorant bastard!"

With deadly speed Will smacked the flat of the hot blade down onto each of the three shoulders from where he stood behind them.

"You're knights!" he snarled. "So here's a knighting to remind you of what that ought to mean!"

As the three shrieked with pain as the blade seared through their clothing, the cloth began to smoulder and smoke, making them cough as well.

"Not so funny breathing smoke, is it, you fat, pampered little pigs?" the burly smith growled, looking for all the world like some pagan demon from the pits of Hell itself, as he stood wreathed in smoke with another glowing blade in his hand.

"Jesu save us!" squeaked one of the two men who weren't Richard de Cuckney, but who were both called Robert.

"I think he's busy at the moment, consoling the grieving families you left behind," Gilbert shot back at them, just as Malik said,

"Allahu Akbah. God is great, in your tongue. Insh'allah. God wills it. Do not call upon the Lord to save you when you do not repent of your evil deeds, for he may reply in way you do not expect!"

"Like me!" Will growled in Cuckney's ear, and was rewarded with the sound of running water as this squire to one of the ringleaders at York pissed himself again in fright.

In tremulous tones, Richard de Cuckney now babbled out how his master, Richard Malebisse, with William Percy, Marmaduke Darell and Philip de Fauconberg, and their respective squires, had orchestrated the whole thing with the connivance of Sheriff John Marshal. The callous indifference of the leading four to the suffering they had caused almost broke Guy's control over Robin and the others. Their anger had reached almost combustible levels, and with great difficulty he got them to move down a floor to regain some control, leaving the quaking trio of squires still bound to the oak chairs on the first floor.

"They will pay for this," Guy told them vehemently. He put his hand on the Torah which Malik still held. "This is evidence," he said tersely. "It will go back to Nottingham, and then when the sheriff's done with it I shall personally take both items back to the rabbi in Lincoln for him to return to anyone who might be left from York. But you have to back off now and let me do this legally!"

Luckily, having been signalled by James that they had taken the keep, the others had by now come in behind the palisade, except for the Nottingham soldiers who were still in the village. So on the castle's entrance level were the calming influences of Tuck, John,

Hugh and Thomas, and now they joined forces with Guy, insisting that the six crusaders leave it at that.

"You wanted the peace and law of England when you were in the East," Hugh reminded them. "I know how hard it is not to take matters into your own hands, but think on this, if the sheriff of Nottingham gets them, and then they appear before justices who will be other sheriffs, then all of England will know what they've done. If you kill them now, their families will be able to twist things until they sound like martyrs themselves, and surely that would be even more insulting to the memory of those who died at York, and to Much's family?"

To Guy's great relief those words, if not his own, sunk in.

"Very well," Robin agreed grudgingly. "But we're not quite done yet! York they will answer for, but what about Norton? Who's going to give a rat's arse about Norton apart from us?"

"I want to see them," Much's quavering voice said from behind Guy, and he came round to face him. "I want to see their faces."

"Very well," Guy sighed. He hadn't the heart to deny Much that. "Pull your hoods up, you lot. Everyone else, stay out of sight and keep quiet."

"Guy?" Marianne's voice was full of worry. She could see the strain of holding this all together was beginning to tell on her friend. Then was even more startled when Guy's face suddenly broke into a feral grin.

"Come with us Marianne! Make your Hospitaller's uniform visible. And you, Tuck!"

And before they could protest, he started back up the stairs again. By the time Marianne, Much and Tuck had caught up with the seven, they were standing in an arc around the three terrified squires – Will once more by the fire and whistling with chilling jollity as he heated the sword-blades again.

"Norton," Guy said flatly.

"Oh Christ, not that again," whimpered one of the Roberts. "We told you, it was just some place."

"Just some place," echoed Robin icily. "Except it wasn't 'just some place' for the people who lived there." He waved Much forward. "You took this man's family from him. Took their lives and their livelihood."

Much stepped inside the semi-circle.

"Why?" he asked in despair. "Why did you do it? What had we ever done to you?"

The three born to such privilege looked back at him in incomprehension.

"Answer him!" Will snarled, moving behind them with another blade glowing red.

Gilbert, at the other end of the arc, clipped the nearest Robert around the ear. "I'd speak up if I were you, boy, or you'll get another 'knighting'!"

"I don't understand," babbled this Robert in terror.

"What don't you understand?" Robin demanded. "That you should have to answer for what you did?"

"No," Guy interjected, his own anger rising now. "He doesn't understand why he should have to have a reason for what he did beyond his own petty, mean and spiteful fancy! That's it, isn't it? They were just peasants. Not even people in your eyes. Just something to be used for sport, like a cat with a mouse. That's your view of the natural order, isn't it?"

De Cuckney managed to work up a sneer of a smile, but the two Roberts were now visibly shaking. Said with all of Guy's venom, their view of the world suddenly didn't sound so secure or unquestionable. Even more terrifying, Guy was standing in the middle of the seven with Siward on his left and Robin on his right, and their two hooded heads now whipped round to look at Guy, mirroring one another, and exclaiming, "What?"

As if some malevolent and demonic triptych had come to life, these three indistinguishable figures shot forwards and each gripped one of the squires by the throat in vice-like grips.

"There's a priest here," Guy snarled, barely able to stop himself from crushing de Cuckney's windpipe in his anger.

"I'd confess if I were you!" Siward spat out from his left into Robert's face, while Robin just shook the other Robert so hard he went a strange puce colour.

"Now, now, brothers, they can't confess if you choke them," Tuck reminded them calmly, yet his apparent acceptance of these strange apparitions only rattled the squires more. "Let them speak. And when you three make your confessions, you should know that you do in the presence not only of myself, a true priest, but in the presence of these Templar's and this Hospitaller sister."

As Marianne stepped into the arc starring at them coldly, the Robert in Robin's hands gave up the fight to hold onto the world which was shifting all around him and passed out. Without a word, Robin loosed him and stepped back, but Marianne moved to in front of him and then slapped him hard. The first slap didn't work, but the second brought him round, although not for long as one look at her face and he was gone again.

Meanwhile Guy twisted de Cuckney's face sideways to see what was being done. "This woman has survived Jerusalem and Saladin's army," he hissed into the youth's ear. "I wouldn't count on any womanly sympathy from there if I were you!"

Marianne flickered him a glance then looked down into the seated de Cuckney's face. "You are the most despicable beings I've ever come across!" she snapped. "You will tell me and the brother here, in every detail, what you did at Norton. I won't say 'may God have mercy upon your soul'. I hope He, in His infinite glory, makes you suffer for every pain and injury you inflicted!"

That was the last straw and suddenly de Cuckney was tripping over his own tongue to tell her.

"We thought we saw men from York. We thought they might have seen us. We couldn't let them live!"

"Why?" growled Will in his ear, brandishing the red-hot blade again.

"The hundred courts!" squeaked the remaining conscious Robert, eyes ricocheting all over the place as he tried to see which of these dreadful demons might come at him next.

"The hundred courts," Guy repeated icily. "And why was that? Pray tell us what three such fine young men might have to fear from the hundred courts?"

De Cuckney snuffled his running nose as tears of fear began running down his cheeks. "They could tell. Tell the sheriff."

"The sheriff?" Robin wondered. "What have you to fear from fitz John?

"No! Sheriff Marshal!" de Cuckney blubbered. "He told us we had to keep quiet! Threatened us with what he'd do to us if anyone found out he started all this! We couldn't let him know we might be brought to court!"

"But you didn't even know if these men you *thought* you saw were even *in* Norton," Marianne snapped in disbelief. "Are you saying that you put a whole village to the torch just because you thought someone who *might* have seen you *might* be passing through it?"

"Yes," snivelled de Cuckney.

"Burn in Hell!" Will snapped, and slapped the red blade against de Cuckney's cheek. As the squire howled in agony he added. "Wear that brand to remind you every day of what it feels like to burn!"

"You'll not find a bride so easily with a face like that!" Siward laughed viciously.

"And it'll remind you of the hell-fires to come when you die!" Robin growled.

The sound of James saying calmly to Much, "Are you satisfied with that?" mercifully broke the spell which had seemed to hang over everyone in the room.

Guy turned to Tuck and said softly, "Get everyone outside, then we'll take these three down to the cellar for the night." He was more than a little shaken at how close he'd come to losing control over himself, let alone the others, and knew it would be safer if the three remained out of sight overnight.

The three prisoners were taken and locked in the secure cellar storeroom, still bound hand and foot, and then left to their own devices for the night. Meanwhile, Thomas and Piers liberated some of the castle's stores and got food going for everyone while Guy, back in his usual dress, went and found Ingulf and his men, and found those who normally worked at the manor to question them as to their master's whereabouts over the last few weeks. No doubt the young squire's father would be less than delighted when he returned and found out just what his son had been up to in his absence.

As they all squeezed into the castle that night, Guy caught Robin staring pensively into the flames.

"Penny for your thoughts," he said, plonking himself down on the bench beside Robin and handing him a flagon of the castle's best ale.

Robin blinked, then smile back at Guy. "Just thinking about our plans."

"Oh?" Guy was glad that it wasn't about how to wreak further revenge on their prisoners, but he hadn't the will or energy to start arguing with Robin over any other wild scheme.

"This felt right today. The fate of Much's family is never going to get much time even in the hundred court, is it?"

Guy shook his head. "Not without witnesses, no. The loss of the village and the mill will be recorded, but with no-one to tell how, I suspect it'll just get put down as more widespread damage from the riots."

"And how many more times will this happen?" Robin asked softly. It reassured Guy that at least at the moment Robin was calmer. The almost manic edge had gone, maybe dissipated by the chance to let out some of the buried anger earlier. Would Robin ever be free of that burning fury over the losses in the East? Guy feared not, so maybe it was better that he might have something to channel it into.

"Quite a lot, I'm sorry to say," Guy sighed. "The courts worked wonderfully under King Henry, but it all hinges on whether the king cares enough to take an interest in their workings. Oh the system will keep on going – it's too well ingrained in the government of the country now. Sheriffs will ride out to other shires on eyre and hear cases brought before them, but we've lost the fair and even-handed men like Ralph Murdac, and got idiots like fitz John in their place. Men with money, but no experience nor the desire to gain it."

"Then Robin Hood must be the means of gaining justice for the lesser folk," Robin said with a far-off look in his eyes.

"You can't wage war on the sheriff!" Guy warned as his heart did several rapid skips.

Luckily Robin just smiled easily. "No, not war, Guy. Or at least not the war you're thinking of. But between the two of us we must surely be able to do some good when things do go wrong?"

"Me on the inside and you on the out-, you mean?"

Robin grinned mischievously. "Robin Hood and Guy of Gisborne, it has a certain ring to it, don't you think?" and the others around them laughed with them.

Meanwhile, in the cold cellar, amongst the turnips and this week's brew of beer, the three imprisoned young noblemen heard the uproarious laughter and feared for their lives.

In the morning it was almost comical to see the faces of the three to find six totally different men escorting them into Nottingham. Osmund had been briefed as to the significance of the candlestick, while Guy himself took charge of the Torah, and would present it to the sheriff as his find. As the only literate one of the seven going back it had to be him, so that he could point out to the sheriff that the holy book was written in Hebrew – hardly a language any of the three prisoners, or fitz John for that matter, was familiar with! Everyone else retired into Sherwood, promising Guy that this time they really would be heading over to the sanctuary of the Loxley river valley until it was clear that no army was heading their way.

However, it was amazing how easily the whole plan worked, for the three prisoners continued to try to worm their way out of any blame once they were securely within Nottingham Castle, so that they were utterly discredited by the time they tried to say that Guy had had different men with him when making the arrest to bringing them to Nottingham. Sheriff fitz John was placated over Guy taking so long to come back when he realised that, out of everyone he'd sent out, only Guy had produced any results from the search, thus saving face for him. And that saving was necessary at the end of April when Longchamp himself rode in, with an army at his back led by his brother Henry, on the way to York. It wasn't quite the force Guy had feared would come north, but it was large enough that he was glad that the rest of his family and friends were well off the route they would be taking – given that with that vast number of men, they would be hunting wide of their marching route, if only to provision themselves with fresh meat to supplement what they brought in the supply wagons.

Fitz John was like a cat with a bowl of cream by the time Longchamp had congratulated him on his speedy reaction, and for once Guy was more than happy to let the young lord take the credit for an action not his own. He was just glad to see the back of young Richard de Cuckney and his two cronies. Longchamp took them north with him to bring Malebisse to justice, and no-one at Nottingham was particularly concerned over their fate, although all were more than a little disgusted when they later found out that they had suffered only heavy fines for their parts in the tragic events.

So you see, Brother Gervase, that night in March of 1190 was very significant! I was utterly appalled at the fact that the rich got off so lightly, when a poor man would have lost his life for a great deal less. Yet it was not only me it had a profound effect upon. My dear cousin, now very much Robin and not Baldwin, had come to a turning point, and from that time on his role as Robin Hood was the main focus of his life. Can you see, Brother, that it was as if we were pushed into those roles by some great and invisible hand? His utter revulsion and anger that a sheriff, of all people, should turn upon the people in his own town was something he would never forget. Never again would Robin Hood have an iota of faith in the men of the law, of whatever rank.

In his eyes the justices who allowed the rich to buy their way out of trouble – as those at York would do – were as culpable as the ones who had hounded those innocent souls to their deaths. From the top to the bottom he saw the justice system as warped and corrupt beyond redemption. The only person who did not come in for his scathing criticism was the king himself. For some reason, then and for some years to come, Robin saw King Richard as the successor to King Baldwin, perhaps because of his commitment to retake Jerusalem, and no more as likely to act ignobly. It bothered me, Brother, for I could foresee there would come a time when the truth of our king's indifference to England would force itself upon my cousin, and what the consequence of that would be upon his state of mind I could not foretell, but for now I would not argue with him on the matter.

My extended adopted family did as I had hoped and went and lay low in the Loxley valley for a few months, while I struggled on with the dreadful Sheriff fitz John. That summer of 1190 seemed very long to me, that much I do remember clearly, even though nothing outstanding happened in the greater scheme of things until well into the autumn. Oh there were rumblings of Prince John trying to worm his way into being allowed back into England – rumours I quite believed had a basis in fact, but our eyes were kept closer to home for the most part.

Longchamp, now gripping the reins of power even more tightly, appointed his brother as sheriff of Northumberland to add to the collection he already had his hands on, and in the meantime the people of England tightened their belts and emptied their purses as Longchamp squeezed everyone's resources tighter and tighter. John Marshal was relieved of his post by Longchamp, and that post too fell into the hands of his brother. Such shameless nest-feathering behind the king's back left most of us speechless. On the few occasions I got away to meet the collected outlaws, we all wondered how much longer this could be expected to go on for. Would the people rise up against the king's man? Could we expect anything better if the barons backed Prince John once King Richard was farther away on crusade? All we had was questions and no answers.

I must rest for a while now, Brother, for this has taxed me sorely and I wish to have enough breath left to tell you the whole story. I need a good night's sleep before I can continue again. However, I will leave you with this hint of what is to come. Robin became the unquestioned leader, as everyone now knows, but that was less obvious at the time, given that he was by no means the oldest of the outlaws, nor the most experienced soldier. For all of his charisma, the leader's mantle could well have migrated over time to Thomas or Hugh, or to Will or Malik, all of whom had the experience and no more of the obvious leader's temperament.

Ah you wonder at that! Well, Gervase, let me tell you that if the country had settled down into the kind of stable existence we had known under King Henry, I think it likely that Robin would not have lasted as the leader, for if he had a fault it was that he was easily bored, just as Allan was – a family trait I fear. Without constant strife to tax his ingenuity I am sure he would have taken himself off to serve in some other foreign land, but as it was, the events of March had drained his need for excitement for many months to come and he was temporarily content, or at least as content as he was ever going to get.

Their happy band made me quite envious, you know, for at least they all had company. I, on the other hand, had to be very careful not to be seen to be too friendly with my chosen men-at-arms. The sheriff and my fellow knights expected to see a proper separation between those of us of noble birth and the lesser folk of the castle, and would have been more than a little scandalised by my preferred associates. Our meeting place soon became the stables, under the watchful eye of Harry and his men. They had needed no recruiting to our rebel group being already implicated in my schemes!

Fitz John had been even worse than they had feared during those first months of his tenure, ordering two more of the original horses slaughtered because they did not fit his ideas of what was handsome. Wilf came to me in a state one day, begging me to bring in some bloody meat he could throw to the dogs for others to see instead of the horses. He and Harry were planning to smuggle the two out to Loughborough market with Harry's brother, but fitz John's kennelman had to have something for his lordship's dogs. This I did, culling a couple of the fallow deer in the park that night, and feeding their flesh and bones to fitz John's hounds, then took the horses out to the forest to await their re-homing. So Harry and the stable men had nearly as much to lose for being found out as I did!

To the knights, I could excuse my forays to the stables as my already known and proven love for animals, and my loss of Fletch and Spike (true in that I had lost their company even if they lived still) allowed me to go to fitz John's hounds in the adjoining kennels without question. Our haughty young lord had a beautiful pack of Talbots, but was only interested in them when he went out to hunt, so I made much of going to keep an eye on them for him. A ruse he fell for in his idleness, for anything which saved himself the trouble of doing much mundane was, I discovered, an easy way to manipulate him. He liked to play the great lord, but without too much effort, although appearances were everything to him.

And in that kind of matter I soon scored another tiny victory over him. It was petty, I know, but it amused me no end that fitz John's four graceful greyhounds took one look at me and proceeded to follow me everywhere I went. He could yell until he was hoarse, but they would not stay with him unless I stayed too! This meant that whenever anyone whom he wished to impress came to visit, I would have to be in or around the Great Hall so that the elegant dogs would complete the lordly picture under the great beamed roof. I got no favours for doing this – much to Sir Henry's disgust, as he would have liked to have found a way to turn any such favours back on me – but it did put me in a marvellous place to observe and listen.

Because I kept quiet and made no attempt to ingratiate myself into any company, unlike Sir Henry, Sir Walkelin and Sir Fredegis, Sheriff fitz John frequently forgot I was even there. Those three, who so deeply sought to curry favour, made such nuisances of themselves that they were often dismissed more swiftly than they might have been from any but the broader gatherings. Whereas I sat silently in the corner, and like a dark spider began to spin my web!

There, Brother Gervase! Is that more to your tastes? An admission of deliberately spying on my lord for you to add to my confession? I might not have been in Sherwood, in amongst the big old oaks, or up in the hideaway up in the Peaks, but I was very much one of the outlaws in spirit and intent. For that first summer we did far less than we would do in the coming years, not least because we were still cautious of bringing down some dreadful retribution on both ourselves and any villagers who helped us. However, as we move into King Richard's reign you will hear of how desperation made us more resolute.

For now, though, you have the genesis of the great legend of Robin Hood! His faithful followers Little John and Allan of the Dales were, you now know, his cousins and friends from childhood. The five knights from the east – Will Scarlet, Gilbert of the White Hand, Siward of Thorpe, James of Tyre and Malik of Ibelin – were to be vital to the success of the outlaws when things turned violent, for in them we had men who had experienced real battles. No amateur soldiers, they had the advantage over mere sheriff's men-at-arms, who more often than not had drilled and trained but never raised a hand in anger except against unarmed villagers. Without them the outlaws would have been far less successful, for Hugh of Barnby could not have trained them to such a standard all by himself. Thomas and Piers Cosham happily joined Malik in teaching all of them archery, but it was the others who provided the sword and quarterstaff skills.

With them remained Algar of Costock and Walter of Fiskerton, neither of whom had ever raised a weapon in anger before, and to be honest were never going to make particularly good soldiers. Much (the miller's son, as he was later to be known) and Bilan Cosham swiftly became close friends, and took to the training they were given with relish. Red Roger was less keen, and he and Allan were often thought to be setting Much and Bilan less than a good example! Yet even this mischievous pair were to find their niche in the outlaw gang, even if they only fought when everyone was roped in for one of the larger schemes.

And then, of course, there was the redoubtable Brother Tuck, who looked after this strange flock of his as if born to the role. He not only ministered to their spiritual needs, he and Marianne were the ones who had a good knowledge of healing herbs, and of what was needed so that they would not become sick. I think that if left up to men like Will and Walter they would all have lived on a diet of nothing more than venison and boar! It was Marianne who, with Tuck's firm backing, insisted on taking time to gather fruits from the hedgerows and dry them, and to find caves and other niches where caches of food could be left without being disturbed by other men or animals. They would not have lasted long without Tuck and Marianne, even if they do not get such credit in the legends.

So there you have it, Gervase, a band of outlaws and Robin, and many of them experienced fighters even before they took to the greenwood. None of them had ever set out to be deliberately lawless men, but God, Fate or whatever you care to ascribe our destiny to, had other ideas. For my part I subscribe to Tuck's philosophy and believe that a kindly divine hand of some sort thought us a fitting tool to use in redressing the balance of injustices perpetrated on the innocent ordinary folk of the three shires – Nottinghamshire, Derbyshire and Yorkshire – for Loxley was on the border and there were times when we plagued the sheriff of Yorkshire just as much as we did my masters in Nottingham!

We shall rejoin them later in 1190, but for now I must pause and get some rest, Brother. Have your pen and parchment ready for tomorrow, for there are tales aplenty still to come, and I am not ready to die just yet! God willing, you will have the full tale!

THE END

Thank you for taking the time to read this book. Before you move on to the notes which give you a bit of background to the story, I would like to invite to to join my mailing list. I promise I won't bombard you with endless emails, but I would like to be able to let you know when any new books come out, or of any special offers I have on the existing ones.

Simply go to my website www.ljhutton.com

Also, if you've enjoyed this book you personally (yes, *you*) can make a big difference to what happens next.

Reviews are one of the best ways to get other people to discover my books. I'm an independent author, so I don't have a publisher paying big bucks to spread the word or arrange huge promos in bookstore chains, there's just me and my computer.

But I have something that's actually better than all that corporate money – it's you, my enthusiastic readers. Honest reviews help bring them to the attention of other readers better than anything else (although if you think something needs fixing I would really like you to tell me first). So if you've enjoyed this book, it would mean a great deal to me if you would spend a couple of minutes posting a review on the site where you purchased it.

Thank you so much.

Historical Notes

In the perennial quest to find the 'real' Robin Hood, there has been much speculation and digging through historical records. However, the real man has never been pinned down, and with so few surviving records from the period, is never likely to be. Yet this has not prevented there being copious works about him, and also of the man seen as his main companion, Little John.

What is more surprising is that little attention has been paid to the real sheriffs of the periods in which the legend appears – and which of whose years are questionable too. Surviving poems from the medieval era focus on the latter end of the Wars of the Roses as a time for Robin Hood, as well as the Anglo-Norman era, but the later poems seem to refer back to an already known legend. So for this story I have opted to focus on the late twelfth and early thirteenth centuries, and have used the real sheriffs who held office at that time. All of these men were sheriffs of the two shires of Nottinghamshire and Derbyshire together – no sheriff just had Nottinghamshire.

However, whoever Guy of Gisborne might have been, he has remained remarkably free of historical investigation! I therefore had to find him a role which would allow him to interact with these sheriffs and to have some longevity of office, and have consequently made him a forester. The world of the foresters in the real royal forests was a complicated business with its own courts and fines, the explanation of which would take a chapter all by itself. Forest in this sense did not necessarily mean woodland, but could include open farmland subject to its laws.

As for the legendary forest of Sherwood, it is a matter of record that until Henry II's reign it was known as the Forest of Nottingham, and only covered a lozenge of land running down the central belt of the shire. He then brought virtually all of the rest of the shire of Nottingham under forest law, intending it to provide an income for his favourite son, Prince John. Yet this state of affairs only lasted until the end of John's reign, by which time the great barons whose lands had been engulfed by royal forest hated these laws almost as much as the ordinary people. At the time of Magna Carta, therefore, there was also issued the Charter of the Forest, which returned vast swathes of 'forest' back to its original legal status and took it out of royal hands. Consequently the massive royal forest which so ground down huge numbers of people with its terrible impositions only lasted a matter of decades, but if there was ever a real Robin Hood, then this would surely have been the time and place for him!

I have made Ranulph de Blundeville, Earl of Chester, older by several years in this book – in 1185 he was all of fifteen and hardly likely to be escorting Prince John anywhere, although he had become Earl of Chester in 1181 at the tender age of eleven. However, this is a novel despite being grounded firmly in history, and so he becomes a major player somewhat earlier than expected! In 1188 or 9 he married Prince Geoffrey's widow, Constance, which resulted in several clashes with the royal family and shows a certain ambition, which I have exploited. The earls of Chester were always significant in this period by virtue of the huge landholding they had on the sensitive Welsh border, meaning they were rarely ignored by kings even if they were not popular.

Prince John did take several stabs at going to Ireland, none of which lasted more than a few weeks, nor were any successful in establishing the prince as a great lord over there, let alone as king of Ireland as his father wished. The de Lacys, on the other hand, very successfully carved a major lordship out for themselves, especially as lords of Meath. As far as I can tell, Prince John did not veer off his proscribed route to south Wales in 1185, although something certainly had him unexpectedly turning back to London.

We have no records of who exactly held the castle of The Peak, or the royal forester's role, during Henry II's reign except for the fact that they were under the sheriff of Nottingham's rule. On this matter there are no names in the Pipe Rolls, although later constables are recorded.

As for the crusades, Balian of Ibelin was a very real hero, although much older than he was portrayed in the film *Kingdom of Heaven*, when he really did command the defence of Jerusalem against Saladin. Faced with the near impossible task of defending the Holy City with all of two knights, his decision to then knight sixty lesser men was startlingly modern given the rigidity of medieval social structures. What may also come as a surprise is that there actually were female Hospitallers working in the order's huge hospital in Jerusalem – Marianne's role is not fiction!

And if anyone is surprised at the mention of groves of almonds and pistachios in the Holy Land, you may be interested to know that one of the many reason why the Turks' overlordship was so hated by the start of the twentieth century was because of the wholesale destruction of these groves. The Ottman Empire's reach into the Middle East was extensive, and with the coming of railways they found a means of faster communication. Therefore the woods were plundered for every scrap of timber to build new rail tracks, to the extent that the entire region became deforested. But back in the time of the crusades, the unrelenting swathes of desert that we know now were a long way in the future, and in springtime the blossom from these trees must have made large areas of modern-day Isreale and Jordan as pretty as any English orchard.

Most people call the sheriff who took office after Ralph Murdac Roger de Lacy, but that became his name well after the period of this book when he inherited the de Lacy properties around Pontefract, not from his father, but from grandparents. Before that he is properly called Roger fitz John, and this is the name I have used.

There was only one Christian casualty in the massacre in York – a hermit whose hysterical ravings against the Jews took him too close to the castle walls and a falling rock! However, for literary purposes I have allowed Eudo to meet a sticky end there and also the two boys, Peter and Tumi. The truth of what happened in York is hard to decipher, but clearly some word got out to the Jewish community at large since it is recorded in medieval Jewish texts as well as English chronicles. What is beyond doubt is that John Marshal, as sheriff, was seriously implicated in causing the riot, and the ringleaders I have mentioned are the names of those who were actually involved.

Clifford Tower in York – the later stone keep of the castle – has a memorial plaque to the Jews who died on 16th March 1190, but the arm of the river which formed its moat has long since been filled and the river culverted. Also town walls were not to appear across England until nearly a century later, which is why I have not mentioned any around York. And for ease of following the action, I have used surviving street names in Nottingham and York, although they undoubtedly weren't fixed or in use at this time.

The famous English longbow made of yew did not come into service until the late thirteenth century in the reign of Edward I, and so didn't appear for another century after our story here. The more common bow for soldiers in the twelfth and early thirteenth centuries was the crossbow, and for hunting it was the smaller wood bow. Recurve bows were known via the crusades, but were not used in wet climates like England since the glue for the laminating wouldn't hold fast. However, as early as the mid twelfth century the longbow, made of elm (and often specifically wyche-elm) not yew, was known as weapon of the Welsh.

Only in 1251 in the reign of King John's son, Henry III, was it made law that the men of England should be capable of mustering with a bow and arrows, and it was in the same reign that we start to see the guilds forming – bowyers and fletchers. Prior to this, bows and arrows would have been made locally and to varying standards –

it was very much up to the buyer to know what he should be looking for and choose appropriately! Therefore our outlaws and soldiers would have been making their own arrows and fletching them as best they knew how, and Malik and Thomas would have recognised each other's work.

And finally, a little word on clothing. Many novelists who write on this era have men of all social strata wearing *chaussés* – which if you've not come across the term before, refers to the cloth 'stockings' which look a little like cowboy's chaps. However...! The main source of reference for these are medieval manuscripts, particularly the Lutterell Psalter, but the Lutterell Psalter was not produced until c.1320-40 – in other words, more than a century after the time we are talking about here. You would not look at an 1850s book and take it as evidence for the 1700s, and we should not do that here. Times change and fashions change.

Also, you disregard at your peril the waspish humour of that marginalia. When priests with impossibly large phalluses can be found romping with monkeys, we really should view images of effete young men, prancing through corn fields in courtly dress, in the same light as we would a modern cartoon of a model wearing Jimmy Choos walking through a similar field. In the 14th century *chaussés* were a fashion item at court, but to force them back to the late 12th or early 13th centuries, and through all layers of society, on the basis of these illustrations is historically unsound.

But more than that, you have to take into account the fact that the only archaeological remains of *chaussés* found have been made of silk, and therefore would have been the clothing of only the wealthiest. Also, to get such a garment to hang correctly, you absolutely have to cut it on the bias of the material – in other words, crosswise – otherwise the 'stockings' simply ride up in leg-gripping wrinkles, and that makes them very wasteful of cloth. Now given that King Richard's reign at least coincided with, and may have caused, crippling inflation, when people were struggling to even afford the grain to make bread, excessive use of cloth would have been a very long way down the list of expenditures for everyone. Even more telling is the fact that very little survives for these particular decades of clothing of any description, hinting at even the wealthier having to make do and mend, with worn out adult clothing being cut down for children. Hosen – in other words something approximating to very thickly woven pantyhose – were a garment of the period, but again something much more likely found at court than in a peasant's cottage, and for the same reason that they would absolutely have to have been cut on the bias, too, and were equally as wasteful of cloth.

And finally, if you need any further convincing that Robin Hood and his men were not tripping around Sherwood in tights, you need to concider whether any sane man would have ridden in the saddle for a whole day with nothing between it and his family jewels but his linen braes (undergarments)! The very idea takes heroic to a whole different level! However, 'trews' – in other words very basic trousers made of two 'legs' of cloth connect by a band of cloth to make the gusset, with a drawstring top – have been found going right back through Viking times and back to the Romans. The idea that ordinary people would just have 'forgotten' how to make such simple garments is ludicrous. Therefore Guy and all of the other men in this story wear trews of varying kinds, with *chaussés* being consigned to the royal courts of the future where they belong.

With all of King Richard's reign to mine for adventures and King John's beyond that, Guy and Robin will appear again!

The next book in the series is ***Outlawed***, out now.

Printed in Great Britain
by Amazon